Broken

Kings Reapers Box-set Books 7-9
Surviving Storm
Raven's Place
Playing Vinn
Nicola Jane

Copyright © 2021 by Nicola Jane.

All rights reserved.

No portion of this book may be reproduced in any form without written permission from the publisher or author, except as permitted by U.K. copyright law.

Meet the team

Cover Designer: Charli Childs, Cosmic Letterz Design
Editor: Rebecca Vazquez – Dark Syde Books
Proofreader: Jackie Ziegler
Formatting: Nicola Miller

Disclaimer:
This book is a work of fiction. The names, characters, places, and incidents are all products of the author's imagination and are not to be construed as real. Any similarities are entirely coincidental.

Spelling:
Please note, this author resides in the United Kingdom and is using British English. Therefore, some words may be viewed as incorrect or spelled incorrectly, however, they are not. I'd also like to point out that some words, like Cop, is used in the UK as well as in the US, so try not to get too hung up on the origin.

Acknowledgements

A quick thank you to everyone who has read and loved the Kings Reapers so far. Thanks to each and every one of you who left a review or rating or spread the word and recommended the series to your friends and family. I've been overwhelmed with how much people have loved Riggs, Cree, Chains, Blu, Blade, and Lake, so I hope you like Storm, Raven and Vinn just as much.

To all the amazing people who have battled, and continue to battle, self-harm and mental illness. Your strength amazes me. Keep fighting, you're doing great! And remember two things, this feeling is temporary, and always take one day at a time.

A note from the Author

If you've come this far, you probably don't need to read my warnings. However, if you're new to the Kings Reapers, you should take caution before entering.

The following stories cover a range of topics from mental health to domestic abuse. Please only read if you're not triggered easily.

Contents

Surviving Storm

Raven's Place

Playing Vinn

Surviving Storm
Kings Reapers MC - Book 7
Nicola Jane

Playlist

Stay Away - Mod Sun ft. Machine Gun Kelly
Heavy - Linkin Park ft. Kiiara
I'm Not Mad - Halsey
Don't Waste My Time - Post Malone ft. G-Eazy
Beauty in the Struggle - Bryan Martin
Sorry Not Sorry - Demi Lovato
Shattered Glass - Britney Spears
Animals - Maroon 5
I Knew You Were Trouble - Taylor Swift
Issues - Julia Michaels
What Other People Say - Demi Lovato ft. Sam Fischer
I'm Gonna Show You Crazy - Bebe Rexha
Crazy Love - Halsey & Post Malone ft. G-Eazy
No More Drama - Mary J. Blige
I Hope - Gabby Barrett
Hate The Way - G-Eazy ft. blackbear
Man! I Feel Like A Woman! - Shania Twain

Chapter One

LOTTIE

Mental health. Everything comes back to mental health. I stare blankly at the counsellor. She's got no interest in me. They never have. I could spill my guts out to this woman and never see her again, then I'd have to tell the exact same story tomorrow to the next one. It's a pointless game we keep playing.

"So, you're telling me this was an accident," she says doubtfully.

I nod. "What can I say, a TikTok video gone wrong." I shrug, and she stares at me for a few seconds before signing the paperwork.

"I'm gonna check on you tomorrow," she says. "Will you be at this address?" She holds up the clubhouse address.

"Yes," I mutter.

"And who is collecting you today?"

"I'm not sure," I say. "My brother or one of his brothers." She frowns in confusion, but I ignore her and send a text off to Sara, my real brother's ol' lady.

Me: Can you come get me from the hospital? Small accident when making a TikTok, nothing to worry about but don't tell Lake.

Sara: I can't lie to your brother. I'll send someone to get you now. Wait at the main entrance.

Me: It isn't lying, it's just not telling him.

Lake's been in my life for a few months now and we're working on our relationship. It's not perfect by far. Our mum left us both, although I spent longer with her. She had Lake young and gave him up for adoption. I was born a few years later, and she tried to be a mum but got it so wrong, so I ended up in care just like Lake.

I stand outside in the cold. It's freezing today, and I came here in pyjamas. Hearing the rumble of a bike, I sigh with relief, but that soon vanishes when Storm, the newest club member who transferred from Nottingham, stops at the kerb and takes off his helmet to assess me with his dark eyes. I reckon my counsellor would take one look at this hot mess and tell me he's a psychopath. It's something in his eyes.

He steps off the bike and moves towards me with the stealth of a lethal animal. Without a word, he grabs my arm. I try to pull away, but he's strong and his grip is bruising as he pushes up my sleeve. He stares at the bandages and then, without any questions, tugs and unwinds the sticky tape. I'm either too shocked or too mortified to object.

He stares at the deep lacerations across my arm with interest, pressing his thumb next to the deepest one. Spots of blood pool on the surface and it coats his digit. "What are you doing?" I whisper, almost as mesmerised as he is.

His brow furrows because I've interrupted his trance-like state, and he wraps the bandage back around my arm. I gasp when he pops his thumb into his mouth to clean my blood away.

Storm gets on the bike and pushes his helmet on, offering me the spare. I climb on, trying not to press myself against him, but my efforts are futile because he grips me by the knees and tugs hard, so I don't have a choice. He holds me there for a second, making sure I don't move. Satisfied I'm staying put, he kicks the bike to life and drives us home.

When we arrive back, Sara is waiting for me. She's holding Leo against her chest and pacing. "What happened?" she demands to know, the second I step inside.

"I hurt my arm when I was learning a dance. Fell into my mirror," I say. It's not strictly a lie—the mirror did break.

"Shit, why didn't you wake me? I would have come with you."

"I'm a big girl," I say, smiling. "It's nothing, just a small cut. I didn't want you to tell Lake cos he'd laugh, and I'd never hear the end of it."

"True," agrees Sara. "Thanks for getting her, Storm. I owe you."

I don't sleep well that night, so it's no surprise the following day, when I'm staring blankly at the large screen television in the main room of the Kings Reapers MC clubhouse. The women have put on some kind of rom com, but I don't take notice. I can't stop thinking about yesterday and my ex's announcement over social media—his girlfriend, my former best friend, gave birth to their child. It was like a punch to the gut.

"Lottie!" Tiny yells, and I glance over to where he's standing at the entrance. "Visitor," he adds, opening the door to let her in as my eyes widen. I'd forgotten! I dive from the couch and rush over to Doctor Welsh.

"Can we do this outside?" I hiss out.

Lake comes up behind me and places his hands on my shoulders. "I'm Lake," he says, holding out his hand for her to shake. She does, smiling. "Charlotte's brother."

"She mentioned you," says Welsh, showing off her perfectly white teeth. "I'm Dr. Welsh."

"Shall we go outside?" I push.

"No need for that," says Lake. "The office is free."

"Lake, it's a quick chat. It's fine," I say.

He fixes me with a hard stare. "Now, Lottie," he says firmly. Tears form in my eyes, but I swallow the lump in my throat and follow him, smiling awkwardly at Welsh.

"If this is a bad time," says Welsh as Lake takes a seat in the office, "I can come back." He points at two seats, so I take one.

"Why are you here?" asks Lake, and Welsh side-eyes me.

"Just to check on her dressings."

"And?" Lake questions, clearly not buying it. "We've never had a private visit from a doctor, and we've had a lot of dressings need changing in this place."

"I really can't discuss my patients," she says hesitantly. "I think Lottie would prefer we speak in private."

Lake arches his brows at me, and I stare down at my feet. "You wanted to build our relationship, so shouldn't I know everything?" he snaps.

"Maybe you two should talk and then Lottie can call me when she's ready," suggests Welsh.

"Lottie?"

"It's nothing," I snap. "I cut myself by accident, and she thinks I tried to hurt myself."

Lake stares at me for a long minute. "Start talking," he hisses.

"I have a history," I mutter. "But it's been ages since I . . ." Trailing off, I sigh heavily. "Things get a bit much sometimes," I whisper, and my eyes fill with tears again. "But I never . . . I didn't mean to . . . I don't . . ." I give up, burying my face in my hands and sobbing.

Lake stands. "Stay here," he orders. "Me and you need to talk," he says to Welsh, and she follows him from the room.

Seconds later, Storm comes in, stopping mid-step when he sees me. "Lake sent me in to watch you," he says.

"Oh," I mumble, wiping my eyes on my sleeves. This is exactly why I didn't want to tell Lake. He'll watch my every move, and then when he sees I'm too crazy, he'll kick me out . . . and I wouldn't blame him—he has enough on.

Storm sits in the chair opposite me. "Serious shit when the shrink does a home visit," he says. I watch the way he leans back in the chair. His large, well-built frame is mesmerizing. How does a man that big get around without knocking into shit? His muscles bunch as he leans forward, resting his elbows on his knees. "And now your secret's out."

"I don't have any secrets," I mutter.

"Oh, you do," he accuses, his brown eyes narrowing like he's trying to read my mind. "So many, you're ready to break," he adds thoughtfully.

I look away, unable to stand his assessing eyes. "I want to go to my room," I say.

"No," he replies firmly.

"You can't stop me," I snap. "I'm not a prisoner."

"Try it," he says, leaning back again and smirking. "Go on. Try." I frown, glancing from him to the door. "I'm waiting," he says. I push to my feet and run for the door. His hand slams against it as I pull it, and it closes with a sharp bang. Both his hands rest above my head, my back to his front. "You can't escape me, little broken butterfly," he whispers into my ear, and I shudder. "Shall we sit back down?"

"I want Lake," I whisper.

"Sit down, Charlotte," he says more firmly. I duck under his arm and take my seat. "You can't keep running," he says. "It'll just follow you."

"I'm not running," I snap.

"You are. Things are good and you think you're cured, then you have a bad day and wanna run. But it'll happen again. The bad days will always come."

"Stop trying to get in my head," I hiss.

"I'm already in it, butterfly. And that's dangerous for both of us."

STORM

Fuck, fuck, fuck. Now what! Why the hell was I sitting on my ass in the club yesterday? If I'd have gone out with Taya and Seb like she'd asked me to, I wouldn't have ended up picking Lottie up from the hospital. When Sara asked me, I could hardly say no. I'm trying to make a good impression around here, hoping to stick around for Seb's sake.

I pace back and forth in my room, tugging at my hair like I always do when I'm stressed. Lake specifically warned me off his sister. I can't ever go there if I wanna stay. And I wanna stay. I like it here, but damn if I can't stop thinking about the little broken butterfly.

I dial her number. I know I shouldn't, and she probably won't answer, but it doesn't stop me hoping. When it connects, I hold my breath as if she'll guess it's me just by hearing me. "Hello?" she answers. Everything stops. My racing heart, my fucked-up thoughts . . . it all stops just because of her. "Hello?" she repeats. I can't answer. I shouldn't. "Storm," she says hesitantly. "Storm, is that you?"

"Laura," I mutter and hear her intake of breath.

"You shouldn't be calling me," she whispers.

"I'm sorry. I just . . ." I pause. What do I say to explain why I've broken the restraining order for the second time within two months?

"Are you trying to get yourself arrested? If Tommy knew, he'd call the police." I clench my jaw at the mention of her fiancé's name. "This is your fresh start."

"I just needed to hear your voice," I explain. "To stop the noise."

"Bullshit. You can't keep leaning on me like that. Find something else to stop the noise." She disconnects the call, and I stare at her number. There's no point in deleting it because I know it by heart. The judge advised her to change it, but she'd never do that because her brother went missing years ago and she lives in the hope he'll turn up one day or remember her phone number. I used to tell her she shouldn't cling to that hope. Mainly because I knew he wouldn't ever come back. He crossed the MC and we disposed of him. Of course, I never told her that part, but I don't regret it because it led me to her.

My sister, Taya, hands me a beer. "Seb was really unsettled at bedtime," she says. I'm distracted, and she sighs when I don't respond. "What is it?"

"I fucked up," I mutter.

"Again?" she asks, raising her brows.

"I called Laura."

Her eyes widen. "You did what?" she snaps. "That's so far past fucked up!"

"I know," I hiss. "I wasn't thinking straight."

"Did she pick up?"

"Yes."

She buries her face in her hands, groaning. "Storm, I don't know how to help you."

"It was a slip-up. It won't happen again."

"That's not good enough. We've moved to start again. I've given up my life to help you, and you keep fucking up. You have to stop."

I nod. "I know." I slide my phone across the table. "Riggs is gonna keep hold of this for a while. No temptation then."

"What if there's an emergency with Seb? How will I get hold of you?"

"I don't know the fucking answers, Taya. I'm trying to make it harder for me to pick up and dial her damn number. What do you suggest?"

"You're right. Sorry." She looks around the clubhouse. "I should make an effort with the women here," she says. "If we're sticking around."

"We are," I confirm. "I told you, I like it here."

"What's her story?" Taya asks, nodding towards where Lottie is sitting, staring at the wall. All the other women are chatting, but she's not paying any attention. "Didn't you pick her up from the hospital yesterday?"

I nod. "She said she fell into a mirror."

"The club girls were talking about her. They think she hurt herself on purpose. A doctor turned up here earlier."

I scowl. "Club girls shouldn't be talking about her. Lake would have a fit. Why are you listening to club girls anyway?" I snap.

"They were just talking, and I happened to be in the same room. I can't turn my ears off." "Next time, pull them up on that shit."

"I can't pull rank in a new place, Storm. What's your problem anyway? You don't even know these people."

"I want us to make a home here, and that starts with defending our own."

Chapter Two

LOTTIE

"Are we gonna talk?" asks Lake, breaking my daydreaming.

"There's nothing to talk about," I say, smiling. "I'm fine. I promise. Everyone has down days . . . it's just sometimes mine are a little extreme."

"What caused your down day?"

"I don't know," I lie. "Sometimes, I overthink. That's why I like to keep busy. Speaking of which, did you ask Riggs about a job for me?"

Lake sits next to me. "Do you think it's a good idea?"

"Yes, it's a very good idea!"

"Just with everything . . ."

"Argh!" I stand, taking him by surprise. "You don't have to wrap me in cotton wool. I. AM. FINE." I march towards the exit, needing air.

I fling the door open, letting it hit against the wall, and then I clench my fists and stamp my feet. It's a childish thing to do, but I'm so frustrated, and I learnt it from a therapy group I once attended. When pressure builds, release it, much like a pressure cooker.

"Nice. Are you gonna throw yourself on the ground next?" I start at the sound of Storm's deep voice. "I'm only asking so I can film it. 'Grown woman throwing a tantrum' will be a hit on the internet."

"I have to get out of here," I say, tugging on the collar of my shirt. I feel like I'm suffocating.

"You want me to get someone?" he asks, glancing at the door. I ignore him and head for the gates. "Lottie, don't go off on your own," he yells after me.

I'm almost at the end of the road by the time Storm's bike slows beside me. "Get on," he snaps.

"I need some space," I say.

"You need to get on the bike." He kicks the stand down and gets off the bike, but I keep walking until he grabs my arm. It's the bandaged one, so I wince. "You like the pain, don't you?" he asks, keeping hold of my arm. "Doesn't it make you feel better?"

"You have no idea," I snap, pulling free.

"I know a place. Somewhere you can go to be alone," he mutters, and I see a hint of vulnerability in his eyes. "I'll leave you alone once we're there. You don't have to talk to me."

We stop on some wasteland. There're dumped piles of unwanted household items everywhere. I slowly turn and take in our surroundings. "It doesn't look much, but I promise, it's quiet and no one comes here," he smirks, "apart from when they wanna dump shit."

"You sit amongst people's unwanted waste?" I ask, arching my brow.

"No, I sit in that," he says, pointing to a rundown caravan. The tyres are flat, and it's rusting on the outside.

"So much better," I mutter, following him towards the heap.

Inside, it's better than I pictured. It's clean, and there's seating and a small table. On the counter are a few empty bottles of whiskey, which Storm quickly collects and disposes of in a waste bin. "I have coffee," he says, pulling two cups out of a cupboard and placing them near a kettle.

"Who owns this heap?" I ask, taking a seat.

"I dunno," he shrugs. "No one ever comes in here, so I just use it."

I stare at him with my mouth fully open. "Storm, this could be someone's property. I don't know how you do things in Nottingham, but here in London, you can't just rock up and use someone's caravan."

"No one ever touches the stuff I leave laying around here, so it can't be occupied."

He hands me a coffee, then takes his own and sits in the doorway of the caravan. I stare at his back for a few seconds. "It's kinda weird sitting here together with your back to me," I say.

"We ain't here to chat. You need some thinking time."

"Were the whiskey bottles yours?"

"Again, we're not here to talk," he mutters.

"I just feel a bit weird sitting here not talking," I say, tapping my fingers on the table. "It was three bottles, that's a lot for one person."

"Who said I drank them alone?" he spits.

"No need to get defensive. I'm not judging."

"You can't when you cut yourself for kicks," he mutters.

"Ouch," I almost whisper. "Fine, you win. No talking."

We sit for a few minutes. Eventually, he clears his throat. "You been doing that shit long?" He stares straight ahead.

"Long enough to know it doesn't help," I say. "But I still do it."

"You wanna die?" he asks.

"Sometimes," I admit, then steel myself. Why am I opening up to this guy? If he tells Lake, he might send me away. My heart aches at that thought. I love the MC and I love being around Lake, Sara, and Leo. "Where's Seb's mum?"

"Fuck, you're nosy."

"It's a talent," I say, smiling.

"Do you get help for it?" he asks, referring to my cutting.

"Did she die?"

"Cos you should. Lying and telling people you did it by accident won't help."

"Sara said Seb's got special needs. What's that mean?"

"I ain't explaining my life to you, especially when it comes to my kid."

"Fine. Stop talking then," I snap. "Don't ask me shit and not expect to answer any of my questions."

We fall silent again. This time, I press my lips closed so I'm not tempted to ask him anything else. Not one to sit still, I eventually slide past him and take a walk around the dumping ground.

STORM

I watch her move around the piles of waste. She's beautiful. Her long hair is tied up into a messy pile on top of her head. She's wearing leggings that fit snug to her rounded ass, and I can't take my eyes off it. She bends down behind an abandoned mattress, and when she doesn't reappear, my curiosity gets the better of me and I head over. "Look," she whispers, standing with a small bundle of fur in her arms. "It's a puppy."

A pair of black eyes and a wet black nose stare back at me. "Fuck, Lottie, put that thing down. You don't know where the hell it's been. I bet it's got fleas!"

"He's scared," she says, hugging the puppy closer.

"You can't take that back to the club," I say. "Riggs will have a fit."

"I can't leave it here," she hisses. "He might die."

"Sometimes that's the way. Survival of the fittest and all that," I say, heading back towards the caravan.

I hear her steps behind me. "Are you kidding me? You really want me to leave this puppy here to die?"

"What if it belongs to the owner of the caravan?" I suggest.

"You said there was no owner."

"Riggs hates having Diesel around the place as it is. He ain't gonna take kindly to a flea-ridden puppy chewing shit up."

"Bet the kids will love him," she says, smiling as the puppy snuggles against her chest. "I think I love him already," she adds, and I roll my eyes. I'm not a fan of animals. Seb wanted a puppy right after everything with his mum, but it was one thing I never gave in on.

"We can't take it on the bike anyway. Leave it here, and if it's still around the next time I come, I'll bring it back." It's a lie, and she doesn't fall for it. Instead, she tucks the puppy against her stomach and zips her jacket up, leaving just his head out, which he soon tucks away too. "You've got to be kidding. Lottie, I can't have a fucking live animal on the back of my bike. What if he gets loose?"

"He won't. Please, Storm. I can't abandon him. He looks so sad. Maybe he'll be the thing I need to take my mind off shit," she says, making me groan. Using that is a low blow but one I know I'll give in to. Anything to stop her hurting herself. I try not to think too much about why I feel that way.

"Tell me why you did that yesterday," I say, nodding towards her arms, "and I might consider it."

She hesitates. "It's so stupid," she almost whispers. "I feel so stupid."

"I won't judge. I don't do that."

"I saw some stuff on social media. It got to me. I haven't hurt myself like that for ages and I just had a bad day."

"What did you see?" I push.

"Why do you need to know?" she wails, and the puppy sticks his head back out her jacket.

"So I can make sure it never happens again."

Her mouth opens and closes a few times before she finally sighs. "My ex had a baby with my best friend. It was born yesterday."

I walk towards my bike without another word, and she follows. That's all I need for now . . . until she trusts me.

I take the puppy from Lottie once we're outside the clubhouse. She gives a questioning look. "Well, if Diesel wants to eat it, at least he'll bite me to get it and not you," I explain, and she smiles.

"Careful, I'll start to think you care."

Inside, there's an audience. Riggs and Anna are at the bar with Cree and Eva. Diesel marches right up to me, sniffs the puppy, then walks off like it's nothing. "Aww," says Lottie, smiling. "He likes him."

I present the puppy to Riggs, who eyes it suspiciously while the women gush over how cute he is. I let Lottie explain why the fuck I'm holding this flea bag in the club, and when she's finished, Riggs rolls his eyes. "You couldn't fucking lose it on the way back here?" he asks me, and I shrug. Anna playfully nudges his arm with hers.

"It is kinda cute. It's not like you'll have to look after it," she says, placing a kiss on his cheek. "And you do owe me."

"You're gonna use that again?" he asks, and she nods. "Fine, it's one less thing off the list," he says, and Anna smiles at Lottie, who does a small happy dance before she heads off towards the stairs.

"List?" I ask.

"I've got to give in to Anna ten times to make up for being an ass. Malia's idea. So, that dog is number four ticked off. Six more to go, baby," he says, smacking Anna on the ass.

Chapter Three

LOTTIE

I'm in the main room watching television with Seb and Malia. It's a kids' film, but it takes my mind off other things. The puppy is sleeping curled up between the kids.

Storm's sister, Taya, joins us. "Have you named the dog yet?" she asks.

I shake my head, and Seb looks back at me. "I like Bently." Malia nods in agreement.

"That's kinda cute," agrees Taya.

"I like it!" The kids cheer. "I gotta get him food and stuff," I say.

"I don't think you need to bother," says Taya, nodding towards the door.

Storm is carrying some bags towards us, then he dumps them at my feet. "Let's go wash that thing before he infects the kids."

"I checked him," I say, laughing. "He doesn't have fleas." "Still," he mutters, scooping the puppy up and then the bags. Taya winks at me, and I follow Storm upstairs to his room. He empties the bags onto his bed. "I got shampoo. A leash. Some bowls. Food." I stare at the haul, which also includes some puppy toys, and I smile.

"What do I owe you for all this?"

"Nothing," he says, heading to his bathroom.

"But you hate him," I accuse, following. He's filling the bath with Bently under his arm.

"Hate is strong. I just didn't want you to catch anything or get your heart set on keeping him for Riggs to say no."

Once there's enough water in the tub, he puts Bently in, and I pass him the dog shampoo. He baths him expertly, and minutes later, he's wrapping him into a large fluffy towel and carrying him back to the bedroom. I watch from the doorway as he rubs the puppy, smiling when he tries to lick Storm's face.

"Where did you live before coming here?" he asks.

"I've been around. I was looking for Lake for a long time and I spent the last year going from biker club to biker club. Before that, I lived in Norfolk."

"That where your boyfriend lives?"

I nod. Just thinking of Justin hurts my heart. "We had a place together."

"Did you split before he bedded your best mate?"

I place a handful of the dry food into Bently's new bowl as Storm places him on the floor so he can eat. "No. We all lived together. I let her move in because she'd had a nasty break-up. She lived with us for around eight months, and for six of those, they were creeping around behind my back."

"That's real shitty," he mutters.

"Whatever." I shrug. "I'm glad they found happiness."

Storm arches a brow. "Really?"

"God, no, I was trying to tone down the bitter ex bull," I say, smiling.

He takes my arm and stares down at the bandage, unwrapping it again. It's healing well, the redness much calmer than yesterday. "I drink," he mutters, rubbing his thumb over one of the wounds. "When I can't cope, I turn to alcohol. My biggest downfall. It's caused a lot of problems."

"Is that why Seb's mum left?" I ask.

"She didn't leave," he mutters. "Not by choice." He begins to wrap my arm again, but once he's done, he keeps a hold of my hand. "I'm not good at relationships."

"I thought I was," I say. "Seems not. I didn't even see it when they were cheating right under my nose. It only came out because she got pregnant."

"What did you do when you found out?"

I stare down at where his hand holds mine. "Something stupid as usual. It didn't work. He just got mad and tried to have me sectioned."

He places his finger under my chin and tilts my head up to look at him. His brown eyes stare straight into mine. "Don't be ashamed of struggling. We all do stupid shit when we get hurt."

"I love too hard," I mutter. "It's what Annabell used to tell me. Maybe she was trying to get me to back off right before stealing him."

"How can you love too hard?" he asks. "Love is love—you don't control how you feel it."

"I do these days," I say, smiling. "I avoid it."

He grins. "Me too. Works out much better that way."

Turns out Bently hates to sleep alone, which is why I ended up putting him in bed beside me in the middle of the night. He'd spent the first few hours sleeping, then whimpering for an hour, until I eventually gave in. Now, at five in the morning, he's decided he's had enough of sleep altogether and is pacing the room, crying. I pull on some joggers and take him downstairs. Maybe a walk around the yard will settle him.

I'm around the side of the club watching Bently sniff the dirt when I hear voices. Pausing, I listen to make sure it's club members and not strangers.

"Why are you out here so early?" It's Taya's voice.

"Couldn't sleep," comes Storm's voice. "You?"

"Seb had an unsettled night. He's finally gone off, and now I'm wide awake."

"Sorry, you should have come and got me," he mutters.

"It's fine. You heard anything from Laura after your call?" There's silence and then she sighs. "At least the cops haven't turned up. Maybe she didn't report you."

"The whole thing is bullshit," he mutters.

"You can't go to prison, Storm. Not over her. How come you and Lottie were out together?"

"She needed a break from this place."

"Just be careful there, Storm. Let's not let history repeat itself," she mutters.

"Taya, get off my back," he snaps. "I'm not gonna fucking break every time I see a woman I like. I told you I'm not looking for anything and I meant it."

Bently yaps, and I panic, running away from where I'm standing, and then I turn and stroll back towards them like I've been walking all along. Storm comes around the corner and his eyes narrow in on me. "What are you doing?"

"Walking the dog," I say, frowning. "Obviously."

Bently fusses around Storm's feet, and he strokes him, eventually picking him up. "You want company?"

"Sure," I say.

He glances back to where Taya must be standing. "Catch you later."

We walk in silence for a few minutes. "Taya spends a lot of time looking after Seb," I say.

Storm nods. "She's his legal guardian." I wasn't expecting that and I must look shocked because he smiles, nodding again. "She's an amazing sister. She took him on when I had to go away for a while."

"Where to?" I ask.

He hesitates before eventually saying, "Prison."

"For?" I ask.

He laughs. "Enough story time from me." We fall silent again. "So, since your ex,

there's been no one else?"

I shake my head. "Nope. I've given up on men."

"Liar. Lake told me you were interested in me," he says, winking. I gasp at Lake's betrayal. "He was worried I'd sweep you off your feet and warned me off."

"He did what?" I snap.

"Relax," he soothes. "I'd do exactly the same if a guy like me was sniffing around Taya. He knows bad news when he sees it."

"I can make my own decisions."

"I'm sure you can," he mutters. "It's a good job we've both sworn off relationships," he adds.

"Did you go to prison for killing Seb's mum?" I ask, and he frowns. "Well, you won't tell me, so I have to make up my own story," I say, smiling.

He laughs. "Your imagination is wild."

STORM

Fuck, she's everywhere I turn. I've lost count of the cold showers I've had to cool myself off, but she's stuck in my mind twenty-four-seven. Taya's following me around, watching me extra closely in case I 'make a bad choice' as she likes to call it.

"Storm, you need to watch Seb today," Taya says.

"Why? What are you doing?" I snap. She always watches Seb for me. It's like an unwritten rule.

"I'm having a day off," she says, sounding equally pissed.

"A day off?" I repeat. When she doesn't break a smile, I realise she's deadly serious. "I can't. I have shit to do," I say, heading to Riggs' office. The door is open and he glances up. "Ain't that right, Pres?"

He looks between us, then nods. "Yeah, that's right. Vinn needs manpower today."

"You need to give me some notice when you just wanna take off," I say, arching a brow. Taya huffs and marches off. "Thanks, Pres. I owe yah."

"I'm serious. Vinn's asked for manpower. You can head to his house now."

I groan. I was looking for an excuse, not a damn job.

Vinn wasn't kidding when he said he needed manpower today. I slam my fist against the guy we have tied to a chair in Vinn's club. It's closed, being the middle of the day, but there's staff around the place, stocking up for tonight. They don't even look over as we lay into this guy.

Vinn's leaning one elbow on the bar, casually watching with a smirk on his face. This guy is three times my size and weight, and it's taking everything I have to get this motherfucker to bleed. When he eventually spits a tooth out onto the floor, I want to do a fucking celebratory jig. Lake pats me on the back. He's just as knackered as I am. "Alright!" The guy growls. "Jonah Delonghi sent me."

"You only lost one tooth," I say. "You're gonna give it up after one tooth?"

"Shut the fuck up, man. I'm done with this. If I have to carry on, I'll die before he does," snaps Lake, and I smirk.

The door bangs and we all look up as Lottie enters. I swear, I almost gasp at the sight of her. She's wearing a skirt shorter than is even possible. There's no way she can bend without showing us everything. Her top is low cut and her tits are spilling out over the top. Her heels click as she walks towards Vinn. Once she's closer, I see she's wearing makeup and I frown. For a second, dread fills me. What if she's on a date with Vinn? I glance at Lake, but he looks just as confused as me. "What are you doing here?" he snaps.

"I'm here to see Vinn," she says with a confidence I've never witnessed from her.

"About?" he asks.

Vinn smirks, placing a hand on Lottie's lower back and leading her towards his office. "I'll take care of her, don't worry. Get on with what I pay you for," he says. The door slams shut behind them, and Lake looks ready to combust.

"Are they dating?" I growl out, unable to keep the anger from my voice.

Lake eyes me suspiciously. "Why are you fucking asking?"

"Cos it's Vinn!" I snap like that explains everything. "I watched him cut someone's tongue out last week, and now, he might be fucking Lottie. She's part of the club, she shouldn't be in bed with the mafia . . . literally."

"Shut the hell up," growls Lake. "She ain't fucking Vinn." He slams his fist into the guy's face hard enough to bust his nose. Blood spurts out and the guy lets out a string of curses. "At least, I don't think so," adds Lake. "It's not like she tells me anything."

It's an hour before Vinn reappears with Lottie. The guy has taken a bad beating, partly cos me and Lake took our anger out on him. He's passed out with blood pouring from his face. Vinn assesses the scene, shaking his head. "Jesus, what the fuck happened? I asked for information, not a kill."

I throw a piece of paper on the bar top. "All there," I mutter, letting my eyes roam up and down Lottie. She doesn't look flustered or just fucked.

"Are we good to go?" snaps Lake.

"He is," says Vinn, pointing to me. "You're not. I need a package delivered, and you went before."

Lake growls, rolling his eyes. He glares at me. "Get Lottie home."

Outside, I stop by my bike, but Lottie continues on past. "I gotta get you home," I say.

"I have shit to do. I'll make my own way," she says.

"Why you always gotta do the opposite of what you're told?" I snap. "Just get on the fucking bike."

She spins to face me, looking me up and down. "You're covered in blood," she snaps. "You want me to hold on to you while you're covered in some guy's blood?"

I glance down at my stained shirt. "What's your problem with blood? You like to see your own but not other people's?" It's below the belt and I feel bad the second it leaves my mouth, but I'm pissed. All I can think about is her with Vinn and it boils my blood.

"Fuck you," she hisses before turning and stomping off down the street. I watch her ass sway. She walks different in heels, and fuck, it turns me on.

I roll my eyes before running to catch her up. "Sorry. That was out of order."

"Leave me alone," she mutters.

"Don't let something I said piss you off. I'm a dick. Sorry." We walk in silence for a few minutes, then she stops outside a bar and peers through the window. "Who are we looking for?" I ask, peering through too.

"Just go home. I'll see you there."

There's a group of men inside. They're all drinking and cheering. It looks like a celebration. "Who is that?" I ask. "Who are you looking for?"

"Storm," she growls. "Go home." Whatever she's doing here, she doesn't want me around, so I shrug my shoulders and nod. Then I head back the way we came. I glance back over my shoulder in time to see her go inside the bar. I wait a few seconds before returning and looking in the window. Lottie is talking to one of the drunk guys. He looks angry, and she looks like she's desperately trying to explain something. Suddenly, he grabs her arms and pulls her towards the exit, dragging her into the street, and she's sobbing.

"You're fucking crazy," he's yelling as he shoves her away from him. She stumbles, falling onto her ass. "Stay the fuck away from me," he spits out. I catch him off guard, hitting him on his jaw as he turns to go inside. His head bangs against the wall and he hisses. "What the fuck?"

"You touch her again and I'll slit your throat!" I warn.

"No," cries Lottie, jumping and rushing to stand in front of me. "Leave him," she yells.

"Is this your new man?" asks the guy, laughing. "Mate, if I was you, I'd run a mile. This chick is crazy." He storms back inside.

"Why did you do that?" she cries, pushing hard against my chest. "I told you to go."

"Was that your ex?" I ask, gripping her wrists to stop her pounding them against my chest. "Did you come here to see him?"

"You wouldn't understand," she sobs.

I keep hold of one wrist and pull her away from the doorway of the bar. I'd understand way more than she thinks. "Let's go."

"I wanna be alone," she yells, trying to pull free. People start looking to see what the fuss is.

"Lottie, we've been here before. You can't get away from me, so just do what I fucking say," I hiss. She's attracting attention, and the last thing I need is the cops turning up when I'm covered in another man's blood.

She gives in, letting me lead her back to my bike. I drive us to the caravan since I can't take her to the club in this state. At least here, I can keep an eye on her. I sit in the doorway of the caravan, and she wanders around the discarded piles of rubbish. She lets out an ear-piercing scream, but I don't react. She needs this. Eventually, she drops onto an old mattress and stares out over the horizon. I go inside and pull out the bed. I've slept here numerous times when I've been blind drunk so Taya wouldn't discover I'm still doing it. I find the bottle of whiskey I've hidden here and place it on the table, taking a seat and staring at it. Taya thinks I have a problem . . . I don't. I can stop, I can turn it down, but sometimes, I like to sit here and get wasted to forget. She read somewhere that drinking alone is a sign of alcoholism, but I think it's a sign of sadness.

I snatch the bottle and unscrew the lid, taking a large gulp. As it burns through my chest, I relax, then take another drink. I can see Lottie through the window. She's still staring out at nothing, but at least she ain't screaming anymore. I drink half the bottle before my eyes feel glazed and I'm completely relaxed. I sway when I stand, holding the table to steady myself. Heading over to Lottie, I come to a sudden stop when I lay my eyes on her. "What the fuck have you done?" I g rowl.

Chapter Four

LOTTIE

The noise has stopped, so I stare down at the thick, sticky liquid covering my entire arm. "I said, what the fuck have you done," yells Storm. "I don't have my phone," he growls. "Riggs has my phone. Have you got yours?" He grabs my upper arm and pulls me to stand. I don't know why he's so mad. He marches me towards the bike, but he's unsteady on his feet and stinks of whiskey.

"You can't drive," I say dryly. "You've been drinking, and no, my phone is dead, and I haven't got a charger."

He glares at me, his chest heaving up and down. "You stupid bitch, what the hell were you thinking?"

"What were you thinking?" I counter. "I thought you had a problem with alcohol, so why are you keeping stashes of it around here like a fucking treasure hunt? And don't call me a bitch!"

"Yeah, well, it's been a fucking stressful day!" he snaps.

"I've only opened old wounds, relax," I mutter, heading back to the caravan. I open the cupboards, searching for a first aid kit. I've been doing this a long time, and a nurse once showed me how to take care of my cuts and keep them clean. The kit is basic with some bandages but no cleansing wipes. I find a bottle of vodka—that'll do.

Storm swigs from his bottle of whiskey, his eyes fixed on me as I unscrew the vodka cap and hold my arm over the sink, pouring the liquid over my cuts. I cry out. It's unavoidable as the alcohol stings my wounds. "How dysfunctional are we?" I ask, smirking.

"Why'd yah go and see Vinn?" he mutters. "Why did you turn up to see your ex, and how did you know he was there?"

"Why does your ex have an injunction out on you?" I ask casually. His eyes narrow, and I smile innocently. "I overheard you and Taya talking."

He stands, pushing his body against mine and levelling his eyes with me. "Because I'm fucking crazy," he hisses.

"Aren't all the best people?" I ask, squaring my shoulders. I refuse to be scared by him, even if his eyes look more cold and deadly now he's drunk. "You shouldn't try and gain my interest, Charlotte," he growls. "I'm not a nice guy."

"Well, I'm used to bastards," I mutter.

He takes the bandage and rips open the package. "You keep appearing," he mumbles, "like some bad fucking dream I can't escape. I can't get you out of my head. You know how frustrating that is?" he snaps. It's like he's rambling to himself rather than me, so when I push my lips against his, he freezes. We stare at each other in surprise, our lips still pressed together.

Then, as if his brain catches up, his hands drop the bandage and push into my hair. His mouth moves against mine hungrily, taking everything I have as he grips the roots of my hair. It's hot and fast paced, desperate and hungry. I didn't know how much I needed it until this moment.

I'm lost in his kiss, in the feel of his strong body pressed against mine, so when he pulls away, I feel the loss immediately. He slams his fist into the cupboard above my head, and I duck in shock. "No," he growls. "We can't happen!" I watch as he stomps out the caravan, slamming the door behind him.

I pick up the bandage and carefully wrap it around my arm. It's still bleeding badly, and I'm sure I'll need it stitched, but seeing as I'm stuck here the night, I kick off my shoes and lie on the bed.

I'm still awake when Storm comes in an hour or so later, but I close my eyes so he doesn't know. The last thing I need is to face him after what happened. I can't take any more rejection right now. I feel him carefully take my arm and lift the bandage. It's loose because I couldn't tie it off properly. "Jesus," he whispers. "You stupid girl. Why would you hurt yourself over him when you're so much better than that? Damn, you could have your pick of men and you chose that ass." I feel the bandage tighten as he ties it off. His hand gently strokes my hair. "You're so fucking beautiful. Why didn't I meet you years ago?" I keep my eyes closed but feel him move closer, and then his lips gently brush my own. This time, he's gentle and careful. When I respond, I expect him to pull away, but he doesn't. He cups my cheek with his large hand and joins me on the bed, propping himself on his elbow without breaking the kiss. His hand runs down my side, resting against my exposed thigh. My skirt is practically non-existent. "I can't stop myself from wanting you," he mutters.

"Then don't," I whisper back.

"We're not good for each other," he says.

"Let's think about the serious stuff tomorrow. Right now, let's distract ourselves. I need distracting so fucking bad."

Storm kisses me again, moving his lips along my jaw and down my neck. I close my eyes as he tugs my top down, exposing my breasts. His tongue flicks over one, then the other, as his hand pushes my skirt up. His finger brushes over my opening, and I gasp. It's been so long since anyone touched me, and it feels amazing. "Once we do this, it'll complicate everything," he says. I gasp as his finger enters me.

"You think too much," I whisper, squeezing my eyes shut as he inserts another. His thumb presses against my sensitive bud and pleasure shoots through me. I grip his shoulders, and he takes my hardened nipple in his mouth again. With his fingers thrusting and his tongue licking, I can't concentrate on anything other than the build-up of warmth spreading through my body. When I begin to shudder, he releases my nipple and watches me. I've never been watched while I orgasm, but his intense stare only adds to the excitement, and as I cry out, he smirks down at me, clearly pleased with his efforts. "Fucking gorgeous," he whispers, kissing me gently. He removes his fingers and places them in his mouth, closing his eyes and humming his approval. "Now sleep."

"Sleep?" I repeat, rubbing my leg against his raging hard-on.

He grips my thigh, digging his fingers in. "Yes, sleep."

"But don't yah wanna—"

"Of course, I do, but I can't," he says.

"I have condoms and I'm on the pill," I say, blushing.

"Not the reason, but why the fuck do you carry condoms around?"

"Safety," I mumble.

"You carry condoms for safety but not a fully charged mobile," he mutters, shaking his head. He pulls himself to sit up, grabbing the whiskey bottle and taking a mouthful. I lie my head against his stomach. "You slept with a lot of men?" he asks.

I rub my hand over his erection, and he grabs it, holding it against his leg instead. I smirk—I like challenges. "None of your business," I say. I lift my top over my head and throw it to the floor. "I can't sleep in clothes," I explain, pushing my skirt down my legs and adding it to the floor. His eyes narrow as I unfasten my bra and finally lie back down against his stomach in just my panties. "You don't mind, do you?"

"Why were you seeing Vinn today?"

"He's fucking hot," I joke, and I'm suddenly on my back with Storm hovering over me. He narrows his eyes again. "I was kidding," I say, smiling. His eyes roam over my naked breasts. "But I wouldn't kick him out of bed if he offered it," I add, laughing.

He pushes his erection against my panties. "Don't say shit like that when you're in my fucking bed," he growls.

"You think you're the only man I fantasise over?" I ask, grinning.

"I mean it, Lottie," he warns.

"If I was lying next to Vinn, naked, do yah think he'd walk away?" I add.

He kneels between my legs, ripping his belt open. "You want me to fuck you?" he growls, and I nod, smiling innocently. "You want this?" he snaps, gripping his huge, erect cock in his hand and stroking it. I press my lips together and nod again. He keeps his eyes locked on mine as he lines himself up at my entrance. He likes to watch me. Gripping both my hands in one of his, he holds them above my head as he eases himself into me, and I gasp. "You only fantasise about me from this second onwards," he growls. He slams the rest of the way in, pushing me up the bed. His head hangs once he's fully inside me, taking a second to compose himself. "You got that, Lottie?"

I nod, slightly freaked but equally turned on by his demands. "Okay."

STORM

I can't get enough of her hot little body as she screams through her second orgasm. She digs her nails into my hands, and I welcome the burn as I slam into her over and over. The blush on her cheeks and her hooded eyes send me spiralling over the edge with her. I come on a roar and then collapse beside her, throwing my arm over my eyes. We didn't use a condom, so without looking at her, I ask, "You definitely on the pill?"

"Yeah," she mumbles sleepily.

I reach for her, bringing her towards my chest. "Sleep now, butterfly." It feels good to have her snuggled against me. It's that same feeling I used to get when Laura would lie in bed next to me—the constant buzzing noise in my head has gone and I feel settled. My eyes drift closed.

I wake the next morning with a headache and dry mouth. Somewhere in the distance, I hear singing. Realising Lottie isn't next to me, I sit up and look around the caravan. I follow the sound of her voice and find her sitting outside nursing a cup of coffee. "How's the head?" she asks, keeping her eyes fixed on the horizon.

"Bad." She offers me her coffee, and I take it gratefully, sitting down beside her. "How's your arm?"

"Bad."

"We should get back and have the doc take a look at it," I say.

She shakes her head. "I'd rather keep it between us."

"Sure, you would, but how do we fix it if we keep it a secret? Maybe that shrink can help."

"No one can help. I just wanna forget about it. I won't do it again. Seeing him just . . . well, it just threw me."

"Why is he in London? I thought he lived in Norfolk?"

"He's on his stag weekend. I have some of his friends on social media and saw he was nearby when they tagged themselves at that bar."

"What happens the next time you see him? Or the next time you're upset? You need help, Lottie. That shit doesn't just stop."

"Like drinking?" she says, arching her brow. "I bet you don't want Taya knowing about last night."

I smirk. "Are you threatening me?"

"I'm just saying, if Lake asks why you didn't take me to the hospital, I'll have to explain *everything*."

I take a handful of her hair and tug her head back so I have access to her smart mouth. "What sort of war would that cause?" I whisper, pressing my lips to hers. She thrusts her tongue against my own, and I throw my leg over her, so I'm straddling her. I push her to lie back on the grass and lift the shirt she stole from me. She's naked underneath. I run kisses down her body, parting her legs and burying my face between them.

I love outdoor sex—the riskier, the better—and as I lie back on the grass, watching Lottie ride me like a fucking queen, I'm happier than

I've been in months. We've spent the day at the caravan sleeping and fucking. When she falls against my chest panting and sated, I run my hand up and down her back. "We have to go back," I mutter.

"I wish we could stay here forever," she mumbles.

"You and me both, butterfly, but Riggs is probably already after my balls for being gone all night and day. Not to mention Taya. She's had Seb on her own and she'll be pissed. Anyway, Lake will want to check on you."

We get back to the club and everyone is gathered in the bar. They all turn towards us as we walk in, and Lake rushes forward. "Where the fuck have you been?" he yells at Lottie. She takes a surprised step back and glances at me.

"We took some time out," I say. "Sorry, brother. I should have called."

"Called?" he repeats. "Last thing I said to you was take her fucking home!"

"It's my fault," says Lottie. "I needed some headspace, and Storm was helping me out."

"You forget to check in, brother?" asks Riggs, glaring at me.

"You have my phone, remember? And Lottie's died."

"Even more reason to get on your damn bike and come home!" yells Lake.

"Stop yelling," snaps Lottie. "Christ, we're adults. We can spend a night out if we want to."

Lake narrows his eyes, looking back and forth between us. "Did you fuck her?" he asks me.

"Look, Lake—" I begin.

"You piece of shit," he shouts, shoving me hard. I stumble back a few steps and the other brothers rush to get between us. "I told you to stay the hell away from my sister."

"It ain't like that," I explain. I spot Taya by the bar, and she's shaking her head with sadness in her eyes. She walks off towards the stairs. "Taya, wait," I shout, but she ignores me.

"Lake, you're not my keeper," snaps Lottie. "I can do what I like."

"There's a fucking code," he yells back. "He broke it."

"You all need to calm the fuck down," says Riggs. "Break it up."

Cree pats Lake on the chest, leading him outside. Everyone else clears the room until it's just me and Lottie. "Well, that went well," she mutters.

"Yeah."

"I'm sorry he yelled at you."

"I was expecting it. I shouldn't have gone behind his back like that. I'd have killed anyone who did that with Taya."

"I'm an adult," she snaps. "I can do what I like."

"A vulnerable adult. You're Lake's sister, and he's responsible for you in this club."

She scoffs. "Vulnerable? That isn't what you said last night or today every time you fucked me."

"Jesus, Lottie, watch your mouth," I growl. "Let me sort it out with Lake. Until then, let's take it easy. I don't wanna rub his face in it." She looks at me like a wounded puppy, and I sigh. "Just until I've spoken to him properly."

"Fuck you," she mutters, then I watch her stomp off towards the stairs. Things were so much easier a few hours ago.

Chapter Five

LOTTIE

It's been two days since we got back from the caravan. I've avoided Storm. I can't handle the way his eyes watch my every move, like he's constantly hungry for me, yet he won't touch me because of Lake.

He can't avoid talking to me for much longer, though, because I'm working at Vinn's club for a trial shift tonight. I haven't told anyone in the Kings about it, apart from Raven, and she only knows because she works for Vinn. When Lake and Storm find out about this, they'll be raging with anger.

I stare at myself in the mirror. I'm unrecognisable when I overdo my makeup like this, but it's necessary for the show. Raven joins me, taking a seat next to me and staring at my reflection. "Are you nervous?"

"A little," I admit. "Not because of the show, just cos I know the Kings are in tonight."

"Sometimes I think Vinn does this shit on purpose, inviting them when he knows you're starting a trial," she says. "You'll be fine. Your audition was amazing, so you'll smash it out there."

I nod, smiling with a confidence I don't quite feel. It's not the first time I've danced on stage. Before I turned up here looking for Lake, it's how I made money. Travelling around was costing a fortune, and it was a quick way to make what I needed to feed and clothe myself. I check my arms, making sure the makeup I've applied is covering my wounds. It's not perfect, but from a distance, it's hard to see the ugly marks.

I'm next up on stage, the third act of the evening, and as my name is announced, I shake my body to loosen it up. Then I paste a wide smile on my face, saunter out onto the stage, and take a seat. The spotlight hits me, and the music begins. I part my legs, unable to see anyone because the light is shining in my face.

The split in my red dress goes the length of my leg, revealing a glimpse of my red panties. As the thumping beat picks up, I begin to move towards the pole. The cheers get louder, and as I grip the pole and lift myself, the light dims slightly and I catch sight of Riggs and Anna. She looks positively beaming, and I hear her whistles and shouts of encouragement. I tip myself upside down, wrapping one leg around the pole and freeing my hands. My eyes connect with Storm for a brief second before I force myself to look away. He looks livid.

The rest of my dance passes in a blur. I can't think about anything but him and how he'll react. When the song comes to an end, I drop back to my feet, collect my dress from the stage floor, and race off.

"That was fucking amazing," gushes Raven, handing me an envelope of cash. "You made a killing from just that dance."

Clutching the envelope to my chest, I smile awkwardly as I rush to the change rooms. I pull on my jeans and jumper, hanging the dress Vinn provided in the closet. The door crashes open, and I spin to face Storm.

"You can't come back here," I mutter feebly.

His hand goes to my throat and he gently pushes me backwards until my back hits the wall. His mouth crashes against mine in a fast, bruising kiss. He tugs at the button on my jeans until it opens, then he shoves them down my legs. Spinning me away from him, he bends me over, ripping my panties with a sharp tug. His hands dig into my hips as he enters me in one swift movement. I push my hands against the wall to steady myself as Storm slams into me over and over. He comes in minutes, roaring loud enough to let the girls in the other rooms hear us. Reaching around to my front, he rubs circles over my clit, burying his face in my neck. His heavy panting sends me over the edge, and I shudder through an intense orgasm.

Apart from our breathing, the room falls silent. He eventually pulls out of me and tucks himself away. He grabs a box of tissues and takes a handful, wiping between my legs and throwing them in the bin. He pulls my jeans back into place, and I fasten them, turning to face him. "You got naked on stage," he mutters, and I nod. "Don't do that shit again," he adds before walking out, slamming the door behind him. I stare after him in shock. I was expecting a full-on argument, but maybe that will come when I refuse to let him boss me around.

I find Lake and Sara at the bar, and Sara hugs me. "You never said you could pole dance," she exclaims. "Anna and I want lessons. I'm asking Riggs to install a pole at the clubhouse." I smile, nodding. Lake's got his back to me, and Sara smiles apologetically. "Ignore Mr. Grumpy Pants here. He's moody."

"Why didn't you tell me you needed money," he snaps.

"I don't. I have a job here . . . well, hopefully."

"No, Charlotte. You can't work as a stripper. No way."

"Lake, come on," says Sara, sighing.

He gets off his stool. "I said no!" he snaps, stomping off into the crowd.

She rubs my arm. "He'll come around. I thought you were great."

"Have you seen Storm?" I ask, looking around.

Sara shakes her head. "You still got a thing for him?"

"He's waiting for Lake's approval. I don't think that'll ever happen."

"I'll talk to Lake," she offers. "He's getting used to having a little sister, but it's taking some time."

"I've never had a brother, and it's nice to have someone who cares, but he's taking it too seriously. I need him to back off."

She nods. "Noted."

Vinn joins us, and Sara makes an excuse to leave us alone. He pours me a glass of wine. "I liked what you did up there," he says. "Raven's drawing up a contract."

"Contract?" I repeat. Usually, things aren't so formal.

"I like to do things properly. I can offer three nights a week. Any extras are forbidden, but you can dance in private rooms. You decide to give extras, that's your business, but if you get caught, it's an instant dismissal." He slides a business card across the bar. "That's my number if you—"

Storm's hand slams down on top of the card before I can take it, and Vinn smirks. "She don't need it. Just like she don't need your job."

"Storm," I hiss, feeling my cheeks redden with embarrassment.

"You sure about that, biker?" asks Vinn. "She approached me."

"Yes, I want the job. Storm, stop," I snap.

"You're not fucking stripping for other men like some kinda whore, Lottie. It's not happening."

I stand on wobbly legs, rage rushing through me. "You are not my boss," I growl. "I can make my own decisions and there is nothing wrong with my job choice."

"Me or the job, that's your choice," he hisses, holding up Vinn's business card.

I glance at Vinn, who looks like he's enjoying the altercation. I swallow the lump in my throat before plucking the card from his fingers. "I'll be in touch about my hours, Vinn. Thank you." I turn on my heel and head for the exit.

It's late, but Bently was whining and wouldn't settle, which is why I'm walking around the club grounds wrapped in one of the guys' oversized jumpers I found on the back of the couch in the main room.

It smells like Storm's aftershave, and I bury my nose into the material as I round the back of the clubhouse.

I yelp when hands pull my arms behind my back and I'm pressed against the wall. "You don't get it," hisses Storm, and I sag in relief. "I can't just walk away from you now." He lifts the jumper and pushes his erect cock into me.

"Storm, you can't keep fucking me against walls, then yelling at me and stomping off."

"I can't keep away from you," he pants.

I smell the whiskey on his breath and frown. "You've been drinking," I say.

He clamps a hand over my mouth and quickens his pace. "Less talking." This time, he comes and pulls out, not bothering to take care of me. Not that I need it—I've had my share of orgasms tonight.

"Why have you been drinking?" I ask quietly.

He shrugs, staring down at the ground. "I only had a couple."

"Are you meant to have a couple?" He's not exactly said he's a raging alcoholic, but he gives me the impression he shouldn't drink.

"My head's all over," he mutters.

"Why are you making it difficult? We like each other, don't we?" I ask, and he nods. "Then let's give it a go."

"I can't sit back knowing other men are watching you dance like that. You're mine. My broken butterfly. I can't have them wanking over you, looking at you."

"It's just a job. I like dancing. I won't do private dances. I won't let anyone touch me and I won't interact with customers up close. I'll dance, I'll get my money, and I'll come home. I'd like to come home to you."

He stares at me with hope in his eyes. "I'm a mess," he says. "I don't know if I can be the man you need."

I take his hand. "Let's be a mess together."

STORM

I've woken with a hangover every day since I started drinking that night in the caravan. Taya eyes me across the breakfast table as I push the bacon around my plate.

"We need to look at a school for Seb today," she says. "He's missed too much." I nod, not bothering to look up. "I've rang three schools."

"Can't you go and choose?" I ask.

"No, I'm not his mum. Maybe if you weren't hungover, you'd be more enthusiastic," she snaps sarcastically.

"Get off my fucking back, Tay," I snap. "You're like a nagging wife."

"We need to have a conversation sooner rather than later," she says. "I can't take much more of this."

I push my chair back and lean towards her. "Then fucking go," I yell. "If you can't support me, then just go."

A look of hurt flashes over her face. "Maybe I will." She rushes from the room, and I groan, sitting down and burying my face in my hands. I have to get my shit together. I can't look after Seb without her. Since his diagnosis of autism, I've not been able to cope. His hour-long meltdowns and obsession with bikes drive me nuts. I was never good with him, not like his mum was. Her face appears in my head again, and I close my eyes. Some days, when she appears like this, so clear, I feel like I can reach out and grab her. She's wearing the floppy straw hat I brought her the last summer we had together. A light touch on my arm brings me crashing back into the room, and I scowl at Lottie. "You okay?" she asks.

I nod, getting up. "I've got some shit to do. I'll see you tonight." I kiss her on the head and leave. I need a cold shower to get me out of this mood.

"We have a sensory room," says the head teacher, opening a door. Seb claps in delight and rushes inside. Taya joins him, leaving me alone with this woman, and I smile awkwardly. "Any questions?" she asks, but I shake my head. It looks the same as the last two schools we looked at. "We have some other children here from your club," she says with a smile. "They're doing very well, and Seb would be in their class."

"Right. Let's sign him up then," I mutter.

After, as we head to the car, Seb slips his hand into mine. I glance at Taya, who looks just as shocked as me. It's not like we don't touch. He lets me pick him up and carry him when needed, although these days, he's a little old for that. But he hasn't held my hand in a long time. "Malia comes here?" he asks, and I nod. He smiles. "Good."

"I think he's like you when it comes to women," whispers Taya on the drive home. I give her a side glance. "Obsessed."

"I don't get obsessed," I say. "I get serious."

"Same thing," she says. "I've seen how he gets with Malia. He doesn't like Ziggy around her."

"Kid's obsessed with all kinds of shit," I say. "It'll pass."

"I'm sorry for earlier. I'm just worried." She looks up at me through her eyelashes, just like she did as a kid, and my heart melts.

I take her hand in mine and squeeze it. "I'm gonna be okay," I say. "I promise. I know I don't say it enough, but I appreciate everything you do for me and Seb. We'd be lost without you."

Chapter Six

LOTTIE

I haven't seen Storm all day. I climb into bed and fall into a deep sleep, only waking when the bed dips and I smell his aftershave. He doesn't waste any time burying himself inside me until I'm crying out into my pillow. When he's finished, he wraps himself around me and his light snores fill the room. I feel disappointed. All we seem to do is fuck. I wanted to talk with him about last night and about my job choice, but he doesn't seem too keen on talking lately.

It's still dark outside when he enters me again. I don't have the energy to argue, so when he falls asleep straight after again, I get up and shower. It's almost six a.m. and Bently needs a walk.

When I return, Storm is awake and showered. "I thought we could go job hunting today," he says brightly.

"You need a job?" I ask.

"For you," he says, chuckling. He heads out the room and downstairs with me hot on his heels. Looks like we're having that conversation after all.

"Storm, I have a job."

The breakfast table is full, and I regret starting this right before we joined them. "We talked about it, and you're not working in some damn strip club."

The chatter dies down a little, and I feel myself blush. Lake watches us closely. "I'm a dancer, it's what I do."

"Not anymore," says Storm. "No ol' lady of mine is getting her tits out for other men to look at." There's a few audible gasps from the women in the room.

"At last, someone talking sense," mumbles Lake.

"Please, don't you start," I mutter.

"Have some respect for yourself and for me. What will people say if I let you strip?" snaps Storm.

"They'll think you're a lucky son of a bitch," says Leia.

"You want money?" he adds, completely ignoring Leia. "I can give you whatever you need." He pulls out his wallet and dumps a wad of cash in front of me.

My face reddens further. "I don't want your money," I state.

"And I don't want you to strip."

"We'll talk about it later," I say firmly.

"My mind won't change."

Everyone is now paying attention to our argument, and I feel more and more embarrassed and insulted by the second. I slide the money back to him. "Then we can't be together," I say, "if you can't accept my decision."

Storm glares at me, his nostrils flaring. "I need some air," he growls, storming from the room.

"Wow. I thought he was gonna explode," whispers Leia. "He looks murderous when he's mad."

I take a seat at the table, my whole body trembling. After a few seconds, everyone gets back to their conversations, and I glance at the door, wondering if I just did the right thing.

It's my first official night working for Vinn and I'm nervous for two reasons. One being it's always nerve-racking to get up on stage and dance, and two, because I haven't seen Storm since he went off at breakfast in a mood.

I half expect him to be blocking the doorway when it's time for me to leave, but he isn't there, and I'm not sure if that makes me happy or worried. Lake's watching as I pass. He eyes the heels I'm holding in my hand. They're my favourite pair to dance in. "So, you're going ahead with it?"

"Yes," I say, pushing the door to open.

"I was against you and Storm, but after seeing he agrees with me on this, I'm more inclined to agree to whatever is going on between you."

I stop and turn to face him. "There's nothing going on anymore. And I don't know why you think you have a right to control my life," I say. "I was doing just fine before I found you."

Lake scoffs. "Didn't you fuck your way through other MC clubs?"

I gasp. "No, why would you think I did?"

"Impression I got. Weren't you hanging out with Cobras when you got brought back here?"

"That doesn't mean I was a whore!" I snap. "I was looking for you." I pinch the bridge of my nose and sigh. "I don't wanna fight. I'm so glad I found you, I really am, but stop interfering in my life. I don't like it."

"If you're hooking up with a biker, then get used to it. No man wants his woman getting naked in front of a room full of men. Storm will likely be waiting there for you."

Lake's right. As I pull into the carpark, I see Storm's familiar figure leaning against his bike. He approaches my car before I have a chance to get out, then he opens the door and braces his hands on the roof. "Don't step out of there," he mutters.

"Storm, we went over this. It's just a job. I love dancing and I'm good at it. You can watch and see I don't let anyone near me."

"Don't make me lock you up, Lottie. It'll break me to see you sad."

I narrow my eyes. "Are you drunk?"

"I told you we aren't good for each other," he slurs. "That's where you went? To drink yourself stupid because I wouldn't do as I'm told?" I snap. I'm mad he'd turn to drink as soon as things got heated. I pull out my mobile and call Riggs.

"What are you doing?" he asks, trying to take my phone. "Riggs, you need to come and get Storm. He's at Vinn's club really drunk and he's been driving. He'll get hurt or kill someone," I say. Riggs tells me he's on his way, and I check my watch, noting I have twenty minutes before I have to be on stage.

Getting out of the car, I feel around in Storm's pocket, confiscating his bike keys. He smirks. "You ever done it out in the open like this, somewhere this busy?"

"You're drunk. Riggs is coming to get you, and I need to get into work." I take his hand and pull him towards the club. Vinn can watch Storm while I do my thing.

Vinn looks mildly annoyed when I explain, handing him Storm's bike keys. "Riggs is on his way. I'm really sorry," I say.

"Go and change. I'll keep this arsehole under control."

By the time my first dance is up, I'm so anxious, I feel sick. I'm the reason he drank today. I'm the reason he got himself into a mess. Guilt eats away at me, and I practically run off stage to change and head back to Vinn's office. Riggs is there already.

"Are you okay?" I ask Storm, but he turns his head away from me. Riggs gives me a sympathetic smile. "Storm?"

"You did it," he mumbles. "I asked you not to, and you did it anyway. I'm done." He stands on wobbly legs as Riggs steadies him. "Let's go," he adds.

"That's it?" I snap at his retreating back. "Just like that?"

"Looks that way, butterfly." And then, he's gone.

I turn to Vinn, who's smirking. "You made a good choice," he says, shrugging. "An independent woman will go far. You don't wanna be relying on a man for money. And, once you give in on one thing, he'll have you giving in to everything. Before you know it, you'll be stuck at home with six kids hanging off you, wondering when you stopped making your own decisions."

"Would you let your girl dance?" I ask, and he laughs, throwing his head back.

"Not a fucking chance."

Anna curls her legs underneath her. She was awake when I finally finished work at three a.m., tending to her baby. I drop down beside her. "I don't know how I finished my shift," I say. "All I could think about was Storm."

"These men have a way of getting inside your head and heart without you knowing."

"He ended it, and I don't blame him," I mutter. "It's been nothing but drama since we got together, and even then, he never really said the words. I told him to give us a chance, and then I went and got a job I knew he'd hate."

"Don't be so hard on yourself. It's your life and you can choose what you do with it. If he truly likes you, he'll find a way to work past this."

"It's a lot to ask, though, isn't it," I point out.

"Your relationship is still very new," says Anna. "Does he have a right to make demands?"

"I really like him," I admit. "Then dance in a nightclub with your friends, leave the stage. It's not like you can't go back if things don't work out."

I nod. "It was the principle—I don't like being told what to do," I admit. "But when it comes down to it, I'd rather be with him than dance, I guess. And I hate that I made him sad enough to reach for the bottle."

"I'm sure we have bar work available if you want to make your own money," says Anna, and I smile gratefully. "And Sara is always looking for extra hands at her place."

I head upstairs feeling much better. I'll make things right with Storm properly in the morning, but right now, I just need to feel him beside me, so I head straight for his room. I push his door and stick my head in, freezing as my eyes land on the figure next to him. I flick on the light, and he covers his eyes with his arm, groaning. One of the club girls sits up, the covers falling away to reveal her naked chest. I arch my brow. "What the fuck?" I yell.

Storm bolts upright, his eyes falling to the girl and then to me. "Shit," he mutters.

"I was gonna pack the job in. I was coming in here to apologise," I shout. Anna comes rushing up the stairs. She observes the scene before her and takes me gently by the arm.

"Come on, it's not worth it," she whispers.

STORM

I lift the sheets and see I'm naked too. Groaning, I flop back onto the bed. "You said you two were done," Trudy says, running her fingers over my chest. I still her hand. I haven't turned to a club girl in months. Damn the fucking drink.

"We're done," I mutter. "But that don't make this right. Get out."

"After the things we just did," she snaps, "that's how you're gonna be?"

"Get out!" I yell, and she jumps in fright, throwing the sheets from her naked body and storming from the room, leaving her clothes behind.

I feel like history is repeating itself. If Laura could see me now . . . I shake my head, laughing with disgust. I'm a fucking mess.

I wake suddenly from the banging at the door. "What?" I yell.

Taya storms in. "I'm done. Get up, get showered, and come take care of your kid. I'm going shopping."

"Huh?" I mumble, confused.

"You have to start taking care of Seb because I can't do it alone. You're his dad. I found out you were drunk again last night. I'm here watching Seb, and you're hitting the bottle and fucking whores. So, take this as your warning—start helping or I will take him away and you won't see him again," she snaps.

I glare at her. She has legal guardianship over him, so she can take him if she chooses. "You're threatening me?"

"Damn right, I am. Now, get up!"

Seb lines his colouring pens up in rainbow order. I used to find those quirks so irritating, but as I watch the concentration on his face, I find myself smiling. He eventually chooses the red one and colours in the picture of a bike. We walked to the park and had some lunch. It went smoothly, and I realised how far he's come since those early days where he'd spend all our time together screaming. I never knew what to do to make him stop. His sock wasn't on right, or his shoe rubbed, then he hated the buzzing sound of the light that only he could fucking hear, I just couldn't cope with all his demands, so I just gave up. My phone flashes up a text, but when I open it, I see it's from Laura and I frown.

Laura: Stop calling me. I had twenty missed calls. I will tell Tommy if this continues. You're breaking your order and I will send you back to prison.

I delete the message. I must have called her when I was drunk. I got my phone back from Riggs after getting with Lottie, like I was somehow fucking cured. Glancing up as Lottie passes, she looks hot in jeans and a tight top. "Can we talk?" I ask, but she ignores me.

"Is Lottie mad at you?" Seb asks, and I nod. "Draw her a picture. Malia loves my pictures," he says, handing me a pencil. I smile. If only it was that simple. But Seb stares at me until I put pencil to paper, so I write a quick note, asking her to give me just five minutes of her time to explain. Seb folds it extremely carefully, lining up the edges, before excitedly running over to give it to her. She smiles brightly at him when she takes it, giving me some hope, but it's soon dashed when she reads it and rolls her eyes.

"I don't think it worked," whispers Seb as she stuffs it in her pocket. "Malia always kisses my cheek when I give her my pictures."

"Maybe I need to try harder?" I suggest.

"Balloons," says Seb. "Every girl likes balloons."

I love the way he's so invested. "Looks like we're going to buy balloons," I say.

He claps happily as we walk to the florist a few streets away. The young girl behind the counter hands me a dozen foil balloons tied together by a small heart-shaped weight. As we head back to the club, I get some strange stares. I feel like a fucking idiot, but if it makes her talk to me, I'll gladly look an idiot.

"She's in her room," mutters Anna coldly.

We place them outside, knocking on the door and rushing to hide. She looks at the balloons, rolls her eyes again, and closes the door. We watch sadly as the balloons dance in the backdraft. "That didn't work either," mutters Seb.

"We won't give up, kid," I say, ruffling his hair. "It was a great idea, and I'm sure she'll talk to me eventually."

"I have a job on," announces Riggs in church. "Vinn needs a man in front of the stage tonight. All you gotta do is sit there when the dancers are on—"

"I'll take it," I say quickly before anyone else can jump in.

Riggs' eyes narrow in on me. "You sure, brother? I don't want any drama with you and Lottie."

"It's all good, Pres."

He nods. "Okay, fine. Don't let it become an issue."

After church, it's time for me to head straight to Vinn's club. It won't be easy watching Lottie up onstage, but if it means I'll be close to her, then it's what I have to do. Maybe she'll even start talking to me again.

The club is a hive of activity when I arrive—girls are walking around half-naked, security is doing radio checks, and Vinn's at the bar tapping away on his laptop. He glances up and rolls his eyes. "You," he mutters.

"The one and only."

"And Riggs thought you were the best man for the job?"

"I offered, he accepted."

"I wonder why you offered," he says, closing his laptop. "Are you gonna cause me any problems?"

I shake my head. "No, sir."

"Lottie is one of my best girls. You cause her any problems tonight, I'll kick your ass out myself." He stands, getting the attention of the barman. "No one is to serve this guy alcohol, understand?" The barman nods.

I take a seat on a stool next to the stage. It's facing out to the crowd, so I don't have to watch Lottie do her thing for other men. I'm thankful for that, at least.

Chapter Seven

LOTTIE

"What?" I almost yell with surprise into my phone.

"Yep, Riggs just told me now," says Anna. "Apparently, Storm's there tonight. I just thought you'd want the heads up so it's not such a shock when you get out there and see him."

"Thanks, Anna," I mutter. Suddenly, my nerves are off the scale.

I take a deep breath in and release it slowly. I have to focus on the crowd, not him. I can do this. I step onto the brightly-lit stage. The music starts before I'm ready, and I almost stumble my first few steps. I glare at the backstage team and the music stops. Taking a seat with my back to the crowd, I spread my legs, placing my hands on my knees and lowering my head. I push all thoughts of Storm from my mind as the beat begins once again.

STORM

With the music stopping and starting, I turn to see what's going on. My breath catches in my throat. Seeing Lottie in a purple corset and tall heels is breathtaking. But then I remember everyone else in here can see her, and as she takes her position, I grip the edge of my stool to keep me from pulling her offstage and locking her away. I focus back on the crowd, but somehow, that's worse. Seeing men's eyes glued to the stage where my woman dances half naked, I shake my head. I can't blow this, or she'll never speak to me again.

I fix my eyes to the ground because it's the only place I can look without wanting to rip someone's head off. Some of the guys at the front table begin chanting the word 'off'. It looks like some kind of stag party. I glance to the head of security, and when he nods, I approach the table. "You gotta keep it down, boys," I say firmly.

"Sorry, we'll behave," says one of the guys, who then proceeds to shush the others. *See, I can do this. I can act like a grown man.*

When I turn back to my seat, Lottie is closer to the edge of the stage than I realised. She's now in panties, stockings, and suspenders, and her hands are covering her breasts. I lock eyes with her. She doesn't get fully naked, she told me. There's a twinkle in her eye and a smirk on her lips as she removes her hands, placing them in her hair instead, and pouts sexily at the group of men. They all go wild, whistling and cheering as the music dies. She turns and heads backstage, her ass wiggling with each step, while my jealous eyes burn holes into the back of her head.

LOTTIE

"Shit, Lottie, you made a killing," says Raven, handing me a bunch of cash. "I thought you didn't like to get naked," she adds.

"There was a drunk group up front. I knew they'd tip more."

"They certainly did. Even asked if you do private dancing," she says.

"Really?"

"They seemed keen. You wanna do it?" I chew on my lip. I hate private dancing in case they get too hands-on. Raven senses my dilemma. "The no touching rule applies, and security can watch through the one-way mirror if you feel they'll be too much."

"Okay, why not? I have twenty minutes until my next show."

"I'll set it up. Red room in two minutes."

"Not Storm," I say to her retreating back. "Get someone else from the security team."

I dance my ass off. All the guys are given the rules by security before they come in, so they're all sitting on their hands like good little boys while I shake my ass for all it's worth. I don't know when I became so into dancing—I just remember always doing it. I frown as a flashback of me as a kid enters my mind, but as quick as it comes, it disappears. I shake the memory away and continue to dance. "This one's getting married next week," says one of the guys.

I smile at the groom-to-be and move closer, placing my hands on his shoulders. "Don't do it," I joke.

"I said yes so I could have the stag party," he admits, and the other guys laugh.

The dance comes to an end, and even though the guys have already paid up, they stuff notes in my hand. I agree to see them at the bar for a drink.

STORM

The stage light goes out, and I stand, stretching my legs. There's a five-minute interval before the next dance, so I head towards the bar to order a Coke. I spot Lottie at the end in her underwear, chatting to the rowdy group. She sees me glaring and turns her back to me, which only pisses me off more. "Ouch, she's really testing you," says Vinn. "Getting naked onstage, private dancing, and now at the bar with a groom looking to have one last night of freedom."

"Private dancing?" I growl.

"Yep, she just took that whole group in the red room for a five-minute show. Man, she made almost five hundred for five minutes of work."

I make a move towards Lottie, but Vinn pulls me back. "Should I get someone to fill in for her? She's next up."

"No, I'll have her back in time," I grit out.

"Remember what I said—no drama," he adds.

Lottie looks at me, her expression bored. "We need to talk," I say.

"Take the hint," she mutters. The men shift uncomfortably.

"Lottie, don't make me carry you outta here," I warn.

"Hey, man, relax," says one of the guys, tapping me on the shoulder.

I snatch his hand in mine and bend it backwards. He yelps. "Don't put your hands on me again," I snarl.

"Fuck," hisses Lottie. "Fine, we'll talk." She stomps off towards the exit, and I follow.

It's freezing outside, but she folds her arms and glares at me. "Make it quick."

"I'm sorry for what I did," I begin.

"For getting blind drunk? For turning up at my job two nights running? For sleeping with someone the first chance you got?"

I sigh. "All of the above. Technically, we'd had sex a few times, but we weren't really official so—" Her eyes widen, and I realise I ain't making the situation any better. "I fucked up. More than once. I'm sorry, okay."

She shrugs. "Okay."

I smile with relief. "That's it? We're all good?"

She nods, pulling the door open to head back inside. "Yep. Enjoy the rest of the night."

"I mean, are we good, me and you?" I ask, following her inside.

"Yes," she repeats.

I take her wrist, turning her to face me, hardly believing it was that easy. I pull her towards me, and she frowns, placing her hands against my chest and stepping back. "Oh, you meant are we okay as in carrying on from where we left off?" she asks, and I nod. A smile pulls at the corners of her mouth. "Then, no, baby. We ain't fine."

LOTTIE

I grin at Raven. "You are a star," I say.

"It was Anna who brought them over," she says. I stare at the foil balloons Storm brought for me earlier today, like balloons can make it better. The fact he even thought they could makes this revenge all the more sweeter. "You want them onstage?" she asks.

I nod. "Yes, please, all part of the set."

As I pass the music tech guy, I hand him a note with my new song choice. He grins, shrugging and tapping the song title into his laptop.

Once out onstage, Demi Lovato's "Sorry Not Sorry" begins to play, and I smile as I start to move to the music.

I have Storm's full attention, and he must be wondering why I've put the balloons onstage. He's standing at the front, watching me move, looking mad as hell with each word that Demi sings. I lip sync the words, which only causes him to look more and more annoyed. Taking a balloon from the bunch, I move sexily down the steps and towards the crowd, handing it to a woman sitting near the front. I proceed to hand out the balloons one by one, smirking each time I pass him.

As the song comes to an end, I take the last balloon and move towards Storm. His ice-cold stare burns into me as I place my hand on his shoulder and move against him. The last words echo around the room, and I grip the foil balloon, turning away from him and pushing my arse against his groin. I dig my nails into the foil hard, until it pops, then I drop the deflated globe by his feet, take a bow, and head back onto the stage, feeling satisfied with my little performance. Fuck Storm.

I sit in the change room, slowly wiping off the layers of makeup that hide the marks on my arms. I always cover them before a performance because there's always one ass wanting to point them out or ask questions. I run a finger over the angry red welts. The newer ones are still healing, and I gently press my nail against the join. It splits easily and I watch the crimson bubble surface. When the door opens with a bang, I jump in fright and hide my arm behind my back. Storm is glaring at me, his nostrils flared and anger pouring from his body. "I'll take you home," he growls.

"I have my car," I say.

"Tiny took it," he mutters, and I grab my bag to search for my car keys. "You took my keys?"

"Be ready in five minutes," he snarls, slamming the door closed. My heart beats hard in my chest. I wasn't expecting to have to get on his bike right after I angered the beast inside of him. *Fuck.*

I find him leaning against his bike. "Don't do that again," I say coldly. "Don't take my things without my permission."

"Are you proud of your performance tonight?" He sneers.

I nod. "I made plenty of money, so I think there were a lot of people pleased with my performance."

He throws his leg over his bike and pushes his helmet on. I take the spare and do the same. "I'm gonna sit back and let you do this," he says, his voice crackling through the speaker in the helmet. "Because I can't let you go."

"Are we forgetting about the whore in your bed this morning?" I snap. "You think you can give me your blessing like I need it? Get your head from up your arse."

I hear his growl as he turns the bike into oncoming traffic. Cars screech, beeping their horns, and I grip onto him and squeeze my eyes closed. When I reopen them, I see he's driving in the opposite direction from the clubhouse. "Storm, what are you doing?"

"Doing what I've been wanting to do for days."

We stop at Storm's favourite place—the caravan. I shove my helmet against his chest. "This is crazy."

"We're staying here until you hear me out. I deserve a second chance."

I scoff at his boldness. "Who the hell do you think you are? The king? I decide if you get a second chance with me, not you!"

He grabs hold of my wrist and pulls me towards the caravan. I try to pull free, but his grip is strong, and even though I drag my feet, I end up in the caravan with him. He locks the door and stands in front of it while I look around at the empty bottles. "Party for one, was it?"

"I was here alone, if that's what you're asking," he says bluntly.

"Like I trust your word." I scoff, sitting down.

"Ask me anything," he says desperately. "I'll answer all your questions." I eye him suspiciously. There's so much I want to know about him, but now doesn't feel right to ask. I'm here against my will, and he's acting crazy. I pull out my phone, and he snatches it from my grasp. "No phones."

"Storm, you're starting to freak me out," I mutter as he shoves it into a lockable cupboard.

"Seb's mum died."

I suck in a breath as Storm takes a seat. "My real name is Jaxon Michaels. They call me Storm because I go in full-on. I just storm on in there. Like I've done with you."

"You don't have to tell me this," I mutter. "It won't change anything."

"She died when he was still small. She had cervical cancer. It was quick—they told us and a month later, she was gone. She hadn't even started treatment. She had died the same day Seb had his diagnosis for autism, and I was so pissed. I thought it was something we did to him, and I walked out in anger. Everything was going to shit and I lost control. I hate not having control, so I went off and I drank. I got so shitfaced because I wanted it all to go away. When I came back, she was gone. Just like that."

My heart aches for him, and I reach across the table, gently placing my hand on his arm. "I'm so sorry," I whisper.

"I can't sit here and tell you Lucy meant nothing. She was my world, and I loved her so hard. Losing her was the most painful thing I ever went through and I'm barely out alive. I started drinking more after that. Taya had to come in and take over with Seb cos I couldn't do it. I didn't know fuck all about sensory overload or meltdowns. That was her thing, she knew all that shit. I didn't know why he'd only fucking eat certain chicken nuggets or why the fuck he wouldn't just . . . stop . . . screaming. He'd cry all the time, and I'd lock myself in my room so I didn't have to watch him fall apart. He wanted her too, and I couldn't bring her back for him, for us. Taya couldn't get help for him with the medical services and shit, and since I wasn't around and Lucy was dead, she had me sign papers to take custody of him. It was best for Seb at the time."

"She's done great with him. Seb's an amazing kid."

"Then I met Laura. Things got better for a while, but she didn't like me drinking. She hated my possessive streak, and wouldn't listen to why I tracked her phone or turned up where she was. She saw it as stalking, while I saw it as love because I wanted back what I had with Lucy. Lucy was like me. She liked that I loved her so much, and maybe people were right, maybe it was toxic—the fights, the drama—but it worked for us. Then she was gone, and those same behaviours wouldn't work with Laura, so she eventually kicked me out, said I was too full-on. She got a restraining order after she met her new guy, and he couldn't deal with me calling her and checking in."

"And you still contact her?" I ask.

He nods. "Every time I drink. Sometimes when I'm sober. I'm a fucking mess."

"You're heartbroken, Storm. It's not your fault."

"When I drink, I try to forget. It's not an excuse, but taking the club girl to my bed was a way to forget. I'm sorry I fucked up."

I pull my hand back. "Thanks for sharing. I get it, I really do, but I have my own shit to deal with and I'm not strong enough to deal with yours too."

He nods, avoiding my eyes. "As long as you know I'm sorry. That's all I wanted to say."

It's on the tip of my tongue to spill my life story, but I hold it in. He needs to talk, and he needs me to listen. My heart is too torn to let him in with all his emotional baggage. And I know, just from how I feel after a few weeks of knowing him, that I'll fall madly in love and it'll only end one way—me with a blade and him with a bottle.

Chapter Eight

STORM

I feel lighter. Telling someone else I'm a mess makes it easier to deal with. Lottie didn't judge me or look at me with pity. I took her back to the clubhouse as soon as we'd cleared the air, and we're speaking again. It's all I wanted.

The next morning, Taya leaves Seb with me again. She also seems happier, and I wonder what she's doing when she's away from us. I watch Seb run around with Bently nipping at his heels. He loves the dog, and Lottie agreed to come for a walk around the yard with us.

"You're wearing long sleeves," I say, nodding to her covered arms.

She gives an uneasy smile and pulls them down over her hands. "So?"

"You haven't worn them since your last hospital visit."

"I feel chilly today." She shrugs.

"Or you cut yourself last night."

"I really didn't. Let's just enjoy the walk."

"Show me," I say. She stops walking, and I turn to her. "If you haven't, then show me." I carefully reach for her arm, and she watches as I begin to roll up her sleeve. Touching her gives me all kinds of thoughts, but I try to dampen those down because this is not the time.

"Jax . . ." I glance up at the sound of my birth name and frown in confusion as Laura totters towards us in six-inch heels. She takes my breath away, and I drop Lottie's arm.

"Laura?" She reaches up and wraps her arms around me, which only confuses me more. "Is everything okay?"

"I was passing and I remembered you saying you were staying here and—"

"Passing from Nottingham?" I ask sceptically.

"Details, details," she says, waving her hand in the air. "Seb, my darling boy," she adds, rushing to Seb and kissing him on the head. He pulls away slightly, hating that she touched him without warning. He'll only let people he's comfortable around do that. *Why wasn't that ever a warning sign to me before?*

"This your ex?" whispers Lottie, and I nod. "She's not what I was expecting," she adds, arching a brow.

"What were you expecting?"

"Someone a little less," she pauses to think of the right word, "trophy wife." Laura is exactly that. I was drawn to her blonde hair and stunning face. Her makeup was always perfectly in place, and she wouldn't be caught dead in anything but designer. It was refreshing at the time and totally the opposite of what I'd always gone for previously.

"Can we go for a chat?" asks Laura.

"I have Seb," I mutter.

"Oh, I thought she was the nanny or something," she says, glaring at Lottie, who laughs and smacks me on the shoulder in a friendly yet hard whack.

"You go and rekindle your love. I'll watch Seb." She walks off before I can object. "Come on, Seb, let's walk the hound," she adds a little too joyfully, and Seb claps his hands and runs after Bently.

"We're not meant to be near each other," I say. "What happened to you wanting that?"

"Things with Tommy and me have ended," she replies, her eyes fixed to the ground. "I just needed to see you."

"So I can help you get over him?" I snap.

"Don't be like that, baby," she says, pouting. "I can have the restraining order cancelled."

I cast my eyes to where Lottie and Seb are running around on the grass. "You can't be here."

"I don't have anyone else," she wails. "Can't I at least stay with you for a few nights until I find somewhere else?"

"What's wrong with Nottingham?"

"I've outgrown it. I'm here to make a career for myself," she says. "I'm in contact with a modelling agency."

I roll my eyes. "I'm not sure you staying here is a good idea."

"Please, just two nights. I have an interview tomorrow. It's the least you owe me."

"I owe you?" I snap. "I didn't do anything but love you and look how you repaid me. Tommy is a photographer, so did you use him to get some pictures done?" I'd suspected it at the time, but she always denied it. Now, she gives a sheepish smile.

"Please, Jax. Just a couple of nights while I get the interview done."

"Look, I'll ask the Pres, but he might say no. I've caused him enough drama as it is."

"No," says Riggs firmly.

"Come on, Pres. Two nights," I push.

"Are you stupid?" he snaps. "It could land you in prison. You're breaking a court order. Why the hell is she here anyway? She thought you were bad enough to get the order, yet she turns to you for help?"

"She's got a job interview or some shit. But I feel guilty, I owe her this."

"Two nights?" he asks, and I nod. He sighs. "Just two nights. If the cops come, you're on your own. I'm not bailing your ass out for your own stupidity. She's in your room, you sleep with her or on the couch, I don't care. But make sure she doesn't go snooping around."

I smile gratefully. "Thanks, Pres."

As I'm heading for the door, he calls me back. His expression is serious. "Look, I agreed to have you here. I heard you were a single dad and that spoke to me. It's no secret I want to expand the club and new members come with that, but I'll be honest, you're causing me more headaches than anyone here right now." He rubs his forehead. "I like you, Storm. I see myself in you. But you gotta get your shit together. For Seb, for Taya, for yourself, and for the club. And fuck, even for Lottie, if that's how you wanna play it. Lake won't let you mess his sister around, and this club's had way too much drama on that front."

I nod. "I hear yah," I mutter.

"You hear me, but are you listening, brother? Get it together or you're gone. I got charters all over crying out for new members, and I'll move you on."

"I'll sort myself out, I swear on Seb's life."

"One last thing," he says. "Is Lottie okay? Anna is worried about her."

"She will be," I say.

LOTTIE

"Hasn't he told you about her?" whispers Leia.

I shake my head and pop another grape in my mouth. Since walking with Seb earlier, he hasn't left my side, so we're at the kitchen table colouring pictures of bikes. "All I know is she got an injunction out against him, so I figured that's the reason he moved here."

"I don't like her," says Frankie. She slices the onions a little too hard and almost cuts her finger. "Shit," she hisses.

"You don't even know her," says Raven. "She looks nice enough."

"Is she club material?" asks Frankie, arching her brow doubtfully. "I think not."

"You said that about me," Anna points out.

"Different circumstances," says Frankie. "Riggs is my son, so I have a duty to hate all new women in his life. And actually, I really liked you. I was just worried about your ex."

"But my point is, everyone deserves a chance. She might be really nice, and she might fit in just right," says Raven.

Leia offers me a sympathetic smile. "Just what you need to hear, right," she whispers, and I return the smile. I can't complain. I told

Storm straight I can't deal with his shit right now, so he's free and single.

"Well, Riggs said she ain't stopping long. Storm asked for two nights. She's got an audition for a modelling job," says Anna.

"She's moving to London?" I blurt out, and all eyes fall to me.

"I don't know. Maybe it's a one-off job?" says Anna.

"It doesn't matter either way. You're over him, remember?" Leia snaps. "He treated you like crap."

"I know," I mutter. "I'm just not quite at the 'let his ex move in' stage yet."

The kitchen door opens, and Laura walks in. We all fall silent and busy ourselves as she looks around the room. "Storm told me to come in here and introduce myself," she says.

"We know who you are," snaps Frankie.

Anna stands. "Frankie," she hisses. "Hi, I'm Anna."

"I'm Leia, this is Lottie, and that's Raven." We all offer a small smile as Leia introduces us.

"And the miserable bag in the corner is Frankie," jokes Anna.

"I'm just wondering why you turned up here when you're not allowed to be around Storm," Frankie blurts out.

"Stop," hisses Anna, glaring wide-eyed at her.

"It's fine," says Laura. "Storm was obsessed. He was following me and being over the top. My boyfriend at the time encouraged me to go for the restraining order, but I wish I hadn't. It was a huge mistake."

"So, now you're here to claim him back?" asks Frankie.

"I don't know, I haven't decided. I want to take it slow."

Frankie scoffs. "You haven't decided, wow, it must be nice to have so much control in Storm's life."

"Like I said, he's obsessed with me."

"And let me guess," Frankie continues, placing the knife on the chopping board, "you need a little pick me up, some attention, and that's why you're here. Did your boyfriend dump you?" Laura's eyes fall to the floor, and Frankie laughs. "I've seen your type before. You swan in here like the queen bee you think you are and flutter those pretty false lashes, shove your tits in his face, and he's like a love-struck puppy. You'll let him follow you around and boost your ego until someone else comes along."

"Frankie," says Raven, sighing, "give her a break."

The door opens and Riggs enters. We all exchange sheepish looks as he assesses the room. "You ladies being friendly?" he growls out. His eyes narrow in on Frankie, who's gone back to chopping.

"We're just getting to know each other," says Anna.

"I need you," says Riggs, snatching Anna by the hand. "It's urgent."

"You dirty dog," says Leia, grinning. "It's the middle of the afternoon."

Riggs drags Anna from the kitchen, smirking at his sister. "Watch the baby," he orders.

Laura sits in the seat Anna vacated. The other women have changed the subject, and I pull my sleeves over my hands. I've been covering my body for so long, now it's become a habit. "Have you and Storm got a thing?" she asks in a low voice.

I shake my head. "No."

"Good. I just wanted to warn you if there was."

"Warn me?" I repeat.

"Well, it's clear you like him. I saw the way you tried to hide the hurt when I showed up here and took his attention. But that'll always be the way. It doesn't matter what happens between us, he'll always come back to me. He's crazy. He's obsessive and possessive. He'll never let me go." She looks smug, and I bite my lip. Her words hurt me more than they should.

I gently ruffle Seb's hair. "I've got things to do," I tell him. "I'll catch up with you later." He nods without looking up.

"You okay?" Storm's voice makes me jump, and I drop my hand from my bedroom door. I keep my back to him. Tears are brimming, and I can't let him see me like this. "Lottie?"

"I'm fine. Tired," I mutter.

"I was gonna ask if you wanted to go for a walk with Seb and the pup again. I enjoyed it earlier, well, until Laura showed up."

"I can't. Take the pup, though. Seb loves taking him out." I open the door, and Bently shoots out, jumping up my legs and barking playfully.

"Nah, it's fine," says Storm.

"Storm, take him. Seb would appreciate the quality time."

He scoffs. "What's that supposed to mean?"

"Nothing." I sigh. "I just think you should spend some time together. He's a great kid and—"

"You don't think I fuckin' know that?" he snaps, and I'm taken aback by his harsh tone. "I just thought you'd wanna join us." Bently sits by Storm's feet. "Forget it." He stomps off with the pup at his feet.

I blink and it releases a tear. I let it run down my cheek before swiping it away. She's been back two minutes, and he's already changing. What the hell is wrong with me? I slam the bedroom door and take a few deep breaths, glancing at the drawer beside my bed. I know it's there, that's the problem. I pull the drawer and stare at the small metal tin for a few seconds before closing it again.

I go to the window, pushing it open and taking a few deep breaths. I never wanted to feel anything for Storm. I fancied him the second he got to the club, but it wasn't supposed to turn into anything. I wasn't meant to like him properly. It wasn't supposed to hurt when he rejected me because that was always going to happen, so I should have seen it coming and prepared myself better. Even the club whores have more to offer than me. I look down at my arm and see blood through my sleeve. Without realising, I've scratched the old wounds, opening them up. My tears fall harder because as much as I want to stop this vicious cycle, seeing that blood gives me so much relief. Voices from below grab my attention. I see Bently running around on the grass with Seb chasing him excitedly. It brings a brief smile to my face, which soon fades when Storm and Laura follow on behind. They look good together. She's pretty and perfect and I'm . . . well, I'm just not.

I slam the window and rush back to the drawer. Fuck Storm. The second I pick up my tin, I feel better.

Chapter Nine

STORM

Laura's twisting my ear about some bullshit excuse for her and her boyfriend splitting up. I'm not stupid—he left her ass, and now she's back here looking for a fill-in. It ain't happening. We were done the second she called the cops on me.

I hear a bang and look towards the direction it came from in time to see Lottie move back from her window. I frown. Shit, she probably thinks Laura and I are down here making up. "Seb," I shout, and he turns around. "Come on, kid, we gotta go back inside."

"What?" asks Laura. "Why?"

"Something I gotta deal with."

I ask Leia to keep an eye on Seb, then I take the stairs two at a time. I have a bad feeling, and when I push open Lottie's door, my heart sinks. She looks up, her expression panicked. She begins to grab the sharps surrounding her, but it's too late, I've seen them. I slam the door shut and drop to my knees before her, gripping her bleeding arm. "What have you done," I whisper. There's a closed first aid kit beside her, and I flip it open. "Why do you keep marking your perfect skin?" I take out some antiseptic and unscrew the cap with my teeth, spitting it out and pouring the liquid over her arm. She hisses, watching the blood mix with the antiseptic and drip onto her jeans. "It won't stop you from hurting." I rip a bandage open. "If it did, you'd be all healed now." I start to wrap the wound. It's not too deep that it'd need stitches, but it's deep enough the doc will need to take a look.

"It does help," she whispers, and I stare into her red, swollen eyes. "For just a second or two."

"What are you running from, butterfly?"

She hangs her head, and her shoulders begin to shake. Tying off the bandage, I pull her into my arms, wrapping myself around her and letting her cry against my chest. We stay like that until my arse goes numb and Lottie's soft snores fill the room. I carefully pull her closer so I'm cradling her like a child, and I stand, sighing with relief as the blood rushes to my numb places. I lay her on the bed and unbutton her jeans. They're wet from the antiseptic and take some tugging to remove, but she hardly shifts. Slipping out of my kutte and jeans, I climb into bed beside her. I don't know if she wants me around, but my heart's telling me to stay. I don't want her to wake alone.

I lie awake with her against my chest, picturing her bloodied arm over and over in my mind, and my heart aches. It ain't like I ain't seen blood before but seeing hers drip from the wounds she put there, that feels different. After an hour, Lottie begins to stir. She sits up, looking around the dark room before peering down at me. The moonlight shines over her perfect face and that familiar ache returns. "You okay?" I whisper.

"You stayed?"

"Where else would I go?"

"Why?" she whispers.

I hook my little finger around hers. "Why not?" When she doesn't answer, I push myself to sit. "Do you want anything? You fell asleep before I could get you any painkillers." She shakes her head, avoiding eye contact. "You don't have to be ashamed," I mutter. "I'm not judging."

"I don't know why I do it," she whispers, and her words are laced with pain. She bows her head, and I run my fingers up and down her spine. "I get this knot in my stomach and nothing gets rid of it. That first cut," she pauses before sucking in a breath, "it releases the knot."

"Why was the knot there today, Lottie?" I ask. Her shoulders lift and fall in the shadow of moonlight. "Was it because of me?" She doesn't answer. "Because I was talking to Laura?"

"I'm a psycho, right?" She scoffs. "A guy pays me a smidgen of attention and I'm planning the fucking wedding. What's wrong with me?"

My heart swells a little. "You're not a psycho."

"Feel free to run. I get it. I'd run too if I was you. This," she holds up her bandaged arm, "is because I'm weird. It's not your fault. Just get out of here. I totally understand—"

I cut off her words, jumping over her and pushing her to lie back. "I don't wanna run," I whisper against her lips, and her breath hitches. "Nothing you said just then made me wanna go anywhere. I'm sorry I made you doubt what I feel for you. I was helping Laura out, but if that makes you feel like this, she'll be gone first thing."

"No," she objects. "I'm being crazy."

I press my lips against hers, and she opens for me, allowing my tongue to sweep against her own. I take my time, tasting her sweet mouth until my erection is painfully hard. "You're not crazy. If you had an ex staying, I'd kill him."

She smiles. "No chance of that ever happening, seeing as he's with my best friend."

"Good. Means you're here with me . . . where you belong."

Her face suddenly falls serious. "Storm, what happened before, with the club girl—"

I cut her off again, kissing her hard. "Won't happen again. Ever."

"Is this a bad idea?" she whispers, her eyes full of worry. "We're both so . . . broken."

"We'll fix each other," I say, running kisses along her jaw and down her neck. I push her shirt up, kissing my way down her stomach. Hooking my fingers in her lace panties, I drag them down her legs. "Promise me something," I say, pushing her legs apart. I run my tongue the length of her opening without warning, and she hisses, her hands gripping my hair. "You feel that knot again," I press my tongue against her swollen clit, sucking and nipping, "tell me. Don't reach for the blades."

I don't let her answer. Instead, I go to town on her pussy until she's writhing and panting on the bed beneath me, unable to get her words out. "We'll find new ways to release that tension," I promise her. I push my finger into her wetness with ease and hook it slightly until I feel her tense. Keeping up the pressure against that spot, I watch her perfect face flush with colour as her orgasm pulses through her. I lick her juices from my fingers, and she screws her face up, laughing. "Best taste ever," I say, smacking her arse. "Now, get some sleep. We gotta tell your brother about us."

LOTTIE

"Lake, you got a minute?" asks Storm.

Lake looks up from his phone. "Depends what for, brother," he mutters, his eyes going back and forth between me and Storm.

We take a seat on the opposite couch. "Lottie and me." Lake's face instantly morphs to anger. "We wanna make it work," Storm continues.

"Right, weren't you fucking Trudy a few nights ago?" snaps Lake. I lower my eyes because it still stings thinking about those two. "Trudy, get over here."

"Shit, brother, don't be an ass," mutters Storm.

Trudy sashays over with a smirk on her red-painted lips. "You and him?" asks Lake, pointing to Storm. "You fucking?"

"We did," she says, shrugging. "You both wanna join me?"

Lake shakes his head. "I have an ol' lady," he snaps. "Show some fucking respect."

"Why are you asking me who I'm fucking then?" she snaps impatiently.

"When was the last time?"

She shrugs. "A few nights ago." She glances at Storm for confirmation, and he shrugs, looking helplessly at me.

"This is ridiculous," I finally snap. "Lake, stop being a dick. We came here to ask your permission—not my idea but Storm's. As far as I'm concerned, I can make my own choices, but he doesn't want to cause bad blood between you both."

"Will you quit dancing?" asks Lake.

"Yes." I nod, and both men look at me surprised. "I respect you, and it makes you uncomfortable," I explain to Storm. "I don't want to be the reason you feel like that. I'll find something else." His bright smile is a big enough reward, and I'm happy I made that decision this morning after we made love for the second time.

"So, you're claiming her?" Lake asks coldly.

I feel panicked, waiting for Storm to answer. He never said those words when we talked about us being together. Claiming someone is practically agreeing to be with that person forever, and Lake's backing him into a corner. "If you'll give your blessing," Storm answers with ease, and I raise my brows in surprise. The fact he wants to claim me makes me happy. Now, it's clear we belong to each other, and the club girls can keep their grubby hands off him.

"If she wants you, who am I to say no," mutters Lake. "But take care of her, brother, because I don't wanna have to kill you." They shake hands, and Lake stalks off.

I turn to Storm and smile. "That was easier than I thought it would be."

"It's official," he says, pulling me onto his lap. I wrap my arms around his neck and kiss him slowly. When he pulls back, he's got that hungry look in his eyes again, and I laugh. "You can't keep kissing me like that, butterfly. We'll spend forever in bed." He scoops me up, and a surprised squeal escapes me. He marches towards the stairs with purpose but stops abruptly when he sees Laura coming down towards us. Her smile fades. "Laura, we need to talk," he mutters, lowering me to my feet and taking my hand in his. "Is now good for you?"

Her eyes fall to our joined hands. "Not really. Maybe later."

"It won't take long," he persists, and she rolls her eyes and flounces towards the couches in the main room.

"Shall I leave you to it?" I ask uncomfortably.

"No, you're my ol' lady and I want you to see that I'm serious."

"So," Laura says with a bored sigh, "you and little miss perfect are a thing?"

"Don't be rude," Storm says coldly. "But yeah, we're a thing. That means you can't stay here. You gotta go."

Her face reddens, and I'm not sure if she's upset or angry. "You said I could stay a few nights," she hisses.

"I said two nights, but things have changed. It ain't fair on Lottie."

"Last week, you were phoning me and leaving me messages telling me how much you miss me. How you can't find anyone who makes you feel like I made you feel," she snaps. "Now, you're moving on like I'm nothing to you?"

"I was drunk when I left those messages," he says.

"No surprise there then," she says dryly. "You always spoke the truth when you were drunk. Now, what was it you said?" She taps her chin thoughtfully. "That fucking me was the only way to stop yourself spiralling. Has that changed now? Is she your new whore, or is she like me, someone you depend on to keep you thinking straight?"

I absentmindedly rub my arm, liking the scratchy feel of the bandages against my wounds. Storm carefully places his hand over mine, forcing me to stop. "I don't know what to tell you, Laura. Yes, you helped me forget my problems, but they never went away. And when we ended, you made things worse for me. So much worse that I had to fucking move away. And now, here you are, following me to London and trying to set up home here, and I don't know what you expect me to do with that. I'm claiming Lottie, I'm serious about her, and that means you have to leave."

"Where the hell am I supposed to go?" she yells.

"A hotel?" he suggests, and she scoffs like that's absurd.

Laura stands and straightens her shirt, brushing off imaginary fluff. "A word of warning," she says quietly before fixing me with a hard stare. "He'll reel you in with a sob story about his dead ex, you'll bend over backwards to make him feel good, even pack in your job because he hates a working woman, and then, he'll treat you like a prisoner. He'll track your phone, check up on you, suffocate you. If I was you, I'd get out before you get in too deep."

I watch her stomp off. "I knew she'd take it badly, but Christ, she's so dramatic," says Storm. I smile, but it doesn't reach my eyes because her words are ringing in my ears. He sighs and hooks a finger under my chin, turning my face up to look at him. "Ignore her. She's just annoyed. If I was that bad, would she have come here to me for help?" I shake my head, and he places a gentle kiss on my nose. "I'm gonna talk to Riggs. I'll come find you when I'm done, then we can do something together?" I nod in agreement.

"That was intense," says Leia, joining me on the couch once Storm's left. "Is she leaving?" she asks, nodding towards Laura, who's passing us with her bags. I nod. "Ouch. No wonder she looked mad."

"She was mad because Storm told her he's claiming me."

"Shit!" Leia's eyes widen. "That's out of the blue, right?"

I shrug. "We've been going back and forth for weeks."

"He messed up badly, and now he's claiming you?"

"You think it's too soon?" I ask, rubbing my arm again.

"No, not at all. Everyone feels love differently, right? If you know, you know. Storm seems nice, and if he makes you happy . . ."

I nod, smiling. "He does. But Laura said something and it's playing on my mind."

"She's the bitter ex, so I wouldn't take any notice."

"She said he's full-on. He'd check up on me, track me, make me pack my job in."

Leia smirks. "Sounds like most of the guys in this place. Some say it's too much and others don't mind it. You gotta see it from their point of view." She pauses when Anna joins us and briefly fills her in. Anna grins. "These guys are mainly ex-army, right? They come from regimented backgrounds, and they've seen too much. Yes, they're over-the-top protective, but it's because they love us so much. And Anna can vouch for this," she says, winking at Anna, "ol' ladies have broken the rules in the past, thinking they knew better. They've gone off without telling their OGs and gotten themselves into whole heaps of shit. Who comes running to save you? That possessive guy who tracked your phone."

"She's right," says Anna. "It can take some getting used to. You're not new to club life and you know the dangers. Enemies target us, so our guys want to keep us safe. So what if he checks up on you? So what if he tracks your phone? Does he beat on you? Does he lock you away from everyone?"

"And the work thing?" I ask. "Because he didn't like my job, and I told him I'd quit."

"Hey, Chains," shouts Leia, causing Chains to glance up from the bar. "Would you let me work in Enzo's as a dancer?"

He scowls. "You wanna take your clothes off for other men?" he questions, narrowing his eyes further.

"No, I'm asking if you'd let me do that?"

"Why the fuck you asking me that? Don't I give you enough money? Aren't you happy being a mama to Grace? You wanna leave our daughter to go and shake your ass for other men?"

Leia laughs. "No. It's a hypothetical question."

"It's a fucking stupid question."

"See," she mutters to me. "None of them want to share. It's like they missed that lesson at school."

Riggs and Storm come from the office. "You heard this, Pres?" asks Chains. "Your sister wants to strip for money."

Riggs glares at Leia, and she rolls her eyes. "That's not what I said."

"So, I spend a fortune on getting you a nursing degree, and you wanna shake your ass for strangers?" Riggs growls out.

"That's what I said," Chains says smugly.

"Jesus, you guys are overreacting. I do not want to strip for strangers. I was asking a simple question, and you got all cavemen on me," she argues.

"Like Vinn would let you anyway," adds Riggs.

"I'm sure he'd be front row to see you naked." Anna grins as all the men glare at her. "Kidding," she whispers.

Chains pulls Leia to stand and leads her towards the stairs. "'Scuse us, we need to have serious words," he mutters.

Chapter Ten

STORM

I kiss Lottie on the cheek. It feels like the most natural thing in the fucking world, and now Lake knows my intentions, it feels like all the pieces of the puzzle are falling into place. I spot Taya coming in with some shopping bags. She's next on my list. "I have to speak to Taya about this before we make any big announcement," I tell Lottie, and she goes to stand. I still her and wince. "Actually, do you mind if I tell her on my own? I think she's gonna stress out." Lottie lowers back onto the couch and nods, looking slightly hurt. "She worries. I don't want her to push all her negativity onto us when we're both happy about this."

I take the bags from Taya and follow her through to the kitchen. "Seb is getting fussier with his food," she mutters, opening the fridge and putting some things away. "I told Frankie I'd shop for him because I feel bad making her get all this."

"I need to talk to you," I say, taking a seat.

"Is this about Laura?"

I shake my head. "No, she's gone. I told her to leave."

Taya goes back to putting the shopping away. "Thank God for that. I had nightmares you'd get back together. She's nothing but a bitch."

"I'm not getting back with her. That'll never happen."

"Good, because she'd be a terrible stepmother to Seb."

"What do you think of Lottie?" I ask.

Taya stops and turns to face me. "She's nice," she says carefully. "Good with Seb."

"And you? Do you like her?"

"Yeah, I guess. Is she what you wanted to talk to me about?"

I nod. "We've decided to give it a go. I like her and—"

"You haven't known each other long," she mutters.

"I know. But sometimes, you just know. With her, I feel . . . happy."

"That's good. I'm happy for you, if this is what you want, but just be careful. You have a habit of going in there full steam ahead, and I don't want to see you hurt."

"That's the other thing," I say. "I've kinda claimed her."

Taya's eyes widen. "Christ, Storm, that's huge."

"I know, and I get you're worried, but can you try to act happy for us? Lottie is . . . delicate. She needs reassurance and to know I'm serious."

"Delicate how?" she asks through gritted teeth.

"I don't wanna talk about her like that, but she needs to know I'm serious about her and that seemed the only way."

"Fuck, Storm, there's loads of ways. Just keeping your dick in your pants is one of them. Have you done this to make up for the fact she caught you with Trudy?"

"No," I snap. "Just trust me."

"What about Seb? You're barely looking after yourself, let alone him, and now, you're throwing a woman into the mix. One who will also need looking after. What if you're not strong enough?"

"I will be," I say firmly. "I'll have to be."

Taya shakes her head, and her eyes are full of uncertainty. "You're putting yourself under too much pressure. This will end badly."

The kitchen door opens and Riggs comes in. "Brother, stay calm, but the cops are here. They wanna take you to the police station."

"What the hell?" I growl as four cops march in.

"Hey," yells Riggs. "I asked you to wait while I talk to him."

Two of the cops grab my arms and twist them behind my back. "Jaxon Michaels, I'm arresting you on suspicion of breaking a court order . . ." The rest of the words blur together as my wrists are cuffed, and he reads me my rights.

"I'll get a solicitor to the station," says Riggs.

Lottie watches sadly as I'm led through the main room. "Don't worry," I tell her. "It's a misunderstanding. Be strong," I say, my eyes conveying what I mean by that. "For me," I add, and she nods.

LOTTIE

The girls try desperately to distract me. They get their kids to bed and make me join them in the club bar to relax and unwind. Riggs sent the club's solicitor to the police station, but we've heard nothing. "Do you think it was Laura?" asks Leia.

"We agreed to avoid the subject," says Eva.

"Sometimes it helps to talk about these things," says Leia, shrugging. "I think she called them to spite him. She wasn't happy earlier when he asked her to leave."

"Surely, it won't stick. She came here, to his home," says Anna. "She came all the way from Nottingham."

Taya sighs heavily. "She's a twisted cow. She'll lie, and they'll believe her because she has this way of making men do whatever she wants."

"Like Medusa?" asks Leia, and Taya laughs, nodding.

"I just want him home," I mutter, and Leia smiles sympathetically.

"He didn't get a chance to make the announcement," says Eva.

I catch Taya's grim expression and wonder if he had a chance to tell her. She sees me looking and gives a small smile. "Shall we go for a walk?" she asks.

We get outside, and I take Bently's leash off so he can run around the yard. "Do you think he's okay?" I ask to break the ice.

"He's a big boy. He can take care of himself."

"Did he cope well with prison before?" I ask because he never went into detail about that.

Taya presses her lips together. "He told me he plans to claim you." I notice she avoided the question, but I nod because she clearly has things she needs to get off her chest. "He said you're delicate."

I suck in a surprised breath. She's direct, and it unnerves me. "Did he?"

"What does he mean?"

I shrug and tug my sleeves down over my hands. "Not sure."

"Because he is too," she says. "He won't tell you because he wants to be seen as the strong one. He would rather struggle than tell you he needs help."

"I'll pay close attention," I say. "Watch for signs."

"And then what will you do?" she asks bluntly. When I don't answer, she stops walking and glares at me. "When you see the signs, what will you do?"

I shrug helplessly. "I'm not sure."

"How will that help?" She begins walking again. "What happens if you're both struggling?"

"I don't know."

"Lottie, I don't want to come across as rude, but it doesn't fill me with confidence when you have no idea how to support or help my brother."

"You just said he was a big boy," I mutter, and she narrows her eyes. "I can't give you answers I don't have. I like him . . . a lot . . . and I'll help him the best I can, but until we reach that point, how will I know what to do?"

"He drinks," she says, ignoring my comment. "He thinks I don't know, but I do. At least he takes it away from Seb these days."

"Is he an alcoholic?" I ask.

She shakes her head. "I don't think so. He can live without it, but when things are hard and he's not in a good place, he disappears for days on end and drinks. He comes back relaxed and calm, and we have some good weeks. Then the cycle repeats . . . and it *always* repeats," she says pointedly.

"What exactly are you saying, Taya?"

She shrugs. "I don't know. I just feel like this is moving so quickly, and if it falls apart, I have to pick the pieces up again. And frankly, I'm sick of it. It'll be us who have to leave when it all goes wrong because Lake won't kick you out."

"You want me to walk away now?" I ask. "Tell him it's over?"

She shakes her head, looking conflicted for a moment. "I'm so tired," she finally mutters, "of not living my own life. I know it sounds so fucking selfish, and I feel like a bitch for even saying this out loud, but I'm caring for a kid I never asked for. And I love Seb, I really do, but Storm seems to live his life, and I just follow him around, looking after him and his child, and I can't help but get pissed when shit like this happens. I don't want to move away again. I want to settle down. I want to make friends and maybe meet someone myself."

I suddenly feel bad. I hadn't looked at things from her point of view. "I'm so sorry, Taya. It doesn't sound fair. Have you talked to Storm?"

She shakes her head. "No, and I don't want you to tell him either. I love him and Seb, and I wouldn't want him thinking I resent him, because I don't. I just want to avoid anything or anyone who's gonna cause drama."

"Let's make a deal. I'll try not to cause drama. I'll try and help with Seb and Storm, and if it all goes wrong, I'll leave. I don't want to be the reason Seb has to move again, so I'll go. I promise."

Taya smiles sadly. "That's so sweet, Lottie. I can see why he likes you. Let's take each day as it comes. Just remind him that life isn't a race. He doesn't need to declare his love, marry you, and get you pregnant all within the first week," she says, and I laugh, nodding in agreement.

"I'll slow him down."

Anna fills my wine glass to the brim. "I really shouldn't have another," I mutter, checking my watch. It's almost ten in the evening and there's been no word from Storm.

"Last one," says Anna, winking. "Seeing as she won't join in," she adds, glancing at her best friend, Eva.

"I can't be bothered listening to Cree nag at me," mutters Eva. "He's really serious about making babies, and if I hear one more lecture on my body being a temple, I might gouge his eyes out."

I almost choke on a mouthful of wine, laughing at her statement. "You don't want kids?" I ask.

"I do," she mutters. "We've been trying a long time, and I'm starting to worry there's a problem. He must think the same because he's suddenly on this health kick and he's big on me not drinking."

"And he's watching her every move," whispers Anna, nodding in the direction of where Cree is watching from the bar.

"I keep telling you, there're loads of kids around this place, just take one of them," jokes Leia. "I never thought I'd see the day Cree wanted kids."

"I think seeing everyone else popping them out has affected him," says Anna. "He's realised he ain't getting any younger."

"Did Chains cool down after earlier?" I ask, and Leia smirks.

"I had to show him my actual dancing for him to see no one would ever employ me to do it professionally."

"Did you have to strip?" asks Anna, giggling.

"I tried, but he was too busy laughing at my dancing to take an interest."

I'm draining the last drops of wine when Storm finally walks in. I stand to greet him, but he barely looks my way as he stomps towards

Riggs' office. "Let him cool off," says Anna, gently patting my arm. "He'll be in no mood right now."

"It's hard," says Eva sympathetically, "and it takes some getting used to, but let his brothers handle him right now. They can deal with the mood, and you can soothe him later."

"Don't ya think Hannah and Taya are looking very cosy lately?" muses Leia.

I glance over to where Hannah, Blu's ex, and Taya are laughing together. "Leia, just because Hannah is bisexual doesn't mean she's into every woman she speaks to," says Eva. "We're all laughing together, but does it mean we're having sex?"

"I wasn't suggesting anything," says Leia defensively. "But that's the fourth time this week I've seen them whispering together. She's so wrapped up in their conversation, she didn't see Storm come in!"

"Hardly whispering," says Anna. "They're very openly sharing a joke."

"Is Storm's sister straight?" Leia asks me, and I shrug.

"How would I know? I'm still getting to know Storm. We've hardly spoken about his family."

"Lottie," calls Storm from outside Riggs' office. He's glaring at me through narrowed eyes.

"Make him wait a second," whispers Leia. "Play it cool."

"Don't be stupid, Leia. Stay out of it," hisses Anna.

I stare back and forth between the pair, unsure what to do. Storm's eyes widen. "Didn't you fucking hear me?" he yells.

"Oh no he didn't," Leia says, looking outraged.

I glare at him, and he sighs, looking down at his feet. "Sorry . . . tough day. I just wanna go kiss my kid and get into bed with my woman."

I melt slightly, but Leia rolls her eyes. "Go be with your man," says Eva. "Ignore her. She'd have gone running the second Chains walked in. She pretends to be hard-faced."

STORM

I gently kiss Seb on his sleeping head and pull the sheets over his tiny body. He looks so peaceful as I stare at him for a few minutes before heading to my bedroom warily. Lottie is lying on her stomach, staring at her mobile. She smiles when I slap her ass. "You were gone a long time," she says, placing her mobile on the bedside table. "What happened?"

I pull at her pyjama shorts, revealing her naked ass. I climb on the bed, kneeling behind her and running my hands up her thighs. "I don't wanna discuss today," I mutter, gripping her hips and tugging her so she's on all fours. I unbuckle my jeans.

"I wanna know why they arrested you," she says, glancing back at me over her shoulder. I rub my hand between her legs, and she moans, dropping her forehead and resting it against the bed.

"Later," I mutter, pushing my finger inside her. "All I've thought about is this

moment," I add, lining my erection up. I sink into her, pausing halfway to get control of myself. The urge to fuck her hard and fast is overwhelming.

"Stop being gentle. I'm not gonna break," she pants out.

"Don't say that, butterfly. You have no idea how rough I wanna be right now," I mutter, gripping her hips. She begins to meet me thrust for thrust, forcing me to slam into her. "Fuck," I mumble, wrapping her hair around my hand and tugging her head back to give me more leverage. Moving faster, I chase the impending orgasm. I feel her pussy clench my cock as she cries out. I feel her wetness between us and pull out, pushing her to lie down on her back so I can bury my face between her legs and taste her pleasure. She tugs at my hair.

"No more," she eventually groans, trying to push me away. I grin down at her flushed face.

"I hope you don't think we're done," I tease, arching a brow. Lottie smiles, pushing herself to sit. "That's more like it," I add when she takes hold of my erection and runs her tongue along the shaft. My head falls back as she takes me into her wet mouth. She sucks me greedily, and I hiss each time I hit the back of her throat. "I'm gonna come," I groan, warning her, but she doesn't let up, cupping my balls and sending me over the edge. I release into her mouth and watch as she swallows every drop.

I flop down onto the bed, and she joins me, cuddling into my side. "I missed you today," she mutters.

"You didn't cut," I note, and she shakes her head. "Good."

"Was it Laura?" she asks.

"Sleep, butterfly," I murmur, stroking her hair sleepily.

"I don't want to sleep, Storm. I was worried all day," she says, propping her head up on her hand. "What happened? Why were you arrested."

I twist a lock of her hair around my finger. "I've gotta go and do a job for Riggs," I say, and she frowns in confusion. "I was gonna tell you, but I wanted an hour of drama-free," I add.

"What's going on?" she asks, pleading with her eyes. "Why won't you tell me anything?"

I smile, pushing myself to sit. "Don't worry, butterfly. I'm fine. Everything is fine. You get some sleep, and I'll be back before you know it." I sit on the edge of the bed, and she wraps her arms around my neck, pressing her cheek against my back. "Lottie, I promise, I'm fine."

"You've been gone all day, and now you're going again. You won't tell me what happened. Something doesn't feel right."

"Sometimes club business is between the brothers. This is one of those times," I explain.

"I think you're leaving me to go and drink," she mutters, and I twist around to face her.

"I swear, I'm not. On Seb's life. I have a job on for Riggs. Ask him yourself."

"He'll lie for you," she says, and she's right, he would, but in this case, I'm not lying to her.

"They arrested me for breaking the injunction Laura took out on me," I finally say, telling her half the truth. "My solicitor got me released on bail. I have to report to the station every day at ten in the morning while they are investigating, but it's pretty obvious she came to see me. She even took the train, so there's proof. I'll deal with it." I kiss her until she melts against me. "Now, I have to go before Blu comes looking for me."

We arrive in Nottingham in the early hours of the morning and head straight for the clubhouse. The President of the Nottingham Charter is expecting us, so when I walk in to find him waiting for us, I'm not surprised. "Pres, this is Blu," I introduce as he shakes our hands.

"Good to meet yah," says Deano.

"You talk to the brothers?" I ask, and he nods. "And?" I push.

"And there were no witnesses. We burned everything, including the body. There ain't no way they have anything to pin this shit on you or anyone else in this club," he snaps. "I told you that bitch was poison, and now she's coming for us!"

"We gotta get our story straight," I say, ignoring his outburst.

"I'll give you the alibi. It goes without saying. That night, we had a huge party to announce one of the brothers taking an ol' lady," he says.

"Which brother? And who's to say I didn't sneak out? It's gotta be solid," I say.

"Right, well, can't we use your current ol' lady?" suggests Deano, but I shake my head.

"Nah, I don't want her involved."

"There's always Raven," says Blu. "She's good at this stuff. She'll hold her own with the cops, and it ain't the first time she's stepped up to help a brother."

"That could work," I say.

"You met her a few months back at a club get-together and you stayed in touch and hit it off," Blu suggests.

I nod. "But what about the whole stalker thing? Will they believe it when Laura was accusing me of stalking her?"

"Who gives a fuck. It only implies you're innocent of that. It's a good, strong alibi. We'll get the brothers on side and make it watertight," says Blu. Damn Laura and her stupid punk ass brother. I'm beginning to regret ever meeting them.

Chapter Eleven

LOTTIE

"He was supposed to report to the police station at ten," I snap, and Riggs rubs his forehead warily. "Just tell me where he went."

"Anna!" he yells, and she appears in his office doorway. "Get her the fuck outta here before I do something stupid and piss off Lake and Storm."

"Come on, Lottie," says Anna gently. "He'll be back soon."

I roll my eyes, stomping out of the office and crashing into a solid chest. Storm's arms circle my waist, and I sag against him with relief. "Thank fuck for that," snaps Riggs. "She was driving me crazy."

"Where were you?" I demand. "I was worried."

Storm looks mildly pissed and pulls me to one side. "Butterfly, you can't be going around harassing the Pres. I told you I was on a job. Sometimes these jobs can take days, so you gotta get used to that."

"You said you had to report to the police at ten." I look at my watch. "It's eleven. I was worried you'd miss it."

"I'm an adult. I took myself there at ten." He narrows his eyes. "Have you hurt yourself?" he hisses, gripping my blood-soaked bandage. I shake my head as he pulls the bandage away.

"It was old wounds," I say quickly. "Not new ones."

"I don't give a fuck," he yells, dragging me towards the stairs. "I told you to stay calm. To wait for me. You don't have to do that shit anymore."

"It's not that easy," I protest, feeling the sting of tears as he shoves me into my bedroom. He goes to my drawers, and I watch in horror as he pulls them open one by one and rummages through them.

He finds my tin and holds it up. "It's very easy. Get rid of this." I try to take it from him, but he holds it above his head, making it impossible. He grips my chin hard and glares at me. "No more," he hisses. "No fucking more."

I watch him leave, slamming the door hard enough to shake the windows. Taking my tin was like unplugging my life support—I can't cope knowing it isn't there, and I feel my heartbeat thumping in my chest.

Leia rushes in. "Are you okay?" she asks. I shake my head, unable to find the words. "Did he hurt you?" I shake my head again, *at least not physically.*

"You know what you need? Some girl time," she suggests, taking my hand. "Let's get out of here."

I don't think Leia was exactly right about the girl time thing. It's great they want to be there for me, and for the first time since arriving here, I feel part of their circle. But right now, all I want to do is curl up in bed and forget about today. "You get used to it," says Anna softly, keeping her voice low enough for only me to hear. "His moods and stuff," she adds. "They're all like that—one minute they're treating you like a queen, and the next, they're growling at you like some rabid beast. Don't get me wrong, sometimes that's sexy as fuck, but it's also pretty fullon."

"He's pissed at me," I mutter.

"You wouldn't know," she says sarcastically, adding a grin. "You're here all sad and shit, and he's over there brooding."

I glance over to where Storm sits with Cree and Lake. "When I first came here, Lake told me if I had any problems, I should go to you cos you're like the head of the women around here."

Anna scoffs. "I am not. Frankie owns that title, but she's as hot-headed as the guys, so if you want level-headed responses, I guess I'm the woman for you."

"I have some . . . issues."

"Don't we all," she mutters. "Talking can help." I look down at my covered arms, trying to find the right words. "Is it to do with the scars?" she asks. "I've seen them, when your sleeves have risen up."

I nod, staring down at my hands. "That's why he's mad."

"He just found out?" she asks, and I shake my head. "So, if he knew, why is he mad now?"

"Because I can't stop."

"Have you tried getting help?"

"Yeah, but nothing helps. I've been doing this so long, it's hard to explain why I do it. And when I see the mental health nurse, it's never the same one, and I hate explaining the same shit over again. They tell

"Not because I want to do it, but because it makes me feel safe having it around. It's in my head, I know that, but I feel better knowing it's there. The nurse told me to keep clean sharps, so if you take that tin and I break, I'll use anything and that's not good."

"The nurse told you to keep a tin of sharps?" he snaps, and I nod.

"They don't tell you not to do it. They try and help you find ways to cope so you don't turn to cutting, but so far, those things haven't worked."

"I want us to go and see someone," he says. "Doctor Chapman works with the club. Some of the guys see her. She's supposed to be good at listening. I thought we could give it a try." He unfastens my bra and adds it to the pile. "I need you naked tonight," he explains when I raise my eyebrow. "Will you come with me to see her?" he asks. I nod, because how can I say no when he's distracting me with his hands?

STORM

I lay awake thinking back to that night. It was a simple job—take out the little shit who had stolen a hundred grand worth of crack cocaine. I'd never met the fucker before, just some street rat wanting to make it big in the criminal world. He'd failed at the first hurdle by screwing over the Kings Reapers. It took Deano less than a day to pinpoint Steven Aspling as the culprit. He'd been working as a security guard at the docks and knew our shipments came in regularly. He'd joined up with a small-time gang on the promise they'd make some big money once he'd shifted the gear. They killed two of our guys and took the shipment, so when Deano gave three of us Steven's name and address, it was a straightforward job.

Meeting Laura, Steven's sister, was pure chance. She came to us looking for him because someone had tipped her off that he wanted to be a part of our club. She was a distraction for me, and my brothers had all joked at the time that she was out of my league. I wanted to prove them wrong. Turns out, she was really great at distracting me. But now, the stupid bitch has gone all detective and told the cops I'm responsible for her missing brother.

I gently move some stray hair from Lottie's sleeping face. I meant it when I said I love her. I've only ever said those words and meant them to one other person, but between us, we're fucked up so bad, even I'm worried it'll ruin us. I need her well in case this all turns to shit and I end up inside for murder. I'm pinning all my hopes on the doctor tomorrow. Cree reckons there ain't no one she can't fix.

"What sort of things will she ask us?"

I take Lottie's hand. "I don't know, butterfly. We just gotta be honest."

I look around the doctor's office. It's a good likeness to the sort of shrink's office you see in films. The door opens and a female walks in. She's hot—Cree never mentioned that part—though not as hot as my ol' lady, of course. She shakes our hands, smiling kindly before taking a seat.

"Sorry to keep you waiting," she says, pulling out a notepad. "I had a telephone crisis. How are you both?"

"Good," I say.

"I'm Eleanor Chapman. You're Jaxon Michaels and Charlotte Murphy?" she asks, and I nod. "So, what brings you both here today?"

"We wanna be together," I begin, "but we have issues to work through."

"And you need help to sort those out?" she asks.

"Yes."

"Okay. Charlotte, why don't we start with you?"

"I'd rather we didn't," mutters Lottie, squeezing my hand.

"I drink," I say, taking the doctor's attention away from Lottie. "Not all the time, but when I feel like I can't cope, I take myself off and I drink. I can be gone for days." The doctor scribbles something down on her notepad. "And Lottie, she cuts herself," I add.

The doctor's eyes roam over Lottie and land on where she's holding her sleeves over her hands. "Okay. That's a good place to start. Have either of you ever sought help before?"

"No," I say. "I don't see it as a problem." I pause. "I mean, I do, but I don't let it affect anyone around me, so I don't see it as a big issue. I'm here more for Lottie."

"How do you feel about Jaxon drinking, Charlotte?" she asks gently.

"He hasn't done it a lot since we've been together. His sister worries."

I turn to Lottie. "You spoke to Taya?" I ask. She nods, and I frown. She hadn't mentioned that. "Why?"

"She wanted to talk to me," says Lottie, shrugging her shoulders.

"About?" I push.

"About me and you," she says impatiently. "Can we just get this over and done with?"

"You don't want to be here, Charlotte?" asks the doctor. Lottie shakes her head.

"You didn't tell me you didn't wanna come here," I say.

"Why did you come," asks the doctor, "if you didn't want to be here?"

"I want things to work with Storm. He gets angry when I cut myself."

"Do you think you have a problem?"

"It makes me feel better. Sometimes I feel guilty afterwards, but that's because I know he'll be upset."

"When he gets upset with you, how does that make you feel?"

"Like crap," mutters Lottie. "I hate people being mad at me. I hate to disappoint."

Doctor Chapman scribbles more notes. "Overall, are you happy together?"

"Yes," we both reply at the same time and smile at each other.

"It can be hard to have a relationship when you're both battling your own demons. Sometimes these sessions run better one on one. I'd want to go through your past, dig up old skeletons to find out why these behaviours are present. That can be hard for the other person to listen to."

"We're doing this together," I say firmly.

"Charlotte?" the doctor asks.

"I don't want any secrets," Lottie quietly answers.

"Okay. Let's start with you," she says, looking at me. "When did you start to drink?

Chapter Twelve

LOTTIE

I replay the information I've just learned about Storm over in my head. Hearing how much he loved Seb's mum was heart-warming. His face filled with love whenever he mentioned her and losing her so quickly to cancer sounded brutal for all of them. I see why he lost his head for a while after her death. The doctor made him see that his relationship with alcohol isn't healthy. She's given him some coping strategies to try before our next meeting in a week's time. Then it'll be my turn to talk, and that fills me with dread.

"What did Taya say to you?" he asks. I knew he'd not let it go once I'd let it slip.

"Just girl stuff," I say.

"Butterfly," he says, his tone warning, "I don't have time for games." It's almost ten and he needs to be at the police station to check in.

"I'll come with you," I say, but he shakes his head. "Come on, you'll be late if you don't go directly there, and I know you won't let me walk home alone."

"Damn straight," he utters, handing me my bike helmet.

"Let me come. Please."

He relents, which surprises me, and we head in the direction of the police station. We get as far as the door before he turns to me. "Wait here." I agree, letting him go in ahead of me before following without him noticing.

"How can I help?" asks the desk sergeant.

"Jaxon Michaels answering to bail," says Storm.

The officer types away on his computer. "For the charges of?" he asks.

"The disappearance of Steven Aspling."

An audible gasp leaves my mouth, and Storm's head whips around to me. "You never told me that," I snap. "You never said that."

I rush out, taking the steps two at a time. He has to sign the bail paperwork and can't chase me, so I get a good head start. When I get into the park, I slow down. I drop down on a patch of grass knowing he won't find me here because it's too busy. Disappearance in club terms means murder, but he told me it was because of Laura. Murder means a long time in prison if he's charged. My phone rings, and I stare at his name but don't answer. It's followed by a text message.

Storm: Answer the phone, Charlotte. It's not as bad as you think.

I send him a text telling him I'll make my own way to the clubhouse. I need some time to let it sink in, but the second I step out of the park, I see him standing by his bike with his strong arms folded across his chest. "You think you can just walk home alone?" he asks, shoving my helmet towards me. "Not happening."

"I just needed some space," I snap. "When were you going to tell me they're investigating a disappearance?" I hiss.

"I didn't want you to worry," he mutters, getting on the bike.

"What if they charge you? What if you go to prison?" I growl. "You'll be inside for years."

"They haven't got any evidence. It's Laura stirring up shit. I never even met her brother."

"Her brother?" she snaps, placing her hands on her hips. "Sounds a lot like this is club business, so you wouldn't tell me even if you have made this guy disappear. And honestly, I don't give a crap. But if you go inside for this, what will happen to me?"

He stares at me for a long minute before turning away. "Get on the bike, Lottie."

We get back to the club, and Seb rushes over with Bently's leash. I smile sadly. How will Seb cope without his dad? "Okay," I say, taking the leash.

"Lottie, we gotta talk," snaps Storm.

"There's nothing to say. You didn't want to talk until I caught you out, so why bother now?"

"Don't be like that," he mutters. "I didn't want to worry you."

"Well, I am worried, and now I know you keep the truth from me, it makes it worse. That huge secret will affect me. You should have told me, so I knew what I was getting into."

We walk Bently with Storm following a few feet behind. "Are you mad at my dad?" whispers Seb.

I grin down at his cheeky little face. "Maybe a little."

"Shall I have a talk with him?" he asks, his expression serious.

"What will you say?" I ask, playing along.

"That he's got to be really nice to you from now on because I don't want you to take Bently away."

My heart melts. I stop walking and lower to his level. "Seb, don't ever worry about that. I won't take Bently away from you, I promise." He smiles, a look of relief on his face before he darts off after the dog.

"What was that about?" comes Storm's gruff voice.

I turn to look him in the eye. "I'm mad because the thought of losing you when I've only just found you, scares the shit outta me," I confess.

He hooks his fingers in mine and tugs me towards him. "I ain't going nowhere," he mutters. "I promise."

STORM

My mobile rings and I snatch it up when I spot Laura's name. Lottie is asleep, and I don't want the ringing to wake her, so I rush out of the room. "Yeah?" I answer.

"Were you ever going to tell me the truth?" spits Laura.

"What about?" I head down to Riggs' office where he's working away and mouth her name to him before hitting speakerphone.

"About my fucking brother, you arsehole," she yells.

"Have you had a drink?" I ask. She always yells when she's had too much wine.

"It's what you've driven me to," she mutters.

"I don't know anything about your brother, Laura. I don't know why you think I do."

"I know it was you," she screams, ending her words with a sob.

"Who told you that?"

"It doesn't matter. What did you do with him? Where's his body? You at least owe me that much."

"Sweetheart, I don't even know your brother. I haven't met him. When we met, you told me he was missing."

"And you knew all along where he was. You let me cry on your shoulder when you knew he was dead."

"I didn't."

"Tommy paid a private investigator. He's got evidence," she snaps.

I lock eyes with Riggs. This is fucking news to me. "Why's Tommy wasting his money when you two aren't together?"

"He hired him before we split up."

"You know those guys rip you off, right? He'll have nothing because there's nothing."

"Photographs of you and my brother together."

"Laura, that's bullshit. I never met your brother."

"We'll soon see. I've sent everything to the police. They'll be arresting you again soon, and hopefully now, they'll charge you."

She disconnects, and I stare at Riggs. "Sounds more complicated than we thought," he mutters.

"Before that night, I never met her brother. Where the hell would this guy have photographs from?"

"Try not to worry about it. I'll call the solicitor first thing tomorrow and see what they can find out. I'm sure it's nothing. Like you said, you never met him until that night. And now we know what they've got on you, we'll prepare."

"It'd be simpler to take Laura out," I mutter.

"Don't do that, brother. You know the rules—we don't hurt women or kids. She's a grieving woman trying to get justice. There's nothing tying you to him. Besides, the cops would have been banging down the door by now if they had anything solid."

"I don't know what it'll do to Taya and Seb if I go down over this, Pres. And then there's Lottie."

"Let's make sure it don't happen then. Anna wants to organise a party tomorrow night to celebrate you and Lottie. I said no, but maybe it's what we all need, some light relief."

I nod. "It'll cheer Lottie up," I agree. "I'll book us in for the tattoos ASAP."

Lottie remains on the bike, and I stare at her, confused. "What?" I ask.

She stares, eyes wide, at the tattoo shop door. "I can't go in there."

"Why?"

"Tattoos hurt."

I laugh, like really laugh. "Butterfly, are you scared of needles?" She nods, and I laugh some more, holding my sides. "But you . . . oh God, I can't take it. You cut yourself all the time."

"I know," she mutters. "That's different."

"How?" I scoff.

"I don't know, it just is."

I lift her from the bike. "Baby, it's tradition. You're my ol' lady, and I want that mark on your skin, so pass out, sleep, whatever makes it bearable."

Inside, she watches warily as I get her name on my arm. The cursive writing is large, taking up most of the space on my forearm. I went with Lottie and underneath, in smaller writing, the word 'Butterfly'.

When I'm done, she backs towards the door. I catch her arm and pull her back into the room. "Close your eyes," I say. "It'll be okay." She wraps her arms around my neck and nuzzles into me, then she wraps her legs around my waist tightly. "Baby, you gotta let go," I snigger, kissing her neck.

"You want me to do this, then I'm staying like this. Mr. Stabby over there will have to work with it."

"Mr. Stabby," Ink, the club's best tattooist, laughs, "never heard that one before. Lower back?" he asks me, and I nod. I sit in the seat with Lottie wrapped around me like a baby monkey. I lift her shirt up, giving Ink enough room to work. Lottie hisses when the needle first hits her skin, and I smirk, wondering how the fuck she cuts herself with blades but doesn't like needles. After a few minutes, she begins to kiss my neck gently.

"Butterfly," I whisper-hiss. "Not now." My erection stands to attention the second her teeth nip at my skin, and I feel her chest shake against my own when she laughs. Her hand slips between us, and she grips my length through my jeans. "I'm warning you, baby. Don't tease me ."

"It's punishment for making me go through with this."

I grin. She doesn't know punishment . . . not yet.

Ink stands back to admire his work. Lottie twists so she can look at it in the full-length mirror and grins. "I love it."

The delicate butterfly sits on her lower back with 'Storm' written below it. It's perfect, and seeing my name on her skin gets me all kinds of turned-on. I practically drag her from the shop and onto the bike, then I head straight for the caravan. I haven't been there for over a week. I haven't needed the quiet time since being with Lottie.

I pull off my helmet but stay seated on the bike. Lottie gets off. "Why are we here?"

"Lose the jeans," I order.

She smirks, looking around. "Here?" I nod, and she doesn't make me ask twice. She kicks off her boots and slips off her jeans, then I wrap my hand around the back of her neck and pull her in for a kiss. She melts against me, and I lift her, sitting her over the bike. She wraps her legs around me and her arms around my neck.

"You're a tease," I whisper, tugging the lace material of her panties until it gives and falls away from her. I unfasten my jeans and release my cock. "Now, you better make up for it."

She grips me, rubbing the head of my erection through her folds. When she's wet enough, she lines me up and sinks down on my cock, throwing her head back and moaning aloud. I lift her shirt over her head, careful not to catch her new tattoo. Having her naked out in the open and on my bike is like a fucking wet dream come true. Lottie lifts herself and slams back down. I rub her nipples, and she moves faster until I still her, squeezing her thighs for her to stop.

"I wanna see my name on your skin when I come," I say, lifting her from me and standing her beside the bike. Bending her over, I place her hands on the leather seat. "You're officially mine," I growl, staring at the tattoo as I fuck her.

"And you're mine," she pants.

Damn straight, I am.

Chapter Thirteen

LOTTIE

Turns out the tattoo is a bigger deal than I thought. Everyone wants to see it when we finally arrive back at the club. I'm distracted from the fact the women have decorated the clubhouse bar with balloons and banners. "We don't usually go all out for this sort of thing," I say to Anna.

"We need a celebration," she says, shrugging. "Everyone seems a little down lately, so it'll do the club good to celebrate. Leia's got an outfit ready for you upstairs. She's in your room."

When I get upstairs, Leia is waiting to pounce with makeup and curlers. It's not long before Anna and Eva join us with wine. I let them pamper me, and when I finally look in the mirror, I hardly recognise myself. "Now for the outfit," says Leia. "I wanted to go girly with a summer dress, but Anna wouldn't let me. She said you hate showing too much skin." I smile gratefully at Anna. I could cover my scars with makeup, but the girls would see them first and that'd put a damper on this whole makeover experience. "Which I find really odd for a stripper," she adds.

"Dancer," corrects Eva sharply.

"Same thing," says Leia. "Anyway, she forced me to go with this, but I still love it so . . ." Leia holds up a tight-fitting, short minidress with long, off-the-shoulder sleeves. There's no back to it, so it'll show off my tattoo, which will please Storm as he's obsessed with it. I head for the bathroom to slip into it. When I return, their smiles tell me I look good. "Storm is gonna go wild when he sees you in that," says Leia.

When the rest of the girls are changed and we've helped Malia and Molly into their dresses, we head downstairs. I wasn't keen on this party, but now it's here, and I feel like a princess, I'm excited.

The second I enter the room, Storm's eyes find me. It's full of bikers and it's noisy as hell, but it's like he sensed me coming. He's standing in front of me within a few seconds. He cups my face in his hands and kisses me so hard, I stumble back a couple steps. "Butterfly, you look fuckin' stunning."

"It's just something I threw on," I say, twirling.

He grips my arm and turns my back to him. "Jesus, where's the back of the dress?" he hisses.

"You like it?" I ask, looking over my shoulder and smirking at his shocked expression.

"How the hell am I not supposed to kill every man in here tonight?" he growls, hooking his finger in the material just above my ass and peering down my dress. His eyes bug out of his head when he sees the string of my thong. "Are you trying to give me a heart attack?"

"It's all for you, baby," I whisper, turning and kissing him gently. "Only you."

"You wanna wear my kutte?" he asks, placing his hand over my lower back. "It's pretty cold in here."

I smile. "I'm good."

"I can't get it out of my mind," he murmurs close to my ear. "I'm not gonna last long in a room full of people when all I wanna do is—"

"Lottie, you look amazing," says Riggs, cutting Storm off mid-sentence. "Storm tells me you got your tattoo?"

"Yeah, it was totally worth the pain," I say, trying to turn around to show him. Storm pulls me against his side tightly so I can't move. I frown at him, but he stares at Riggs like nothing's wrong. "Erm, maybe I'll show you another time," I say, shrugging.

Riggs grins, giving Storm a knowing smile. "You wanna offer her your jacket, brother? It's pretty cold down here." Chuckling, he heads off to speak to Leia.

"That's it, put on my kutte," he mutters, shrugging out of it and slipping it over my shoulders.

"What difference does it make if I show him now or tomorrow? It's not moving from my lower back."

"You turn in that dress that barely covers your arse and every man in here will be taking a mental photograph."

I roll my eyes. "You're acting crazy."

I'm relaxed. The wine's flowing, and the girls are making me howl with laughter at some of their stories. For once, I feel like I belong. I add a layer of gloss to my lips and take a step back from the mirror to check I'm presentable. The toilet door opens, and Storm fills the doorway looking charged and ready for action. I smirk. "This is the ladies'," I remind him.

"Shut up and bend over the sink," he growls.

I laugh, shrugging out of his kutte and holding it out for him. "You need it back?"

"Bend over," he repeats, snatching the jacket and hanging it over the stall door. He unfastens his belt, keeping his eyes on me like a predator about to pounce.

I laugh, turning to face the mirror again, lifting my dress, and leaning over the sink seductively. "Like this?" I purr, and he slaps my ass, making me flinch.

He roughly runs a finger over my opening before lining his erection up and easing into me. I bow my head as he fills me. "It's all I can think about," he growls. "Your fucking pussy."

"Good."

"Seeing all my brothers drinking and knowing I can't is making it harder."

I hadn't even considered he might struggle around everyone. He wraps his hand around my neck and adds some pressure as he slams into me, grunting with exertion. It's fast and hard, and we come together in minutes. He pulls my thong into place and straightens my dress. "Don't you feel able to have a couple drinks?" I ask. He told me he wasn't an alcoholic, and Taya confirmed that.

He shakes his head. "One leads to two, and before you know it, I'm passed out. It's best if I avoid it."

I kiss him slowly, standing on my tiptoes. "I'm proud of you."

He looks thoughtful for a second. "No one ever said that to me before," he admits.

My heart aches for him. "Well, they should have."

We head back inside, and I excuse myself for ten minutes so I can sneak off upstairs to clean myself. Storm tells me he's had the brothers move my things into his bedroom. There really wasn't a lot, just a few clothes and some books.

I go into the en-suite bathroom and smile at the sight of my things just dumped beside the sink. I put my shampoo by the shower and my makeup bag under the sink. I open the medicine cabinet and freeze when I spot my tin. My hand hovers over it for a moment. I don't need it, but I feel safer having it, and Storm has probably forgotten about it anyway, so I don't see any harm in keeping it at the back of the drawer in the bedside cabinet. Cleaning myself up, I run a brush through my hair and head back down to the party.

STORM

The party was a good idea. Everyone seems more relaxed when we join them for breakfast the following morning. "Why don't we take Seb to the park today?" Lottie suggests, and my heart swells even more for this woman. She's fucking amazing, and I feel her light slowly warming my heart. Glancing around the busy table, Taya's nowhere to be seen, which is unusual.

"If you're looking for Taya, I think she got lucky last night," says Lottie with a wink.

I frown. "What are you talking about?"

"Someone spotted her and Hannah looking cosy. Leia reckons they fancy each other."

"Means nothing," I snap. "You shouldn't be gossiping about my sister."

Lottie narrows her eyes. "Can we have one day where we don't argue?" she mutters. "Hannah's really nice and she deserves some happiness. She lost her previous partner. Anna told me she was a cop. You want Taya to be happy, don't you?"

"I want people to stop talking about my sister," I mutter. "I've got a job on for Riggs. I'll probably be gone most of the day. Don't forget we have to see Doctor Chapman tomorrow." I kiss her on the head and leave her to eat breakfast. She looks pissed as hell, but I have to find Laura today and speak to her about her brother.

I press the buzzer to Laura's flat. It's the only address I have for her since she left the club, and I'm praying she's still here. "Hello?" her voice crackles through the intercom.

"Laura, it's me."

"Not today, Storm," she snaps.

I sigh heavily. She's already testing my patience, and I haven't got up to her flat. I press the intercom of one of the other flats and they release the door without speaking. Taking the steps two at a time onto Laura's floor, I try the door and it opens. I smirk to myself. Who the hell leaves their door unlocked these days? Laura jumps up from the couch, outraged when she sees me. "I said not today," she yells.

"You gotta stop this witch hunt, Laura," I say. "I didn't kill your brother."

"The police seem to think you did."

"Then why am I walking around free? If they have evidence, they'd charge me."

"I know he stole drugs," she mutters.

"I know nothing about that."

"From the club in Nottingham," she continues. "The private investigator found that out."

"But it's got nothing to do with me!"

"Why won't you just tell me?" she wails. "You've seen what this has done to me. I've spent months trying to find him. How could you let me cry in your arms knowing he's dead?"

"Jesus, don't you listen? I don't know him, I didn't kill him, and I don't know where the fuck he is now."

"It was Tommy who suggested you. Said your club does that sort of thing."

"Baby, you were around the club. When did you ever see anyone murder another?" I ask. "Do you think Tommy was pissed because you still loved me?"

She scowls. "I dumped you."

"But you came back several times," I remind her. "From his bed to mine. Then you spring an injunction on me like I'm crazy," I snap.

"You realise tracking my phone and turning up unannounced to my place and my work isn't normal, right?"

"In my world, it is," I mutter.

"In my world, it's called stalking. We were over and you turned up where I was."

"We were still fucking," I growl out. "You remember the party?" I ask, and she looks away. "Your new boyfriend was with his mates, and where were you, Laura? What were you doing?" When she doesn't answer, I laugh. "You were on your fucking knees choking on my cock in the bathroom. You called me that night, a booty call cos you were horny, and your man was busy with his boys."

"I'm not doing this with you," she hisses. "Get the fuck out."

I open the door. "I just want you to know, if you keep this up, messing up my life, I'll have no choice but to put a stop to it."

"A stop? Are you threatening me?"

"I'm happy, Laura. I've got myself an ol' lady and I wanna move on and forget about you. Stop dragging me back in. Let me go."

She scoffs. "I let you go a very long time ago. Don't flatter yourself."

I go to the police station to sign my bail, then meet Lake to grab a shipment at the docks. We're halfway through loading the stock onto a lorry when my mobile starts blowing up with calls from Lottie. "Leave it," mutters Lake. "We gotta get this load moving before the cops come sniffing around. Vinn's expecting us right after this to help with security at the club."

"Fine," I say, sighing. "I'll call her later."

Chapter Fourteen

LOTTIE

He never answers his phone. Coward. I scowl at the picture message I received an hour ago from an unknown number. It's Storm, naked, asleep in someone's bed. I stare at the bedside drawer longingly. The urge to cut is so strong right now, but I'm trying to avoid it simply because Storm is making the effort to not drink, and I should do the same. Maybe if I just hold the tin, the cold feel of the metal will bring me a sense of calm.

I reach inside and take it, holding it to my chest and closing my eyes. A nurse once told me to take deep breaths and count them, so I give it a try. The bedroom door opens, surprising me, and the tin flies from my hand and clatters to the floor, scattering the contents. Seb looks down and then at me.

"Sorry, Seb, you scared me." I drop to my knees and collect the blades up, dropping them back into the tin and shoving it away in the drawer. "Everything okay?"

"That's a cool tin," he says. "Can I see it?"

"It's nothing. Let's go for a walk with Bently," I say, distracting him. He agrees, and I guide him from the room, thankful he didn't walk in and find me cutting.

I wake with a start to find Storm standing over me. I slowly sit up and blink a few times, realising it's dark outside. I glance at my bedside clock—two in the morning. "Why are you in here?" he growls.

"It's my bed," I mutter. There was no way I was gonna sleep in his room after those pictures and a whole day and night of radio silence from him. "Where have you been all day?"

He flicks on the bedside light, and I stare at his blood-soaked shirt. "Busy."

"Too busy to answer my calls?"

"Yes. I told you before, I have work to do that could keep me away from you. You can't be calling me all the damn time."

"Right," I mutter, pulling my sheet back over me and lying down. "Thanks for clarifying. Goodnight."

"You're not sleeping in here. Get in our bed."

"No. I'm happy here. Close the door on your way out."

"Don't fucking test me tonight, Lottie. I've had a day from hell, and I want my woman in our bed."

"You weren't too fussed earlier about me so . . ."

He growls before scooping me in his arms, marching me back to his room, and dumping me on the bed. "I need to shower. Stay there."

I glare at him angrily. He thinks he can just take what he wants whenever he wants? I'm not that kind of girl. Once he's in the shower, I storm back to my room, only this time, I lock the door. *Arsehole.*

I hear his heavy footfalls on the landing a few minutes later, then he bangs on the door. "I get that you're mad at me, butterfly, but I still need you in my bed. We'll talk about it tomorrow."

"Where were you today?" I repeat and hear his heavy, impatient sigh. "Only, I got a message telling me, so I suggest you be honest with me now."

"I was with Lake. Go ask him."

"Before that? Lake didn't leave until a couple of hours after you."

"I had a job on. Lottie, I told you this already. Open the fucking door."

"Did you see Laura today?" It's a random guess, but I don't know any of his exes apart from her. There's a long pause. "You're an arse," I mutter.

"I went to see her, yeah, but I had to speak to her about this bullshit she's spinning for the cops."

"And how exactly did you do that?" I ask. "Did you fuck her?"

"What?" he asks. "No fucking way. Butterfly, I'd never do that to you. Open the door."

"You've done it before so . . . anyway, I saw the picture. You were naked in her bed."

"Show me," he snaps. "I can't defend myself if I haven't seen the evidence."

I snatch my phone off the bedside table and unlock the door. He takes it from my grasp and stares at the picture. "It's an old picture."

"Right," I mutter.

"It's an old picture," he says more firmly and points to a tattoo on his chest. "I had this done two months ago. It's not on my chest in this picture." I stare back and forth, feeling my face flush. How did I not notice that? "Get your arse in my bed right now," he growls. "We'll talk about this tomorrow."

I take the phone from him and sheepishly head for his room. He slides into bed beside me, gently pushing me onto my stomach and kneeling between my legs. He rubs his hand over my opening, and I push my face into the pillow to muffle my whimpers. He guides himself into me, growling with each slow thrust. "I love you," he murmurs in my ear. "Always and forever. You can trust me."

I nod. "I love you too." We come together, and I fall to sleep with his strong arms wrapped around me. I feel stupid for doubting him, but for once, I didn't cut when the going got tough, and that makes me smile. *Progress, right?*

"Sometimes, self-harm is used as a way to be in control," explains Eleanor. "Tell me a little about your history. Do you have a good relationship with your parents?"

I shake my head. "I didn't know my dad and my mum was an addict. I was taken into care when I was around six years old and . . ." I pause, wondering if I say the words out loud, it'll change how Storm feels about me. He smiles, encouraging me to continue. "I was abused when I was a teenager. Groomed by a gang." I feel Storm tense. "I didn't see it at the time. I thought the guy loved me, but he reeled me in and then passed me around his friends. They weren't his real friends, of course, but that's what he told me."

"You said your mum was an addict. That's past tense. Don't you see her now?"

I shake my head again. "She's dead, and I'm okay with that. I made peace with it. She didn't give me up voluntarily, social care took me from her. Addiction is an illness, so I don't blame her."

"And so, you met a man and you were in a relationship?" she asks.

"Yes. He brought me trainers and a mobile. He'd pick me up in his BMW, and I felt grown up. I was fifteen, so all my friends were envious of me. After a couple of months, he took me to a party, and I got drunk. I'd never drank before, so it hit me really hard. I woke up in bed with Ali and another man. They were touching me and stuff. . ." I trail off, hanging my head. "Anyway, that became a regular thing. He'd say if I loved him, I'd help him out by being nice to his friends."

"That's pretty tough. How did you escape that?" she asks, writing notes in her book.

"I met Justin." I smile at the thought. "He was at one of the parties, and I was talking to him. I think Ali must have approached him and asked if he wanted to have sex with me. That's when I realised he was charging people, selling me. He said yes, and once we were in the bedroom, he helped me out the window. We left Leeds after that and moved around regularly. He stuck with me."

"And then he left you for your fucking friend?" snaps Storm.

I nod. "He got tired of me. He said he didn't know how to help me anymore. I don't blame him. The truth is, I didn't want help because I didn't see it as a problem. It made me feel better."

"Did you get help after what happened to you?" asks Eleanor.

"No. I was happy with Justin, so I didn't think I needed it, and the cutting helped."

"How long were you with Ali?" she asks.

"Three years. I was eighteen when Justin found me."

"And you've been cutting ever since?"

"Yes. It makes me feel better when things are too much."

"Did you cut last night?" Storm snaps. He grabs my arm and roughly pulls up my sleeve. Eleanor frowns, biting on her pen. When there's no fresh cuts, he releases me. "Was that because I've taken your blade?"

"Why have you taken it?" asks Eleanor.

Storm glares at her like she's lost her mind. "Because I don't want her to hurt herself."

"Mental pain can sometimes feel worse than physical pain," she says.

"So, you think I should let her continue?"

"I think you shouldn't take her choices away without giving her another coping mechanism."

"I'm fine," I butt in. "It's okay."

"Then tell me what to do," growls Storm. "Tell me how to fucking help her instead of asking her about some bastard who sold her for sex." His voice is raised, and I flinch.

"If you're finding this hard, you can have separate sessions," she suggests calmly.

"But then I wouldn't know any of this, would I?" He turns to me. "Why haven't you told me any of this?" My heart sinks. He's disgusted.

"How do I drop that into a conversation?" I ask quietly. "I didn't want you to hate me or see me for the dirty whore I was."

Storm's face softens and he crouches before me, taking my hands in his. "Butterfly, I don't think that, and I definitely don't hate you. I'm so mad right now, but not with you, with the bastards who laid their hands on you, on my beautiful butterfly. I want to hunt them down and rip them apart. I just wish you'd told me."

Eleanor is smiling. "It's clear you have support, Charlotte. We need to work through the things that happened to you, and we need to find a way for you to cope without reaching for a blade. But for now, I want you to read this." She hands me a leaflet. "I know you've probably heard all this before, and until we go over the reasons you feel so out of control, you'll probably think this information is crap. But read it. And between now and next week, I want you to write down every time you get the urge to self-harm. If you feel able, write what happened right before the urge so we can identify any triggers. Then, I want you to try and delay that feeling. So, tell yourself, I'll go for a twenty-minute walk first, or I'll see my friends first. If you delay, the urge may pass."

I nod, tucking the leaflet into my bag. "We're going to get you through this," she adds, and for the first time, I feel like I've found a professional who gets me.

STORM

"I gotta find these arseholes," I growl, pacing back and forth. We're in church, and I had to tell the brothers what happened to Charlotte. We have to find the paedophile ring and end it.

"Let me tell you the good news before you go and get yourself involved in another murder investigation," says Riggs. "I got a call from the solicitor. The police have dropped the charges against you. Raven gave her statement, saying she was with you on the night of

Steven's murder. She told them exactly what we practised, and with the Nottingham charter all saying the same, that you were all partying to celebrate you taking Raven as an ol' lady, the cops have no choice but to drop the charges. The investigation is ongoing, but without a body and no evidence, they have nothing."

I breathe a sigh of relief. "Thanks, Pres."

"I'll do some digging, see if I can trace this bastard and his gang," says Brick.

Lake's staring straight ahead at the wall. "You okay, brother?" I ask.

"She never said," he mutters. "She didn't fucking tell me."

"She doesn't want anyone to know. I couldn't keep this from you, though. These bastards could still be doing it. She said they always had girls around."

"I'm glad you told me," he says. "I just wish she'd told me herself. She wanted to talk when she first got here, but I was always avoiding her. I feel like a shitbag for it now."

"You and me both," I mutter, "but if it's of any consolation, she said she's dealt with it."

"Dealt with it?" he repeats, scowling. "Brother, she cuts her own flesh open. That ain't somebody dealing with it."

I find Lottie sleeping. The counselling took it out of her, and she's been washed out since we got home. I gently kiss her cheek, and she stretches out, smiling up at me. "Get showered and dressed, we're going out to dinner," I say.

An hour later, when she steps from the bathroom, she takes my breath away. She's wearing a short red dress and heels, and her hair hangs in loose curls around her shoulders. Her makeup is minimal, but she doesn't need that shit cos she's naturally beautiful. "Wow," I mutter.

She grabs her cardigan, but I shake my head. "No, you don't need to cover your arms," I say. "If anyone stares at you, I'll kill them."

She smiles. "I won't relax."

"Baby, you got naked on stage," I remind her.

"And I covered them with makeup."

"They're on the insides of your arms, no one will notice." I kiss her wrist and along her arm. "I want you to feel comfortable with me, scars and all."

She takes a deep breath. "Okay," she whispers.

We go to one of Vinn's restaurants, the one his dad ran right before he was killed. "The women always talk about this place," she says as we're seated. "Apparently, it does the best carbonara."

"I'm a newbie to this place too," I say. I don't wine and dine women, not because I'm an arse, but romance like this ain't really my thing. But after today, I thought Lottie needed to see how I feel about her.

"Wine?" asks the waitress. I screw my nose up, so she hands the wine list to Lottie instead. Wine's never been my thing, even when I was drinking heavily.

"Just water for us both," says Lottie. "Thanks."

"Butterfly, you can drink," I offer.

"I don't want to. I want to remember every second of this date because I don't think it's something you do very often," she says, grinning.

"True. First time in a candlelit restaurant," I admit. "I like steak houses and burger joints."

"I've never really been wined and dined. It's always made me feel uncomfortable, like I don't belong. Give me a burger joint any day," she says.

"Lottie, you can walk in any place and instantly belong. These people aren't better than us because they sit down and eat posh food over a candle. I just wanted to show you how much I love you. Leia said this place is perfect for romance."

"I appreciate it," she says softly. "Today was hard on us both, but I don't want it to change us. I'm not a delicate little flower. I won't break."

"You were brave today, saying all that personal stuff in front of me and a stranger."

"It doesn't haunt me like it used to. I understand it wasn't my fault, though it took me a long time to see that, but I don't think about it like I used to. I've moved on."

"I guess we both have a shady past, but we'll talk about it in time," I say.

"We've got forever, right?"

"Right." I smile. "Now, let's address the picture you got."

"I should have trusted you," she admits.

"Yeah, you should. I'm not gonna cheat on you. I'm not Justin."

"If you do," she starts, and I try to protest, but she holds her hand up to shut me up. "If you do, be honest. Tell me straight away, so you don't blindside me. It'll hurt but not as much if someone else tells me."

"Okay," I mutter, "but I won't cheat."

"We didn't talk about your drinking today with Eleanor," Lottie says.

"You stole the limelight with your little tale," I joke, and she grins. The candlelight flickers, illuminating her face. "I want us to marry . . . I want kids . . . I want the whole thing," I blurt out, and she raises her eyebrows in surprise. "It's soon, I get it, but I want you to know that's my plan. I'm not going anywhere. Being my ol' lady isn't enough—I want it all."

"Let's sort out our demons first," she says, gently placing her hand on my own. "We've got forever, remember."

"In other news, the cops have dropped the charges. Raven gave me an alibi."

Lottie smiles wide and relief floods her face. "We really will have forever then."

Chapter Fifteen

LOTTIE

"It was lovely," I admit, and Anna smiles.

"I'm so glad you had a good night," says Leia. "We stayed in again." She scowls at Chains, who groans.

"We have a fucking baby, where the hell do you wanna go?"

"Anywhere but this damn club," she mutters, marching off.

"Women," Chains hisses, drinking his beer down in one.

"Make the most of the honeymoon period, because it soon ends up like that," says Anna, grinning.

"I take you out," says Riggs, "and we have three kids between us."

"Don't rub it in," snaps Chains. "Maybe if you didn't have me working my ass off in the garage and then sending me on runs, I wouldn't be so tired. You realise I'm not the only brother in this MC, right?"

"Perks of being my brother-in-law," says Riggs, patting him on the back.

"You can't punish me for marrying your sister forever."

"Watch me," Riggs utters with a smirk.

Hannah joins us, taking a seat on the couch next to Taya. I see Storm eyeing her questionably, but she shrugs it off, causing him to scowl. I wonder if he's okay with her sexuality. I haven't asked him because he clearly doesn't want to talk about it. Last time I tried to make light of it, he bit my head off, but rumours are circulating amongst the club girls that Taya and Hannah are seeing each other.

Everyone begins to split off, having conversations amongst themselves. I turn to Anna. "Storm mentioned marriage," I whisper, and she smiles wide. "Don't you think it's a bit soon?" I ask, frowning.

"You know what these guys are like, Lottie. When they want something, they go above and beyond to make it theirs. If you like each other, I don't see the problem. Did he say he wants to march you down the aisle tomorrow?"

"God, no," I gasp.

"Then stop overthinking. He's just letting you know where his head is at. Future plans," she says, shrugging.

It's not that I don't wanna marry him. I've never thought about it. But that's the problem, right? I've never thought about it because we're so new. And Storm comes with a lot of baggage. Seb is great, he's a cute kid, but I can't even sort my own head out, let alone look after a kid.

Storm takes my hand and pulls me to stand. "Let's go to bed, baby. I gotta work off that dinner." He winks and leads me away. Tonight has been perfect, and I'm not gonna overthink, like Anna pointed out. I'm gonna take each day at a time and enjoy what we have so far. It can only get better now we've finally admitted our feelings.

It's a week later when Storm raises the subject of marriage again. We're sitting out back on a blanket, watching Seb play with Bently. It's a hot day, and I'm lying with my head in Storm's lap, letting the sunshine warm my face. "Have you thought about marriage?" he asks.

I keep my eyes closed. "Erm, not really."

"I thought all women did that shit from being a kid. Planned the big day, pictured it in their heads."

"Not me," I say, shrugging. "I climbed trees, pretended I was a parkour champion."

I feel his body shake as he laughs. "I can't wait to see mini Lotties running around doing just that."

"You don't want kids with me," I say lightly. "I was trouble, always doing something wrong."

"I don't believe that for one second, but hearing it makes me want kids with you even more."

"It's literally been a few weeks," I mutter. "We're going from zero to a hundred." I feel him stiffen, so I open one eye. "I'm just saying, let's enjoy what we have right now."

"I am. I'm just letting you know where we're headed."

"The future isn't promised, Storm."

"Ours is, butterfly. Ours is."

"Don't make promises," I almost whisper, sitting up.

"Is that what's wrong?" he asks, moving my hair over my shoulder. "You think I'm gonna let you down?" I shrug again. "Baby, I'm not going anywhere. We're together. It's real. We both turned up at this club for a reason, and I think it was because we were meant to be. I love you, Lottie. I ain't leaving."

"That's what all men say. I can't get through another break-up. I thought we were a bit of fun, and now we're serious and you're talking kids and marriage. Fuck, slow down."

He pushes to stand, looking annoyed. "Haven't we had the best week? We've been together every minute and look how happy we are. You haven't cut once, and I haven't picked up a bottle. That shit's real. We're real."

"Why are you getting so mad? I just want us to slow down, take one day at a time."

"I don't go slow, baby, in case you hadn't noticed." He sighs heavily. "I need to be away from you right now."

I watch as he heads back inside. A few minutes later, Seb runs over. "Where's Dad going?"

"He's too hot out here. He needs a break from the sun," I lie.

"Can I go inside too?"

I nod. "I'll be in soon."

Bently runs after Seb, and I watch them disappear inside. They're becoming good friends. I lie back down on the blanket and close my eyes. Thoughts of marriage and babies infiltrate my mind. Why's he gotta get so serious about us all the time? I'm not saying I don't want that stuff, but I just want us to concentrate on one day at a time. Eleanor understands where I'm coming from. At counselling this week, I was open about my fear of being hurt again, and if we were to hurt each other, what that would mean for both of us mentally. It's a lot of pressure.

"Lottie! Lottie, wake the fuck up!" I sit up with a start, almost head-butting Anna.

"Fuck," I hiss, looking around in a panic. The sun is setting, I must have fallen asleep out here. "What time is it?"

"There's been an accident," says Anna. "Seb got hurt, and Storm's taken him to the hospital. We gotta go." I stand quickly, running with Anna towards her car. My heart is pumping fast outta my chest and my adrenaline is spiked from being woken like that. "The others have already headed to the hospital," she adds. "I've been looking for you."

"Is Seb okay? What happened?"

"I don't know. I was shopping when Riggs called me. All he said was to find you and get to the hospital."

We arrive and head straight for Paediatric Accident and Emergency. Riggs, Cree, and Eva are waiting outside a side ward. The second Riggs spots me, he rushes over, looking furious. "You gotta get her outta here," he mutters to Anna.

"Me?" I ask, confused. "Why?"

"You told me to bring her," says Anna, looking just as confused.

"I sent you a text. Why don't you ever check your fucking phone?" he snaps.

Anna opens her messages, and her mouth forms an O shape. "Right, we better go," she whispers, backing up.

"Why? I don't understand what's going on. Is Seb okay?"

The curtain pulls back, and Storm glares at me. His face is a picture of anger. "What the fuck are you doing here?" he growls.

A few nurses look up from their workstation. "What did I do?" I ask.

"Storm, leave it. Get back in here," comes Taya's voice from behind the curtain. I hear Seb begin to cry, and a pained look passes over Storm's face.

"Is he okay?" I repeat.

"No thanks to you. Get out of my sight before I do something I'll fucking regret," he snaps, before turning his back to me and pulling the curtain into place.

"I'll update you," Riggs tells Anna, and she nods as she gently takes my arm and leads me away.

We drive back to the club in silence. "I don't understand what just happened," I eventually mutter.

"Riggs didn't say. In his text, he just asked me to keep you away from Storm because he was pissed at you."

"I was asleep. How could I have hurt Seb?"

"I don't know, sweetie, but I'm sure Riggs will call soon. Why don't you go and lie down, and I'll come and find you when he calls."

I go to my old bedroom, pausing at the door. All my stuff is in Storm's room, but after the way he was just now, I don't think he'd want me there. I go inside, knowing Storm will find me if he wants me in his bed.

Minutes turn to hours, and soon, my arse is hard from sitting by the window, staring out across London's skyline. A million thoughts go through my head, but nothing prepares me for the minute Storm returns.

I hear him before I see him, stomping along the hall. He stops outside my door, then pushes it open. He stands in the doorway, staring hard at me. He still looks mad as hell, so I keep my mouth closed. "You not gonna ask how he is?" he grits out.

"How is he?"

"In fucking pain," he yells, and I flinch.

"I don't know what I did," I whisper, my eyes brimming with tears. He can't seriously be this mad over our earlier disagreement.

He sniggers and it's cruel. He moves towards me quickly, grabbing the top of my arm and pulling me from the window. "I'll fucking show you, shall I?" He drags me towards his room, flinging the door open. The floor is littered with open bandage packaging, some blood-soaked, some clean. In the middle of it all sits my cutting kit. It's laying open in a pool of blood, the blade carelessly thrown to one side. I gasp, covering my mouth. "No," I whisper, shaking my head, my tears falling freely.

"My boy cut his arm from here," he pulls my arm out so it's straight and places a finger roughly at my wrist, "to here," he says, making a straight line to the crux of my elbow. Storm's hand grabs my face, forcing me to look at him. "Tell me, butterfly, how the fuck did my seven-year-old kid find your dirty fucking blade when I hid that away?"

"I'm so sorry," I murmur.

His fingers pinch my jaw tighter. "How?" he yells.

"I found it and hid it in the drawer," I cry.

"Why would he go in the drawer?"

"He saw me putting it back one day. He asked me about it." I sob uncontrollably, and Storm shoves me away. I stumble back out into the hall.

He swoops down, picking up the bloodied blade. "You want it so badly, fucking have it," he yells, throwing it to my feet. "Make it count," he growls.

I grip my chest. The pain is unreal as I make my way back to my room, locking the door behind me, and sliding down until I'm sitting in a broken heap on the floor.

STORM

I press my hand against Seb's sweaty forehead. The doctor said he was fighting an infection and that's why he's running a temperature, but this is the third day and I don't see any improvement. He hasn't eaten and now they have him hooked to a drip to get fluids in. The worst thing, I can't make any fucking decisions because Taya is his legal guardian. The doctors will only speak with me when she's here. That shit needs to stop.

When she returns with two coffees, I clear my throat. "I'm ready," I say.

"For?" She looks so tired. How had I never seen it before?

"Being his dad. I'm ready."

She grins, placing the coffees down. "Good. You gotta sign some paperwork and have social services approve it, but I don't think that'll be a problem."

"I'm sorry it took me so long."

"You just needed time. What are sisters for? I knew you'd get to this point eventually. I'm proud of you." I smile, because she's never said that to me before. She sips her coffee as she fixes her eyes on me and says, "I heard Lottie is leaving." I frown. Since putting my hands on her the way I did, I haven't seen her. I'm ashamed, but fuck, I was mad. I've never felt my blood pump like it did that day. Seeing Seb like that, lifeless and bleeding out, it sent me crazy. "Lake is devastated. She's talking about leaving London."

"Probably for the best," I mutter, stroking Seb's hand.

"You really think that?"

"Don't you?" I ask. "You weren't keen on me seeing her anyway."

"Yeah, at first, I had my doubts, but she's grown on me. I was worried you were jumping from heartbreak to heartbreak, but she looked at you like you were her saviour. I thought you'd save each other."

"In a way, she has. If Seb hadn't found her shit, I wouldn't be here now realising how badly I want to be his dad. Maybe it was all to lead us to this point." We fall silent for a few minutes before I add, "She been okay though?"

Taya shrugs. "I don't know. Lake's been with her a lot. She spent two days locked in her room and refused to see anyone. Lake got that counsellor to come to the club and talk to her, and she eventually opened her door. But nobody's told me anything, I've just picked up shit the club girls have been saying."

"I'm surprised Lake hasn't been on my ass about her," I mutter.

"Your son got hurt badly. The guys get it. Most people would react how you did. But you don't stop loving someone just like that. Accidents happen."

"It was an accident that could have been avoided. I didn't even know Seb had followed me back inside that day. I moved her tin to stop her cutting, and she put it back in the drawer. Not only that, she knew Seb saw it and didn't move it out of his reach. Kids are curious. She should have hidden it," I snap, feeling my temper rise again.

"She doesn't have a kid, Storm. People don't think about stuff like that when they haven't had kids around. You knew she had issues when you decided to claim her. Are you going back on that now?"

I shrug. "It's for the best. She's right—we're both too fucked up to be happy together. I need to concentrate on Seb from now on."

"Are you going to tell her it's over?" she asks.

"I think she got that memo already," I respond, "but sure, I'll go see her."

"Just stay calm. She'll be just as upset about Seb as you are. She didn't mean for this to happen."

When I get back to the club, I find Lake standing outside Lottie's door like some kind of guard. He eyes me warily. "She said she promised your sister that if things went wrong between the two of you, she'd be the one to leave," he snaps. "I only just got her in my life, and now she's fucking leaving."

"Let me talk to her," I say. He sighs, stepping aside, and I knock on the door. "Lottie, can we talk?"

A few seconds pass before she opens the door and I step inside. Her suitcase is open on the bed and she's folding clothes neatly. She looks tired, her face is pale, and she's got dark circles under her eyes. "Is Seb okay?" she asks quietly, her voice hoarse. "I've been checking in with Taya for updates," she adds. "I didn't want you to think I haven't been checking on him."

"He's got an infection, he's on a lot of pain meds, and he lost a lot of blood, so they're keeping him in until he shows signs he's improving."

She stuffs a makeup bag in the case. "How long for?"

"I don't know. They tell me he's doing good, but I don't see it." I watch her stuff some more clothes into the already full suitcase. "Where are you gonna go?"

"I've got some friends in Liverpool. I'm gonna head there for a while, then probably move on." She shrugs her shoulders. "I don't really know after that."

"You don't have to go," I mutter. "If you wanna stay, it's cool with me. We'll avoid each other."

"I was thinking of moving on anyway, so no time like the present," she says brightly. "I found Lake and I'll always have him in my life, I don't have to be here for that. Besides, I love Liverpool."

"You got enough cash?" I ask, pulling out my wallet.

A choked sob leaves her throat, and she smiles painfully, turning her back to me. "Mm-hmm," she mumbles.

"Cos I got some savings I can give you, and here's some to get you started." I hold out a bunch of folded notes.

She shakes her head and looks back at me, her smile forced. "I'm good, thanks. I have some savings and I can get bar work when I get there."

"It's my . . ." I pause, frowning and staring at the wad of cash. "I mean, it was my job to provide for you, so this money is as good as yours for putting up with my moody arse." I force a smile so she gets the joke, but she keeps packing her bags and shakes her head. I stuff it back into my wallet. "I shouldn't have grabbed you the way I did," I begin, but she waves her hand like it's nothing. "No, I really shouldn't have. I'm sorry about that. There's no excuse apart from I was crazy worried about Seb and I lost my mind for a few minutes." I place my hand over hers to stop her packing, but she flinches so I withdraw it quickly. She's fucking scared of me, and now I feel like an even bigger arsehole. "Butterfly, I—"

"Please," she whispers, turning to look me in the eye. That's when I see the finger bruises on her chin, and I wince.

"Fuck," I hiss. I take her hand and push her sleeve up. She immediately withdraws it when my eyes widen. There are big, ugly, red cuts crisscrossing over her arm. It's hard to see the skin through them.

She pulls up her other sleeve to reveal the large bruises I caused. "If these are what you're looking for, then here," she snaps, shoving her arm in my face. "But I deserved it."

I scowl. "You didn't fucking deserve that, Charlotte. Don't say that shit. I shouldn't have grabbed you like that. I'm an ass, and I am so sorry." My phone rings and I pull it out my pocket to check it's not the hospital. I frown, confused when I see it's Ink, the tattooist the club uses. "Yeah?" I answer.

"Brother, I gotta check an appointment with you. Your ol' lady booked in later today for a cover-up. That right with you?" he asks.

My eyes connect with hers and a stab of hurt hits my chest. Of course, she wants the tattoo removing, why the fuck wouldn't she. "Yeah, thanks for running it by me, Ink. Put it on my tab. I'll settle it later."

"If you're sure, brother."

"One hundred percent," I mutter, disconnecting. "The tattooist," I say, and she presses her lips together. "You hate needles . . . you want me to come?"

She shakes her head. "I'll be fine."

"Butterfly," I begin, and she squeezes her eyes shut before sighing.

"Please stop calling me that," she whispers.

I nod once. "Lottie, you need to get help. The cutting is out of hand. Stay, see the counsellor. You said you liked her, that she's the only one you've ever liked."

"I'm gonna be fine, Storm. I survived before you and I'll survive after you." Bently jumps up on her bed, and she smiles, rubbing his neck affectionately. "There's no room for Bently, since I might have to couch surf for some time. I'd like Seb to have him. Bently's lost without his BFF, and I promised Seb I'd never take him away." Her voice breaks and she swipes away her tears. "Please tell him I'm sorry . . . for everything."

I nod, and our fingers brush as she hands me Bently's leash. "Take care, Lottie. If you need anything—"

"You too," she says, cutting me off. "And I won't . . . need anything, that is. Not from you."

Chapter Sixteen

LOTTIE

I spin the keychain around my finger. Standing in the centre of the room, I slowly turn three-sixty to take in my surroundings. After leaving the MC, I couch-surfed for three months in Liverpool before going to a homeless women's shelter, and now, finally, I have my own place. I allow a smile to creep onto my lips.

"Where do you want this?" asks Kyla, holding up a box.

"I wrote the room names on the box. You were there when I did it," I say, rolling my eyes. She grins before dumping it on the coffee table.

"This place is perfect," she says.

I nod in agreement. "Finally, things are coming together."

"How do you feel about being back here permanently?" she asks.

I shrug my shoulders. It's not ideal. I met Kyla at the women's shelter in Liverpool, but she's originally from North London, so when she said she was coming back here, I decided to follow. I figured it was far enough away from the club, and you only really bump into the bikers when you know where to hang out, so I'll avoid those places at all costs. "I'm far enough away to not bump into *him*, and besides, I miss my brother. We've spoken regularly, but it isn't the same. I want to see him, and eventually, I'd like him to meet this little one," I say, peering into my daughter's Moses basket. Her brown eyes stare back at me, and I sigh. "If he can keep it to himself, that is."

"I'm sure he will if he wants you to stick around. You said it yourself plenty of times that he wanted to come and see you."

"They're really close at the MC. It'll be hard for him to keep this from Storm."

"Maybe he isn't there anymore. He wasn't originally from London, so could he have gone back to his roots?"

I nod, but deep down, I know Storm will be at the club. He was settled there, and so were Seb and Taya. I make sure I never ask about him when I speak to Lake or Sara, but I must have picked the phone up a million times to call him. I wanted to tell him all about his daughter and the way she smiles just like him, but then I'd remember what happened and how he looked at me that night he found Seb, and it's enough to make me put the phone away. We're not good for each other. If we were, it would have worked out.

It's almost nine in the evening when I finally sit down and pick up my mobile to call Lake. I smile when he answers. I miss him so much. "Hey," I say. "How are you?"

"All good, little sister. How are you?"

"Same. Guess what?"

"You've seen sense and you wanna return to the MC?"

I smile again even though he can't see me. "You say it every time I call, and my answer will always be no. I'm happy where I am."

"And where is that exactly?" he asks. Again, it's the same thing he asks on every call, only this time, I plan to tell him.

"I'm in London," I say quietly and hear his intake of breath.

"Where? I'll come get you."

"Actually, Lake, I've been back for some time."

"Are you shitting me?"

"I wanted to tell you, but I wasn't ready."

"You haven't seen Connor or Leo in a year. Don't you miss them?" he snaps.

Guilt creeps in. "Of course, I do, Lake. You know I do. But things have been tough. I had to get my head straight and sort myself out." I glance at the scars on my arms. I no longer cover them because I'm not ashamed. I still have my down days, and that's okay, but I haven't reached for a blade since everything happened.

"Can I come and get you?" he eventually asks.

"I was thinking you could bring Sara and Leo to see me, and Connor if he isn't too busy. I'm in Enfield. You could stop over. I have my own place and I'd love you to see it."

We make plans for them to visit the upcoming weekend. "One last thing," I add. "Please don't tell Storm. I don't want to see him. Not ever."

STORM

"Seb, get back here," I say playfully. He runs back and grabs his school bag. "Have a good day, kid."

His teacher greets him at the door, and I watch their interaction with a grin on my face. He's so happy at this school, I've never seen him so animated. As I turn to walk away, I spot Emily leaning against her car parked directly behind my bike. Her kid goes to this school too. She looks hot in a summer dress and boots. "You waiting for me?" I ask.

"I don't have to be in work for another half-hour," she says, raising her brow suggestively. "Meet you at the club?" she adds, opening her car door. I smirk, throwing my leg over the bike.

Hannah and Taya are just leaving as I drag Emily past them. "In a hurry?" Hannah asks, grinning.

"Morning. Emily, wasn't it?" asks Taya.

I don't give Emily enough time to answer because we're already taking the stairs two at a time. I slam the bedroom door, and she tugs at my belt. We've been hooking up for weeks, but I'm starting to notice the way she looks at me—it's with a longing for something more, something I can't give her. I ain't ever settling down again. Not after Lottie. *Fuck no.*

Fifteen minutes later, I'm standing in the doorway waving Emily off. Voices come from behind me, and I pause to listen. "He didn't say exactly, just that she's in London."

"Why wouldn't she tell him that? He's her brother, for goodness sake."

I pretend not to hear Anna and Sara's discussion. Instead, I step farther out the door so they can't see me. "She said she's been back months. Lake's missed her so bad, I felt sorry for him," continues Sara. "She hasn't seen Leo in a year. She's missed so much."

"I guess she must have felt really bad after what happened with Seb. Guilt's an awful emotion. Then there's Storm, of course. They didn't exactly part on great terms," says Anna.

"I know, and I get all that, I really do, but it doesn't make sense. She wouldn't have been forced to come back to the club. She could have asked Lake to go see her, but she refused to even say where she was staying. Don't you think that's weird?"

Bently whines at my feet, and I pull the door fully open like I've just returned from his walk. The women whip their heads round. "Morning," I say brightly.

"Morning," they chorus.

"Why'd you both look suspicious?" I ask.

"No reason," says Anna. "We were discussing Riggs' birthday."

I head for my room. I don't appreciate the lies, but clearly, I'm not supposed to know Lottie is back in London. The news shouldn't bother me. It's not like I still think about her every day . . . well, maybe just for a fleeting minute, but not like I used to. I scrub my hands over my face and pull out my mobile. "Eric," I growl. I met him at my first Alcoholics Anonymous meeting nine months ago, and we agreed to sponsor each other, a decision I regret almost daily whenever I hear his joyful tone.

"What's up, bud?" he asks, and that simple sentence makes me wanna reach for the bottle even more.

"I need a drink."

"One of those days, huh?"

"It's why I'm calling," I grate out, irritated by his Mr. Nice Guy routine.

"Talk me through it, big guy," he says, and I roll my eyes.

LOTTIE

I pace nervously, glancing through the window every ten seconds. When Lake's car finally stops outside, I let out a nervous breath. Kyla offered to be here, and I told her I'd be fine, but now I wish I had taken her up on it now.

I wait until they're walking up the path before opening the door and smiling wide. "You made it." I embrace Sara, then look up at my older brother, who's holding their son in his arms. "Wow, he's so big," I say. "He doesn't look that big when we talk on video call," I add, laughing. Lake hugs me, and I lead them inside.

"This place is fancy," he grunts.

"I moved in last week," I say, showing them into the kitchen.

"We've missed you so much," says Sara. "Why didn't you tell us you were here?"

I flick on the kettle. "It's a long story. Tell me all your news first."

"We're here to hear the long story," growls Lake. "Get talking."

I swallow hard. Some things never change, like his bossy tone. "You might want to take a seat," I mutter, heading back to the living room where Elsie is sleeping. I carefully lift her from the basket and go back to the kitchen. They both stare at me for at least a minute before Sara stands and moves towards me.

"What the hell?" She whispers, "You had a daughter?" I nod.

"No fucking way," snaps Lake. "You had a fucking kid and didn't tell me?"

"I wasn't ready," I mutter.

"We're your family," he yells, and Elsie jumps along with Leo. Sara takes her son from Lake and moves to the window to distract him. "How the fuck could you hide something so fucking huge from us?"

"I didn't mean to. I didn't find out until I was five months, and then I could never find the right time. I was worried you'd make me come back to the club."

"You couldn't drop it in conversation? We spoke every couple of weeks, and you couldn't say, 'by the fucking way, I've got a kid'?"

Sara slowly turns, her eyes wide. "Oh my god! She's Storm's?"

STORM

I grunt as my fist smashes into the guy's ribs. He winces but no sound escapes him. I know that fucker hurt, so he's got a good poker face. I hit the same spot a second and third time, and on the fourth time, he hisses. "Fuck, I thought he was an alien for a second there," says Blade, sounding relieved.

"You make me fucking sick," I growl in the guy's face.

"Please, I served my time," the pussy cries.

"No, there's only one place you deserve to go after what you did."

"I have a family to go to," he mutters. "I have kids."

"Do they know what you did? The truth of how you raped girls? Have you got daughters? Shall I pass them around my brothers?"

"Man, they were in it to make money. Those bitches lied about us grooming them," he argues, and I hit him again.

Blade pushes his knife into the guy's eye, and he screams out. "Fuck, brother, a little warning," I snap. He always does that shit when you're least expecting it.

"I'm bored. How many more of these shitheads have we got on the list?"

"Two," I say, grinning.

It's taken a year to track down every member of the gang involved in the paedophile ring that Lottie was groomed by when she was a teenager. I was mad after we split, but when Brick told me he'd managed to track down some of the gang members, I told myself I was doing it for Lake. After all, it was his sister they hurt, and he's joined me on every kill so far. Today, he had something on. I suspect that involves Lottie, but it's not my business.

So far, we've caught up with every single member. Now, we just have the ring leaders left, Rashid Mohammed and Ali Mosafo. Ali groomed Lottie and passed her around to grown men against her will. We've saved him until last. For that murder, I'll be waiting for Lake.

Chapter Seventeen

LOTTIE

"You have to tell him. Secrets like that never go down well in the club, Lottie. This is fucking huge," gasps Sara.

I shake my head, alarm in my expression. "No, please, you can't tell him. We're not good together. We've learnt to live without each other, and I can't have him back in my life."

"It's not just about you, Lottie. Fuck, he's her dad and he deserves to know about her," she argues. I take a deep breath. I knew this was a bad idea. "I'll run," I mutter. "I'll leave London completely." Lake's eyes burn into me. It's a low blow, but I'm desperate. "That's a shitty move," hisses Sara. "We haven't seen you in a year, and you know we've missed you. Now you're threatening to up and run?" "I'm sorry. I can't deal with Storm." "Seb has a sister. You're being selfish," she hisses. "Don't you care that your daughter has a whole family and you're keeping her from us?"

"I'm protecting us all. You saw how I was before—" "That wasn't Storm's fault," snaps Sara. "We were both dependent on something.

I self-harmed, and he drank himself into oblivion. Together we're a mess."

"He doesn't drink anymore," mutters Lake. "But he will. With me on the scene, I'll drive him to it."

Lake shakes his head in disgust. "You have no clue what he's done for you. The lengths he's gone to." I frown because I have no idea what he's talking about, but I don't want to get into it right now. "I can't keep this from him, Lottie. It's too big. He's my brother," Lake continues.

"And I'm your sister. Your actual blood sister!"

"You know the bonds of the club. I have to tell him."

I grit my teeth. "Fine," I mutter. "But let me do it."

Lake takes a pen from the worktop and scribbles something on a scrap of paper. "This is his number now. He changed it after you left."

I smirk. "That's how happy he'll be to hear from me. He went to all that trouble to change his number."

"He'll want to hear this," says Sara.

"Is he," I pause, "seeing anyone?" They exchange a glance that tells me he is. "Won't this mess it up for him?"

"I don't think it's serious. It's only been a few weeks, but she's nice. I think she's into him. They both have kids, so maybe it won't make a difference," says Sara, shrugging.

"Come back with us to the club. Tell him face to face," Lake commands.

I shake my head. "I don't want an audience. I'll tell him, and as soon as I do, I'll let you know."

I smile gratefully at Kyla. "Are you sure you don't mind?" I ask for the hundredth time.

She rolls her eyes. "You know I love being with this princess. You go do what you have to do. Call me if you need me," she says. I kiss Elsie on the head and grab my keys.

I haven't called Storm, but I know where he'll be, so I'm not surprised when I pull up in the yard where he once took me to cool off and see his bike outside the rusty old caravan. I check my hair and makeup in the mirror before stepping out and heading to the caravan. The door is open, and I stop in my tracks when I spot Storm with his jeans around his ankles and a woman on her knees practically choking on his erection. I gasp, which gets his attention, and when his eyes land on me, he visibly scowls. "What the fuck are you doing here?" he growls.

I turn my back on the pair, giving them time to compose themselves. My face is on fire with embarrassment. "Sorry, I just wanted to talk to you," I mutter feebly.

"Jesus, you finally see Lake after all this time and you're straight back here to see if I'm still pouring whiskey down my throat over you?" he scoffs.

"God, no," I say a little too quickly. "I have something to discuss with you."

"I'll get someone to come get you," Storm mutters to his lady friend.

I turn back to face them. "I'll go. I should have called."

"I changed my number," he mutters, tapping out a text message on his mobile phone. "Blade's gonna come and take you back to the club," he says, gently taking the woman by the back of the neck and pulling her to him so he can kiss her. I avert my eyes again. He looks really into her, and I can't help the stab of jealousy. Since him, there's been no one. It took me this long to stop crying every time I remembered what happened to Seb.

I take a walk around the yard, giving them time alone until Blade comes. It feels uncomfortable and Storm clearly isn't happy to see me. I didn't expect him to be, not after everything, but I guess a small part was hopeful he'd at least have a twinkle in his eye.

Blade finally arrives, and I watch from my place across the yard while Storm kisses her with the same amount of force he once kissed me. I rub my aching heart and wait for her to leave before I head back towards him.

"So," he mutters coldly, "what did you wanna talk about that's not been important enough for the last year?"

"How have you been? How's Seb?"

He glares at me, and I pray for the earth to open and swallow me whole. "Why are you here, Charlotte?"

"What I'm about to tell you might be a shock," I mumble, scuffing my trainers in the dirt. "And I don't want it to change anything. I'm telling you because Lake said I had to, but I don't expect anything from you. In fact, I'm quite happy to go back to my life and never see you again," I add. Storm sighs impatiently. "After I left—"

I turn as three black cars come screeching into the yard. It all happens so fast, Storm grabs me and pulls me behind him. He pulls out a gun and backs us into the caravan. "Fuck," he hisses. "Get my phone out of my pocket," he orders. "Stay behind me and text Riggs now. Tell him the last two guys have found us, he'll know what that means. Tell him you're here with me."

I place my shaking hand into his back pocket and shrink behind him while doing exactly what he's instructed. "Now, turn it to silent and tuck it into your knickers."

"What?" I hiss, peeking out over his shoulder. Men are now out of the cars and walking towards us with guns raised.

"Do it now. Riggs can track us, and they won't check your underwear."

I roll my eyes. I've not had this drama for over a year and here I am shoving a phone into my underwear within five minutes of being in contact with Storm.

"You found me," says Storm, as the guys circle the caravan. "You kind of pissed on my parade cos I was coming for you later, and now you've beat me to it," he adds.

"I was always too impatient to wait for anything," says one of the men. "Who's your friend?"

"No one important. She's just leaving."

"Not anymore. Put the gun down and step out here for me, Storm. We have some things we'd like to discuss."

"Let my friend go, and I'll happily do whatever you want."

"Don't be stupid. You're outnumbered. You'd be dead before you managed to pull the trigger," says another man, and I frown. I recognise that voice, yet I can't seem to place it.

Storm flicks open his gun and empties the bullets out onto the ground. "What the hell are you doing?" I hiss.

"You have to stay calm. We're gonna go with them. We don't have a choice," he whispers back. "Riggs will find us."

"Are you crazy?" I almost shriek. "I'm not going with them. This has nothing to do with me."

Storm throws the gun out and reaches behind to find my hand. I let him take it. "Be brave, butterfly," he whispers, stepping out of the caravan doorway and leading me with him.

"Good choice. I really didn't want to kill you out here when I'm wearing my best suit," says one of the men. "Again, who is your friend?"

Storm pulls me to his side, and my world tilts when I lay eyes on Ali Mosafo. How the fuck is he here? He recognises me the exact moment I recognise him, and a smirk pulls at his lips. "Is this who it's all about?" he asks, grinning before breaking out into a laugh. He pats the shoulder of the man beside him. "Fuck me. You remember Charlotte? Fucked-up kid. We called her 'Irish'."

His friend grins in recognition. "Christ, she had a mouth like a vacuum," he sniggers.

I feel my face redden, and for a second, I'm thrown back in time to being fifteen years old and feeling that shame wash over me as they leer and make fun of me.

"You're telling me all this hassle is over this bitch?" asks Ali.

"Her pussy must still be fucking amazing," adds his friend.

Storm almost growls as he lunges forward and punches Ali's friend in the face. Four large men rush and seize Storm by the arms, bustling him towards a car. "You can ride with me, Irish." Ali smiles and grabs me by the wrist, dragging me towards a separate car.

Ali leans over and pulls the seatbelt around me. The same aftershave assaults my nostrils just like it did back then. Just the smell of him makes me want to vomit. He runs a finger over my bare knee, and I shudder, staring hard out the window and doing my best to angle my body away from him. "Now, you know the routine, Irish. I'll need your phone." He holds out his hand, and I pull my phone from my pocket, pressing it hard into his palm. "Good girl."

A million questions race through my mind, the main one being how the hell Ali and Storm know each other. Is it pure coincidence or is the club involved in something with these guys? My stomach churns. To think, I almost told Storm about Elsie.

We travel for at least a half-hour before we pull into a carpark. It's to a block of high-rise flats. Ali was big around this area when I was a kid, which is why I was so easily impressed. It seemed like everyone knew him. "Welcome back to my palace," he says, clipping a handcuff around my wrist and attaching it to his own. "We're going inside without a fuss. If you draw attention to us, I'll begin shooting parts of your boyfriend until he bleeds out." It's not an idle threat. I once watched him use a spoon to pop a man's eyeball out of the socket.

Storm is also handcuffed and flanked by several men as we enter the high-rise and Ali calls for the lift. He pulls me inside while Storm is left with the others as the doors close and we ascend to the tenth floor.

We go into the same flat I used to come to all those years ago. Nothing's changed. There are still men hanging around. The carpets and walls are still stained and filthy. The rooms have mattresses thrown on the floors with no bed sheets. "Make yourself at home. I need to talk to the boss about you." Ali uncuffs himself, then cuffs my wrists together. When he shoves me into a room, I lose my balance, falling hard onto a dirty mattress. I screw my face up and wriggle myself into a seated position. A minute later, Storm is also shoved into the room, his hands also cuffed.

Storm leans against the wall. His chest is rising and falling at a rapid rate, and he looks pissed. "How do you know Ali?" I ask quietly.

"Riggs'll never find us in here," he whispers angrily. "He'll get a signal to this building, but there must be three hundred flats in here."

I glance nervously at the open bedroom door. There are two men leaning against the opposite wall with guns in their hands. Riggs will get shot the second he enters.

"This place is exactly the same as before," I mutter. "Tell me how you know each other," I almost plead.

STORM

There's no way around this. I have to come clean, but before I can, Ali fills the doorway.

"It's been a long time, gorgeous. You're still as beautiful as ever." He smirks at Lottie, and she shies away. "Come on, baby, I know you ain't shy. I remember those parties we had. You were wild."

"I was a scared kid," she mutters.

"There was nothing childlike about you." He sneers. "I gave you a good life, and you ran away like an ungrateful bitch."

"A good life?" she repeats, scoffing. "You're deluded. You're a paedophile, Ali. I was never here because I wanted to be."

He marches towards her and hauls her up by her upper arm. I move forward, and he laughs at me. "What are you gonna do with your arms behind your back?"

"Touch her and you'll find out," I growl.

"Man, I did more than touch her back in the day. She fucking loved it. She could entertain a whole room of men." He sneers, and my head crashes against his before he manages to finish his sentence. His nose bursts and blood splatters across his face, splashing over Lottie's white top. The two men from outside the room rush in and grab me, shoving me hard against the wall and holding me there. Ali smiles, his white teeth coated with crimson fluid. "Just for that," he hisses, "I'll give you a private show of my friends and I showing your girl a good time."

"I'll fucking kill you, just like I did your friends," I yell, pushing against the two men who struggle to keep me against the wall.

Ali laughs, wiping his nose on the sleeve of his jumper. "We spent weeks trying to figure out who was coming for us. If I'd have known it was over this little whore, I'd have killed her and her kid," he spits.

"Elsie," gasps Lottie, and my eyes fix on her scared face.

"Don't worry, sweetheart, she's safe for now."

Lottie loses her shit. Her face changes and she uses her cuffed hands to shove Ali hard. He stumbles back, sniggering, and she rushes him again, hitting her hands against his chest. "You leave my daughter out of this," she screams. "I'll fucking rip your heart out if you hurt her."

Ali steps away, his confident smile faltering. "Do as you're told, and I might spare her from the life you should have had," he snaps, tipping his head to the men holding me. "But you mess me around, and I'll sell her within the hour."

They all leave, and Ali locks the door behind him. I stare at Lottie in disbelief. She had a kid?

Chapter Eighteen

LOTTIE

Storm's eyes are wide. "I meant to tell you," I mutter feebly. "It's why I came to see you."

"So, what, you're married? Single? You were only gone a year. That's quick work. You can't have known the kid's dad long," he says, confusion on his face. I realise he hasn't worked it out and my lips form an O shape. "I mean, I didn't expect you to stay single or never move on," he adds. "But you said you didn't want all that. Was it with me you didn't want it or . . ." he trails off, looking sad and lost.

"That's why I came to see you. Elsie is our daughter, Storm. She's yours." His eyes narrow and he swallows hard, and I watch his throat bob up and down. When he doesn't speak, I fill the silence by rambling. "But like I started to say earlier before these idiots showed up, I don't expect anything from you and I'll happily go back to my life. Lake said I had to tell you—"

Storm cuts in. "And if he hadn't, would you have?"

I pause for a moment, then shake my head sadly. "No, probably not."

"You fucking selfish bitch," he mutters, turning away from me.

"I thought it was best for all of us," I explain. "We were so messed up."

Storm kicks the door, and someone unlocks it and opens it slightly. "I want a different room, away from her," growls Storm. I roll my eyes, because now he's being stupid.

"Tough shit. This ain't a fucking hotel," snaps a man the other side of the door before slamming it closed again.

He keeps his back to me. "I can't change the past, but now you know the truth. She's gorgeous, Storm. She has big brown eyes and your dimples," I say softly.

"Get the phone out," he mutters coldly.

"We were too toxic together. I'd probably still be self-harming and you'd be drinking. Lake said you've stopped. That's really great, by the way."

"Fuck, Lottie, I can't think straight. Shut the hell up and get the phone out," he growls.

I struggle to get my cuffed hands into my underwear, but when I eventually do, I grip the phone and throw it down on the mattress. I kneel, and Storm stands behind me, watching as I press the screen to light it up. There's a message from Riggs saying they're tracking us. "Press call," orders Storm, and so I do. "Now hold it to my ear."

I hear Riggs answer and say a few words to Storm. "Yeah, it's the tenth floor. I have a feeling all the flats on this floor belong to these guys. It might be best to tip off the cops. There's gonna be girls here." He pauses for Riggs' response. "There's at least fifteen men in this place. All armed. Fuck knows how many more are hanging about. Hit it when it gets dark. We can hold out till then."

When he's finished, I hide the phone back in my underwear. "What if Ali comes for me before dark?" I ask.

"He won't," he snaps. "You're too old for him now. He was never looking for you in the first place. You shouldn't have showed up today."

"I had to tell you about Elsie," I say. "How could he have known about her?"

"I don't know, Lottie. I don't fucking know," he mutters, sighing. "How old is she?"

"Three months," I say. He glares at me, his eyes cold and mistrusting. "I didn't find out until I was five months pregnant. I hurt myself pretty bad," I explain, holding up my arms so he can see the scars. "I was taken into hospital, and they discovered it when they did blood tests. I wanted to call you then, but I was ridden with guilt over what happened to Seb and there I was still doing it. It made me sick to my stomach knowing I could have taken my own life as well as our baby's. From that moment on, I stopped."

"You should have called me," he mutters.

"As time went on, I found excuses not to. Were you still drinking? Was Seb well again? Would Taya try and take her away from me?"

"Why would Taya do that?" he snaps.

I shrug. "I don't know, but that's the sort of thing in my head at the time. We were hardly fit parents."

"I asked her to take legal guardianship over Seb—which I now have back, by the way—so I could get help for the drinking. I've been sober for nine months," he says.

"That's great," I say, beaming. I'm genuinely happy for him.

"But I can't deny that when I found out you were back in London, I wanted to drink again. You're right, we're not good for each other, but just cos we have a kid doesn't mean we have to be together. I've got a new life now. Maybe things will work out with Emily. Who knows? But they didn't work out with us, and there's no point raking over it all again. We'll get out of here and meet up to discuss co-parenting and shit," he says, and my eyes widen. "What?" he snaps. "You think you can drop that bombshell on me and walk away? She's my daughter. I want to see her."

"And I'm happy for supervised contact to take place, but co-parenting—"

"Supervised visits?" He scoffs. "Are you fucking with me?"

"You've never met her. She doesn't know you," I protest.

"And whose fault is that?" he growls.

My blood rushes around, making me dizzy. I'm not ready to share my baby girl, not even with her father. "You've kept her from me for three months, Lottie. You won't make this difficult for me," he says, his tone warning.

The door opens and Ali steps in. "Let's go, beautiful," he says firmly.

"Where?" I ask, glancing at Storm.

"To paradise." He grins, gripping my arm and pulling me towards the door.

"Storm?" I plead.

"Not even he can help you now," Ali says, sneering.

STORM

I pace the small room. She's been gone hours. It's starting to get dark outside, and I regret telling Riggs to wait for nightfall. I was convinced nothing would happen until then, and why would they take Lottie? She's out of their preferred age bracket. I twist my wrists again, wincing when pain stings where I've already tried to pull them through the tight metal cuffs. When the door finally opens and Lottie is shoved onto the mattress, I breathe a sigh of relief. She waits for the door to be locked before slowly rolling onto her back. I gasp. She's taken a beating so bad, her eyes and face are swollen and bruised. "Jesus," I hiss.

She holds her arms out in front of her and blood pours from open cuts along each one. "They cut me," she mutters, staring as the blood drips onto her jeans.

"Christ, Lottie. Did they . . . do anything . . . else?"

"No," she mumbles. "They beat me in front of some young girls. They wanted to scare them into doing as they say. They did the same when I was fifteen."

"Fuck," I growl. "If Riggs doesn't get here soon, you're gonna bleed out." Peering closer, the cuts go the length of both arms and they're deep. "Shit."

"I'm feeling light-headed," she whispers. "I need to lie down."

"Butterfly, don't go to sleep. Talk to me," I say, kneeling beside her.

"I'm not your butterfly," she whispers, smiling sadly. "Not anymore."

"You'll always be my beautiful, broken butterfly," I mutter. "Keep talking. Tell me about Elsie."

She smiles again, her eyes fluttering closed. "She's so pretty. I know all mums say that about their babies, but she really is. She's such a happy baby. Everyone says it."

"Yeah?" I say, grinning. "She must take after me."

Lottie gives a weak laugh. "She's stubborn like you. I went a week over her due date."

Sadness hits me, because I should have been there for her birth. "You hate pain," I mutter.

"I miss Seb," she mumbles. "I'm so sorry for everything."

"Don't apologise like it's the last time you're gonna get a chance," I snap. "Stay awake."

"I'm too tired," she whispers, closing her eyes.

"I killed them," I say, and she flutters them open again. "Every fucking bastard who was involved in this paedophile ring is dead apart from the last two. Stay with me, because they'll be dead before the sun rises. I promise."

She closes her eyes again. "Thank you," she mutters, "for caring enough to go after them. I wish I knew you years ago. You would have saved me so much pain."

"After today, you'll never feel pain again. Not like this. I'll make it right."

We fall silent for a few moments, then her eyes open again. "Storm . . . she has a pink stuffed elephant. She can't sleep without it. She likes the movement of the car when she can't settle. And she hates waiting for her morning feed, so be on that shit right away." She gasps, and I squeeze her hand harder in panic.

"Baby, you can show me all of that when we get out of here, okay?"

I watch Lottie's chest move up and down. She hasn't opened her eyes for fifteen minutes now, and it doesn't matter how much I nudge her with my foot or shout her name, she's out cold. Her blood is soaking into the mattress despite the dirty rags she's got pressed against her wounds. I hear a loud bang and freeze. Rushing to the door, I press my ear to it, grinning when I hear Blade's familiar voice. "Motherfucker, that hurt," he snaps.

"Blade, in here," I shout, moving back from the door. A second later, it busts open, and Blade pokes his head in. "Brother, it's so fucking good to see your ugly ass face," I say.

"Shit, you look like you've done a few rounds in the ring," he observes.

"We gotta get Lottie out of here. She's unconscious." I move to the side so he can see her on the mattress. Pulling out a set of keys, he unlocks my cuffs. I don't bother questioning why he's got a set of handcuff keys. I scoop Lottie up in my arms and follow Blade out the room.

There's chaos in the flat, men fighting and dead bodies strewn across the floor. Raven is by the door, and I pass Lottie to her. "Get her to the hospital," I order.

"Shouldn't you be with her?" she asks uncertainly.

"I have some unfinished business here," I say, turning back to the chaos.

I spot Riggs with Ali. He's got him by the throat. "How happy are you to see me again?" I ask, grinning.

"You must love that whore to go to this amount of trouble." Ali grins, spitting blood at my feet.

"I just can't stand people like you," I say. "You see that man there?" I add, pointing to Lake, who's just slit the throat of this arse's accomplice. "That's her brother, and he's super-pissed about the whole situation," I say.

"You think I'm scared of you? Any of you?" he asks, smiling. "Only God can judge me."

I take a knife from Blade. "Wrong," I say. I hold his little finger to the side and slice the knife to the bone, snapping the rest. He howls in pain, and I shake my head. "Not even God would protect scum like you. Right now, I'm your judge and jury and I say you belong in hell." I stick the blade into the palm of his hand, and he wails. Riggs stuffs a towel into his mouth to muffle his screams as I stab the blade into his other hand.

Brick comes over, holding his mobile to his ear. "Pres, the cops are on their way."

I roll my eyes. Trust law enforcement to show up when I'm just getting warmed up. "Go set off the fire alarms, give everyone a chance to evacuate before we send this place up," orders Riggs.

I stuff the knife into Ali's stomach, and his eyes widen. I love that look in the second they realise they're actually going to die. I pull the blade along his flesh and step back as his guts spill out. He tries to hold them in, sliding down the wall and clutching what he can. "Rest in hell," I mutter.

Cree is splashing petrol around the flat. We step out, and Riggs throws a cigarette back inside, lighting the fuel instantly. He closes the door and we make our way down the stairs along with other residents who are leaving the building in response to the blaring fire alarm.

Chapter Nineteen

LOTTIE

"I didn't try to kill myself," I hiss.

The doctor looks doubtfully over at Anna. "Let me talk to her," she says and waits for him to step outside.

"Lottie, he's never gonna believe you didn't do this, not with your history," she says carefully. "Just get him to sign the damn paperwork and you're free to leave."

My eyes widen. "Free?" I repeat. "That's not exactly true, is it?"

"Would you rather they section you?" she asks.

"I'd rather we all just tell the truth," I snap.

"You know that can't happen. The guys will get sent down for murder, arson, and god knows what else."

"But I'll be free," I hiss.

"You want Lake to go to prison?" she snaps. "I know you think this is unfair, but this was all for you. Be thankful you're alive. Agree to the release terms and come home to your daughter."

My heart squeezes. Since waking up in hospital three days ago, I haven't seen Elsie. The doctors think I tried to kill myself, despite my bruises and obvious assault. Now, my choice is get released into the club's care or go into a mental hospital for three months of intense treatment. "Riggs pulled some strings to have you released to the club. It's your best option," says Anna, her eyes pleading for me to listen. I sigh heavily and nod. Fine, I'll sign the damn papers. Three months at the club with Elsie is better than being locked up in a hospital.

I stare at the clubhouse doors. "It's gonna be okay," Anna whispers gently. "Everyone's been so worried about you."

"Is he good with her?" I ask, referring to Storm and Elsie.

"He's really good with her. He's been doing her night feeds. I think she's been unsettled without you."

"He didn't come to the hospital," I point out. "I thought he'd bring her to see me."

"He had to deal with social care. They were asking all kinds of questions. Things have been a little crazy."

I nod. Social care agreed to let Elsie stay with Storm, but it wasn't easy convincing them he hadn't beaten me and that was the reason I'd tried to kill myself. I guess that would have been easier to believe than the truth. "If you need anything," says Anna, "you can always come to me. Nothing's changed."

I push the door open and step inside. "Everything's changed," I whisper.

I'm greeted by the ol' ladies. They're all pleased to see me, and I feel slightly more relaxed. Even Frankie seems happy as she embraces me. I spot Storm watching me from across the room and make my way over. "She's sleeping," he says bluntly.

"I need to see her," I say desperately.

"You can, once she's awake."

"You don't understand," I whisper, tears filling my eyes. "I've never been apart from her, and now, it's been four days. I have to see her."

"Now you know how I feel not seeing her for the first three months of her life," he snaps.

"That's not the same," I hiss. "You didn't know about her."

Anna gently places her hand on my shoulder. "Storm, let her pass. She's been through enough."

He glares at Anna, then sighs, stepping to one side. I rush upstairs to his room and burst into tears when my eyes finally land on Elsie. I scoop her into my arms and bury my nose into her soft body, inhaling her baby smell. "I've missed you so much," I mumble against her. "I love you."

A woman, the one from the caravan, steps into the room from the bathroom and stops when she sees me. "Does Storm know you're up here?" she asks, glancing at the door.

I nod, swiping at my tear-stained face. "I'm her mum," I explain.

"I know," she says, "but he said not to let anyone in."

Ignoring her, I take a seat in the middle of the bed and lie Elsie down in front of me so I can stare at her peaceful face. The door flies open and Seb runs in. "You're back," he screeches, and I smile wide. He seems happy to see me. "Guess what, I have a sister," he adds excitedly. He climbs on the bed and lays next to Elsie, gently running a finger over her tummy.

"I know," I say. "How cool is that?"

"Really cool," he says. Bently joins us, curling up on the other side of Elsie. I smile down at all three of them. I ignore the niggling voice telling me this could've been us, if I'd have given Storm the chance to be a part of Elsie's life.

"Seb, shall we walk Bently?" asks the woman.

Seb shakes his head, taking my hand in his. "I want to stay with Lottie," he says.

"Too bad. You need to walk the mutt," comes Storm's voice, and Seb rolls his eyes.

"I'll be here when you get back," I reassure him, and he nods, following the woman from the room. Storm catches her hand in his as they pass, and they share a brief kiss. I stare down at Elsie, ignoring the squeeze to my heart.

"I thought you were gonna die," he mutters, taking a seat on the end of his bed.

"It would have worked out better for you if I had," I say, straightening Elsie's little pink dress. "With me out the way, you could play happy family with your ol' lady and my daughter."

"She ain't my ol' lady."

"Yet," I say.

"How's this gonna play out?" he asks.

"I'll stay out of your way," I mutter. "Three months will fly by, then I'll be outta your hair."

"Taking my daughter with you," he says coldly.

"I never asked for any of this," I snap. "I wanted to go home and live my life, but I had to lie to keep you all from going to prison. I didn't ask you to get involved, so why did you go after Ali and those men?"

"For you," he growls, standing and pacing the room. "I couldn't stand what they did to you. They had to fucking pay."

"It was over. My life was moving on. I have a nice place and a future. You've dragged me back into this life, and now I have to stick around here for three months watching you with her—" I clamp my lips shut. I didn't mean to say that.

"She isn't living here. She came to see how I was doing."

"It doesn't matter. You have your life too. It's why I never wanted to tell you, but Lake made me and now look." I suck in a breath.

"You should never have kept it from me. I know I lost my mind after everything with Seb, but if you'd have told me, I would have supported you. We had it good, didn't we?"

"I don't wanna talk about the past," I mutter. It's too hard to go over what could have been. "I made my choice and I can't change it. I'll stay out of your way, and when it's time for me to leave, we'll sort arrangements out for Elsie then." I scoop her against my chest and get off the bed. "Nothing's ever simple with us, is it?" I add. "We attract drama. I don't miss that."

STORM

Watching Lottie be a mum to our baby girl is both hard and amazing all at the same time. It's been two weeks since she arrived and her bruises have slowly faded to pale yellow. Leia has been in charge of the bandage changes and she tells me the deep cuts to Lottie's arms are healing well, and the stitches are due to be taken out any day now.

"It changes things, doesn't it." Riggs takes a seat beside me on the grass. "When Anna told me she was pregnant with Willow, I was so pissed. I remember thinking, how the fuck do I tell this woman that

I might not be around to help raise our kid. I'd only just found out about the cancer then, and I was a mess. I'd go to visit Willow and see Anna with her and my heart would ache, brother. Seeing her be a mother to my kid, fuck, it changed everything. I found a new respect that wasn't there before. She carried my child and was raising her on her own like a fucking queen. Even with all the shit I was throwing her way, she still got on with it."

I nod, keeping my eyes fixed on Lottie as she cradles Elsie against her chest and laughs at something Anna is telling her. He's right. Something possessive is growing inside of me, and every time I watch them together, it gets bigger. "She can't wait to get out of here," I say. "If it wasn't for Lake, I wouldn't even know about Elsie."

"Do you blame her, brother? Man, she came back to see you and within an hour she was handcuffed in a room by a man who molested her as a kid."

I snigger, shrugging my shoulders. "What's your point?"

"There was a time when you claimed her as yours, brother. The way I see it, you both fucked up along the way, but now you're both in a better place, and you have that beautiful little girl to raise. What better excuse do you need to give it a go?"

I laugh. "I think she'd rather gouge her own eyes out than ever have my name tattooed on her again."

"You're a Kings Reaper, since when did we ever take no for an answer. You want her, go get her."

"And what about Emily?"

"You ain't claiming Emily," he scoffs. "She's a tight pussy to help you out on a bad day, but she ain't ol' lady material and you know it. That there," he says, pointing to Lottie, "is your future."

"Careful, Pres, you almost sound wise."

Riggs laughs. "I've always been wise," he says. "I just hide it well."

I watch Lottie apply the finishing touches to her makeup. "Why are you wearing all that if you're just drinking in the club bar?" I ask, rocking Elsie gently. I said I'd watch her while Lottie got ready for a girls' night, and even though she's not actually leaving the club, I'm still scowling as she applies a coat of lip gloss.

"It's nice to feel attractive sometimes. Especially when you've just had a baby. I spend my days covered in milk spit," she says, laughing. Over the last few days, things have been easier between us. We've gradually spoken more and more and even shared a joke or two.

"You wanna meet someone?" I ask, trying to look nonchalant.

"Who the hell would I meet here, Storm? Everyone's got an ol' lady, and those who haven't, are single for very good reasons."

"I haven't got an ol' lady," I say, feigning insult.

She rolls her eyes. "It's been months since I had a drink and even longer since I spent quality time with the girls. I'm looking forward to relaxing and not worrying about Elsie." I place a kiss on Elsie's head, and she stirs. "If you're sure you don't mind watching her for me," she adds.

"Of course not. Since you've been back, she's slept like a dream," I say, and Lottie's eyes bug out of her head.

"How would you know? She's in here with me."

"I'm right next door. I hear every whimper coming from this room." I raise an eyebrow, and she blushes. "So, just remember that tonight. I'm gonna put her down in her crib. Have a good night." I head towards my room, where I've got a crib set up for Elsie. I plan on keeping a close eye on her *and* her mum tonight. There ain't no way I'm sitting in my room knowing Lottie is down in the bar looking this good with men like Vinn likely to stop by.

Chapter Twenty

LOTTIE

I've made no secret about the fact I'm mad as hell to be back at the club, but sitting here chatting with the ol' ladies is something I've definitely missed. Leia tops up my third glass of wine, and I take the glass and keep my hand over the top so she can't do it again. I haven't drunk in such a long time and it's going straight to my head.

"I like Raven," argues Leia, "but she's always with the guys. I'm surprised Riggs hasn't made her a club member," she adds.

"They don't take girls," says Eva. "I asked already."

Anna laughs. "You want to be a club member?"

Eva grins. "I was winding Cree up. Told him I want to get a bike and join an MC. He freaked the hell out. We spent all day in bed that time," she says, winking.

"What would your road name be?" Anna asks.

"Something really crude like 'Wet Pussy'," she says, and Tillie giggles. "Just so I could see the shock when I said my name to some of these guys."

"You're going off subject," argues Leia.

"Because we don't wanna talk about your crazy obsession with Raven," says Eva.

"Why doesn't Riggs let any of us go on runs? He had Vinn showing her how to use all kinds of guns. He'd never ever dream of letting any of us use a weapon."

"I don't want to use a weapon," says Anna.

"That's not the point. It's wrong he has rules for some of us and not others."

"Then raise it with your brother," Anna suggests. "Riggs is reasonable, he'll explain why Raven is more like a brother than an ol' lady."

"Are you all happy that she goes on runs with your men? What happens when it's a long run? Where the hell does she sleep?"

Eva groans. "For goodness sake, Leia, stop. Has something happened to make you freak like this?"

Leia shakes her head. "I just think it's weird."

"We're not talking about this anymore. Talk to Riggs about it," says Anna firmly, then she turns to me. "How are you?"

"Good," I say, smiling. "Still not happy that I've effectively been sectioned, but I'm getting over it. I missed you guys."

"We missed you too. It's so great to have you back. Just like old times," says Sara.

"But not for long," I remind her, and she pouts.

"Would you consider staying if you and Storm can work past the hostility?" asks Eva.

"Actually, the last few days we've been civil, friendly even," I say, "but it won't last. One of us will say or do something to upset the other, usually me." I feel Storm enter the room. My skin prickles, and our eyes connect as he crosses the bar and joins Riggs and some of the others.

"Looks like he's made an effort this evening," Anna notes. He's wearing a white button-down shirt and his usual Levi's. She's right—he looks hot. Leia clicks her fingers to gain my attention, laughing when I start.

"Earth to Lottie," she jokes.

I blush. "I have my own place. I like the independence I have. I'm out of here as soon as the three months are up and the doctor clears me."

The main door opens and Emily enters. Anna groans. "What's she doing here?"

I take a sip of my drink and pretend I don't care. "She is his girlfriend," I point out, forcing a smile. "Don't you like her?"

Anna nods. "I guess she's alright, but she isn't exactly club material. And she's not you."

I smile affectionately. "He's allowed to move on. We ended almost a year ago." I down my glass of wine, wincing at the bitter taste. This time, I push my glass towards Leia for a top-up. The women talk, but my attention keeps going back to Storm and the way he's got his arm possessively around Emily's shoulder. And the way he looks down at her, giving her a crooked smile every time she speaks to him. I roll my eyes, shaking my head. He catches me and narrows his eyes like he wants me to explain. I give him a fake smile and turn my attention back to the girls. "We need another bottle," I say, standing a little too quickly and gripping the table to steady myself. "I'll get it."

I waltz over to the bar, brushing past Storm, who's in my path. "Sorry," I mumble, gripping his waist as I squeeze past. I lean over the bar waiting for Frankie, who's already pouring someone a beer. I feel him behind me as he leans close to my ear.

"Everything okay?" he asks.

I nod. "Elsie asleep?" He wiggles the video monitor in front of me to show Elsie sleeping in her crib. "If Emily is staying over tonight, I can have her back in my room. I'll just stop drinking now."

"Look at us being civilised parents." He smirks.

"We've both grown up, a little," I say, smiling.

Frankie hands me two bottles of wine. "Do you want me to have Elsie back?" I ask, showing him the two bottles of wine.

He shakes his head, smiling. "No, butterfly, you have a good night." His nickname for me stings, but I return his smile and head back to the girls.

The jukebox kicks to life and the girls cheer their approval. Frankie gives us the thumbs up, and Anna blows her a kiss. "Now, it feels like a party," she says, topping up our glasses.

"The guys look like they want to evacuate," says Eva, laughing. Little Mix blares out of the speakers, and we move to a table-free space so we can dance.

"We can't dance to Meatloaf," says Anna, shrugging. "They'll have to suck it up for one night."

I laugh as Leia throws some crazy moves, and I try my best not to fall as I sway to the music. Five glasses of wine is clearly my new limit as the room wobbles around me. I catch Storm watching over Emily's shoulder and give him my best sultry look as I move my hips. "Girl, you're flirting!" accuses Anna.

I grin. "I shouldn't, right, not when his girlfriend is right next to him, but something about him makes me wanna do crazy shit," I admit.

"You can only flirt if he lets you, and right now, he's looking pretty intrigued."

"You should be reminding me about girl code," I say.

"Girl code goes out the window when we've had way too much wine, and she's not a part of the club. Until he claims her, I don't have any loyalty towards her."

It's like a cold bucket of water washing over me. If he claims Emily, I'll be the outsider, not her. I spin into a hard chest. I feel the taut muscles under my hands, and my eyes eventually look up into Vinn's. "Well, well, well, the wanderer returns," he says with a smirk.

"Vinn," I say, and it comes out breathy.

"It's the perfect time to kiss you," he says, and I suck in a surprised breath, "and I'd love nothing more than to piss your ex off. I can feel his eyes burning into my head. But I have business to attend to. I don't have time for club drama." I stare at him like a rabbit caught in headlights. "Don't pretend you wouldn't love the opportunity to wind him up," he adds with a wink.

"He's with his girlfriend. He's not interested in me," I whisper.

Vinn's hands go to my arse, and I yelp as he tugs me hard against him. "Dance with me," he says, slowly turning us until I see Storm's face full of anger, staring directly at where Vinn's hands squeeze my arse. "Can you imagine what he'd do if I tipped you back like this," he adds, dipping me back slightly. I grip his shoulders, staring wide into his mischievous eyes. "And kissed you."

"Why do you like winding these guys up so much?" I ask.

He chuckles. "It's fun to see them explode. They know they can't touch me and it makes it even more satisfying."

"Why can't they touch you?" I ask.

He moves his face closer to me, his lips inches away. "Because I'm untouchable, *farfalla*," I frown at his Italian word, and he grins before standing me back straight. "Butterfly," he explains. "Thank you for the dance."

I watch as he strolls towards Riggs' office. "What the hell was that about?" asks Anna.

I shrug, my mouth still open in shock. "I'm not sure, but I need some air."

Anna laughs. "He has that effect on women. He's a modern day Casanova."

I notice Storm and Emily have disappeared as I break out into the carpark and take a deep breath of cold air. Christ, Vinn is so intense. I laugh to myself. He never misses an opportunity to piss off the guys. "It's just not working," I hear Storm's voice and edge to the side of the building, ducking behind the large bins.

"But you were fine just a minute ago and now you're dumping me?"

"Emily, it's not you. It's me." I wince as I hear the sound of a slap. "Fuck," hisses Storm, and I stifle a laugh. "I never said we were serious."

"Did you invite me here to make your ex jealous?" she demands to know.

"No, why would I do that? I told you, we're not like that. She's moved on, and so have I."

"You'll regret this," she shouts, and I hear the sound of her heels clicking as she walks away.

"How long are you gonna hide down there?" asks Storm as he steps in front of me.

I slowly rise to my feet. "Sorry, I didn't want it to look like I followed you out. I just wanted some air."

"Not surprising after the little show you and Vinn put on in there," he mutters.

I sway, steadying myself against the wall. My head spins and I close my eyes briefly. "He was winding you up."

"I had my hand on my gun," he says, and I grin.

STORM

Lottie wobbles forward, and I catch her arm to steady her. "How much have you had to drink?"

"Way too much," she mutters. "I think . . . I might . . . oh god . . ." She doubles over and vomits over the floor. It splatters over her shoes. "Fuck," she whispers.

"You couldn't do that ten minutes ago all over that Italian prick?" I ask, lifting her hair back while she vomits again.

"Please go inside, this is so embarrassing," she cries.

"And miss this?" I ask, laughing. "Let's get you to bed."

"Now is hardly the time to proposition me," she wails, and I laugh harder.

"Butterfly, trust me, I ain't propositioning anyone. Especially not someone who I've just watched throw up two bottles of wine."

Leading her inside, I wave to Anna, indicating I'm taking her to bed. Anna gives me the thumbs up. We get to the stairs, and I bend, throwing Lottie over my shoulder. "You want me to take her?" asks

Vinn, appearing from Riggs' office. His arrogant face bothers me more than it should.

"And why would I want that?" I ask.

"Well, you aren't a thing anymore, so maybe she doesn't want you helping her up the stairs. Especially when she's passed out from drinking."

"She's the mother of my kid. I'll always look after her."

Vinn shrugs. "The offer is there if you ever need me to distract her."

"Ain't it about time you got your own woman instead of leering round the club's ol' ladies?" I snap.

"Only she isn't an ol' lady, is she?" he sneers. "She's free and single."

I shake my head, muttering the word 'dick' as I head upstairs. I stop outside Lottie's room, hesitating. What if she's sick during the night? I don't want her choking. I take a step towards my room, then stop and turn back to hers again. It's not really responsible to leave her alone all night. I sigh and head for my room. Elsie is flat on her back with her arms above her head. I smile. Laying Lottie on my side of the bed, I take off her shoes, screwing my face up and taking them to the bathroom to wash off.

When I return, Lottie is curled up under the sheets. I take in the scene before me . . . my daughter and her mum, both in my room. My heart swells with love.

I climb into bed beside her, leaving my clothes on, and prop myself on my elbow to watch her sleep. She's beautiful. I gently brush some hair from her face and lean closer, pressing a gentle kiss to her cheek. She stirs and rolls onto her stomach. I run my finger over the healing scars on her arms. The stitches have left ridges over her skin, a harsh reminder of what that bastard did to her.

Her shirt has ridden up, and I peer at the tattoo poking out from under it. Carefully lifting her top, I get a better look, curious to see what cover-up she went with the day she left. The lamp isn't bright enough for me to get a good look, so I use the torch on my phone. A large, brightly coloured butterfly sits over where my name once was. It's surrounded by smaller butterflies. Above them, the words 'Surviving the Storm' are written in script. I trace the outline of the butterfly, my heart heavy for everything we've lost.

Her name still sits on my arm in large letters—I didn't have it in me to cover it up.

I wake as a warmth spreads throughout my body. It takes me a second to realise the room is in total darkness and that warmth is from Lottie as she rides me. "What the fuck?" I pant, flicking the lamp back on.

She looks at me with panic. "You want me to stop?"

"I . . . what . . ." I glance at the bedside clock. We've only been asleep an hour, so she's still drunk. "Shit, Lottie, you'll regret this in the morning," I say, gripping her waist and trying to slow her down.

"I haven't had sex in a year," she whispers. "It felt like the right thing to do." She braces her hands against my chest and pushes herself up, then sinks down slowly, releasing a low moan.

"Don't you think this will just complicate everything?" I ask.

"Yes, but right now, I don't care." She begins to rock back and forth, shuddering with each stroke. "I'm not on the pill," she adds, guilt on her face, but it's too late, I'm already squeezing her thighs as I come, staring up at her in horror.

I wake with a start, glancing around the room and feeling down my body for my clothes. Everything is still in place, including my jeans that are crushing my erection. "Thank fuck," I whisper to myself, relieved it was a dream.

"You okay?" asks Lottie. I spin my head to where she's sitting up in bed, feeding a bottle to Elsie.

"Erm, yeah. Sorry, I didn't hear her wake," I mutter, grabbing the covers to hide my erection.

"It's six in the morning. That's great for her," she says. "I feel like I've had a sleep in."

"No bad head?" I ask, lying on my side and watching Elsie guzzle her milk.

"No. Did I vomit all over my shoes?" she asks, blushing.

I nod. "That's why you're here. You were really drunk, and I was worried you'd choke or something," I explain.

"How embarrassing," she mutters.

"Everyone's allowed to drink until they throw up at least once as a parent," I joke. "I'm just glad you didn't throw yourself at Vinn."

Her blush deepens and she groans. "Oh god, I remember that. He was dancing with his hands on my arse."

"Don't remind me," I mutter.

"Oh god, you dumped Emily?" she gasps. "Why did you dump Emily?"

I shrug. "Things weren't working out. I wasn't looking for anything serious."

Lottie bites her lower lip, and my erection strains harder. "And she slapped you," she says, smirking.

"You could look a little less pleased about that part," I say, arching my brow. She giggles and it warms my fucking heart. I missed that sound. "What about you? Did you meet anyone in Liverpool?"

She shakes her head, glancing down at Elsie. "I had other things on my mind. Men were the furthest thing from it."

"Where did you stay? How long were you there?" I ask.

"A few months. I went into a women's shelter once I discovered I was pregnant. They help you get a place to live, only there weren't many nice places in Liverpool. I met my friend. Kyla, there. She was moving back to London, so I came with her and the shelter managed to find me a place right away."

"And you never thought about coming back here?"

She shrugs. "Maybe a few times. It would have been the easier option, but I wasn't strong enough. I had to fix myself. I couldn't do that here."

"Because of me?"

"Because of lots of things. Lake, Conner, everything I ever wanted was here, and walking away took a lot. I didn't want to face them again until I was strong enough. What happened to Seb—"

"It wasn't your fault," I blurt out, and she looks at me with surprise. "I was angry and I lashed out, but it wasn't your fault. It was an accident. I should never have put any of that on you."

"I'm just glad he's okay."

"We messed things up every time," I mutter. "We had so many chances and we always fucked it up."

"We can't regret it. We have Elsie."

I nod in agreement. She's been in my life for almost four weeks now, and I love her like she was always a part of it. Seb is completely taken with her, and it'll break his heart when she leaves the club.

Chapter Twenty-One

LOTTIE

I watch Storm's mouth move as he speaks to Riggs across the breakfast table and all I can think about is feeling his lips against mine. The demanding and forceful way he kisses me with his hands at the back of my neck, holding me in place while his tongue dips into my mouth. I release a slight moan, and Storm glances at me before continuing his conversation.

He eventually turns to me. "You want sex?" he asks, and my eyes widen.

"Huh?"

"I said, have you sent that text?" he repeats, frowning at me. "To your friend. You said she'd be worried if you didn't make contact soon."

I smile awkwardly. "Yes, I sent it earlier." I've been in contact with Kyla several times to explain what happened, but I promised to check in with her regularly.

"Have you told her you're staying here for a while?" he adds, scooping more eggs onto my plate. I scowl, and he raises a brow. "You've lost a lot of weight. You need to eat."

"I think I look good," I say, glancing down at myself. "It took some hard work to lose the pounds I gained from Elsie."

"Maybe you should give up your new place. We can find you somewhere once your time here is up. Somewhere closer," he suggests.

"I like my new place," I say.

Storm holds up a forkful of eggs and waits for me to open before shoving it into my mouth. I frown. He's way bossier than I remember. "How will I see Elsie every day if you're that far away?"

"It's a twenty-minute drive," I argue.

"In an ideal place with no traffic. It'll take me forty minutes to get to you, and that means Seb won't get to see her as often. I won't be around to fuck you every night."

I glare at him, glancing around to see if anyone else heard. "What?"

He frowns again. "I won't be able to tuck her in every night. I want to be there to do normal things like read her a bedtime story or tuck her into bed at night."

I laugh at myself. I'm driving myself nuts. "We'll talk about this later," I say. "I need a shower." A cold shower.

He watches me in confusion as I rush from the table. Lack of sex hasn't bothered me at all, but being back around him is getting me all kinds of fired up. I check that Elsie is still asleep. She always goes back to sleep after her morning bottle. I leave the bathroom door open in case she wakes and I turn the shower on to cold.

Lathering myself in soap, I shiver as my hands brush over my skin. Fuck, when did I become such a horny cow? I stare at the shower head, biting on my lower lip. It'd only take a second, and I have to do something about this sexual tension. I reach for the shower head and hold it in place, smiling as it hits the spot. Pinching my swollen nipples, I throw my head back and pant as I climb closer to my orgasm.

"Butterfly, I was think—"

I drop the shower head and water spurts up in my face as the head dances about. Storm stares at me with his mouth wide open, unsure what to do as I try desperately to get a hold of the shower head.

"I was . . . I just, erm . . ." I try to explain.

He nods stiffly and turns, leaving the room. My face burns with embarrassment. How the hell will I ever face him again? To top it off, I didn't even get to dim the fucking buzz.

I dress Elsie, taking my time so I put off seeing Storm. When I eventually head downstairs, he's on the couch with Seb watching a cartoon. His eyes burn into mine and this time, they're full of heat. I look away, embarrassed. Every time I picture the shock on his face, I feel a little more mortified. Frankie breezes in and holds her arms out for Elsie. I hand her over, confused. "Aren't you going out with the girls today?" she asks.

"Not that I know of," I say.

"Of course, she is," says Anna, "I just have to let Riggs know we're off. Give me two minutes."

"What's this?" asks Storm. "We're taking Lottie out for a few hours," says Anna.

"Since when? Who okayed this?"

"I did," snaps Anna.

"Not with me, you didn't," growls Storm, narrowing his eyes.

His scare tactics don't affect Anna, and she rolls her eyes. "I don't have to clear it with

you. I cleared it with Riggs. And seeing as Lottie isn't claimed, she's under Lake's care, so I also cleared it with him."

"Where are you going?" he asks, clearly pissed by her smartass answer.

"Again, it's none of your business, but we're going to the salon to pamper ourselves."

"Who's watching over you?" he pushes.

"Christ, is Anna my ol' lady or yours?" yells Riggs from inside his office, causing Anna to giggle. "If you're so fucking worried, you can go watch them along with Brick."

"You were sending Brick?" shouts Storm. "He's got the attention span of a fucking fly. How will he keep them safe?"

"That ain't a fucking problem no more cos you're taking your moody ass along for the ride. Maybe you can drop by Lake's club later and get laid, see if some rough sex can't sort that mood out?" Riggs retorts.

Storm shakes his head. "I'm all good in that department, Pres."

I frown. What the hell does he mean by that? I don't get time to analyse it because Anna takes her car keys and grabs me by the hand. "Come on, the others are meeting us there."

It's been over a year since I last visited a salon. The hairdresser lifts my lank hair and examines the split ends closely. "I had a kid," I mutter feebly. "I haven't had time to get it cut properly."

She smiles at my reflection in the mirror. "What sort of colour were you thinking?" she asks. I've spent years colouring my hair and haven't been back to my natural strawberry blonde colour since I was a teenager.

"As long as I leave here looking better than when I walked in, I'll be happy," I say, smiling.

"Let's go for a dark reddish-brown. You have a lovely skin tone and it'll freshen up this drab, washed-out colouring."

While my hair colour takes, I sit next to Leia to get my nails done. "You okay?" I ask, and she nods. "I feel like you need to talk about Raven," I add because the girls shut her down last night and I think she feels like Raven is some kind of threat.

She shrugs. "Since having Grace, I feel crap about myself. I know it's my issue, but I can't help stressing that Chains will look elsewhere. They have a connection. Chains saved her life."

"But he isn't with Raven, he's with you."

"What if that's because of Grace? He came back with Raven and they were sleeping together. I kept Grace a secret from him. Maybe he only got with me because of her."

"I think it's normal to worry like this," I reassure her, "especially after having a baby. I feel like a great big flump most days, but I really think Chains is mad about you. Plus, Riggs would gut him if he messed around with anyone else."

"She's just so . . . perfect," she mutters. "I don't mean it in a bitchy way—I'm genuinely in awe of her. She's brave, she doesn't take any shit from the guys, they turn to her for advice, they even take her out on runs."

"Everything you've just said makes me feel sad for Raven," I say, and Leia looks confused. "The guys see her as one of them. None of the guys see her as ol' lady material, and isn't that the reason most of the women stick around the club? Don't they want to be an ol' lady?"

"Not everyone," says Leia.

"From what I've heard, she's had a few crushes on some of the guys. That tells me she'd jump at the chance to be an ol' lady. Seems to me she gets friend zoned a lot. You're sitting here wishing you were more like her, while she's probably doing the same about you. If you feel crap, dress up, stick some makeup on, dance sexy for your man behind closed doors . . . do whatever it takes to make yourself feel great again."

Leia nods. "Maybe you could show me how to dance?"

"I would love to. Chains won't know what's hit him."

I stare with my eyes wide at my reflection as the hairdresser stands behind me, smiling proudly. "You like?"

"Oh my god, I love it." I run my fingers through the bouncy, deep reddish-brown curls.

"You look amazing," says Anna. "I can't wait for Storm to see you." I glance through the window. It's reflective glass, which means I can see him sitting idly on his motorcycle chatting to Brick, but he can't see me.

"Right, ladies, we have to dance," says Leia, shaking out her own fresh curls and wiggling her ass. A few of the beauticians stand eagerly.

Riggs booked the shop out to us for the morning, so there are no other customers as Leia cranks up the music on her mobile. "Lottie's gonna show us some sexy moves, right?" she adds.

I stand, pushing my chair out of the way. "Let's go."

STORM

"What the fuck takes so long?" mutters Brick.

"Women like to look good," I say, shrugging. It's been hours and I'm curious as to what the hell's going on in that place. The faint sounds of Shania Twain's "Man! I Feel Like a Woman!" and the women laughing and yelling have piqued my interest. "Let's go check it out," I add, getting off my bike.

"Now, we're talking," says Brick, grinning and rubbing his hands together. I open the door and stop. I'm met with women, bent over, their arses in the air, all gripping their ankles. "Let me see," whispers Brick, and I step inside with him hot on my heels.

Lottie stands, smiling wide. "Ooo, men, can we show you our dance?"

I sigh, taking a seat. I feel like I'm about to witness carnage, a bit like when Malia and Molly want to show off a dance they've learnt from some Disney film. "Okay, girls. From the top," orders Lottie.

Shania Twain begins to play again, and I exchange a glance with Brick when the women begin to move. This is no ordinary dance. I suddenly feel like I'm back in Vinn's strip bar, watching the women onstage. They sway and dip, biting their lips and shaking their asses. I shouldn't be watching the brothers' ol' ladies dance like this, but damn if I can peel my eyes away. When the song comes to an end, they all bend over with their asses in the air, and I glance back at Brick, who looks just as uncomfortable as me.

Lottie stands, smiling. "So?" she asks.

"Are you trying to get us killed?" I ask.

"Were we good?"

"Good enough that I shouldn't have watched it. Fuck." I stand and point my finger. "If any of you women breathe a word of that to your old men, we'll deny it. As far as I'm concerned, we didn't even step into this place today," I say stiffly. I head out with Brick right behind me.

"Jesus," he mutters. "Why the hell did we go in there? Now, I gotta go find me a woman."

I snigger. "If you'd seen some of the things I'd witnessed today, you'd have balls dragging on the ground right now." I shake my head, trying to get rid of the image of Lottie in the shower this morning. Seeing her with her head thrown back in pleasure, that shower head doing the job I'm desperate to do . . . shit, I'm a walking bag of horny right now.

The girls begin to file out of the salon. Lottie heads straight for me. "We're going for lunch," she says.

I reach for a curl and twist it around my finger. "I like this," I say, and she blushes.

"Are you following us to lunch?" she asks.

"Damn right," I mutter, kicking my bike to life. She smiles and walks to Anna's car. Not having her on my bike is something else I'm struggling with.

I take a seat at the bar along with Brick, while the women are seated at a booth. "Are you and Lottie—" begins Brick. I shake my head before he's finished. "Is she free?" he adds, sipping his whiskey.

"What kinda fucking question is that?" I snap. "Does Lake know you wanna fuck his sister?"

"Whoa," says Brick, holding up his hands. "Who said anything about fucking anyone? I was just asking a question. Wondering what your plans are, like if you're gonna make her yours again?"

"She's not available," I growl.

"Easy, tiger, I wasn't trying to step in there."

We sit in silence, but his questions rile me. When a woman isn't claimed, it means she's free for the brothers. I can't kill anyone for laying a finger on her because she isn't mine. Usually, she'd be expected to join the club girls and do jobs around the place as well as have sex with the brothers, but cos she's Lake's sister, it's different. She's gonna be around the club for a few months yet and she'll turn heads of the brothers. They'll see her as ol' lady material because of Lake and she's got a kid. I run my hands through my hair and glance over to where she's chatting with Anna. They laugh, and she throws her head back, exposing her throat to me. My cock twitches. Being around her is fucking killing me.

Chapter Twenty-Two

LOTTIE

"I don't think going to Vinn's club is a good idea," I say to Anna.

She scowls. "It's Saturday night, and we have babysitters. What's your problem?"

It's been a week since Storm caught me in the shower and I've not touched myself since. Mainly because I'm terrified he'll walk in on me again. So now, I'm ridiculously horny, not helped by the fact that everywhere I turn, I see that big, handsome, tattooed bastard. "You saw how Vinn was. He goes out his way to annoy Storm, and we're getting on so well, I don't want to rock the boat." It's true that Storm and I have come to a comfortable truce. He even helps with night feeds when he hears Elsie cry.

"Are you going to stay home? Sit with Frankie, Esther, and the kids? Because Storm is coming to the club. I heard Lake ask him." That's even more of a reason to not go, but I find myself snatching the dress she's holding out for me to try on. Damn my hormones.

The dress is short, barely covering my arse. "Perfect," says Anna.

"If it's perfect, why aren't you wearing it?" I ask.

"Cos Riggs would kill me. Storm can't say anything to you, not unless he claims you."

"You're obsessed with that," I say. "Why?"

She shrugs. "I guess I want you two to sort your shit out. You belong together."

"I don't think he sees me like that anymore, Anna. You're wasting your time. This is the longest time we've spent together without arguing."

"And you think that's because he doesn't love you anymore?"

"Maybe. He looks at me differently. The fire in his eyes is gone."

Anna smiles. "He sees you as the mother of his child. His love has changed. It's deeper. There's a respect there now that wasn't there before."

Anna's words play on my mind as we head to the club. A few weeks ago, I would never have thought I'd be back at the MC clubhouse, let alone getting on with Storm. I kept a huge secret, and he forgave me. When I see him with Elsie, it does something to me. I see him through different eyes too.

Vinn greets us the second we step to the bar and tells the bartender to get us champagne. "You had your hair done," he says, taking it between his fingers. I shift my head away, noting that Storm is watching from across the bar where he stands with the other guys. Vinn smirks. "You and him a thing again?" he asks, and I shake my head.

"Stop trying to get under Storm's skin," says Leia, taking the bottle of champagne. "One day, Mr. Romano, you'll meet your queen. Until then, stop trying to steal someone else's."

He grins playfully, "We both know you were supposed to be my queen until that oversized biker stole you," he says warmly. It's no secret Vinn has a thing for Leia. "Enjoy your evening, ladies. Keep your beasts under control."

"Has he always been like that?" I ask Gia, his sister, and she rolls her eyes.

"He's an idiot. Ignore him. He could flirt his way out of anything."

We join the men, and even though I'm talking with Anna, I feel Storm's eyes on me the whole time. Leia nudges me. "It worked," she whispers. When it's clear I have no idea what she's talking about, she smirks. "The dance. I chose my best underwear, no mummy pants in sight, and shook my ass exactly how you showed me, and I felt great. He couldn't get enough of me." Chains' eyes are watching her every move, and I smile. I'm glad she feels good about herself.

"Can I buy you a drink?" A man I don't know approaches me, and I look around awkwardly.

"Can we help you?" snaps Lake, stepping forward.

The guy rakes his eyes over the group of bikers. "Oh, are you with those guys?" he asks me.

"No, she isn't. She's free and single, and of course, she'd love a drink," says Leia, shoving me towards the guy. I look at her helplessly as she gives a little wave.

"Wine?" he asks.

I nod. I feel so uncomfortable and I glance back to the group. Storm is chatting with Riggs, and I'm relieved he hasn't seen me. Leia marches over and hisses in my ear, "Will you relax? Storm needs to realise you won't wait forever."

"I don't want him to get upset with me," I snap. "And I'm happy as we are."

"I see the way you look at each other. I feel like banging your bloody heads together," she mutters. "You'll never get back together if someone doesn't give you a little shove."

"This is not the way," I snap.

The guy turns back to me, handing me a glass of wine. Leia grins before heading back over to the group. "You look amazing," he says. "I'm Colin."

"Lottie," I answer. I glance over to Storm again, and this time, he's watching me with those brooding eyes of his.

"Come with me, birthday boy," says Vinn, approaching Storm. "I have a gift from your brothers. She's waiting up there," he says. I watch as the guys laugh and pat Storm on the back. He didn't tell me it was his birthday. I down the wine as Storm makes his way to the stage. He climbs the steps and sits on a chair already placed centre stage. The guys have moved front stage, cheering loudly.

"Looks like he's getting lucky tonight," Colin comments, smirking.

"Actually," I say, handing him my empty glass. "Thanks for the drink, but I'm here with my friends. I should get back to them."

Leia scowls, but I ignore her. I know Storm, and I know he wouldn't appreciate me flirting with other men, even if I am single. I'm still the mother of his child and that means not annoying him. I clap along to the music and a stripper enters the stage. She does her thing, dancing and shaking around him, getting the crowd whipped up. I miss the buzz from that. "You should totally get up there and dance for him," says Leia excitedly.

"Christ, no one wants to see my saggy tits," I scoff. Since having Elsie, those days are well and truly over. The dancer begins to remove clothing. It's his birthday gift from the guys, but it's hard to watch another woman all over him like that.

"Something tells me he'd welcome your saggy tits any day," says Leia. I look to where she points and find Storm is watching me. I bite my lower lip, a move I know he loves, and his eyes darken.

"I need to pee," I whisper to Leia, before disappearing to the bathroom. I'm washing my hands when the door opens, and Storm appears behind me. "This is the ladies'," I say, turning to face him.

He places his hands either side of my body, resting them on the wash basin behind me. "I can't get you out of my head," he says, his voice low. "I keep picturing you in the shower."

"You didn't tell me it was your birthday," I whisper.

His eyes go to my lips, and I lick them subconsciously. "I don't celebrate birthdays."

"I would have got you a gift, from Elsie and me."

"There's only one gift I want from you," he mutters.

He carefully moves his lips closer, giving me a chance to back out, but when it's clear I'm not going to, he gently cups my face with his large hands and presses his mouth against mine. When he pulls back, I whisper, "Happy birthday." He gives a crooked smile before slamming his mouth back to mine. I push my fingers into his hair, enjoying the way his hands roam my body while he thrusts his tongue into my mouth like a starved animal. I wrap my legs around him as he lifts me onto the counter.

"Fuck, I've missed this," he growls.

STORM

The second I come, I feel a weight lifting. Being with Lottie feels right. This is right. She cries out, digging her nails into my shoulders. I welcome the sting. Fucking her in the bathroom of Vinn's club was not the way I wanted to get back with Lottie, but shit happens, and I couldn't control myself around her for a minute longer. I pull out of her and tuck myself away. "Let's finish our drinks so we can get the fuck outta here. I need to feel you naked against me," I say, grabbing a handful of toilet paper and wiping between her legs.

"It's your birthday, shouldn't you stick around and celebrate?" she asks, arranging her clothing back to its former state.

"It's no fun when you're the only one drinking orange juice," I say, and her smile fades. "I'd rather be with you alone," I add, kissing her on the forehead.

I feel like a boring arse, but when I tell the guys I'm heading back to the clubhouse, they all decide to call it a night too. "We can party back at the club for cheaper," jokes Chains. I don't bother to tell them I'm taking Lottie straight up to bed.

Lottie rides on my bike and it feels fucking amazing to have her wrapped around me again. When we step into the clubhouse, I automatically push Lottie behind me. Something feels off and the rest of the guys aren't back yet. They jumped in cabs and the bike's way faster. I press my finger to my lips, telling Lottie to keep quiet as I carefully take a step forward. It's dark—no one ever turns the lights out in this place. "Don't take another fucking step," comes a female voice followed by the click of a gun.

The light flickers on, and Laura is standing a few feet away with a gun aimed right at my head. "What the fuck?" I snap. I take one step, and she fires the gun at the ceiling. Lottie screams as a bullet ricochets off and hits the wall.

"I told you not to fucking move," screams Laura, waving the gun around.

I wince, reaching behind me and taking Lottie's hands. She grips onto me tightly. "Okay, I'm staying right here. What's going on?"

"You tell me," she hisses. The door opens and the guys pour in. Riggs realises pretty quickly what's going on and holds his hands up, halting the rest. They fall silent, and Laura's eyes dart back and forth between me and them. "Tell me someone's armed," I hear Cree whisper. "You know we don't carry to Vinn's place. It's safe for us there," Chains whispers back.

"Listen, Laura, I get you're mad at me, but let these guys go. It's nothing to do with them," I say calmly.

"You got off with murdering my brother," she yells.

"I told you, I didn't murder him."

"Lies!" she screams, waving the gun around again. The brothers duck, keeping their ol' ladies hidden behind them. I take in her unkempt appearance. It's so different from the woman I once knew. There're dark circles under her eyes, and she looks crazed.

"Shit, man, she's lost the plot," mutters Blade.

"I want the truth," she snaps. Her voice breaks as a sob escapes her. "Is he dead?" she whispers.

"Laura—" I begin, but she points the gun at my chest.

"If I shoot, it'll kill you both. Who will look after your precious baby then?" she asks, grinning maniacally.

"Oh god, where's Elsie?" panics Lottie.

"She's upstairs safe. For now. Maybe I should hurt you like you've hurt me, Storm," she says, tears running down her cheeks. "Maybe I should take someone you love."

"That won't make you feel better, Laura," I say.

"It might," she suddenly screams again, shaking the gun.

"Okay, okay," I hiss. "After the police arrested me, I did some research. I know who killed him." She sniffles, waiting for me to continue. "His name was Cobra. He had an MC here in London, and your brother stole some money and drugs from him."

"Jesus, how many murders can we pin on Cobra?" whispers Blu, sniggering.

A noise from behind Laura grabs her attention, and she spins around, coming face to face with Frankie and a baseball bat. She takes a swing, knocking Laura clean out. "You fucking woke the baby," hisses Frankie. "Someone get this bitch out of here," she adds, turning back to the stairs. "And next time, carry your fucking guns."

Lottie throws herself against me, and I hold her tightly. "I thought she was going to kill you," she cries.

"Call the doc, get this bitch sectioned," orders Riggs.

I kiss Lottie, and a few of the guys cheer. "About time," mutters Cree.

"Let's get you to bed," I mutter. "We've had enough excitement for one night."

I spend the night worshipping Lottie's body, trying to convey exactly what she means to me . . . not just as the woman I love but as the mother of my child. When I finally pull her into my arms, we're both exhausted. "You didn't use a condom," she mumbles sleepily.

"I plan on keeping that belly full of babies for at least the next ten years," I say and I feel her smile against my chest.

"Is it really that simple?" she asks.

"We've spent too long trying to get this right and failed every time. For once, I'm listening to my heart. I love you. I never stopped. Having you and Elsie in my life is all I want, and I'll do anything to make it work."

"I love you too. Do you think our life will always be full of drama?" she asks.

"Seems to be the way in this club," I say, laughing. "All I know, Charlotte Murphy, is we're gonna marry. We survived so much and we have come too far to let what we have slip away again."

She looks up at me, her sleepy eyes full of happiness. I never want to be the reason they look sad again. "We survived the storm," she says, smiling.

"Damn right, we did, baby."

I don't know what the future holds, and maybe the storms will keep coming, but I know we owe it to ourselves and to Elsie, to give us a go. If we can survive mental illness and addiction, and still find our way back to each other, what else can possibly tear us apart?

The End

Raven's Place
Kings Reapers MC - Book 8
Nicola Jane

Playlist

Can't Hold Us Down - Christina Aguilera
Breathe - Blu Cantrell
Heartbreaker - Mariah Carey ft. Jay-Z
Love Don't Cost a Thing - Jennifer Lopez
Tell Me - Diddy ft. Christina Aguilera
Everytime - Britney Spears
Case of the Ex - Mya
Too Lost in You - Sugababes
Playing with Fire - N-Dubz ft. Mr Hudson
Only Love Can Hurt Like This - Paloma Faith
I See Fire - Ed Sheeran
Don't Leave Her (If You Can't Let Her Go) - Chris Young
Please Don't Leave Me - P!nk
Torn - Natalie Imbruglia
Revelry - Kings of Leon
Lead Me to the Water - Nick Wilson
Lips of an Angel - Hinder

Chapter One

RAVEN

I stare straight ahead, ignoring the muffled cries of the gagged man tied to a chair before me. There's a loud ringing in my ears which always comes whenever I'm in this sort of situation. Somewhere in the distance, I hear my name, and suddenly, the ringing stops and I'm back in the room.

"Raven." It's Vinn, sounding unimpressed, and when I eventually look at him, his face is full of anger. He doesn't like being ignored. "Bag the gentleman's fingers and have them sent first class to his lover."

By 'lover', he means Raymond Clay, a powerful crime boss who seems set on stepping on Vinn's toes. Of course, no one knows Raymond is gay, not even his trophy wife of eleven years.

I squat down in front of Martyn James, a city lawyer who never asked for any of this. He just fell in love with the wrong guy. We can all sympathise with that. I pick up his ring finger, one from each hand, and drop them into a plastic bag. I make the mistake of looking into his eyes as I stand. Chains told me a million times to never look them in the eye. He thinks I can't cope with the guilt, but I can, sometimes better than any of the men in this room.

Blade wipes his hunter's knife down his jeans and tucks it away. "Let's see if Raymond loves you as much as he tells you when he's three inches in your arse," says Vinn, adding a smirk. Martyn whimpers, his eyes burning into me, asking, no, begging for my help. I turn away and head for the door. I need to post these before five or they'll end up sitting in the post box, stinking the thing out.

As I pass, Vinn catches my arm. "You okay?" he asks in a low voice, not wanting anyone to know he's checking in on me. I nod stiffly and pull free from his tight grip.

Anna is waiting in the office for Riggs. They have a date night, which I heard her gushing to Eva about over breakfast this morning. She glances at the clear, bloodied bag. "A food bag? Seriously?"

I shrug, smiling. "Vinn's tight with his cash, so he likes to keep costs low."

"Are they gonna be much longer?" she asks.

"Just finishing up. Off anywhere nice?" I make polite conversation as I parcel the fingers up like it's normal, everyday mail. I guess, in my world, it is.

"He promised me a full night of his attention. He's even turning his phone off. I booked a show and dinner," she says, and I resist the urge to roll my eyes. He'll hate it. Then, she laughs, and says, "I'm kidding. We're going to a steakhouse and we'll more than likely end up at the Windsor for a few drinks before he tells me he's tired." She lowers her eyes. "I'm not complaining, he can't help being tired," she mutters, and I smile sympathetically. I'm sure Riggs' recent cancer battle has them both drained.

"Well, enjoy your date. I have a shift downstairs in the club, and then I'll most likely fall asleep to a Netflix show that'll bore the shit outta me." I grab my coat and the parcel.

"You should have a night off," she says as I head for the door, laughing. "I'm serious," she adds. "You're always working. Why don't I arrange something with the girls? We could go for cocktails," she suggests, but I hesitate. It's not that I don't want to, but I've never really gelled well with women. I was the girl at school who all other girls hated, and I just found hanging out with guys easier. And in some ways, that's still the case. "Of course, if you don't want to," she continues.

"That'd be great, Anna. Thanks." I wince as I rush down the stairs. I'll come up with an excuse as to why I can't go, as I always do.

Riggs steps out of the room, and I crash against him. He steadies me, laughing uncomfortably. "Sorry," I mutter.

"Where's the fire?"

I hold up the parcel. "I gotta get this to the post office."

"You did well in there," he says. "I've never let a woman handle business or be a part of it," he adds thoughtfully, "and with you working for Vinn, I guess it's not my call. But you're becoming more and more like one of the guys every day." I smile stiffly, then brush past him. That's me . . . one of the guys.

I work a full bar shift, my feet aching after having been here since ten this morning. I help Vinn in the office during the day, then work bar shifts in the evening, sometimes here at Vinn's club but also for

Anna in her micro-bar. I'm stocking up the fridges when I feel Vinn approach the bar. "You look good on your knees," he jokes.

"What can I get you, boss?" I ask, arching my brow as I look up at him. The other bar staff already hate me because they think I'm his favourite.

"Boss," he repeats, smirking. "Is that how you wanna play it, Corvo?"

I push to my feet. I used to swoon when he called me the Italian word for 'raven'. Corvo . . . it just rolls off his tongue in that sexy way he has. But since he announced the upcoming wedding, *his* upcoming wedding, I feel less and less turned on by his smooth talk. "Do you want a drink?" I ask again, arching a brow.

He narrows his eyes, a smile still firmly in place. "I'll take a scotch."

Grabbing a glass, I pour him a double measure. "Anything else?" I ask brightly.

"Yes, less fucking attitude," he mutters, taking his drink and heading back to his table.

After closing, Brick sits at the bar. He works the security here, so we're almost always on shift together, and since he's also a Kings Reaper, I get a lift home after my shift. "Why are you single, Raven?" he asks thoughtfully.

"Are you offering to marry me, Brick?"

He scoffs. "Fuck no," he says a little too quickly. My eyes widen, and he realises his mistake. "I mean, just cos I don't do that sort of shit, dating and stuff," he finishes, shuddering.

"Relax, I don't do that shit either," I say. "Why do men assume all women want to marry and have kids? You're not the only one who likes to play the field."

"Oh, right, well, if you're on the market for a hook-up, I'm down with that," he says, grinning. I roll my eyes as Vinn slaps Brick on the back.

"Are you hitting on my bar staff?" he asks coolly.

"She was hitting on me," Brick protests, and Vinn's eyes fix on me.

"That's not true," I mutter, shaking my head. "Telling you I like hook-ups over relationships doesn't mean I want to hook up with you," I add.

"I'll drop Raven home," says Vinn. "Get yourself off," he tells Brick, "literally."

Brick looks at me to confirm it's okay, and I nod. What's the point in arguing when Vinn will only cause a scene? He waits for Brick to leave before taking his seat, and I go back to wiping down the bar top. "Corvo, are you going to be mad at me forever?"

"I'm not mad."

He smiles, pushing to stand. "Good. Get your things, the other staff can clean up."

I glance around, hoping no staff overheard. "My shift doesn't end for ten minutes," I point out.

"Don't make me ask twice," he says firmly, heading towards his office. I huff and roll my eyes again. "And don't fucking roll your eyes at me, Corvo," he shouts over his shoulder. *How the fuck does he do that?*

I remain silent on the car ride home. I can tell it's annoying Vinn by the way his fingers tap impatiently on his knee. "I didn't keep it a secret," he mutters, pushing a button next to him so the black glass screen goes up between us and his driver, Gerry.

"I'm really not bothered about it, Vinn," I lie. "Honestly, I'm fine about the whole thing."

"Nothing has to change," he says, sighing heavily.

My eyes bug out of my head as I stare out of the window. "You know what? I really need some air. Stop the car here and I'll walk the rest of the way."

"Don't be ridiculous."

"Stop the car," I repeat, glaring at him. I hate being bossed around, and I've put up with it from this Italian prick for the last four months.

"I can't let you walk, Corvo. Riggs will have my nuts."

"My name is Raven!" I suddenly scream, and he winces. I bang on the dividing glass. "Stop the damn car!"

Vinn lowers the screen. "Keep driving. She's lost her fucking mind." I fold my arms across my chest and lean back in the seat, staring out the window. I refuse to speak another word to this arse.

As soon as the car comes to a stop outside of the clubhouse, I get out. Vinn likes to do the gentlemanly thing and open the door, but I'm so over that bullshit. Music blares out from the club. It's almost two in the morning, I really don't feel like partying, but the second I enter, Chains thrusts a bottle of beer into my hand.

"Here she is," he slurs. It's unusual for the guys to be partying this late. Since most have settled down and had kids, the club's heavy partying days are over. "This is Raven," he announces, turning to the side slightly to reveal two new faces. I hold in the gasp threatening to leap from my throat. "Raven, this is Mac and Ace. Raven is practically one of us," says Chains proudly as I smile awkwardly. I've worked a fifteen-hour day, so I look and feel like shit. "These guys are staying with us. They're from Nottingham, like Storm."

Mac gives a lopsided grin, and I swallow hard. Fuck, he's gorgeous. Most of the guys around here are, but he's everything I'd want in a man if I was to create my perfect match. Suddenly, I feel Vinn behind me. "You'd better get some sleep, Corvo. I need you in the office bright and early."

"I'm taking a day off," I announce, and he scowls. "I've not had a day off since . . ." I pause to remember, then shrug. "Since I fucking came here."

"Then let's do shots," says Chains with a grin. "This girl can drink shots better than anyone I know," he goes on to tell the new guys as he heads to the bar. Vinn grabs my wrist, pulling me to him.

"I get you want to punish me, but don't do anything to jeopardize what we have," he hisses into my ear. "I won't forgive easily." Snatching my wrist away, I follow the guys to the bar. Fuck him. Hypocrite.

MAC

The constant buzzing as my mobile phone vibrates across the bedside table is fucking annoying. I realise drinking shots last night was not a good idea as I struggle to focus my blurry eyes. If I turn the phone off, she'll know I saw her call, so I continue to ignore it.

Following Ace to London was the best thing I ever did. Now, I have to make it work. The plan is to throw myself into the club. The Pres here seems alright, everyone speaks highly of him, and I know he wants to make this charter bigger, so I just gotta prove I can work hard, then I can begin my life again. A new life where she isn't a part of it. The buzz begins again, and I growl in frustration. *When will she get the fucking message?*

Breakfast is crazy in this place. Kids are running around, and there are at least five different conversations going across the table. I spot Storm, and he grins, standing to greet me. "Sorry I wasn't around last night when you arrived. Good ride down?"

I nod, shaking his hand and taking the seat next to him. "Yeah. I haven't been on a run that long in a while, so it felt good to be back on the road, brother. Deano told me you'd settled down?"

He grins. "I have, brother. She's the reason I wasn't around last night. I'll introduce you when she wakes up. What about you and Ruby? Is she following you here?" I take a deep breath and release it slowly, shaking my head, and he winces. "Sorry, have I put my foot in it?"

"We split a few weeks ago."

"Shit, never saw that coming. You were always so tight. I mean, weren't you together since school or some shit?"

I nod, smiling bitterly. "Eighteen years."

"Fuck, sorry, man." He pats my shoulder.

"How's Taya and Seb?"

He smiles fondly, glancing around. "Seb," he shouts, and a kid comes running over. He was smaller the last time I saw him. "Do you remember Mac from the club in Nottingham?"

Seb nods once, watching me through curious eyes. He was always quiet and withdrawn back then. It doesn't look like much has changed, until a female gently runs her fingers through his hair, causing a beaming smile to spread across his face. "Good morning, my favourite boy." She then plants a kiss on Storm, and he smacks her arse before pulling her onto his lap.

"Lottie, meet Mac, my brother from Nottingham."

"Nice to meet you," she says, grinning. "Are you sticking around?" she asks.

I nod. "I think so."

"Well, then, welcome aboard."

After breakfast, I hit church. Riggs is more organised than my president back in Nottingham. He has an agenda and works his way down, telling us what work needs doing, and seeing as I'm gonna step up as Treasurer, alongside Blade, my first job will be to go over the books and catch up. Cree, the VP, hands me what I need. "You can stay in here and get some peace," he adds.

I wait for the other men to file out before I move to a small desk in the far corner and get stuck in. I've always been good with numbers. It was one thing I did right at school. While I got bad reports in every lesson, math was always glowing.

An hour later, the door swings open and the woman from last night, Raven, bounces in wearing exercise clothes and earbuds plugged in her ears. I bite back a grin as she proceeds to sing out of tune along with whatever she has blasting in her ears and begins stretching. She dips her head, snapping it back and letting her long, deep red hair fly wildly around her head before breaking out into Beyoncé's "Single Ladies".

She suddenly stops and growls, pressing a button on her headset. "What?" I realise she's answered a phone call. "No, I'm busy . . . because I have a life, Vinn." She rolls her eyes and turns slightly, jumping back when her eyes land on me. "I have to go." She presses another button on the headset before narrowing her eyes on me. "How long have you been hiding there?"

"I wasn't hiding," I say. "When's Beyoncé signing you to her label?" I snigger.

"It's not polite to hide in corners watching women dance," she snaps.

"Does Riggs know you're using church as an exercise room?"

She huffs, folding her arms across her chest, pushing her breasts higher. My eyes are naturally drawn there, and she huffs again until I make eye contact. "I come in here to hide away from perving eyes."

"Still, I don't think he'd be happy."

"Well, you keep quiet about this, and I won't tell the women you were sneaking around watching me."

I laugh, nodding. "Fine. Deal." We shake on it, and the moment my hand grips hers, I feel a spark. We stare at each other for a few silent seconds before she takes off, closing the door hard behind her. "Fuck," I hiss out loud. That's a complication I don't need.

Chapter Two

RAVEN

After my embarrassing encounter with the new guy, I head over to the Get Go gym. It's owned by Vinn and all employees get free usage.

I'm lost in thought on the running machine, jogging steadily with my earbuds in place, when a hand reaches over and slows the machine to walking. I don't need to look to know it's Vinn, so I stare straight ahead and walk. He tugs the earbud from my ear. "You hung up on me earlier." He has the ability to make me shiver with his smooth voice.

"I was busy."

"With?" he asks, and I furrow my brow.

"How's Sofia today?" I ask lightly. "I booked your table for one-thirty. Don't be late."

"I know, I checked my diary, despite you taking an unexpected day off," he says dryly.

"Great, well, don't let me keep you, Vinn. Have a great day." I smile even though it's obviously forced and fake as fuck. I jump off the machine and grab a fluffy white towel from the nearby shelf before heading for the steam and sauna rooms.

"I've had a long morning, Corvo," he drawls, following me. "Not helped by my assistant avoiding me."

"I'm not avoiding you, Vinn. I'm taking a day off. Fuck knows I need it. Let me recharge and I'll be back tomorrow as normal." I begin to strip off, and he watches me through hooded eyes. I have my bikini on underneath my gym clothes, not that it makes a difference, because he's seen me naked too many times. His eyes track me until I disappear into the steam room, relieved to be away from him.

I lie back on the wooden bench and close my eyes. It wasn't supposed to be like this. Falling for Vinn Romano is one of the stupidest things my heart has ever done, and I'm so fucking mad at it. I always do this. I always find the most unobtainable man and that's who I fall for. I thought I was safe with Vinn since mafia bosses have never really been my type. I hate the way heads turn whenever he enters a room, and I hate the expensive suits and disgusting fizzy champagne he insists on drinking. I'm not the type of girl to look pretty on his arm at expensive dinners, and I certainly don't want to wear red-bottomed shoes and diamonds.

Because that's what he expects from his women—top quality. I'm more budget-friendly. But I liked the way he didn't ask questions. Neither of us is ashamed to admit we love sex. It's the twenty-first century, and a woman can own that shit without being judged. And he didn't, judge me that is. Vinn's only rule was we don't fuck around. We fuck together with no strings, but the second we hook up with another, we walk away like it never happened. I agreed. Sex. Just sex.

I let out a large sigh. "Idiot," I mutter out loud.

"Corvo, don't be so hard on yourself." His voice rumbles through me, and I jump. Opening my eyes, I find him sitting by my feet, completely naked. I didn't even hear the door.

"What the fuck, Vinn?" I gasp. "Someone might walk in," I hiss.

He takes his large, erect shaft in his hand and rubs it with a cheeky smirk. "Then you'd better make it quick."

"Fuck off. You can't just demand that I—" I inhale sharply when his fingers brush over my bikini bottoms, applying pressure. I'm instantly wet.

"Take them off," he commands. I shake my head, and he laughs, slipping a finger inside and running it along my wet opening. I gasp as he retrieves it and places it into his mouth, grinning as he licks it clean. "Now, Corvo, before I become impatient." I hook my thumbs either side of my bottoms and lift my arse, sliding them to my ankles, where he removes them completely and gives a satisfied smile. He places his hands on both my knees and pulls my legs apart, taking a second to stare at me laid out before him. I lie back on the wooden bench and close my eyes.

Vinn might be a complete selfish bastard in general, but when it comes to sex, he knows exactly what he's doing, and I'm too fucking weak to say no. I try . . . I really try, but there's something about the way his mouth crooks up at one corner and how his eyes darken when he's in the mood to fuck. And the way his toned body moves over me, owning me in ways no one ever has before. It's hard to say no to a man so fucking perfect, it's ridiculous.

He grips my thighs, digging his fingers into my flesh as he eats my pussy like he's starving. The little groaning noise he makes at the back of his throat whenever he's turned on is a personal addiction of mine. When I'm ready to burst into a thousand tiny pieces, he pulls away, wiping his mouth unapologetically on the back of his hand before grinning down at me. Slowly, he crawls over my body like a hungry panther, he looks down between us, lining himself up with my entrance and slowly easing himself in. I press my hands against the wall above my head. It's fucking hot in here and our bodies are dripping wet. As he slides into me, I stare into his eyes, willing him to kiss me. It's the one thing he never does, and it drives me insane.

He crooks his mouth up. "You ready, Corvo?" I nod, not trusting myself to speak. He buries his face in my neck, biting me gently before bracing his arms either side of my head and withdrawing inch by inch before slamming back into me hard enough to make my fingers slip against the wall. I struggle not to bang my head as he slams into me over and over.

Deep groans escape as he begins to lose control. And then, just as I can feel that build-up again, he stops and tips his head slightly at the sound of male voices outside. I panic, trying to push him away, but he grins wider and begins to move again.

"Vinn," I hiss, "they're gonna see us." He puts his foot against the door, using it as leverage to fuck me harder. I bite my lip to stop me crying out as the voices get closer.

"How good does it feel, Corvo?" he whispers in my ear, then proceeds to nip along my jawbone. "To know you have me on my knees, begging for your pussy. To have me come find you because you hung up on me. Do you like having the power?"

"Vinn," I mumble as warmth builds in my stomach.

"Do you think about my cock, Corvo, like I think about your wet pussy?" If only he knew how much I thought about us like this, doing exactly this. Someone tries the door of the steam room, but with Vinn's foot against it, it holds. "You need to come, Corvo," he whispers. "I'm not stopping 'til you've come on my cock."

There's a knock on the door. "Excuse me," shouts a man, "I think the door is locked. Can you open it from the inside?"

"Come, Corvo," he pants, twisting my nipple gently between his thumb and finger. I shudder, gripping his shoulders as I convulse through a powerful orgasm. It rolls through me over and over until the voices outside sound distant. Vinn places his hand over my mouth as a muffled groan escapes.

"I'm going to get a member of staff," the man shouts.

Vinn slams harder, and I watch his beautiful face as he closes his eyes and growls, stilling as he releases into me.

I'm so hot, I feel lightheaded as he climbs from me and slips my bikini bottoms back into place. He wraps his towel around his waist and sweeps his hair back from his face before pulling the door open. Two disgruntled men and the female receptionist are on the other side. "About time," snaps a balding, overweight man. His eyes dart between us, then narrow in on me. "Have you been having sex in here?"

"That's really none of your business," says Vinn, taking me by the hand and pulling me to stand.

"It is when I've got to sit in here. It needs a deep clean," he adds, glaring at the receptionist.

She smiles at Vinn, blushing slightly. "Mr. Romano," she salutes, nodding.

"Please close the steam room for a deep clean," he says with authority. She nods and closes the door, turning the sign already hanging there to 'Out of Order'.

"Mr. Romano?" the man repeats, swallowing hard. "My apologies."

"And arrange for these gentlemen to receive some free drinks in the bar after their session today," he throws over his shoulder. Vinn leads me out of there and to the showers, and I watch in awe as he hangs his towel and steps under the cool jet of water. When I haven't moved, he glances at me. "What?"

"You're naked. People come in here."

He laughs, soaping his body quickly and rinsing it. He turns the spray off and grabs a fresh towel. "You worry too much. I'll meet you outside."

"No, it's fine. I've planned to go shopping."

"Then meet me outside and I'll have Gerry drop you in central London."

He breezes past me, and I shake my head in agitation. He'll only force me into his car if I refuse, and I don't want anyone else to stare at me with curious expressions today.

Once I'm showered and changed, I step out of the gym and spot Vinn leaning against his car, staring down at his mobile. He opens the door and waits for me to slide in before joining me. "Central London, Gerry, please," he says before pressing the button that puts a black glass screen between us and Gerry. He pulls out his wallet and tries to hand me a credit card. I stare at it, waiting for an explanation. "For shopping," he offers.

"I have money," I mutter.

"So, do I. Take the card, Corvo."

"No." I hate this part, where he makes me feel like fucking Julia Roberts in *Pretty Woman*. And I get it now . . . I get why she was so pissed when Richard Gere offered her a nice apartment and fancy clothes. He'd still get to keep the pretty little woman at his beck and call, just like Vinn's trying to do with this offering.

"Take the card."

"No."

"Take the fucking card," he yells, and I jump in fright, snatching the card and stuffing it in my pocket. I won't use it. "And if you don't use it, I'll buy you something ridiculously expensive." I hate waste, he knows I do. "I'll buy you a diamond bracelet and matching earrings." I shudder because I also hate anything in the least bit showy. "What are you shopping for anyway? You hate shopping." *I hate shopping alone.*

"Anna invited me out with the girls. I thought I'd treat myself."

"You're going out with the girls?" he repeats, laughing. I nod, staring out the window at the busy streets. "Why?"

"Because she asked."

"You'll cancel. You always do." I narrow my eyes. Like he fucking knows me. "Leia said you never go out with them." Of course, Leia would tell him. She hates my guts for reasons out of my control. Her husband, Chains, helped me escape a life of hell, and we became close. It was before she got with him, sort of, and Chains is like my best friend. Yes, we hooked up while we were thrown together, before he came back to the club, but it was a mutually agreed hook-up, just like Vinn and me.

"Have you told Leia about us?"

"Why would I?" he scoffs.

That stings and I stare harder out the window. He's always so quick to dismiss any talk of us, which I guess isn't a bad thing. I know where he stands. "Are you spending the afternoon with Sofia?" I ask, then instantly regret it. I feel like the harder I try to convince us both I don't care, the more I look like I care.

"Why are you asking?" He keeps staring at his mobile while tapping away.

"I'm just making conversation, Vinn. You made me get in the car with you. I'm being polite."

"I have a meeting with her father. You'd know that if you were at work today." Her father, also Italian, is setting up business in London with Vinn's help. The marriage will be good for Sofia's family from what Gia tells me. Vinn's sister said that her family is huge in Italy, so it's a mutual agreement to tie two good families together. I don't know the date for the wedding, Vinn hasn't told me, but I know she'll be expected to be pregnant soon after they marry.

The car comes to a stop and Vinn gets out. I wait patiently for him to open the door, even though it pisses me off every time. I'm not one of those jumped-up rich bitches he's used to. I can open my own damn door, but I don't because he'll only cause a fuss.

I get out, but he braces his arms either side of me, stopping my escape. "I know this is hard, Raven, but it's out of my control."

"It's not hard," I say, faking a smile. "Who said it was hard?"

He runs a finger down my cheek, eyeing my lips like he's desperate to taste them. I wish to God he would. "Your face says it's hard."

"Have a good lunch," I say briskly.

"Would you like to meet for dinner this evening?"

I smirk. We never have dinner. "No, Vinn. I'm going out with the girls, remember?"

"Maybe tomorrow evening?"

I shake my head. "Why?"

He shrugs. "We never have dinner together."

"Because we're just fucking, so why waste time having dinner?" I ask, grinning.

He grips my chin and stares hard at my lips. I know he wants to kiss me—I can sense it. "I have something I want to run by you, Corvo. Something that might make us both happy."

I'm intrigued, of course, but at the same time, I'm scared that whatever he has to say will only ruin what we have, so I shake my head. "Let's stick to the rules, Vinn." I duck under his arm and head for the nearest shop.

MAC

"Why don't you just change your number?" asks Ace with a sigh.

"Cos everyone I know in the entire world has this number. Why should I change it?"

"Because the constant fucking calls and texts are distracting." He's right. Ruby still isn't giving up, and I've only been gone a couple of days. "Just fucking talk to her or I will," he adds.

"She'll get the message eventually."

"Something tells me you're wrong about that." He lights a cigarette. "How are you finding it here?"

I grin. "Good, brother. It's the fresh start we both needed."

"Damn straight," he says, also grinning. "And the women here are H.O.T."

"Anyone in particular?" I ask, the redhead immediately jumping to mind, but I shut it down.

"Are we talking club whores or actual ol' lady potential?"

"Either or?"

"All I'm saying is the whore with the short blonde hair has a mouth like a damn vacuum."

I glare at him. "Damn, brother, first night and you're already testing them out?"

He laughs. "Maybe you should give it a go, get that stupid bitch out your head." I give half a smile. If only it was as easy as that.

"Are you fuckers gonna work or not?" asks Chains, shoving a box into my hands. I take it and place it in the van.

"Sorry, brother. We were just talking about the blonde with the good mouth," says Ace, and Chains grins.

"She's new. Brick said the same. Unfortunately, I don't get to sample the delights these days."

"You are missing out!" says Ace.

"Having my ol' lady in my bed every night, knowing she's all mine, nothing beats that shit."

"Bullshit." Ace laughs. "Different pussy every night, nothing beats it."

"I remember saying those words too, brother, but trust me, when you have what I've got, you'll never look again." I stay quiet because Chains is right. When you think you've found that one person who beats all others, you never look elsewhere.

"I'm trying to convince soppy bollocks here to get out there, and you're not helping my cause," says Ace, nodding towards me.

"You got an ol' lady?" Chains asks.

"Would I be trying to convince him to play the field if he did?" Ace jumps in, saving me from an awkward conversation.

"Maybe you'll find new pussy tonight. Pres is putting us on woman watch."

Ace rubs his hands together. "I like the sound of that!"

"Trust me when I say that excitement will soon vanish. The ol' ladies are hitting the town tonight, and we get the wonderful job of making sure they're safe at all times, they don't get too drunk, and they return to their men in the same condition they left them in. It sounds easy, but it ain't. Leia is the ringleader, and she'll cause us trouble all night."

"Isn't Leia your ol' lady?" I ask.

"Yep. I love her, she's the reason I get up every day, but fuck me, she's a pain in the arse."

"What's the story with Raven?" asks Ace, and my ears prick up as I load more boxes.

Chains laughs. "You don't stand a chance. She's like you, doesn't wanna settle down, doesn't want kids and marriage. She's even started to get in on some of the club business. She's more like a brother than an ol' lady."

"Is she a lesbian?" Ace asks, and I slap him upside the head.

"Just cos she don't want kids and marriage, don't make her a fucking lesbian," I snap. "And actually, lesbians can have those things these days. Don't be such a cock."

"I was just asking," Ace retorts, rubbing his head.

"She's straight," says Chains with a wink that tells us he knows from personal experience.

Chapter Three

RAVEN

Lottie tops up my glass with white wine. "How come you never come out with the girls?" she asks, sitting next to me. The rest of the ol' ladies are dancing. We hit two bars before this, much to Chains' dismay, and now the alcohol is really starting to hit. "I'm not having a go or anything," she adds quickly.

"It's nothing personal," I say with a smile. "I'm usually working. I like to keep busy."

"You do work a lot."

"I'm an addict."

"We're not so bad, are we?" she asks.

I laugh. "No, not at all. How's things with you and Storm?" She gives a wistful smile, and I find myself smiling along with her.

"He's amazing. I know I should find a fault, just one that makes me less smug, but I honestly can't. I love everything about him. He's great with the kids, he lets me sleep in sometimes to give me a break, and he's always checking I'm okay. I can't complain about anything right now."

It's good to hear. They had a rocky start, but I'm pleased things are going great for her. "Lake missed you so much when you went away, I'm sure he's glad to have his sister back. And I've never seen Storm looking so happy. You need to give me some tips so I can find my own Prince Charming."

"You?" she asks, frowning.

Her reaction isn't what I was expecting, and I smile awkwardly. "Er, yeah."

"I just thought you were happy being single and carefree," she says with a shrug. "I didn't think you were the type to settle down."

"Why?"

"You never give off that vibe. Even with the men. They literally see you as one of the guys."

Leia joins us, out of breath from dancing, and grabs my glass of wine, downing it in one. "What are you gossiping about?"

"Raven was just saying how she wants what I have with Storm."

"Please," grins Leia, "we're all jealous that you have your freedom. Don't disappoint me and give it up for one of these arseholes."

"Jealous?" I repeat doubtfully. Why would anyone be jealous of my life?

"Yes!" Leia exclaims. "You get to do what you want, come and go as you please. You have fifty-thousand jobs," she exaggerates, "and you get to look at Vinn Romano every damn day!" I laugh. I'd never seen it from their point of view. "You get to be with the guys when they're on club business, while we don't get to see that side of things," she adds, and I lower my eyes; she really isn't missing much. "They respect you in a different way."

What I'd give to have the respect and love of just one man. I sigh, grabbing the bottle of wine and topping up my glass.

"How's things going with you and Chains?" asks Lottie, causing Leia to glance where Chains is talking to the new guys.

"Good. Since you taught me to slut drop, he's seen a different side to me," she says, but her smile doesn't reach her eyes, and I frown. Chains hadn't mentioned things were weird between them. "I still feel rubbish about myself, though. I can't seem to lift it."

"Aww, honey," says Lottie, taking her hand, "Chains loves you. Maybe you need more 'me' time? You spend a lot of time with Grace."

"Maybe," she mutters, picking at the edge of the table.

"Well, this looks like the saddest table in the damn room," says Anna, joining us. "Drink up. Some of the guys are at Vinn's club, so we're headed there."

I groan. "I might head home."

Anna shakes her head, hooking her arm into mine. "Not a chance, sunshine. Your dull light needs a spark, and we haven't yet found you the man of your dreams."

Reluctantly, I let her drag me from the bar. I didn't plan on seeing Vinn until I turn up at the office in the morning. I wouldn't usually work on a Saturday, but I felt bad after taking today without notice.

Enzo's was named after Vinn's late father. It's a busy nightclub, well known for miles around. There's never a quiet night, but the weekend is its busiest time, and I'm not surprised when I see the length of the queue outside. We go straight to the front, and the doorman embraces me, kissing the top of my head. Eric's old enough to be my dad, and there are times I wish he was—he'd do a better job than my own ever did.

We go straight to the VIP floor and find Riggs and some of the other guys there. The ol' ladies break off to their men, and I head to the bar. Chloe, the bartender, grins. "You can't keep away."

"Not my idea," I mutter. She hands me a shot, and I knock it back. Glancing around, my eyes settle on him. Vinn is at his usual table, reserved for him to entertain clients and special guests. Our eyes connect briefly before his attention is pulled away by a female sitting beside him.

"I always thought you and he were . . . well, yah know," says Chloe. "But tonight, he put that rumour to bed by bringing in his fiancée," she says excitedly. A strained noise leaves my throat, and I smile. It must come across as painful because she frowns. "Are you okay?" I nod, taking the vodka and Coke she offers. "Are you sure? You look sick."

I take a few mouthfuls of my drink. "The shot was too strong," I mutter.

"Anyway, her name is Sofia. He introduced her to everyone. He looks so in love," she gushes. The rest of her words fade as I watch the way Vinn listens with interest to whatever Sofia's saying. I'm lucky if he bothers to look up from his mobile phone. I'm so lost in thought that it takes me a second to realise he's heading my way. I panic, quickly turning away to face Chloe, who has now stopped talking and is watching him approach.

"Chloe, give us a minute, would you?" he asks politely, and she practically swoons away to the other side of the bar. "Corvo, I didn't expect to see you in here," he says. He doesn't sound happy about my unannounced visit.

I take a breath to steady the churning feeling I have in my stomach. "The girls wanted to come here. Riggs must have told Anna he was here."

"How's your night been?"

"Good, really good," I lie. Remembering I have his credit card, I fish it from my bag. "Thanks. There was nothing I liked."

"Liar. You spent over five hundred pounds today. Two hundred of that was in Tallulah Lingerie." He looks smug with his finds, and I narrow my eyes.

"Stop spying on my bank balance, it's weird."

"My question is, why would you spend that much on lingerie if you weren't planning on seeing me tonight? You turned down my dinner invite."

"I like pretty underwear," I snap.

"Me too. Especially on you. When are you going to show me?"

"Jesus, Vinn, your fiancée is sitting right there," I hiss. "When are you going to realise, this has to stop?"

"It stops when I say, Corvo. Come and meet Sofia." He grabs my hand and tugs me hard behind him. I pull back, trying to protest without making a scene, but he only drags me harder until we're at his table. "Sofia, meet my assistant, Raven," he announces, pulling me from behind him like he's presenting a prize. She smiles, and it's friendly and cute. Of course, it is. She's exactly what I imagined Vinn would go for—dark hair, natural beauty, tanned skin, perfect smile, and amazing hazel-coloured eyes. She's completely the opposite to me.

"Hi, great to meet you," she says with a thick Italian accent.

"And you," I say, awkwardly.

"Join us," she adds, holding out a glass of champagne. Vinn places his hand on my lower back, gently pushing me to take the glass.

He waits for Sofia to be distracted before leaning in close. "Sit down, Corvo."

"Vinn, would you mind if I borrow Raven for a minute or two? She lost a bet and owes me a drink." I stare wide-eyed at the new guy, Mac.

"Just order it and stick it on my tab," says Vinn, irritated.

"But then she wouldn't be paying up on her debt."

Vinn's eyes burn into mine. He isn't happy, and I know he's trying to work out what this guy's game is. "You playing games, Corvo?" he asks. It's a loaded question—he wants to know if I've broken our deal even though he's sat here with his fucking fiancée.

"Enjoy the rest of your evening," I say to Sofia. She smiles before going back to her conversation with Leia. "I'll be in the office first thing," I add to Vinn. I get a step away before his hand wraps around my wrist and I'm pulled back to him. He presses his mouth close to my ear.

"Don't do anything you might regret," he hisses.

"I never have regrets," I whisper back, and his eyes connect with mine, "until you." I pull free and follow Mac towards the bar.

I release a breath and pull myself onto the bar seat. "You looked like you needed to get away," says Mac, and I smile gratefully. "You work for him, right?" I nod. "He seems a little intense for a boss."

"That's Vinn all over," I mutter, "intense and full on."

"Does anyone know?" he asks, and I stare at him quizzically. "That you're a thing?" he adds.

I stutter in shock before replying, "It's not like that."

"It's a gift," he then says with a smirk. "I can read lies easily. I can smell them before they've even left your mouth. I'm also good at reading body language. My mum used to say I was blessed. Little did she know, it's actually a curse."

"Bet it's a barrel of laughs being your girlfriend," I mutter.

"So why the big secret? I assume you were before the fiancée?" He pauses, then realisation hits him. "Unless you're still hooking up?"

"Can we drop it now? I'm grateful for the rescue and all, but seriously, I'm not talking about my life with a stranger."

"Who do you talk to?" he asks, and I frown. "Everyone needs someone." Great, just what I needed, to be reminded I have no one. "It sounds like you're always there for everyone else."

"I'm not paying for therapy," I point out coldly, and he grins.

"Sorry, bad habit of mine."

"I'm really not good company right now, but thanks for the help." It's a hint for him to leave but he stays put.

"If you ask me, he's a dick."

"Oh god," I groan, "please don't hit on me."

His eyes widen. "God, no, I wouldn't dream of it," he says a little too quickly. I'm offended by his obvious repulsion towards me, and he jumps in to correct his error. "Sorry, I don't mean it like that. I know you like a good time and shit, but I'm really not looking for anything ... at all."

"A good time?" I gasp.

"Er, fuck, I keep putting my foot in it."

"Who told you that?" I practically wail.

"Look, this isn't how I wanted this conversation to go. I'm really sorry."

I sigh heavily. This night just keeps getting better. "Come on," I say, standing. He looks confused. "You're buying me cheesy potato wedges or something equally as calorific to make up for your awkward conversation and irritatingly accurate views of me."

MAC

I watch Raven shovel food into her mouth like she's not eaten in weeks. She catches me staring and slows down, pressing her lips together. "Sorry, I'm always hungry after I've had a drink."

"No, please, carry on. It's like watching a nature show with David Attenborough," I say, grinning. She knocks her shoulder into mine and smiles. It's nice to see her smile.

"Why London?" she asks.

"Why not?"

A rowdy group of men pass, and we fall silent for a few minutes. "We have this agreement," she eventually says. "We hook up, but if there's anyone else, we stop."

"I think he's made it pretty clear he's met someone else." She nods sadly. "Maybe it's time you did the same. That way, there's no going back." She nods again.

"How do you forget someone? How do you stop thinking about them?"

I smirk. "Fuck knows, but when you find out, let me know."

"Who are you trying to forget?"

"We're not here to talk about me."

Raven's mobile lights up and silently flashes in her hand. She stares at it. "It's him," she says. It stops flashing briefly, only for it to start seconds later.

"Ignore it. He's got a fiancée."

A text message appears, and she shakes her head as she reads it. "He wants me to go to him."

"Do you want to?"

She nods. "But I shouldn't."

"You really shouldn't."

She hands me her phone. "Keep it for me, then I can't answer it." I tuck it in my pocket and stand, holding out my hand to help pull her up. The second we connect, it's exactly the same as before and that buzz of static shoots up my arm.

Chapter Four

RAVEN

Mac keeps hold of my hand, and I let him, because right now, I need that connection to remind me that I still get that thrill when a handsome man touches me. I spent years chasing the buzz I feel whenever Mac touches me. He's completely different to Vinn, with his huge frame and tattoos. He's got a dark shadow across his jaw, whereas Vinn likes to be clean shaven. He wears jeans and a t-shirt that shows off his defined chest muscles, and I know without looking that he has a six-pack, maybe even an eight. Vinn has a good body too, but they're completely different in shape, with Mac being stockier.

We're passing the club when my mobile must ring again because Mac pulls it from his pocket. Before I can object, he's pressing it to his ear, and I watch in horror as he grins.

"She's busy. What do you want?"

"Mac," I hiss, trying to take it from him. I get it and glare at him as I hold it to my ear in time to hear Vinn's threats of violence if Mac doesn't get me to the phone.

"It's me," I say.

"I suggest you get in the office right now, Raven." He disconnects, and I stare at the handset.

"Why did you do that?" I cry.

"Because he needs to think you've moved on. You'll always be at his beck and call if you keep giving in to him."

"Actually, he wants me to go to the office, so it's probably work-related," I say, knowing it's bullshit.

Mac shrugs. "Go ahead, but don't say I didn't warn you."

We both go back into the club, and Mac goes to find the others. I find Vinn leaning against his desk, his arms folded over his chest and his eyes fixed on me as I hesitantly enter. Before I can say anything, his hand is at my throat, and I'm pushed against the wall. "Don't say one fucking word unless it's my name," he hisses. His free hand squeezes my arse, and I feel his erection pressing against me.

"Did you fuck him?" I shake my head. He doesn't get it—I can't fuck anyone else because I'm crazy about him. "If you're lying to me, Corvo," he hisses.

"I'm not," I whisper. I want to scream 'what about Sofia', but instead, I close my eyes as he places rough kisses down my neck and across my chest.

"Then we still have a deal," he growls.

"Do we?" I ask.

"Neither of us has had sex with anyone else, so yes," he says pointedly. A small part of me feels relieved. I know he hasn't spent a lot of time with Sofia, but I'm surprised he hasn't had sex with her. He's got a higher sex drive than me, and that's saying something.

Vinn keeps me pushed up against the wall, and we're both fully clothed when I feel him pull my panties to the side and push his erection into me. It's an instant relief. The ache in my heart dulls, and I don't think about anything but the way this man makes me feel whenever he's buried inside me. "I can't stop," he growls, slamming into me, and I don't know if he means this thing between us or his explosive orgasm that comes seconds later. He roars with each thrust, digging his fingers into my thighs. He rests his head against my collar bone for a second to catch his breath before beginning to move again. He always makes sure I orgasm, sometimes coming twice himself in the process. I've never had a man who could keep going after orgasm.

"I have a place," he mutters against my temple. "No one knows about it, not even Gia." I close my eyes, concentrating on that warm feeling building below. "I want this to continue," he pants, moving faster when he feels me squeezing his cock. "I'm not ready to let you go." It's like ice water being poured over me as the warm feeling disappears. He must feel the change because he slows. "I didn't plan to ask like this," he mutters. "I wanted to take you to dinner."

"Get off me," I whisper.

He shakes his head. "Not until you come, Corvo."

"Now, Vinn," I snap, and he instantly pulls away, tucking himself back into his trousers. I adjust my underwear and skirt and straighten my just-fucked hair.

"I know you like living at the club, so I'm not saying move in. But it's a place we can go instead of sneaking to hotels and bending you over my desk."

"A fuck pad," I state.

"If that's what you want to call it," he says with a shrug. "I'd like you to choose the furniture and décor, make it yours."

I laugh, but it doesn't reach my eyes. "Jesus," I mutter, realising just how much my life is becoming like *Pretty Woman*.

"You're not ready to walk away either, Raven. I see the jealousy pouring from you like fucking poison. This way, we still get to be together."

"Together," I scoff. "Together in your fuck pad."

"Together in a place of our own, instead of stealing moments like this," he snaps. "You might like the seedy fucks against the wall, but I have more class." My hand hits his cheek before I've had a chance to see sense, and I immediately pull it back and hold it against my chest. My palm stings as I stare wide-eyed at Vinn, waiting for his reaction. His head stays to the side for a second while he processes what's just happened. Then, I'm back against the wall with his hand around my throat and his face pushed into my own.

"You ever fucking do that again and I'll remove it," he hisses. "Understand?"

"Yes, boss," I snap angrily.

"I'm offering something more than this," he growls.

"Thank you for your kind offer," I spit out, "but I'll leave it. It's over."

"It's not over until I say it's over."

"Unless you're planning on raping me, Vinn, we're done."

He steps back, releasing me, and for the first time, I see a flicker of hurt in his eyes. "I have to marry her. I don't have a choice."

"There's always a choice, Vinn. Always."

"Not in my life . . . not for who I am. You don't understand. If I backed out of this marriage, there'd be a war."

"And I'm not worth the fight, right?"

"People would die. I might die . . . or Gia. I can't just walk away, Raven. I have a responsibility."

"So do I," I mutter. "I have to protect myself. I'm sick of being second best."

"That's not what you are, Corvo. This wasn't supposed to be anything more than a fuck to stop the itch. I went and bought a flat outright because I couldn't stand the thought of ending us. You're not second best, but I can't stop this marriage."

"You've never even kissed me, Vinn. What we have isn't real. It's exactly what you wanted it to be—a fuck."

"You know that's bullshit. Look me in the eye and tell me you're not crazy jealous when you see me with her," he snaps.

"I'm not doing this," I mumble, heading for the door.

"Just like I can't look you in the eye and tell you I didn't wanna fucking rip Mac's head off tonight for walking out of here with you. The thought of you and another man," he pauses, shaking his head, and when he next looks at me, his eyes are dark, the way they go when he's just killed someone.

"So, what happens if I move into this flat, Vinn?" I ask. "When Sofia gets pregnant, when your first child is born, when you get the son you desperately want. What happens to us?"

"I don't have all the answers, but I'm trying to find a solution to suit us both."

"It's to suit you," I yell. "It's to suit you. Because I'll tell you what happens in the end, shall I? You walk away with your life and pretend this never happened. And I will have put my life on hold for you. So, when you leave with the perfect family, I'll have nothing. I know the ending because I've seen it before."

"I can't let you walk away," he whispers.

I smile sadly. "It's my choice."

MAC

I happen to glance up just as Raven is rushing towards the exit. Vinn's not far behind her, but when she doesn't respond to him shouting her name, he gives up, looking pissed. I catch his eye, and he scowls before heading back to his office. She shouldn't be leaving alone, so I head after her. It's the right thing to do, and I'm annoyed at Vinn for leaving her like that. She's almost at the end of the road when I spot her. Jogging up behind her, I shout her name, but she ignores me, just like she did Vinn. "Hey," I yell, "wait up."

"I'm fine, go back inside," she mutters, marching ahead.

"You're not fine. What happened back there?" I place a hand on her shoulder, and she spins to face me.

"I'm not like the others, Mac. I can look after myself!" she snaps. She's angry and needs to shout to release it, so I smirk.

"Sure, you can. You think because you've stood around while the men do their shit, because you clean up a little blood, you're all equipped to scare away the bad guys."

"What is it with you fucking men?" she yells. "Why do you assume women are these little creatures you have to protect when the only thing we need protecting from is you?"

"You're right," I say, shrugging. "We're natural predators, and you're natural prey."

She scoffs, her eyes wide. "I am no one's fucking prey!"

"Not even mafia god's back there?" I ask, grinning. "If you ask me, you're definitely easy prey. He only had to send you a text, and you went running."

"Well, maybe he has something worth running for."

"Yeah, a flashy car and a big bank balance. And if he's all that, why are you out here right now looking ready to cry while he's back inside with the woman he's gonna marry?"

Raven pauses, gathering herself. She looks upset. "He has to marry her. It's not his choice," she mutters.

I roll my eyes, breezing past her. "Everyone has a choice, Raven, and he's chosen her. Save yourself the drama and forget about him."

"What, so I can move on to men like you?"

I laugh, glancing back. "Don't flatter yourself, darling. I'm not after anything from you. I like my women . . ." I pause, then shake my head. "Forget it."

She rushes after me. "No, tell me."

"Just, yah know, like ol' lady material."

"Right," she mutters, keeping in step with me. I have the feeling it isn't the first time she's heard that line.

"No offence," I add because she does look offended.

We walk in silence for another five minutes before she stops outside a small bar. There's low lighting and a mellow tune drifting from the open doors. "One for the road?" she asks. I find myself nodding, even though I've managed to convince her I'm not interested in her. This will only make things worse for me, but damn, I can't stop the pull.

We sit by the window, and a waitress comes to the table to take our drinks order. This isn't my kind of bar, but Raven seems relaxed.

"What is ol' lady material?" she almost whispers while avoiding eye contact and picking at the tablecloth edge.

"I guess it's different for everyone. We all look for different qualities in a partner."

"Well, tell me what you're looking for. I know it's not me." She blushes. "I'm not trying to hit on you or anything."

"Why do you want to know?"

She shrugs, looking embarrassed before sighing. "I'm never the one they choose. I'm the good time girl or the part-time girl but never the one they take home to meet their mum or the one they cuddle up to at night, and I don't know what's wrong with me."

In that moment, under the flicker of the orange low light, she looks so beautiful, it almost takes my damn breath away. So vulnerable and broken, I have to stop the alpha in me demanding I pull her into my arms and take care of her. "There's nothing wrong with you, Raven," I say. "You just haven't met the one."

She rolls her eyes again—it's becoming my favourite thing to see. "What if I never do? Am I supposed to settle for second place all the time?"

"What's the hurry? What are you, like twenty-something?"

"Thirty this year," she mumbles, and my eyes widen. Not because it's old, but because she's closer to my age of thirty-five than I thought. "Most of the women I know have kids already and they're younger than me."

"I don't think anyone knows you feel like this, Raven. The guys seem to think you're happy just doing you. The impression I get is that you're too busy for dating because you're always at work. Chains told me you're not the settling down type, that you're having fun and working hard."

She lowers her eyes as the waitress places our drinks on the table. Once she's gone, Raven takes a large gulp of her wine. My mobile rings and I glance at Ruby's name on the screen, then I cancel the call. "Wife?" asks Raven.

"I don't have a wife or an ol' lady."

Ruby immediately calls back. "Seems pretty desperate to get hold of you."

"Are you and Vinn done?"

"Are you and Ruby?"

I smirk. "He'll never treat you how you deserve," I point out, but I know she already knows that.

"He bought us a flat."

"Wow, charmer."

"It was supposed to be a bit of fun," she mutters miserably.

"But you fell in love."

"I think he did too. He got the flat and said he can't let me go."

I laugh, rolling my eyes. "Raven, listen to yourself. That's not love. If he loved you, he'd never give you up. He'd do whatever he could to keep you. Marrying Sofia wouldn't be on his to-do list. He wants to have his cake and eat it. Do you seriously want to spend the rest of your life answering to him when he has a wife? Eventually, he'll have a kid, and then you'll always be second best. Don't you want kids and marriage?"

She bites on her lower lip. "Maybe I could live like that. It's what I'm doing right now."

"And look how miserable it's making you. Look, you don't know me, so maybe that makes it easier for me to say this, but he's a dick and he's laughing with his pretty wife on one arm and his dirty little secret on the other. Dump his arse. You can do better."

"Did Ruby cheat on you?" she asks.

I drain my drink, standing. "Let's get back."

Chapter Five

RAVEN

Working on a Saturday wasn't my best idea. I woke with a cruel hangover and a dry mouth, which resulted in me heaving over the toilet for at least half an hour. I couldn't eat breakfast, so I left twenty-minutes late with an empty stomach.

I'm thankful Vinn's nowhere to be seen, and I get stuck into a pile of filing that's been building up for weeks. I then make some calls to potential new dancers for Vinn's strip club. That business is doing so well, he hired a club manager to take over the daily running and he now puts most of his time into this place. I arrange some interviews, and I'm still in Vinn's office putting them in his diary, when he arrives. My stomach does somersaults, which adds to the hangover, and I feel physically sick.

Vinn hangs his jacket by the door, unfastens his cuff links, and rolls his sleeves. He'd do this right before he was about to pin me down and fuck the life out of me, so the somersaults soon turn to butterflies, but then he takes a seat at his desk, paying no attention to me. "Can you do that later?" he asks coldly. "I have calls to make." He's never asked me to leave his office. Never. I nod and make my way out. "Close the door," he adds. Another thing he's never done.

I sit at my desk and pretend to tap away on my laptop, but in truth, it's not even switched on. My heart aches. I never got like this when I was with Chains. Sure, I liked him, but not like this. I knew Leia was right for him the second I saw them together. Then when I had the stupid fleeting crush on the Pres, I found it easy to turn my feelings off once Anna told me straight to stay the fuck away from him. But this, with Vinn, it's different, and I hate he's ignoring me. I hate his distance. I occasionally glance through the window to his office, seeing him in deep conversation on the phone. I decide to occupy myself with work, because I can do this. I can get over Vinn Romano.

It's almost eleven o'clock when he surfaces from his office. He stands at my desk, holding out a piece of paper, and I glance up from my computer. "This is Sofia's list of things still to do for the wedding. I thought I'd take some of the pressure off and finish it." I take it and stare at the scribbled list. "If you could make it a priority."

I stare wide-eyed. "You want me to do it?"

"Yes, you are my assistant," he says dryly.

"I don't think it would be appropriate," I say, handing it back.

"In what way?"

"Vinn," I sigh, "I know you're mad at me, but punishing me by rubbing my face in your wedding plans is a little childish, especially for you."

He glares at me, and I'm reminded of why men cower at his feet. "Raven, I pay you to do a job. If you can't do it, then stop wasting my time."

I gasp. "I do a damn good job, but planning your wedding isn't in my job description. Hire a wedding planner. You can afford it."

He places his hands on my desk, leaning closer. "I think you may have forgotten who the fuck I am. You do what I tell you to," he hisses. "Now, get your coat. We have business to attend to."

I stare at him a few seconds, thinking of all the ways I want to tell him to get fucked, but instead, I smile sweetly, grab my coat from the back of my chair, and stand. "Great. Let's go."

I bite the inside of my cheek so hard, I taste blood on my tongue. "I hope you're not too hungover." Vinn smirks as he drops the lump of flesh to the floor. It splats and I swallow the vomit threatening to appear any second. Gerry holds out the man's arm, as he's too weak to put up a fight, and Tommy slices another chunk of flesh. I didn't bother to listen when Vinn listed the guy's wrongdoings. It's usually a drug dealer on Vinn's patch or someone trying to move in on his deals. Vinn wipes his bloody hands on a cloth before straightening his tie and shrugging his jacket back on. "Next job." We leave Gerry and Tommy to deal with the man.

Vinn drives like a maniac, darting in and out of traffic. I miss Gerry's driving when he's like this. "You're very quiet," he notes. When I don't respond, I feel him look over, his eyes assessing me. "Are you not well?"

"Just tired," I mutter, staring out of the window.

"Drinking until three in the morning with a stranger can do that."

I spin my head to look at him and instantly regret it because of the nausea. "You were spying on me?"

"Checking you were safe, Corvo. There's a difference."

"He's with the club, why wouldn't I be safe?"

"He's unstable. His brother just died."

My mouth falls open. "How do you know that?"

"I'm Vincent Romano, I know everything."

"Don't spy on me. I don't like it."

"I'll always watch over what's mine."

My heart squeezes. I wish those words were true. I wish I was completely his and that he was completely mine. His wedding list pops into my head, and I sigh. It's just another reminder that we'll never be together, not properly.

We stop at the docks, where Chains and Mac are waiting. Chains throws his arm around my shoulder. "You look sad, what's up?"

"Hangover," I mutter, and he smiles.

"I was just giving Mac some abuse about keeping you out until late."

"We were just talking," I say defensively, mainly because I don't want Vinn to think anything happened between us.

Chains smirks, nudging into me. "Yeah, sure. I know what you're like." It's said in a playful tone, but I'm instantly pissed off.

"Jesus Christ," I hiss, "I don't drop my knickers for every man I meet, yah know!"

Chains looks taken aback. "I was kidding."

"You've already talked shit about me, telling Mac I don't do relationships. How would you even fucking know? Just because I didn't want to settle for you, doesn't mean I'm gonna be like that with everyone. And just because you've been in my bed, doesn't mean you fucking know me."

"What's crawled up your arse?" asks Chains, confused.

"I'm so sick of men!" I snap, storming away from them.

I find a quiet spot looking out over the choppy waters and sit down, dangling my feet over the edge. The dark, murky abyss below suddenly looks inviting, and I shake my head to clear the fog. Maybe I should move on. I came here with Chains because I wanted to settle in a safe place, and the Kings Reapers have been that for over a year now. I have a good amount of savings in my bank, still not as much as I'd like but enough to set me up in a new place.

Ten minutes have passed when Chains joins me, lowering himself beside me and looking over the edge at the water below. "Sorry," he says.

"Me too."

"You wanna talk about it?" He never asks me this question. It's become normal for me to listen to him and some of the other brothers. When he was avoiding Leia, it was me he turned to for advice, and when Riggs discovered he had prostate cancer, it was me who sat in his office late at night and spoke with him. I'm the one who gives advice and listens to their problems. But they're men, so they never think to ask if I'm okay, and when they do, it isn't because they really want to know, it's just an empty question.

"Am I a club whore?" I ask.

Chains furrows his brow. "No."

"But I'm not ol' lady material?"

He shrugs. "I don't know."

"I'm not. None of the guys think I am."

"Where's all this coming from?"

"I guess I'm feeling like it's time to settle down. I'm sick of being on my own."

"You're never on your own . . . you have us."

"You know what I mean, Chains. I want what you and Leia have, or Riggs and Anna. I'm sick of being alone. I want to feel special and loved."

"You know I love you, Raven. You're my best friend, and if you're unhappy, then I am too. I'll find you a suitable man, if that's what you want."

I laugh. "I don't trust you with such an important job."

"Hey, I'm a good judge of character. Obviously, he won't be as good-looking as me, but you can't have everything."

"You don't know my type," I point out.

"Anyone who looks like me," he says, shrugging.

"You're not my type," I protest.

"We had sex . . . a lot," he says.

I laugh again. "It was just sex. There's a reason we didn't settle down."

"Because I had to break your heart for Leia."

"Don't flatter yourself." I grin. He always manages to cheer me up.

"Corvo," says Vinn from behind me, "are you ready?"

I check my watch. "Actually, I'm gonna call it a day, if that's okay. I'm not feeling well at all, and I've done all I needed to at the office. Text me that list and I'll start it on Monday," I say brightly.

"Fine," he mutters before heading off.

"Did something happen with you two?" asks Chains. I lower my head, and he groans. "Fuck, Raven. Of all the men, you had to choose that prick? You know how I feel about him."

"I know," I mutter. "It's over now anyway. No harm done."

MAC

Chains approaches hand-in-hand with Raven. She looks a little happier. "You don't mind if Raven tags along for the ride, do you?" asks Chains, and I shake my head.

Our next job is collecting from a shop owner who owes Vinn protection money. Apparently, he's always late paying and now he's beginning to get into debt. Blade is already waiting for us inside. The shop owner is agitated, and Blade is trying to negotiate, all while throwing and catching a knife. "Why are we here again, Matt?" asks Chains, casually picking up a cannabis tin. There're all kinds of drug paraphernalia that he sells legally, but his problem is the hardcore porn he sells out back. Locals hate it, and he's often threatened or gets his windows smashed. Since Vinn helped him out with protection, that's all stopped. "I'm bored of calling in here week after week. People might start to think I'm buying that bullshit you sell out back."

"I called Vinn, told him what my situation was. I can't give what I haven't got."

"I don't believe you, Matt," says Blade.

Raven wanders out back, and I follow, despite Matt's protests about it being private property. There's wall-to-wall shelving filled with DVDs. Raven walks towards the television set up on the desk, takes a seat, and presses play on whatever's on screen. Moans fill the air, and Raven smirks. "This is low grade, cheaply-made porn. Who the hell buys this shit when you can find it free online?"

I shrug. "Maybe the older generation who can't use the web?"

"No," she mumbles, shaking her head. "Something isn't right. No one would pay for this shit."

Raven pulls a random DVD from the shelf and pops it in the player. Seconds later, a child-like cry fills the room, and Raven's eyes widen. I glance over, and she's covering her mouth with her hands, tears springing to her eyes. On the screen is an older man and a kid who must be no more than eight years old. Raven pauses the DVD and stares up at me with total devastation on her face. My blood boils and I move fast, rushing back into the front of the shop and grabbing Matt by his neck.

"Whoa," yells Chains in surprise.

"You piece of shit," I growl, squeezing Matt's neck hard. I lift him a few inches from the ground, and he chokes, desperately trying to loosen my grip on his throat. "He's a nonce," I tell Chains.

"I'm not," he gasps as his toes skim the floor in his struggle.

"Raven played one of the DVDs. There's a room full of them."

"Not . . . mine," whispers Matt. I land a punch square on his jaw as I release his neck, then he hits the floor with a loud bang. I hear Chains on a call to Vinn, explaining the situation.

Raven joins us. "There's a lot," is all she says before I lay into the scumbag again.

Chains pulls me back. "Relax. Vinn wants to deal with him. He's in the area, so he's heading over."

"Fuck that," I snap.

"I'm with Mac," Blade adds.

"He's the boss, not me," says Chains, shrugging.

"He ain't my boss!" I snap, laying into the fucker again.

By the time Vinn arrives, the guy is a bloodied heap on the ground. Vinn looks from me to Matt, then back to me again. "Which part of wait didn't you understand?" he asks calmly. "Do they not understand that word in Nottingham?"

"I figured I'd get the job done. I don't need you to watch over me whilst I end a dirty fucker like him."

Vinn takes a few deep breaths, then his eyes narrow in on the bloodied heap. "I thought you were going home to rest," he spits out to Raven.

"I was. These guys had to do this first," she mutters, and it pisses me off she's bothering to answer to him.

"Well, we'll let *these guys* clean up, and I'll take you home."

Raven looks hesitant. "I can take her home after clean-up," I say firmly.

Vinn suddenly yells, "I'm sure you can, but seeing as I'm in fucking charge, I'll make the decisions."

I smirk. It'll take more than him raising his voice to worry me. Chains arches his eyebrow in warning for me to shut the fuck up. "In charge?" I repeat.

"Enough," snaps Chains. "Thanks, Vinn, we'll sort the clean-up."

"Bullshit!" I snap. "You're not in charge of me."

Vinn reaches for his gun, drawing it and pointing it at my head. There's an easy look in his eye, like he'd take my life without a blink. I know that look too well—it's similar to my own. "While I'm paying your wage, I'm in charge," he says clearly.

Raven steps between us. "Vinn, there's no need for that," she says with pleading eyes, but he doesn't acknowledge her. I gently pull her behind me, not comfortable with the gun so close to her.

"Clean this shit show up. Raven, let's go!" he growls.

"Do you want to go with him?" I ask, turning my back on him and his stupid gun so I'm looking at her. "It's up to you."

"Who the fuck does this clown think he is?" Vinn shouts.

"It's fine," mutters Raven. "I'll see you later." I shake my head angrily. She's just trying to keep the peace, but I'd happily take this arsehole on if she gives me the nod. Instead, I step aside, letting her pass. Vinn grabs her by the arm, and it pisses me off even more.

The second they're outside and the door closes, Chains shoves me in the chest. "Are you fucking stupid? What did I say to you about showing respect?"

"If you ask me, it's about time someone challenged him," mutters Blade.

"Well, no one asked you," Chains snaps. "Riggs will go mad when he finds out about this."

"I don't care," I say, checking the body for a pulse. "He's still alive," I add. Blade rolls his eyes and lunges forward, pushing a knife into the guy's eye. I screw my face in disgust. "As far as I'm concerned, I answer to Riggs. He's my President, not Vinn. And if you were a good friend to Raven, you'd have intervened there. She's heartbroken, and she didn't want to go with him."

"Raven and Vinn?" asks Blade, and I nod.

"She told me it wasn't serious and that it's over now anyway," says Chains.

"Well, she's hurting pretty bad. If I can see that, why can't you?"

"Are you looking for something with her?" Chains asks accusingly.

"No!" It comes out sharper than I intended. "I was just around when she was upset and I couldn't walk away. I'm telling you so you take over."

"Brother, I get enough shit off my ol' lady about Raven, I can't spend any more time than I already do. Besides, she's confided in you, so clearly she trusts you."

"She doesn't fucking know me, so stop passing the buck. Look, if you don't wanna deal with her, then that's your problem. I've told you, and if you choose to ignore it, so be it."

"Can't you watch out for her?" he asks.

"I just walked away from all my shit. I don't have the headspace to deal with hers." And right on time, my mobile rings and Ruby's name flashes up again.

Chapter Six

RAVEN

I groan when Vinn pulls into the carpark of one of his restaurants. "I just want to go home."

"You're gonna hear me out, Raven."

I follow him inside as he breezes past everyone without saying a word, which I find rude, so I smile politely at his staff, muttering apologies. "I'll have two steaks brought up to my office. I have a business meeting that may take some time, and I do not want disturbing no matter what!" he shouts to no one in particular.

The nearest chef nods. "Of course, Mr. Romano."

"Actually," I say, staring at the nervous-looking chef, "I'll just take a salad." He glances at Vinn as if to get permission for my decision, and I groan out loud in frustration, pushing past Vinn and heading for the office. I hear Vinn confirm my order. "And this is exactly why we would never work," I say the second we're alone in the office. "I can't even order my own fucking lunch."

"You're overreacting. You just did."

"With your permission," I point out.

"Corvo—"

"Raven."

"Same bloody thing," he hisses impatiently. "Take the apartment."

"No!" I shout. "I don't want to talk about this again, Vinn. I'm tired." I pause to catch my breath, and it's shaky, like I'm about to cry. I blink a few times to chase the tears away. "Just let me get over you."

He takes my hand and tugs me towards him. "I don't want you to." He runs a hand down my face, rubbing his thumb along my jaw. "We have something. You know we do."

I smile sadly. "It isn't real."

He places a kiss on my nose, and I close my eyes. "It's real, Corvo." I hold my breath, feeling his lips close. I open my eyes slightly, and he's watching for my reaction as his lips gently press against mine. It's the first time he's ever kissed me. Even just brushing my lips sends sparks flying around my body. As his hands cup my face and his lips press a little harder, he sweeps his tongue into my mouth and it's all it takes to turn this sweet, gentle first kiss into a hunger I haven't felt in such a long time.

I allow him to lift me onto his desk, not breaking the kiss. He unbuckles his belt, and I unfasten my shirt. It's never felt this real before, this intense. His eyes are dark, his wandering hands desperate to touch every part of me, and I'm crying out for him to take me right now on his desk. But a knock on the door, followed by it opening, has Vinn pulling away fast. It's almost like he sensed Sofia there, or maybe he heard the protests of the waitress. Either way, we all stand quiet for a few seconds, Vinn's heavy breathing filling the silence, while Sofia takes in the scene before her.

The waitress mutters an apology and begins to say how she tried to stop her, but Vinn flicks his hand at her like she's an annoying puppy, and she scuttles away. "I can see you're busy," says Sofia stiffly. I lower my head, feeling like shit. "I'll leave you to it." She spins and rushes out, and Vinn looks at me with guilt before rushing after her. A second later, the chef appears, holding two domed dishes. He frowns in confusion, and I give him a watery smile.

"Mr. Romano has been called away urgently. We won't be needing lunch. Thank you."

I fasten my shirt and pull out my mobile. I try calling Chains, but there's no answer. I could call any of the guys, Riggs would send someone to get me, but I can't face them right now, so I dial the only person I know who will come no question and make me see sense.

Mac answers after the second ring. "Where are you?" is the first thing he asks, and it makes my tears spill over and fall down my cheeks. I reel off the address to the restaurant. "I'm just around the corner. I'll be there in two minutes."

Heading outside, I spot Vinn and Sofia in a heated discussion. I keep my eyes fixed to the ground and sigh with relief when I hear the rumble of Mac's motorcycle. As I climb on, I glance towards Vinn, who's got his eyes fixed on me. He looks torn as we ride away, but he's made his choice, and now, I've seen it for myself. His loyalties are with Sofia.

Mac stops outside a building I recognise as newly built apartments and we get off. I didn't want to tag on to another job, but I can't complain, seeing as he did me a favour. I follow him into the building, and he uses a key card to let us into the lift. Stopping on the second floor, he uses the key card again to open one of the apartment doors.

Inside is basic, and it screams single man with the dark grey couch, small coffee table, and large television.

"I thought you might want to get your head straight before we go back to the club. I kind of made Chains aware you're upset, and he might make a fuss."

I wander through the living room to the kitchen. Again, it's basic with just a microwave, fridge, and kettle. "Is this your place?" I ask. Some of the guys at the club have places they can go to if they need some time out. It can be full on, living with all those people and their crazy kids running around the place.

"It's not mine. Brick gave me the key for you to come and chill out." I smile. The guys all care about me in their own ways and it cheers me up a little. "Vinn doesn't know about it either," he adds with a wink.

"He won't be coming to look for me. He made his feelings perfectly clear."

"Was that Sofia I spotted with him outside the restaurant?"

I nod and my cheeks colour with shame. "She walked in on us."

"Fuck."

"Exactly. He went running after her, leaving me there. I mean, of course, he did, she's his fiancée, so I don't know why it hurt me so much. But it did." I go to the living room and drop on the couch.

"There are other men out there, ones who aren't attached to a shit load of baggage. Why's he marrying her anyway, if he was with you?"

"He wasn't with me, technically. I told you, we were hooking up, not dating. We never went to a restaurant unless it was for business meetings. He never even kissed me until . . ." I trail off, remembering the way his lips felt against mine when he finally kissed me.

"You fell for a man who never kissed you?" he asks sceptically. "Kissing is the connection."

"Maybe that's why he avoided it. I wonder if he's kissed Sofia," I mutter.

"If you're gonna get all mushy on me, I'm off," says Mac. "And I'm pretty sure he's done more than kiss her. They're getting married."

"Apparently, she's untouched. Saved for her husband-to-be," I say dryly.

Mac's eyes almost bug out of his head. "She's a virgin?"

"According to Gia, if the woman is promised, she has to be pure."

"Shit. I wanna marry into the mafia."

I laugh. "So, you're a man-whore?" He falls silent, keeping his eyes fixed to the floor, and a look of pain flashes over his face. Maybe he's been cheated on. At least, that's the impression I get, and he's avoiding Ruby's call, whoever the hell that is. "Speaking of which, did you ever take Ruby's call?"

"Yah know, I brought you here to get your head straight, not to talk about my fuck-up of a life," he jokes, taking a seat beside me.

"Maybe it'll make me feel better to know your life is messier than mine."

He grins. "Nice try. Who was your last relationship before Vinn? Maybe you can go back there to help you get over him?"

I laugh. "Women don't work like that. Besides, Chains was before Vinn, although it wasn't a relationship."

"Another no strings hook-up, huh?" I nod in response. I never wanted more before now. Maybe it's my age or the fact everyone has someone and I don't. "What's your longest actual relationship?" he asks.

I bite my lip. "I haven't had one."

He glares at me. "Never?"

I shake my head. "You?"

He seems to think it over, and I can tell he doesn't want to talk about himself, but he eventually answers. "A long time. I was with her since leaving school at sixteen."

"Jesus," I gasp, "childhood sweethearts?"

"Yeah." He smiles like he's thinking about that memory. "Eighteen years."

"Shit, thinking about that gives me hives," I joke. "How do you heal your heart after that length of time?"

He shrugs. "I don't know if you ever do."

"Kids?" I ask, and he shakes his head.

"Eighteen years and no fucking kids?"

"She couldn't have them," he admits.

"Siblings?" I ask, remembering what Vinn told me about him losing his brother.

"No."

"Me either," I say, to move on. Maybe Vinn got it wrong.

MAC

Siblings. I hate that word. Images of my twin infiltrate my mind, but I shut them down. This is a fresh start. I have to block all that shit out and concentrate on moving forward. "What about your parents?" I hear Raven ask, and I shrug.

"What about them?"

She smiles. "Well, do you speak to them?"

I shake my head. "Do you speak to yours? I can't imagine they're happy about you hanging around the MC."

"I don't have any," she says bluntly. "I was adopted when I was small."

"Oh. Did you have a good childhood?"

She shakes her head. "Not really."

"So, how did you end up at the club?"

"It was just a life I stumbled into when I was on the streets as a teen. Hung around the wrong people and got into situations I had no real control over. Eventually, I was a club whore for Cobra." I raise my eyebrows. Cobra is infamous amongst the other Kings charters as the Pres who went rogue. "Chains found me, got me out of there, and I've been here in London since. I love it here, though. It's nothing like some of the other places I've been."

"My dad was in the club, and his dad before him. I grew up in it," I say. It's the most I've told her and it feels good to talk about it. I loved growing up in the MC. It was my dream to take over my own charter, but that never worked out. Ruby loved being in Nottingham, it's where her family was and she needed them around her. So, I settled . . . I became Treasurer and settled. Until I didn't anymore, and here I am.

"Why'd yah leave?"

"Why do most people move on?" I ask. "Love or heartbreak, and as I don't have an ol' lady with me, you work it out."

"But you did have an ol' lady?" she asks, and I nod. I couldn't be with Ruby for eighteen years and not make her my ol' lady. "And she didn't want to come with you, so she broke your heart?" she guesses.

"Will you always be in this life?" I ask, changing the subject.

"I hope so. I love it. But who knows what the future holds?"

I smirk. That's a true statement if ever I heard one.

❦

I stretch out and open one eye, seeing it's dark in the apartment now. We must have fallen asleep. I glance to where Raven's head is resting against my chest. We talked for hours— mainly she talked as I didn't want to give too much away, but I let her tell me about her teenage years and how the girls at school hated her. It sounds like she went from one boy to the next, looking for love but always being used. I wrap a tendril of her red hair around my finger. It's been a few months since I woke up with a woman next to me like this.

Her mobile lights up, silently flashing Vinn's name on the screen. I carefully reach for it and see she has ten missed calls and a text message from him. Arsehole. He's treated her just like all the men in her life do, used her and dumped her. I open the text message.

Vinn: Where the fuck are you? I've been to the club and you're not there. Call me.

I delete it. It's wrong, but I'm looking out for her and lord knows someone needs to. I'm not gonna let men use her again. Maybe this is my time to put shit right.

❦

I wait until daylight before waking Raven. She groans, and I smile as she blinks her eyes a few times before sitting up in a panic. "Oh shit, what time is it?" She grabs her phone and frowns when she sees no missed calls or texts.

"Relax. It's Sunday. What do you have that's so time critical today?"

She lets out a breath. "Nothing, I guess."

"Wanna hang out?"

She smiles. "Sure. What do you have in mind?"

"Let's start with breakfast. Brick's got nothing in this place."

We find a small cafe just around the corner, and Raven orders a bagel while I order a full English and tuck in the second it arrives. "I've only ever told Chains some of that stuff I told you last night," she admits.

"What can I say, I'm easy to talk to."

She smiles. "Maybe."

We finish breakfast in silence, then her mobile rings. We both stare at it buzzing across the table, Vinn's name flashing on and off. "If I don't answer, he'll keep ringing."

"It's taken him until now to check in on you," I lie. "He deserves to wait." She worries her lower lip. "It gets easier to ignore it, I promise."

"Why are you ignoring Ruby?" she asks, pushing her phone away.

"Too much has happened, and I need to be away from her and everything else."

"Do you still love her?" she asks.

"Maybe. It's complicated." I don't deserve her is what I wanna say, but I don't.

After breakfast, I make Raven take me to some tourist spots. She's loving every minute as she tells me all about Chains doing the same for her when she came here. She missed out on this sort of thing growing up, so she's excited every time we head to the next place.

We're at Madame Tussauds when Riggs calls me, and I step away from Raven while she takes selfies next to the wax statues. "Yeah?" I answer.

"Where are you?"

"Needed some time, Pres," I say. "Everything okay?"

"I just had Vinn here screwing about Raven not answering his calls or some shit. He came looking for her last night too, and I realised you've both been missing since yesterday. He said you screwed up a job."

"I finished a job. It was gonna end that way anyway, and he's just pissed he didn't get the glory."

"Look, Mac, I don't know how things were done in Nottingham, but we're in deep with Vinn. You got a problem with that, come speak to me. Don't go rogue on jobs. Is Raven with you?"

"Yep."

"You know her and Vinn are hooking up, right?"

"They were, not anymore. But it's not like that between us, Pres. You know why I came here—I'm not looking for more drama, I just feel bad for her. She's upset over him."

"Some advice for you, brother, let them deal with it. Don't get involved, especially going up against Vinn. It won't end well."

"Ain't it your job to keep Raven safe? To look after her? She needs the club right now."

"Fuck, Mac. You've been here two minutes and you're already upsetting people. Don't add me to the fucking list. Get Raven to Vinn now. It's work-related."

"I can't do that, Pres. I'm sorry. "

"It's an order, Mac!" he snaps.

I disconnect the call, and Raven rushes over and throws her arms around my neck. "I'm having the best day, Mac. Thank you so much."

I smile. "No problem."

Chapter Seven

RAVEN

I turned my phone off in the end, tired of Vinn's calls and messages. I noticed Mac do the same, and I wondered if that was to avoid the same or if Ruby was still calling him. He's secretive about his past, but it doesn't bother me, simply because knowing everything about the brothers is tiring. It's nice to be intrigued and not have all the answers. He isn't piling his problems on to me.

We spent the entire day sightseeing and it's been amazing. Mac has managed to distract me enough to only think about Vinn fleetingly. He's paid for the entire day, despite my protests, and now, as we ride back to the clubhouse, I can't help but feel sad. Our day has come to an end, and I have to face reality. Starting with work tomorrow.

Gia grabs my hand when I walk into the club. "Oh my god, you've driven Vinn crazy," she says with delight.

"Oh?"

She heads up to my room, and I follow, giving a quick wave to Mac as he heads straight for Riggs' office. She drags me into my room and closes the door. "So, tell me what the hell is going off." She's smiling, so I relax.

"Erm, do you mean with Vinn?"

"Yes, I mean with my brother. Sofia isn't speaking to him. He's tearing London up looking for you. What the hell?"

"I just had a day out with Mac. He wanted to see London."

"Are you and Vinn seeing each other?"

I shake my head, unsure of how much Vinn would want his sister knowing about his private life. "I just work for him."

"Bullshit," she yells, laughing hard. "You're having sex. Sofia told me."

I feel my face redden. "We were but not anymore. He wants to marry Sofia."

"So much so he was fucking you in the restaurant? Oh my god, do you know what he's risking by doing that?" She's still finding the whole thing amusing, and I'm confused by her reaction.

"Are they still getting married?"

Gia shrugs. "More than likely, since neither can really back out. It doesn't mean she won't make his life hell, though. Maybe that's why he's so desperate to see you—he wants to get your stories straight."

My heart aches again. Why did we have to end our perfect day to return to this?

"I won't say anything to her," I mutter.

"She isn't stupid. Didn't he have you on the desk?"

I blush further, nodding. "We ended before that. It was just a moment of madness."

We both jump with fright when the bedroom door crashes open. Vinn is in my doorway, glaring at me, his eyes dark and angry. "Oh shit," whispers Gia.

"Get out, Gia," he growls, and she practically runs to escape.

He slams the door, turning the lock. "I've been calling and texting all night, all day. Where the fuck have you been?"

I take a big swallow. "That's none of your business."

He moves so fast, I don't have time to react before his fingers wrap around my throat, and he's pushing me against the wall. "Where the fuck have you been?" he yells angrily.

I'm not used to seeing this side of him aimed at me and my eyes prickle with tears. His grip isn't tight, but it's threatening. He's mad as hell. "Let go of me," I demand firmly.

"You think you can just go off radar and tell me it's none of my business? You took the tracker off your phone!" he shouts.

I shake my head. I haven't, which makes me wonder who has. "It's for the best. You shouldn't be tracking me. I'm not your priority."

"Were you with him, Corvo?" he asks in a low, threatening tone.

"Did you sort things with Sofia?" I ask, and he instantly releases me and begins pacing the room.

"My head is fucked," he spits. "Why can't I just walk away?"

"It'll get easier."

He shakes his head. "No, no, it won't. I'm not giving up on you. You're coming to look at the apartment I got for us. Once you see it, you'll realise I'm serious." He grips my wrist and pulls me from the room.

I try to tug away, but his grip is too strong, "No." He ignores me, pulling me behind him as we descend the stairs. He's acting crazy, and for the first time, I'm scared. "Vinn, stop!"

Riggs comes out of his office, followed by Mac. "Everything okay?" he asks.

"I'm taking Raven. I'll return her soon."

"I'm not a piece of property. Let me go," I snap.

"Vinn, she's upset," says Riggs, trying to make him see reason.

"She'll be fine. I just need to show her the apartment." Seeing Vinn so unravelled is scary.

"Man, she doesn't wanna go with you," says Mac firmly. "Let her go."

"Stay the fuck out of this!" yells Vinn.

"You're scaring her, let her go!" Mac growls.

"Maybe you need to go into the office, and I'll sort this out," Riggs says to Mac.

"No. Let her fucking go now," Mac yells, pulling his gun.

The room falls silent as Vinn turns slowly to look at Mac. "Have you got something to tell me, Corvo?" he asks me.

"I was with her last night," says Mac. "But that's got nothing to do with you because you've made your choice. Now, let her go."

Riggs moves in front of the gun. "We all need to calm down. Mac, are you claiming Raven?"

"No, but he ain't taking her."

"Brother, you know you can't enforce that, and I can't either, not unless she's an ol' lady. She and Vinn have been hooking up for weeks. I can't intervene."

Everyone's looking at Mac, including me, unable to believe Riggs has put him in that position. He stares into my eyes, steels his spine, and says, "Then I'm claiming her."

I gasp, my throat suddenly feeling too tight, then all hell breaks loose. Vinn releases me and rushes Mac. They end up in a scuffle, with other brothers wading in to pull them apart. Gia grabs my hand and pulls me out the way. "Let them deal with it," she whispers and takes me into the kitchen. We're immediately joined by Anna and Leia.

"Well, that was unexpected," says Anna.

I'm staring at the now closed kitchen door. "What just happened?"

"You just got yourself an old man," says Leia.

"But he's not looking for . . . he isn't . . . I'm not . . ."

"I've never known it to happen like that before," says Leia. "He clearly doesn't want Vinn to have you."

"But what do you want?" asks Gia, rubbing my hand.

"I don't want all this," I mutter. "And I want what you all have, but not because he feels obliged."

"Have you two . . . yah know?" asks Leia.

I shake my head. "No, nothing like that. He's been like a really good friend these last few days. I think I'm in shock."

"It's one way to protect you from Vinn," says Leia.

"Now, the club has to protect you," adds Anna, "as an ol' lady."

I stand. "I can't let him do this."

Anna pulls me back to sit. "He's made the choice. You can't go back out there and throw it in his face. Look, get over whatever that was with you and Vinn, then things will have settled."

"You don't know my brother," scoffs Gia, and Leia nods in agreement.

"There's nothing he can do now without upsetting the club, and nobody wants that," says Anna with confidence.

MAC

Fuck. Frankie isn't gentle when she wipes the split in my eyebrow. I wince, and she rolls her eyes impatiently. "Are you serious about this?" asks Cree, and I nod. "But you don't know the woman."

I shrug. Yeah, it wasn't on my list of things to do today, but neither was sightseeing. "She's like a lost soul, and I feel for her," I explain. It's true—something in her calls to me, and I can't resist the pull to protect her. She's had a shit life and she deserves to be happy. And yeah, it might not be with me, but at least it'll give her breathing room from Vinn.

"But you're not together," says Riggs.

"It don't matter. There's nothing in the rules that says I can't claim an ol' lady unless I fuck her."

"He's got a point," says Frankie.

"I just don't get *why* you'd wanna claim her," says Riggs.

"Because she needs to be away from Vinn. If he had his way, he'd marry the Italian and keep Raven in some luxury apartment on the side. She deserves better."

"Why do you care?" asks Cree.

"I dunno," I mutter. "I just do."

"Look, man," Riggs begins, "you haven't got to punish yourself for what happened back in Nottingham." I glare at him. It isn't common knowledge, but he nods to reassure me he isn't going into detail. "All I'm saying is don't rush into this. You might end up breaking her heart."

"I'll be straight with her," I say.

I find Raven in the kitchen with some of the other ol' ladies. She smiles sadly at me, and I hold out my hand. She takes it, and I lead her out to the back of the club, where there's a field and some trees, and we slowly begin to walk. "That wasn't how I planned the day to end," I say.

"Look, I know you said that to save me from Vinn, and I appreciate it so much, but I don't expect you to go through with it or anything. It's cool to back out."

I glance at her. "I ain't backing out."

"Oh."

"You deserve better than Vinn. Heal your heart and find someone who will treat you good."

"Can I do that if you've claimed me?"

"It's our rules, who's gonna stop us? I just wanna give you a chance to move on. You can't do that with him in the picture. If I have to be the buffer, then so be it."

"Seems a little extreme," she mutters with a nervous laugh.

"Just the way I am," I say. "You'll get used to it."

I walk her to her bedroom when we get back to the club, and she stands at her door awkwardly. "See you at breakfast," I say, gently kissing her on the head. She nods and goes inside, and I head to my room with a smile on my face, feeling like I've done something good for once.

As I'm stepping out of the shower, my mobile rings. I sigh. I have to face her sometime, I know I do, so I press it to my ear. "Mac," she gasps, surprised I've picked up. "I've been trying hard to get hold of you. Are you okay?"

"What do you need, Ruby?" I ask.

"To meet up, to talk?"

I hate the hope in her voice, knowing I have to crush it. "That's not possible."

"I can come to you. Just give me your address and I'll head over."

"I'm not in Nottingham anymore."

"Oh. I thought you were just taking a break."

"No, it's a permanent move. Fresh start and all that."

"Fresh start," she whispers. "I'm glad you've found it so easy. Have you spoken with her?" When I don't reply, she sighs. "Have you spoken to Meghan?"

"No."

"Look, I really need to meet up with you so we can talk. Things have changed. I—"

"It's not going to happen, Ruby. I've moved on. You should too." I disconnect the call, and the feeling I had just minutes ago is now replaced with an ache in my chest.

I had a restless night, tossing and turning, thinking over shit that happened months ago. Things that I can't change, no matter how hard I want to. I tap on Raven's bedroom door, and when she answers, I'm surprised to see her in her work clothes. "You're going to work?"

"Yeah. If I still have a job, that is."

"You can't go back there. You know how it'll end. Raven, you need to not see him for a while."

"It's my job. I worked hard to get it and I'm good at it."

"But he'll reel you back in."

"He won't. Look, Mac, it's the first time in my life I've earned real money in the way other people do. I'm not having to sell myself so I can eat. I have savings for the first time in my life, and I'm not giving that up because I fucked my boss. I have rights, so he can't let me go. I want that job."

I bite my inner cheek. She's stubborn and independent. "Fine. I'll drive you."

"I can drive myself," she says, smiling.

"But as my ol' lady, I'd like to drive you."

She laughs but gives in. "Fine."

I drop Raven at her office, then head back to the club for church. The guys file in, and Riggs stands. "Things seemed pretty settled around here, and then Mac arrived," he says, smirking.

"Shit, what you done now?" asks Ace.

"He's only gone and claimed Raven so he can do a chivalrous thing and protect her from Vinn Romano," says Cree, laughing.

Chains glares at me. "You did what?"

"She needed my help," I say, shrugging. "You said you couldn't do anything because your ol' lady was sick of you two spending time together, so I did what I had to do."

"Christ, Mac. Why the fuck would you lay claim to someone you hardly know?" asks Ace.

"Whatever the reasons, it means Raven is now an official part of the family. We take care of her like we do all the ol' ladies around here. Things with the mafia are good right now, and I hope it doesn't change because of Mac and his surprise claiming."

"And if it does?" I ask.

"We'll cross that bridge when we come to it. I don't think Vinn would let his personal life interfere with business. However, I'm pulling you off any jobs involving him. Strictly club business only from now on." I nod, happy with that.

We go over other business, then I go to find Anna because she wants me to look at the books for her bar. We sit in the main room as I begin looking over the figures. It's a good little earner. "Do you like Raven?" she suddenly asks, and I glance up at her. "Just, it's nice to see her settled."

"I wouldn't call her settled," I mutter. "I'm just helping her through a rough time."

"You know, she latches on very easily, so if you're not planning on making it serious, be careful."

"What do you mean? I thought she hadn't had relationships."

"She hasn't, as far as I know. She had a thing with Chains and they still spend a lot of time together, it bothers Leia. And she had a thing for Riggs."

"Right."

"Well, I'm just saying be careful."

"When I look at Raven, I see a woman needing love. She's surrounded by couples and kids, and she wants that too. She'll never have that with Vinn. I'm gonna keep her away from him until she finds someone."

"Okay," Anna nods, "I'm just worried for her. What if she falls for you and then you walk away too?"

"She won't fall for me. We're friends."

"I hope you're right, Mac. Like you said, she deserves to find her happily ever after."

Riggs heads over, kissing Anna on the head before fixing me with a glare. "Vinn called. He wants you on a job."

"But you said—"

"I know what I said. I tried to get you out of it, but he was hell-bent on keeping things as they are. He said you and Chains are good at the collecting."

"Right. Okay, if you're sure."

"But let me warn you," says Riggs, firmly, "don't mess with him, Mac. Just do what he pays us for and keep your head down and your nose clean. No more ignoring orders or offing people on a whim. You clear shit with me if you have a problem."

I nod. "Yes, Pres."

Chapter Eight

RAVEN

When I arrived for work, Vinn was nowhere to be seen, which was a relief, but I've had knots in my stomach all morning anticipating the mood he'll be in when he eventually shows. So, I'm surprised when he breezes in with two coffees, placing one on my desk. "Good morning."

"Morning," I reply with a small smile. I don't trust him when he's like this. "Would you like to go through your diary now or when you've settled?"

"Now's good," he says, heading into his office.

I gather the diary and follow him. "Mr. Clay requested a meeting this afternoon."

He grins. "About time. I honestly thought he'd be in touch much sooner. The severed fingers didn't quite have the impact I was looking for."

"After that, Sofia's father would like to meet."

Vinn stiffens. "Right."

"Should I order lunch in?"

"No, I don't think he'll be staying long." I want to ask if everything is okay, if Sofia has backed out of the wedding since she saw us together, but I refrain. It isn't my business. "Have you made a start on the wedding list?" he asks.

I nod. "Yes. I've placed the order with the florist and paid the deposit on the cars. And I've sent Sofia's measurements to the dressmaker for the adjustments. Her final fitting will be next week."

He nods. "Thank you." I gather the diary to my chest and head for the door. "Raven, I'm sorry about my recent behaviour. I have a lot going on. It's coming up to the anniversary of my dad's death and my head's all over."

"Sorry to hear that. I hope you're okay."

"You and Mac—" he begins.

"He's just looking out for me, Vinn. And for once, I'm gonna let him, because I'm tired of being on my own."

Sadness passes over his face. "I never meant to fall in love," he mutters, and my heart stutters. "I'm sorry for hurting you."

"Me too," I whisper before rushing away. I head straight for the bathroom, needing to gather myself. When he acts all vulnerable like that, I just want to wrap him in my arms and never let him go.

When I get back to my desk, Mac and Chains are stepping out of the lift. Mac grins and holds out a brown paper bag. "Chains said it was your favourite." I smile, taking it and peeking inside. It's a love heart shortbread biscuit with jam in the centre. My absolute favourite.

"Thank you."

"Is the big man available?" asks Chains.

I glance towards Vinn's office, and he's staring directly at me. "Yes, he seems to be."

The men head in to Vinn, and Chains hands him a bag of cash from the debt collections. "Any problems?" asks Vinn.

"Nope. All good."

"Mac, I'd just like to apologise for my behaviour yesterday. I was out of control, which is very unlike me. Congratulations to you and Raven. I wish you the very best. Have you booked for your tattoos yet?"

I pretend to be busy with my computer. "Not yet," Mac replies.

"Will you cover up Ruby's name or just add it?" My fingers freeze over the keys at Vinn's question. I knew his mister nice act was too good to be true. "Are you allowed two ol' ladies?"

"There are no strict rules," mutters Mac.

"Does Ruby know about Raven yet?"

"Why the fuck are you bringing up Ruby?" snaps Mac. "How do you know about her?"

"I know everything," says Vinn with a laugh. "I'm being friendly."

"Let's just go," says Chains.

"As a goodwill gesture, why don't I pay for your tattoos?" asks Vinn.

"I don't need your fucking money," Mac says.

"I'll give Raven the time off if you want to get them done right away. I know how important it is once you've claimed someone."

Mac turns to leave, his eyes fixed on me. "Great idea," he hisses. "Raven, let's go and see if they can fit us in now."

"Oh . . . erm, is that a good idea?" A tattoo is very permanent and this is a temporary arrangement.

"It's a fucking great idea. Let's go." He takes my hand, and I grab my bag, following him into the lift.

As the doors close, I turn to him. "What the fuck?"

"I know, alright, I wasn't keen on the idea either, but he pushes my fucking buttons. He knows we're not together and wants us to crack. Well, I'm not letting him back into your life, so we're getting the damn tattoos."

"But they're permanent."

"I'll pay for your cover-up. Get a small one."

Tatts isn't busy when we arrive. He's drawing on a sketch pad with music blaring out. "Good to meet you, man," he says, shaking hands with Mac. "Lake was telling me some new guys have joined. Take the chair and we'll get started."

I watch as Mac pulls his shirt over his head and hands it to me. Two things happen—I get a whiff of his aftershave, which smells amazing, and I stare wide-eyed at his hot torso. Of course, he's got an arm covered in tattoos. He turns away from me to take a seat, and I notice they crawl down his back too. Ruby's name sits on his left shoulder in large letters.

"What am I doing, brother?"

Mac pulls up an image on his mobile and shows Tatts. "I want this with Raven's name underneath."

"Not a problem," says Tatts, going over to his desk and sketching it out.

"What are you having?" I ask.

He turns his mobile to me and a black raven stares back. It's nice, and once this madness is over, no one will know that Raven is an actual person. He'll just look like a bird lover. Mac takes a pen from the side and holds out his hand. I place my hand in his, and he turns it over, writing on the side of my wrist. Once he's done, I look at his name in neat, scrolled lettering. *Mac*.

"It doesn't have to be a huge statement," he says.

I gently press my fingers over it. I like it. Way more than I should. Tatts returns and shows Mac his drawing. Once he's happy with it, he presses the design against Mac's skin on his back. There's not much room left, but it looks amazing, like it was made to fit. Tatts sets about tattooing the outline, and I watch with interest. This wonderful man is going to all this trouble for me. I've never had anyone do anything like this before.

Once Tatts is done, Mac admires it in the mirror. He seems pleased, and when I get in the chair, he takes a seat beside me and holds my free hand. I show Tatts where Mac drew the name. "You don't have to have that," says Mac. "I was just showing you an idea."

I smile. "I want this one. I like it."

Tatts takes less than two minutes to run the ink over Mac's name. Once it's done, I admire it. I like it . . . a lot.

Arriving back at work, Vinn is already in his first meeting. He catches my eye, but I take a seat at my desk and throw myself into work. The meeting doesn't go well, and Gerry steps forward a few times to push Mr. Clay back into his seat. It's heated, though I'm not surprised. Vinn is now blackmailing him, using his gay love affair as leverage to get what he wants from Mr. Clay. Only fools would cross Vinn Romano, and this man was a huge fool for putting himself on Vinn's radar.

My mind wanders to Ruby. Mac avoids talking about her, but I'm desperate to know more. Did she cheat? Is that why he moved here? Vinn would know the answers, and if he doesn't already, he could find them out. But maybe it's too soon to be asking for favours.

Mr. Clay storms out the office. "You're too nice to be working here, Raven," he snaps as he pushes the call button for the lift. "I can give you a job and pay double what this arsehole pays you."

"But you won't be able to fuck her like I do," drawls Vinn, and I blush with embarrassment. "Have a good day."

Once he's gone, Gerry leaves with the cash Chains and Mac delivered, and Vinn hovers over my desk. "So?"

"So?" I repeat.

"Did you get it? The tattoo?"

I lay my wrist on the desk, and he peers at the tattoo. "Fuck, you really did. All this trouble just so I can't have you. You must really hate me, Corvo."

"It's because I don't hate you that Mac's doing this."

"You don't think there's an ulterior motive behind his help?"

I shrug. "If there is, I'll deal with it."

"I'll never give up," he says, running his finger along my jawline.

"What did Sofia say?"

His face hardens as he rubs his thumb against my lower lip and his eyes darken with desire. "What could she say? It's not like she can cancel the wedding. We're both stuck in this, whether we like it or not."

"You know, you could just make it work with her, Vinn. There's a choice."

He smirks. "I know." He heads back into his office, and I gently touch my lip where his thumb was.

At six, I head downstairs and find Mac waiting at the bar. I usually go home now and change, ready for my evening job in the club. "Your carriage awaits, madam."

I smile, following him out to his bike. I could get used to this.

Back at the club, I shower and change. I'm straightening my hair when Mac knocks on my door and steps inside. He drops down on my bed. "Don't you get tired of always working?" he asks, thoughtfully. "I've never known anyone work as much as you."

"I like to keep busy."

"Why?"

I shrug. It's too soon to tell him why I can't stop, not even for a second. Because the minute I do, I'm flooded with memories. Memories I can't deal with, still after all these years. "I like the money."

"You live here, do you really need so much?"

I laugh. "Mac, I've been on the streets. I don't ever want to go back there and I know how easily that can happen. One day, your life can be amazing, and the next, something bad happens and it's all gone. I want enough money to never have to worry."

"You're my ol' lady now, so technically, I have to look after you."

"I'll never depend on a man. Not like that." It comes out harsher than I meant it to. "Besides, don't you have to support Ruby?"

He sighs heavily. "Ruby, Ruby, Ruby. Her name just keeps coming up."

"You won't talk about her, so it makes her even more intriguing."

"As a matter of fact, I don't support her. She's still under the club in Nottingham."

"Even though you're not there?"

"Yup."

"So, she's still your ol' lady then?"

"Technically. Like I've already said, it's complicated." I want to push him and ask why he lied when I first asked if he had an ol' lady. But instead, I open my underwear drawer, pull out a black matching set, and throw it on the bed, followed by a tight-fitted dress. Mac picks up the lace garments and rubs the material between his fingers. "Who are you trying to impress?"

"I like nice underwear," I say defensively.

"I bet Mr. Boss-man does too."

I blush. "It's not for Vinn."

"Maybe I'll come along tonight, wait around for you to finish."

"That won't be necessary. I'll be finishing late."

He stands, holding up the underwear and arching a brow. "I'm good with that."

"Mac, seriously, I'm not going near Vinn."

He smiles, dropping the garments back on the bed. "I know that, sweetheart, cos I'm gonna be there watching your every move." He leaves the room, and I bite my lower lip, trying to suppress the smile on my face. I can't help it—I like that he's so invested in watching out for me.

MAC

"Tell me why we're here again?" asks Ace.

I point to Raven, who's chatting to a group of men in business suits. "I wanna make sure she doesn't fall back into bed with that dickhead."

"Why do you care?" he asks, rolling his eyes.

"I don't like him. He thinks he can have what he wants, when he wants, and it pisses me off."

"Is this because he pulled rank the other day?"

"No," I snap. "And he didn't. He thinks he's some kind of fucking Romeo." I glare as Vinn charms a group of women.

"So, this has nothing to do with Ruby, Meghan, or Cain?"

I drink my whiskey and slam the glass down. "Nope."

"You think by wading in there to save some bitch you don't know, it'll make everything right?"

"My brother is dead. It's done. I've moved on."

"Cain died a few months ago. You haven't dealt with it properly and you walked away from a clusterfuck back home. You don't just take another ol' lady and move on. At some point, you're gonna break. I know that, Riggs knows that . . . we're just waiting."

"Nice to know you're all waiting for me to fall."

"You know it ain't like that, brother. I'm worried about you. Making these rash decisions only makes me worry more."

"I'm fine. Everything is good. I bring you to a nightclub full of pussy and you wanna sit here discussing my life? What's wrong with you?"

He grins. "You're right. You're ugly enough to take care of yourself. Now, where do we start?" He looks around, rubbing his hands together like a kid in a candy store.

"Not me, brother. I have an ol' lady."

Ace laughs. "Jesus," he mutters, shaking his head.

Ace brings a group of women over to our table, but I keep my attention on Raven. Vinn made a few attempts to bring her into conversations with important-looking men. He makes a point of touching her in some way all the goddamn time. His hand on her lower back or a gentle shoulder squeeze, it pisses me off, but I continue to watch. When they eventually head upstairs to the office together, I follow. Gerry steps in front of me, a smile on his smug face. "Mr. Romano doesn't wish to be disturbed right now."

"I don't wanna speak to Mr. Romano," I snap.

"Then you have no business going past this point."

"My ol' lady is up there with him."

Gerry laughs. "We both know who Raven really belongs to. This little show of disrespect to my boss is gonna land you in hot water."

I pull out my mobile and dial Raven's number. She cancels the call, and I begin to pace. "If I call Riggs, this will get messy," I warn Gerry.

He sighs just as a scuffle breaks out behind us. He shoves past me to deal with it, and I grin, taking the steps up to the office. I push the door open and stare at the pair as they pull away. Raven immediately blushes, and Vinn smirks. "Doesn't this look cosy?"

"We were just—" she begins.

"Let's go," I snap, cutting her off. She bites her lower lip, and my eyes bug out of my head. She's actually contemplating whether she should follow my order or stay here with him. "Now, Raven."

"You'd better go, Corvo. Now he's your man," says Vinn.

"And don't you forget it!" I growl, taking her by the hand and leading her downstairs. As we pass Ace, I tell him we're leaving. He's got his hands full of a brunette's arse, so I don't expect him to follow.

We break out into the fresh air, and I take a deep breath. "What the fuck was that?" I yell, and she looks surprised. Passers-by glance our way. "Is he that fucking alluring, you can't say no?"

"We didn't do anything, Mac. He leant in to kiss me, and you turned up."

"Well, I didn't see you pushing him away."

"Why are you yelling?" she hisses, glancing around in embarrassment.

"Because you made me look a dick tonight, Raven. You being alone with him, letting him come in for a kiss, it's fucking disrespectful!"

"Sorry," she mutters, "I wasn't thinking."

I grab her wrist and turn it, forcing her to see my name on her skin. "I did this for you and this is how you repay me? If I hadn't walked in, you'd be fucking him right now!"

"I wouldn't," she protests, but I shake my head in disgust. She's lying to herself.

"I'm taking you home."

"My shift hasn't finished," she mutters.

"Get on the damn bike, Raven. If I have to go back in there and look at that smug piece of shit, I'll end up killing him." She nods, taking the helmet I'm holding out for her, then climbs on behind me. The second she places her arms around me, I relax.

Chapter Nine

RAVEN

Mac's angry with me, and I don't blame him. Something about watching Vinn last night had me all heated up, and the second we stepped into the office, I wanted him to kiss me. I need distraction, so after breakfast, I head into Riggs' office. He looks at me with suspicion. "Got time for a chat?" I ask.

"Depends what it's about."

"I need to be kept busy. If I was to drop some hours at Vinn's, could you give me work?"

"What kind of work?"

"Stuff I usually do." I've helped the club out a lot. I'm good at getting enemies to talk. He often sends me to places to scope them out or find someone they need to speak to. I'm less obvious than a big biker.

"I can't let you on club runs no more, Raven. Sorry."

"Why?"

"You're an ol' lady now. It's Mac's call."

"Mac won't care. We both know he's not serious about all this. He's just helping me out."

Riggs goes to the door and shouts for Mac to join us, which he does. "Your ol' lady wants to work for me again. I told her I gotta run it by you."

"Doing what?" asks Mac.

"She scopes places. I've got this guy I need spotting," says Riggs, placing a picture in front of us. "She's good at surveillance."

"Women don't get involved in club shit," says Mac, and I glare at him, burning holes in the side of his head. Riggs shrugs at me.

"I've been involved since I came here," I point out.

"It's outta my hands," says Riggs.

"Are we done here?" asks Mac, standing.

"No, we're not fucking done. You don't get a say in what I do around here."

Mac smiles and it's obvious he's still pissed about last night. "Oh, but I do, Raven. I do."

"This isn't funny," I snap.

"It ain't meant to be," he mutters, heading out the office, and I rush after him.

"Mac, I'm serious. I need distracting."

"To forget a man who treats you like fucking shit?" he snarls, and I back off. "To forget someone who makes you his second best? Fuck, Raven, if you need a distraction to forget someone like that, maybe you need more help than I can offer."

If he knew how true that statement was, he wouldn't have said it in such a cruel way. I blink back tears, which only angers me. I hate crying in front of people. "Well, at least I don't run from my problems. At least I don't ignore the calls to pretend everything is okay."

"You don't know anything about my life."

"And you don't know anything about mine." We're at a standoff. No one's gonna win here, so I head up to my room to dress for work.

When I'm ready, Mac is waiting for me on his bike. "I can drive myself," I mutter.

"Get on the bike," he orders, and I roll my eyes but get on. If he wants to be a damn chauffeur in this fake relationship, let him.

Vinn isn't in when I arrive, but Sofia is. It takes me by surprise. "Good morning," I say as brightly as I can. "I'm not sure what time Mr. Romano is in today. Would you like me to call him?"

"I thought you'd arrive together," she says coldly.

I place my bag on my desk and shrug out of my jacket, trying to work out what to say. "I'm really sorry about the other day," I begin.

"Don't apologise. I've heard all about you, Raven. I know you like to steal other women's men. But let me tell you something, if I'm being forced to marry this man, I'm having him to myself. I know a lot of men like Vinn have other women, but that is not how my marriage will be. So, keep your hands to yourself or I will make sure he fires you."

I'm pretty sure she's already tried that, and he's refused. There's no way he'd let her tell him what to do. "We're not a thing anymore," I say, equally as cold. "I started sleeping with Vinn before you came on the scene. So technically, I didn't do anything wrong. But the second I knew you were in London, I pushed him away. What you walked in on the other day was a moment of weakness. It won't happen again. I've met someone."

She narrows her eyes. "Then we're both clear."

"Crystal."

The lift doors open, and Vinn steps out looking fresh. His eyes dart between us before he leans in to press a kiss to Sofia's head. "Good morning. What a lovely surprise."

"I'm sure," she says sarcastically. "We need to talk. I'm postponing the wedding," she adds, breezing into his office. He mutters something in Italian, then follows her, slamming the office door. I grab my earbuds and connect them to my playlist. I don't wanna hear the argument I know is about to follow.

It's a full twenty minutes before Sofia marches out of the office uttering words in Italian, which I'm sure aren't nice. Vinn watches her leave. "We're pushing the date back," he says to me, and I try to hide my surprise. "Two months."

"Okay." "Sofia will email you a list of contacts and the new date. Call them and make the changes." I nod, and he goes back into his office.

At lunchtime, Leia turns up. She used to pop in to see Vinn a lot, but since having Grace, she hasn't been. She places a paper bag on my desk. "Vinn's in a meeting," I explain.

"I came to see you," she says, and I frown. "Don't look so confused," she mutters. "Chains told me you're having a shit time, so I offered to come check on you."

"Oh."

"I got us lunch," she adds, opening the bag. "You're an ol' lady now, and we take care of each other."

"It's just weird, that's all. You don't like me."

She grins. "I do."

"Bullshit," I say, smirking.

"Maybe it's taken me a while to adjust to you being in Chains' life, but I'm dealing with it. It's hard when a stunning woman turns up with the man you love. What did you expect?"

"You know, I pushed him to get back with you," I point out. "We're just friends."

"Like with you and Vinn?" she asks.

I shake my head. "No, not like me and Vinn at all. I fell in love with him."

"Obviously, he's fit as fuck." She pulls out a sandwich and hands it to me. "But off limits."

"All the good ones are."

"Mac isn't."

"Mac's helping me out. I don't know exactly why, but . . ." I trail off, shrugging.

"Maybe he's just a nice guy."

I nod. "I'm not used to meeting them."

"Chains said Mac's stopping you from doing club work?"

"Yeah. Apparently, women don't do club work."

"They don't," says Leia. "It's shit, but it's how it is. Why would you want to involve yourself in their crap, anyway? If I was you, I'd make the most of being Mac's ol' lady. He's gotta support you now."

"I don't wanna rely on him for anything. Besides, it's not for real."

"He's treating you like that, telling you what you can and can't do." She's got a point, but I wouldn't feel right turning this into a battle. Mac did this for me.

Vinn steps from his office with his associate and walks him to the lift. Once he's gone, Vinn kisses Leia on her cheek and smiles at her fondly. "Good to see you, *mogliettina*."

"Did you just call me wifey?" she asks, laughing.

He smirks. "Your Italian is getting better."

She shakes her head as he goes back to his office. "How do you do that?" I ask. "Keep him at arm's length but still have the flirty fun?"

Leia arches her brow. "I didn't give in to his charms. I'm the one he didn't get, and it kills him."

"That's my problem," I admit, "I give in too easily."

"There's nothing wrong with loving sex, Raven. But if you want a relationship, you gotta keep them on their toes. Giving up the goods the second he demands it isn't what he wants as a wife."

"I didn't set out to be serious with him."

"Well, the next guy who comes along, make him wait, just in case. Men are tricky. They want a goody-two-shoes for a wife and a whore in the bedroom. It's a fine line trying to balance both."

"Vinn offered me an apartment. That way he could have his goody-two-shoes wife in Sofia and me as his whore."

She winces. "Ouch, no wonder Mac wanted to save you. You deserve better, Raven. Start demanding better for yourself. Don't get me wrong, Vinn's a good guy deep down, but he's important in his world and he has to live up to expectations. I'm not making excuses, but he didn't intend to hurt you. You both saw it as fun, and as I understand it, Riggs warned you not to involve yourself with him. Stick with Mac and walk away from Vinn."

I nod. She's right, I know she is, it's just not as easy as that. Riggs did warn me. He saw me working extra hours and realised what was going on. He didn't want my affair to impact the club, and who can blame him? I didn't think then that it would get this far. "I'm gonna cut my hours down. If you hear of any evening jobs, let me know."

Vinn holds out my jacket. "I need you for a job."

"Oh?"

"Nothing too much. I want you to deliver a message to someone. I can drop you home after."

"Erm, I'm not supposed to be doing that sort of thing anymore," I mutter.

Vinn narrows his eyes. "Riggs told me. And I told him, it's your choice. Don't let a man tell you what to do with your life, Raven. While you're on my time, I'll let you choose. Let's go."

I don't point out he's doing exactly that!

Gerry stops the car outside the Chesterfield Hotel. It's huge and guests can spend a fortune just for one night here. "Are you clear?" asks Vinn, and I nod. He's been giving me the rundown since we left the office. I unfasten the top few buttons of my shirt and run my fingers through my hair. "Gerry will be right outside," he adds.

We ignore the receptionist and use Gerry's key card to access the lift. I don't know where he gets this sort of thing, but he can access anywhere he wants.

I knock lightly on room two-twenty and wait for the guy inside to open the door. Gerry stands out of view. "About time," the man says with a grin. He grabs my hand and tugs me inside. He's exactly what I imagined him to be—overweight, thinning hair, and a leering smile that puts me on edge. "I asked for young looking," he says with a grin. "You're spot on." He pulls me against him and gropes my breast.

"Whoa there," I say, pushing his hand away.

"Are you one of those shy types? Do you want it a bit rough, darling?" he asks, grabbing a fistful of my hair with one hand and my throat with the other. I'm so shocked, I freeze. This isn't what I was expecting. Another man steps out from the bathroom and grins. Vinn didn't mention two men and panic sets in.

"She's early," he says, moving towards us, then squeezing my arse. They stand either side of me, grabbing, pulling, and feeling my body. "The agency said you're up for role-play," he pants in my ear, pushing his erection into my back.

"I'm not from the agency," I manage to spit out. "Vinn Romano sent me."

Their hands pause, but they keep me pinned between them. This wasn't how it's supposed to go. Usually, I have the guy tied to a chair before Gerry enters to deliver his threat. It's dangerous announcing why I'm there like this, but what choice do I have? "And why the fuck did Vinn Romano send a woman to do his work?"

"Oh, he didn't," I say with a smile. "I'm not alone."

One of the men laughs, looking around. "Looks like you're on your own to me, sweetheart. Now, where the fuck was I?" He grips my shirt and rips it open. I'm immediately transported back to Cobra and my time with his club. The man's hands grab at my breasts while the other grips my throat and pushes me back onto the couch. "You look like the type of girl to love cock," he whispers, running his tongue across my cheek.

I cry out, trying to get Gerry's attention. Surely, he's realised something is wrong. A hand presses to my mouth, muffling my screams. I bite it, hard, and I'm rewarded with a sharp slap across the face. My throat is squeezed tighter, and I struggle to get enough air into my lungs. I feel fingers in my underwear, then there's a popping sound and the intruding fingers stop. Another pop follows, and the man holding my neck falls onto me, his weight crushing me. He's suddenly ripped away, and I'm staring up into Vinn's eyes.

"We had trouble getting access," he mutters, his eyes raking over the state of my clothing.

"Are you fucking kidding me?" I scream, diving up and shoving my hands hard against his chest. Angry tears fall down my face, and I swipe them away in a temper.

"Raven, I'm so sorry," he says, trying to grab my flailing arms.

"Fuck you, Vinn!"

I storm from the room and press the lift button several times. He's behind me in seconds. "Don't leave like this," he whispers.

"Get the hell away from me," I hiss.

"I'll take you home."

"I'm not going anywhere with you."

I step into the lift, my eyes burning into his. I'm so angry and adrenaline is coursing through me, causing me to shake uncontrollably. "You can't walk back through the lobby looking like that," he says. The doors close, and I sag in relief. Turning to the mirror, I take in my appearance. Black mascara stains my cheeks and my eyes are red from my angry tears. My shirt is open and covered in specks of blood. There's a large red mark on my cheek where I was hit.

Vinn's right—I can't walk out looking like this. I pull my jacket around me and fasten the buttons. Then, I quickly run my fingers through my hair and lick my thumb to clear away the dark smudges under my eyes. As I exit the hotel, I keep my head lowered.

MAC

"I met with Raven today for lunch," announces Leia.

Chains kisses her on the head. "Thanks, baby."

"Was she okay?" I ask, because I haven't heard from her all day, and Riggs told me not to pick her up after work as Vinn was dropping her home. I couldn't argue, since things are rocky surrounding the whole situation.

"Yeah. A little down, but she'll be fine."

I check my watch, realising she finished work over an hour ago. Riggs comes over with his phone to his ear. "Right, thanks. I'll send the guys out to look for her." He disconnects the call, and I know the second he looks at me, something is wrong.

"Stay calm" are the first words that leave his mouth. I stand, already feeling a build-up of anger. "That was Vinn. He took Raven to a job and it went wrong. She's walked out, he can't find her, and she isn't answering her mobile."

"What kind of job? Is she hurt?" I ask.

"She was meant to distract a guy in a hotel room. Turns out there were two of them, and Vinn couldn't get access to the room straight-away. She was trapped in there with two men who thought she was an escort."

I take a deep breath and ball my fists. "Is she hurt?"

Riggs nods. "I think so."

I pull out my mobile and call her, but it goes to an answer-message. "I'm gonna kill him," I warn.

"I'll deal with that. You go and find her. I'll send the others out too," says Riggs.

I spend hours driving around the city looking for Raven. Between the guys, we cover a huge space, but she's nowhere to be found. Anna and the other women called the local hospitals to check she hasn't been admitted. I call her mobile over and over, but each time I get her answer machine. Eventually, Riggs orders everyone back to the club. I'm angry and frustrated, but he's right, she'll turn up when she's ready. It's not the first time she's been out on the streets alone.

I can't sleep, so I bust the lock on her room and head inside. It smells of her, and I instantly relax a little. I pick up her perfume bottle and inhale the sweet smell. I notice a small picture stuck on her mirror and I pull it off, peering closer at the little girl smiling up at an older woman. Maybe this is her and her mum, although I'm sure she said she grew up with her aunt and uncle. I stick it back on the mirror and pull open her drawer. It's full of makeup. Ruby didn't wear makeup, because she's naturally beautiful and hated the way it felt on her skin. Raven's beautiful too. She's got pale skin and it gives her that English rose kind of look.

I wander over to another set of drawers, opening the top one and pulling out a lace garment. It's a red all-in-one bodice. Ruby hated this sort of thing. I laugh to myself at the memory of when I had brought her a set for Christmas, and she accused me of wanting to change her. I bought it to spice shit up. We'd been together a long time and I could feel my eyes wandering. I had to stop it, so I tried stuff to bring us together again. I sigh, dropping the garment back into the drawer and closing it.

"Is there a reason you're going through my drawers?" comes Raven's voice, and I spin to face her. I take in her bruised cheek, her swollen eye, and her torn, blood-splattered shirt.

"Where have you been?" I ask, rushing to her and tugging her against me. She lets me, laying her head against my chest. I bury my nose in her hair and inhale her strawberry shampoo. It's enough to settle the ache in my chest. "I've been fucking worried sick."

"I just wandered around for a while."

"We went looking for you. You've had most of the club out."

"Sorry. My phone died, so I couldn't call, and I wasn't ready to come back here."

I lead her to the bathroom and turn on the shower. "I'll let the guys know you're home."

I sit on her bed while she showers and send a text to Riggs explaining she's back and once I get to the bottom of things, I'll let him know. When she steps back into the bedroom, she looks exhausted. She's wearing a man's t-shirt that comes to her thighs, and when she sees me eyeing it, she shrugs. "It's Chains' and it's comfortable."

I scoff. She's meant to be my ol' lady, and I can't have her wearing another man's shirt to bed. I shrug out of my kutte and pull my t-shirt over my head. I hold the bottom of Chains', and she lifts her arms, allowing me to remove it. I suck in a breath when I realise she's completely naked underneath. I quickly replace the shirt with my own, and she gives a small smile before pulling her sheets back and getting into bed. "What happened?" I ask.

"He was supposed to be alone. He wasn't." A tear leaks from her eye, and I lower onto the bed, pulling her against my chest and holding her. "I was supposed to go in, make him think I was gonna dance for him, tie him up, and then hand him to Gerry," she explains through sobs. "He was too hands-on right from the second I walked in, and then his mate appeared, and it was game over. I couldn't get them off me." I stroke her hair, making shushing noises as she sniffles against my chest. "It was like being back with Cobra. I haven't felt that out of control in such a long time, I forgot how it felt or how to deal with it."

"I'll kill him," I mutter.

"No," she snaps. "I don't want you fighting Vinn. I won't ever go on jobs like that again."

"He went against what I said, Raven."

"I don't care. If you want to help me, you'll leave this alone. I'll deal with Vinn myself."

"You're not to go near Vinn Romano again," I say firmly, and she looks up at me through wet lashes. "If you want me to leave it alone, you'll stay the fuck away from him."

"I work for him," she whispers.

"Not anymore. I'll find you something else. Vinn is bad news and he put you in serious danger tonight."

"Why do you care so much?" she asks.

"Maybe I'm making up for past fuck-ups," I mutter. "This is my chance to make shit right. I'll take care of you, Raven. Stop fighting me."

She snuggles tighter against me, and I wrap my arms around her. Maybe this is why I ended up here in London, why our paths crossed. She needed someone, and that someone, is me.

When I wake with Raven still in my arms and an erection the size of a mountain, I shift uncomfortably. She feels me press against her arse and stiffens. I feel like a prick as I get up from the bed and head for the bathroom. It's the morning after she was almost assaulted, and she wakes up with my cock against her arse. I step in the cold shower, but it doesn't do much to dull the ache in my balls. It's been months since I fucked anyone or had that release. Wrapping a towel around my waist, I return to the bedroom to find her sitting up in bed, looking through her mobile. "I'm gonna get dressed. I'll come get you for breakfast," I say.

Her eyes dart to the semi I'm trying to hide and she blushes. "Actually, I might give breakfast a miss today."

The bruise on her face is dark this morning. Not even makeup's gonna hide it. "Get dressed, Raven. We're having breakfast."

Once I'm dressed, I go back to her room. She's still sitting in bed. "I'm really not hungry."

"I told you last night I'd take care of you, so we're having breakfast."

"Fine, let's go out for breakfast. If I have to eat one more of Frankie's cooked breakfasts, I'll scream."

"You know, avoiding everyone won't make it better. It'll just make everyone ask more questions."

She sighs. "Just give me today."

I nod, holding out my hand. "Fine."

Once she's dressed, we head straight out, avoiding seeing anyone other than a couple of the prospects who are out washing the bikes. I head for a cafe a few streets away. It does a variety of breakfasts, and Raven smiles when she sees the menu and decides to order a fruit selection. Frankie doesn't bother to cook the healthiest breakfasts cos the guys always want bacon.

"What past mistakes?" she asks as I sip my coffee and scan the newspaper.

"Eat something," I say, nodding at her bowl of fruit.

"Please, just tell me one thing about your past. You never tell me anything, but you want me to trust you to look after me?"

I sigh. "I had a brother. His name was Cain, and he died three months ago." It makes me an arse, because when she asked me before if I had siblings, I told her no. Technically, I don't anymore, but at the time, I didn't want to answer her questions, and whenever anyone finds out about Cain, there are always questions.

"Oh," she whispers, looking sad. "I'm sorry. How old was he?"

"The same age as me . . . we were twins."

She gasps. "Oh, Mac, that's awful. Was it an accident?"

I smile. "You said one thing. I've told you two."

She fiddles with the silver ring she wears on her right ring finger. "My mum gave me this. I think I was maybe five when she gave it to me, and it was always too big. I used to wear it around my neck on a chain."

"What happened to her?"

"She gave me away."

I frown. "Just gave you away to strangers or to social services?"

"She told me the man who came to pick me up was my uncle and he was taking me to see my aunty. I was six."

"You hadn't met him before?" I ask.

She shakes her head. "No. He wasn't really my uncle. I'm pretty sure he wasn't anyway because he had these urges, unnatural ones for a relative."

My blood runs cold, and I feel the newspaper being screwed up where my hand grips it too tight. "Did your aunt know?"

She laughs, but it's cold and empty. "Yeah. She was fine with it. She showed me what to do, how to please him, and then eventually, how to please his friends. I guess it got her off the hook."

"Raven, I'm—"

"I haven't told anyone that. Not properly. Keep it to yourself, okay."

I nod. "Of course."

We finish breakfast in silence, both lost in thought. Knowing that information makes me want to slit Vinn's throat even more. She's been through enough. We get on the bike, and I drive us to central London. It's the last place we came where we both laughed and had fun. It made us forget all the shit for a day, and I plan to do the same again.

Chapter Ten

RAVEN

How does Mac know exactly what I need without me saying a word? He drags me around the shops, and I pretend to hate it, but I love every second. He asks me to help him choose some new clothes for himself, which I do. He gets me to decide on a new aftershave, telling me he needs a new start and scent is key to that, then he chooses a new perfume for me, It's fruity, like something I'd usually go for, and he insists on paying as a way to thank me for all my help. We laugh and mess around, and it's what I needed today.

I get a few stares when people notice the huge bruises on my cheek, and I know they're looking at Mac with accusing eyes, but he doesn't take any notice. Instead, he owns it, grabbing my hand in a possessive hold and staring right back at them with menacing eyes. "Let them think what they want," he tells me. "We know the truth."

We sit in Covent Garden and eat ice cream, and then we take a stroll around the market. Mac buys fruit for my breakfast tomorrow, and a gypsy palm reader steps out from the next stall and grabs my hand. He smirks as she tells me I should avoid danger, peering at him with distrusting eyes. She tells me that a knight in shining armour is in my future, and he'll rescue me from evil. I cross her palm with silver just so she doesn't curse me before we rush away, laughing.

We're strolling back through Covent Garden when the heavens open and rain pours down, drenching us instantly. Mac grabs my hand, and we make a run for shelter under a large tree, but it's too late. My summer dress is sticking to my skin and it's obvious I'm not wearing a bra when the material becomes practically see-through. Mac's eyes darken as he takes in my dishevelled appearance. He shakes his head like he's breaking his thoughts and shrugs out of his kutte, placing it around my shoulders. If everything wasn't such a mess, it would be the perfect time for him to steal a kiss.

I bite my lower lip to stop myself smiling. I think back to Leia's words about keeping things low-key and not rushing into anything new. Mac's been hurt too, I can sense it, so maybe that's why he's holding back. Or maybe he genuinely doesn't see me in that way. I've spent so long hiding behind sex, I'm not sure if my feelings are real either. So, I turn away from him and stare out at the people around us, all running to their destinations. It's been a lovely day, but I can't mistake my happiness in this moment for feelings towards Mac.

When we arrive back at the club, Riggs calls me into his office. Vinn is in there, and his presence instantly puts me in a bad mood. He closes the door, and I suspect that's because he doesn't want Mac to see. "We wanted to check if you're okay," says Riggs.

Vinn eyes Mac's kutte that I'm still wearing. "Had a good day?"

"You surely didn't expect to see me at work after last night?" I snap.

"Of course not," he mutters with regret on his face.

"I won't be returning to work, Vinn. It's best if I walk away."

"What?" he gasps. "You can't. I need you."

I stare at the ground. I like working there, but Mac is right, it isn't working out. "I'm sorry."

"Is this him? Is he making you quit?" he asks, moving towards me and taking my hands in his.

I shake my head. "How dare you blame him? You put me in danger last night, and I almost got seriously hurt."

Vinn sighs. "I know. I'm so sorry about that. It was last minute and I didn't think the plan through. It won't happen again." When he sees I'm not wavering, he crouches slightly to look in my eyes. "Corvo, you know I wouldn't let anything bad happen to you on purpose. I killed both those bastards. You know how I feel about you. If you want to take a break from work, fine, but don't quit."

"I don't know," I mutter.

"Quitting is too final. You're upset and angry, and I get that, so don't make any rash decisions right now. Please, Corvo. Just take some time out."

I nod, and he smiles with relief. "Thank you." He leans closer and gently places his lips against my own. He holds the kiss for a few seconds, until Riggs coughs, interrupting us.

"Don't fucking push it, Vinn," he growls.

"We both know Mac hasn't claimed her," mutters Vinn, releasing me.

I turn to open the office door and find Mac staring through the window. He shakes his head in disappointment and moves away. "Shit," I mutter, rushing after him.

"Mac, wait," I shout, making a grab for his shoulder. "I told him I'm quitting. He was saying sorry and goodbye."

"With his lips?" he snaps.

"It wasn't a proper kiss," I argue. "He's only ever kissed me once," I add, like that makes it better.

He spins to face me, and I stumble to a stop. "How did you fall in love with a man who's never kissed you properly?"

I shrug. "I'm used to men not kissing me. It's not what they want me for."

He releases a low growl. "How do you manage to piss me off and break my heart all in one? Fuck, Raven, I hate how you've been treated."

I smile sadly. "It's fine."

"It's not fine. Stop saying it's fine." He scrubs his hands over his face. "You deserve so much better." He pushes a hand into my hair and stares at me for a few seconds. I can see the internal battle he's having with himself. He roughly runs his thumb over my lips, like he's brushing away any trace of Vinn. "Why can't you see it?"

I feel like he's moving in slow motion as he edges closer. I stare into his dark eyes, and as he presses his lips against mine, I suck in a surprised breath. I saw it coming, but at the same time, I wasn't expecting it. He cups my jaw with gentle hands and tilts my head as he sweeps his tongue into my mouth. His body flanks my own as he takes control, and I feel safe to relax while he explores my mouth. When he eventually pulls away, he keeps my head in his hands and stares into my eyes.

"That's how you should be kissed. Every time. If a man doesn't kiss you like that, he isn't right for you." He turns on his heel and heads out of the club, leaving me open-mouthed and staring after him.

"What the hell was that?" asks Eva in a dreamy voice.

I blink a few times, still staring at the door he just exited through. "Huh?"

"That was hot as fuck," says Anna. I nod, unable to find my words.

"She's gone into shock," Leia says, laughing.

I slowly turn to face the women, who all look wistful, like they were the ones just swept off their feet. "He just kissed me," I mutter.

"He *really* just kissed you," says Leia.

Anna leans forward. "Was that an 'I'm a great friend' kiss, an 'I like you' kiss, or just a kiss?"

Leia grabs my hand and pulls me to sit with them. "That was a hot as fuck, 'I want to love you forever' kinda kiss."

I shake my head. "No. He doesn't like me like that. He's a friend. That kiss was a 'let me show you how a man should be kissing you' kiss."

"That's not even a thing," Leia says.

"Did Vinn ever kiss you like that?" asks Anna.

I shake my head. "He kissed me once. Right at the end of our agreement."

"Agreement?" Eva repeats.

"They were just hooking up," explains Leia. "When Raven wanted to call it quits, he kissed her in a last-ditch attempt to keep her."

"But not like that," I say dreamily. "I don't think I've ever been kissed like that. Not outside the bedroom, anyway." I steel myself. I'm getting carried away, seeing things in a kiss that aren't there. Mac's clearly mending a broken heart. He doesn't need me latching onto him after everything he's done for me. "Anyway," I add, determined to change the subject, "I'm taking a break from working for Vinn. So, if any of you have shifts you want covering at any of the club's bars, let me know, I'll do anything."

A high-pitched laugh comes from the other side of the room, and I look up to where some of the club girls are hanging out. Leia rolls her eyes. "There's a new girl amongst the pack," she says. The Kings don't have many club girls these days, not now a lot of brothers are settled down, but the usual three are knocking back shots of tequila in the corner. There's a girl with her back to me. "Her name's Kiera."

"She seems nice," Anna adds.

The club girl turns, and I recognise her from one of the clubs I hung out with years ago, when I was a teenager. "I know her," I say, standing. We were good friends back then, but when I moved on, she stayed. "Kiera," I say, and her eyes widen.

"Oh my god, Raven." We hug tightly.

"It's been years. How the hell are you?"

She shrugs. "Yah know how it is. I like it here, though. Everyone's lovely."

I nod, taking a seat on a nearby couch, and she joins me. "Yeah, everyone's really nice here. How did you end up here?" She was always adamant she'd marry a biker and become someone's ol' lady.

"I tried to settle down," she shrugs, "but it never worked out. What about you?" She plucks at Mac's kutte, and I smile. I'd forgotten I was wearing it.

"It's complicated. I'm not really an ol' lady. The guy is helping me out of a tight situation."

"Oh. Tell me it isn't Brick or Mac and we can still be friends," she jokes. At the mention of Mac's name, I hold my breath. He isn't mine, but the thought of him being with someone else pisses me off. "Oh god," she gasps. "Is it one of them?"

"Mac," I say, shrugging, "but like I said, we're not really a thing, so he's free."

"Oh, thank god," she says, placing her manicured red nails to her chest. "Because I am determined to have a piece of that!" I laugh a little too forcefully and smile awkwardly. I remember the men loving her. She was always easy going and she's gorgeous, not tired-looking or desperate. She always looked after herself, and seeing her now, she still does.

"Go for it," I say. "He's a great guy."

"Are you sure, cos I don't wanna step on anyone's toes."

"No . . . absolutely . . . he's free as a bird."

She nods. "Well, great. Thanks. I'll catch up with you later. I'm getting to know the other girls." I nod, watching her re-join them, then I head back to where the ol 'ladies are sitting.

"How do you know her?" asks Leia.

"When I was younger, we got talking. She's really nice. The guys will love her."

"Brick certainly does," says Leia, nodding towards where Brick is staring over at the club girls.

"I think she has her sights set on Mac too," I say with a bright, fake smile.

"Did you set her straight?" asks Anna.

"No. There's nothing to set straight. He's free."

"Raven," gasps Eva.

"Yah know, I think he's trying to repair a broken heart. I feel for him. He's really nice and he deserves to be happy. Kiera might just be the person who's here to do that. I'm not gonna stand in the way of that."

"She's a club girl, they don't end up being ol' ladies," explains Leia.

"Not strictly true," I say. "I've known club girls who have fallen in love and made it. Let's not write her off before she's been given a chance."

MAC

"I kissed her. I fucking kissed her. Why the fuck did I do that? It's her damn past. The way her eyes go all sad and shit. Fuck!" I'm pacing as Ace watches me through amused eyes. "This isn't funny!"

"Hey, I'm not laughing. I just can't believe you've been here a couple of weeks and you're already in the shit."

"It was just a kiss. It doesn't mean anything, right?"

"Depends what kind of woman Raven is."

"She's independent, a free spirit. She'll definitely not read anything into it."

He grins, resting back against the wall of the clubhouse. "Then why do you look so worried?"

The door opens and Brick steps out, holding a full bottle of whiskey. He slides down the wall, joining Ace. "Why are you out here?" he asks.

"Mac is in crisis mode."

"I am not!" I snap.

"Not surprising after that statement in there, kissing Raven like that."

Ace laughs. "You made a statement."

"It was just a fucking kiss. Everyone needs to calm the fuck down." My outburst makes Ace laugh harder. I roll my eyes and snatch the bottle from Brick. "I'll talk to her."

"What will you say?" asks Ace, chuckling.

"I'll say you dickheads are winding me up and telling me she'll think it means shit that it doesn't." Brick screws his face up. "Don't say that."

"What should I say?"

"I haven't got a fucking clue, brother, but that's a little blunt. I don't see the problem, anyway. She's your ol' lady, right? It's not the usual way, but there's nothing to say you can't fall in love over time. She's a great woman."

"I was just saving her from Vinn, man. I can't give her a relationship. I'm staying away from that sort of thing."

"Oh. Well, for the record, you're not giving off those signals." Ace laughs harder, fist bumping Brick. I take large swigs of whiskey, enjoying the feel of it burning my throat. Raven loves Vinn, so she won't see anything in that kiss. I'll explain, and she'll be fine about it.

I stay with the guys a while longer, drinking whiskey and talking shit to pass time. I'm putting off speaking to Raven. I don't know why. I eventually take a breath and head back inside. She's still with the girls, laughing and drinking wine. I smile when her laugh rings out. I like to see her happy.

A hand presses against my chest, stopping me in my stride. I glance down at the red painted nails and then into the blue eyes of Kiera. "Hey, gorgeous," she smiles.

"Hey."

"You look like you've had a rough day. You need some help to relax tonight?" I glance at Raven, and Kiera runs her nail along my jawline. "Raven told me about you two." My heart stutters. Raven's staked her claim, and for some reason, that makes me smile. "And she said you weren't actually together. She said you were free as a bird." My heart twists. Why? At least, I know Raven understands the kiss meant nothing. *Nothing.* "So, what do you say?" It's been a while since I've shared my bed in that way. The kiss with Raven was the first kiss in months and the most I've actually done. I take Kiera's hand and stare at her pointed red nails. "Imagine them," she says, leaning close and pressing her mouth to my ear, "around your cock." Her words stir something inside.

"Can you give me a minute to talk to Raven?" I ask.

"Of course." She places a kiss on my cheek and heads back to the club girls.

"Raven, can I have a word?"

She stands, smiling, and I lead her to another table. "Everything okay?" she asks.

"Yeah. I just wanted to apologise for kissing you earlier. It was out of order." She blushes, lowering her eyes. "Don't apologise, it's fine."

"I didn't want to give you the wrong idea—"

She cuts in before I can finish, laughing. "It didn't. Not at all. In fact, Kiera just came and asked about us. I told her we're just friends, and you're free to do whatever... you want to do... yah know, because you're free and shit."

"Great, so that's clear then, because the guys were just giving me shit about it, saying you'd see something into it, and I wanted to set it straight. Yah know, cos I know Vinn's already being an arse, and I didn't want you to think I was like him." I'm babbling, and she smiles, placing her hand over mine. I take a breath and laugh nervously. "Sorry, I'm making this awkward."

"Have a great night with Kiera. Make sure you show her how a girl should be kissed." I watch her head back to the ol' ladies. So, that's clear then... she gets it. So, why does my heart ache?

Chapter Eleven

RAVEN

I try not to pay attention to Mac as he takes Kiera's hand and leads her towards the stairs. It's fine. I'm getting over Vinn and I definitely don't feel anything towards Mac, not like that. He's a friend. Just a friend. I'm happy for him. So, I don't understand this knotted feeling in my stomach.

Leia hands me another glass of wine. "Are you okay?"

"Yeah," I say, grinning. "But I think I've had enough wine for tonight. I'm gonna head up to bed."

She smiles sadly. "Okay. Tomorrow, we'll work on a new job."

Vinn steps out of Riggs' office as I pass. "Goodnight, Corvo."

"Night."

"You sure you don't want company?" he asks with a smirk.

I roll my eyes. "No."

"I wish I had your ability to turn my feelings off," he mutters.

I head for the stairs, ignoring him. He's not gonna guilt trip me into falling back into his bed. He'll leave here tonight and not think about me again. I head for my room, turning down the hall, and almost crash into Mac and Kiera. She's pressed against the wall with her legs wrapped around his waist, and they're kissing like they're starving. They're kissing like we just kissed. I blush instantly and stare down at the floor. "Sorry," I mumble, moving around them and rushing to my room.

I close my door, lean against it, and groan. That was awkward. Why was it awkward? I hope he didn't think I was being awkward. A few minutes pass and I get undressed, slipping into Mac's t-shirt, pulling the material to my nose and inhaling like a sad loser. It smells of him, and I flop onto my bed with another groan. *Fuck*.

A knock on the door makes me jump, and I get up to open it as Mac walks in. We stare at each other for a few seconds. "Wrong room?" I ask with a small laugh.

"No. I told Kiera I needed to check on you."

I frown. "I'm fine."

"I kind of used it as an excuse to get away."

I glance at my watch. "Christ, that was fast work."

He shuts my door. "I didn't fuck her. Christ, I can last longer than a minute!"

I laugh. "I'll take your word for it. So, if you didn't do anything with her, why are you here?" There's hope building in my chest, but I try to quash it. I'm reading too much into it.

He shrugs. "It didn't feel right."

I nod, climbing into bed. His broken heart is stopping him from moving on. I'm not surprised—I know the feeling well. "Has there been anyone since Ruby?"

He ignores me.

"Why?"

He shrugs, pulling his shirt off and placing it on the chair. Unfastening his belt, his eyes briefly connect with my own before he rips it from the loops and places it atop the shirt. My thighs clench and I press my lips together. We might not be a thing, but there's certainly some sexual tension flying around since the kiss. "I want to know."

"You want to know how much I suffered as a kid?" I ask, smiling. "Sicko."

He grins, pushing his jeans down his legs and stepping from them. Once he's added them to the pile, he lifts the sheets back and gets into bed beside me. I don't question it. Not once. I don't even question it in my mind. "Do you have any good memories?"

I nod. "I had a tricycle when I was really young, maybe four? We lived in a high-rise block of flats. They were terrible, practically falling down, but everyone who lived there was like a big family. Women would take care of each other's kids, so it was like having fifty mums. My mum was never around. She was a prostitute and would sleep most days and be gone all night. I'd ride up and down the ramps at all hours of the day or night. I loved it."

"Freedom of the bike," he says with a knowing smile.

"Maybe that's where my addiction to this life began?"

"Didn't other women question why such a young kid was out at night?"

I shrug. "I don't remember. It was quiet at night. I liked it the best. Apart from the drug users and prostitutes," I add, laughing.

"So, then your mum gave you up?" My smile fades as I nod. "And she told you they were family, but they weren't."

"I don't think they were. I met all kinds of people in that area, but I'd never seen those people in my life. I think my mum genuinely believed they would take care of me. She was struggling, and this couple must have told her about their nice house in a better area, and she wanted what was best."

"But they didn't give you a great life?"

I shake my head. "No. I felt they didn't want me there at first. They were cold and snappy. I remember thinking they were mad at my mum for dumping me with them. As I got older, my uncle's intentions became clear. He said I had to pay my way for everything they'd done for me."

Mac places his arm around me and tugs me to his chest. I smile to myself and snuggle against him. It feels nice. "If I ever find him, I'll kill him for you."

"You're so romantic."

"I know. Just call me Romeo."

"What about you?" I ask. "How was your childhood?"

"Good."

"Mac!" I want more information than that.

"It was good. My parents were in the club. We grew up with other kids. I was terrible at school and got kicked out when I was a teenager. I got involved in the club really young and could fire a gun with accuracy by the age of eight."

"What's your mum like?" I ask.

"Nice."

"You don't give anything away."

"We don't talk much. She misses my brother, and I find it difficult to deal with."

"It must be hard on all of you. What was he like?"

I hear his heartbeat thumping faster. "He was better than me. At everything. We were inseparable. Really close."

My heart breaks for him. I've read that twins share so much more than normal siblings. No wonder he finds it hard to talk about. I gently run my fingers up and down his chest. "I wish I could make it all better for you."

"You are," he mutters. "Helping you, is helping me."

I smile, snuggling closer into him. I close my eyes and allow myself to enjoy this moment. Mac doesn't need anything from me. He isn't demanding sex, and yet, he's here, cuddling with me. It feels nice.

I wake up some time later to Mac's phone buzzing on the bedside table, and I sit up slightly. He's sleeping soundly with his arm thrown across his eyes. I lean over him carefully and see Ruby's name on the screen. Maybe she feels guilty and she's constantly calling to try and make things right. Or maybe after his brother died, she couldn't reach him anymore. Death can affect people in different ways.

I lie back down, my back to Mac. It disturbs him and he groans, stretching out before spooning me and wrapping himself around me tightly. He's asleep, not aware that he's pressing his erection into my back. I bite my lower lip. It's impressive, and I don't move as he rubs himself against my arse. After a few minutes, he stills, and I hear his light snores. I lie awake, feeling horny as hell and tired all at the same time. When the sun rises, I can't take anymore, so I throw the sheets back and dress in my workout gear. I need to burn off some of this energy.

MAC

"So," whispers Ace, leaning closer into me at the breakfast table, "did you set the record straight?" I nod. "Good. Did you fuck the new girl?" I shake my head, and he narrows his eyes. "Why?"

"I wasn't feeling it."

"You've got to move on from your past, Mac. Go fuck a whore. It's not healthy to behave the way you are."

"Maybe I don't need sex like you do to function," I joke.

"You're a red-blooded male. You need sex." I don't bother to tell him that guilt is eating me alive, and I can't bring myself to take one bit of pleasure. I don't fucking deserve it.

Raven joins us, glowing after her morning run. "What are you doing today?" I ask.

She shrugs, grabbing a bagel and taking a big bite. I love that she eats well. She isn't the sort of girl to shy away from a good meal because she's with a guy. "Job hunting. Maybe."

"Maybe?" I repeat.

"Vinn didn't let me fully quit last night. He told me to take a break."

Before I can argue, the door crashes open, and Gia comes in holding a newspaper. She shoves it towards Riggs, who scans it before raising his brows. "Have you spoken to Vinn?" he asks her, and she shakes her head.

"What's wrong?" Raven asks.

Gia hands her the newspaper, and she lays it out on the table. There's a large picture of Vinn and the headline reads, ***London, Big Dreams or Little Lies?***

"You may as well read it out," says Gia.

Raven clears her throat and begins, "London, the place where all your dreams come true—or is it? The truth is, London is a big, scary place. Take it from someone who knows. From the busy streets to the flashing night lights, London has it all going on. And on the surface, everything looks so glamorous. Take the nightclubs. Everyone who is anyone knows of Enzo's nightclub. Just to look at that place makes my bank balance shake.

"But if you delve deep enough, if you look past the crystal chandeliers and mirrors, you see the special handshakes where men in suits pass their drugs to eager young people, desperate to get off their heads and forget about their stressful London jobs and the high cost of living. You see the owner, Vincent Romano, strutting around the place like he's the king, and, boy, do they treat him like one. I often wonder if men like him are overcompensating for something else . . .

"Women fall at his feet, and if you're pretty enough, he'll pin a gold badge on you that tells everyone in the club that you are his VIP guest. And who wouldn't want that? Endless champagne, and not the cheap stuff, as much white powder as your nose can take, the attention of your very own crime lord . . . every woman's dream, right? Wrong! Drinking in clubs like Enzo's undermines the very thing us women have fought for. Emmeline Pankhurst would stuff Romano's gold pin right where the sun doesn't shine! And who would blame her?

"It's hard to believe places still exist where, if you're young, pretty, and flash a little flesh, you'll be treated like a princess. London will swallow you whole if you let it, so look past the flashing lights and special invites and don't lose focus on your dream. After all, we all want to live the dream, right?"

"Ouch. Someone doesn't like Vinn," says Leia.

"Lots of people don't like Vinn," says Chains with a grin. "Mac, did you do this?" he adds, laughing.

"Seriously, he'll go mad when he sees this," Raven says, folding it up and tucking it under her arm. "I'm gonna go into the office and see if he needs me to do anything."

"I don't think it's a good idea," I begin, but she's already out the door.

"I know he's my brother," says Gia, taking a seat beside me, "but I'm rooting for you and Raven. He has to marry Sofia, and Raven deserves a man who can give her one hundred percent."

"Oh, it's not like that," I begin, but she smiles, patting my hand.

"Of course, it is, you just don't know it yet."

Chapter Twelve

RAVEN

I get to the office and find Vinn yelling into the phone. When he sees me, he hangs up and marches over. "Thank god, you're here," he says, pulling me into his arms and burying his nose in my hair. Suddenly, it feels wrong. I realise it isn't his arms I want to be in, so after a few seconds, I pull back.

"I saw the article. Any idea where it came from?" I ask, ignoring the way he looks confused by my cold retreat.

"No. I called the Gazette. They said it was an anonymous writer."

"So, they have no name?"

"Just a pen name, Revenge!"

"Oh, revenge on you or just in general?" I ask.

"Fuck knows, but right now, it's clearly aimed at me. Let's hope it's a one-off. I offered the editor money to pass all future articles my way next time, but he laughed in my face and said I couldn't buy him off. Who the fuck ever heard of an editor you can't buy?"

"If I was you, I'd step up the charity donations. Make a bigger deal about what you do for the community and shout about it, so it pushes the bad press into the shadows. I'll set up some photo opportunities." I take a seat at my desk.

He smiles. "That's why I need you around."

As he heads back into his office, I call his name, and he turns to me. "This is strictly business from now on. If you cross the line, I'm gone for good." He nods once and closes his door.

I spend the next few hours arranging meetings with charity organisations. Vinn's given me a ballpoint figure to split over three local charities. If I can get him in the news for the right reasons, no one will listen to anything else. The lift pings and Mac steps into the office. I'm happy to see him, and my heart races as he places a paper bag on my desk. "Thought you might need something to eat."

"Thank you. You didn't have to." He glances towards Vinn's office. "I can't lie, Raven. I'm pissed off you came running the second he got in the shit."

My heart twists a little. "I love this job. It's a hard habit to break. And, they slagged off Enzo's. I've been managing that place, so it's my baby too."

"It seems like *he's* the hard habit to break."

"No. It's not like that."

"Enjoy your lunch," he adds, turning to leave.

"Mac, wait, join me. Please."

He hesitates, then reluctantly grabs a chair and pulls it to my desk. I smile as he takes a seat and reaches into the paper bag. "Any idea who wrote it?" he asks, passing me a sandwich.

I shake my head. "Nope. Anonymous."

"He deserves it."

I laugh. "He does not. He's a businessman and he doesn't need some dick writing shit like that. It could harm his business."

Mac stares me down, pressing his lips together in a tight line. "Don't defend him, Raven. He doesn't deserve your loyalty."

"He's my boss. And, yes, he's hurt me, but I'm getting over it. I still like him as a person." Mac's phone rings from his pocket, but he makes no move to answer it. "Ruby still calling?" I ask, and he shrugs. "Maybe you should just talk to her. She might stop if you do."

"I spoke to her once. I said what I needed to and I don't want to speak to her again. It's done. She needs to take the hint."

"Women find it harder to let go. Have you let her explain her side?"

"I'm not interested."

"If she's carrying around guilt for hurting you—" I begin.

"She's not," he snaps. "You don't know anything about it, so just leave it." I wish he'd open up and talk to me about it. After a few silent, awkward minutes, he stands. "I gotta go." I nod sadly. I can't force him to talk, but I hate the ache it causes in my chest when he gets like this and runs away.

When I get back to the club after work, I head straight for the kitchen. Frankie looks up from her stool as I place a bag full of groceries on the table. "What's all that?"

I smile. "I thought I'd make Mac dinner tonight."

"How come?" She pulls the bag closer and inspects the contents, raising her eyebrows with approval. "Steak? Nice."

"Because he's been really good to me lately, and I think he's having a hard time."

"You need any help?"

I shake my head. I haven't cooked a good meal in a very long time, but I want to do it for Mac. Frankie smiles as she passes me to leave. "Shout if you need anything."

"Actually, there is one thing. Do you think you could help Eva set up the table on my balcony? She got really excited and started talking about romance and stuff. I don't wanna send him the wrong signals. I think she even ran off to find fairy lights." Frankie laughs, nodding as she disappears to find her.

Once the vegetables are cooked and the steak is resting, I rush upstairs to shower quickly and change into something more comfortable. The women did a great job setting a table up on my balcony, although I blew out the candle in the centre and rolled my eyes at the fairy lights strung around the plant. I hate to think what it would have looked like if Frankie hadn't stepped in.

I go and get the food and lay it on the table, covering the dishes and rushing off to find Mac. I knock on his bedroom door and wait a few minutes. I can hear him inside talking, and think maybe he's on the phone, so I knock louder. This time, I hear him curse before he rips the door open and stands before me in a towel with a scowl on his face. I spot Kiera lying on the bed naked and wince at my shitty timing. "Sorry, it's not important."

Mac's face pales slightly and his scowl softens and transforms into what looks like regret. His mouth opens like he's about to say something, but I don't give him a chance. I rush back to my room, my face burning with embarrassment. I pace, running through excuses as to why I needed to see him, just in case he asks. Then, I spot the domes of food waiting to be uncovered and I groan. I lift the first and look around for somewhere to hide it, but the door opens, and Mac stares at me. He's got jeans on this time. His eyes fall to the dome, and he curses again.

"I was coming to ask for advice," I say quickly, "about how Brick would like his steak. See, Frankie said medium, but then I panicked and thought maybe he's not a medium kind of guy. Do you know how he takes it?"

"Brick?" he repeats. It's the first name that came into my head. He's single, and if I'd have said Vinn, Mac would have gotten mad. I sigh. I should have said Vinn—it's more believable.

"Yeah. I heard steak was his favourite."

"Christ, you're moving on quick."

"You said I should forget Vinn," I say, shrugging.

"I know but, Brick, really?"

"I mean, it was just an idea. A stupid one. If you're free, maybe you could," I stare at the dome and then the table. I'm so glad I blew the candle out.

He looks uncomfortable, and I immediately regret asking. "It's just, I've got Kiera and—"

I nod, smiling wide and cutting him off mid-sentence. This shit is embarrassing and painful enough without him going into details. "Of course. Sorry. Go and finish . . . her . . ." I turn away, cringing at my choice of words.

"You want me to find Brick?"

I shake my head. Fuck, that's the last thing I want. I wait for him to leave before taking a seat and pulling the cork from the bottle of red wine. I don't even think he drinks wine—what fucking biker drinks wine? I sigh and pour myself a large glass, taking several big mouthfuls and then refilling. I lift the lid on the dome and pop a potato wedge into my mouth. I'm such a loser.

There's a knock on the door, and I pray to God it isn't Brick. I'm relieved when I find Eva there. "I just saw Mac and Kiera together. What happened to having dinner?"

I open the door wider, and she follows me onto the small balcony. "I just assumed he'd be free. Stupid, really."

I refill my glass and then offer her the bottle. She tops up the other glass. "Oh. Maybe if you tell him, he might come and eat with you."

"A pity date, no thanks."

"I thought this wasn't a date," she says, grinning.

"It's not . . . I mean, I just wanted him to open up a little."

"Do you like him, Raven? You can be honest."

I shrug. "He's easy to talk to and kind, and he looks out for me. He's single, which is great because let's face it, my track record isn't good. But he's a friend, and I think he likes it that way. I haven't known him long, and for once, I'd like to just see how things go. I always rush in. I'm still not over Vinn, not really. And now, I feel like a dick for misreading the signals . . . again."

"Hey, you and Vinn weren't serious. It's okay to look at other guys."

"I just found Mac in bed with Kiera. He's not interested in me. I'm an idiot. I cling onto any fucking man who pays me a little bit of attention."

"You've had a tough life. There's other shit behind why you're the way you are."

I bury my face in my hands and groan aloud. "I'm such a desperate loser. He came in here, and I told him the meal was for Brick. Now, he thinks I'm after Brick."

Eva laughs. "Christ, Brick will shit his pants. He's terrified of you."

I grin. "Is he?"

She nods. "He's scared of strong women."

I roll my eyes. "I'm hardly strong."

She grabs my hand. "Raven, you are. Own it. And, if you like Mac, even just a little, fight for him."

"I don't think he's ready. He's been hurt and he refuses to talk about it. Maybe it's not the right time."

"Hunny, if he's moved on to club girls, he's ready. He'll open up, just be patient."

MAC

"Fuck, baby, if you don't stop that, I'm gonna have to take you back upstairs," I hiss into Kiera's ear. She giggles and grinds harder against me. I grip her hair and pull her face down to kiss me. A slap lands on the back of my head, and I release her, looking back over my shoulder to see Frankie glowering at me.

"Where's Raven?" she demands.

"Last time I checked, in her room. Why?" I snap, rubbing my head.

"Cos that's where you should be, dumbass."

"Why would I be in Raven's room?" I grip Kiera's hips to stop her rubbing against my painfully hard erection.

"Eating the dinner she prepared for you the second she got in from work. She is your ol' lady, remember?"

"I thought that was for . . ." Her words sink in, and I trail off. Raven cooked for me. Of course, she did. "Fuck."

"I wouldn't worry. I spoke with her, and she said she's fine about us," Kiera tells Frankie.

"I don't care what her lips are saying, this is technically her man, and no one is standing in the way of it, so get your arse off his cock and go find someone else to fuck." Kiera huffs, getting up and stomping away. No one argues with Frankie. "And you, get back up those stairs and have dinner," she tells me.

I take the stairs two at a time, willing my hard-on to disappear. I tap lightly on Raven's door. She doesn't answer, but I hear her laughing, so I go inside. She's sitting with Eva at the table outside, and they're drinking wine and laughing hard. I watch her for a few minutes before Eva spots me and smiles. Placing her glass on the table, she gets up. "That's my cue to leave."

Raven looks back at me, and I notice she's lit the candle on the table. It flickers, illuminating her beautiful face. "Someone told me about dinner," I say, and her blush returns. "You should have told me."

"It was nothing. Just a dinner to say thank you for being so nice. It wasn't important. Not as important as you and Kiera so—"

"Raven, Kiera is a club girl, she doesn't mean anything. I'd have ditched her to spend the evening with you."

"I know, but I don't wanna be that girl who cockblocks so . . ."

I take a seat opposite her and hold up the now empty bottle. "You got thirsty?"

She shrugs. "Umm, nothing beats a liquid diet. Where is Kiera?"

"I don't wanna talk about Kiera right now."

"You know, she had a good life growing up. Her parents gave her a great upbringing, but she chose to club hop. She finds it fun." Most club girls have shit upbringings, so when Kiera told me her story, it shocked me. Who would choose that life?

"Some people," I joke, rolling my eyes. "So, what did you cook for me?" I ask, lifting the dome nearest to me. "My favourite."

"I know," she almost whispers.

I pick up the steak and tear into it. She smirks. "Perfect," I say, chewing the now cold but tender meat. "I was pissed when you said this was for Brick."

"Really?"

I take another bite to stop me from continuing that sentence. "Did you manage to sort Vinn?" She nods. "And then you came back and cooked your old man his dinner. I like that. I could get used to it."

She laughs. "Don't bother. Temporary arrangement, remember?"

"I might decide to keep you." My eyes burn into her for the briefest of minutes before I take her glass of wine and drain it. "You look great, by the way."

She looks down at her outfit. "Yes, joggers are a good look on me," she jokes.

"How about, I shower and you get into my shirt, and we pretend that we had a great night eating steak and drinking wine?" I suggest. She smiles, nodding. Sharing her bed the last few nights has been something I've looked forward to. It might be dangerous—in fact, I know it is—but I can't help myself. While she's my ol' lady, I'm gonna make the most of it.

I lie with my arm around her, aware her arse is pressed against my thigh. With one slight shift, she'll most definitely feel the erection I'm desperately trying to hide, but it feels good to have a woman lying next to me where there's no pressure or drama. We're just a couple of good friends enjoying each other's company.

"You know so much about me," she whispers, "and I know nothing about you."

"That's a lie. You know I had a brother."

"Was he married? Did he have kids?"

I gently rub my chin against her hair, liking the soft feel of it. "Yeah. Cain had an ol' lady, Meghan. They have twins, Shelby and Rose."

"Wow, you have a niece and nephew?"

I nod. "Yep. Aged three."

"Oh god, that's so young to have lost their dad. They must be heartbroken. And now, you're here, so they've lost you too. Are you going back to see them?"

A pain twists in my chest. "Probably not."

Raven sits up slightly and stares at me wide-eyed. "Why not?"

I shrug. "It's a reminder, seeing me. We looked the same, and I don't want to hurt them any more than they're already hurting. They have the club and Ruby."

"Oh, so Ruby is still at the club without you?"

"Yeah."

"Usually, when an ol' lady is caught cheating, they leave, not the biker."

I twist her hair around my finger. "As I said, it's complicated. Tell me what happened after you left your uncle's house. Did you run away?"

Raven nods. "I got pregnant." She waits, letting that shellshock settle in my brain. "There was no fucking way I was gonna stick around there and bring a child up in their fucked-up world, so I ran away. There was this guy on the estate who had a flat and all the teenagers used to go and hang out there. Looking back, he was clearly some kind of paedophile, but he offered me a bed, and I took it. He paid for me to have a backstreet abortion. It was horrendous. The night I got home, I was in agony, and that piece of shit said I owed him. He raped me." She sighs heavily. "After that, I just went from one bad guy to the next. I was a mess. Sometimes, I think it's karma for aborting an innocent child."

I pull her tight against my chest and kiss her on the head. She's spent so long being used and abused, she thinks it's her own damn fault. "That isn't true, Raven. You did the right thing, and it couldn't have been easy. Look, I know Vinn has hurt you, but you've still got the club. You'll always have a home here."

Chapter Thirteen

RAVEN

We fell asleep wrapped around each other again, so when I'm awoken by Mac pushing his erection against my arse, I'm reminded of how horny I am. I can hear his soft snores, so I know he's asleep. He's been so great that maybe we could turn this into a convenience thing. I mean, he's my acting old man, and it isn't like I haven't been here before with Vinn or Chains.

He shifts against me again and his cock presses right at my opening. I close my eyes, enjoying the feel of him there. I carefully turn onto my back and glance at his sleeping face. He looks hot yet peaceful. His hand travels over my stomach and up towards my breast, where he caresses my erect nipple through his shirt. I let my hand fall against his erection and my eyes widen when I feel the thickness and length. He's huge. He thrusts up into my hand, and I take a firm grip through his boxers. I let him thrust a few more times before I take control. My head's still fuzzy from the wine I drank at dinner, and if he regrets this tomorrow, I'll blame it on that.

I kneel between his legs and tug his boxers halfway down his thighs. He stays sleeping, so I have time to assess the enormous erection as it lays against his stomach. I use both hands to grip the base, and he lets out a groan. I smile, leaning down and running my tongue over the swollen end. Tasting his pre-cum on my tongue, it spurs me on to take him into my mouth. His deep moan sends wetness pooling in my panties. It's been too long.

I run my tongue up and down the length before sucking him back into my mouth and doing my best to accommodate his size. He grips my hair, his eyes still tightly shut as he pushes me to take him deeper.

"Shit," he hisses, "Meg." I pause for a second . . . wasn't that his brother's wife? Suddenly, he thrusts up, almost choking me. The feel of my throat tightening makes me gag and I cough. Mac's eyes shoot open and he immediately looks down at me.

"Fuck," he cries, and before he can say anything else, he comes, filling my mouth until I can't swallow fast enough and it spills out, running down his cock. He looks so horrified, I don't know what to do, so I carefully sit up, wipe my mouth on my hand, and stare back at him. "What the fuck was that?" he pants, pulling his boxers back into place.

"Erm . . ." Words fail me, so I shrug helplessly. I don't understand why he looks so upset.

"I thought I was dreaming," he adds, looking confused.

"Sorry, I thought you—"

"I didn't!" he cuts in sharply, and I feel my cheeks burn with embarrassment. He throws his legs over the edge of the bed and places his head in his hands. "Fuck."

"Oh my god," I whisper, "I'm so fucking sorry." I suddenly feel like some kind of sex predator, and I rush to the bathroom and throw up into the toilet. I fall to my hands and knees, coughing hard until I have nothing left.

"Raven," he says, appearing somewhere behind me.

I hold my hand up behind me to stop him coming any closer. This is embarrassing enough without him watching me vomit. "Can we do this later?"

"Sure," he mumbles. I hear him leave and sigh with relief. I just fucked everything up. I'm the biggest idiot ever.

I dress early for work and leave before the rest of the club is awake. Vinn has a meeting at nine with a woman who runs a charity to support women's refuges. We'll put the pictures out ourselves onto social media and hope the press gets wind of them. A busy day is exactly what I need right now to take my mind off Mac and my fuck-up.

At exactly eight-thirty, Vinn arrives looking smart in a suit and shades. He's hand-in-hand with Sofia, who looks equally as stunning in a white summer dress and sandals. They look great together. My heart aches.

I hand Vinn his morning coffee and give mine to Sofia. Luckily, I didn't drink any yet. "I thought it would be good to have my fiancée in the pictures," says Vinn, and I smile wide.

"Great idea. Well done."

"I want to look like a family man."

"Of course." Sofia doesn't look happy at all. She doesn't bother to fake a smile. Instead, she takes the coffee and sits in the reception area, leaving Vinn to go into his office alone. "Are you okay?" I ask politely.

"I thought you were leaving this job."

I'm taken aback by her stand-off attitude, and I frown. "Erm, well, I was taking some time out, but with the newspaper article, I thought I'd come and help."

"Wonderful. Well done to you for saving the day."

I take a seat at my desk, unsure of how to deal with her. "Can I get you anything else?" I decide that ignoring her bad attitude is the way to go.

"Nope," she mutters, sighing.

By nine, the office temperature is at freezing point and so I'm relieved when Vinn's meeting turns up with the photographer at the same time. I spring into action, making drinks and introducing everyone. Vinn and Sofia sit together on the couch in his office, hand-in-hand. The photographer takes a few snapshots. "I was surprised when I received an email about this meeting, Mr. Romano," says Ms. Stone. "I approached you on numerous occasions for support and donations to the charity."

"I see," says Vinn, glancing at me for help.

"My fault," I say, smiling. "We have a lot of people wanting help for charities, and so you can imagine the decisions I have to make on who gets what. Mr. Romano wishes he could give to everyone, but unfortunately, it's just not possible."

"Right," she mutters. "Well, let me tell you a little about what we do at the women's refuge."

We spend the next hour showing interest and asking the right questions before Vinn smiles and hands over the cheque. They pose for more pictures, then I see Ms. Stone out.

Vinn sees Sofia out, and when he returns, he stops by my desk. "Can you work a shift at the club tonight? I'm short-staffed and need a manager in. I'd do it myself, except I have a dinner date I can't get out of."

"Sure," I agree because it's better than going home and seeing Mac.

I finish at the office and rush home to shower and change. Mac's in the main room, and I avoid eye contact as I dart past. I shower and am halfway through applying makeup when Mac pops his head in. "I need to talk to you."

"Not now, I'm running late."

"For?"

"I have a shift at Enzo's."

"Fuck, I upset you, and you go running back to Vinn," he spits out.

"No, I'm not upset. He's short-staffed." "Well, you're not doing it, so you'd better call him and tell him." He folds his arms over his chest and glares at me.

"I'm a little confused, Mac. For a second there, I thought you said I can't do it."

"You heard right."

I laugh, turning back to the mirror to apply lipstick. "You're not my keeper. I'm going to work."

"I'm your old man, so technically, I am."

"Here we go again," I mutter, "quick to pull that card when you want your own way."

"If you go there, I'll have to come too."

I narrow my eyes. He's right. When the other ol' ladies leave the club, they're accompanied by their men or another club member. I shrug. "Suit yourself."

I spend my shift behind the bar, rushed off my feet. Mac spends it sitting at the end of the bar, watching me the entire time. What does he get out of wasting his evening like this when we're not together? Vinn's given up and hasn't hassled me since I set him straight, so Mac could step away now, and Vinn wouldn't bother.

Just before closing, Vinn shows up. He looks stressed and signals for me to go to the office with him. Mac follows.

"There's another article going out. I don't know when, but I have someone on the inside. They've heard it's attacking my character. When are you putting the pictures from today up on social media?" snaps Vinn.

"I'll do it first thing," I say.

"We need to find the person doing this," he adds angrily.

I gently rub his arm, and his eyes beg me to get rid of Mac. I can't, not while I'm this horny, because I'll end up right back at square one. "We'll sort it out. Let's stick to the plan and post lots of good stuff about you."

He scoffs. "I don't think there's much good stuff."

"Of course, there is. Loads. Try to forget about it tonight. We'll meet tomorrow and go over things."

He glances at Mac, then back to me. "Are you okay?" I nod, faking a smile. "You don't look it. You look sad and upset. And maybe horny," he says, grinning, and I blush. "Yes, definitely horny."

"Stop," I hiss. He's trying to rile Mac, but it isn't working.

"We'll talk about it tomorrow," he says, winking.

"What the fuck are you whispering about?" snaps Mac.

"She was saying how horny she is. Are you not taking care of her needs, biker boy?"

"That's not what I said," I say to Mac. "Vinn!" I add with a tone of warning.

He kisses me on the head. "Go home, Corvo. Get your toys out. I'll picture it in my head."

"What the fuck did you just say?" growls Mac.

"You never showed him all your toys, Corvo? I feel honoured."

I shake my head as I leave. "Toys?" Mac questions the second we step outside.

"He's just trying to get a reaction from you."

"Is that the sort of shit you did together?"

"You're making me feel embarrassed," I mutter.

He hands me my helmet. "You need to buy new toys," he grumbles as we get on the bike. "Ones he hasn't touched."

When we get back, I head towards the stairs, but Mac takes my hand and pulls me in the direction of the kitchen. I'm not hungry, but he makes me sit at the table anyway and grabs some leftovers from the fridge. "I bet you hardly ate today," he says, placing it on the table. I take a piece of chicken and nibble it slowly.

"I wasn't hungry."

"You're upset," he says.

I sigh heavily and drop the chicken back on the plate. "Are we really gonna pretend last night didn't happen?"

"No. Why did you do it?"

I regret asking the question. "I don't know."

He places a finger under my chin and forces me to look him in the eye. "You do know. Why did you do it, Raven?"

"I thought it's what you wanted."

"Did you want it?"

I blush and try to look away, but he holds me in place. "Yes."

"Or did you do what you thought you needed to? Did you think it's what I expected you to do?"

I shrug. "Maybe."

"Fuck, Raven. I don't want anything from you. I'm not hanging out with you because I expect something. You don't owe me."

I nod. "Okay."

"I'm not like the other men from your past. I just wanna take care of you. Please don't do shit like that because you think you owe me."

"Okay," I repeat.

We eat in silence. Once we're finished, he takes me by the hand and leads me up to my room. "Go shower," he mutters. I spend longer in the shower than usual, avoiding him because I feel stupid. Yeah, maybe I thought he'd want me to do what I did, but I also wanted to do it. I like him. Maybe more than he likes me, but I do. And I promised myself I'd take this slow and see what happens naturally. But when he's holding me like that and prodding me with his erection, it's natural to want to explore it.

When I'm done, I slip into my pyjamas, conscious not to wear anything that smells of Mac. He's sitting on my bed, tapping away on his mobile. He glances me up and down, and I can see he wants to mention my choice of bedwear, but instead, he stands, pulling the sheets back, and signals for me to get in. He then leans down and kisses me on the cheek. "I thought I'd give you some space tonight," he whispers. I nod, feeling sad he's resorted to sleeping in his own room. He's probably terrified I'll jump on him again.

MAC

It kills me to leave Raven in bed alone, but I know how it'll end up if I join her for another night. I find Ace in the bar. A good drink is exactly what I need right now. "You've been gone all evening," he states.

"I went to work with Raven."

"I had to go sort the docks on my own," he grumbles.

"She's meant to be my ol' lady, I can't let her work in Enzo's without someone watching her."

"You know, this was meant to be a fresh start and you're heading down the same track you did in Nottingham."

"It's not the same," I argue.

"Your head is with her, all the damn time. We've been here two fucking minutes and you're sharing her bed."

"Not like that," I snap. "Jesus, I just came to have a drink with my brother. I could do without the lecture."

"I spoke to Ruby. Deano called to say things were in a mess. He's only just been made aware."

"You spoke to her?" I growl.

"Seems you're needed there, brother. Meghan ain't coping well."

"She'll learn to," I hiss, drinking a shot of whiskey.

"You're making everything messier by hiding here with Raven."

"I ain't hiding. You said this was a good move!"

"Yes, to clear your head. Now, you're jumping into bed with her."

"Make your mind up, you told me to fuck a whore!"

"A club whore, yes. Someone with no feelings towards you—" He stops mid-sentence and stares past me. I slowly turn to see Raven rushing back towards the stairs.

"Shit," I mutter, going after her.

I manage to grab her halfway up the stairs, catching her by the waist and pushing her against the wall. "Stop," I whisper, "Let me explain."

"Fuck a whore," she spits, throwing my words back at me.

"Not what I meant," I say firmly. "And I haven't fucked you, so it's irrelevant."

She slams her hands against the wall. "Get off me."

"Let's talk about this calmly," I say, slowly releasing her and backing off.

"Let's stay the hell away from each other," she snaps, rushing up the rest of the stairs and heading for her room.

I roll my eyes and follow, sticking my foot in the door before she can slam it in my face. "Why are you up anyway? You should be sleeping."

"Fuck you."

"Raven, you're taking it out of context. I was mad at Ace and snapped. I wasn't referring to you as a whore."

"I heard you," she yells, releasing the door and jumping into bed. I step inside and watch her for a second as she pulls the sheets over her.

"You wanna know why I'm not in your bed tonight?" I ask. When she doesn't reply, I step closer. "Cos I don't trust myself with you."

"Because I'm such a whore," she spits.

"Because every time I lay beside you, it gets harder not to kiss you. When I wake up next to you, all I can think about is fucking you. And I don't wanna ruin what we have. I don't want to fuck this up like all the ones before me." She watches me with interest. I slowly climb into bed, propping myself on my elbow and stroking her hair from her face. "It felt fucking amazing to wake up this morning and see you sucking my cock. I close my eyes and that's all I see."

"Why were you so mad?"

"Because I didn't want you to do it because you thought you had to."

"I did it because I wanted to," she mutters shyly.

"You've gotta be over Vinn before anything can happen with us," I say.

"I don't want Vinn." Her hand rests against my chest and she cautiously presses her lips against mine to test the waters. I cup her cheek before leaning in for another, but this time, we don't pull apart. A million things flash through my mind—Ruby, Meghan, the twins, Cain—but as our mouths work together, they soon fade away.

Chapter Fourteen

RAVEN

The kiss is perfect. As perfect as the first time he did it. I've dreamt of that kiss every night since, and now, I'm finally getting lost in it again. I feel his erection pushing against my leg and I rub against it. I'm so fucking horny, it's all I can think about. "I've been denying myself pleasure for so long, I was shocked this morning. I think it's why I reacted so badly," he whispers against my lips.

"Why have you denied yourself?"

"I don't deserve it," he mutters.

My heart breaks at the sight of his vulnerable expression, and I pull him in to kiss me again. This time, I wrap my leg around him and push him to lie on his back. Climbing over him, I straddle him with our lips still sealed and rub myself over his hard length. "You deserve it," I say.

He watches through hooded eyes as I lift my night-shirt over my head and drop it to the floor. His hands cover my naked breasts, gently squeezing my nipples. "You're so fucking hot," he whispers.

I smile, tugging his belt open, followed by the button of his jeans. Pushing them over his hips, I watch his erection spring free and I wonder how the fuck that's gonna fit inside me. I watch as he reaches into his back pocket and pulls his wallet out. He produces an XXL condom, and I smirk. I take it from him. I've never used one this size, but I'm sure it goes on the same as any other, so I rip the packet open and pinch the tip as I roll the rubber over his cock. My hand barely fits the girth as I smooth it down. He grips my arms and tugs me closer, lining himself up at my entrance. "You're taking too long." He grins.

I take his hands and sit on him, crying out as I stretch to accommodate his erection. "Holy shit," I hiss.

"I was gonna suggest foreplay first," he sniggers, "but you're just as impatient as me."

I press my hands against his chest as I lower myself further, stopping every so often to allow myself time to stretch. When I'm as full as I can take, I lift up. Mac watches me with a fire in his eyes. He wants to take control, but instead, his hands grip the sheets, screwing them up tightly. He's holding back, and I'm glad, I need to adjust to him before he fucks me senseless.

I build a rhythm, moving faster and faster the second I feel that familiar warmth building up. It's so close, and as I climb higher and higher, I begin to tremble. My movements become jerky, and I cry out as my legs shake. I lose the rhythm as my body reacts to the intensity of the orgasm ripping through me. Falling against his chest, I take a minute to catch my breath before sitting up again and moving against him.

"Fuck, that was hot," he whispers. I start moving faster, and he closes his eyes, groaning in pleasure and gripping my waist hard. He stiffens and tenses, then he lifts me from him. He lies still, panting with his eyes closed.

I frown in confusion. "Are you okay?" He nods, throwing his arm over his eyes. "It's just, you didn't . . . yah know."

"I know. It's fine," he pants.

I think back to what he said earlier, about not pleasuring himself because he doesn't deserve it. "What was the point if you didn't finish?"

"The point was, I got to fuck my ol' lady," he says, grinning and reaching for me. I lie against his chest, and he pulls the sheets over us. He removes the condom and drops it in the bin beside the bed. "Now, sleep."

I lie awake thinking, confused and frustrated by his weird behaviour. "Will you ever let yourself orgasm again?" I ask.

I feel his chest shake when he laughs. "One day. Maybe. Technically, I came in your mouth not twenty-four hours ago."

"But that wasn't a choice. I don't get it. How do you just stop yourself? Was I shit in bed?"

He laughs again. "Definitely not. I know you don't get it. I just have to work through whatever crap I've got going on. It's not easy to hold back when I've got a beautiful woman riding me, trust me."

"So, relax and let yourself go."

"One day, baby. One day."

I wake the next morning with his erection pressing at my entrance. I'm on my stomach, and he's lying over me. "Morning, beautiful," he whispers into my ear.

"What a way to wake up," I mumble.

He lifts my leg to the side and pushes into me. "Every woman should start their day with an orgasm," he says, easing in fully. As he withdraws, I push my hands against the headboard. Something tells me I'm gonna need to hold on, though nothing quite prepares me for the way he slams into me, shoving me up the bed. He repeats it, growling as I cry out. "You're so fucking tight," he hisses.

"I don't think I'm the problem here," I groan, pushing my face into the pillow as he grips my hips and continues to slam into me.

"Fuck, Raven, you gotta come," he pants. He reaches around my front, using his finger to rub circles over my swollen clit. "Raven," he grits out impatiently.

Smiling, I remain quiet, determined that I'm not coming until he does. He growls, ripping himself away from me. I feel the loss immediately and fist the pillow in frustration. "I know what you're doing," he mutters, kneeling beside me and gripping a handful of my hair. He keeps my face pressed into the pillow and places a leg over my own, pinning me in place, as he inserts his finger into me. "And it won't work." He rubs frantically, holding me there to take it even though I'm desperately wanting to thrash around in ecstasy.

"Mac," I cry, trying to move away as the feeling builds, becoming too much. He presses his thumb against my backside, forcing the digit into the tight hole. It's enough to send me spiralling over the edge, and I moan into the pillow as I shake uncontrollably. When my body calms down and I begin to relax, he releases me, slapping my arse hard.

"Shower, so we can eat breakfast cos I'm starving," he orders. I roll onto my side, too exhausted to speak. His erection stands proudly, and I smile, edging closer. He watches with amused eyes as I run my tongue up his shaft. "You think you're clever," he mutters, closing his eyes and letting his head fall back when I take him into my mouth. I work my mouth up and down, hollowing my cheeks and sucking with everything I have. I'm determined to see this man come apart again. He fists my hair, occasionally letting a groan escape. Cupping his balls, I feel the way they tighten in my hand. He's almost there . . . and that's when he pulls away, jumping up from the bed and pressing his head against the cool glass of the window. He stays there for a minute, panting with his eyes closed while he regains control.

"Shower," he repeats, and I head that way, smirking as I go. Something about his self-restraint is a massive turn-on. I love a challenge . . . it just adds to the excitement.

MAC

I can't concentrate on fuck all. Not what Riggs was trying to tell me at breakfast, not what Ace was moaning to me about afterwards when we went for a run, and not now while Blade is tying a man to a chair on behalf of the great Vincent Romano. How I landed this job is a mystery, but I suspect it's what Riggs was telling me about earlier when I wasn't listening.

The guy looks like he's recently taken a beating as he struggles against the tight ropes. "Mr. Romano will be with us shortly, so save your energy for then," says Blade, looking bored.

"Remind me again what we're doing here," I ask.

"Man, I know as much as you. I get the guy, I tie the guy up, sometimes I slit his throat, other times I give Vinn the knife to do it. But whatever, as long as I get a fat cheque at the end of it, I don't care."

"If Riggs is turning the club around, why do we still help Vinn out?"

"Ask the Pres, I don't have the answers."

The door opens and Vinn saunters in like a fucking king. Behind him is Raven, and I narrow my eyes. Why the fuck is Raven here? "Mr. Clay, we have to stop crossing paths like this," says Vinn with a smile.

He pulls the gag from the man's mouth. "Fuck you, Vinn. I did what you asked. I gave you what you wanted."

"Imagine crossing my path not once, but twice, and not having the brains to up security. You're a well-respected man, Raymond. Do you mind if I call you that? Good."

"I haven't crossed you again!"

"Raven, be a darling and wipe the man's face. He's sweating, and no man likes that look, especially not a gay man like him." I watch as Raven steps forward and wipes the guy's brow. She shouldn't be here on this kind of business. "While you're there, show Raymond the pictures."

Raven opens an envelope and pulls out some pictures, showing them to the man who begins thrashing around like a possessed demon. "You stay away from them!" he screams, almost head-butting Raven in his struggle.

"Your wife is a stunner, and those kids . . . you're a lucky, lucky man."

"What do you want?" he yells.

"I hear you're a good friend of the editor down at the Gazette?" says Vinn, and I glare at Blade. All this to avoid a bad fucking newspaper article? "You need to warn him not to run any more bad press stories on me. It doesn't look good for me."

"Especially the one today," the guy spits out, and Vinn laughs, pulling Raven into his side.

"Yes, as you can imagine, my wife-to-be isn't too happy about it. Luckily, she knew all about my relationship with Raven, so no damage done."

My eyes burn into Raven, and she gently pulls away from Vinn. "I don't blame you," says the man, smirking and staring at Raven's arse. "I'd tap that if she were my personal assistant."

My fist slams into the side of his head, and Raven flinches but lowers her eyes. "Don't talk about her like that," I growl.

"Now, look what I did, upset the gorillas." He grins, spitting blood onto the ground.

"Go cool off," snaps Vinn.

I storm out of the room, taking the steps two at a time to get out of there. Raven follows, calling my name. I get out into the fresh air and spin to face her. "What story?" I yell.

"There was another one printed. It says he doesn't support the women's shelter as he has no respect for women."

I scoff. "At least they got that right."

"It goes into detail about his fling with me. I'm painted out as some scarlet woman," she mutters, her cheeks turning red with embarrassment. "Falling for a wicked man's charm while his innocent fiancée is left heartbroken."

I sigh, pulling her into my arms. "Why the hell were you in there anyway? You shouldn't be doing shit like that. Look what happened before."

"He's my boss. It's my job."

"No, it isn't, and as your old man, I'm telling you it isn't, or I'll stop you working for him. You do his shitty office work and that's it.

No more being his bitch. I thought we'd already cleared this up several times."

"You give me a couple of orgasms and think you own me," she says, adding a small grin.

I press my lips against hers, backing her to the wall. "Damn fucking right."

Vinn coughs, and I smirk against her lips. I'm glad he's seen us together like this. Maybe now he'll take the hint. "We're done," he says. "Let him go, dump him at the docks."

"She's done doing your dirty work," I say, nodding towards Raven. "From now on, she handles your office work or nothing at all. I don't want her doing shit like that."

Vinn looks at Raven and grins. "That right, Corvo?"

"Her name is Raven. You keep using that fucking pet name for her, and I might have to stop you seeing her altogether."

Vinn holds his hands up in mock surrender. "Okay, no more pet names, no more hard labour. I get it."

I kiss Raven, hard. "See you later, baby." She smiles, nodding.

"Are you and Raven a real thing now?" asks Blade. He takes a sharp left, and Mr. Clay falls onto me. I shove him back into the middle of us.

"You could have made him look less suspicious," I mutter.

Blade grins over at me. "You think the black sack on his head is too much?"

"Yes, Blade. It's worrying that you don't!"

"So, you and Raven?" he pushes, turning into the docks. It's quiet, and we make our way to the far end where nobody bothers to walk their dogs.

"We're seeing how it goes. It's all very new."

"Aww, man, I'm pleased for yah both. She deserves a good man."

I scoff at his words. "I wouldn't say I'm good."

He stops the van, and we get out. I pull Mr. Clay out too, his hands tied behind his back and his ankles bound together. I sit him against a metal container and pull the sack off his head. He blinks a few times, his eyes adjusting to the light, as I cut his hands free. "Don't be so hard on yourself, brother. She doesn't want a law-abiding citizen or she wouldn't hang out with bikers."

"Why didn't we just drop him home?" I ask, cutting Clay's ankle ties. "It makes no sense, dropping him here."

"Following orders," says Blade. "You seem to have a real problem with that."

"You heard what Mr. Romano said," I say, looking Clay firmly in the eyes. "Speak to the Gazette. There's gonna be some real problems for you if they print another bullshit story."

"Yah know," he says, rubbing his wrists, "rumour has it, he really fell in love with your girl. You should keep an eye on her. When Vinn Romano tells a girl he loves her, it's unlikely he'll just walk away."

"Thanks for the advice, but concentrate on sorting your own problems."

Chapter Fifteen

RAVEN

This is what it feels like to be truly happy. As I lie back against Mac, with his arms tightly wrapped around me, enjoying the company of Anna and Riggs, I realise that I finally feel happy. Happy and content. The waitress places a tray of cocktails down for me and Anna to try. She's interviewing for a position at Anna's bar and part of the process is to make cocktails. I sit up, and Mac places a hand on my knee. I love that he's always touching me in some way. It's been a month since we became official, a month since we first fell into bed together, and a whole month of being so wrapped up in each other that this is the first time we've been out of the club on a date.

Riggs sips his whiskey and watches Anna closely as she sips the first cocktail. Her eyes widen and she smiles, offering me a second straw to try. "Why are you always happiest when you're drinking cocktails?" he asks, grinning.

"That's not true. I'm happiest when I'm with you. The cocktails are just a bonus . . . and the fact I have no children hanging from me also helps."

"It must be nice to have the night off," I say.

"I love the kids. Honestly, I do. But they tire me out, and that's with all the help of Eva's mum, Esther, and Frankie. Ziggy and Malia are amazing, they're so mature for their age, but Willow, she's on another level. I swear, she'll send us mental before she's even hit her teenage years."

Riggs pulls her in for a kiss, smiling. "She takes after her mama."

"So, are you guys gonna have any more?" I ask.

"Anna says no, but I'm definitely putting more babies in that belly," says Riggs.

"Hey, it isn't my fault you feel you missed out with Willow. I'm not risking having another child like her."

Riggs leans back in his chair confidently. "We'll see."

"What about you guys?" asks Anna, changing the subject.

"A little early for the kid chat," says Mac, and Anna laughs.

"I mean, what's happening with you two?"

"We're good. Taking it slow. I'm teaching Raven not all guys are dickheads."

I grin, acting surprised. "Oh, really? Is that what you're trying to teach me?"

"Well, you both look really happy," she adds.

Riggs picks his drink up. "I'm done with this chick talk. Follow me to the bar, brother."

I smile, watching them make a quick exit and grabbing a stool at the bar.

"I mean it," says Anna, pulling my attention back to her. "You look happy."

"I feel it," I say, smiling. "I just . . . never mind."

"No, say it, what's wrong?"

"It's like I'm waiting for something to go wrong. I never get the happy ever after and now—"

"Now, you do."

"I hope so. I really like him."

"And has he talked about his past much?" she asks. I'd already spoken to her and Eva about his unwillingness to talk about his past and about Ruby. We've just come to a place where we don't talk about any of that.

I shake my head. "Nope, and he's still denying himself real pleasure," I say, and her eyes widen.

"Are you kidding me? So, in all this time, he hasn't come?"

"Shh," I hiss, glancing back to check he hasn't heard. "I mean, don't get me wrong, we have some fun, and I always . . . yah know. But he just won't let it happen. It can't be healthy."

"You need a plan."

I remember back to me giving him a blowjob without his actual consent and shake my head. "If he's not ready, then I can't force it. Surely, he'll give in eventually. It's just frustrating. Everything about him is perfect except that, and it's not even my issue. It must be killing him."

"I just don't get why he's denying himself. It's like he's punishing himself."

I down one of the cocktails. "Hire this girl, she's good."

I've never witnessed Mac drunk. Getting him and Riggs back to the club was a task in itself, and as I watch him flop into the centre of the bed, I realise there's no way I'm gonna be able to shift him. I sigh, reaching for his boots and tugging his feet free. Standing over him, he's completely passed out as I unfasten his belt. His wallet and mobile are in his pocket, so I remove them, and as I do, I see a text message from Ruby. I can only see the start because the screen lock is on. ***Does she know what you did?*** is the line that stares me in the face.

I place his mobile on the drawers and continue to undress him. The message replays over and over in my mind. I sit beside him on the bed, staring across at the phone. I trust Mac, he's never given me a reason not to, and checking his phone is a massive no. It means I don't trust him deep down, otherwise, why would I be checking? What do I expect to find? Nothing good ever comes from snooping.

Placing a sheet over him, I decide to go downstairs. It was pretty quiet around here when we arrived home, so I'll sleep on the couch.

Ace is watching a game on the large television. He eyes me as I lay a sheet out on the couch and slip under it. "You okay?" he asks, and I nod. "You sure? Where's Mac?"

"He's passed out wasted," I say, smiling. "I can't get in the bed."

He frowns. "Weird. He doesn't usually get in a mess."

"I think he may have contacted Ruby," I lie, watching him for a reaction.

His face remains impassive. "Really, why?"

I shrug. "I don't know. I mean, it's about time, right? He's been avoiding her for a long time."

Ace nods too. "I guess so."

"I know it was hard on him when they split. He's carrying a lot of pain."

"Look, Raven, I'm not gonna spill anything about Mac and his life back in Nottingham. If you wanna know shit, ask him."

"I do. He doesn't answer me."

"Then make him. You deserve to know the truth." He turns off the game and heads for the stairs.

I lay for another hour before I convince myself that it's okay to have a quick peek at his messages to Ruby. Not because I don't trust him—of course, I do—but he won't explain his relationship with her, and don't I deserve to know? I could kid myself and say it's to protect myself before I get in too deep, but what's the point? I'm already in deep.

Mac is still passed out on the bed. His snoring is ridiculous, and I smile as I approach him. He looks so peaceful and carefree without the worry lines creasing across his forehead. His mobile teases me from the drawers with its little message alert light flashing. I reach for it, then snatch my hand away again. What the fuck am I doing? This isn't me. I don't do this crazy shit. It lights up again with a new message, and I automatically read the first part.

Ruby: Please, Mac, please answer.

It's so desperate, so pleading, I almost feel her pain. It's how I felt when Vinn hurt me. And now, she's going through that exact heartbreak. How can Mac soothe my heart and ignore hers? I snatch the phone up and press the home button. It's locked with Mac's fingerprint. Biting my lip, I stare between his hand and his phone. Fuck it. One look and I'll never do it again. I carefully take his forefinger and hold it over the home button and it opens. There's no going back.

I scroll to the top of the messages. It begins with Mac texting Ruby tonight at ten o'clock. He was in the bar with me and Anna then, already very drunk.

Mac: Stop calling me, Ruby. I'm not going to answer. I've moved on. You should too.

Ruby: What does that mean? Have you met someone???

Mac: Yes

Ruby: Wow, you really are a piece of work. You've left utter carnage here and you're setting up a new life fuck knows where like nothing happened?

Ruby: Did you speak to Ace? I talked to him over a month ago and explained how important it was I speak with you.

Mac: I told him the same as I'm telling you. We're done. I've moved on. Now leave me alone.

Ruby: Tell me where you are!

Mac: Why?

Ruby: Because I need to speak with you one last time. I need to tell you something important.

Ruby: Does she know what you did?

Ruby: Please, Mac, please answer.

She's so hurt. I don't understand it. I always thought that maybe she'd cheated. He's so set on treating women right, it can't possibly be him. But maybe no one cheated, and maybe he just ended it. He said she couldn't have kids, and they'd been together a long time, so maybe he just fell out of love. That would explain her hurt. But whatever happened, she's blaming him, and I'm desperate to know why.

Something in my broken heart feels for her. She needs closure. And so, I do something so stupid, it makes me feel instantly sick. I send her the address. I tell her where he is and then immediately regret it. I bite my lip so hard, I taste blood. *Fuck. Fuck. Fuck.* What if this gets them back together? What if she turns up here and he sees her and realises how much he loves and misses her? I drop the mobile on the bed like it's poison. Why did I do that? A message comes through, and I hesitantly pick it up to look.

Ruby: Mac?? Is that you?
Mac: No. I shouldn't have done that. Please delete it.

I know she won't, because it's a stupid request to ask a broken heart to forget the information she's been asking for. My mind turns crazy. What if she's stalking him, and I've just given him up?

I wait a further ten minutes, but no text messages come through. I delete the ones I sent. It's a cowardly move, but I'm still praying she'll leave it now she knows where he is. Maybe it was just a curiosity thing. I curl into Mac's side and lie awake, thinking of all the shit things that might happen now I've fucked up.

It's a long night. I know the minute Mac awakens because he curls his body around mine, pushing his erection against my thigh. "Morning," he whispers. I close my eyes, pretending to sleep. His hands wander across my body, lifting my nightshirt and rubbing my arse. "Baby, wake up."

I don't respond. I might vomit from the guilt if I open my mouth. He rises to his knees and gently tugs my legs apart, slipping my panties down. The thought of him pleasuring me and not himself makes me feel worse, so I turn away, pushing his hands from me. "Raven?"

"I'm tired," I mumble, forcing my voice to sound sleepy.

"You don't have to do a thing," he says, burying his head between my legs. I shove him away, gently at first but rougher when he doesn't take the hint. "Did I do something wrong?" he asks.

Tears fill my eyes and I turn away, shaking my head. "No."

"Are you mad because I passed out?" The bed dips as he settles behind me, burying his face into my neck. "I'm sorry."

"I'm not mad at you," I say.

"Raven, you have one of the hungriest sexual appetites I've ever known. Something is wrong if you're turning me down."

"Not everything is about sex, Mac. Maybe I just don't feel like it," I snap. I'm being a bitch, and it's because of the guilt, but I can't stop myself.

"Okay," he says, kissing my neck. He sits up, and I hear him grab his mobile. He stays silent for a minute, so I turn back to face him. He's reading his messages.

"Everything okay?" I ask.

"Yep."

"It's just your phone was pinging a lot last night."

He glances at me, frowning. "So?"

"I just thought maybe it was urgent."

"Raven, I've got nothing to hide. Do you want to see my phone?" he asks, and I shake my head. "No, here, check it." I shake my head again, but he grabs my hand and places his mobile in it. "I'm not hiding anything, baby."

I glance at the messages from Ruby, the ones I've already checked, then drop the phone and dive from the bed, rushing to the toilet and vomiting. I hear him approach behind me. "Shit, are you okay?"

"I'm not feeling great," I mutter, keeping my head over the toilet bowl.

"I'll go get you some water."

When he's gone, I fall back onto my arse and bury my face in my hands. I'm an idiot. A fucking idiot. And I have to tell him what I've done.

MAC

I watch Raven brush her teeth. She doesn't look too well, but I tell her she's beautiful, even when she's vomiting. She smiles sadly and heads back to bed, and I follow. "What do you want to do today?" I ask.

"I think I just need to stay in bed and rest," she mumbles. I nod, lifting the sheets and climbing in. "You don't have to stay," she protests, but where the hell else would I go when she's feeling this bad?

I grab the television remote and turn on Netflix. Pulling her to lay on my chest, I find a chick flick I know she loves. "You don't think . . ." I pause, unsure how to say it, "that you might be pregnant?" She sits up, staring at me wide-eyed. "I know you're on the pill and shit, but it happens still, right?" We stopped using condoms weeks ago because Raven takes the contraceptive pill.

"But you never come inside me," she says, and there's a look in her eyes that tells me this is her problem right now. She's mad at me because I don't come.

"Is that why you didn't want me this morning?"

"Jesus!" she cries, and I wince.

"Okay, so it's not the reason, that's fine," I quickly add.

"But while we're on the subject, I don't see the point of having sex when you never come. I find it insulting, to be honest."

I watch her for a second. She sometimes has an outburst, then regrets it, and we laugh about it, but right now, I see she's not gonna laugh this off. "Okay, so this is an issue?"

"Wouldn't it be for you?" she asks. "You insist on making me come, but you never do. Maybe I should stop myself too, see how you like it."

I smirk. "You have no self-control." This only angers her more, and I rush to correct myself again. "Baby, stop this. I get pleasure from your pleasure."

"You can't even see how weird this is!" she cries.

"I told you, I'm just going through some shit." I don't tell her that recently I've found it impossible to finish. It's not always a choice for me. I read up on it and it's probably due to stress.

"Then tell me about that. Tell me about the shit, so I can understand."

I throw my legs over the edge of the bed. "Why do we need to drag all that up when we're getting on so well?" I ask.

"Because it's stopping you from coming!" she yells.

I spin around, gripping her shoulders and pushing her to lie back. Climbing over her, I kiss her hard and fast. "You want me to come, fine." I pull at her nightshirt, tugging it over her head and throwing it to the floor. I just want her mood to be done so we can get back to being good again. I line myself up at her entrance and thrust forward. She cries out, her nails digging into my back. It's hot and fast, and after she comes, she pushes me to lie on my back and climbs on top. She looks fucking amazing, riding me hard with her cheeks flushed pink and her lips swollen from our kisses. Reaching back, she cups my balls, and I close my eyes, feeling the build-up as she fucks me. And just as I release into her, a low growl escaping me, the door opens, and Ace rushes in. He doesn't pay any attention to the fact that Raven is lying over my chest, panting hard.

"Brother, there's a problem."

Chapter Sixteen

MAC

"Jesus, Ace, can't it wait?" I pull a sheet over us to hide Raven's naked body.

"No. Ru—" he begins.

"Get the fuck up right now," yells a voice from behind him. I lock eyes with Ruby as she storms in like a raging bull. "We need to talk." Raven rolls from me, taking some of the sheet.

"Do yah think you could wait outside and let me dress?" I snap. I'm in shock, nothing ever gets under my skin, but seeing Ruby here rattles the hell out of me. How the fuck did she find me? Everyone was sworn to secrecy. My brothers back home in Nottingham would never have given me up like that. Not because they owed me any loyalty, but because they were glad to see the back of me. Most of them made it pretty clear their loyalties were with my twin, even after his death.

"It's not like I haven't seen it all before," mutters Ruby before stepping out with Ace.

I grab my jeans and pull them on, keeping my back to Raven. "How the hell did she find me?" I mutter, more to myself than her.

"I'm sure she just wants to clear the air so you can both move on," says Raven.

"She's here to rake up shit that I wanna forget. I came here for a fresh start. She needed that too."

"Maybe she's hurting and needs closure," she suggests.

I groan and bury my head in my hands. Just when things were going well. Raven kneels behind me and rests her head against my shoulder. "Just talk to her. She's obviously in pain. Some things need to be settled face to face."

"You don't get it," I mutter.

"She just sounded so hurt, like she needed to see you to get things straight in her head."

I frown, pulling away slightly to look at her. Her eyes widen and her mouth opens like she's about to talk but nothing comes out. "What are you talking about?"

"When . . . erm, when she texted you. When you showed me her texts."

"You hardly looked at my phone when I showed you those." Her expression fills with guilt. "Unless you'd already read her messages?" I add. She doesn't respond. Instead, her cheeks flush pink and she looks away. "Raven?"

"Oh god," she mutters. "Okay, I checked your phone and I feel so bad for it. I just wanted to know who was texting, in case it was urgent." She sighs, shaking her head. "That's a lie. I was checking your phone to see what she wanted."

"Raven, you don't have to sneak around checking up on me. If you wanted to see it, you could have asked."

"I know. I felt awful when you showed me earlier. I'm so sorry. You avoid talking about her, and I was curious when she kept texting you."

I'm not mad at her for being curious. She's been through a lot, and I don't blame her for not trusting men. I pull her in to kiss her. "I texted her back," she whispers, and my lips freeze inches from hers. "I am so sorry, Mac."

I pull back, staring in disbelief. "You told her where I was?" She nods, and I stand, feeling the sting of her betrayal. "Why would you do that? You know nothing about my situation with her."

"I felt like she was hurting badly, and I could relate to that, so I was trying to help. I thought if you'd just see her and explain—"

"Explain!" I yell, taking her by surprise. "Explain what? You don't know what happened! You can't make that decision without the facts!"

A tear leaks from the corner of her eye. "I thought I was helping, like you helped me."

"Bullshit. I've done nothing but be patient and kind to you, and this is how you repay me? By contacting the one person you knew I was avoiding without knowing any of the facts. You've just made my life so much worse, Raven. You have no idea what you've done."

The door opens, and Ruby stands there. "Can you have your domestic another time? I've been waiting months for this."

"You shouldn't have come," I snap.

Ruby smirks. "That would suit you, wouldn't it, Mac? That way, I couldn't come here and tip your life upside down like you did mine." Her eyes land on Raven and she arches a brow. "So, this is the one you've met?"

Raven stares down, and Ruby places her hands on her hips. "You know he's a fucking two-timing cheat? It won't be long before he's ripping your heart out and running out the door." I groan. Raven's head snaps up to look at me. "Oh darling, he's been keeping so much from you." I grab Ruby by the arm and march her from the room as she laughs. It's the reaction she was hoping for as I push her along the passage towards my room. "How serious are you two?" she asks, still looking amused.

"She's my ol' lady," I mutter, pushing her into my room and slamming the door.

Ruby laughs sarcastically. "Christ, you really are an arsehole."

"You came all this way to tell me that?"

"You haven't told her anything, have you?"

"Why would I? I came here to forget it!" I yell.

"Well, while you're here 'forgetting it'," she says, using her fingers as air quotes, "your brother's wife is falling apart. We can't get her out of bed, let alone to look after the kids. She just cries or stares into space."

"Then call a doctor!"

"They'll section her, take the kids!" she shouts.

"Maybe that's for the best," I growl, and she slaps me hard. It stings, and I hiss as I rub my cheek.

"Cain would be turning in his grave right now if he could see you."

"He wouldn't even be in a grave if it wasn't for me!" I yell back.

"Well, we both agree on that," she snaps.

RAVEN

"How the hell did his ex get his address?" asks Leia.

As soon as Mac dragged Ruby away, I sought out Anna, who just happened to be with Leia. "I gave it to her," I admit, and then I fill them in on the text messages. They both stare at me in shock. "I know . . . I fucked up. I instantly regretted it, but it was too late."

"You knew he didn't want to speak to her," says Leia.

"I just thought maybe he was hurting. It sounded like she'd cheated on him."

"Raven, what the hell were you thinking?" asks Anna, sighing.

"He should have told me the backstory. If I'd have known, I wouldn't have been so curious and I wouldn't have read her messages and I wouldn't have felt sorry for her."

"Does he know?" asks Leia, and I nod. "Shit. Was he mad?" I nod again. "Let's hope your plan works and they make friends and live happily ever after." Somehow, I don't think that will happen, and by the look on Leia's face, she doesn't either.

"Anyway, she said he's a cheat."

"Oh my god," they gasp in unison.

"He always talks like he disagrees with cheating. I don't get it. I know he was unhappy with Ruby, they were together a long time, but why didn't he correct me when I said she cheated?"

"No man would admit to that crime," says Leia.

"But to try and heal me, to make out he's a good guy when actually he's done the same thing to his ol' lady? It doesn't make sense."

I stay in the main room for an hour, and Mac makes no appearance, so I eventually decide to go to bed. Mac will find me when he's ready.

I wake with a start, sitting up to find Mac's silhouette looking out my bedroom window. I turn on the lamp, but he keeps his back to me. "What time is it?" I ask, my voice croaky from crying.

"Six a.m."

"Are you okay? Has Ruby gone?" He shakes his head. "No, you're not okay, or no, she hasn't gone?"

"Both. We need to talk."

"Okay." I rest against my headboard, my heart beating out of my chest.

"I have to go back to Nottingham." I stare, waiting for him to say he's taking me with him or he's just kidding, but he doesn't bother to look at me as he adds, "I'll pay for your tattoo cover-up and anything else you need until you get sorted. It's the least I owe you."

I frown. "What?"

"It's not fair for me to keep you waiting here when I don't know how long I'll be or if I'll even come back."

"I don't understand," I whisper.

"It's not gonna work between us, Raven."

"Bullshit. It's been working just fine."

"I thought it was too until I find out you're going behind my back, checking my phone and texting my ex."

"I was trying to help," I wail.

"Well, you didn't."

"Are you getting back with her?" I ask.

He gives a sarcastic laugh. "No."

"I need more than that, Mac. Don't just tell me it won't fucking work with no real explanation."

"I can't give you a damn explanation, Raven. I have shit to sort out."

"Did you cheat on Ruby?" I ask, and he nods, still keeping his back to me. "Why didn't you tell me?" He remains silent. "You let me think she hurt you!"

"It was easier that way."

"On who, you?" I yell.

"Yes. Yes, Raven, on me, because I'm a piece of shit, okay. Would you have trusted me if I'd have told you? Would you have let me help you?"

"Yes," I snap. "Everyone makes mistakes, Mac. You could have told me anything, and I would have given you a chance."

He spins to face me. "And that's why you'll always get hurt," he hisses. "You haven't learnt fuck all. Stop letting men walk all over you. I don't deserve a chance. When you find out the truth, you'll see that."

"I don't care about the truth. This is a fresh start, you said it yourself. We can get through anything. You can be a different person. You can choose to be better."

He smirks, shaking his head. "I fucked my brother's wife," he spits, looking me dead in the eye. "I cheated on my ol' lady and fucked his." He glares at me with a cold expression. I've never seen this side of him and my heart shatters. "Are you happy now, Raven? Can you forgive that? Can you trust me now?"

I shake my head, tears filling my eyes. "No. You wouldn't cheat. You hate cheating."

He laughs, and again, it's without humour. "I charmed Meghan into my bed. I did everything I could, and then, one night, she'd argued with Cain and guess who she turned to."

"I thought you were close to him," I mumble through tears.

"I was. That's why finding out killed him."

I take a shuddering breath. "Was it one time?"

He rolls his eyes. "You think I'd risk it all for one fuck? No, Raven, it went on for months. I got a thrill from it. The sneaking around, the brief touches while he was standing right fucking next to her."

I don't recognise this man. This cold, unapologetic man. "That's why your parents don't have contact with you?"

"Meghan won't get out of bed. She isn't looking after the twins, and Ruby's come here to take me home. To face my mess and sort it out. I'll be leaving later today."

"So," I mutter, wiping my cheeks, "you fucked up, but that doesn't mean we can't work. You've left that life. We can start over and carry on just like we were." It comes out desperate, and I hate myself for it, but I can't let him go. Not like this.

"You don't get it. Cain died, Raven. He fucking died because of what I did." He pauses to let the news sink in. "And now, I have to go back and sort out my mess."

I shake my head, grabbing his arm. "No, you don't. It's done. Stay here and start again."

"I thought you wanted me to face up to it. Isn't that why you told Ruby where I was?"

"I didn't know the truth then," I cry.

"No, you didn't, and you interfered anyway."

"Then I'll come." I grab his arm, kneeling on the edge of the bed.

He shakes his head, pulling away. "You've done enough."

"You'll need someone on your side. I can help."

"Right now, I don't want you near me." I flinch at his words. "I was happy, Raven. For the first time in years, I was happy. Now, that's all gone."

"I'm sorry," I cry. "I'm so sorry. Please, don't just leave. We can be happy." I hate that I'm begging, but this hurts so much more than it did with Vinn.

"Fuck, Raven. I've just told you I cheated on my ol' lady of eighteen years with my brother's wife. His fucking wife! And you're here begging me to stay with you. My brother died because of me. He died! And you're willing to still be with me."

"It happened before us. We can move forward from this. Everyone deserves a second chance."

"I don't. I thought I did. I wasn't supposed to fall in love with you. I wanted to help because I wanted to be better. I thought by helping you, it would somehow make up for all the shit I'd done, but it doesn't. It comes back to bite harder. Now, I have to walk away from you and finish what I started back home."

"Love?" I repeat. "You fell in love with me?"

"It doesn't matter. I don't deserve to be happy."

"That's why you'd never come? Because you think you don't deserve pleasure or happiness? How long will you punish yourself?"

He sighs, rubbing his brow. "Do you know how Cain found out? He walked in on us. I was in his bed with his wife. Fucking her so hard, she was screaming my name. He ran out of there without a word, got on his bike, and hit a forty-four-tonne lorry at fifty miles an hour. He was dead on impact. That should have been me. I should be dead, and he should be here with a wonderful woman like you. I'll never stop punishing myself. The coroner put accidental death on his death certificate, but he said he couldn't actually rule out that Cain didn't drive at that lorry on purpose. How do I forgive myself for that?"

"So, what's your plan? Go back to Nottingham, drag Meghan out of bed, and force her to look after her kids?"

The bedroom door opens, and Ruby enters. "Shouldn't you make a move on packing or something?" she asks, glaring at Mac. She rakes her eyes over me. "He told you then?"

"Give us a minute," snaps Mac.

"We need to hit the road."

I wipe my eyes and wrap the sheet tighter around myself. "Let me come with you, Mac."

Ruby scoffs, rolling her eyes. "I've done you a favour. See this as a lucky escape."

"Everyone makes mistakes," I mutter.

"Just leave us, Ruby!" Mac demands.

"Christ, you're one of those women who take cheaters back time and time again, aren't you? Or do you think you'll be the one to change him? I'm not judging cos I was like you once. This piece of crap cheated on me so many times, I just got used to it. How many of my friends did you sleep with?" she asks, glaring at Mac. "Three, maybe four, and that's only the ones I knew about."

"Ruby, please," he mutters.

"But this time, he really did good. His own brother's wife. He'll always need that rush, that thrill of the chase. He'll never settle down."

"So, why would you want him back at the club in Nottingham?" I snap.

"Oh, trust me," she hisses, screwing her face up in disgust, "I don't. I've been sent to get him back to try and help Meghan. We're all out of ideas."

I scoff. "And you think taking Mac back after everything that happened will help?"

"No, I don't. But when she gives birth, he needs to step up." I gasp. "Oh, you didn't tell her everything then?" Ruby adds, smirking.

"Fuck, Ruby. Get the hell out of here. I'll find you when it's time to leave."

"Your old man's gonna become a daddy."

"Ruby!" he yells. She laughs and heads out. "Raven," he begins, but I get off the bed, head for the bathroom, and turn on the shower. Mac watches me in silence. I feel numb, like someone suddenly switched everything off inside me. He lingers in the doorway, watching. "I was gonna tell you," he mutters. I close the door in his face, making sure to lock it.

Chapter Seventeen

RAVEN

I spend a good half-hour in the shower, crying. I cry until my chest hurts and my eyes are swollen. Wrapping myself in a large, fluffy towel, I step out into the bedroom, where Mac is sitting on the edge of my bed with his head in his hands. He glances up, and for a second, I get a glimpse of the Mac I know. "You should pack," I say, rummaging through my drawers to find underwear.

"I just wanted to check if you were okay."

"Don't forget this," I add, handing him his t-shirt.

"Raven—" he begins, but I cut him off by glaring at him.

"Take care, Mac. It's been fun."

He stands, his eyes darkening. "It's been fun," he repeats coldly. "Fun?"

"I hope everything goes well in Nottingham."

"Suddenly, you don't want to come?" he asks, smirking. "The cheating and lies didn't put you off, but the baby has?"

"Does it matter which part put me off?" I ask, grabbing a dress.

He watches as I pull on my underwear under my towel. "What I said about you being pregnant," he starts.

"I was sick out of guilt and worry," I cut in. "Because of the text I'd sent to Ruby. It's nothing else."

"You don't know that."

"I do. I can't have kids."

"Raven, you don't know that. You're guessing because of the backstreet abortion. Nothing is impossible."

"Jesus, Mac," I cry, dropping my towel. "I'm not pregnant, and even if I was, I'd be heading straight for the abortion clinic. I'd hate to complicate your life any more than it already is. So, please, go and pack, start your life with Meghan or Ruby or whoever the fuck you want. But trust me, you'll never hear from me again."

"What changed? You just sat here begging me to stay."

"You've made it clear how you feel. You don't love me. If you did, you'd never have kept any of that from me. If you knew me at all, you'd have trusted that you could tell me all of that, and I wouldn't have judged you. And that isn't because I'm weak. It's because I love the idea of love. It makes me a fool, and it makes me misjudge people, and it gets me hurt over and over, but I'll never change because I'm a good person."

"I wanted to tell you so many times."

"You should have. We all have a past, and I never expected yours to be squeaky clean."

"I'm too ashamed to talk about it," he admits.

"And you don't think I was ashamed sharing my past with you? You think it was easy to tell you about all those men and what happened to me as a kid?"

"No, but that's different, Raven. You had no control over any of that. I did. What I did was my own selfish choice."

We're going around in circles, arguing over whose decisions are worse, and I'm done. I send a quick S.O.S. text off to Anna. It's what all the girls use when they need rescuing, and it works because within a minute, she's at the door. "I made plans with Anna," I tell Mac. "You should go now."

He glances at his watch. "At seven in the morning?"

"Yes."

Anna nods awkwardly. "Gym."

I button my dress and grab my gym bag from under the bed to make the lie believable. He presses his lips together, clearly wanting to out me on my lie, but instead, he nods. He grabs his t-shirt and places a gentle kiss on my head. "I'm sorry, Raven."

"Me too," I mutter, and he leaves, taking my heart with him.

MAC

I've felt pain like this before. The way my heart twists in my chest and the sick feeling in the pit of my stomach. I didn't intend to hurt Raven, and knowing that I have makes the ache so much worse. I want to go back to last night. I want to go back to being happy in the bar with the Pres and his wife. I want to be laughing with Raven about something stupid she's said or done. I don't want to be here with Ruby, parking up my bike in the same spot I used to all those months ago.

Ace decided to stay in London. I don't blame him. He had his own issues with this place, so returning wasn't an option. I place my helmet under my arm and follow Ruby inside. There're a few brothers around who nod their head in greeting but don't bother to make a fuss. Why would they? They fucking hate me. My eyes lock with my mum's. She's wiping down the tables in the bar, pausing for a second, and then she looks away and continues her work.

I knock on the office door and wait for the President, Deano, to call me in. When he does, he stares at me for a solid minute before pointing to a chair in front of his desk. "Sit." I do. He's a big bastard and not someone I want to get on the wrong side of . . . again. "Didn't think you'd come," he adds.

"Almost didn't."

"I would have called you sooner if I'd known how bad the situation was. I didn't know until Ruby left for London. I mean, I knew about Meghan and her refusing to get out of bed and shit, but I didn't know about the baby. I just thought she'd come around in her own time."

"How's things been since I've been gone?"

"Weird. It ain't the same without you, Cain, and Ace causing me problems," he says, adding a smirk. "Quiet without the three amigos." Hearing his nickname for the three of us makes me feel sick to my stomach.

"How's Mum and Dad?"

"They're surviving, that's about all. I keep sending your pops out on runs, but he ain't how he used to be. More quiet and withdrawn, I guess."

"I'll try to keep a low profile. See if I can help with Meghan. I don't intend to be around longer than I need to be."

"I know feelings are running high around here, brother, but at the end of the day, you're a Kings Reaper. Always have been and always will be. Ain't no brother here who's perfect or hasn't been caught with his dick in something it shouldn't have been in. You stay here as long as you need to."

I give a small, sad smile. If only it was that easy. "Can I go up and see Meghan?"

"Of course. You're in the room next to her. Thought maybe being close might help her."

I take the stairs to the second floor and find my room. It's basic, which is all I need for now. I chuck my bag on the bed and go to Meghan's room, knocking once before entering. She's sleeping, so I take a seat on the rocking chair beside the bed and watch her. She looks pale and thin. There're dark circles under her eyes, and her hair is dull and greasy with dark roots showing through her blonde locks. It's a far cry from the Meghan I once knew. She'd never be caught without makeup or shiny blonde hair.

RAVEN

The women are fussing and it's driving me nuts. I'm sad, heartbroken even, but all the fussing is making me worse. I had to escape to the office for a few hours just to breathe. It's Sunday, and Vinn isn't around, which I'm grateful for. I lose myself in paperwork and try to push thoughts of Mac out of my mind.

It's almost lunchtime when Vinn turns up, surprised to see me. "Sunday," he says, as if I didn't know what day it was.

"I was at a loose end and thought I'd come in and catch up on all this charity bull," I say. Since Vinn gave to charity, I've been buried in figures and publicity and other charities asking for money.

"You and your lover boy have a fight?" I shake my head and continue to stare at my laptop. "Liar."

"I'm finishing up here and heading home," I say.

"Actually, if you're at a loose end, I could do with you for a business lunch. It's at the golf club, and they serve a very nice roast dinner," he says. I want to keep busy, so I nod. It's not like I have anything else to do.

MAC

Meghan wakes after an hour of me watching her like some creep. She blinks a few times and her brow furrows. "Cain?" she whispers. I shake my head and pain washes over her face. "Mac?"

"Ruby told me you weren't looking after yourself."

"Go away," she whispers, tears filling her eyes.

"She said the twins miss you and you won't see them."

"Please," she cries.

I shake my head. "Get up. You need a shower. When was the last time you fucking showered?" I rip the sheets back, and she screams angrily. She's wearing one of Cain's shirts, but it looks dirty, and I wonder if she's worn this since he died. I grab her wrist and pull her to stand. Her swollen stomach protrudes, and I stare at it. "Shower, now."

"No!" she yells, trying to pull free.

I keep hold of her, dragging her kicking and screaming to the en-suite bathroom, then I turn on the shower. She's sobbing so hard, her thin body is shaking. "Get in the shower, Meg, or I'll put you in it." She's still trying to pull free, so I take her by both arms and move her under the warm jet of water, soaking her shirt through. "No," she cries, staring down at the shirt. "It smells of him." Each time I release her, she tries to escape, so I step in with her.

"Meg, calm down. If you stop, I can take the shirt off for you." She stills, and I carefully release her. When I'm sure she isn't going to run, I take the hem of the shirt and lift it over her head. She stands like a child, her hair sticking to her face and her arms by her sides. I throw the shirt in the sink. "I'm gonna wash you now." I reach for some shampoo and squirt a good amount into my hand. I don't think she's washed it in months. I gently lather her hair, and she closes her eyes, relaxing as I massage it into her head. I take the showerhead from the wall and begin rinsing. My mind wanders to Raven and how we'd wash each other in the shower. I miss her already and it's only been a few hours.

When we're done and she's fully washed, I wrap her in a towel. Cain's t-shirt is too wet to put back on, so I sit her on the bed. "I'll be back," I tell her, but she looks at me blankly.

I go back to my room and change into joggers and a fresh t-shirt. Next, I head up to Cain's room. He had another bedroom for when Meg had the kids in bed with her. The twins would take hours to settle some nights. The second I open the door and smell his aftershave, I shudder. How is it possible it still smells of him when he's been gone months? It's untouched. His bed sheets are still scrunched on his bed, and there are clothes strewn over the chair. I search through and find a used shirt. As I leave, I glance in the mirror and catch a glimpse of my guilt-ridden face. Stuck on the mirror is a photograph of me and Cain, side by side. Fuck, I miss him.

RAVEN

Mac's been gone a few days, and it's not getting any easier like the girls promised it would. In fact, it's getting harder. I can't sleep, eat, or smile, all things he made possible by just being around. Vinn places a sandwich on my desk. Since he realised Mac's left, he's been really good, keeping me busy and bringing me lunch. "Thanks," I say as brightly as I can.

"You look tired, Corvo."

"I'm fine."

"That's all you say when I point out truths. But you're not fine. I can see you're not fine."

I sigh. "I'll be fine, in time."

"You want me to have him killed?" he offers.

I smile. "No, I don't want him killed. People survive worse things than a little heartbreak."

"Doesn't make it hurt any less, though," he says, taking a seat at my desk. "Look, why don't you reconsider this evening. I know you don't feel in the mood for a party, but you'll be missed, and Leia really wants you to go." It's Gia's birthday, and Vinn's arranged a lavish party at his club. He's gone all out and everyone from the club is going, but the thought of having to smile and make idle conversation all evening makes me feel ill. Since Mac left, all I do is work and sleep. Netflix has become my new best friend. "I could do with you there to keep everything organised, even if you just come for the first hour or so."

"We'll see," I say, knowing full well I won't show.

Leia is waiting for me when I finally arrive home. I dropped by Vinn's club on my way to check everything was running smoothly, which it was, so I figured I could come back here and make the most of the quiet night while they're all out partying. Only Leia isn't having any of it as she lays out a new dress on my bed. "This is perfect for you." The short, flared, red dress is pretty and something I'd choose if I was to buy it. Teamed with the heels she's holding up, it's a stunning outfit.

"I have a headache. I'm just gonna go to bed."

"And watch reruns of *Friends* on your own? Snap out of it, Raven."

"I'm gonna sleep. An early night will do me good."

"You're coming, whether you like it or not. Chains will carry you over his shoulder if I tell him to," she threatens.

"Leia, seriously, haven't you ever had a break-up so bad you can't stand the thought of making small talk all evening?"

"Yes," she says firmly. "When Chains left the club, I was devastated, but I carried on. And now, you have to."

I sigh, and she pulls me in for a hug. "It's taken a long time for me to like you, Raven. Don't piss me off now." I smile against her shoulder. She has such a way with words.

MAC

The two people who don't hate me around here are my niece, Rose, and my nephew, Shelby. When they first saw me four days ago, they were over the moon. Rose kept touching my face and telling me how much I looked like her daddy. It was sad and cute all at the same time. They've recently turned four and they don't quite understand why their mummy is hiding away from the world. The brothers are civil towards me, not exactly friendly, but they're not ignoring me either, which is fine by me, I get it. My parents avoid me at all costs. Mum can't bring herself to look at me. I guess having me here is a reminder of what they've all lost.

That's why I can't stay here. Once Meghan is feeling better, I'll go, but not back to London. Hurting Raven after getting her to trust me has been an all-time low to add to my collection.

I settle on the picnic blanket next to Meg. It's taken four days to get her from the room and into the fresh air. The twins are playing with a ball, and she watches them with tears in her eyes. She hasn't spoken to me, not since the shower incident four days ago, but each day I've sat with her, forced her to shower and brush her teeth, and brought her food, even though she hardly eats it.

"Meg, we have to talk about the baby," I try for the third time. "You need a scan to check it's okay and to find out how far along you are." She stays quiet. "I booked it. We're leaving in ten minutes." This snaps her out of her trance, and she glares at me. "We need to know whose baby it is," I say bluntly.

"It's mine," she whispers.

"And maybe mine," I say, pleased she's finally spoken.

"We'll never know, though, will we?" she mumbles.

The chances of doing a DNA test and getting an accurate result are slim since me and Cain were twins. "We will if the dates don't add up."

"Look at me," she hisses, leaning back to show her small bump. "I could only be a few months. He's been dead for three."

"You've lost a lot of weight. It's hard to tell."

Mum approaches us. I'd asked Ruby to ask her if she'd have the twins while we go for the scan. She looks past us to the kids. "Thanks for this, Mum," I say, but she doesn't acknowledge me. I sigh, standing and holding out my hand to Meg. She pushes herself up without my help, and I roll my eyes, heading for my bike.

"Do you have any idea how far along you might be?" asks the sonographer with a gentle smile. I'd already explained on the telephone that Meg's husband had recently died, and so she's not been in touch with the doctor or a midwife. Meg shakes her head and stares blankly ahead at the wall. The sonographer gives me a sympathetic smile and goes about setting up the machine.

"You'll need to pull your top up," she adds, but Meg stays still, completely ignoring her. Instead, I roll up Meg's top, and the sonographer squirts a clear liquid on her stomach. She spends a few minutes silently rolling the scanner over Meg's bump, occasionally giving an awkward smile. "Meghan, you're due," she says carefully. "Your baby is full term. It could arrive any day."

Meghan sucks in a surprised breath, then bursts into tears, sobbing into her hands. I begin pacing, hardly believing my ears. The baby isn't mine. It can't be mine. "Oh, sweetie," says the sonographer, handing her some tissues. "Would you like to know what you're having?" she asks, and Meg nods. "It's a boy."

I feel Meg's body shaking all the way back to the club as she lets her tears flow. We go inside, and she sweeps the twins against her and kisses them over and over. Mum looks on in annoyance. Meg leads the kids away, and I take a seat. Dad is on the couch also, so it's the perfect time to talk.

Chapter Eighteen

RAVEN

I slip out of my heels and rub one of my feet. Leia was right—coming to the party was a great idea. I haven't thought of Mac for at least three minutes. I smile to myself and press the champagne bottle to my lips, taking a swig. I hate this stuff, so I screw my face up but take another drink regardless.

Vinn sits beside me and takes my foot, placing it in his lap and rubbing it. I groan aloud, unashamed by the fact I'm enjoying this so much. He grins, shaking his head. "Are you having a good night?"

"Yes." I swig another mouthful and hold the bottle up as if this explains my good time.

"Glad you came?"

"Where's Sofia?"

"She'll be here later. She's at a family meal first." The wedding is just three weeks away now, after Sofia delayed it. I haven't spoken to Vinn about it at all, and apart from making the odd phone call to check up on things, I've had little to do with it. "Have you heard from Mac?" he asks, taking my other foot and rubbing it.

I shake my head. I've picked up my phone to call him a dozen times but talked myself out of it. In a moment of weakness, after he first left, I texted him to see how he was, but he didn't reply. That was enough to tell me all I needed to know. I refuse to be like Ruby, calling constantly only to be ignored.

"I'm not hitting on you," says Vinn warily, and I narrow my eyes. "Promise," he adds. "I just wanted to let you know that the apartment I bought is still empty. If you need a place to get away, you're more than welcome to stay there."

"Why have you kept it?"

He smiles sadly. "Heartbreak is a funny emotion." Placing my foot on the floor, he stands gracefully. He produces a key from his pocket and stares at it for a few seconds. A look of conflict passes over his face before he reaches down and takes my hand. He presses the key into my palm, looking me in the eye.

I glance down. The address is on the key tag, and it's not far from the office. I love being at the club, I really do, but lately, I feel like it would be nice to get away. Maybe I'll go check it out tomorrow.

I stumble as I feel my way along the wall. Maybe the whole bottle of champagne was a little too much. Giggling to myself, I carefully climb the three steps that lead to the brightly lit apartment complex. I pull the key tag closer to my face, frowning at the small writing. The cab dropped me right outside and promised this was the right place. There's a man sitting behind a large concierge desk, and he smiles as I enter. "How can I help?"

I dangle the key Vinn gave me, and the man nods, standing. He presses for the lift and guides me inside. "Maybe I should help you to your apartment," he adds, laughing.

We get out on the top floor, where there's one door opposite the lift. He leans me against the wall and takes the key, unlocking the door and helping me inside.

I stare wide-eyed at the large open-plan apartment. It's amazing. Nothing like what I expected. "Whoa, this place is fucking huge," I gasp, and the man laughs again.

He points to a white keypad on the wall. "If you need anything, dial number nine and I'll try to help." He leaves, closing the door behind him.

I wander around in awe. The decor is classy and exactly the sort of thing I'd pictured Vinn to have in his own place. It's nice, completely out of my league, and so quiet. After years at the club, this place is tranquil and exactly what I need right now. There's a door leading to the bedroom, which is also big with an en-suite bathroom.

I flop on the king-size bed and kick off my shoes. Taking my mobile from my bag, I snap a picture of myself smiling. I send it to Vinn with a text to say I like the apartment.

My finger hovers over Mac's name. Maybe I should call to see how he is. It's almost two in the morning, so he'll probably be asleep anyway. I chew on my lip, contemplating what to do when Vinn texts back with a smiley emoji. It makes me jump and I almost drop the phone. When I catch it, I press 'call' by accident.

"Fuck," I whisper, sitting up. I let it ring a couple of times and I'm about to cancel when he answers.

"Raven?" His growly voice sends a shiver down my spine.

"How are you?" I mutter.

"It's two in the morning. Why are you awake? Is everything okay?"

"I've been to Gia's birthday party."

He falls silent for a minute. "Did you have a good night?"

"Yeah. How are you?"

"Where are you now? It's quiet."

I look around the freshly painted bedroom. "In an apartment."

"Whose apartment? Where?" he asks, sounding worried. It pleases me he's worried, it means he still cares.

"Just an apartment," I say, not wanting to confess to being in Vinn's place. "What are you doing?"

"Are you alone?" he asks.

"Are you?" I counter.

"Mac?" I hear a woman say his name and wince.

"Coming," he replies. "Sorry, I have to go," he adds to me.

"Sure. Sorry, I won't call again. I don't know why I did really, too much champagne," I mutter with a laugh.

"Champagne?" he repeats. "You're at Vinn's place?" he guesses because who the hell drinks champagne at the MC bar?

"Take care, Mac." I disconnect as my heart races in my chest. I shouldn't have done that. It doesn't help my heart.

MAC

I place my phone on my bedside table. "Everything okay?" I ask Meghan. When she doesn't answer, I go to my bathroom, where she's sitting on the toilet. "Meg?"

"I think my water just broke," she announces, looking up at me with shock.

"Seriously?" I gasp, panic setting in, and she nods. Since the scan earlier, she's been different, more relaxed. She came to my room half an hour ago to say she felt unwell, so I made her a sandwich and a glass of milk. "What do I do?"

"I packed a hospital bag, it's in my room on my bed. I need that and my phone."

I rush off to get them, and when I return, she's pacing the room. "Shall I get someone?" I ask.

She scoffs. She's just as much hated as I am. "I need to call the hospital and tell them about my water." I wait while she calls ahead, and they tell her to wait until her contractions are two minutes apart before setting off.

<hr />

It's another three hours of her pacing and panting before her contractions get to almost two minutes apart. I rub her back, rinse her cold flannel, and play song requests. When it's time to leave, I knock on my parents' door, and Dad answers looking tired and groggy. "Sorry to wake you," I say. "I'm just letting you know Meghan's in labour. I'm gonna take her to the hospital." He nods, not bothering to use words. I tried to talk to them earlier, but it ended in yelling, so I walked away.

When we get to the hospital, her contractions are a minute apart and she's rushed straight onto the labour suite. They help her change and get her on the bed to examine her. I try to leave, but she grabs my hand and holds me there. It feels wrong being here, it should be Cain. But I stay, because I know he'd expect me to step up, despite what I did. And he wouldn't want her to go through this alone.

I stand by the side of her bed, her hand gripping mine tightly. "It's time to push," instructs the midwife. "When you feel the next contraction, go for it." She then turns to me. "Dad, you can help by—"

"He's not the father," Meghan pants, "thankfully."

I smirk. "Cheers, Meg."

The midwife nods. "Okay, whatever. Let's just get this baby here."

Meg makes a grunting sound and squeezes my hand until my fingers turn white. "You're hurting me," I whisper, close to her ear.

She presses her chin to her chest but opens one eye. "Are you fucking kidding?"

I swallow as her nails dig into my skin. "Yep, totally kidding, squeeze away," I mumble, wincing. She groans louder, wrapping her arm around my neck and pulling me closer. "Headlock, perfect," I mutter.

"Oh Jesus," she cries, her nails digging into my shoulder. "I can't do this." She suddenly bursts into tears, and I look to the midwife for help.

"You're nearly there, Meghan. One more push and the head will be out."

"Hear that?" I whisper, brushing her hair from her face and smiling. "One more push and your son's head will be out. You can do this, Meg, you pushed the twins out with no problem. Cain told me they flew out like rockets."

She gives me a watery smile. "I miss him so much."

I nod. "Me too."

She sucks in a breath, squeezing her eyes together and making that deep, growling noise again. "That's it," I say encouragingly. "Nearly there." I glance down to where the midwife is looking and gasp in amazement. The baby's head is almost out. "You're doing amazing."

"Get back up here," she hisses, grabbing my hand and yanking me away from that end. I smirk, apologising.

By the time Cain Junior arrives, I'm in awe of Meghan. She gave birth like a boss. I've never thought about birth and the process. You see pregnant women all the time and then they just appear with a baby in their arms. I never considered the amount of pain or stress it takes to bring it into the world, but now I've seen it with my own eyes, I'll never forget it.

Meghan has to stay in hospital overnight, so I head back to the club. It's strange without her because we've literally spent every second together, even though she never spoke to me, but with everyone either avoiding us or ignoring us, it was easier to form an alliance.

Mum is with the twins. She looks up when I approach. "How is she?" Her voice is low, like she doesn't want anyone to hear her.

"She's good. Cain Junior is healthy and feeding well. She should be home tomorrow."

"Cain Junior?" she repeats.

"Yeah. She said it the second she held him."

"Did you stay for the birth?" she asks. I nod, not sure how she'll feel, but she smiles, nodding.. "Good."

"Yah know, when she gets home, she'll need you and Dad to support her." Mum glances past me to where Dad is sitting at the bar. "It's

Cain's baby, and he isn't here. You need to help her. I got her out of bed and washed, you need to help her look after her kids."

"It's not that easy," she mutters.

"It is. You just help her. She can't do it alone. She's grieving and heartbroken."

"And so she should be," comes Dad's voice as he approaches. He stands behind the couch where Mum sits and rubs her shoulders. "It isn't our job to bring her kids up."

"They're Cain's kids too."

"So she says," he mutters.

"Are you serious?" I hiss angrily.

Mum stands. "Let's take this away from the twins."

I follow them into the kitchen, close the door, and glare at Dad. "Those kids are Cain's. All three of them. Meghan is part of the family, and she needs you."

"She ruined this family," growls Dad.

"*We* did," I say, nodding. "*We* fucked up and *we* wrecked everything, and we have to live with what we did forever. I think about it every single fucking day and that's the least I deserve, but Meghan, she doesn't deserve your hate. I pursued her. I talked her around. It was my fault. I've been on self-destruct for as long as I can remember, and if I could change anything, it would be that I was the one hit that night, not him. But I can't change it. And I can't run from it anymore."

"Do you know how many times I've wished it was you?" Dad asks, and Mum gasps, covering her mouth in shock. "Thanks to you, his kids will grow up without him. They went from having a great dad and a fun uncle to losing both." He almost chokes on a sob, and I feel his pain hit my chest. He's never cried, not in front of me anyway.

"And then I get angry at myself for wishing my only son dead. And I don't know what's worse," he takes a breath to hide the sob, "having you alive and hating you or having you gone from our lives completely, but either way, we lose. We lost Cain, and then we lost you."

Mum places a hand on his shoulder, her own tears flowing freely. "I'm trying to look at you how I used to, but it's fucking hard, Mac. What you did was so selfish and reckless that I can't get my head around it. All the women in this place and you chose her. Cain worshipped her. She was his world."

"I know," I mutter.

"Did he do something?" I shake my head. "Was it jealousy?" I shrug. "That's not enough!" he suddenly yells, slamming his hands on the table. "Help me understand it, so I don't feel like it was completely senseless."

I lower into a chair and put my head in my hands. "It wasn't about him. Not really. I was unhappy with Ruby. And so fucking depressed I hated myself, which made me hate her. And then Meg came into our lives and she was like a breath of fresh air. It wasn't the first time I'd met her. I'd seen her out and about in town, and we even chatted a few times, but she wasn't available then. When Cain brought her home, something inside me clicked. I guess I thought maybe it was meant to be. But then she got pregnant with the twins."

Dad and Mum join me at the table. "She struggled, and Cain was always out on runs, desperate to escape baby duty. I helped out, we got close. It wasn't intentional then, it was coincidental. Old feelings came back, and I convinced myself it was okay because I was unhappy. If I'd have known that it would lead to months of sneaking around, I would never have gone there. I thought I needed a night to get her out of my system. Turns out, I couldn't let her go."

Mum wipes her eyes on a tissue. "Did you love her?"

I nod. "A lot."

We fall silent, all thinking about my confession. We'd never sat and spoken about any of it. When Cain died, Meg couldn't handle the guilt, so she confessed all to the cops who were investigating, and it all came out. My parents were too busy yelling and grieving to talk rationally about it or understand. We even had to stay away from his funeral. But I see now that leaving wasn't a solution, it just prolonged the pain.

"Your mum thinks Cain wouldn't want us to cut you from our lives," Dad mutters. "She wanted to reach out to you so many times, but I just couldn't. I couldn't forgive you, and I don't know if I ever can. But knowing that you loved her, I guess that makes it a little easier to understand."

"I don't expect you to forgive me. I can't forgive myself. All I'm asking is that you forgive her. Help her to raise Cain's kids because he'd want that. He'd want you to look after his wife."

"Are you and her?"

I shake my head. "No. Neither of us can handle our guilt, and Meg regrets everything. She's so cut up over Cain, I don't know if she'll ever move on. For her, it was an escape from the boring housewife she thought she'd become. She felt unattractive and unloved. Knowing Cain Junior is his baby is a huge relief for her."

Dad nods, and Mum takes his hand. "Where did you go?" he asks.

"London."

"Are they expecting you back?"

I shake my head. "No. I kind of fucked up there too."

Dad rolls his eyes almost playfully, and it reminds me of how we used to be together. "A woman?"

I nod. "Yep. Broke her heart to come back here."

"If she loves you, she'll forgive you," says Mum, patting my hand.

Chapter Nineteen

RAVEN

I'm becoming great friends with the concierge guy who looks after the apartments. His name is Cyril and he's like the grandpa I never had. He greets me warmly each time I get home, and if I'm laden with bags, he'll take them and walk me to the apartment. He has eight grandchildren and a wife named Susan. I imagine they spend Christmases together laughing over a giant turkey and piles of presents. We often spend time chatting in the reception. They have a red chaise lounge where I'll sit, and he makes me tea from a little kettle he has behind his desk.

Tonight, we're so deep in conversation, it takes a second for either of us to look at Vinn when he enters. He's dishevelled, far from the man I'm used to seeing. "Hey, are you okay?"

"No," he mutters.

I glance at Cyril as he raises his bushy eyebrows and shrugs his shoulders. "I'll catch up with you later. Thanks for the tea." I place the cup on the desk and head for the lift.

We step inside the apartment, and Vinn grabs my wrist, spinning me to face him and hauling me against his solid chest. I'm so shocked, I freeze, and as his lips crash against mine, I make a choked sound in the back of my throat because this all feels wrong. He realises I'm not responding and pulls back, frowning. "Kiss me!" he demands.

I shake my head. "No." His behaviour seems erratic, and it puts me on edge. "What's going on?"

"I'm getting married," he yells, his face frantic. "Married."

I step from his arms and head for the coffee machine. "This isn't new news," I say.

He grips the counter and hangs his head. "What if it doesn't work out?"

I smile, turning to face him. "Vinn, it will. I mean, maybe not if you keep kissing other women, but embrace marriage and the rest will flow naturally."

"It's not me. I'm not the kind of man who gets married."

"Well, as of Saturday, you are."

My mind goes to Mac, as it often does. It's been three weeks since I last spoke to him on the phone. I've heard nothing since, and I've refrained from making an arse of myself a second time by calling or texting him.

"Fuck," mutters Vinn, burying his head in his hands. I pour him a black coffee.

"It's just last-minute nerves. They'll pass. You said yourself, you don't have a choice in this, so make the best of a bad situation and suck it up. How's Sofia feeling?"

"I don't know. She hardly talks to me. Good start to a marriage, right?"

"Because of us?"

"Partly. I think she's just as unsure as me. But I've got to man up and make her think I'm confident in us, that we're doing the right thing."

I smile sympathetically. "You're overthinking this. If anything, I feel bad for her. She caught you kissing me, so she's not going to trust you. And since she's moved from Italy to London, I bet she's having major doubts right now."

"Maybe she won't turn up, then it isn't on me."

"What happens if she doesn't show?"

"I get to walk away with my head held high, and she will be shipped off to fuck knows where for embarrassing her father."

"Wow, that's unfair after what you did."

"We did," he corrects. "Riggs arranged a stag night. I bailed."

"Why? You should make the most of others wanting to hang out with you. I don't suppose you get that often?" I smirk, and he laughs.

"I wish we'd worked it out," he mutters.

I press my lips in a tight line. "Things happen for a reason, Vinn. We were never going to work. I'm rooting for you and Sofia; I hope you're both very happy together." And I realise I actually mean that. I'm over Vinn Romano and it feels good.

MAC

I lie back against the headboard of Meghan's bed. Cain is sleeping against my chest, and Meghan is taking a shower. She's been amazing. These last few weeks, I've seen a huge change in her. Cain, or CJ, as we've been calling him, is a chilled baby, and the bond they have is tight. My parents have been helping her, and I think that's a huge weight off Meg's mind. I don't know if the guilt of our decisions will ever go away completely, but we're slowly moving forward. And that's why I've decided to move on.

Meg steps into the room and smiles at the sight before her. "Cute," she mutters.

"I'm gonna hit the road in the morning," I announce, and she bites on her lower lip. "You have my parents back on side, and they'll help with the kids."

"Have you told Ruby?"

I shake my head. Since returning, she's avoided me, and I'm happy with that. Dad seems to think she's moved on to another brother and that's fine also. I hurt her and I was a coward. I want her to move forward and meet a man who'll take care of her the way she deserves. "I'll call and check in with you. If you want me to."

She nods. "Are you going back to London? To Raven?" We've spent countless nights talking about Raven and mistakes I've made. I shake my head again. "Why?"

"You know why. I hurt her. She deserves better."

"For goodness' sake, Mac, stop punishing yourself. If Raven loves you as much as I think she does, she'll forgive you. Your head must have been all over, thinking I was pregnant with your kid, and then Ruby turning up like that. She'll understand."

"I need a fresh start."

"You said she was sick when you left. You thought she might be pregnant. Shouldn't you go back and find out?"

I kiss Cain on the head. Since being at the birth, the thought of Raven having my kid warms my cold fucking heart. The thought of filling her with my babies is the best feeling in the world. "She said it was down to stress. Anyway, she'd call me if she was."

"Would she? After everything?"

I let that seed of doubt sit in my mind. Raven never spoke of wanting kids. Would she keep my baby now that I've moved away? She'd mentioned abortion already.

It's almost ten when I get back to my bedroom. I stare at Raven's name on my phone for a good minute before calling her number. I'm about to give up when it connects. "Hello?" It's a man's voice, and for a second, I don't know what to say. Maybe she's moved on.

"Is Raven around?" I eventually ask.

"Nope."

"Vinn, what the hell are you doing?" comes Raven's voice. There's a rustling sound and she comes to the phone. "Hello?"

"It's Mac," I say, feeling like an idiot. "Vinn," I repeat with an unamused laugh.

"It's not like that," she says.

"You said that once before to me, turned out it was exactly like that. Isn't he getting married in a couple of days?"

"Mac, it's really not like that, but I don't have to explain myself to you. Why are you calling?"

"Never mind. It wasn't important." I disconnect.

My mobile begins ringing, and Raven's name flashes up. I reconnect. "How dare you hang up on me? I am not fucking Vinn. In fact, I was really proud of myself tonight because I realised that I'm over him. So, don't you dare call me up for no reason and make me feel like shit."

"Raven, I—"

"No," she yells. "You can't keep popping in and out of my life. If you call me, it should be for a reason. Don't get my hopes up and then disconnect." She groans. "I'm making an idiot of myself. I have to go."

"No, Raven, pl—" It's too late. She cancels the call.

I pull the rucksack from under my bed and begin packing up my clothes. If I turn up in person, there's no way she can hang up on me.

I waited for morning before setting off to London. I had to say goodbye to my parents and Meghan. When I left before, it was under a cloud, but this time, it felt less black and heavy.

Ace and Brick are outside when I pull up. They greet me with smiles and slaps on the back, completely different to the brothers back in Nottingham. This feels like home. We head inside, and I go to see Riggs in his office. "Are you here to stay?" he asks, pouring me a drink.

I shrug. "If Raven will have me."

"Brother, she's hardly been around. She told Chains she's enjoying time on her own in some apartment near her office."

"Vinn's apartment," I mutter, wondering if she lied to me on the phone last night.

Riggs smirks. "I don't blame her. I'd love some fucking peace and quiet."

"I'll wait until the wedding," I say. "Surprise her."

"You're a braver man than me."

Chapter Twenty

RAVEN

It's the day of the wedding, and Vinn's been non-stop calling me to sort out last-minute problems. I find myself rushing around with my heels in my hand, at the London's Mayfair Hotel, where the bridal party is staying, trying to locate a missing bride's bouquet.

I'm pretty sure this is why the bride has a maid of honour and the groom has a best man, but Vinn seems to think I'd be better at it. While I'm waiting at the front desk for the receptionist to check the back room, an older, Italian-looking man approaches me. "Sorry, I overheard you telling the receptionist that you're Vinn's personal assistant?" I nod, adding a smile. "It's just that I have a problem and I need your help."

I glance around. "Erm, I'm not sure I can."

"I'm Sofia's uncle. She's currently locked herself in the bathroom just over there, and if I tell anyone in the family, well, it probably won't end well. Maybe you could speak to her?"

I feel the colour draining from my face as I shake my head. "That's really not a good idea. I don't really know her, and Vinn would go mad at me if I mess it up."

"Please," he whispers, desperation clear on his face. "I don't want to tell her parents about this."

I groan and roll my eyes. "Fine. I'll try, but I don't think it'll make anything better."

I step into the bathroom. It's huge with large mirrors on the wall and gold wash basins. There's a deep red couch in the centre, and I take a seat. "Sofia?" I hear a sniffle. "Your uncle asked me to come in here. It's Raven, by the way." When she doesn't answer, I sigh. "You probably don't want to speak to me. I wouldn't want to if I was you." I pause for her reply but receive nothing. "You must be really nervous. Marriage is a big step."

"I don't even know him," she mumbles, sniffling louder.

"It does seem odd marrying a man you don't know. And it's not like Vinn's the most loving, romantic person."

"He's rude and bossy," she admits.

I smile to myself. "He is. And so arrogant."

"Are you still sleeping with him?" she almost whispers.

"No. I told you, it was over ages ago. I moved on."

The lock clicks, and she steps from the toilet. She's wearing a silk robe and her hair is pinned into a beautiful style of curls with small pearls. Her makeup is in place and she looks flawless. "Wow."

She smiles a little and joins me on the couch. "I'm worried it won't work."

"Understandable. You don't know each other, you've moved here with no friends, and you're not in love."

"Aren't you supposed to be talking me into this wedding?"

I grin. "But I can tell you that once you get to know Vinn, he's fantastic. He puts on a front, but underneath it all, he's kind and loving and possessive, and he'll love you so hard, you'll never want anyone else."

Sofia falls silent, staring down at the large diamond engagement ring. "It's not like I have a choice, is it?"

I shrug. "I guess not. Look, I know we got off to a terrible start, but if you ever need anything, I'm here. Marrying Vinn might not be as bad as you think."

Sofia doesn't look convinced but stands. "I should finish getting ready." She looks at her watch. "I'll see you in half an hour."

The receptionist finds the bouquet, and I hand it to Sofia's uncle, who rushes to her room to give it over. I check the seating in the room where they'll be exchanging vows and check everything is right, then I straighten the chair ribbons. "Thought I'd find you here." I spin to face Mac. I suck in a surprised breath. "You look like you've seen a ghost."

"You're back," I mutter.

"Yep. Thought I'd cheer Vinn up by attending his wedding." I'm too surprised to respond with a smile, so I just stare at him. My heart's beating wildly in my chest, and I don't know if I should laugh or cry. Is he back for the wedding, or is he back to see me? I have so many questions. He shifts uncomfortably before holding out a small package. "I got this, just in case."

I take it, frowning, and gasp when I peer inside the bag. "What the fuck?" There's a cough from the other side of the room, and I glance apologetically at the vicar. I grab Mac's arm and move him towards the door. "Why have you gotten me a pregnancy test?" He came all this way, and this is the first thing he offers me? Not an apology, or even a 'how the hell are ya', but a damn test.

"I want you to take it. You were sick when I left."

"I was sick with guilt for checking your phone. Seems I shouldn't have felt so bad, though, because I'd still be in the dark about your past, wouldn't I?"

"At least rule it out."

"Christ," I hiss, pressing the package hard into his chest until he takes it back. "That's why you came back? To make sure I wasn't carrying your child? How is Meghan, by the way?"

"Her kid isn't mine."

I laugh sarcastically. "I don't trust a word that comes out of your mouth."

"Call her . . . call Ruby . . . call my parents. The baby is Cain's. She was full term, pregnant way before I went there."

I roll my eyes in disgust. "Congratulations, you're off the hook."

"That's the weird thing, cos it made me see how badly I want kids," he explains.

I take a step back. "And you thought you'd turn up here, on my boss's wedding day, with a test?"

"Seeing CJ born was amazing, and I want that with you. I wanna see you give birth to my baby." I screw my face up. He's lost the plot. "I know I sound crazy." He pauses to take a breath. "Fuck, I'm messing this up. What I meant to say was, if you were pregnant, I wouldn't run a mile. I'd be really happy, Raven."

I shake my head, laughing at his absurd rantings. "First of all, who's to say I'd want your baby? And second of all, who's to say I'd want you in my life? You left, Mac. You made me trust you and feel safe, and then you left and you broke my heart." Tears threaten to leak from my eyes, so I put more distance between us. "What you did, was so much worse than Vinn. I have to go."

"I'm sorry, okay. I'm sorry I left—"

"Me too." I rush outside just in time for Vinn's car to arrive. I wipe my eyes and straighten my hair. Other guests are milling around, and I smile at a few people I recognise. Vinn steps in front of me, Ignoring everyone else. He narrows his eyes. "You're upset."

"I'm fine. Long morning. Are you ready to marry Sofia? She looks amazing."

"I think so. Too late now, anyway," he says, smiling. It fades as his eyes stare past me. I know he's seen Mac because his brow furrows. "He's back?"

"Seems so."

"Corvo, don't let him upset you. That offer still stands," he says, glancing around. "There's at least fifty people here right now who could dispose of him."

I laugh and straighten his tie. "I'm good. Thank you, though."

MAC

I watch the way she straightens Vinn's tie and laughs at whatever he's saying. Jealousy burns through me, but her words are playing on repeat in my head. I hurt her worse than Vinn ever could.

I make sure I'm sitting right behind Raven during the ceremony. She needs to know I'm not going away, despite the angry looks she keeps throwing my way. I want her to do the test, and I want her to accept that I'm back for good. Seeing her again only confirmed how I feel. I love her, and I'll spend the rest of my life making up for what I did to her.

Once the ceremony is over, we head through to the bar while the bride and groom have their pictures taken outside. I wait for everyone to be busy, then I slip into the dining hall and stare at the large seating plan by the entrance. There are three tables reserved solely for the Kings Reapers, and I'd called Gia yesterday to ensure I was included too. Raven is seated over the other side of the room, which annoys me. She's one of us, and technically, she's still my ol' lady. I take her name card from the board and move it next to mine, then I re-join everyone at the bar.

Ace is bending my ear about Nottingham, but I can't stop watching Raven. My body aches for her as she gracefully walks around the room, speaking to people as if I wasn't here. I hate not being on her radar, and I hate not having her attention. "Man, are you even listening to me?" snaps Ace. I shake my head, and he follows my gaze. "Leave her alone."

"I can't. I'm back here for her. I need her, brother."

"You need to stop obsessing over women. It only gets you in trouble."

"She's worth it."

"Mac, she isn't even living at the club. Vinn's got her some posh apartment, and we ain't seen her in weeks."

"Then help me get her home where she belongs."

"Or we could just let her do what she wants to do," he suggests.

"Not my style," I say, smirking.

The bride and groom enter the room and people begin clapping. I have an idea that I relay to Ace, so he can slip off and put it into action. It's crazy and probably won't work, but it's got to be worth a shot.

Vinn and Sofia stand at the entrance of the dining hall, greeting each and every one of us as we pass them. I stand behind Raven and watch her glance over the seating plan and frown. She must have known she wasn't sitting with us. "Well, look at that," I say in her ear, noticing the way she shivers at my voice. "It's my lucky night."

Anna sits on the other side of Raven, which gives her the perfect opportunity to ignore me and speak to her. She tells her about the wonderful apartment she's staying in. She's talking extra loudly so I can hear every detail, which only pisses me off. "Are you gonna ignore me all night?" I eventually ask.

"Yes, that's the plan."

"I know you, Raven, and I know you miss the club. You miss me."

She scoffs. "You really think you're something."

"And I missed you . . . so fucking much. Seeing you today, and not being able to touch you, is killing me."

"Well, lucky for you, I've wished you dead at least three times in the last ten minutes so—"

"Lies."

"You're good at those."

"Take a test."

"Fuck you."

I take the package from my inside pocket. "Raven, you're pregnant. Take a test."

"Suddenly you're a doctor?"

"Your tits are bigger. You've lost weight from not eating, but they're bigger. And you have a bump, a small one, but it's there. I know every inch of your body and I'm telling you, you're pregnant."

"Jesus, you're full of compliments. I'm due on my period, actually, which explains it."

"If you're so sure you're not, take a test."

Angry, she turns to face me, her eyes are blazing. "Okay, Mac. What do you think will happen if I find out I'm pregnant?"

I swallow hard. I know by her tone that whatever I say will be the wrong answer. "You'll forgive me, say you missed me, move back into the club, and we'll live happily ever after?"

"No." She arches her brow. "I'll book an appointment at the nearest clinic and sort the problem out."

"You don't mean that. You're hurting."

"You think I'd have a kid with you?"

"I've made mistakes, Raven. I never said I was an angel. But I know I want this. I want you. I love you." She stares wide-eyed. "I love you," I repeat. "I'm gonna tell you every day until you forgive me and say it back. And even if you're not pregnant now, you will be soon, because you're mine, Raven, and we're gonna spend forever together. I love you."

"I need the bathroom," she mutters, rushing off.

RAVEN

When I return, Mac is gone, and I breathe a sigh of relief. How dare he ruin today for me with his incessant nagging. I rub my hand over my stomach, wondering if I look fat. It's impossible, I've hardly eaten a thing and I've been sick loads. Not because of pregnancy, but from heartbreak.

The food is being served, so I take my place and chat with Anna while waiters work around us. Minutes later, Mac returns looking smug. "I love you," he says, sitting down. I ignore him and continue talking with Anna.

"Did he just say what I think he said?" Anna whispers. I nod, and she grins. "Is he staying in London?"

"He said he is."

"Isn't that a good thing?"

"No."

"She doesn't mean that. She loves me too," says Mac. "And I love her. And our baby." He places a white stick in my hand, and I glare at him. "I dipped your pee. Not sure how accurate that is with toilet water mixed in, but it's the only way I could get the test done."

"You followed me!" I hiss. He nods to the stick, and I look at it. Two blue lines fill the little window. "This isn't accurate. Someone could have peed before me. Are you the reason the toilet wouldn't flush?"

He nods proudly. "I had Ace tamper with the flushes."

"Oh my god, you've lost your mind. This is next level stalker behaviour. I am not pregnant. That test will not be accurate."

"Then do this one," he says, handing me another package. "Put your mind at rest."

I snatch the package angrily, reeling from the lengths he's going to, and stomp off to the bathroom. I'll have no trouble peeing a second time because I'm constantly peeing lately. And that doesn't mean anything, I tell myself. Nothing at all.

I pee on the stupid stick, then check my stomach in the large mirror while I wait for the result. I'm standing side on and rubbing my period belly when the door opens, and Mac comes in. "This is the girls' bathroom," I snap.

"And the mother of my child is here, so I have to be wherever she is."

"Don't call me that! It freaks me out, and I'll call security if you don't leave."

He grins. "Let's see if they can remove me."

I sit on the red couch and sigh. "Why are you doing this to me?"

"I told you, I love you."

"You don't love me, or you wouldn't have left. You'd have taken me with you."

"I regret it. I wish I had, but my head was a mess. I'd just seen Ruby for the first time since my brother died, and then she told me about Meg, and I was panicking. And I was ashamed. You finally knew what I'd done, and I couldn't stand to see the way you'd look at me."

"If you knew me, you'd know I wouldn't judge you like that."

"But I couldn't see that at the time, Raven, because I hated myself for it. I was so ashamed that I thought everyone would feel like that. And then I shut down my feelings before you realised what a dick I really was. That way, it wouldn't hurt so much when you dumped my cheating arse."

"I was working on getting over you," I mutter. "Just a few more weeks and I'd have cracked it. I've thrown myself into work, and I love the new apartment, but now you're here, messing it all up."

He takes the stick from the side and then joins me. "I am so fucking sorry for leaving you behind with no hope I'd come back. And I'm sorry I lied and that I hurt you. But I mean it, Raven . . . I love you. And I'm not saying I won't fuck up ever again. I will. But I'll try my hardest not to hurt you again, and I won't ever leave you. I promise. I wasn't gonna come back. I didn't want to face up to you, and that makes me a fucking coward. I rip things apart and run away. But the thought you could be having my kid means the world, and I had to face you, make right what I did wrong."

When I don't reply, he turns the test and smiles before showing me. "Oh fuck," I mutter when I see the two lines.

"You're not gonna forgive me easily, and I'm prepared for that. I'll work my arse off to prove myself, and I'll do whatever you want if it means you give me another chance."

"I'll make a terrible mum," I whisper, dread running through me.

"You'll be amazing," he says, lifting my chin to look into my eyes. "Fucking amazing."

"I don't know how to do it."

"We'll learn together."

"What if you leave again? I can't bring a child up alone."

"I'll never leave. I'll marry you right here and now to prove it."

I laugh nervously. "People leave marriages all the time."

"I'll stay by your side twenty-four-seven," he says. "You can cuff me to you."

"Then I'll be the one running away," I joke.

"Please, Raven. Please give me a chance to prove myself. I'm begging. You can punish me however you like. I deserve it. I'll let you check my phone, screen my calls, check in with me whenever I leave your side." I sigh, glancing at the test again. "Your place is in this club with me, Raven. We belong together. Think about how happy we were before I screwed it all up. There're no secrets now, nothing to get in the way. I'll do whatever you ask. You're in control, you're calling the shots."

I've always been weak when it comes to men, and him begging like this is something I always fall for right before I get hurt again. "A baby is a huge step."

"One we're gonna master. I know you're nervous, but we'll have help at the club, and I'll be there every step of the way. It's okay to worry. All mums feel like that."

"But I didn't have a mum to learn from."

"I did, so I'll help. Raven, you know how to love. You love so hard and fast, it gets you into trouble. When you hold your baby, you'll feel it, and you'll love him or her. The rest we'll figure out."

"I can't just forgive you like that. You really hurt me, Mac. We have to take it slow."

He nods eagerly with hope in his eyes. "Slow, okay."

"And we keep this between us."

"Anna already knows. She'll have told the girls."

I groan. I'm not sure how I feel about people knowing. Mac takes my hand and gently kisses it. "It's going to be okay. I promise." And somehow, I believe him. He's right—the only place I've ever felt at home is at the club with him by my side. *He* is my home. My place is here with Mac . . . with Mac and our unborn child.

As if sensing my resolve, he leans in and kisses me. I close my eyes and marvel in the feeling of having him with me again. I've missed him so damn much, and I'm kidding myself if I thought I'd ever get over him, because he is it for me. My love, my world, and everything in between. I might not turn out to be the most amazing mum, but the thought of raising our child together gives me hope. Hope for our future.

"Slowly," I repeat, and he nods. It'll take some work to trust him again, and it won't be smooth sailing. I'll need to know everything, every last detail, even if he thinks I won't like it. Then we can begin to move forward to build our future.

I've finally found my place in the world, and it's never felt more right.

The End

Playing Vinn
A Mafia Revenge Romance
Nicola Jane

Playlist

Maybe Don't - Maisie Peters ft. JP Saxe
    Favourite Ex - Maisie Peters
    Tell Me You Love Me - Demi Lovato
    Love Don't Cost a Thing - Jennifer Lopez
    Picking Up the Pieces - Paloma Faith
    Arcade - Duncan Laurence
    Gangsta - Kehlani
    Foolish - Ashanti
    Flames - MOD SUN ft. Avril Lavigne
    Please Don't Say You Love Me - Gabrielle Aplin
    Little Did I Know - Julia Michaels
    Hate That I Love You - Jonathan Roy
    Playing With Fire - N-Dubz ft. Mr Hudson
    Do I Wanna Know? - Arctic Monkeys
    Lost In Your Light - Dua Lipa ft. Miguel
    Dancing With The Devil - Demi Lovato
    Hate The Way - G-Eazy ft. blackbear
    Good Guy - Eminem ft. Jessie Reyez

Chapter One

SOFIA

I wake, stretching out on the king-sized bed and running my hands over the cool silk sheets. I hate silk. I glance around the white room, I groan aloud. White walls, white furniture, and white silk sheets.

I make my way to the en-suite bathroom, which is twice the size of my family bathroom back in Italy. *Italy.* Damn, I miss it so much. I step into the walk-in shower with white tiles adorning the walls and stare with hatred at the white towels hanging innocently on the white wall radiator. I hate white.

Next, I open my wardrobe and run my hand along the many items of clothing hanging there. Some things are mine that I brought with me from my home, but the rest, well, who knows where the rest came from. Obscenely-priced shops, mostly. I glance at a price tag on a cream trouser suit and arch my brow. Who the hell would wear this unless they're over sixty? I close my eyes and pull out the first thing my hand lands on, it's a game I've played every day since I came here. I laugh at the low-cut, bright orange summer dress. It's short and way too revealing. He'll hate it. I smile as I pull it on.

Downstairs, I pass the usual security men, I call them Bill and Ben after an old

television show my mama loved, but I have no idea what their names are because no one bothered to introduce us. They nod in greeting, and I smile politely. I hear pots and pans banging as I head for the kitchen, and Josey looks up as I enter. She's sweating and looks flustered. "Sofia," she says, smiling and wiping her head on her forearm, "did you sleep well?"

I pull myself up onto a chair at the breakfast bar, where no one ever seems to sit. "Yes, thank you. Did you?"

"Yes. Breakfast?" I shake my head and reach for the coffee pot instead, pouring myself a cup. "You really should eat something."

"I'm not really a breakfast person," I admit.

"Vincent came looking for you this morning. He wasn't happy that you didn't eat with the family again." I lower my eyes. What does he expect? I never know when he's here or away on business. We communicate through his staff or occasionally through his mother.

It's hard to believe we've only been married a week.

It was an arrangement made by our fathers years ago. His father died, so you'd think that would release me, right? Wrong. My papa still reached out to Vincent Romano and asked him to marry me. It's his name that makes him hugely desirable—not to me, of course, but to many men who have daughters. Connecting your family with the Romano name can open all kinds of opportunities, and when you're part of the mafioso, opportunities are everything. "Anyway, he said to tell you he's in his home office today and he'd like to see you." When I remain quiet, she moves to where I'm sitting and places her hand over mine. "It gets better, Sofia, I promise."

As I approach the ground floor office, Gerry is just leaving. He looks surprised to see me, so I guess I've been hiding away in my room a lot. "Good morning, Mrs. Romano."

I shudder, hating that name. "It's Sofia," I mutter. He leaves the office door open, and I step inside. Azure, or Blu, as everyone calls him, is pacing back and forth, and Vincent, my husband, looks angry. Both men turn to glare at me.

"You should knock before entering," barks Vinn. I roll my eyes and step back over the threshold, raising my fist and banging on the door. Blu almost cracks a smile but recovers fast when Vinn stands angrily. "I don't find you amusing, Sofia."

"Josey said you wanted to see me. I can go, it's fine."

He takes a deep breath and turns to his brother-in-law. "Blu, leave us." Once he's gone, I step closer to the large oak desk. "My mother is offended," he begins. "You don't join us for breakfast . . . or any meal, come to think of it."

"How would you know, you're never here yourself."

He stares at me, unblinking, "I have to attend to business, it can't be helped."

"Okay," I say, shrugging. I turn on my heel and head for the door.

"What does that mean?" he snaps. "Will you be joining us for lunch?"

I check my watch. "No. I have a date."

His laugh is cold. "Really? I'll see you in the dining room at one o'clock. And change your dress, unless you want my men dreaming about you."

I head out, not bothering to answer.

Zarina spots me entering the restaurant at one o'clock exactly. I hate to be late. She stands to greet me and hugs me excitedly. "You look amazing."

"So do you," I say, holding her at arm's length and taking in her beauty. It's all natural, from her long black lashes to her pedicured toes. She's stunning. Zarina is my cousin and closest friend. She was also a bridesmaid at my wedding, the one condition I had when the event was arranged. She knows everything about me, and when she discovered I was moving to the UK, it was the perfect opportunity for her to check out what London had to offer. Her father is my papa's underboss, and it took some convincing to allow it, but he eventually agreed she could stay here for three months. Secretly, I think he's hoping Vincent will find her a nice Italian man.

"So, tell me everything," she demands.

"Like?" I ask casually.

"Like how is married life? What's Vinn really like? Is he as scary as his reputation?"

"For this conversation, I need a drink," I mutter, catching the attention of the waitress.

"Drink," repeats Zarina. "You never drink."

I order a white wine and lemonade. I've heard some of Vinn's sister's friends order it and always wondered what it tastes like. Zarina sticks with water. "It's awful, Zee," I whisper, glancing around like I'm going to be heard. "I'm always on my own. It's like I'm a prisoner. I had to sneak out today just to see you."

"You did what?" she hisses, her eyes wide.

"I told him I had a date for lunch, but he didn't believe me. And why should I tell him my business? I know nothing about him. He leaves before breakfast, and God only knows when he returns. Is this it? Is this my life forever?"

Zarina offers a sympathetic smile. "Sofia, we talked about this a hundred times. You have got to make this work. For you, for your family, and most of all, for Mario."

My heart twists at the mention of my brother's name, and I nod. She's right—this marriage will make everything right again and Mario will be able to come home where he belongs.

VINN

I tap impatiently on the dining table. "Vinn, please," whispers Mother.

I check my watch and sigh heavily when I see it's almost ten minutes past one. "Get her," I order Conner, one of my men. He heads up to Sofia's room, where she's always hiding out since moving here. It doesn't bother me—the less I see of her, the better, so I can forget the marriage and all that comes with it. But it's upsetting my mother, and I can't allow that to happen.

Conner returns without Sofia. "Boss, she isn't there."

I frown. "What do you mean, she isn't there?"

"I checked her room, her bathroom, and the library, all places she usually goes. She isn't there." "Then check the other rooms. She'll be here somewhere."

"Actually," comes Josey's voice from somewhere behind Conner, "she said she was having lunch today with her cousin."

Conner visibly swallows. "Did you know this?" I ask, and he shakes his head. "Who was watching her today?"

"The new guy."

"Bring him to me now."

Mother pats my hand. "She'll be fine, Vinn. It's just lunch."

I nod stiffly, not wanting to snap at her. "But I told her to be here."

"It's nice she's going out and enjoying herself. If she's staying in London, she'll need a life." I snort. "She has a life here, in this house. It's my job to keep her safe."

Conner returns with the new man I hired two weeks ago. "Well, you're not with her," I state, "which means my wife is out there alone."

"I'm sorry, Boss, she never said she was going out. I checked her diary and everything," he explains.

"It's not an excuse," I reply, trying to stay calm.

"But I'm not a mind reader," he snaps, and Conner nudges him, telling him to shut up.

Blu enters, and when he feels the tension in the air, he stops and looks back and forth between us. "Everything okay?"

"This clown just spoke back to me, Azure. Get him out of my sight before I kill him."

Blu doesn't need asking twice before he takes him by the upper arm and guides him out.

"I'll go find her now, boss," says Conner.

"Don't bother," I snap, grabbing a set of car keys. "I'll go myself."

Sofia's cousin responds to my text message immediately. I like her, she's obedient, why the fuck didn't I marry her? Arriving at the restaurant, I spot the pair inside, eating lunch and chatting animatedly. When I step inside, the waitress rushes to greet me, but I pass her, ignoring her extra nice greeting, and head straight for Sofia's table. Zarina keeps her eyes downcast, her expression filled with guilt as Sofia glares at her accusingly. I sit down, shoving her farther along the booth. "You never said you were meeting your cousin."

"Yes, I did. I specifically told you I had a lunch date."

I push my face into hers, and she backs up against the seat. "No, *mia cara*, you told me you had a date, and I thought you were making a joke. I should have known that wasn't the case, since I don't think I've ever seen you crack a smile."

Sofia squares her shoulders, defiance in her eyes. "Firstly, I am not your darling. Secondly, pay attention when I talk next time."

My tongue runs along my lower lip while I try to gain control of my boiling rage. Twice in one day I have been spoken back to. It's a new record, and I wonder why the fuck everyone suddenly thinks it's okay. "Zarina, my driver will take you home. Please join us for dinner tomorrow evening. I'll have you collected at eight."

Zarina nods, sliding from the seat. "But we haven't finished eating," hisses Sofia.

I swipe my hand across the table, sending everything clattering across the floor. "Now, you have." She gasps, glaring at me like I've lost my mind. She's lucky I didn't throw it across the room to release some of this anger rushing through me. "Get your things."

She's angry too, breathing in through her nose sharply. Good. Maybe it's time we cleared the air. I stand, and when she doesn't, I grab her upper arm and force her to her feet. I take a bunch of notes out of my wallet and drop them on the table, apologising to the waitress about the mess as we leave.

It's beginning to rain and she's wearing the damn summer dress I told her to change out of. I offer her my coat, but she turns away, so I shrug and grab her by the arm again, marching away from the restaurant. As we pass men in the street, they stare at her with appraising expressions, and I glare at every goddamn one of them until they avert their eyes.

The orange dress is now a darker shade as rainwater soaks into it. Her hair looks matted, sticking to her face and chest. She's practically popping out the top, showing way too much skin for a married Italian woman. I look away, tempted to forcibly wrap my damn jacket around her body. We reach Enzo's, the nightclub I own, and she stops abruptly. "I'm not going in there."

"I have work to do."

"Then I'll go home. I'm not sitting in your office while you make eyes at your assistant."

I smirk. She found me kissing Raven a few months back and hasn't stopped reminding me of it since. She even delayed our wedding because of it. "Sofia, as much as I'd love to stand here in the pouring rain, discussing my assistant, I don't have time."

"I'm not going in there."

I growl, bending and tossing her over my shoulder, and she screams angrily. "Like I said, I don't have time." Raven looks up as we enter the office, mainly because Sofia is hitting my back and shouting curse words in Italian. I dump her back on her feet. "Watch her. If she tries to leave, tie her up."

Raven laughs. "Vinn, I'm not tying up your wife. That's your job."

Ignoring her, I head into my office and slam the door. I close the blinds, so I don't have to see either of them, and then I sit at the desk and stare at the picture of my father. "This is your fault," I mutter. "You and your stupid promise to your stupid friend. You said I should always honour a promise, and I did, Pops, but shit, you owe me big for this."

SOFIA

I fiddle with the hem of my dress. "So," says Raven, "things going well?"

"Perfectly," I mutter.

"Look—" she begins.

"You told me he was a nice man," I butt in accusingly.

"In all fairness, you were locked in the bathroom, refusing to come out and marry him. The alternative was to let carnage happen amongst the two families, and I'm sure you didn't want that." It was my husband's mistress who talked me into marrying him on the morning of my wedding. Ironic, right? I never wanted this in the first place, and when it came down to it, I was terrified to walk down that aisle towards a man I didn't know. But it was Raven who convinced me to do it . . . that and the fact I had no choice. My father needed this marriage. I sigh, looking around the office. "Why does he like white so much?"

Raven looks around too. "I dunno. Maybe cos it's clean-looking?"

"Or maybe he's just boring."

"Boring?" Raven chuckles. "Vinn Romano is the least boring person I know."

"In or out of the bedroom?" I quip, and she blushes. I shouldn't be unkind, because she was just as hurt by Vinn. Besides, she's been nothing but nice to me, and she and Vinn are well and truly over. She's happy with her new man. "Sorry," I mutter, taking a breath. "I hate it here," I admit, and her eyes soften. "His house is so . . . cold and lonely. He's never there. How am I supposed to get to know a man who's practically invisible?"

"Have you talked to him?" asks Raven.

I shake my head. "I don't think I want to. He looks at me like I'm an annoying bee buzzing in his ear. Neither of us are happy."

"Sofia, you have to talk to him. You're both in this whether you like it or not, and if you feel the same, air it and find a solution."

I glance at the office, seeing the blinds are still closed. "I'm going to the bathroom," I say, and she eyes me suspiciously.

"You're not gonna run, are you? He'll kill me."

I shake my head, not wanting to lie out loud. I take the stairs but pass the bathroom and continue to the ground floor, where I head for the exit. There's no way I'm hanging around here all day. I have shit to do.

The house is quiet when I get home, apart from the usual house staff. I head for my room and send a text off to Vinn, letting him know I'm home safely. I don't want to get Raven into trouble, and there's no point in antagonising him by letting him think I've wandered off and am roaming the streets of London alone.

Opening my laptop, I go to my secret files, load the document I've been working on, and smile. The trouble with Vinn Romano is, he thought I was quiet and maybe a little stupid. He might think he's the boss in every sense of the word, and he might even think I've forgiven him for ripping me away from my family while fucking his personal assistant, but he's about to discover I'm not who he thought I was.

Chapter Two

VINN

I glance at the text on my phone. Why can't she do as she's fucking told? Raven knocks on the door, and I see her silhouette through the frosted glass. "If you're coming here to tell me she's gone, I already know," I say dryly.

She steps inside. "Actually, no. I just got a call from my inside woman at the London Daily Spy and your number one fan has made contact." I sit a little straighter. "Contact?"

She nods. "Bad news, Vinn, they're running the story."

"Are you fucking joking me? What's the story?"

"I don't know, she's trying to find out. All she knows is it's going on the gossip page."

"That whole newspaper is a gossip fest. Nobody buys it, anyway, so I'm not worried."

Raven leaves, and I turn my chair to stare out at the busy streets below. Some dickhead had taken it upon themselves to write to the press about my life. They've accused me of being a chauvinistic pig, exposed my affair with Raven, even though Sofia was already aware, and now this. I need to find them and put a stop to it before it gets serious. I don't need bad press when I'm trying to expand businesses, and who knows what they'll uncover if they keep snooping into my life. Maybe this is the reason people suddenly think it's okay to disrespect me.

"Word on the street is you're going into the gossip pages tomorrow," comes Blu's amused voice from behind me.

I slowly turn to face him, annoyed by his smug expression. It's a permanent fixture on his face ever since he married my sister. "Word travels fast."

"Raven told me," he says sheepishly. "What gossip could they have on you?"

"It's probably a lie. Newspapers don't give a shit as long as it fills a column."

"Maybe this person is a disgruntled ex?"

I shake my head. "I don't have any, not that were serious. There's only . . ." I frown. "Well, just Raven, but she wouldn't."

Blu glances over his shoulder to see Raven on the telephone, then he pushes the door closed. "Are you sure about that, Boss? You hurt her pretty badly."

I shake my head. "She wouldn't dare. Besides, she came running when the first story hit the Gazette and sorted all the positive PR bullshit. It's what got her to come back to work for me." "I'm just saying, don't rule her out too quickly. Women are clever, and revenge is a dish best served cold." He sits and places his feet on my desk. I eye his boots with a scowl. "Anyway, how's married life?"

"You ask me every time I see you, and every time, I tell you the same thing. It's fine."

"Things good between you two?"

"Why do you ask?"

He sighs. "I'll be honest, Boss, your sister is worried about you both."

"Gia needs to stop worrying and concentrate on her own marriage. Maybe she could teach you some manners," I say dryly, pushing his feet from my desk. "Now, if you don't mind, I'm busy."

He checks his watch. "We have a meeting in ten minutes."

I glance at my diary. Fuck. My head is not in the game right now. "Mr. Hicks. Right."

"Gia thinks Sofia is miserable and that she's missing home."

"Impossible. She's at home right now."

"You know what I mean. Italy. Plus, you're never together."

"We were together this morning."

"Look, Boss, I don't wanna have this conversation either. I told Gia to keep me out of it, but you know what she's like when she gets going. She wouldn't leave it. She's gonna speak to Sofia today and see if she's okay."

"I can assure you, she's fine."

"Gia mentioned—" I groan, and he sits up straighter, grinning. "Hear me out. She said you have separate bedrooms." I stare at him. There's no way we're discussing this. Blu's eyes widen, and he laughs. "You're shitting me, right? You mean to tell me you haven't . . ."

"That's none of your business. You're overstepping."

"So, shoot me," he says, relaxing in the chair.

"You're not safe just because you married into my family."

"You're the boss, the top man, and you haven't—"

"Azure!" I suddenly yell, but he doesn't jump in fright. It's in his blood not to react. It's the way he was trained, just like me.

"Look, you have a reputation to uphold, and as your second in command, I'm telling you, you need to sort this out. She's your wife, and that comes with responsibility. Isn't it time you taught her that?"

"I'm not gonna force myself on her."

"You already did when you married her. You have to go through with it, Vinn. Back in the day, the families would have checked the sheets to make sure you'd consummated." He laughs. "Things have changed, but still, you need to complete the marriage. How the fuck are you gonna have a son?"

"It's temporary. I'm letting her settle in."

"You're letting her think she's the boss. If this gets out, people will think you're an *omosessuale*, that you're hiding behind a fake marriage. It's not the first time a mafioso boss did that. People will think you're weak." I hear Raven greet our guest, and I sigh with relief. "Hicks is here. Concentrate on making us money and securing this deal, and forget about my marriage."

SOFIA

I smile as I press the telephone to my ear. "Oh my god, Sofia. You can't send that story," yells Zarina.

I emailed her my undercover story just minutes ago. "There's no way you've read that fully, I only just sent it."

"I don't need to. The headline says it all." I hear her suck in a shaky breath. "Sofia, have you lost your mind? What if he discovers the truth? What if he finds out the mysterious 'Revenge' is you? This is out of hand now."

"He won't."

"He'll kill you. You can't fuck over men like him."

"Zee, relax. He won't find out. Besides, what else am I supposed to do, sitting in his fucking white tower every day, bored out of my mind?""You do what housewives do, Sofia. You make friends. Have lunch out. Go to the damn library. But you don't write shit about a mafia boss."

"He underestimated me. He shouldn't have." I'm angry she's defending him when she knows how unhappy I am.

"So, you want to write shit about him? Embarrass him just because he underestimated you? Christ, Sofia, listen to yourself. He married you to help your family. Think of Mario. If Vinn finds out about this, Mario might never come home."

"I don't understand why you're defending him, Zee. Anyway, you're killing my vibe. He won't find out."

A few stories in a gossip rag are hardly gonna bring down the great Vincent Romano. Maybe when the Gazette were printing my work, I'd have stood a chance of getting under his skin, but since he shut that down with his violent threats, I've had to go to less known news outlets. Now, it's just a bit of fun.

I head down for dinner at six, the same time as almost every evening. Josey and Lorenzo share dinner duties. Lorenzo once had his own restaurant and he's an amazing chef. Josey mainly sticks to breakfast and lunch as well as housekeeping. Both are fantastic at what they do.

I'm surprised when I step into the dining room to find Vinn seated at the head of the table. He glances up from his laptop, and when he sees it's me, he closes it and moves it to the side. "You're home," I say.

"I thought you might want to spend time with me," he says, smirking. I take a seat away from him, and he sighs impatiently, then pulls out the seat to his left. "Here," he demands, so I move. "You seem to want my attention, *mia cara*. No?"

"Why would you think that?"

"You keep defying me. I can only assume it's because you want more attention."

I roll my eyes. "That's the opposite of what I want. I like eating dinner in the kitchen and chatting with Josey."

"And Lorenzo," he chips in.

I laugh. "You're not going to ban me from speaking to your oldest employee, are you?" It bothers me that he knows what I do when he isn't around. How does he know my every move? I glance around the room, looking for cameras, but see nothing obvious.

"Why did you leave the club today?"

"Because I was bored."

"So, you'd like something to keep you busy when I'm not around?"

"No, I can amuse myself," I say, arching a brow.

"I can get Gia to show you the local salons or the best places to shop," he suggests, and I inwardly groan. This arrogant arse is a chauvinistic dick.

"I'd rather you didn't."

"What else would you like to do, if not shop?"

"You know, Vinn, not every woman is a shopaholic with an addiction to lip fillers and facials."

He smirks, nodding. "I feel like I've been tricked," he murmurs, and my heart rate picks up a little. "Your father portrayed you as a quiet virgin, but now, I see you have your own opinions and an unruly mouth."

"Shocker," I mutter sarcastically.

"Let's hope some of what your father told me is true."

His eyes are burning into me. I feel the colour drain from my face, then sigh with relief as the food is brought out. Once the food is set before us, the waitress leaves. "Where were we?" asks Vinn.

"My mother taught us not to talk at the table."

"Did she teach you how to be a good wife?"

"What's that supposed to mean?"

"Well, we've been married for a couple of weeks, maybe it's time you moved into my bedroom?"

I almost choke on my own saliva. It's not what I was expecting him to say. "That's not happening," I manage to splutter.

"We are married," he repeats.

"And that means shit," I snap, and he narrows his eyes. "I don't even know you. You haven't spent any time getting to know me at all. We went on a three-day honeymoon where you spent the entire time glued to your phone and laptop."

"So, you want to spend more time together?" he asks.

"No . . . yes . . . no! I don't know," I cry, frustrated and flustered all at the same time.

"You know, eventually, we'll have to . . ." He leaves the sentence open, but we both know what he's referring to. I drop the white napkin on the table and stand. "Where are you going? You haven't touched your food."

"I've lost my appetite." I head for the door.

"Am I that repulsive?" he yells. "There are other women out there who would love to share my bed!"

"And I'm sure you'll let them. I haven't forgotten about Raven," I snap. "How can you expect me to act like a real wife when it's been a sham from start to finish?" I spin back to face him, suddenly feeling the need to get everything off my chest. "I never agreed to this marriage. I was happy in Italy. I had a life that I've been ripped away from and brought here to live in this . . . this big, empty place that is too white and has far too much silk." I take a deep breath. "I don't love you, Vinn, and I can't ever be the wife you want me to be."

He stands slowly and his eyes darken. I'm suddenly reminded of why men are scared of Vinn Romano. He moves towards me menacingly, but I refuse to take a step away. I will not bow down to a man who forced this life on me. "You have a responsibility, Sofia."

"If you want me to bear you a son, it'll be through force, no other way."

He sniggers, his face so close, I can feel his warm breath on my cheek. "You *will* have my child. It's not up for discussion. But I won't force you, Sofia. You'll come to me willingly and you'll beg before I lay a finger on you," he whispers.

My head feels light, and the second he leaves the room, I grip the back of a chair for support. I hate him, so why the hell do I find his words hot? I let out a slow breath, glancing around the large room to check there were no witnesses to that moment of madness I'd just experienced. I scoff. "Beg him, please, not if he was the last man on Earth," I say aloud.

VINN

I like the sound my shoes make as they crunch over the dusty floor. It's deathly silent, apart from that sound, and I feel like it sets the mood for what's about to happen. Blu removes the black sack from my guest's head, and I smile. "Good evening."

The man's eyes widen and terror fills them. Before this moment, he probably wondered what the hell was going on. Before this moment, he probably thought he'd be able to talk his way out of whatever trouble was awaiting him. But now, as he makes annoying noises behind his tight gag and struggles against the thick rope binding him to the chair, he knows this will be his last night on Earth. Because nobody crosses me and gets away with it.

"I hate that it's come to this," I say, and I mean it. I'm sincere when I say those words, because if I wasn't, what kind of a monster would that make me? "But I tried to be kind. I sent my men to talk with you and explain everything. Didn't you understand the terms of our agreement?" He nods wildly, desperate for me to hear him out. "Then I don't understand where it all went wrong." I like a dramatic pause, so I wait a moment before continuing. "Wait, I know." I pull out a piece of paper and hold it up. "It was around the same time you emailed Raymond Clay and offered up information about my organisation." My captive makes more stupid noises, and I roll my eyes and wave my hand for Blu to remove the gag.

"I swear, Boss, I didn't. He wouldn't leave it, put money into my account. It's a set-up."

"So, these emails are not between you and him?"

"It wasn't how it looks—"

"Really, Carlo? Because it looks pretty bad from where I'm sitting. I moved you up in the ranks. You're a made man, even though everyone around me thought you weren't good enough. I thought you were worth the risk because I liked you, Carlo. You had fire in those eyes, and I knew you'd run the soldiers with no problem. But then, you screwed me over, you screwed the mafioso over. You know I can't let that slide."

"Please . . . please, Vinn, I didn't mean to. It was a mistake, and I fucked up, but I'll make it right. I'll do anything."

"There's no way back."

"I gave my life to you," he suddenly yells, and I smirk. The begging is over because he knows it won't work, so now, the hate is pouring from him. "I killed for you," he hisses.

"You killed for the family. You wanted in, and I gave it to you," I growl out, pushing my face close to his. I feel the darkness lingering as I crack my neck from side to side. "I gave you everything, and you fucked it up. Now, you have to pay."

I hold out my hand for Blu to pass me my knife. Gripping Carlo by the throat, I dig my fingers into his clammy skin. He stills, accepting his fate, and I slowly push the blade into his eye. He begins to scream and thrash around. I close my eyes, absorbing his cries of pain, and inhale the stench of his dirty blood pouring from the wound.

I took this kid in when he was seventeen and taught him everything he needed to know. Making him part of my clan was a big deal. He wasn't from a family I knew well, and I took a big risk, one that didn't pay off because his loyalties were too easily bought by my enemy.

The crimson fluid turns black as it mixes with brain matter and trickles down his lifeless face, and Blu is already on the phone arranging a clean-up. I remove my gloves and throw them in a nearby metal drum, followed by my jacket, the material now soaked by blood splatters. Blu runs an ultraviolet torch over me to check for any lingering evidence. There's nothing, so I head back to the car where Gerry is waiting.

"You might want to look at this," he says, passing me an iPad. It's open on an article. The picture of Sofia and me standing apart screams unhappy, and as my eyes take in the headline, I grip the tablet so hard, the screen cracks.

Gerry drives me home, and as I take the stairs two at a time, my head is full of rage. I push Sofia's bedroom door open, slamming it hard against the wall. She sits up, dazed and confused, blinking through tired eyes. Grabbing her wrist, I haul her from her bed, causing her to scream out. She stumbles as I drag her across the landing, open my own door, and shove her inside.

"From now on, you sleep in here," I yell, slamming the door closed and locking it. Sofia stares at me, her whole stance ready to fight. Her breathing is rapid, and her fists are clenched. "Do it," I hiss, pushing her to carry out her attack. "I dare you."

"I'm not scared of you," she says through gritted teeth.

I smirk, moving close enough to feel the heat from her body. "Oh, you should be, *esuberante*."

"I'm not feisty," she hisses. "I'm an enraged woman, and I'll never be scared of you."

I take in her shorts and low-cut vest, the swell of her breasts taunting me for the second time. I might be a bastard, but I won't ever force myself on her. "Go back to sleep."

She turns, looking at the super-sized, four-poster bed. "It's not white," she mutters.

I head to my bathroom, ignoring her.

Chapter Three

SOFIA

The deep red cotton blankets are a nice change from the cold white silk. I slip in and close my eyes. The bed is soft and comfortable, but the thought of sharing it with Vinn has me wide awake and alert. I hear the shower stop and turn onto my side so my back is to him. When he steps into the room, he pauses for a minute before passing me to go to his walk-in wardrobe. I open one eye in time to see his naked arse disappear. When he returns, he's wearing bottoms. I watch as he rubs his wet hair with a towel, taking in his large, muscled physique. I can see why women drop at his feet—he isn't exactly ugly.

Vinn throws the towel into his laundry basket and climbs into bed. I lay frozen, awake and hardly daring to breathe, for the rest of the night. When the sun finally rises, I feel Vinn stir. Without a word, he disappears back into the bathroom, showers and dresses, then leaves the room.

I sit up, staring at the closed door. He always seems to be mad about something, and now, I realise he even wakes up like that. Biting my lower lip, something tells me it's about to get a lot worse when he sees that article today.

Downstairs, I hear Gia and Blu. I join them at the table, taking my seat beside Vinn, who is staring at his mobile as usual. "Good morning," says Gia brightly.

"Good morning." "What are your plans today?"

I shrug. "She's spending the day with me," says Vinn coldly.

We all turn to him, but he continues to stare at his phone. "Doing what?" I ask.

"Smiling for the fucking cameras," he snaps.

My heart drops. He knows about the story. "Cameras?" I repeat.

"Ignore him. He's got his panties in a twist over some gossip in the paper. It's nothing."

"Nothing?" yells Vinn, looking up. He snatches the nearest newspaper and opens it. "High-flying businessman Vincent Romano is living a lie," he reads.

"Come on, Vinn, nobody reads that paper," says Gia.

"The business mogul who recently married Italian Sofia Greco is living a lie. It's not the first time a man of his status has married to keep their love life secret. Our source revealed he has yet to consummate his marriage to the Italian beauty, leaving everyone wondering if it's female company he really desires." Vin throws the paper across the room, and it spreads over the wooden floor as it lands. "Whoever the fuck this 'Revenge' person is, I want him found."

"Vinn, you have a million enemies. It could be anyone," says Gia.

"Then I'll kill every single one of them."

"What if it's not an enemy?" asks Blu. "What if it's someone closer to home?"

"I told you, Raven wouldn't do it," snaps Vinn. "She's not like that." It annoys me how he jumps to her defence, but I feel some relief they're not looking in my direction.

"You did hurt her," I mumble.

"We sorted that out and moved past it."

I arch a brow. "And how exactly did you sort it out?"

We stare at each other angrily, and I feel Gia shift uncomfortably. "Anyway," she continues, "I thought we could spend the day together."

"I told you, she's coming with me," snaps Vinn.

"Maybe I don't want to."

He takes a calming breath. "You're my wife, and you will act like it."

I scoff, folding my arms over my chest. "Fine." He wants a wife, I'll fucking be the doting wife.

Vinn's mother enters the room, and we all fall silent. She takes in the newspaper scattered across the floor. "Keep your head, Vinn. Do not respond to negative lies and show a united front with your new wife. It will die down." Then, she calmly takes a seat.

When we arrive at Vinn's office, Raven is already yielding calls. She smiles sympathetically. "It'll blow over."

"It's not that." He glances at me. "Let's go to my office," he says to Raven, releasing my hand. I ignore the sting of hurt in my chest. Why should it bother me that he can talk to her? After all, she knows him much better than I do. Instead, I head for the stairs. "Where are you going?" asks Vinn, but I ignore him.

I'm halfway down before I hear him chasing after me. "Sofia," he hisses angrily.

"I'm acting like a wife," I say, forcing a bright smile. "Isn't that what you wanted?"

"You're not leaving!"

"You just asked the assistant you were fucking to step into your office so you can open up to her about how hurt you are," I say, mimicking a baby voice and sticking out my bottom lip. "Do you think a wife would react well to that?"

"She's my P.A., and I have business to discuss."

"Great, then I'll be on my way."

"Sofia," he shouts as I take another step away.

"You told me to act like your wife, so I am. I will not be made out to be a fool. Unless the story is true," I accuse, narrowing my eyes.

"Don't be ridiculous," he barks.

I close the gap between us, a smug smile on my face. "Is that what you need to talk to her about? Does she know the real you?"

He moves so fast, I don't see it coming until his hand is around my throat and his lips are an inch from my own. "You'd like that, wouldn't you," he whispers, "a reason to get out of this marriage." I swallow. His thumb idly rubs along my jaw as he stares at my mouth. "Just say the word and I'll prove it isn't true." His other hand takes mine and he holds it against his pants. His erection pushes against my palm, and my eyes widen. "Say it," he whispers.

I pull free. "Never."

He grins, his eyes still fixed on my lips. "Never is a long time." Our heavy breathing fills the silence and then he steps back. "Now, get back upstairs, Sofia."

VINN

"I can't let anyone think I'm gay, Raven. I can't lead the organisation like that. I'll have men trying to say I'm not up to running it. They'll think I'm weak.""That's bullshit. Gay men aren't weak."

"I know that, but things are different in this life. There are beliefs. I must have a son. It's expected."

She shrugs. "If you ask me, it's all outdated crap. You're the boss, change the ways."

I laugh. "If only it was that simple."

"Then get her pregnant, shut them all up."

"That's proving a little more difficult than I imagined," I mutter.

"She can't have kids?" gasps Raven.

"I wouldn't know. We'd have to try to know that."She stares at me for a few seconds, absorbing what I've said, and then she laughs.

"You're kidding. You haven't had sex?"

"I don't know why this news shocks everyone. Blu laughed too."

"Well, it's just you're so . . . well, let's just say you're insatiable. It's been weeks . . . months since you and I . . . so where are you going?"

"I'm not going anywhere else. I'm married," I say, defensively. "I'm waiting for my wife."

"Oh. I bet that's hard." She laughs at her pun, and I roll my eyes.

"How're you and Mac?" I ask, changing the subject.

"Actually, there's something I should tell you. It's early days, but as my employer, you should know. I'm pregnant."

My mouth falls open. "Pregnant? Since when?"

"Since before Mac left for Nottingham. I did the test at your wedding."

"Shit," I stand, and so does she. "Erm, congratulations."

She smiles, and I wrap her in an awkward hug, inhaling her strawberry scent. "And it's definitely his?"

She hits my chest playfully. "One hundred percent."

I nod again, not wanting to push too much. Would she even tell me if I was this baby's father? As if reading my mind, she smiles softly. "This baby is Mac's, not yours. I'm only eight or nine weeks, and it was months ago for us."

I ignore calls all day. The other Capos want to speak with me, but the fact they'd even question these lies makes me want to kill them all. "There's nothing else for it," states Blu when I turn up at the Kings Reapers clubhouse later in the day. "You'll have to get her pregnant."

"It doesn't mean anything," says Riggs, the club's president. "People deny they're gay all the time. They lead full lives with the opposite sex and come out later in life."

"How about I shoot every man who asks me if it's true?" I ask, staring hard at Chains. He grins wide. "Go on, try me," I tease. We're always looking at ways to piss each other off.

"Chains, don't," warns Riggs. "If Vinn kills you, my sister will kill me."

"It might be worth it," Chains replies, smirking.

"Better still," I murmur, standing just in case my next words touch a nerve, "let's ask your wife." I turn to where the women are chatting with Sofia. "Leia?"

"Jesus, Vinn, she's my little sister," snaps Riggs.

"Don't push me for a fight because some nutcase ex is selling shit about you," drawls Chains. "I got the girl, get over it." He's right, I need a fight and I'm pushing him. Leia would never forgive me if I hurt her husband, and when she joins us and snuggles into Chains' side, he winks at me, reminding me that he did in fact win the girl.

"What's wrong?" she asks.

"Vinn's in a mood cos of the story in the paper today," says Chains. "And he isn't getting any."

"Any what?" she asks innocently.

"Any of what we did an hour ago," he responds, smirking.

Riggs shoves him hard. "Some shit is private," he hisses. He hates any talk like that about his sister, as would most men, but Chains laughs and kisses Leia on her head. They have a kid together, so Riggs can't exactly do anything about their relationship.

"It's nice you've brought Sofia over," says Leia, and I nod. "She's really lovely."

"Just say what you really need to say, Leia," I mutter.

She kisses Chains before taking my arm and leading me away from everyone else. She's the only person I'd let drag me around like a damn puppy dog. We sit down at a table, and she clasps her hands like she's about to get serious. "She looks so sad, Vinn."

I glance over to where Sofia is sitting with Anna, Riggs' wife. I've never really taken the time to watch her, but I guess I can see sadness there. Her smile doesn't quite reach her eyes. "There's nothing I can do about it."

Leia arches her brow. "Nothing?"

"Yah know, I did her family a favour. They're hardly up there in the family ranks. By giving her my name, her father went to the top. She acts like I forced this on her, but she should be grateful."

"Sheesh, if you say shit like that to her, no wonder she's miserable. You know she had a boyfriend back in Italy, a life with friends and a career?" she asks, and I narrow my eyes. It's new information, and Leia wouldn't understand the gravity of what she's saying. Our lives are not the same, and we have expectations. Sofia was promised as pure, saved for me. It was her father's job to keep her safe until the day she married. There should never have been a boyfriend.

"So, she's pining over some boyfriend?" I snap.

She gasps. "God, no, that's not what I meant. I just wanted you to understand she had a life, and now, suddenly, she's here with you. It's a huge change."

I stand and straighten my tie. "I married Sofia because my father was a good friend to her father and he set it all up. It's not a marriage for love but for convenience. We both have to get on with it."

"Vinn," says Leia, trying to grab my hand, "it doesn't have to be like that. You could be happy together."

I scoff, shaking my head. "This isn't a fairy tale, Leia. It's life. I'm not the kind of man to love or to be loved. As long as my bloodline continues, my job is done.""Bullshit," she snaps. "I know you, and I know you could treat her so good. You could fall in love and be happy."

"Nobody truly knows me, Leia. You know what I allow you to." Hurt passes over her face and her hand falls in her lap. I feel a pang of guilt as I step away. Diesel, the dog I bought Leia, rushes past me to get to her, and she makes a fuss of him. "I know you, Vinn. I don't care what you say," she mutters from behind me, and I smile to myself.

We're in the car heading home when Blu calls me. "You're not going to be happy," he greets, and I brace myself. "Planning permission for the apartment complex was turned down."

I grit my teeth. "How? That was supposed to go straight through without any hitches." I've sponsored an entire campaign for the local councillor, costing me thousands, all so this planning permission would go through smoothly. "Today is the gift that keeps on fucking giving," I utter, leaning towards Gerry, who's up front driving. "Take me to see Councillor Jones."

"I'll meet you there," says Blu. I disconnect and note the annoyance on Sofia's face.

"It won't take long," I explain. As the car slows to a stop outside Jones's small office, I take a deep breath. "We have dinner with your cousin. Afterwards, we'll talk." She doesn't respond. Gerry opens my door, and I direct her, "Stay in the car. I won't be long."

Blu's already waiting, and he bangs on the door. Jones isn't popular amongst the locals, hence why he keeps his office door locked. He appears at the other side of the glass, looking mildly irritated when he spots us. "How hard would it be to hide his death from the public eye?" I mutter as he unlocks the door.

Blu smirks. "I'd make it work."

"Gentlemen, I'm about to head home," Jones says, faking a smile.

"Too bad." I shove my way in, and Blu follows. "Azure just delivered some very upsetting news," I drawl, picking up a photograph of his wife from his desk.

"Yes, well, as I explained to Azure, it can't be helped. If I was allowed to vote alone, I would pass it. You know that, Vinn. But there are twelve people on the board, and all of them had reservations."

I place the photograph down and turn to face him. "I don't think you understood the assignment. Your mission was to quash the reservations."

"Vinn," he gives a condescending chuckle, "throwing your toys out the pram won't get the planning permission granted." I glance at Blu, hardly believing my ears. I've spent years listening to my father tell me I should always show respect, ask nicely, and reach agreements with as little violence as possible. But this is one dick too far today, so when my hand wraps around Jones's throat and I force him to take a seat, it's almost a natural reaction, and I wonder which Vinn is the true me. "I have been very patient," I seethe. "I've helped support your ridiculous campaign."

"Vinn," he whispers, choking when I squeeze harder.

"You told me it wouldn't be an issue. You said you had a strong say on the panel."

"I'll talk to them," he croaks. I release his throat and hold my hand out as Blu passes me a small knife. "Our next meeting is in a month," he splutters.

I grip his leg, and he frowns, confused. I take the small, sharp knife and push it into his thigh, twisting it. It's painful, and it'll take a hospital visit to close the wound. When he realises what I've done, he opens his mouth to scream, but Blu shoves a handkerchief in there and it muffles the noise. "I have had enough of people thinking they can take the fucking piss. You have twenty-four hours starting now. I want that planning permission."

I withdraw the knife, and he cries harder, gripping the wound. Blood pours through his fingers as he looks at me with panic in his eyes. "If I was you, I'd call an ambulance. That's pretty deep. It'll need packing and stitches." I pat him on the shoulder and hand the knife to Blu, then I wipe my bloodied hand down Jones's jacket. "You should be more careful using knives when opening your mail. I'll have my P.A. send you one of my company letter openers."

Outside, Gerry and Sofia are leaning against the car, chatting. I narrow in on the way she's smiling as she watches him smoke a cigarette. As if my day's not bad enough, I have to contend with her breaking all the fucking rules. "Get in the car," I growl. My voice makes her jump. Gerry flicks his cigarette and gets into the driver's side without a word. Sofia utters something under her breath as she gets in the back seat, slamming the door.

Blu's behind me. "Remind me again, what exactly did her father tell you about her?" he asks.

"That she was a good girl."

"She's a fiery one, that's clear."

"She's pushing me too far, Blu. I'm gonna snap." He pats me on the shoulder. "Sometimes it's easier to work with them. Gia is much calmer when I agree to whatever she wants."

"Sofia wants to be in Italy with her old life."

"Oh. Well, show her it's better here, with you."

I shake my head, getting into the car. I don't have time to settle her in, she's just got to suck it up and stop being such a spoiled brat.

I arranged for dinner to be on the terrace this evening. It's a warm evening and with this being Zarina's first visit to our home, I thought we should make the effort. If I can win over Sofia's cousin, maybe she can talk her into making my life easier and complying.

Sofia smiles wide when Zarina arrives, and I watch as they embrace. They're close, it's obvious. I stand and kiss each of Zarina's cheeks. "Your home is so beautiful," she gushes, and I smile.

"Thank you." It's something Sofia has never commented on apart from the other night when she made a confusing statement about it being too white and full of silk. I got the impression it wasn't a good thing.

The waiter pours us wine as we settle into our seats. "How long are you here?" I ask.

"Three months. My father agreed to a short-term arrangement, although I have fallen in love with London and would love to make it a permanent thing."

"Yes, it's magical on the first visit. What do you do for a living?"

"In Italy, I'm a beautician."

I smile wider. "Yes, it shows." She blushes under my compliment. "Maybe you can give my wife some tips. We have a charity dinner tomorrow evening."

She glances towards Sofia and offers a guilty smile. "Actually, Sofia is amazing at make-up. She taught me."

I smirk. "I have yet to see that side of her."

"I am actually sitting here," Sofia says brusquely.

"Oh, I'm aware," I drawl, sipping my wine. "Tell me, did she show that side of herself to her boyfriend?" They exchange a look, and I drain my glass. "Your father never mentioned it."

The waiters bring out the food. "This smells wonderful," says Zarina, relief in her voice. I stare at the homemade salmon pasta, Lorenzo's speciality, then we eat in silence.

Afterwards, the women make polite conversation with each other while I check emails on my phone. I'm angry at the thought of Sofia with someone else. Not because I'm jealous, although I am, but because her father lied to me, and now, I have to deal with that.

I finish the bottle of wine seeing as both women stick to one glass. "What did you do back in Italy?" I ask Sofia, interrupting the conversation they were having about a fashion designer.

Sofia stares for a second before replying, "Why?"

"Why can't you ever just answer a fucking question?" I yell, taking her by surprise.

"I was a hooker," she spits, smirking when my eyes blaze with anger.

Zarina stands. "It's been lovely, but I should go," she mutters.

"I'll see you out," says Sofia, leading the way to the exit.

I remain seated, tapping my thumb on the table and counting silently to try and calm myself. When she returns, she stays on the other side of the table and rests her hands on the back of her chair. "You can't even be nice for one dinner. Isn't it exhausting being so angry all the time?"

I stand abruptly, knocking my chair back. "Who was the boyfriend?"

"Nobody important."

"Did your father know?" She stares at me blankly, which angers me more. "Think about your answer, Sofia, because it could get someone killed."

"It was a stupid fling, nothing important. Why does it matter? You don't even like me!"

I stalk around the table to her, and she stands tall, keeping her eyes locked on mine. "It matters if your father lied to me, *moglie*."

"Why do you do that?" she yells, throwing her hands in the air. "You have pet names for every fucking woman in your life, but you refer to me as 'wife' or something equally as distant and unaffectionate."

"Answer my question!" I shout, slamming my hand on the table.

She swallows. "Yes," she whispers. "Yes, he knew."

Chapter Four

SOFIA

Vinn closes his eyes briefly, and when he opens them again, they are darker than I've ever seen them. "Did you have sex with him?"

"I don't have to answer that," I sputter, feeling my face heat. This wasn't the plan. Papa never said what to do in this situation. "I need to speak to my papa."

He shakes his head, sneering. "No."

"Then I'm going to my own room," I hiss, turning on my heel.

His arm cuts across me, stopping me. "Did you have sex with him?" he repeats. When I don't reply, he growls and spins me until I'm facing the table. His hand wraps in my hair and he shoves me over the table. "Should I find out for myself?" he yells. I close my eyes, trying to hold back the tears. *Don't show fear.* I repeat it like a mantra in my head, zoning out from Vinn as he holds me pressed against the table and kicks my legs apart. "Tell me!" he shouts.

"Yes," I mutter, digging my fingernails into the cotton tablecloth. "Yes."

He shoves away from me, but I remain where I am, scared if I move, he'll carry out his threat. I hear each heavy breath as he falls into his seat. "Get out," he mutters. It takes me a second to realise what he said. I glance up, and his eyes are now cold and vacant. "Get out," he repeats. I slowly push up from the table and straighten my hair, tears leaking from the corner of my eyes. "Go to your own room," he adds, and a pang of hurt hits my chest.

I lie awake. Maybe I should tell him the truth just so he doesn't look at me like I'm dirty, but he might see it as a green light to do what the hell he likes to me. Maybe my papa is right, and he'll use it as an excuse to disrespect me further. Mama said men like Vinn don't forgive and forget. She said he'd look at me like dirt forever, like my papa looks at her. I wipe another tear. I don't want to be like her, yet here I am, stuck in this marriage with a man who hates me. Eventually, he'll do exactly what papa did to her—he'll spend his nights with other women and return when it's convenient for him. He already spends as much time away from me as possible, and now he knows about Dante, it'll always be that way.

Maybe it's good I've kept him at arm's length, at least his rejection can't hurt me.

As predicted, I eat breakfast alone. Gia breezes through but tells me she has a busy day, so she doesn't have time for breakfast. Josey tells me

Vinn's mother requested to eat in her room, so I tuck into pancakes and coffee and chat with her about her life outside of here.

When Vinn saunters in, I almost choke on my mouthful of pancake. "Phone," he says coldly, holding out his empty hand. I stare at him, waiting for an explanation. "Give. Me. Your. Phone."

"Why?" I notice Josey rushing out to give us privacy.

"Make me ask again," he warns.

"I wanted to call my mama today."

"Then you'll call from my office, in front of me."

I narrow my eyes. "Why?"

"That word is banned from this point forward," he snaps as I place my phone in his hand. "You question me again and you'll regret it."

He clicks his fingers, and a male and female enter wearing grey suits and shades. I smirk because it's almost like a comedy sketch with the way they obey his clicky fingers and stand together with stony expressions. "Frazer and Ash are now your personal guards. Everywhere you are, one of them will be there too." He flicks his hand, and they leave as quickly as they appeared.

"What's going on?"

He grabs a handful of my hair and tugs my head back. "Did you question me, *puttana*?" His use of 'whore' sends another dagger to my heart. I wince as he tugs harder. "You'll be pleased to know we're flying home to Italy at the weekend." I keep my mouth closed, not daring to question him. "I have business to attend to there. In the meantime, you need to do this test," he says, pushing a small box into my hand. He releases me, and I glance at the ovulation test. My blood runs cold. "Now, *puttana*."

"I . . . what do I . . . I don't know what to do."

"Pee," he hisses, grabbing my arm and hauling me to my feet. He gives a small shove out of the kitchen, and I move forward.

"I don't need a pee," I mumble feebly. He follows me to the downstairs bathroom, holding the door open for me as I enter. He also steps inside. "You're staying?" He folds his arms across his chest and watches me coldly.

I sigh, opening the box and emptying out the contents onto the sink unit. Glancing over the instructions, I find it hard to concentrate with his moody arse glaring at me. With a shaky hand, I open one of the pee sticks. "Could you at least turn around?" I ask, and he rolls his eyes, turning to face the door. I will myself to pee but only manage a dribble. Fuck knows if it's enough, but honestly, I'm past caring. How dare he make me feel so fucking cheap and worthless? I put the cap on the stick and slide it across the marble floor until it hits his shoe. He glances down at it, then at me with an arched brow. "Apparently, you're looking for a smiley face," I snap.

He lowers gracefully and swipes the stick from the floor. He stares at the small window. "Looks like you're off the hook, for the next two nights anyway. We'll test again before we fly to Italy."

"What happens?" I ask, and he pauses to look at me. "When we get a smiley face?"

A grin spreads across his handsome face. I don't think I've ever fancied and hated someone all at once. "You'll spend the night in my bed."

"Why would you want a child with me when you hate me so much?"

"Because something good has to come out of this fucking nightmare that you and your father trapped me in." "Trapped you?" I repeat, hardly believing my ears. "I didn't trap you. This was you and my father. I'm the one trapped!"

"Two days, *puttana*."

"Stop calling me that!" I scream, clenching my fists.

He laughs. "I thought you wanted a pet name." I glare after him as he leaves. My mama was right—he looks at me differently now. Imagine how he'd be knowing the truth. I rush to my bedroom, needing to get my words down on paper. It's the only way to release the hatred I'm feeling.

VINN

"What's with the mood, Boss?" asks Blu warily.

I glare at him. "Maybe I'm just sick of everybody questioning me." "Hey," he says, holding up his hands in defence, "I ain't questioning you, I just haven't seen you so angry and agitated."

"Get used to it. It makes me feel better."

"Is this something to do with Sofia?"

"She isn't a virgin," I blurt out, and he raises his eyebrows in surprise. "Her father told me she was." "Maybe he didn't know?"

"Or maybe he took me for a mug."

"Is it really important to you?" he asks carefully.

"You're missing the point," I snap, speeding up the running machine.

"I much prefer running in the park than in this sweaty gym," he complains, starting up the machine beside me. "So, what's the point I'm missing?"

"Her father lied. She told me he knew about it. He lied and let me marry her. Why would he do that?"

Blu shrugs, "Maybe to get her off his hands? She's a mouthy one."

I shake my head. "No, there's a reason he wanted her to marry me. He fed me lies to agree. He said she was quiet, shy, a virgin who never left the house. It was bullshit. He sold me a dream wife, and I got her."

Blu laughs. "Is she that bad?"

"Worse."

"Why do you think he wanted her to marry you? It could just have been the deal he made with your father back in the day."

"He's practically an outcast in Italy. The families don't trust him. I agreed because it's what my father would have wanted. Diego was his closest friend at one point."

"Are you gonna tell him you know?"

"Damn straight."

"And what will you do if he laughs in your face, Vinn? You're married now, there's nothing you can do." "We haven't consummated, so we can get the marriage resolved." Blu slows his machine until it stops, and I feel his eyes on me. I glance over to him. "What?"

"You'd seriously resolve the marriage? Why?"

"We're not right for each other. I want someone I trust to raise my son, and I don't trust her. She's keeping secrets from me, and her father lied." "Did you ever ask her if she was a virgin, or did you take her father's word for it?"

I shake my head. "It doesn't matter."

"I just think you're overreacting, Boss. You weren't exactly pure when you met her. What if she wanted a pure man?"

I laugh. "Are you coming to Italy or not?"

"Of course. Where else would I be when my boss is starting a war with an Italian mobster?"

SOFIA

I'm not used to travelling in style, so when the car drives directly onto the tarmac at the airport and Ash opens my door, I stare out at the private plane. "Are you sure this is right?" I ask her. It's only been a couple of days since Vinn hired the duo to follow me around, but I quite like Ash and she's growing on me.

"Yes, ma'am."

"It's Sofia," I remind her again, and she smiles.

I head up the steps of the aircraft. Vinn avoided me for two days straight, and I was instructed to meet him here at six p.m. for our flight to Italy. It's now five-forty-five.

Gerry is seated at the front of the plane, tapping away on a laptop. He nods in greeting. I'm not sure if I'm imagining it, but he seems off with me these last few days, just like Vinn. Gia and Blu are in the next seats. She's resting her head against his shoulder with her eyes closed, and he's staring out the window. He doesn't acknowledge me, so I slip into a seat in the next row.

Five minutes later, the curtains at the back of the aircraft open and Vinn steps out, grinning. He's followed closely by the air hostess. His eyes land on me and his smile fades. "You're early," he mutters. I roll my eyes and turn to stare out the window. And he has the nerve to call me a *puttana*? He slips into the seat beside me, and I shift further towards the window to get away from him. "Have you eaten?"

"I'm not hungry." I haven't joined him for any mealtimes these last two days, not wanting to be in his cold company for a second longer than I have to. But Josey has made sure I've eaten by bringing food to my room.

"You need to look after yourself if you're going to carry my child."

"What does that mean?" I snap.

"You're welcome to use the gym I own."

I spin to face him. "You think I'm fat?"

He scoffs. "I think it wouldn't hurt to hit the gym."

My eyes widen. "I think it wouldn't hurt for you to keep your opinions to yourself." I straighten my shirt, glancing at my stomach. I'm not overweight, not even a little. I've always been lucky enough to eat what I want and never gain a pound, but hearing someone say I need a workout offends me.

"Sofia, I just meant—"

"Stop talking to me," I hiss, turning back to the window. I hate him so much.

I spend the next hour watching the air hostess as she flutters her lashes and constantly touches Vinn's arm or shoulder as she serves him whiskey and laughs at his stupid remarks. I hate him. I hate him. I hate him.

I can't help but compare her tiny waist to my normal one. I buy size ten to twelve, and she must be a six, if that. Christ, maybe I am overweight. I rub my stomach subconsciously. Why do I suddenly feel so unattractive? Gia's the same size as me and she's gorgeous. I sigh heavily, and Vinn glances at me. "Are you hungry?"

"No," I snap. "Christ, I don't eat that much."

"I didn't say you did," he mutters.

"But you think I'm fat?"

Blu glances back at us, a warning look in his eyes aimed at Vinn. "No, I didn't say that," Vinn says.

I stand. "Why am I letting you make me feel like this?" I ask aloud even though I'm talking to myself. I pass him, wondering if my arse looks as fat to him as I do. Oh god, what's wrong with me?

I go into the small bathroom and stare at myself in the mirror. "Jesus, woman. Sort your head out. Why do you care what that Italian prick thinks of you? You're gorgeous. Stunning. He's lucky to be sitting next to you," I say aloud to myself. "Now, stop doubting yourself. Own your curves." The door opens, and I yelp in surprise. Vinn steps in, pushing me back against the wall. "Who were you talking to?" he asks, placing a hand either side of my head and staring down at me like a predator about to eat his prey.

"Myself."

We stare at each other for a moment. Every so often, he glances at my lips, and I subconsciously lick them. His eyes darken when I do. "I wasn't trying to insult you back there. Apologies," he whispers. "You're beautiful. I read that mothers-to-be should work out to keep fit, that it helps their bodies go back to normal after birth. I should have explained myself better." He moves in closer, sniffing my neck, and I shiver, closing my eyes and willing myself to be strong. "You smell amazing," he mutters, his nose brushing my hair.

"We should go back out," I squeak.

"Actually, I have this," he says, holding up an ovulation test. I stare at it, then reality washes over me and I snatch it. For a second there, I thought we were making progress.

I sit on the toilet, not bothered that he's watching me this time. I pee on the stupid stick and push it into his hand, not caring it's wet with my urine. He glares at it with disgust. There it is—the look I'm used to. I wipe myself and as I stand, he smiles, turning it to face me. "Oh look, it's smiling." I feel the colour drain from my face as the smiley face mocks me. "And just so we're clear, nothing happened with me and the air hostess."

I scoff. "And I should believe you?"

"Yes. I don't lie." His words cut deeper than they should as I head back to my seat.

Chapter Five

VINN

I forgot how ridiculous the heat gets in Italy this time of year. Add in the mountains and winding roads, and by the time we reach Sofia's parents' house, I'm too hot and very irritable. I'd booked a hotel in the same village, but I'd also agreed to a welcome dinner with her parents, and we're already late, so there was no time to change.

Her father greets us at the door, which is unusual, but I let it slide. Maybe he gave his staff the night off. He kisses Sofia on each cheek, smiling proudly. She flinches slightly as he booms his greeting like he wants the whole damn village to hear. "Go through, your mother is so excited," he adds, pulling her inside. He holds out his hand, and I shake it, eyeing him cautiously. He's nervous and jumpy, glancing behind me as I step inside.

"Is everything okay?" I ask suspiciously.

"Fine, just tired. Flying back and forth to London is hard work." He set up his property development business in the UK, hoping to get more work. He's built his business here in Italy, but like me, he follows the money. He's already working on a few of my projects, including the apartment development that was finally agreed on earlier this week by the council.

"We should go over the property plans for the apartments while I'm here," I suggest.

Sofia is talking in a low whisper to her mother, Angela, and she stops abruptly when I enter the room. "Vincent, how lovely," her mother greets, standing. She grips the chair and winces like she's in pain.

Sofia shakes her head, glancing away like it hurts her to see her mother struggle. "Are you okay?" I ask, catching her hand.

"Yes, my hips are acting out."

I kiss her cheeks, and she lowers carefully back into her seat. "I'll make us some drinks," says Sofia, disappearing into the kitchen.

"How are you both?" asks Angela as Diego joins us.

"Good," I lie. "Will Mario be joining us for dinner?"

They exchange a look at the mention of their son. "Not this evening," says Diego, the lie rolling off his tongue. "He's very busy."

I nod. "Are we eating here or out?"

"We're joining some of the other families up on the rooftop," says Diego. "Everyone is looking forward to seeing you."

Sofia re-joins us with a tray of iced tea. "Dinner on the rooftop?" she repeats. "I thought we agreed we'd have a family dinner this evening?"

Diego glares at her, and she lowers her eyes. "The families are our family."

"Of course," she mutters.

"Is there somewhere I can freshen up?" I ask, and I'm pointed to the downstairs bathroom. Pulling out my mobile, I call Blu, who headed straight for the hotel with Gia and Gerry. "Look into Mario Greco, he's missing."

"He didn't attend the wedding either, right?"

"Correct. They said it was a passport problem. I didn't care to question it, but for him not to see his sister at all since . . . I want him found. Also, Diego was acting shifty when I arrived. He's arranged for dinner on the rooftop this evening with the families."

"Interesting. You'd think he'd want to spend time with his daughter." "My thoughts exactly. He's showing us off, wanting everyone to know we're here. I'm delaying my conversation with him about his lies."

"Probably for the best. I'll check out Mario and let you know what I find."

Rooftop dinners have not changed. I remember them from when I was small. Everyone from the village gathers for tapas and drinks. It's a regular occurrence, one I sometimes miss, and it's a good way for the families to keep an eye on each other. The main man of this part of the organisation, the capo, isn't here, and it surprises me. If he was to come to London, I'd make sure I was available as a show of respect. It leaves me questioning how happy they are to have me here in Italy despite having two connections, one through Gia and Azure and now through Sofia.

I make polite conversation, occasionally looking over to where Sofia sits with her mother and some other older ladies. She takes a limoncello from the centre of the table and knocks it back, taking a second and doing the same. I've never seen her drink apart from the occasional glass of wine.

SOFIA

I wince as the sweet, sticky liquid slithers down my throat. It doesn't even taste that nice. Why do people insist on drinking this stuff? "Are you okay?" whispers Mama. I nod, taking my fifth drink, and she watches me warily. "Are you sure?"

"Yes. Are you?" She knows what I'm really asking. "Hips." I scoff.

"What did you expect me to say? That I fell down the stairs? That old cliché?"

I sigh. "Have you heard from Mario?"

"He's doing well, Sofia. Please don't worry."

"I haven't seen or heard from him in months. I miss him. When can I talk to him?"

Papa joins us, shifting his chair closer to mine. "Why are you here?" he whisper-hisses.

"I have no idea," I snap. "He announced the trip two days ago and took my phone so I couldn't warn you."

"Have you argued? Have you told him anything you shouldn't have?" I shake my head, my mind wandering back to my conversation with Vinn about Dante. Papa eyes me warily. "What, Sofia?"

"You told me to say I had a boyfriend, right?"

He nods. "Yes, if he questions your virginity."

"Well, he did. Sort of."

Papa leans even closer, his eyes full of rage. "What happened?"

"He asked if you knew, and I wasn't sure what to say. He took it like you did and got mad." Mama squeezes my hand. "Why didn't you use your brain and tell him I didn't?" Papa hisses.

"Because I'm not good at lying. I told you that."

He shakes his head angrily. "You had one job," he hisses.

Vinn's shadow falls over us. "Sofia," he says sharply, and I look up guiltily. He holds out his hand, and I take it. "I just need to speak with my wife for a second," he tells Mama and leads me away. I snatch a glass off a nearby table as I pass, drinking it fast before Vinn notices.

The alcohol is making me lightheaded, so when we stop at the terrace edge, I grip the wall to steady myself. "What's going on?" asks Vinn.

"Going on?" I repeat.

"I'm not stupid, Sofia. I can see something isn't right. Tell me now, because if I have to find out for myself, it won't end well."

I shrug, and he narrows his eyes. "I don't know what you're talking about. Why are we here, Vinn?"

"Here on the rooftop or here in Italy?" he asks, his face serious. "I have things to discuss with your father."

"Because he lied?"

"Is your boyfriend here, Sofia?" he asks, looking around the crowds, but I shake my head. "Tell me who he is."

"It's in the past, leave it there."

"Did you love him?"

"Do you care?" I counter.

"I could kill your father for lying to me like he has."

"He didn't know," I blurt out, and Vinn laughs.

"Get your story straight, did you, when you were just chatting?"

"He didn't lie."

"Gerry is on his way to collect you. He'll take you back to the hotel."

I panic. "But I thought tonight was . . ." I swallow, not wanting to say the words. "You know, the night."

Vinn smirks, running a finger down my bare arm. I shiver. "I'll join you later. I have business to attend to."

I grab his arm, desperate to make him listen. "Vinn, please, Papa doesn't know about Dante, I swear it."

His face darkens. "Dante?" he repeats.

"Shit! Fuck," I hiss. "Danny . . . I meant Danny."

Vinn removes my hand from his arm and glances at his mobile. "Gerry is here. Go."

"Please," I try one last time, "don't hurt my family."

"Then tell me what you're hiding."

I take a shaky breath. "Papa is the reason Mama is hurt. He's violent. But she loves him, and without him, she'll die. I love her so much. Please don't hurt him, or he might take it out on her."

"That's not the secret, Sofia," he says, smirking. "Try again."

I glance to where Papa is watching us. "There're no secrets."

He looks past me. "Take her back to the hotel, Gerry."

I glance back as Gerry makes a move towards me. I grab Vinn's arm, and he stares at my hand with disgust. "Vinn, please," I beg desperately.

"Good night, *puttana*."

At the use of that name again, I spit at his feet. It's a huge insult to spit at the feet of a capo, but I want to distract him from my papa. His hand dashes out fast, gripping my hair and pulling me close to him. People nearby are staring wide-eyed. Disrespecting my husband is one thing but disrespecting a capo in front of everyone cannot be ignored. Vinn's eyes are blazing with fury. "For that, *piccola vagabonda*, I'll be extra hard on your papa," he warns, shoving me towards Gerry, who catches me.

"Little tramp," I repeat, laughing in his face. "At least I've had sex. I'm beginning to wonder if the news story was true." I'm antagonising him in the hope he takes me back, leaving my papa here, alive.

Vinn takes a deep breath, forcing a smirk in place of the seething anger. "No more alcohol, Sofia. You can't handle it. Take her now."

Gerry wraps an arm around my waist and lifts me from the floor, carrying me to the car. "That was stupid," he hisses in my ear. "What were you trying to achieve?" I begin to sob. "He's going to hurt my papa. You have to stop him."

"You know as well as I do, I can't stop Vinn Romano. Nobody can. Disrespecting him like that in front of the families was a huge mistake. He's going to make you pay."

I break free, almost stumbling. "I'm already paying with my life," I yell. "I'm tied to that monster forever."

Gerry shakes his head, his expression full of disappointment. "I thought you'd be the one to change him, but I was wrong."

"What's that supposed to mean?"

"He wasn't always this harsh. Since his father passed, he's..." Gerry trails off as he unlocks the car. "Well, let's just say he's not as calm as he once was. I put it down to a broken heart."

I scoff. "He'd have to have a heart for it to be broken."

"And I thought you'd heal it. Heal him. But you're causing more drama than is needed."

"I can't just take it lying down. I didn't want to be in this marriage, and then I caught him cheating with Raven and God knows who else."

"I have no time for your dramatics. Something is going on here," he says, pushing me to get in the car. "And when he finds out, which he will, we'll all suffer."

VINN

I invite Diego to sit away from the families. Most of the women have gone, leaving the men to drink. "Why did you lie to me, Diego?"

He looks almost bored, but it's forced, and it only confirms what I already know—he's hiding something. "Lie?" he repeats. "I haven't lied." "You're lying to me right now. You know what the punishment is for lying to me?"

"Can you be more specific?"

"Who's Dante?"

He sits straighter. "Who?"

I slam my hand on the table angrily. "I am trying to be patient for Sofia's sake, but if you don't start talking, I'm going to kill you right here," I hiss through gritted teeth. Diego glances around before sighing. "I didn't know until after the wedding," he lies. "I still don't know the whole truth."

I take out my gun and lay it on the table, resting my hand on it. He eyes it warily. "Sofia lied to me too. I only found out because Angela slipped it out," he says. "Is that why you beat her?"

Diego pauses, his nostrils flaring. "What happens between a man and woman in their marriage is private business."

"I feel like I've been taken for a fool, Diego. I promised my father I'd help you, should you ever need it, and I upheld that promise. The least you owe me is the truth."

"He's Colombian," he mutters reluctantly.

My eyes widen at his confession. "But not mafia? Surely not the Colombian mafia?"

His eyes flick to mine before landing on the gun again. "I don't know how she met him or what happened. She's yours now, he's not around."

"You handed me used goods, and not just any used goods, Colombian used goods!" I snarl and click off the safety on the gun. "Give me a reason not to kill you."

"Sofia will hate you."

"She already hates me," I yell, pointing the gun to his head.

He stares me in the eye, and I respect that he's showing no fear. "Teething problems. All marriages have them. Take her to dinner once in a while, buy her flowers."

"I don't need relationship advice from a man who lies and beats his wife," I snap. "Why me?" I demand, pushing the barrel of the gun hard against his skull. "Why didn't she marry him?"

"Italian and Colombian? I'd have been cast out."

"That's all that matters to you, isn't it? And now, you have my name to help you climb that ladder a little bit higher." I slam the gun against his head, and he hisses as blood trickles down his cheek.

"Vincent, Benedetto would like to see you," says a voice from behind me. I turn to find three men in suits waiting patiently. They lower their heads in greeting. Benedetto, the Capo of this Italian clan, is my age, having taken over from his father recently. If I was still here, he'd be my capo too, but since my father made it alone, we have our own clan back in London. It's respectful to agree, so I follow the men to a waiting vehicle, where Benedetto is seated in the back. We shake hands.

"Apologies I wasn't there this evening," he says, handing me a whiskey. "I had things to discuss."

"Not a problem. I was going to come and see you tomorrow."

"I hear things have been heated this evening."

"Nothing I can't handle."

"Diego Greco and his daughter, Sofia?"

"Like I said, nothing I can't handle."

"There were rumours about Sofia," he says, sipping his drink. "And then she was shipped off to London."

"What rumours?" I ask.

"That she was fucking the Colombian mafia."

I swallow the liquid in one. "I hadn't heard."

He chuckles, leaving me feeling uneasy. "Strange. I thought you'd do your homework before committing. Rookie error."

"My research didn't bring anything back," I say through gritted teeth. "Diego goes way back with my father, as he did with yours. I was honouring an old agreement."

"Yes, to tie the Romano and Greco families together. With your ties to the Rossi family too, it makes you very powerful."

"Are you worried I'll take over?" I ask, smirking.

Benedetto laughs, but it doesn't reach his eyes. "You wouldn't want Italy. You have your hands full with London. Besides, if the rumours are true and your wife is fucking the Colombian mafia, you'll have bigger problems."

I place my empty glass down. "It was great to see you, Benedetto. We'll talk soon."

"I look forward to it." He smirks, and I exit the car.

Gerry is parked up behind. I pull the door open with more force than is needed and get in. "Jesus, what a night."

"I don't think it's going to get any better, Boss. Sofia found a bottle of Jack back at the hotel, expensive stuff left for you from someone in the village. She wasn't in a good way when I left, so I hate to think how she'll be when we return."

I sigh. "Fucking great."

Music is playing loudly from our hotel room, and I find Ash standing by the door inside. "Where is she?" I ask.

"Bathroom," she says.

"Thanks. Get some sleep."

She nods once and leaves. I lock the door and go to the speakers to turn them off. Sofia comes scrambling into the room wearing only underwear. "What happened to the music?" she wails. She freezes when she sees me. "Vinn."

"Hi, honey, I'm home."

"My dad?"

"Is alive."

She sags with relief. "Thank you."

"I didn't do it for you."

I shrug out of my jacket and loosen my tie. "I'm not a bad person," she almost whispers, but I ignore her. "Why do you hate me?"

"Colombian?" I ask, and she pales. "You were fucking Colombian mafia?"

Her mouth opens and closes before she finally mutters, "It wasn't what it seemed."

"I can't even look at you," I spit.

"It wasn't how everyone is saying," she snaps.

"Where is your brother, Sofia?"

She shrugs. "Working. He's on the oil rigs."

"More lies," I yell, unhooking my cufflinks. "You keep lying. You disrespected me in front of everyone," I throw them on the table, and they skid off, hitting the floor. "You're making me out to be a fool."

She rushes to me, gripping my arm. "I'm not. I don't mean to."

"Get some clothes on," I snarl in disgust. Hurt passes over her face. "You look like a whore."

She covers her mouth, and I wait for her tears to flow, but instead, she bends slightly and vomits down my front. I stare at the bright yellow fluid as its warmth soaks the thin cotton and clings to my skin. "Oh shit," she croaks. She scrapes her hands down my shirt, trying to scoop the vomit off. It splats on the floor, and I suck in an irritated breath. "Sorry," she whispers.

Chapter Six

SOFIA

I wait patiently while Vinn showers, my head pounding. Why the hell do people drink regularly if this is how it makes them feel? I've spent ten minutes on my knees scrubbing my own puke from the floor and trying my hardest not to repeat the incident.

When he returns, Vinn snatches a pillow from the bed and heads for the couch. I watch as he lies down. "I'm sorry, Vinn." He doesn't reply. "I'd understand if you wanted to divorce or leave."

He scoffs. "Maybe I should let the Colombian have you."

"If it makes you feel any better, I hate myself."

"Don't!" he hisses, glaring at me. "I'm not gonna feel sorry for you. How the fuck did you meet a man we consider to be an enemy?"

"Vinn, do you trust me?"

He laughs, shaking his head. "I don't trust anyone. Trust gets people killed." I nod sadly. "You're probably right. I trust the wrong people. That's why I'm here, in this mess." I lie on top of the blankets, turning my back to him.

"And don't think I don't know why you got drunk this evening," he snaps.

Part of me wanted to test what kind of a man Vinn is. Would he still force himself on me if I was drunk? It would have been easier on us both. He thinks I've drank in the hope he'd leave me alone, but in reality, it was to numb the pain I'm going to feel the second he lays down with me. It's not that I don't find him attractive, I do. And it's not because of Dante, fuck no. It's because making love, having a family, should be about choice, and I am so sick of having my choices taken away.

When the sun rises at exactly five-thirty, Vinn is banging around and making as much noise as possible. I groan, throwing an arm over my eyes. "Up," he orders, ripping the sheets from me. His eyes linger a second on my body, then he turns away and begins rummaging through a suitcase. "Now," he adds, throwing some clothes at me.

I sit up and hold my spinning head. God, I feel awful. "Where are we going?" Taking in Vinn's running gear and trainers, I groan and flop back on the bed. "No, I don't run."

"I'm still extremely pissed about your father lying and I'm undecided how to make you both pay for tricking me into marrying you. I suggest you do exactly what I ask before I go on a rampage and take half the families out." He says it so casually that it takes a second for his words to hit my brain. "Running is a good cure for a hangover," he adds more softly.

Ten minutes later, we're standing outside the hotel while Vinn stretches. "Even in this heat?" I complain.

"There're other ways I like to burn off my anger," he says, raising a suggestive brow, "but I don't think you'll handle that, so running it is."

He begins to jog away, and I groan. Why didn't I marry an overweight, ugly, out of shape Italian? Then at least when he says things like that, I'd be repulsed instead of . . . well, instead of not.

After thirty minutes of me constantly stopping and complaining, we reach a clifftop. I bend, placing my hands on my knees, and try to suck in more oxygen before I pass out. When I look up, there's a car approaching. It stops beside Vinn, Blu steps out, and they shake hands. "What's going on?" I ask warily, glancing around. It's pretty secluded here, and we haven't passed a house in ten minutes.

Gerry steps out from the driver's side and opens the back passenger door. He reaches inside and struggles for a second before dragging a man from the back. The man's hands are bound and there's a black bag over his head. Gerry shoves him hard towards Blu, who pulls him to the cliff edge. Vinn smirks at me as he removes the sack from the man's head, and I gasp as my papa's pale face stares over the cliff edge. He doesn't move, doesn't make a sound. My screaming pierces the silence, causing birds to fly from the trees in panic. Gerry wraps his arm around my waist, holding me back. "Now, *cagna*, start talking," whispers Vinn with a satisfied look in his eyes.

"Bitch? Oh, the names get better," I yell. "But nothing sweet yet, I'm disappointed." He laughs. "Your precious papa is about to go over the edge. You have five seconds before I give the go-ahead."

"You can't kill him without Benedetto's permission," I shout.

"Five . . ."

"You'll be killed yourself . . ."

"Sofia, keep your mouth shut! This piece of shit cannot threaten me!" my papa shouts.

"Four . . ." says Vinn in a sing-song voice.

Blu moves closer to the edge. "Vinn, be reasonable. I'll give you whatever you want. A son, a family, whatever."

"Three . . ."

I shake my head, tears wetting my face, and I plead with my eyes for him not to do this. "You don't have permission. You'll never make it out of Italy," I whisper.

"What makes you think I don't have permission?" he asks, grinning. "Two . . ."

A silence falls over us all, the sound of my heavy breathing echoing, then Vinn nods to Blu. "One—"

"Okay!" I scream, and Blu pauses, glancing at Vinn for confirmation.

"Sofia, no," my papa yells.

"I was attacked," I continue. "The Colombian raped me." Vinn's mistrusting eyes narrow. "It's true," I add. "I saw a private doctor. There were notes, you can check."

Vinn tips his head in the direction of the car, and Blu drags Papa away from the edge. "You stupid girl," he snaps as he's shoved back in the vehicle.

Vinn steps closer, and Gerry releases me. "Tell me everything." I hesitate, and he arches his brow in warning. "I can get him back out here."

Gerry and Blu leave us, waiting in the car for their next order. "Mama said it was best to keep it to myself because it would start a war." I tangle my fingers together in a nervous knot. "Benedetto doesn't even know." "How did this happen? How did they get to you?"

"I was taken from my uncle's private boat. We'd spent the day at sea, me and Zarina with some of our other cousins. They took me during the night."

"You were on a boat with no security?"

"Papa is struggling financially. He had to let the staff go. Nobody knows," I mutter.

"He's setting up in London," says Vinn, confused. I shrug, unable to explain where Papa got all the money from for a new business and flights back and forth. He doesn't share that sort of information with me. "And your brother?"

"Papa said he's working on the oil rigs, but I don't believe him. I haven't spoken to Mario in months, not even on my wedding day. Papa said he didn't want to have him return in case he found out about the attack and started a war."

"Who knows about the attack?"

"Just my cousin. A video of the attack was sent to Papa. He says they are blackmailing him and that's why he has no money. The marriage to you was supposed to put an end to everything. They wouldn't want to war with you, or so Papa thought."

"Blackmailing him how?"

"I don't know. Papa said if word got out, I'd be accused of working for the Colombians, and Benedetto would have me killed."

Vinn sighs, nodding to Gerry for them to leave. Once the car has gone, he pulls me against him and wraps his arms around me. I stiffen, surprised by his show of kindness, and then I relax, letting him hold me. Suddenly, I'm tired . . . so very tired. Vinn scoops me into his arms and heads back down the path as I rest my head against his chest and close my eyes.

VINN

I carried Sofia back to the hotel, putting her straight to bed. Now, I'm watching her sleep as her eyelids flutter occasionally, her dreams clearly not good because she whimpers and flinches. Blu stands behind me. "You believe her?"

I shrug. "Find the doctor."

"Already done it," he whispers proudly. "He's meeting us here in thirty minutes."

"It doesn't add up. Why would they blackmail him over Sofia? Unless he's hiding something?"

"You think she was taken as a warning?"

I nod. "I want to know who this Dante guy is. We need to dig deeper into Diego Greco. We're also taking her mother back to England, so make sure she has a passport."

"And if Sofia's lied again?" asks Blu.

I stand, grabbing my jacket. "No more chances. I will kill her."

The doctor shakes our hands and takes a seat. The barman brings over a tray of espressos. "These are the notes," he says, handing me a file.

"Tell me," I say coldly, and he nods.

"Ms. Greco—"

"Mrs. Romano," I correct him, and he nods again.

"She was assaulted sexually and physically." He opens the file and lays out a few close-up photographs of Sofia, bruises on her face, her thighs, and her neck. Her lips are swollen, and her eyes are bloodshot.

The doctor uses his pen to point to her red eyes. "Consistent with choking. These marks on her neck are rope burns. She was held for six hours and raped repeatedly. Internal bruising was extensive, but she healed well and there should be no lasting scars."

"And this was definitely an attack?" asks Blu. "Yah know, it couldn't be consensual, rough sex?"

The doctor shakes his head. "Very rarely do I see anyone with these kinds of bruises. Mrs. Romano was extremely lucky. The culprit didn't care for Sofia, and he made sure to leave traces of who he was." He pulls out another sheet of paper. "He left DNA behind, which is very unusual in cases like this. It's almost like he wanted her to know who he was."

I stare down at the name. "Dante Arias," I say aloud. I pass over the envelope of cash, and the doctor tucks it inside the file. "Thank you."

When I get back to our room, Sofia is sitting on the bed with her knees pulled to her chest, staring out the window. "We fly home this evening," I say.

She starts at my voice. "Can I see my parents before we go?"

"No."

"But my mama—"

"We're having dinner with Benedetto and his family. Dress."

"I don't feel like—"

"Dress, Sofia!" I snap impatiently.

She slowly rises from the bed and heads for the bathroom, slamming the door closed. That's better. I can handle things when she hates me.

Benedetto's home is much like my father's used to be. There're men hanging around playing cards and drinking whiskey, and the atmosphere is light and jovial. When I replaced my father, I changed things. I decided to keep my family close, and although I still have my closest men hanging around, it's not how it was before, not like this.

Benedetto greets us like long-lost family, ushering us inside a quieter room with a table laid out with tapas and wine. I'd forewarned Sofia to act like my wife today, so her hand is firmly gripped in mine, and as we're introduced to Benedetto's wife, Caterina, I release her so she can make small talk.

"Did you ask your wife about the Colombian?" he asks, pouring me a glass of dark liquid.

"I want to tell you, Benedetto, I really do, but I don't trust you," I tell him bluntly.

"If you were in Italy, you'd be under me and you'd have no choice but to confess all. Vincent, this is my family, and I'll do anything to protect it."

"I hope you're not talking business," says Caterina, smiling and seating herself on Benedetto's lap.

I smirk. Sofia stands awkwardly beside me, and I hook a finger around hers, guiding her towards my lap. I pull her down and wrap an arm around her waist. "You're right, apologies," I say.

"I was just telling Sofia about my pregnancy," she adds, holding up a grainy image. "We had the first scan yesterday."

"Congratulations," I drawl, rubbing my hand along Sofia's thigh.

"We've been married for a month and weren't expecting to catch so quickly, but we're excited," Caterina says.

"Any news for you two?" asks Benedetto. "Everyone is wondering after that ridiculous story in the news."I laugh. "It's hardly news, Benedetto. It's a gossip page for bored idiots. I'm sure we'll make our own announcement in time." I grip the back of Sofia's neck and pull her down for a kiss. Her eyes widen as I press my lips lightly against her own. "Right, *bellissima*?"

SOFIA

I shudder when Vinn addresses me with the same name he uses for Leia. I don't know why it annoys me, but it does, and as he pulls away, I place my hands on his cheeks and kiss him back, only I take it deeper, sweeping my tongue against his and taking my time to taste him. It's our first proper kiss, and as I pull back, I feel my cheeks flush. For the first time, I see heat in Vinn's eyes instead of anger. There's desire and maybe even a little shock. Turning back to the couple, I smile, gasping when I feel Vinn's erection pressing against my arse.

"That's right," I manage to squeak out.

"Wine?" asks Benedetto.

"Not for Sofia," Vinn cuts in before I reply. "We're flying home this evening."

"It'll help me sleep on the flight," I say, taking the glass offered to me.

Vinn removes it and places it on the table. "We have plans for the flight," he warns, and my cheeks burn again.

We eat while Vinn tells Benedetto about London and some of his businesses. It's boring really, but I do find out more about his property plans that my papa's drawing up. Vinn needs him, so there's no way he'd have pushed him over the cliff today.

I'm nervous for the flight home, so when I climb aboard the private plane and see my mama sitting beside Gerry, I'm in shock. "What's going on?"

"A visit," says Vinn, moving past me and heading for whatever is beyond the dark blue curtain at the back of the craft.

"Are you okay, Mama?" I ask, crouching before her and taking her hands in mine. She nods, glancing at Gerry nervously. "Have you hurt her?" I snap, glaring accusingly at him.

He smirks. "I've been a gentleman."

"We'll talk," I whisper to her, then I storm after Vinn. "What are you doing?" I hiss.

He looks amused, and I take in the small kitchen area as he pours himself a drink. "I'm having a drink."

"I mean about Mama."

"I told you, she's coming to visit."

"She's never away from Papa," I snap. "What did he say?"

Vinn slams his now empty glass on the counter and pushes his face close to mine. "Your papa didn't have a choice," he growls out. "I call the shots.""What could you possibly want with her?" I wail.

"Maybe I did it for you."

I scoff angrily. "You don't do anything for me, Vinn."

His hand wraps in my hair at the base of my neck and his lips almost touch mine as he smiles. "I'm gonna set the world on fire for you, *ragazza dolce*."

"Sweet girl?" I repeat in a low voice. It's the first nice thing he's said to me and meant it.

"Men will burn, Colombia will fall, and it'll all be for you, *cara ragazza*."

I suck in a sharp breath. Nobody has called me 'dear girl' since my nona. "That's not for me, Vinn. It's for you. It's to save your reputation."

His nose brushes mine and his eyes stare at my lips. "Think that, if it makes you hate me more, but I know the truth." His lips press against my own in a slow, careful movement, almost like he's waiting for me to pull away. I don't. I wait, and as he tilts his head and his thumbs angle my face perfectly to connect with his, I close my eyes and let him kiss me. It's the kind of kiss that curls your toes and makes you press your legs together to ease the building ache.

Vinn's lips move across my mouth and then my cheek. He brushes the hair from my shoulder and runs his lips down my neck and across my collar bone, occasionally nipping the skin. His hands skim my stomach, which is on show thanks to the cute, cropped shirt I chose to wear, and then they travel underneath, his thumbs drawing circles as they make their way up to my bra-less breasts. He guides the shirt up and leans down to trail kisses over my chest, towards my pebbled nipple. I grip the counter behind me, throwing my head back when he takes my nipple into his warm mouth and circles his tongue over the sensitive nub.

His hand tugs at the button to my denim shorts, and when he slips it inside, I gasp, feeling slightly exposed as he runs his fingers through my wetness and smiles. He moves his finger in circles, and I jerk as sparks zap through my body. His other hand gently wraps around my throat, and he tears himself away from my breast to thrust his tongue into my mouth, kissing me with hunger.

Vinn rubs his erection against my leg, groaning into my mouth as he pushes a finger into me. My hands grip his wrist, trying desperately not to cry out in pleasure when he presses his thumb against my swollen clit. Knowing there are people just on the other side of the curtain is as much a turn-on as the thought of getting caught.

He pulls his hand away, and I resist the urge to grab it and put it back in my knickers. He holds his glistening fingers between us and grins before sucking them into his mouth. "Are you ready to beg yet?"

I stare open-mouthed. "Huh?"

"I told you before, *moglie*, you need to beg me, because I'll never force myself on you."

His words hit me like ice water. I straighten my clothes and take a deep breath. "I don't beg, *marito*. Ladies don't beg."

He laughs. "Very well. I'll sort this myself." I watch as he loosens his trousers, and my eyes widen. "Are you going to watch?" he asks, amused. I shake my head, backing out of the kitchen area and almost crashing into the air hostess. Vinn smirks, opening a door behind him and disappearing inside. I leave the curtain open just so I can keep an eye on the hostess, who sets about making drinks as I take my seat.

"Mama, what happened?" I whisper, leaning across to her.

"Vinn told me I was coming to visit London," she says with a shrug. "Your papa wasn't impressed." "I'm so sorry," I murmur. Vinn returns looking relaxed as he slips into the seat beside me.

"Are you looking forward to your visit?" he asks.

"Very much," smiles Mama politely. I can tell by her fake expression she's nervous and wondering what the hell is going on. I turn to Vinn, making sure my mama can't hear.

"Please don't hurt her, Vinn. She knows nothing about my papa and his dealings, she won't be able to tell you anything." "Relax, it's just a visit."

"Why?"

"Did I not warn you about questioning me?"

"Swear on Gia's life," I whisper.

"I won't hurt your mother, Sofia," he says firmly, but I note how he didn't swear it on his sister's life. "Don't you want some company at home?" I nod. "Then be happy."

Mama loves London. She always has. She'd visited before the wedding and then again for the big day. Her eyes light up at all the hustle and bustle, and even being followed by Ash and Frazer doesn't dampen her mood.

We've been here for three days, and we've spent every single daylight hour sightseeing. Ash knew all the best places to go despite Frazer's reservations of safety issues. We finish our day with a coffee in our new favourite cafe.

"You don't spend much time with Vincent," Mama remarks, stirring her latte.

I half smile, "I've been spending time with you." "I spoke with Josey, and she said you seem unhappy."

"Mama, don't let Vinn hear you're checking up on me with the staff," I hiss, groaning. "He'll send you home." Despite her reservations about coming here, she's really enjoying herself, and honestly, I think the break from Papa is doing her a world of good. It's the first time in a long time she's walked straight without cowering or wincing in pain.

"I have to go home one day, or your papa will come looking for me. Why aren't you happy?"

I shrug, picking up my napkin and tearing pieces from it. "It's a big change."

"We talked about this already. Vinn will keep you safe."

"Mama, he can't stand me. He isn't going to keep me safe."

"He will. You'll have his child, and then he'll have to."

I avert my eyes, and she places a hand on my cheek. "Sofia, what's wrong? You are trying for a child?"

"Not exactly," I mutter, and she gasps, looking around like it's a shameful secret someone might overhear.

"Dear girl, Vincent is your safety net. He was your way out of Italy. Don't let him slip through your fingers. You're his wife!"

"Like I said, he hates me."

"It doesn't matter, Sofia, he'll learn to love you. Just be yourself and the rest will come naturally, but you have to give him a child."

"Did you learn to love Papa?" I ask, and she stares down at the table.

"It was a difficult relationship from the start. My family was poor, and I didn't have the novelty of choosing a man like Vinn. Your papa was just a soldier back then. He worked hard to become a made man. Benedetto's father gave us a chance to be who we are, and I'm grateful.

I don't have to eat from the garbage these days." She laughs. "I love your papa, but he's a complicated man with a lot going on."

"You could stay here, with me."

She shakes her head. "I have a duty to him, until death do us part. Italy is where I belong."

"I'll need help with your grandchild one day."

She smiles, taking my hand. "Good girl, you'll make me proud."

"Mama, why did Papa choose Vincent?"

"He knew his father, you know all this."

"Just... he seemed so insistent on it. Vinn said he hadn't seen Papa for years before they met to discuss the wedding. I wondered if there was another reason."

"It doesn't matter either way. You have a decent man, so look after him like a wife should."

Chapter Seven

VINN

It's late when I finally climb the stairs to bed. I'm so exhausted, I can hardly see straight, and the bottle of whiskey I shared with Blu didn't help. As I open the bedroom door, I pause. Sofia is asleep on top of the blankets in a sexy nightdress. It's short, riding up her thigh, and it's shaped around her breasts. I frown. She's been sleeping in her own room since I yelled at her and told her we'd only share a bed when she was ovulating. She'd not even attempted to step one foot in here let alone dressed like that.

I carefully strip down to my shorts and sit on the edge of the bed. She looks peaceful, and even though my cock is screaming at me to fuck her until she wakes, I know I can't. So, I lie down beside her stiffly, trying not to disturb her.

I wake sometime later, feeling too hot. Glancing down, I find Sofia nuzzled against me with her leg over mine and her arm resting across my stomach. Her head is laying on my chest, angled up so I can see her beautiful sleeping face.

I brush my finger over her cheek, and she mumbles to herself. I smile—she's cute when she isn't talking back and asking questions. I gently kiss her lips, and she mumbles again, this time clearer. "*Frazer.*" I stiffen and it disturbs her, causing her to wake with a start. She glances around, takes in the way her body is wrapped around mine, and scoots away like I've burned her. Maybe she was expecting someone else, I think to myself angrily. Jealousy burns through me at the way her cheeks flush and her lips are slightly apart. "Vinn," she whispers, sounding confused.

I climb from the bed. "Sorry to disappoint," I snap.

"I waited for you, but you were late," she mutters, tugging her nightdress strap back to her shoulder.

"Why are you dressed like that?" I ask, and she blushes deeper and shrugs. I grab her ankle, tugging her until she's flat on her back, and she lets out a yelp. I climb over her. "Who were you waiting for?" I take her tiny hands in my own and hold them above her head.

"You," she whispers.

"Then why the fuck were you dreaming about Frazer?"

She frowns. "I wasn't."

I grip her chin in my free hand and push my face to hers. "You said his fucking name."

"I-I don't know... I don't think I was dreaming about him. I can't control my dreams."

I run kisses along her jaw, and she closes her eyes. "Maybe I've left you alone too much and now you're fantasising about other men."

"I have spent a lot of time with Frazer," Sofia reminds me.

I grip her throat, not enough to hurt but enough to let her know I'm pissed. "You don't wanna bring out that side of me, Sofia. I can't control him."

I tug the strap of the nightdress down her arm until her breast is exposed. She's breathing fast and watching me through hooded eyes as I go back to kissing along her neck and collar bone. I avoid the one place she's desperate to feel my mouth, and she whimpers every time I move around her breast. "What do you want?" I ask, smirking. She presses her lips together, refusing to answer me. I grin and go back to teasing her.

I move down her body, releasing her hands, but she keeps them above her head and occasionally strains her neck to watch me kiss across her stomach, over the soft material of her nightdress, and down her thigh. I gently part her legs, taking one foot in my hand to rub it. She groans aloud, and my cock twitches. I run my hand up her calf and over her knee, almost to the top of her thigh, before running it back again. She fidgets impatiently. "Tell me what you want, Sofia."

"The same as you," she whispers.

"Which is?"

When she doesn't answer, I laugh at her stubbornness. Without warning, I rip her panties, exposing her to me. She tries to close her legs, looking shocked and just as turned on as me, but I pin her knees to the bed and lean closer. She smells amazing. I press my tongue against her opening, and she cries out in surprise. I run it over the bundle of nerves and concentrate on teasing the sensitive bud. She grips her fingers into my hair.

"Say it," I whisper, but she still doesn't answer. I place my hands underneath her arse and lift her pelvis slightly. "You just have to say the words, Sofia." I suck her pussy into my mouth, lapping her juices. I rub circles over her clit with my thumb, and when I feel her clench, I pull away.

Sitting back on my heels, I wipe my mouth on the back of my hand. Sofia stares at me with a lost expression. "Just say the words." I crawl over her, placing a hand either side of her head, and I flick her nipple with my tongue. "Say them." She bites on her lower lip. "Do you trust me?" she asks.

I frown. She asked me this already, and again, I shake my head. "I told you, I don't trust anyone." I roll from her, hating that I feel the loss immediately. "Do you trust me?" I ask.

"No."

"Probably for the best," I admit, turning onto my side and pulling the sheets over. I hear her sigh as she lies back down.

SOFIA

I'm not sure if I'm sad or angry. I dressed sexy, and he didn't show until God knows when because I fell asleep waiting. Then, I give into his sultry smile and his skilful tongue without so much as a fight, and he leaves me wanting more, so much more. I know what I have to say if I want him to finish what he's started, but there's a fear deep inside me that worries I'm asking for more than sex. I was adamant, from the second I knew I had to go through with this marriage, that I wouldn't give him that part of me. At least not willingly, and yet here I am, hooking my leg over his half-naked body and sleeping on his hard, muscled chest like some wanton whore. I roll my eyes. I'm an idiot . . . a desperate one.

When Vinn's alarm rings an hour later, I'm still awake, feeling frustrated and annoyed. Vinn showers and dresses for work like he didn't come home stinking of whiskey in the early hours. How does he do that?

"We're attending an important dinner this evening. Get a cocktail dress," he orders, throwing his credit card on the bed. "And maybe get your hair done?" I narrow my eyes behind his back. *Dick.*

Once he's gone, I dress and head to the library. It's on the top floor of the three-story home and it's the only place, as far as I can tell, where there are no cameras and his men won't bother me. I've yet to explore the rest.

I curl up into a cosy armchair and open my laptop. Vinn still has my mobile phone, and I won't give him the satisfaction of asking for it back. I open my emails. My heart beats faster when I spot the editor from the Daily Spy has sent me something. I scan my eyes over the email, picking out the important bits, and then clap my hands in delight. Just wait until I tell Zarina.

I arranged lunch for me, Mama, and Zarina, and it's the perfect time to tell Zarina my exciting news. I wait for Mama to go to the bathroom before leaning across the table and grinning. "Guess what, the editor loved my story. She said it was Tweeted about loads. She wants me to write another." "Oh, Christ, please tell me you said no."

"Are you joking? Of course, I didn't. Can you imagine if this becomes my career? I could be a journalist like I always wanted." It was a dream Papa squashed, saying no one from our community would trust us. "Or the decomposing ex-wife of a mob boss," says Zarina, shrugging.

I laugh. "It's gossip. No one cares about gossip."

"Vinn will care that his wife is the one writing it," she hisses. "You're crazy if you think he'll laugh this off."

"I can't pass up this opportunity. Do you know how long I've waited for this? He shut down the Gazette, and that was huge. The editor at the Spy doesn't seem to give a crap what Vinn says. She's a female editor and all for women's rights."

"Will she campaign when you're dead?"

"I won't die. You worry too much." I spot Mama heading back to the table. "I haven't told her, so keep quiet."

After lunch, we head back to the house. It still doesn't feel like home and I'm not sure if it ever will, but Zarina is so enthusiastic about the large, cold rooms and flashy decor. She didn't have a chance to really be nosy when Vinn was here before, so she takes full advantage and rushes off with Mama to check out some of the other rooms.

I bite my lower lip as a stupid idea enters my head. There doesn't seem to be many staff hanging around, and I can hear Josey banging around in the kitchen, so I know she's busy. Ash has gone off to do whatever she does when she knows I'm safely locked away in the house, and since I apparently dreamt of Frazer, Vinn's had him moved to his mother's team of security.

I take a tentative step towards Vinn's office. I've only ever been in once, and he was here. I tap lightly on the door and press my ear against the thick, dark wood. There's no answer and I can't hear movement inside, so I push the door and huff in annoyance. It's locked. Taking a step back, I stand on my tiptoes so I can reach the top of the door frame and run my fingers across it. Nothing. My eyes fall to the group of three small flowerpots hanging on the wall with beautiful flowers cascading over the sides. I check each one, digging my fingers into the soil until I feel the key. Smiling triumphantly, I pull it free and insert it in the lock. I glance around to make sure the coast is clear before sneaking inside and closing the door behind me.

I take a second to steady my breathing, leaning against the back of the door and looking around the large office. It's an old man's kind of place, and I guess he hasn't bothered to redecorate since his father passed. I make my way over to the desk, closing the blinds so patrolling security outside can't spot me. Vinn's desk is one of those oversized, dark wood things that you imagine a lawyers to sit at. Pulling the top drawer open, there's nothing but a half-drank bottle of whiskey and two glasses. I feel around the back and pull out a pair of silk knickers. They aren't mine, so I drop them like I've been burnt, screwing up my face in disgust.

The next drawer has some paper files inside. The first has my father's name on it, so I open it and find bank statements and other financial paperwork. I guess after what I told him, he's dug deeper. It doesn't surprise me to see Papa's not as wealthy as he pretends to be. I slam it closed, not wanting to know the extent of his mess.

The next file is about me. Inside has my personal bank details, where I went to school, and my doctor's details. There's an open envelope and I peek inside, finding the doctor's report from after my attack, along with pictures. I stuff them back inside because I don't need reminders of what I went through. I work hard to keep it locked away, which isn't difficult seeing as I spent most of it drugged so the memories aren't vivid. But seeing those might bring it all back.

There's a gun laying at the bottom of the drawer, standard in Vinn's world. I sigh. There's nothing in here that the Spy would be interested in. As I put everything back, I notice a file splayed open on his desk. It shows the plans for some buildings, and when I take a closer look, I realise this must be the new project he's been working on. It's small apartments, lots of them, being built on green space. I grab a piece of paper from his notepad and scribble down the address. This is what he had the council pass through without the public knowing. Maybe the Spy could expose it. I'm pretty sure people will be furious that they'll lose a green space to a bunch of apartments. London is already full of buildings.

I'm locking the door when Mama and Zarina return. "We found a lot of bedrooms and they're all decorated the same," complains Zarina.

"Let me guess, white?"

"Yeah." She laughs. "What have you been up to?"

Mama heads for the kitchen, saying something about an espresso, so I grab Zarina by the arm and pull her into the sitting room. "I found something for a story."

She groans. "No, Sofia. No."

"It's not big, but I think they'll like it."

"What exactly do you get out of this?"

"Apart from my dream to work for a newspaper?" I ask, rolling my eyes. "I can make something out of this, Zee. I could be an undercover reporter. Think of the things I could expose."

She laughs like I've lost my mind. "Listen to yourself," she hisses. "Most women would love this life," she adds, looking around the living room in awe. "He's sexy, powerful, and he's got a great home and a nice family. Why can't you just be happy?"

"Because I want more," I snap. "And maybe that sounds spoiled and bratty, but this isn't enough for me. I don't want to wake up one day and realise I'm trapped here forever. My mama did that and look at her, desperate to get home to beg forgiveness from the man who's spent years mistreating her."

Zarina looks concerned. Maybe because we never speak about my parents and what happens behind closed doors. "Does Vinn hurt you?"

I shake my head. He's scary in a dominant kind of way, and although he's pinned me down and held my throat, I've never felt threatened. Images of his head buried between my legs assault my mind and I shake my head to remove them. "No, but it doesn't mean he won't. We don't know each other, and he's got a temper. He's ruthless. You saw how he knocked the plates from the table in the cafe."

"So, you want to punish him just in case he hurts you?" she asks sceptically. "Because I have to say, that's crazy. What if he turns out to be the most loving husband ever? What if he makes the best father to your children?"

I shake my head. "It won't happen. He doesn't like me in that way. I've seen how he looks at his assistant. He doesn't look at me like that, in fact, he barely looks at me because he's never here. He'll have other women on the side. He probably already has."

Zarina takes my hand and smiles sadly. "It's almost like you're trying to prevent the hurt by dismissing the idea that he could actually be a nice guy. You're pre-empting something that might never happen. You can't live life like that or it's not living."

"Why should I sit around and play the good wife while he's out there doing God knows what with God knows who? If this job works out, I can earn money and save, just in case something bad does happen. I can be financially independent. That's a good thing. Planning ahead for every eventuality."

She sighs, nodding. "Right, well, don't say I didn't warn you."

I tap away on the laptop, smiling to myself. This is gonna be a good story. Suddenly, the library door crashes open and Gerry stands there, looking annoyed. He takes in my pyjamas and messy bun and his eyes bug out of his head. "Why aren't you dressed?" I stare back, bewildered. "The dinner?" he snaps. "Vinn's already at the gala waiting, and he sent me to collect you."

I slam the laptop closed, jumping up in panic. "Fuck, I forgot."

He buries his face in his hands. "At least say you have a dress."

My heart slams hard in my chest. Vinn's gonna be pissed. I shake my head, and Gerry groans, muttering something behind his hands that's inaudible. "It's fine. I have dresses, I'll just grab anything."

"It's a gala. You can't rock up in one of those ugly summer dresses you wear," he hisses.

My mouth falls open. "I didn't choose those," I snap. "They were already in the wardrobe. Besides, I have some of my own clothes."

"Vinn specifically asked you to have your hair done today." At the reminder of Vinn's rude words this morning, I smirk. This is another opportunity to go against the grain. "Don't give me that smirk," warns

Gerry. "I'm not in the mood for games. Dress now, you have ten minutes before he loses his shit and starts blowing up my phone."

All the way to the gala, Gerry glances at me in the rear-view mirror, shaking his head in annoyance. He wasn't impressed when I came down to the car, but we were out of time and Vinn was already calling Gerry. We stop outside a large country manor. It's lit up and there are other sleek black cars parked out front in a neat row. Ash gets out the front passenger and opens my door, smirking. I think she finds my rebellion amusing. "He's waiting over there," she points out quietly.

Vinn's staring down at his mobile. As I approach, he glances up, and as he takes in my short, low-cut red dress, anger passes over his face. "What the fuck?" he hisses.

"You don't like it?" I ask, slowly spinning to show off the back that cuts so low, I couldn't wear underwear.

"It's a gala. You wear cocktail dresses to galas," he mutters, glancing around like he's expecting this to be one big joke.

Raven steps out of the grand building and comes to an abrupt halt when she spots me. "Oh," she gasps. Of course, she's in a floor-length, fitted black dress that clings to her curves perfectly. Her hair is neatly plaited to one side and her diamond earrings glisten.

"Oh indeed," repeats Vinn.

"I was just coming to tell you we're being seated for dinner."

VINN

I follow Raven inside, Sofia trailing behind me. "I'm sure there's an explanation," Raven whispers.

"I'm not interested in explanations."

"Give her a break. Besides, the dress does look good on her."

"Yes, if she was a hooker, the dress would be perfect for this evening," I snap, storming ahead.

"I hate this bullshit," complains Blu when I reach our table. Gia pats his hand, smiling. He hates being part of this life, but since marrying my sister, he doesn't have a choice.

I sit beside Gia, who stands to kiss Sofia's cheeks in greeting. "You look amazing," she gushes, glancing at me with confusion as she embraces her.

"Thanks." Sofia suddenly doesn't look as confident as she did when she first spotted me. Maybe it's because the entire room looked her way as she entered. Being the only person to wear red to a black-tie event is gonna have that effect.

Raven sits opposite me, alongside her husband, Mac. I inwardly curse, like I do every time I see her. She's wearing a long black dress that shows her tiny baby bump. That could have been us. Why the fuck did I mess it up? I sigh heavily, getting everyone's attention around the table. "What?" I snap, and they look away.

Dinner gets underway and I eat in silence, too annoyed that Sofia defied me again to bother engaging as Blu and Mac make jokes about club life. After dinner, Sofia mutters something about the bathroom and marches off with Ash close behind her. Raven moves to the vacated seat. "Christ, get over the dress," she says.

"It's not about the fucking dress," I snap. "It's about her doing as she likes, not listening, not doing as she's . . ." I trail off. Raven's the wrong person to speak to about this.

She arches her brow. "Told?" she finishes. "She isn't a dog."

"You don't get it," I mutter.

"She's your wife. Treat her with respect and she'll do the same." Raven's phone buzzes and she opens an email "Great," she utters. "Another story is hitting the Daily Spy tomorrow."

I pinch the bridge of my nose, willing the dull thumping in my head to go. "It'll be another pile of shit. Ignore it."

"Maybe we should meet with the editor," she suggests, but I shake my head. I've done my research—the editor has no family, no one close, and nothing for me to threaten. She screams about women's rights and animal cruelty. I have no doubt she burns her bra at conventions condemning men. She's not the kind of person to listen and the sort of person who will smile at my threats before printing them all in her cheap rag of a paper, causing me more harm than good.

Sofia is heading back so Raven returns to her seat. The dress is sexy, and I'd appreciate it if it was on my bedroom floor rather than in a place like this, where rich men offer girls dressed like that good money for a night of pleasure. As she sits, the dress rides up higher. If she was to bend over, it would reveal everything. My cock twitches, and I'm reminded why I can't shift my shitty mood or the thumping head—I need sex. It's been months and I'm not sure how much willpower I have left.

"Sorry for—" she begins, and I stand abruptly, cutting her off.

"I should mingle," I mutter, walking away.

SOFIA

Vinn's been gone ages, mingling with the rich arseholes filling this room. Gia has spent the last twenty minutes eating Blu's face off while they whisper and giggle together like horny teenagers, and Raven and Mac have disappeared. I still have Vinn's bank card, so I make my way to the bar. It's not busy, as most people have table service, so I grab a stool and order a white wine and soda. Not being a big drinker, I never know what to order, so I stick to safety. I'm halfway through my drink when a man takes the seat beside me. He smiles, and Ash steps forward. "You can't sit there," she says.

I'm embarrassed and my face shows it. "Ash, it's fine," I hiss. "Honestly, I'm okay."

She steps back, and the man smiles wider. "Are you sure? I can move."

"It's fine."

He looks around. "I hate these events and I felt suffocated sitting over there. Thought a walk over here might help, and then I spotted you and thought you must be feeling the same."

I smile, nodding. "Something like that."

He holds out his hand. "Raymond," he introduces.

"Sofia," I say, shaking it.

"How come you're sitting here alone?"

"Same as you, needed a bit of space."

"Not surprising in that dress," he says, grinning. "You made quite a statement."

"I didn't mean to. I didn't get the memo."

He laughs. "I'm sure Vincent was happy about that."

"You know him?"

He laughs again. "Everyone knows him." The barman comes to take his order. "I'll take a whiskey, neat. Sofia?"

"I'm fine. I can't drink much without making a fool of myself," I say, smiling.

"In that case, let's have some shots." He proceeds to order drinks I've never heard of and hands over his card. "What's a party without making a fool of yourself? Maybe you can top the dress incident," he jokes, and I laugh, feeling at ease.

"I really shouldn't." I glance around, but there's no sign of Vinn.

"I'm a forty-eight-year-old man, not after anything but company. What's the worst that can happen?"

A tray of different coloured shots is placed before us and Raymond smiles. "Let's drink the first to a happy marriage," he says, taking a green one. I do the same, and we clink glasses before knocking the drinks back. I wince at the taste of bitter apples coating my tongue. "Okay, that wasn't the best one. Try this," he suggests, chuckling. I take the pink shot. "This time, you choose."

I think for a moment. "Good company at boring events." This one goes down easier.

"So, how is married life?" he asks.

"Different," I mutter. "London is much busier than where I come from."

"I bet." He hands me a blue shot, and we drink to Italy. "My wife moved here from Canada. She took a few months to settle. She hated it at first."

"Does she like it now?" I ask, desperate to cling to the hope I might settle here and feel happier.

"She wouldn't leave."

He points to the empty tray, and the bartender tops up the glasses. "Let's do one after the other."

"That's definitely not a good idea." I smirk. "I'll be carried out of here."

"I bet Vincent likes you to stay prim and proper," he sniggers.

"I'm my own person," I mutter, frowning.

"I hear he likes his women to be compliant and well behaved."

"I don't think that's true." I suddenly feel like I need to defend the husband I hate.

"Really? Does he listen to your opinions? Do you get to do what you wish?" I take a shot and swallow it, followed by another, and Raymond smiles. "I stand corrected."

"Vincent Romano doesn't tell me what to do!" I say bravely, holding up my empty glass.

"Is that right?" Vinn's voice rumbles from behind me, and I almost fall off the stool. Raymond grabs my hand to steady me. He looks amused.

"Vincent," he greets, smirking.

Vinn's eyes linger where Raymond's hand touches mine. "Let's go," he says firmly, ignoring Raymond.

"I'm not finished," I spit, lifting another shot from the tray. Vinn's hand wraps around my wrist, halting me just as it touches my lip.

"Now, Sofia."

Raymond arches his brow in an 'I told you so' way and stands. "Maybe I should go."

"You'll be seeing me soon, Raymond. Make no mistake," mutters Vinn in a deadly voice, and I shiver.

"Look forward to it," Raymond responds as he walks away.

Vinn pushes his face to mine. "Too far, Sofia," he whispers, his eyes dark and dangerous. His hand runs along my shoulder, and I freeze as he places it calmly around the back of my neck. "Drink the shot," he orders. My hand shakes, causing the blue liquid to run over my lower lip, where it's still positioned. "Now," he growls, and I jump with fright, spilling some of it down my chin. I slowly tip the glass, swallowing it. "Are you feeling the warm buzz?" he whispers, spreading my legs and standing between them. He reaches behind me and produces another full shot glass. He must have ordered more, and I wince, my stomach rolling at the thought of another. "Next," he says, smirking.

"I don't want any more."

"So, you'll drink for Raymond Clay but not your husband?"

"I've had enough."

"You'd had enough when I told you we were leaving, but you were insistent on finishing your little party." He squeezes my throat a little tighter, and I grasp the edge of the stool. "You ask me if I trust you and then drink cheap shots with my enemy."

"I didn't know," I croak, my eyes beginning to water as he applies more pressure.

"Is that how you met the Colombian, *puttana*?"

It's too much, the word 'whore' and then him daring to bring up Dante after I opened up and he saw the doctor's report with the disgusting pictures. I see in his eyes he regrets it the second the words leave his lips, but it's too late. I release a frustrated cry and shove him hard. He only stumbles back a step, but it's enough for me to stand. My hand hits his cheek, and the sound seems to echo as we both glare at each other, processing what just happened.

"I am not a whore!" I hiss, clenching my fists. "I'm not a whore," I repeat, tears stinging my eyes as I rush past him and head for the exit.

Gerry catches me in his arms as I fly down the stone steps, sobbing angrily. He holds me for a second until he spots Vinn and releases me. "Let's get you home," he whispers kindly.

"It's not my home," I sniffle, sliding into the back seat of the car.

Vinn joins me, and we stare out of opposite windows in silence as Gerry pulls away from the house. I remember the underwear in his draw. "Do you love Raven?" I ask, my throat hoarse from crying. He doesn't answer. "You look at her like you do," I whisper.

We get home and I head straight for my own room. We need distance, which is a joke considering we're never together.

Chapter Eight

VINN

I scan my office. "Gerry!" I call, and he appears. "Someone's been in here."

He frowns. "Is something missing?"

I shake my head. "No."

"Maybe Sofia had a wander around?"

"It was locked," I say, and he shrugs.

"No one could have walked in off the street, Boss, but I'll check the cameras."

I settle behind my desk and open the drawers. Nothing is missing, but things have been moved. I hook the knickers on my finger and hold them up. I forgot about these. I drop them in the rubbish bin as memories of Raven spread on my desk assault my already horny brain. Sophia's question plays over in my mind. Do I still love Raven? I scrub my face and let out a loud groan. Fuck, why is it so complicated? I don't love Raven. Of course, I don't. I don't love anyone. But do I still want her? Every fucking second of every day. My body craves her. She was my last decent fuck, and now, I've had to resort to sorting myself out in the shower because I'm married. And the most interesting thing about that is even though Sofia drives me nuts, it was her I thought about this morning when I couldn't concentrate at work and needed to relieve myself. It was her taste on my tongue and her scent burnt into my brain. I slam my hand on the desk in frustration. Seeing her chatting with that piece of shit, Raymond, like he was a long-lost friend tipped me over the edge. I didn't like it . . . not one bit.

SOFIA

I clean the makeup from my face and stare at myself in the mirror. I don't smile anymore, not like before. Vinn didn't answer me when I asked about Raven, and it hurt. Why the hell did it hurt when I hate him? Maybe because I know I'm tied to him. Maybe because I'm a little jealous. I sigh. Raven is beautiful and elegant. She walks into a room and people stare. And yes, they looked my way this evening, but only because I was half naked. Who the fuck did I think I was, dressing in red to a black-tie event? I groan. Why do I even care?

The shots are making my brain fuzzy and it's making me think I'm hurt, but maybe I'm not. Maybe it's just the drink. I pat my face dry with a towel while making my way to the drawers, then I rummage through to find comfortable underwear. I laugh to myself. It's all new stuff—lace, silk, sexy, thongs—but nothing remotely comfortable. I pull out a lace bodice and grin. Christ, I've never worn anything so revealing and sexy. I hold it against my torso and stare in the mirror. It won't hurt to try it on. After Vinn's recent remarks about my appearance, it might be the boost I need.

I stumble around, trying to get the thing on, and then stare at my reflection. I look good, hot even. The alcohol makes me brave, and I pull a pose fit for Instagram, laughing to myself. I turn to check out the back as the bedroom door opens. I let out a squeak of panic as Vinn glares at me. His expression is dark, but it's not anger for once. No, this look is full of desire. He likes what he sees.

"We're married, we should be in the same bed all the time," he says, not taking his eyes from me.

"Right," I mutter. I follow him like this is what I always wear for bed, and I don't even bother to put up a fight. Why aren't I putting up a fight? We get into his room, and I stand awkwardly while he loosens his tie, still watching me through hooded eyes.

Vinn begins to unbutton his crisp white shirt, and I bite my lower lip as he peels it from his body. My gaze follows his hands as he unfastens his belt, ripping it from the loops so it makes a snapping sound that causes me to jump in fright. He opens the button on his trousers. "I want to," I blurt out, and my cheeks instantly burn with embarrassment.

He slowly moves towards me, his eyes fixed to mine. "You want to what?"

My breathing is heavy as he gets closer. "I want to . . . I want . . ."

He stops so close, my breasts brush against his chest. "Show me," he whispers, taking my hands and guiding them to his zipper.

I slowly pull it down. I can feel his erection desperate to be released. I keep looking up into his eyes as I lower to my knees. I'm not experienced, but Zarina and I once watched a porn film for a laugh. Pulling down his trousers and shorts, I stare at his hard cock. It's big. I don't have much to compare it to, but it looks too big. I tentatively run my tongue over the tip, and he hisses as it jerks. "I'm not sure . . ." I begin.

"You're doing great, baby," he whispers, stroking a hand down my hair. It's pathetic that this one kind word has me smiling, and yet I know he's only saying it because I'm on my knees, about to suck his cock. How shallow does that make me?

I hold the base, wrapping my hand around it, and lick him again. He continues stroking my hair as I carefully run my tongue underneath and along his shaft. He's breathing deeply, and I revel in the fact I'm the cause of that. I open my mouth and suck it in like a giant lollipop. Vinn moans and it spurs me on. I suck, moving my head back and forth, careful not to scrape him with my teeth. My jaw aches from his sheer size and there's no way I can get him all in my mouth, but I keep going until he pulls me back and crouches to my level. He kisses me hard, slowly pulling me to stand.

"The first time I come, I need it to be inside of you," he murmurs, leading me to the bed, but I shake my head.

"No," I mutter, and he frowns. "I don't want you to be soft and slow. Fuck me." This needs to feel like what it is, a fuck, a means to an end. We're not making love. I peel the straps from the bodice until my breasts are revealed, distracting him from overthinking my last statement. It works because he sweeps me up in his arms and slams me against the wall, sucking my breast into his mouth. I arch my back, desperate for him to ease the ache between my legs. He reads my mind, moving the piece of fabric between my legs to one side and lining himself up.

"You're sure?" he asks. I nod, gripping his shoulders, and he doesn't double check. Instead, he slams into me, and I cry out, shocked by the intrusion. He pauses, resting his head on my shoulder. "Fuck," he whispers. After a minute, it starts to feel more comfortable. "Are you okay?" he asks, and I nod. He kisses me, distracting me as he withdraws to the tip and slams in again. This time, he doesn't pause, just repeats it. His hands squeeze my arse as he pumps into me, grunting with each forceful movement. I can feel a warm tingle in the pit of my stomach, and he senses it too because he sucks my nipple into his mouth and the feeling intensifies. "Hang on, Sofia, don't come yet," he pants. He moves us over to the bed and withdraws, laying me on my front. He rubs my arse, then slaps his hand against it and rubs it again. I flinch, but it doesn't feel like a bad pain, and when he does it a few more times, I have to clench my legs together because the ache is worse.

VINN

I slap her perfect, tanned arse a few more times, rubbing between each strike. Her skin turns a peachy red, and I run my finger between her legs. She's drenched. I lick her juices from my fingers and line myself back up with her pussy. Gripping her shoulders, I ease back into her. She feels so fucking good, I'm barely hanging on. I push her arse cheeks together to give more friction even though she's already gripping my cock like a damn vice. She buries her face into the sheets and moans. It's sexy as fuck, and I slam harder, slapping her thigh. It sends her over, and I feel her pussy clenching around me as she quivers. Her body shakes as her orgasm washes over her and her tiny fists grip the sheets, screwing them up.

I could watch her all night, but she's too much and too new to this to go the distance. I pull out and turn her over, wanting to see her face when I come. I place one of her legs over my shoulder and guide my cock back to her wet pussy. She watches me as I strain to hold back. I wrap her hair around my fist and tug gently, pushing harder with each thrust. I close my eyes, growling when I release into her. My legs go weak, but I keep moving until I'm completely empty.

I brace myself over her while we stare at each other and try to catch our breath. Sofia was better than I'd imagined, and as I take in her dark eyes and rosy cheeks, I feel a flicker somewhere deep inside my chest.

SOFIA

Vinn is distant again. It came suddenly, right after we'd done what we did. He doesn't make it obvious, though. Instead, he kisses me on the head and removes the bodice from my aching body. He discards it and pulls the sheets back, guiding me into bed. I wonder if it's a part he plays, the gentleman, but his eyes tell the truth, and right now, they're full of regret. "I have some things to finish in the office," he mutters, then places another kiss on my head. "Goodnight, *bellissima*."

Once he's gone, I wrap the sheet around my body. I need to delete the email I was going to send to the Daily Spy. Mama is right—I should make this work, and there's no reason why I can't. Seeing the kind, caring side of Vinn is nice, and maybe it's just because I gave in to him, maybe it's because he might finally get his child, but I want more of it. I want more of him.

I creep back to my bedroom and sit on the bed with my laptop open. I have a private file stored under the name 'coursework' but before I get a chance to open it to delete the articles I've written so far, an email pops up from the Spy. I stare in disbelief as I read it. It's confirmation that my story will appear in tomorrow's paper. Front page! But I didn't send it... unless... I open my sent items and groan. I must have hit 'send' when Gerry stormed into the library earlier today and made me jump. *Fuck.*

When I wake, the bed is empty. I don't know if Vinn even bothered coming back at all. I dress and head down for breakfast. Vinn's pacing as Gia reads something aloud. I recognise it as the article straight away.

". . . the planning permission was seemingly passed through without public input. The space is currently a green space used by many locals and even includes a children's play area. With so many properties already crowding the estate, it's no wonder residents in the area will be angered by Mr. Romano's latest business venture. People may also question the integrity of the local councillors and not for the first time. Jones has been investigated previously for—"

"Stop," snaps Vinn, and she places the paper down.

"That's not good," she mutters.

"We need to call a meeting," says Blu, standing and pulling his mobile from his pocket.

"Everything okay?" I ask, taking a seat.

"Ask me again if I make it home alive," mutters Vinn as he storms from the room and Blu follows.

"What happened?" I ask.

Gia glances at the door to make sure they're both out of earshot. "That Revenge person wrote another story. Vinn's got a project to build apartments on the Dale estate. He's got a lot of investors and if it falls through, it's his neck on the line."

"He can't help if it falls through," I say.

"They won't see it like that, Sofia. You know what these men are like. It mentions dirty money being invested and suggests a backhander to the council." "That's kind of true," I point out.

"These investors will not want to be outed like that. It puts them at risk of the cops looking more closely at where their money is coming from. They trusted Vinn to protect their names as well as their investments. They're gonna be coming for Vinn. Plus, these apartments were to help house women escaping violent relationships. He came up with it after his meeting with some woman who raises money for women's shelters. His heart was in the right place." I remember that woman because I was at the meeting. She told us some harrowing stories of women who have now made something of themselves after suffering many years of abuse. I feel a stab of guilt. Maybe he does have a heart after all.

Mama and my mother-in-law enter the kitchen, laughing about something. They've really hit it off and it's nice to see her laughing again. "Who died?" asks Rose, taking a seat beside Gia.

"Another story," explains Gia, pushing the newspaper towards her. She glances over it, then passes it to Mama.

"Who would want to make up those lies?"

"Vinn will sort it, Mum. Don't worry," Gia reassures her.

"I know he isn't innocent, but he does some good from the bad."

VINN

"Get me the editor on the phone," I order Raven.

"Is that a good idea?" she asks. She's trying to help, but I'm too wound up. When I glare at her, she nods, picking up the phone. She puts the call through to my office.

"Mr. Romano, I've been expecting you." The editor sounds smug, which only adds to my bad mood.

"You know I can have you for slander?"

"You could if it were lies."

"It is lies!" I yell. "That's why real newspapers won't print it. It's bullshit."

"Other newspapers won't print it because you scared them with threats. Editors talk, Mr. Romano."

"I'll speak with my solicitor, and I suggest you do the same!"

"I'll require proof to make a retraction," she says coolly.

"I don't need to prove shit."

"Fine, but my solicitor will tell you the same thing."

I disconnect, muttering in Italian. "We've gotta take this Revenge fool more seriously," snaps Blu. "We underestimated him."

"Damn right."

"The council might retract the permission if residents question it. They can put it on hold while an investigation takes place."

"I can't put it on hold," I growl. "There's too much riding on it."

"I know but keep your head. We've got to meet with the investors and explain what's happened."

I stand, pulling my jacket on. "Fuck that. I'm Vinn Romano, I don't have to explain shit. I want to pay Raymond Clay a visit."

"Raymond?" he repeats, following me.

"He hates me since I cut his lover's fingers off. It makes sense."

"You can't go in there," yells the secretary stationed outside Raymond's office. I ignore her, marching in and coming to an abrupt stop at the sight of his fingerless lover on his knees sucking Raymond's cock. Blu sniggers.

"Don't let us stop you," I drawl.

Martyn James tries to stand, but Raymond places a hand on his head and keeps him there. "I won't," he snaps, jerking himself off. I roll my eyes and move towards the couch. Gerry keeps watch at the door, while Blu stays in the corner. Seconds later, Raymond tucks himself away and pours himself a drink. "I'd offer you one, but I don't like you so . . ."

I smirk. "Are you writing stories about me, Raymond?"

He laughs. "Do I look like I have time to write stories?"

"Honestly, yes. You must have plenty of time on your hands, seeing as I just caught you getting your cock sucked."

"Everyone has time for sex, it's a stress reliever. Clearly, it's not something you have a lot of. Is that why your new wife looks miserable and drinks with strangers in bars?" He sits at his desk. "Have you tried looking closer to home?"

I glance at Gerry, giving him the signal. He moves to Martyn and wraps an arm around his neck. "Yah see, the thing is, I keep my circle tight, Raymond." Martyn panics, his feet sliding over the floor, trying to relieve the pressure on his neck. Raymond doesn't bat an eyelid. "So, I don't need to look closer to home."

"It was just a suggestion, no need to get upset."

"If I find out it's you, Raymond. I'm going to kill you, your wife, your children, and Martyn." Gerry drops Martyn, and he falls to the ground, coughing violently. "If I was you, I'd find a new lover. This one keeps getting you into bother," I say to him as I head for the door.

I spend hours placating the investors, assuring them I'm on top of this deal and they won't lose out. By the time I find my local councillor, I'm even more than pissed.

I take in the large house with four cars on the driveway and shake my head. I must have paid for most of this with the amount I put into his back pocket. I ring the doorbell and a young woman in her twenties answers. She blushes when I smile. "Helen, right?"

"Yes."

"Aren't you stunning," I admire, and she blushes deeper. "Is your father around?"

She nods, opening the door wider and letting us in. She disappears and returns with Damien Jones. He pales. "Gentlemen, let's go into my office."

"Blu, keep Helen company," I order, and Damien shifts uncomfortably. I slap him hard on the back and smile. "Relax, Jones, she'll be fine. Blu's a gentleman . . . most of the time."

I follow him to his office with Gerry close behind me. "We have an emergency meeting first thing to discuss your project," he explains, pouring a drink with a shaky hand.

"I don't want to hear that, Damien. I want to hear that there's no problems."

"Vinn, we've been getting complaints all day. This can't be brushed under the carpet. You'll be lucky if they let it go ahead at all now." I pick up a silver pen and admire the intricate pattern before casually slamming it into Damien's shoulder. It pierces the skin like a butter knife, ripping his pale blue shirt. He screams out, reaching for it. Gerry shoves some material into his mouth to muffle his cries, and I grip his hand that's holding the pen. "Don't pull it out, Damien. That's the worst thing to do when you impale yourself on a sharp object. Now, you let your little friends on the council know that I'll come for each and every one of them until this project gets the go-ahead." Sweat beads on his head and he makes a muffled attempt to agree. "I don't want to have to go to all the trouble of fucking your daughter and having her involved with me, because honestly, I'm a fucking mess. Just ask my wife. But I will, Damien, if I have to. I'll fuck her and have little Vinns with her so we can be one big, happy family. Imagine that, me joining you for Christmas. Now, just so we're clear, the planning is to stay and I'm going to start the build next week. If anything goes wrong, I'm coming for you and all your little jumped-up friends on the council. I won't stop until I get what I want." He nods, and I pat him on the back. "Good man." I pull the pen from the wound in a swift movement and drop it on the desk. "Oops, you'd better get that seen. We don't want you to die before the meeting, and blood loss is a savage way to go."

Sofia is asleep when I get back, so I kick off my shoes and pull the sheets from her. She wakes, sitting too fast and looking around disorientated. "You're alive," she whispers sleepily.

I wrap her hair around my hand and tilt her head back towards me so I can get access to her mouth. "You're not naked enough," I growl, pinching her nipple. The pink lace panties are sexy but not needed right now.

"You have blood on your shirt," she points out.

"It's been a bad day." I gently tug her hair until she stands. "Now, get naked."

She shimmies out of the knickers, and I release her hair, taking a seat by the window and watching as she pours me a whiskey. She brings it to me and kisses me before crouching before me and pulling my belt open. I watch through hooded eyes as she releases my erection from my pants. She takes me into her mouth, and I suck in a breath, tipping my head back and closing my eyes as I revel in the feel of her wet tongue lapping at my cock. Seems Raymond was right—it does relieve stress.

Chapter Nine

SOFIA

The noises Vinn makes spur me on to take him as deep as I can to the back of my throat. There's something sexy about a strong man groaning because I'm driving him wild. He grips my head and stills me, then a long, low moan escapes him, and I feel his cock swell before he coats my tongue with his cum. He flops back in the chair, his arms hanging limply and his eyes closed. I wince as the taste in my mouth threatens to make me throw up. I stand and head for the bathroom, then use my hand to scoop water into my mouth. When I return, Vinn is in the same position in the chair, so I climb back into bed.

"Sorry," he murmurs, "I should have warned you."

"Did you sort business out?" I ask, staring up at the ceiling.

He gives a light laugh before rising from the chair and crawling up the bed until he's staring down at me. "Marriage, sex, and now small talk."

"You were so mad this morning, I was checking you're okay."

He places a kiss on my nose. "Careful, *bellissima*, I might think you care." His mouth slams over mine before I can respond, surprising me with a toe-curling kiss. He trails kisses back down my body, stopping with his head between my legs. He cups my arse in his hands, angling me towards his mouth before taking his time to taste me. Every lick, every suck, takes me a step closer to that delicious feeling I'm quickly becoming addicted to. He doesn't let up until I'm panting through an intense orgasm. He gives a satisfied smile, slapping my thigh and getting up from the bed. "Sleep."

"Where are you going?" I ask.

"Business," he says, fastening his trousers.

I'm woken a few hours later by Vinn's intrusion. I'm flat on my stomach, and he's spreading my legs and easing into me before I've realised what's happening. The man is insatiable. He doesn't go easy, slamming into me with force and grunting like a caveman. It's hungry and animalistic, exactly how I imagined him to fuck. I orgasm within minutes, and as I come down from the high, he pulls me against him, sitting back on his heels. Guiding my legs either side of his, he gently pushes between my shoulder blades until I'm leaning forward and supporting my weight on my hands. He leans back on his hands.

"Fuck me, *bellissima*," he pants. I'm a little self-conscious, knowing he's got a good view of my arse, but his hand crashes against my thigh, shocking me into movement. "*Sai quanto fa caldo*?" he growls. *Do you know how hot that is?* His words of encouragement boost my confidence and I move faster. He grips my hips, thrusting up to meet my movements. "Fuck, fuck, fuck," he cries, coming hard. He falls beside me on the bed, his arm laying over his eyes while he catches his breath. I crawl beside him and tentatively rest my head on his chest. I feel the way he stiffens slightly, and he makes no move to touch me. After a few seconds, he kisses me on the head and stands. "I need a shower."

Breakfast is much quieter today. Gia and Blu are at the clubhouse. With Blu being a Kings Reaper, he splits his time between them and Vinn. Gia explained that even though Blu—or Azure Rossi, as he's known in our world—is part of the mafioso, he only got back into it to save Gia, but before that, he'd walked away, which is unusual. Once you're in, you're in, and the only way out is death. Mama and Rose are planning a shopping trip, and I sit beside Vinn, quietly eating some toast. For once, he isn't staring at his mobile, but he isn't speaking either. I'm quickly learning he doesn't like intimacy after sex, and he hates small talk. I can't complain, I did, after all, tell him to fuck me, because the thought of him making love was too scary. I laugh to myself, earning an eyebrow raise from Vinn.

"What are your plans today?" he suddenly asks.

"Oh, erm, I thought I'd look for work." Our mothers fall silent, and I feel their eyes on me too. "I just thought it would be nice to do something," I add, shrugging.

"No," says Vinn firmly.

"Just something local," I add, ignoring him. "Maybe some office work."

"No."

"It would be helpful to have my phone back so I can make calls."
""Which part didn't you understand?" he suddenly bellows, glaring at me. "You're my wife, what will people say if they see you working? They'll think I can't look after my family. They'll think I'm having money problems."

"I don't think anyone will take much notice, actually," I mutter. "Nobody has to know."

"I'll know. My answer is final." He stands, heading for the door.

"I wasn't asking your permission," I mutter, and he freezes, spinning around and marching back towards me.

"Leave!" he yells to our mothers, and they do as asked. His hand wraps in my hair, but it isn't gentle like before and I wince. He pushes his face into mine and holds a bunch of cash next to my cheek. "You want money, take it," he hisses, slamming it on the table. "I'll pay you for sucking my cock with that pretty little mouth and laying on your back while I fuck you. How about that?"

"I'm not your whore," I snap, trying to get free.

His grip gets tighter. "You think because you're in my bed, you suddenly have power?" He laughs coldly. "Nothing changes because I crave your damn pussy."

I grin. "Who are you trying to convince, me or yourself?"

"It's just sex," he snaps, "a means to an end. A way to get a son."

"What are you scared of, Vinn?"

"Nothing!" he snaps, releasing me. "I'm not scared of anything."

"Except feelings. It scares the shit out of you that you might actually like me." The realisation makes me smile, but he narrows his eyes.

"You asked me before if I still loved Raven."

I shake my head. "Don't say it, Vinn, because you'll regret it and you can't take the words back. You're lashing out because it scares the shit out of you, so you're trying to convince yourself that you feel nothing. Is it because she hurt you?"

"Listen to yourself," he sniggers. "You think having sex makes us real?"

I scoff. "No. I think we're both making the best of a bad situation. Sex is sex, you're nothing special." I stand. "Just because I don't have your experience, doesn't mean I can't go anywhere to have sex. You're just convenient."

I race up the stairs, and he's behind me within seconds. I try to slam the bedroom door in his face, but he gets his hand in there and pushes it open with ease. He uses his large body to push me against the wall. "Convenient?" he repeats, shoving my shorts down my legs. "I'll show you fucking convenient."

VINN

It's hard and fast. Over in minutes. A fuck. Just a fuck. We dress in silence, the sound of our heavy breathing filling the air. She's right in some ways, it's convenient because we're married, and even though we're clearly not happy in this marriage, I can't cheat. The vows meant something, but I'm also a red-blooded male and I need that release.

"You'll come with me today," I say firmly, leaving no room for argument. It's so I can make sure she doesn't do anything silly, like get a job. Fuck, if my mysterious revenge stalker discovers my wife is working, it'll feed his gossip page. "Meet me downstairs in two minutes." I leave, slamming the door behind me.

We reach the office just as my mobile rings. I smile when I see Damien Jones's name flash on my screen. "Good morning, Damien. How's the shoulder?"

"Fine. I'm just letting you know the meeting went well and nothing has changed. Go ahead."

"That's fantastic news. Glad we sorted that out." I disconnect and relay the news to Gerry. "Now, I can concentrate on finding out who the hell keeps trying to ruin my name."

"I'm sure they'll get bored soon enough," says Sofia.

"I'm not waiting around for that to happen."

"What will you do?" she asks.

"What I do best . . . ruin them."

SOFIA

"Can I use that laptop?" I ask Vinn as he settles behind his desk and eyes the laptop perched on a small shelf. "I'm bored, and I can amuse myself with the internet." He nods, and I smile, taking it and curling up on the couch. I open my emails and see there's another from the editor of the Daily Spy. I glance at Vinn occupied with his computer. There's a mobile number to call her urgently and my heart races in my chest. What could she possibly want? I can't call her without my own mobile, but I grab a pen from Vinn's desk and make note of her number.

I wander through to Raven, closing Vinn's office door. She watches suspiciously as I take a seat. "Can I ask something personal?"

She shrugs. "Sure."

"It's about you and Vinn."

Regret passes over her face. "I'm not sure it's appropriate. We've all moved on." "Did he ever lay with you, yah know, after . . ."

"Like did we cuddle and talk into the night?" she asks, adding a laugh. I nod. "Then no. I don't even think we did it in a bed. Vinn and I were hooking up, it was nothing serious and there was certainly no lovemaking with cute cuddles." She pauses. "Why are you asking?"

"No reason. Any chance I can borrow your mobile?"

"You don't have one?" she asks, surprised.

"Vinn took it. I just wanna check in with my mama. She's out shopping with Rose, and I need some things picked up."

Raven fishes it from her handbag and hands it to me. "Don't tell Vinn. I don't want to get it in the neck."

I smile gratefully. "I'll just go to the bathroom and make the call, in case he comes out of his office."

I lock the door and dial the number, making sure to withhold this number. A woman answers on the second ring. "Hello, Jessica Cole speaking."

"Hi, you emailed me and asked me to call."

"Revenge? Nice to put a voice to the name. I wanted to arrange to meet you."

"That's not a good idea."

"I have an interesting offer for you."

"And you can't make that over the telephone?"

She laughs. "I could, yes, but I like to know who I'm working with."

"It doesn't matter. I can't write anything else about Vincent Romano, so whatever your offer is, I can't accept."

"Has he threatened you?" she asks, suddenly sounding interested.

"No, he doesn't know me," I lie.

"Right. So, what's your problem?"

"If he finds out who I am, he'll come for me. You know who he is and what he does, right?"

"Not exactly, I know everyone is scared of him, but I thought you were different. I finally thought I'd found someone to expose him. He hides behind this facade of a businessman, but I have a feeling you know the real man behind the suit."

"I can't go there, I'm sorry."

"Okay, listen, forget meeting. Let's just stick to how things are. You get me something good on Vinn Romano, and I'll pay you."

"I can't, I'm sorry."

"I'll pay a thousand per story. The bigger the story, the more I'll pay."

"I don't need your money."

"What do you want?" she asks. "Everyone wants something. Why did you write the article in the first place?"

It's a loaded question. Why the hell did I? Revenge, anger towards him or maybe my father. Somehow, they all seem like stupid reasons now. "I guess I wanted to write. I always wanted to be a journalist, but I wasn't allowed to."

She pauses. "Then be a journalist. You're perfect for the Spy."

I laugh. "You want me to write from behind my mask?"

"Yes, why not?"

"Do all my stories have to be about Vincent?"

"For now. Get me something big and I'll consider sending you the names of people I'm interested in."

"Why the fixation on him?"

She laughs. "He tried to threaten me. No man threatens me."

Chapter Ten

VINN

"Where is she?" I ask.

Raven glances up from her computer. "You took her phone?" she asks accusingly.

"Where is she?" I repeat.

"And you treat her like a cheap fuck?" she adds.

I glare angrily. Why the hell is Sofia talking to Raven about us? "I'm gonna ask one more time."

"She's your wife. You can't fuck and run, Vinn."

The door opens and Sofia walks in, and upon seeing me, she shoves her hand behind her back innocently. She smiles awkwardly. "What's behind your back?" I ask.

She rolls her eyes and hands Raven a mobile phone. "Thanks."

"Who did you call?"

"My mama. I needed some things picked up."

"Like?" he demands to know.

"Women's things," she snaps, pushing past me to go into my office.

I follow her. "You might be pregnant," I suggest.

"I doubt it. We missed my fertile days, remember?"

"Still, we'll get a pregnancy test just in case." Something about the thought of her being pregnant makes me happy, an emotion I'm not used to. "You spoke with Raven about us?"

"I spoke with Raven about you and her," she corrects.

"Why?"

She shrugs. "I guess I wanted to know if you fucked all whores the same."

I narrow my eyes at the way she implies I'm treating her like a whore. "And did you get the answer you wanted?"

"Yes."

I sigh. "I'm trying, Sofia."

"You don't need to. There's no point." I watch as she pulls a book from the shelf and sits on the couch.

"No point?"

"We're making the best of a bad situation, right? Sex is natural and we shouldn't look elsewhere in case your stalker finds out and sells the story. We wouldn't want the world to know about this sham."

"I'm interested to know why you think you have such a bad deal in all this?" I ask.

"I'm not in love," she says simply. I feel a twinge where my heart should be. "And now, because of you and my papa, I'll never know what that feels like."

"That's not true, Sofia," I murmur. "You'll feel it when you have our child."

"It's not what I meant, and you know it," she mutters, going back to reading the book.

I send Sofia home with Gerry and head to the Kings Reapers clubhouse. I don't have friends, but Riggs, the president of the club, is the closest fit. There's Blu, who I trust to advise me and protect my life, but I can't talk to him at the risk of him relaying things to Gia. I've never been in this situation before, where I've felt the need to discuss my private life or get advice. I keep things simple and focus on business and keeping the mafioso happy. I know how to do that.

Riggs looks up from his desk when I knock on his office door. "Did we have a meeting?" he asks, frowning. I shake my head and take a seat. "So, you're here because?"

"Remember when you were dealing with shit and you turned up at Enzo's? I gave you a bottle of Jack and sat quietly while you consumed the whole thing. Then, I sent for my driver to deliver you safely to your own bed, next to your wife, so you wouldn't wake up with regrets." He nods. "I'm there, at that point."

Realisation passes over his face, and he pulls a bottle of Scotch from his drawer. "This to do with the story in the newspaper yesterday?" he asks.

I sigh with irritation because he clearly didn't hear the part about sitting quietly. "No. I sorted that."

"So, if business is good," he says, pouring two glasses, "it must be a woman on your mind."

He slides a glass to me. "I thought it would be simple," I admit.

Riggs laughs. "There ain't nothing simple about women, and just when you think you got it all figured out, they switch it up and you're back on your arse again, wondering what the fuck happened."

"It was for my father, a last request from him to help his friend. I underestimated her."

"Did she do something wrong?"

I shake my head and drain my glass, holding it out for a refill. "I don't know how to do relationships. I thought we could get married and things would just carry on as normal. I didn't expect to want to abide by the vows I made or that I'd feel this overpowering need to keep her to myself."

Riggs gives a knowing smile. "It hits you out of nowhere. I swear, it's voodoo magic, brother."

"How do I stop it?"

"Stop it?" he repeats. "Why would you want to?"

"It's impossible to be happy in my position. There will always be someone waiting to fuck it up, and she's at risk from my enemies."

"So is Gia, so is Rose. If your enemies wanted to target you, they'd go for anyone you love. It's a risk we take."

"If it was Gia, I could kill Blu for not protecting her. Who do I blame when it's Sofia?"

"Brother, you can't live life waiting for something bad to happen. You're gonna have a kid, right, that's the reason you agreed to this whole thing? Don't you think your kid will be the biggest target?"

I rub my tired face. "You don't get it," I mutter.

"It's not her safety you're worried about, Vinn. It's your heart."

"Bullshit," I spit. "I don't have one."

He smirks. "You being here, just talking about this, tells me otherwise."

SOFIA

Vinn gave me my mobile back. He's put a tracker on it, but I can live with that. The second I get home, I go to my room and call Zarina. I know she disagrees with what I'm doing, but she's the only person I've talked to about it and I desperately need to get this off my chest. I relay what Jessica said. After a long pause, she laughs. "That's the funniest story you've ever told me."

"I'm serious, Zee."

"You can't be, because if you were, I'd have to think you'd gone mad. Maybe the marriage was all too much, and now you've gone insane."

"What have I got to lose?"

"You mean apart from your limbs, or worse, your life?"

"Stop being dramatic. I need honesty here."

She growls angrily. "You don't want honesty because you're choosing to ignore my advice. If you don't want Vinn, just say, and I'll happily slide into his bed." Her words bother me, but I shrug them off. I know she doesn't mean it.

"He's using me for a son. He treats me as his personal whore. He's a complete, controlling dick," I list.

"You seem to think these are bad things," she cuts in.

"Zee, be on my side with this," I beg.

"I'm sorry, Sofia, but I can't. You're making a mockery of marriage and the wishes of the mafioso. Your father was right when he told you the families would treat you like a spy. If Vinn doesn't kill you, they might."

"They won't find out it's me."

"Look, you wanted my support, and I can't give it to you. Don't tell me anything else about the Daily Spy or I'll have to tell Vinn the truth.

Not because I don't love you, I do, but I can't sit back while you ruin his name."

"Why are you so invested in him, Zarina?" I demand, angry at her words.

"Maybe I see what you don't. You're lucky, Sofia, and you're wasting the chance to make a real go of it. Do you know how many girls want to get away from our village? You got to move to London with a well-respected man. You're stupid for wasting it. Grow up." She disconnects, and I stare wide-eyed at the phone. Zarina's been like a sister to me. I can't believe how she's just spoken to me.

VINN

Blu pulls out his iPad. "Sofia is right, her papa is deep in the shit," he begins. "I've been through every account he owns because, trust me, there were some hidden ones. He's been sending money to this account," he says, turning the screen to me. "It's overseas and connects to the following accounts." He clicks a screen and several more accounts appear. "This is why it's taken so long to trace, because every time we find an account, it's a cover for a different one. The trail stops with Angelo Diaz, an accountant in Colombia."

"So, Sofia was telling the truth, he's being blackmailed?"

"Blackmail is a possibility, but these sums of money are regular payments of around the same amount. Look . . ." He shows me another screen which breaks down the payments. "The hidden accounts I told you about," he adds, showing another screen, "one in particular stood out. It's in Mario Greco's name, and I balance is one-point-six million."

"He's working with them?" I state, and Blu shrugs. "Did you trace Mario?"

"No. This account hasn't been touched. There's another account that's accessed a lot but in Italy and London, which tells me it's Diego using it."

"Why is he letting Sofia and Angela think he has no money?"

"To hide what's really going on."

"I need to question Angela about Mario."

"I've already got Rose on it. Why do you think they're so close lately?" I smile, liking the fact he's thinking ahead. "Someone's gotta run shit around here while you're chasing Sofia," he jokes with a laugh.

"My mind has been taken with her and Revenge. Apologies. Thanks for stepping up, although I pay you well for exactly that."

SOFIA

Ash delivered a message from Vinn two hours ago instructing me to be ready by eight. We're attending another black-tie event, and after last time, I decide I'm going to stick to the rules and dress appropriately. If I want information on Vinn, I need to play the doting wife and gain trust.

As I descend the stairs in my ankle-length designer dress and matching heels, the appreciation shows on Vinn's face. He crooks his arm for me to slip my hand in and leads me out to the waiting car. "You look stunning," he says as Gerry drives us. I stare out the window so he can't see my smile. It shouldn't warm my heart, but it does.

The council house is huge. I hadn't paid much attention before, but as we step inside, I'm amazed at its beauty. The stained-glass windows and lavish decorations set the scene for an exclusive event held by local councillors. Apparently, the place will be crawling with top police chiefs, which is why Vinn wanted to attend. My papa is the opposite to Vinn—he'd avoid events like this so as not to throw himself in their path. But Vinn almost taunts them. They must know who he is and what he does, but they still nod in greeting as he passes them, sometimes even stopping to shake his hand.

We find a quiet table and sit, just the two of us. We've never done this, and I look around uncomfortably, trying to think of conversation that might interest him. "Sofia, what job did you do back home?" he asks.

"I wanted to write, but Papa wasn't a fan, so I helped Mama around the house. Sometimes I was allowed to help in his office, filing or answering calls, but as the business got quieter, there was less need for me to help out."

"What would you do if you could choose?"

I smile. "I'd like to be a journalist." His brow furrows, and I realise I've made a mistake, letting my mouth run away. "Just so I could write good stories," I rush to explain. "The news is full of bad things. I want to report the good in the world. There's a lot of it."

He smiles. "You want to lift people's spirits?"

I shrug. "I guess. If someone is feeling low and they pick up a newspaper, they're not gonna go away feeling happier. Maybe filling the stories with good things will spread hope."

He gives me an admiring look, nodding. "I never thought of it like that."

"What did you always want to be?" I ask, thanking the waitress as she sets two drinks down.

"Like my father," he answers quietly.

My heart melts a little. "You never dreamed of anything else, outside of this?"

He nods, taking a drink. "Of course, but I knew this would be my life, so what's the point in thinking about it?"

"It's not fair, is it? We never asked to be born into this life, and yet here we are, carrying out the sins of our fathers."

"It's just the way it is. What would you rather, work a nine to five, then fall asleep in front of the television surrounded by kids and a man who's barely providing?"

I smile, shrugging. "It doesn't sound so bad, if he loved me."

A look passes over Vinn's face, and I'm reminded of our situation. "Love gets you hurt."

"Well, I wouldn't know about that."

He finishes his drink. "Have you tried contacting Mario?"

I'm thrown by his sudden change in subject. "Of course, in the early days, but he never picked up the phone."

"And did you question your father?"

I nod. "Yes. He said he was working the oil rigs and couldn't be reached."

"I don't think he's working the rigs, Sofia."

I bite my lip. I knew deep down it was lies, but in our life, you learn to trust things get sorted, and asking questions never gets any real answers. "Will you tell me when you find him?" He nods once.

Suddenly, a female approaches. She's tall, almost Vinn's height, and pretty, like really pretty. Her skin is tanned to perfection and she's thin, way slimmer than me. I subconsciously place my hands around my waist to hide the slight period swell of my stomach. Vinn stands to greet her with a kiss on each cheek. They speak another language,

French I think, but either way, I don't understand. He eventually turns to me and smiles. "This is Sofia, my wife."

The woman proceeds to speak in French, and Vinn laughs, shaking his head. "Sofia doesn't speak French. Italian and English only."

"Oh," she says smugly. "I don't often meet people who don't speak a variety of languages. What school did you go to?"

"She was schooled in Italy," Vinn replies.

They go back to speaking in French, occasionally laughing, and it pisses me off. I stand, getting Vinn's attention. "Bathroom," I mutter, marching off.

On my way back, a hand catches my own and I stare into the eyes of Raymond, the man Vinn warned was his enemy. He smiles kindly. "Sofia, how are you?"

I glance to where Vinn is still talking to the rude woman, seeing she's got her hand on his arm. "I'm great. How are you?" This man was nice to me, so why the hell should I be rude?

"Are you really great or pretending?"

I suppress a smile. "Okay, I'm getting there."

"Your husband is making waves with these new apartments," he goes on to tell me, taking my elbow and guiding me towards the bar. "Pushing it through and threatening council members."

"I don't know anything about—"

"Of course, you don't," he scoffs. "You're his pretty little wife. You don't get told all that."

I resent the label he's placing on me, and I narrow my eyes. "So, why are you talking about it to me?"

"Because I can see you're not stupid. You hate being the controlled little wifey and you want to rebel."

I start to move away, making eye contact with Ash, who steps forward. "I should go."

"Back to your husband who's talking to his former lover?" I hold my hand up to signal Ash to wait. She stands nearby. "Oh, you didn't know? He occasionally uses her when he needs things pushing through quietly. Bars, strip clubs, night clubs . . . she's the head of licensing. But that's Vinn all over—if he can fuck his way out of something, he will, and if he can't," he points to another man nearby, "he'll threaten them, their families, and anyone else who gets in his way. Poor Councillor Jones has sent his daughter into hiding after a visit from your husband."

I swallow, my mouth suddenly dry. "Why?"

"He didn't like the way Vinn flirted with her, suggesting he'd hurt her if Jones didn't pass the planning for the apartments."

"Hurt her how?"

Raymond shrugs. "Who knows? Rape, murder . . . nothing is past Vincent Romano. He said he'd get her pregnant so he's in their life forever. The lengths he'd go to for power is crazy."

"Why are you telling me this?" I croak.

"Because you deserve better. You're a nice girl, and he's a thug."Vinn spots me and his face morphs into anger. He says something to the woman and then moves around her, making his way towards me. I need time to process what Raymond said, so I head to the bathroom, almost running to put some distance between us.

I slam the door, then lean against it and close my eyes. "Are you okay?" asks a woman watching me through the reflection of the mirror.

"Yes, sorry, I'm not feeling well."

"It's stuffy out there."

I recognise her voice, but before I can place it, the door is shoved hard, and I stumble forwards. Vinn fills the doorway looking more pissed than ever. "What the fuck, Sofia?" he growls.

"I was saying hello, being polite."

"Vincent Romano," the woman says with a smile, and I roll my eyes. Of course, she knows him. She smirks when he fails to recognise her. "Jessica Cole, the Daily Spy," she adds, holding out her hand. Vinn stares at it coldly, and I stare at it in shock. That's how I knew her voice. Fuck, what if she knew mine? She eventually retracts her hand, laughing. "Enjoy the rest of your evening."

Once she's gone, I sag against the sink. Panic fills me at the thought of her knowing who I am. For a second, I forget Vinn's even here until he appears behind me, watching me through the mirror. "I don't like you talking to other men."

"Who was that woman?" I snap.

"The editor of—"

"Not Jessica! The other woman, the French-talking rude woman."

"An old contact."

"Have you got any bars waiting to be licensed?" I demand and watch as realisation that I know about her passes over his face.

"Christ, how long were you talking to Clay for?"

"Long enough to know you and she fuck."

"Not anymore. There's been no one since I married you." Vinn runs his hands over my shoulders and stares into my eyes through the mirror. "I didn't like the way it felt, seeing you speaking to Raymond." He rests his forehead on my shoulder. "I was jealous," he admits quietly.

I hold his stare. "I was just being polite," I whisper.

"You don't need to be polite to men like him, *tesoro*."

I like the way he calls me sweetheart. After months of hurtful names, this one word makes me want to throw myself into his arms and reassure him that he doesn't need to be jealous because my heart is slowly beginning to beat solely for him. That realisation hits me hard, and my eyes burn with more tears. He turns me to face him and brushes his fingers along my jaw and into my hair. "Do we have to keep on hating one another? Couldn't we just try it, yah know, the other way?"

"Other way?" I repeat.

He brushes our lips. "Yes, enjoying each other." He cups my face and pulls me in for a soft, slow kiss.

Chapter Eleven

VINN

I take Sofia by the hand and lead her from the bathroom. Something's changed between us. We've reached a truce and it feels good. Maybe now I can get back to business and focus . . . starting with Raymond Clay. As I pass Gerry, I lean into his ear. "Cause a scene. I need everyone to be distracted."

"Clay?" he asks, and I nod.

"Sofia, take a seat at our table, I'll get us a drink," I tell her. She nods, releasing my hand. Gerry speaks briefly with Ash, who nods and moves into the crowd, pulling a hood over her head.

Gerry suddenly pulls me to the side, yelling about a man with a knife. Nearby, someone screams, and panic descends over the room. People grab for their partners and rush for the exit. Gerry makes a show of guiding me as far as the doors before I yell at him to get to Sofia. He heads back, and I make my way out as the hired security runs inside yelling into their radios.

Gerry appears shortly after with Sofia, and I pull her against me. "I think Ash is inside," she says, panicking.

"Ash will be fine, she's trained."

Minutes later, Ash steps out with another man who I recognise as Clay's security. Her hands have blood on them, but the other guy still shakes her hand and thanks her before heading back inside with a paramedic.

"What happened?" Sofia gasps.

"A man's on the ground. I tried to give first aid, but it didn't look good," Ash explains, her expression grave.

"Let's go," I suggest, keeping my arm around Sofia's shoulders.

"Interesting," comes a female voice from behind, and I turn to where Jessica Cole stands. "Raymond Clay has been stabbed." I feel Sofia tense, but her face remains impassive.

"What a shame. Is he alive?" I ask dryly.

"At the moment, but wasn't he just speaking with your wife?"

I glance at Sofia, who nods. "Yes, I hope he makes it," she says.

"If you don't mind, I need to get my wife home."

"Won't the police need to speak to everyone?" she asks, smirking.

"I'm sure you'll inform them who was here," I mutter, guiding Sofia away.

The car ride is silent. We get into the house and Sofia mutters something about bed, but I snatch her wrist, halting her from escaping. "Not so fast."

I pull her to my office and lock the door. "Talk."

"Did you do that because he spoke to me?"

"Yes."

She covers her mouth, her expression horrified. "It's my fault?"

"No. We have a long history. He'll live, don't worry."

"How can you be sure?"

"Because I didn't order his murder, just a wake-up call." I pull Sofia against me and close my eyes. I like the feel of her body against mine and my cock reacts immediately.

I run my hands over her arse, squeezing the flesh before pulling her skirt up inch by inch until my hands are full of the material. "This is a pretty dress," I mutter, pulling the material hard so it splits. She gasps, her eyes wide. "I'll buy you another."

I push her over my desk and admire her perfect arse, slapping my hand against it and rubbing the redness. I waste no time sinking into her, fisting her hair and flanking her body with mine, using the jealousy I felt earlier to fuck her hard. Maybe this marriage won't be so bad after all.

SOFIA

We fuck . . . it's primal and urgent, exactly what I needed after watching him with that French bitch earlier. The need to claim him burns in my blood, and when I drop to my knees and take him in my mouth, his eyes light with admiration. It doesn't take him long to come, and as he calls out my name, shuddering and growling, I feel a sense of pride. I can make this powerful man come undone and it feels good.

He kisses me on the head as I straighten my clothing. "Go to bed. I'll be up soon."

My heart twists and I hook a finger around his. "Actually, why don't we go together?"

He hesitates, and I can see his mind running overtime, but we've both admitted jealous feelings for one another, and we've had sex more than once. What's so hard about coming to bed with me? He seems to reach the same conclusion as he leads me upstairs.

I lie on my side, watching as he undresses and climbs in beside me. "I like this truce," he admits, lying on his back with his arms behind his head, staring up at the ceiling.

"It's much easier and a lot less stressful," I add. "Tell me something about you," he says. "Something nobody knows."

I bite my lower lip, thinking about his question. "I don't have anything," I mutter.

He glances my way. "There must be something."

I shake my head. "I led a quiet life and was never allowed out. Not without Mario, anyway. What about you?"

He sighs. "I have so many secrets, *bellissima*, it's hard to choose just one."

"How many women have there been?"

He laughs. "Too many to count."

His admission stings a little. "How many times have you been in love?"

"How long has your father been mistreating your mother?"

I feel disappointed he ignored my question. "As long as I can remember. It's always been that way. I thought everyone's parents were like mine until Zarina came to stay once when they were fighting. She told me her parents never argued let alone fight physically."

"You and she are close, no?"

I smile. "Yes. She's like my sister."

"Your uncle wants her to marry into the mafioso too." He says it as a statement rather than a question. "Maybe we can find her someone and she can stay here in London."

"Vinn, how long is Mama staying?" It's been playing on my mind, and I know Papa will be going out of his mind without her.

"As long as you want her here."

"I've never seen her so relaxed. She's happy, but I know given the option, she'll choose him."

"Then don't give her the option. How does that make you feel?" Vinn turns onto his side and watches me closely.

"Sad. Angry. Since being here, I'm starting to wonder who Papa really is. He never used to be like this. He's changed so much recently."

"In what way?"

Maybe I shouldn't tell Vinn about my papa, he'd be so angry if he ever found out. Family business is private, but while we're here, getting along, I feel the urge to let the words tumble out, so I do. "He has become much angrier. More distracted, less tolerant. When I told him I didn't want to marry you, he threatened to call the Colombians and have me sent there."

"You didn't want to marry me?" he repeats with a playful smile. I find myself smiling too. He kisses me, slow and almost loving, and when he pulls back, he smiles again. "Sleep now."

When I wake the next morning, I hear the shower. Feeling beside me, I note the bed is still warm and I smile to myself. Vinn stayed all night. I pick up my mobile and see an email from Jessica Cole. I open it, sitting up and wrapping the sheets around me.

Hi, Revenge. It was great to finally meet you. Tell me, when will I get my next story?

I feel sick. It burns the back of my throat, so I rush to the toilet, falling to my knees and vomiting. Vinn steps from the shower, wrapping a towel around his waist. "Are you okay?"

I nod, flushing away the evidence and trying desperately to hide my embarrassment. "Yeah, it must have been something I ate."

"Or you're pregnant?"

Those words chill me to the bone. "No, honestly, it's just an upset stomach."

He reaches into the drawer and produces a pregnancy test. I glare at him. "I had some brought in."

"I'll do it later," I mutter.

He smiles, but I see the dangerous glint in his eye warning me to do as he says. I snatch the box and push to my feet. He won't let me out of here until I do it, and I have to speak to Jessica. I pee on the stick with Vinn watching. I'm past being embarrassed—he just saw me vomit, and not for the first time. I place the test on the sink unit and go back into the bedroom.

"You don't want to wait for the result?" he asks, frowning.

I snatch my phone from the bed. "I'm sure you'll tell me."

"Suddenly, it feels like the truce is on hold."

"Because I can't even vomit without you questioning my state. Everything comes back to the baby. Everything," I snap, then take a calming breath. "Sorry," I mutter, "I know that's the whole point." He stares at me for a few seconds before going back into the bathroom to brush his teeth. My heart sinks. A part of me desperately wanted him to reassure me it's not the only reason I'm here.

When Vinn returns, I'm half dressed. He throws the test down beside me on the bed. "Negative."

Relief floods me, though I'm not sure why. I'm not against giving Vinn a baby, not like I was in the beginning, but now we have a reason to keep our truce. He still needs me, and while he's being kind, I'm going to drag it out as long as I can.

VINN

I take breakfast into work. I couldn't stand the thought of sitting with Sofia this morning. I can't hide the fact I'm disappointed she's not pregnant. After the news story, I need to set records straight. I hand Raven a coffee and pastry, and she smiles gratefully but is busy on the phone, so I go straight into my office. There's a scribbled note about a video conference call with Benedetto at lunch today. I frown just as Raven pops her head in. "He called and left a message to say he'd be video calling you at noon and he expects you to answer."

I nod. Why the hell does he want to speak to me? He'd never email, as it was drummed into us that the 'e' stands for 'evidence' and so video calling is the favoured form of contact when you can't get face-to-face meetings.

The morning drags. My mind is stuck on this damn conference call, and Blu arrives to join me just as I'm connecting my laptop. He takes a seat in the corner, out of view.

Benedetto's name flashes on my screen, and I accept, leaning back in my chair like I'm totally relaxed. "Benedetto," I greet, smiling.

"Apologies for the last-minute arrangement. It's important. Are you alone?"

"Yes." "You're looking into Diego. Why?"

Of course, he'd know, I'm not even surprised. "I have my reasons." "Vincent, now isn't the time for vague bullshit. He's in my organisation, and I want to know why you're searching in his financial dealings."

"I'm suspicious," I admit. "He pushed for the wedding between me and Sofia, and I haven't seen Mario for a long time. I feel like you're both keeping things from me."

He narrows his eyes. "Mario is dead."

I try not to look too shocked, but I wasn't expecting that, and I glance at Blu. "Sofia doesn't know," I say.

"Nobody does, but I thought Diego would tell you." I shake my head, anger bubbling inside at being told this information by Benedetto. He must think I have no control. "Look, I think we should come together on this," he begins, and I lean closer. "I have my suspicions about Diego and I'm keeping an eye on him."

"You didn't mention that when I saw you in Italy."

"Why would I? You know as well as me, it's not in our nature to share that sort of information. But your men are running checks and it's flagging up to Diego. He came to see me to say he thinks someone is watching him."

"I think you need to start being honest," I snap.

"I know about Sofia," he says. "I know she was attacked. I think the Colombians also killed Mario."

I shake my head. "Why?"

"Because Diego made a deal with them and didn't pay up. I don't know exactly what the deal was, but I'm working on it."

"Working on it?" I growl. "You're supposed to know what your men are doing!"

"It was before me, when my father was in charge. I had my suspicions before, but my father wouldn't hear of it."

"Have you tried reaching out to the Colombians?"

He nods. "It's a slow process. To talk to me, they want to make deals."

"Maybe I should go there and make deals. Maybe I should kill them . . . starting with Dante Arias, who raped Sofia while she was under your care."

He shifts uncomfortably. "Again, it was months before me. I'm tidying up my men. Starting with Diego. If I was you, I'd keep Angela there in the UK."

"Technically, Diego is part of my family now. Any new findings should be run by me and any plans to tidy up will also come through me."

Benedetto nods once before disconnecting. I slam my laptop closed. "What the fuck?"

"Mario is dead?" repeats Blu, just as shocked as me.

"That stays between us," I say. "There're only two things the Colombians would fight for—power and money. Dante had to have made some kind of fuck-up that involved one or both of those.""We're gonna have to bring him in, Boss. Before Benedetto gets to him and feeds us some bullshit."

I pull out my phone and call Diego. He wasn't happy when I took his wife from under his nose, only calling him once she was in London. He answers on the first ring. "Vinn."

"You're coming to London," I tell him. "I'll have Raven book the flight and send the details. It's important for your safety that you don't tell anyone, including Benedetto."

"Is Angela okay?"

"Yes. If you tell anyone about the flight or you don't get on it, she might not be."

SOFIA

I lost Ash in the centre of London. I feel bad, and even worse, my phone is stuffed between the seats in the back of the car, which means Vinn will be more than pissed. I couldn't risk bringing it with me and him tracking me here to Jessica.

I push the button to the second floor like she instructed me, and when I get to the hotel room, I knock on the door. She answers with a bright smile and invites me in like I'm her best friend. As soon as the door closes, I spin to face her. "Are you trying to get me killed?"

She laughs. "I'm not the one writing stories about Vincent Romano."

"And you didn't think you could just keep it to yourself? Sending that email was stupid. He could have seen it."

"But he didn't, and that's why you're here."

"I'm here to tell you I can't write anything else. Especially now you know who I am."

"That's disappointing, Sofia. I thought you were stronger than that."

"Stronger?" I repeat, laughing angrily. "You know enough to know what I did was stupid and dangerous. Things have changed. I can't write anymore."

"You're giving up on your dreams for a man?" she asks, arching her brow. "Wow."

"It's not like that."

"You told me you wanted to be a journalist. To do that, you need to take risks."

"I wanted to write pieces that would make a difference, that would help make people smile," I argue. "I didn't want to be the person who upset everyone."

"Vinn has thick skin, he can take it."

I shake my head and slowly walk back to the door. "I'm sorry, I can't be involved. Please don't contact me again."

"Actually," she says, and I pause, "it won't be as simple as that unfortunately."

"What do you mean?"

"I don't like Vincent Romano. I don't like what he stands for or how he behaves. I especially don't like the way he tried to threaten me. So, I need more on him, and you're going to get that for me."

"But . . . I just told you . . ."

She tips her head to one side and pouts mockingly. "I know you did, sweet pea, but that's not gonna work for me so—"

"If he finds out, he'll kill me."

"And that would make a great headline, but I'd rather keep it low key, maybe something about how he manages to get people to do exactly what he wants. How exactly did he get the permission for those apartments even after we exposed him?" I shrug, too shocked to reply.

"Get me something and then we'll talk again about you giving up your dreams for a man like him."

Chapter Twelve

VINN

I meet Angela outside the cafe right across from where I intend to build luxury apartments for women trying to escape abusive relationships. She glances at me nervously while I pour us each a cup of tea from the china pot the waitress brought over. "I wanted to talk to you today about a couple of things," I begin. "Firstly, Mario." Her face stays blank, and I smile. She's got a good poker face. "I need to know if you know the truth, because if you don't, then what I'm about to say may sting a little."

"I know he isn't coming back to me, if that's what you're asking."

I nod. "But you didn't tell Sofia?" She shakes her head. "Because?"

"I didn't know for certain. Diego didn't tell me. I just guessed when he made no contact. It wasn't like my son to not check in with me for so long. And when you're a mother, you know if your child is no longer on the same planet."

"I also needed to tell you that you won't be going home anytime soon." She visibly swallows but chooses not to question me. Why isn't

Sofia this compliant? "Benedetto wouldn't keep you safe there, and as I am now your family, it's up to me."

"Will Dante be joining me?"

I shake my head and from my expression she knows what that ultimately means. "He's flying into London soon. If you'd like to see him, I will arrange it."

"Are you going to tell Sofia?"

I shake my head. "Not yet. And you won't either." I open a brochure showing what the apartments will eventually look like. "You're welcome to stay in my home with Sofia, I think my mother loves having you around, but if you want your own place, there will be an apartment spare for you." I slide a credit card across the table. "This is yours. Raven will send you details of the account and your allowance. I'm sure it will meet your requirements, but should you need more, please let me know."

She nods, slipping the card into her bag. "You're a good man, Vinn. I know my daughter is having a hard time settling down, but she will, eventually."

I nod. "As will you."

My mobile rings and I pull it out to see Ash's name. "What?"

"I can't find Sofia, Boss. She gave me the slip."

I stand abruptly. "Where was she last?"

"Central London."

SOFIA

I hand over my credit card to the barman. My vision is blurred, but it feels good. If I'm going to die, I may as well do it drunk. "Another one, please," I mutter, and he pours me a whiskey. It's foul-tasting, and when I took my first mouthful earlier, I almost threw straight up. It gets easier with each glass, but fuck knows why Vinn likes it so much.

It's a rowdy bar. Lots of office types are pouring in for after-work drinks, and I move towards the back of the bar. I watch the men and women laughing and talking loudly to be heard over everyone else. Why couldn't my life be normal like that? "Now, you look like a woman drinking to forget," says a smiling man as he takes a seat opposite me. I hold up my hand, showing him my wedding ring, and take another drink. "You're drinking to forget your marriage?" he asks.

I grin, shaking my head. "No, I'm telling you I'm married."

"Happily?"

I pause, my eyes flicking to my diamond wedding band. Am I? I think I could be, in time. "Yes."

"I used to be," he tells me, "until she left for someone else."

"Oh, sorry to hear that."

"Don't be, she was a bitch." We both smile, but when I look across the bar, it's into the eyes of Vinn.

"Oh shit," I hiss, pushing my drink towards the man. "You have to go."

"Did I say something?" he asks, looking around.

"No, but if you don't hurry, you may never talk again." I stand as my moody husband approaches looking pissed, with Blu and Ash at his back. "Hey," I mumble, giving a small wave.

Vinn glances at his watch. "Where have you been for the last hour?"

"Hour?" I gasp, gripping the table to steady myself. "It didn't seem that long."

His eyes narrow. "You're drunk?"

I hold my fingers up, showing a small gap between them. "Maybe just a little."

"Who's your friend?"

I glance at the guy still sitting at my table and shrug. "Who knows."

The man grins, holding out his hand to Vinn. "Clive, pleased to meet you." He's unaware of the dangerous man ready to rip the limb from his body. Vinn grabs it, twisting it up the man's back. He cries out, and I wince, unsure of how to make this better.

"Vinn, stop!"

"Clive, you should gather your things together and leave the bar," he hisses. Clive nods, looking ready to piss himself in a panic. Vinn shoves him towards the exit, and Clive practically runs. "Gerry is waiting in the car," he adds without looking at me, then he takes me by the hand.

"Wait, you're not mad?" I ask.

He stares straight ahead, leading me from the bar. "Oh, very mad, Sofia, but I can't do what I want with a hundred witnesses." I swallow, hoping it was a sexual innuendo.

Outside, it's begun to rain. I tip my head back and smile. I love the feel of it on my skin. I break free of Vinn's grip, and he glances back. "What are you doing?"

"I want to walk in the rain," I say, spinning and almost crashing into someone. I laugh, grabbing Vinn's arm. "Let's walk."

"Sofia, get in the car," he snaps.

Blu and Ash watch on as I continue to walk, Vinn following me. "Come on, don't you ever get fed up with being so fucking boring?"

He looks taken aback. "Boring?"

"Always bossing everyone around and scowling. You know, when you smile, you actually look handsome." I skip, keeping my arms out for balance. "You never laugh."

"Sofia, you'll get the flu. Let's go home."

"See, boring. When was the last time you skipped in the rain?"

"Nobody over the age of three skips in the fucking rain, Sofia," he snaps impatiently, and I laugh.

"Maybe they should."

He continues to follow me, and when we get to the end of the road, I spot a park and head that way. "Really?" he hisses in disbelief. "This suit cost a lot of money."

"Nobody ever melted from rainwater," she says, rolling her eyes. "Let yourself go for once."

VINN

I scowl. I'm fucking wet through, and she wants me to skip and dance through the park. It's empty, with everyone rushing off to find shelter as the rain gets harder, but she's lost her mind. "Live a little. Laugh a little," she continues. There's a patch of trees off to the left, and I grin to myself. She's still lecturing me as I scoop her up in my arms, taking her by surprise. She squeals as I march towards the trees, dumping her on her feet once we're out of view and pushing her up against the nearest trunk. I tug her hair so she's looking up at me and close my mouth over hers. Peace . . . that's more like it.

"You want me to live a little, Sofia?" I whisper against her mouth. She nods. "You want me to relax and laugh more?" She nods again. I shove my hand down her trousers and find her already wet. She hisses, jerking as I roughly rub my hand over her pussy. "Is this more like it,

Sofia?" She closes her eyes, her small hands holding onto my shoulders as I push my fingers into her. "You went off radar today," I hiss. "I was worried."

"Sorry," she mumbles. She's so wet, it's hard to pull away, but I do, just as she's about to come apart. Her eyes shoot open. "What are you doing?"

"I thought you wanted to dance in the rain?"

She follows me back into the park. "I'd prefer to—" I arch a brow, daring her to say it out loud. "Oh, that was punishment for going off?"

"No, *bellissima*, that will come later. That was me shutting you up for five minutes."

SOFIA

The second we get home, Vinn takes me upstairs and works on my punishment. If you can call a shower with a sexy man followed by hours of fucking a punishment.

By morning, I'm tired and hungover. Vinn wakes me with breakfast in bed, which surprises me. He's not usually so attentive. "I'm very busy today. Call if you need me, but only in an emergency. Ash will be right outside," he says, kissing me on the forehead.

I frown. "Outside?" I query.

"The door," he says, smiling.

"I don't understand."

He straightens his tie. "She'll be right outside the door," he repeats, pointing to the bedroom door.

"Why is she waiting for me?"

"She isn't. That's where I've told her to stay until I return this evening."

I laugh, taking a bite from my toast. "You're talking in riddles." He leans closer to me again, taking a bite of the toast and winking playfully. I smile because I like this side of him. Then, suddenly, his eyes darken, and his grin turns cruel. "Remember yesterday, when you decided to take yourself off on a little detour of London?" I nod, slowly realising where this is going. "Well, that won't be happening today."

I watch as he heads for the door. "Vinn, what are you doing?"

He holds up a key and pushes it into the lock on the other side. Panic takes over and I scramble from the bed, my plate crashing to the floor and shattering. Just as I get to the door, he closes it, and I hear the lock click in place. "Vinn!" I yell, slamming my hands against the thick wood. "Vinn, you can't lock me away!"

"Oh, *tesoro*, there's still so much you don't know about me," he says through the door. "I told you there would be a punishment."

"I'm your fucking wife," I scream, stamping my foot. A sharp piece of pottery slices the skin underneath and I cry out, dropping to the floor and gripping it. "Shit," I hiss as blood rushes to the surface.

"Which is why I have to keep you safe. I can't trust you out there when you're always slipping off. Why were you at the Parkfield Hotel?"

My breath catches in my throat. "Sorry?"

"You heard me, *tesoro*. Don't make me repeat myself."

"I wasn't."

His hand slams against the door, and I jump with fright. "Don't fucking lie to me." "I was in the bar, having a drink." "Who bought it?"

"Me."

"More lies!" he yells. "I found you yesterday because I traced your fucking credit card, Sofia. You didn't buy a drink in the hotel."

"Because it was busy. I went in and left straightaway." I hear him laugh. It's low and menacing. "I have to go. When I return, you will be here, waiting, exactly where I left you. Preferably naked."

"Fuck you, Vinn," I mutter angrily.

"You will, when I return."

My foot aches. I wrap it with one of Vinn's expensive white cotton shirts to stem the bleeding, but I'm pretty sure it needs medical intervention. I prop it up on Vinn's pillow and pull my laptop onto my knee. He isn't the only one who can dish out punishments. If he wants to end our truce, that's fine by me.

VINN

Raven goes to lunch, and the second she disappears, the door buzzer rings. Why the hell does it always do that when she isn't at her desk?

"What?" I bark into the intercom.

"Mr. Romano, you wanted to see me?" It's Sofia's cousin, Zarina.

I buzz her in and sit back at my desk. She arrives looking fresh, like she's just had a workout. "Thank you for coming on such short notice." It was Blu's idea—Seduce the cousin and see what she knows. "Please, take a seat," I say, pointing to the chair opposite me.

"Is Sofia okay?" she asks, looking around the office.

"She's fine. Haven't you spoken with her?" She shakes her head, and a sad expression passes over her. "What's wrong?"

"Nothing. We just . . . had a slight disagreement. It happens." She shrugs.

"Look, Zarina, I asked you here because I need your help."

"Oh?"

"I'm worried about Sofia. I think her father is involved in things he shouldn't be and," I pause for effect, "I'm worried." She fidgets and avoids eye contact, so I move around to her side of the desk. "Zarina, it's very important that you tell me if you know something."

"I don't," she insists, "not really. Only what I've heard."

I rest my hand on her knee, crouching before her to make eye contact. She blushes. "Go on," I push.

"I heard her papa on the telephone. I think it was with Mario. He told him not to come back to Italy because he was ashamed of him. I don't know what he meant by that, but he was yelling, saying he disowned him."

"Have you told Sofia or anyone else about this?"

She shakes her head. "No. I shouldn't have been listening in."

I kiss her cheek. "Thank you. If you ever need anything, let me know."

"Actually," she begins, and I inwardly kick myself for being too polite, "my papa has arranged for me to meet a man here in London. My mama's uncle will escort me tomorrow. His name is Darias Marino. Do you know him?"

I try to keep a straight face. The guy's an arse, overweight, useless, and far too rich for his own good. "Yes, I do."

"Is he a good man?"

"I'm sure if your father chose him, it was for a good reason."

She sighs. "How did Sofia get so lucky?" she whispers.

"I'll see if I can find any eligible Italian men. There's plenty in London better than Darias Marino."

She stands, smiling. "Thank you." On her tiptoes, she presses her lips against mine. I instantly pull away, staring at her wide-eyed. "I appreciate your help," she adds, turning to leave. I know she and Sofia are close, but I don't think Sofia would be happy to share me with her cousin. I laugh to myself thinking about how mad she was this morning and I already have a punishment in mind if she isn't naked when I get back.

SOFIA

I admire Vinn's blood-soaked shirt and pillowcase. That will teach him for having white. Josey brought lunch and made such a fuss about my foot that I let her clean and bandage it, even though I wanted to leave it for Vinn to see what he made me do. I stare bitterly at the email right before I hit send. Fuck Vinn Romano.

It's a few hours later when I hear the key in the lock, and I straighten my woolly jumper. Vinn wanted naked, but I've given him fully clothed with at least three layers. I smile smugly when he sets eyes on me. "Josey said you hurt yourself."

"It was your fault, actually," I snap, and when he hears my tone, his face hardens.

He sniggers, marching over to my wardrobe and pulling it open. He removes the clothes, gathering one big armful and carrying it from the room. I don't need them anyway, I have layers. He then removes the contents of my underwear drawer. He returns looking pleased with himself. "Are you going to take the clothes off or should I remove them for you?"

"You wouldn't dare," I hiss, glaring at him. He takes my wrist, bending and throwing me over his shoulder. "Vinn, I swear, stop this. You're being stupid."

"I gave an order, and you didn't follow it."

"I am not one of your men!" I yell, hitting his back, but it doesn't bother him. He takes me into the bathroom and turns on the shower.

"It would be so much easier if you were, Sofia, because I could just kill you."

He dumps me in the shower, and I gasp as freezing water hits my face. "You're crazy." "Thank you." He smiles. "Now, take off the clothes."

"I'm not having sex with you," I snap angrily.

He laughs. "Firstly, I don't want you to, trust me. Secondly, I call the shots."

I pull the wet jumper over my head and throw it at him. He catches it, grinning. "The truce didn't last long," I mutter.

"All you had to do was play nice."

"All you had to do was let me live a little."

"In hotels, picking up guys in bars?" he yells.

I remove the next layer and drop it on the floor. "That's not what happened."

"Clive seemed to think so."

I remove the final shirt and drop it. "I'm so sick of this."

He waits until I'm completely naked and shivering before turning the shower off.

"I am sick of you giving my men the run-around. I am sick of having my day interrupted with tales of your insolence and your immature behaviour. If I give you an order, you follow it, do you understand yet?" His teeth are gritted and his face angry. I suck in a deep breath and nod once. "Good. Get dried. I will leave you clothes for dinner. We're eating alone this evening. You have ten minutes." He marches out the bathroom, slamming the door.

When I exit the bathroom, there's a dress on the bed. It's flowy and short, ideal for dinner, but there's no underwear. I glance at myself in the mirror. I like my body. It's not too thin or too fat, but just right, with womanly curves where they should be. My size C-cup breasts are perky, and I've never thought about surgery or Botox.

I take a deep breath. He told me to be naked, right? I pull the bedroom door open. Ash isn't there. In fact, it sounds unusually quiet. As I make my way along the hall, I hear pots and pans banging and smell the irresistible scent of Lorenzo's homemade pasta and secret sauce.

My wet bandage leaves a print as I descend the stairs. The office door opens and Gerry steps out. His mouth falls open and he quickly turns his back to me. "Sofia, what are you doing?"

"Vinn told me to follow his orders, and his orders were to be naked."

"Something tells me you're about to piss him off."

I grin, passing him. "Oh, I really hope so, Gerry. It's my most favourite thing to do."

Connor is heading my way but turns and rushes into the kitchen when he spots me. I smirk. Why are they all acting like they've never seen a naked woman before? "Mrs. Romano," hisses Ash as I approach the dining room door, "what are you doing?"

"Relax, Ash, I'm proving a point."

Vinn has his head down, reading something on his phone. I'm almost at my seat by the time he looks up. His nostrils flare and he glances around the room, spotting his two security men already leaving. "What are you doing?" he hisses.

"Following your orders," I say, smiling sweetly.

"This is not funny," he growls, unbuttoning his shirt. He shrugs it off and holds it out to me.

"But you said—"

"Put the fucking shirt on now, Sofia," he yells, slamming his hand on the table.

I take it, struggling to keep the smirk from my face. "Careful, you'll hurt your hand."

"Why does it have to be so difficult with you?" he asks, slapping my hands away and taking over the buttons. "What do I have to do to make you behave?"

"Stop telling me to behave, for a start. I'm not a dog."

He fastens the last button just above my cleavage and keeps his hands there. He stares into my eyes. "You push every damn button in me," he mutters. "And I tell myself every day to ignore you, to let you have your tantrum, but then you step it up until I can't."

"Mama always said I was hard work."

His hand cups my cheek. "You certainly don't know how to follow orders."

"Careful, Vinn, it sounds like you're starting to warm to me."

His mouth crashes against mine in a desperate kiss. "I'll deny it if anyone asks," he whispers, spinning me away from him and bending me over the table.

Chapter Thirteen

VINN

Suddenly, Zarina is everywhere I turn. I told Sofia to call her and sort things out, mainly because I need to keep her close right now to build trust. I feel like she knows more than she's letting on. Once Zarina trusts me, she'll open up more because she's desperate to be liked. More than that, she's desperate for me to find her a better husband than who her father suggested. So, when Sofia announced her cousin was staying with us for the rest of her trip, I wasn't surprised. Apparently, she managed to convince her mama's uncle that my home was a better option than his.

It's been two nights since my men saw my wife walking naked through the house. Every single one of them has avoided eye contact with me, in fear I might gauge them out. I smirk at the thought of her boldness. It's highly irritating but also addictive, and I find myself excited to see what she'll do next.

I'm in my office when there's a light knock on the door and Gia steps in. She's holding Alfie, my nephew. I take him from her, and she sits. "I want you to stay calm," she begins.

"Gia, you can't start a sentence like that. Is this why you brought Alfie in here?" She knows he's the light of my life.

"Maybe," she shrugs, smiling. "Listen, Revenge has struck again." She produces a newspaper.

"What? How did I not know about this? Raven usually gets a heads up."

"When you hear it, you'll understand why it was kept quiet."

I brace myself as she holds the paper. "Front page?" I snap, and she nods.

"Vincent Romano, sex predator or businessman?" she reads before diverting her eyes to her son as if to remind me he's here. "When I wrote my first article all those months back exposing Vinn Romano and his overpriced club, little did I know how right I was. I told you about his glitzy nightclub and all it had to offer, provided you were young and gorgeous. I've spent months uncovering the seedy tales behind the bright, white smile. I wasn't short of people ready to spill their guts about the businessman who has been linked to the Italian mafia—"

I grip one fist on the chair, and Gia eyes me cautiously. "That's never been mentioned before," I grit out.

"It gets worse," she mutters before continuing. "They wanted to remain anonymous. All from fear that the great Vincent will come for them. What exactly does that mean? I hear you ask. Well, for starters, he has links everywhere—the police, the court system, even our local councillors. Vivian Blackwell will dazzle us with her fake smile and tell us that new nightlife is just what London needs as she signs off another bar license. She forgets to tell us just how big a payment Vincent Romano slipped her—think inches, not cash—and when I approached her secretary, Blackwell wasn't available for comment. Silence speaks volumes, Ms Blackwell.

"And let's not forget his latest project. I recently exposed his plans to build in an already over-populated area. The planning permission was withdrawn pending investigation. Seems less than a day later, it was pushed back through. Would that have anything to do with Vincent's threat towards Councillor Jones's twenty-year-old daughter? Or could it have been the injury Jones received and attended hospital for?

"Vincent Romano is a powerful man, in that there is no doubt. It's time we stood up to bullies who use sex and violence to get what they want. As women, we spend our lives fighting to be heard against people like this, it's time you listened."

I stare for a good minute, processing what she's just read to me. "It's a woman."

Gia nods. "Seems like it."

"Jesus."

"Make a list of all the women you've hurt and start there." She takes Alfie from me. "Well done for staying calm."

I wait until she's left the office before grabbing the nearest empty whiskey glass and throwing it across the room. It shatters against the wall, but I don't feel any better.

Blu comes in and takes in the broken glass. "Gia said you'd taken it well."

"This is well," I snap. "I haven't killed anyone. I want to find this piece of shit who's writing about me. My father spent years building that club up and this arsehole might bring it all down, not to mention the fact they brought up the mafioso!"

"I'm working on it, but it's hard. I asked Vivian, and she swears she hasn't spoken to anyone recently from the press. This is an inside person."

"If you start banging on about Raven again, I'll hurt you."

"What about the cousin?"

"Zarina? No, she's not the type. She's too quiet."

"She's suddenly hanging around a lot."

I sigh. "I'll bring her in and see how she reacts."

SOFIA

"What's going on?" asks Zarina, closing her bedroom door.

I sit on her bed. "I'm not sure."

"I mean this," she snaps, throwing a newspaper on the bed. I glance at the article and wince. I didn't write those exact words. Jessica changed it, but I gave her the information.

"You told me not to talk about it with you," I point out.

"Now isn't the time to be a childish dick, Sofia. I thought things seemed good between the two of you."

I nod, my guilt showing clearly on my face. "It is. I feel terrible. But that's the last one, I swear."

"This could ruin his businesses. He might get investigated by the police."

The door opens and I spin around to find Vinn. "I need you," he mumbles, and it's the first time he's ever looked vulnerable. He takes my hand and leads me to our own room, where he kicks the door shut before wrapping his arms around me. "I need you so much, Sofia."

"Okay," I mumble against his chest.

He kisses me, but it's not like any of the other times. He's slow and gentle, caressing my cheeks with his thumbs with each swipe of his tongue. He slowly walks me back until my knees hit the bed, then before he lays me down, he peels off my dress. "You make it feel less crazy in my head," he mutters, trailing kisses over my shoulder and back up my neck. "No one's ever done that for me." My heart dances as he climbs over me. "I don't know what you've done to me, but I like it," he adds, lining his erection up at my entrance.

He rests his weight on his elbows and gently pushes inside, taking his time to make sure I feel every inch of his cock. He kisses me as he withdraws and then repeats it. His long, drawn-out movements are like heaven, causing my body to come alive with warmth. I feel like electricity dances between us, zapping back and forth. This time, when he comes, it's not hard and fast. His neck strains and a sound so primal and satisfied leaves his throat in a growl. It's a turn-on, and I follow him over the edge, gripping his arms and crying out into his chest.

Afterwards, Vinn pulls me into bed, wrapping his arms around me and holding me tightly. "I know neither of us wanted this marriage," he begins, "but lately, I've started to realise it isn't so bad." I run my fingers back and forth over his arm that circles my chest protectively. "Me too."

"I've asked your mother to stay here in the U.K. Benedetto may not welcome her back in Italy, and I don't think she'll be safe. She's part of my family now, and we all know Benedetto and the other families barely tolerate me. I've offered an apartment, or she has the option of staying here with us."

"With Papa?"

He kisses my head, inhaling my scent. "No, *bellissima*."

"What's he done wrong, Vinn?"

He sighs heavily. "I don't know exactly, but I don't think it's good." And for once, I don't argue or ask him for more, because deep down, I have my own suspicions about Papa.

We sleep wrapped around each other, and when I wake, it's with Vinn nuzzling my neck and pushing inside of me. We make love for a second time, and even though I have a dread in the pit of my stomach, part of me hopes this will last. Maybe over the next few days, he'll forget about the news story. These sorts of things blow over, and now Jessica has her big story, maybe she'll leave me alone?

VINN

I rub my brow, trying hard to remove the stress. "Fine, whatever," I mutter, dismissing Raven's concerns over the declining VIP bookings in the club. "It'll go quiet for a short time until this blows over and then they'll be back."

"Maybe," mutters Raven, not looking confident. I brought Zarina into the office with me today. She's shadowing Raven for some office experience. Her plans to stay in London are looking more likely, which means she's looking for work until she finds a suitable husband. "What exactly do you need me to show Zarina? Does she know about the other businesses?"

"Stick to legit things. Just general office admin."

"Also, Dave Cline from a local news station wants to speak to you about an interview."

"Absolutely not," I snap. "I've had enough of fucking journalists."

"Actually, I thought maybe we could put a spin on it to work in your favour. I did some research, and Dave has history with Jessica.

He was her editor when she was training. She accused him of sexual harassment, which turned out not to be true. He's got his own axe to grind."

I grab her and kiss her on the head, relief flooding me that we finally have something. "This is why I love you," I blurt, and she laughs, pushing me away.

"Behave or I'll tell Mac you're hitting on me."

Later, when I get home, Sofia is in the kitchen cooking. I lift the lid on a pan and inhale the smell of chilis and garlic. "What's all this? Is Lorenzo sick?"

"No," she says with a smile, "I gave him the night off so I could cook for you."

I smirk. "You can cook?"

She swats me with a towel. "Yes, I'm actually very good at it. How many times have you cooked in this kitchen?" she asks, stirring a sauce that looks amazing.

I take a seat. "Never. I have people for that."

"Don't you get sick of people running around for you?"

I laugh, loosening my tie. "No. But you look good in my kitchen. Sexier than Lorenzo."

"How was your day?"

I laugh harder. "Really? We're at that stage already?"

"You know, you should do that more . . . laugh. It looks good on you."

"Well, if you'd had a day like I've had, you wouldn't feel like smiling either."

I watch with interest as she moves around the kitchen, occasionally humming along to the radio. I find myself smiling. Somehow, I've grown to like Sofia. "At the risk of sounding like a real wife, why have you had a bad day?" she asks with a grin.

She passes me to go to the fridge, and I grab her hand, pulling her to stand between my legs. I tuck her hair behind her ears and stare into her large brown eyes. She's beautiful. Natural and perfect. "I don't think I ever told you," I whisper, placing a gentle kiss on her nose, "you're stunning."

She blushes. "Thank you."

"I hate we wasted time being so angry with each other. This is way better."

"It took you a while to see how amazing I am," she jokes, and I grin, kissing her on the lips.

"It did," I admit. "But now I know, we can stop wasting time pretending to hate each other and admit how we really feel." She breaks eye contact. Maybe I'm moving too fast. "It's okay if you're not sure how you feel. We'll take it slow. I'm just happy we're getting along."

SOFIA

Vinn causes pain in my chest with each word. He's right, we're heading in the right direction and becoming more amicable every day. Last night showed me what it could be like if we keep this up, and I want to keep it up, desperately.

I serve dinner, a homemade pasta with Mama's amazing sauce. I'm aware I'm doing this to ease my own guilt, but as we tuck in and he groans in pleasure, a stab of happiness hits me. I realise I want to make him smile . . . all the damn time.

Zarina steps into the kitchen and halts at the sight of us eating at the worktop. "Oh, sorry," she mutters.

"Join us," I say lightly. It's rude to send her away.

"No, I shouldn't," she says, smiling awkwardly.

"It's fine," says Vinn. "This is amazing, try it." She glows under his words and smiles brightly, pulling up a chair as I go to grab a bowl. Vinn watches her as she tries the pasta. "It's good, right?"

She nods. "I'll have to make my specialty for you," she says, and Vinn glances at me. She blushes. "For you both," she corrects. It's not surprising she's developed a crush on him, he's been kind to her, so I laugh it off. I'm just glad she's talking to me, and I want her to find a nice husband. I'm pleased Vinn's finding someone for her. Maybe coming to London isn't such a bad idea for all of us, Mama included. She's been much happier here than with Papa in Italy.

"Where have you gone, *bellissima*?" asks Vinn, lightly touching my cheek.

I blink, grinning. "Sorry, I was thinking about London and Mama." I shrug. "How maybe it's the right move for us all." He leans over and kisses me on the head.

"Did you get any further investigating the Revenge person?" asks Zarina, and I glare at her. She shrugs like she doesn't get what I'm pissed about.

Vinn groans. "No, although I might have a way to discredit Jessica Cole."

"Oh?" I sit up, paying close attention.

"Raven secured an interview tomorrow with a journalist she falsely accused of harassment. I hate to think what lengths she'd go to for a story."

"But you're still trying to find the identity of Revenge?" Zarina asks.

"Yes. Unfortunately, I can't let that one go. She is causing me some real issues with investors and people are cancelling bookings with the club. I can't let it slide."

I almost choke on my pasta, grabbing my water and gulping. Vinn rubs my back with concern. "What will happen to her?" pushes Zarina, and I will her to shut the fuck up.

Vinn grins. "What usually happens to people when they cross the capo of the mafioso?"

"You think it's a woman," I say. "You can't hurt a woman."

"Don't worry about it, it's not your problem." He stands. "Thank you for an amazing dinner. I have work in the office to finish up. I'll find you at bedtime," he says with a wink, and I nod.

The second he leaves, I glare at Zarina. "What the hell was that?" I hiss in a whisper.

"Don't you want to know if he's looking for you?"

"No, I want him to forget. I told you already, I'm not writing anything else. I've seen a different side to Vinn."

"You're deluded if you think this Jessica woman won't want to repay him for whatever he is planning. She won't go down without a fight and she's got you exactly where she wants you."

The sickness in my stomach returns. "Maybe I should just come clean."

"Maybe you should just run."

"Run?"

"Yes. Take some money and make a run for it before he finds out."

I shake my head. "I can't. I don't want to."

"It was only a few months ago you hated his guts and refused to marry him," she reminds me.

"Like I said, things are better between us. We're learning to get along, and I know I've made it harder on myself, but actually, I really like him, Zee. I can't just walk away."

She rolls her eyes. "You can if it's a choice between life and death. He's going to find out, Sofia, and then what?"

"Maybe I can come to an arrangement with Jessica, make her see I can write better stories, ones that make people smile instead of tear them down."

Zarina stands, shaking her head. "This is going to end in a mess. You should run."

Chapter Fourteen

VINN

I wake with Sofia in my arms. It's becoming my favourite way to start the day. I decide to work from home today. I have a surprise for Sofia, and I know she's going to be really excited, so Raven's organised for Dave Cline to interview me here. It seemed more appropriate to give the impression of a relaxed family man.

There's more good news when Blu tells me Diego is booked onto a flight. He'd been dragging his feet and making excuses as to why he was delaying. I regret not flying to Italy and sorting this out there, but there's no way I could have forced information out of him in another boss's territory.

I take Sofia's hand and lead her into my office. "I have a surprise," I announce, pulling her to sit on my knee. She looks worried, and I laugh. "Relax, it's a good surprise."

"I'm not used to this," she reminds me, and I kiss her, hoping that will relax her since she seems on edge lately.

"You said you wanted something for you, like a job," I say, and she nods. "So, I picked these up and thought you could maybe enrol." I point to the university brochures on my desk. "Journalism or whatever course you'd like to take." She stares at the colourful brochures, lost for words. "If you don't want to, it's fine. We can look for something else." I'm learning to accept she wants a life outside of us.

"You want me to go to university?" she whispers.

"If that's what you want."

She nods, tears forming in her eyes. "Yes, I'd love that. I thought being a journalist was out of the question."

"I never said that, your father did. I don't have a problem, despite hating journalists," I say with a wink. "I liked what you said about making a good difference. The world of news needs someone like you. And if you're still serious about it after you graduate, we'll get you a great role with a respectable newspaper."

She throws her arms around my neck. "I don't know what to say," she whispers. "I'm so grateful. I can't believe you listened to me when I told you my dreams."

"I've always listened to you, Sofia. It was you who never listened." She giggles, placing kisses along my jaw.

Dave Cline is in his fifties. He has two grown children with his ex-wife, and he explains how he hired Jessica Cole as his junior a few years ago. "She was always too big for her boots," he mutters. "Had big ideas she'd change the world. I was happy to encourage her, but then she started writing trash. I couldn't print that shit, I'd have been sued. She didn't get that and accused me of being sexist. Anyway, in the end, I let her go. I couldn't put up with her crazy accusations and bad attitude.

Next thing I know, the cops are banging on my door and arresting me for sexual assault. She told them I'd touched her inappropriately several times. I told them that was impossible, that I'd left my wife the year before for my gay lover, and I wasn't bloody interested in her. She eventually admitted she was lying but not before having me arrested and putting me through a trial for unfair dismissal."

I raise my eyebrows and take a deep breath. "That's quite a story."

"Yes, one she never writes about," he points out. "I hate her newspaper. It's not even a real newspaper, it's a gossip rag. So, I want to give you a chance to put your side forward."

I nod, giving him my best poker face.

"Jessica is an ex of mine," I say, and he gasps. "She's angry that I married Sofia and is hell bent on painting me as the villain, when in actual fact, my only crime was falling in love. Some people can't stand to see others happy, especially when they're successful."

He scribbles some notes down. "Right, let's screw the bitch over. We'll go over the questions and practise the answers, and then, if you're happy, I'll record the interview on my phone."

I nod, giving a satisfied smile. I have no choice but to discredit her stories. My club is suffering, and my apartments could go the same way if this carries on. Investors are getting itchy feet, wanting to pull out.

SOFIA

Vinn's story went on the newspaper's social media page. Jessica Cole's been emailing me since, demanding I call her, but I ignore her messages. Vinn's in a great mood and we're currently surrounded by his biker friends at the Kings Reapers clubhouse. Blu insisted we all watch the news here together, and I have to admit, Vinn was good.

He came across like he was concerned for Jessica's mental health and insisted he was only speaking out so that other men with disgruntled exes harassing them would speak out too and seek help. Now, I just have to avoid Jessica and pray she doesn't tell Vinn what I've done. I want this all to go away so we can move on.

Anna hands me a glass of wine. "Tell us about university," she demands excitedly. The men are by the bar, and I catch Vinn's eye and smile.

"He surprised me with uni brochures. We're going to check some of them out next week."

"I knew he had a heart," she says, smiling.

"It took us a while to get to this point, and there were times I wanted to kill him, but I'm glad I didn't because when he's being like this, I think I could fall in love."

"Could?" Leia repeats. "I hate to break it to you, but you're already there. I can see it in your eyes." I blush. I'm most definitely falling for him, which is why I hate lying to him. "And he is too. Look how he keeps glancing over here."

"I'm happy for you both," says Anna, patting my hand. "You make a great couple, and I can see the change in him already. He's smiling more." "How is the baby-making going?" asks Leia, and Anna hits her in the arm. "Come on, we all want to know," she laughs.

"We did a pregnancy test not too long ago and it was negative."

Anna smirks. "I guess it means you can keep trying."

"Actually, I still haven't had my period. I didn't mention it to him because he was disappointed with the negative test. I'm going to do another test tomorrow."

"That's so exciting," Leia gushes. "He'll be so happy if you are."

"Just keep it between us for now. He's a private person," I say, and they agree.

Chapter Fifteen

VINN

Sofia touches my arm. "I think we should go home. Zarina is drunk," she whispers, and I nod. Zarina is dancing on the table with Raven and Gia. I go over and hold out a hand to help her down. She takes it, smiling seductively. I'm pretty sure Sofia's noticed the way her cousin is around me, but the way she's looking at me now has me worried she's going to hit on me, so I call Gerry over to take over.

We get home and I head to the office, telling Sofia I'll be with her soon. I have emails to catch up on and I've also got a location on the Colombian that hurt Sofia, so I need to do my research.

An hour later, I'm lost looking at maps of Colombia when the office door opens and Zarina enters. I inwardly groan. This isn't going to end well. "Everything okay?" I ask.

She stands before me, resting her hands on the desk and making sure her arms push her breasts up over the silk slip she's wearing. "I was wondering if you managed to find me a husband yet?"

"Maybe we can talk about that tomorrow." She bites her lower lip and stares at me from under her lashes. She's pretty and sexy. If I wasn't obsessed with Sofia, I might be tempted to go there. "Goodnight, Zarina," I add sternly. "Yah know, I told Sofia how lucky she is to have a guy like you."

"Thank you," I mutter, going back to my laptop.

"I don't know why she caused you so much trouble." "Well, we're all good now. We've moved forward."

"Have you?" she asks, wobbling as she moves around to my side of the desk and rests her arse against it. "Because if you weren't one hundred percent happy, there's always another option."

I smile, wincing slightly and feeling embarrassed for her. "That's great but totally inappropriate. You've had a lot to drink, Zarina. Go to bed." She runs a finger over my arm, and I pull away. "Please."

"Fine," she mutters. "Could you help me? I'm not very steady on my feet."

I hesitate but close my laptop and stand. She hooks her arm through mine, and I lead her upstairs. "Why do you have to be so perfect?" she whispers.

We stop outside her door. "Believe me, I'm not. Far from it, in fact."

"To me, you are," she says, and then unexpectedly, she throws herself at me. I stumble back and turn my head away to avoid her lips. She hisses angrily. "She doesn't fucking deserve you."

"I don't deserve her, and I don't want to do anything that will ruin what we've finally got. You can't behave like this in my home."

Zarina stamps her foot like a spoiled brat. "She's lying to you!"

I pause, working out if this is the drink talking. She keeps her eyes locked to mine. "Her whole family fucking lie. Her papa is the master at it."

I grab her upper arm, marching her into her room and closing the door. "You told me you didn't know anything about him!"

She swallows, looking away. "I don't, not really, just what my papa says about him always lying. But I know about Sofia." "What about Sofia?"

"Maybe I shouldn't say," she murmurs.

I'm losing patience. I grip her chin hard and glare at her. "You have five seconds before I lose my shit."

"It's her. She's the one lying about you."

"What are you talking about?"

She tries to remove my hand, but I pinch tighter. "Revenge," she cries, and I instantly release her, stepping away like she's punched me. "She's Revenge."

I stare open-mouthed, then shake my head. "You're lying."

"I'm not. Check her emails. I told her not to get involved."

"She wouldn't."

"I'm sorry. I told her I'd tell you if she carried on. I'd never have done that to you. She really doesn't deserve you."

I grab her again, "Don't breathe a word of this conversation to anyone, especially her, or you'll be at the bottom of the Thames. Am I clear?" She nods, and I storm out.

I take a deep breath before opening the bedroom door. Sofia is naked in bed, fast asleep on top of the sheets. I stare down at her with my heart aching. Zarina must be lying. Maybe she thought I'd give in to her advances. I carefully take Sofia's laptop from the nightstand and go back to my office.

I open it and check the inbox. There's nothing but junk mail, just as I suspected. I go to the sent box and it's empty. I relax a little. Opening her address book, I scroll down and pause when I see Jessica's name. My heart rate picks up again and I close my eyes briefly, the realisation hitting me that she could be Revenge. The pain that follows is like a fire in my chest. I open some of her files, finding nothing of interest, until I stumble across a file labelled 'coursework'. I keep the cursor hovered over the file, knowing that this could well be a turning point because Sofia doesn't do coursework.

I glimpse at my father's picture and shake my head. I can't ignore this. If Sofia has betrayed me, I need to know.

SOFIA

I stretch out and open my eyes. The space next to me is still empty and cold, which means Vinn didn't come to bed. I sit up and almost scream in fright when I see him sitting at the end of the bed watching me. I laugh. "You scared me." He doesn't speak but gives a small laugh. "Are you okay?" He nods. "Are we playing a game?" I ask, grinning. I get on all fours and slowly crawl towards him. "Should I guess what you're doing here in last night's clothes, watching me sleep naked?" I kneel beside him and run a hand over his thigh. When he still doesn't speak, I lean closer, placing a kiss next to his mouth. "Were you thinking of all the ways you were gonna fuck me?" I throw a leg over him so I'm sitting on his lap facing him and I rub against him.

"Something like that," he mutters.

I smile. "I like the sound of that."

He takes me by the waist and lifts me from him, practically dumping me on the bed. "Shower. We have things to do today."

"Oh?"

"University, remember?"

"Today?" I ask, excitement building.

He heads into the bathroom, and I dive up to follow him. He undresses quickly. "Can we both get in there?" I ask, wiggling my brows. He shakes his head, and I frown. "Are you okay?"

"Yep, just got a lot on my mind."

I smirk and step into the shower. "Well, let me help you."

I make a grab for his cock, but he snatches my wrist and holds it tightly. "No, Sofia. Not right now."

I step out like a wounded puppy he's just kicked and wrap a towel around myself. He hasn't been this cold in a long time, and I hate it. He washes quickly and gets out. "Meet me downstairs when you're ready."

I wait for him to leave and shut the door. Taking a pregnancy test from the cabinet, I sit to pee on it, then I get in the shower.

VINN

"What's wrong with you this morning?" snaps Gia.

"Nothing. I just want to eat in peace." I feel Sofia's eyes on me. My mood clouds the entire room, and it's obvious to everyone I'm pissed about something. "I think I'm closer to finding out the identity of Revenge," I add, and Sofia tenses.

"Good, kill them and move on, I'm sick of it already," says Gia, and I scoff. Would she say that if she knew the truth? Zarina keeps her head lowered, not speaking or making eye contact with anyone.

"You're very quiet this morning," I point out. "Nothing to say?" She shakes her head. "Hangovers are a real bitch," I mutter. I don't know why I'm so pissed at her. Maybe a part of me wishes she'd never told me.

After breakfast, I tell Gerry to stay at the house to keep an eye on Zarina. He knows me too well and he'll spot my turmoil. I'm not ready to answer questions yet and could do without him hanging around me, so I drive us to the university with my usual security tailing us from a distance.

I was going to cancel the visits, but I want her to remember what she almost had, so I'm going to show her the university and get the enrolment forms because having hope and losing it is soul-crushing. I smile to myself. I can't wait to crush her.

We look around and it's obvious Sofia loves it. She grabs my hand and practically drags me to the huge library. I never really saw the appeal of university. I got where I am through hard work, so it's possible to be successful without a degree and a shitload of debt for the privilege. "I love it," she gushes, kissing my cheek. "Thank you so much for this." I take the enrolment forms from the office assistant and fold them.

"There's a deadline," she tells us. "Those forms will need to be in by the end of the week." I nod. It's not a problem because Sofia won't be filling in any forms.

On the way back to the car, she slips her hand in mine, and I resist the urge to let go. When she touches me now, it burns. "You're really quiet today, Vinn. Is everything okay?"

I nod. "If you've changed your mind about this, it's fine," she continues.

"I haven't."

"Did I do something wrong?"

I meet her eyes across the top of the car. "I don't know, Sofia, did you?" Her eyes linger on mine for a second too long before she ducks into the car and I follow.

"I don't think I did," she continues. She's got fucking nerve lying to my face again and again after everything I'm doing for her.

"Then don't look so worried."

I drop her back home, following her inside to get Zarina. I don't want to risk her confessing all to Sofia before I'm ready, so I insist she come with me for more work experience. Sofia grabs my hand, letting Zarina walk ahead to the car. "You know she likes you, right?" I nod, and she looks worried. "So, it's probably not a good idea to encourage her to spend time with you."

"Are you jealous?" I ask with a smirk.

Her brow furrows. "I don't have to be jealous to not like it, Vinn, and I don't like it. What's going on with you today? Did something happen between you two?"

"Why would you think that?"

"Because you're acting weird. I don't understand."

I push my hands into her hair and stare down at her. Even now, after what she's done, she takes my breath away. Maybe that's why the betrayal stings that little bit more. "You don't have to worry, *bellissima*, I love you." The words leave my mouth so easily, I almost believe them myself. She gasps, and before she can answer, I kiss her. I take it slow so I can enjoy the taste of her one last time. Our final kiss needs to be perfect.

SOFIA

I watch Vinn drive away, still confused by his odd behaviour. I know he's dealing with a lot, but the way he's pushing me away while still holding me close is messing with my head. I tell myself it's the guilt of everything weighing me down, that I'm seeing things that aren't there.

I go back inside and head for the library. I need to make that call to Jessica before she does something stupid. A man answers her mobile, and I consider hanging up but find myself asking for her. "I'm sorry, she's unavailable," he says.

"Erm, it's actually really urgent I talk to her. She was trying to get hold of me yesterday."

I hear him speaking with someone else in a low whisper before he comes back on the line. "Are you a friend?"

"Yes," I lie.

"Can I take your name?"

"What's going on? Where is she?"

"I'm sorry to inform you that Jessica was found dead in her apartment this morning." I freeze, unsure of what to say. Thoughts race through my head so fast, I have to lower into a nearby seat. "I don't understand," I whisper.

"I shouldn't really say anything else," he whispers back.

"Was it accidental or was she ill?"

He hesitates. "They're saying she took her own life."

I disconnect the call. My hands are shaking so bad, I struggle to press the correct button on my phone. Vinn didn't come to bed last night and he's been acting weird, but it's not like I can ask him, or he'll wonder how I know before the rest of the world.

I sit for a while thinking over the last few hours. Vinn's odd behaviour. He's too clever to make it look so obvious, he only did the interview yesterday. Did she kill herself? She seemed so strong and ready to take on the world. It doesn't make sense.

Gia interrupts my thoughts. "I've been looking everywhere for you."

"Sorry, just processing the university and how huge a life-changing decision it is."

She smiles. "You're going to love it, I'm sure. Anyway, did you do the test?" she asks.

I nod. "I haven't spoken to Vinn yet. He didn't seem in the mood this morning."

"You mean—" I nod, and she squeals, rushing over to me and hugging me. "That's so exciting!"

"Please keep it to yourself. I'd like to make a big deal of the announcement, but I want to wait until he's in a better mood."

"Of course."

Chapter Sixteen

VINN

I get the call to say Diego has landed and Blu's taking him to the lockup underneath the house. It's something my dad had adapted when he originally bought the place. He had the cellar knocked through to make it bigger and then sectioned it into two areas. They're heavily soundproofed, so a gun could be fired down there and it wouldn't be heard in the house. There's also a separate entrance around the side of the house, away from prying eyes.

When I arrive, Gerry drives straight into the underground garage so I can go into the basement without being seen. Blu is with Diego, who's pacing back and forth. "Thank God," he says when he sees me. "Have you got somewhere safe for me?"

I hold my arms out and look around the space. "Is this not what you had in mind?"

"Benedetto will find me here."

"No one knows about this," I say dryly.

"Do you know why he was looking into me?" I used what Benedetto told me and twisted it to make it look as though I wanted Diego to come here so I could protect him.

I shake my head, shrugging out of my suit jacket and handing it to Gerry. "He doesn't trust you."

"Why?" Diego half laughs like he can't believe Benedetto wouldn't trust him.

"Maybe the money exchange between you and the Colombians?"

He stops pacing and his expression gives away the second he realises why he's here. "I don't know what you mean."

"You do."

"Look, let's talk this out. I can explain everything. It's simple, but I understand how it looks."

I unclip my cufflinks and hand those to Gerry too, then take my time to roll up the sleeves of my designer shirt. "I'm waiting."

His body language gives away the fact he's nervous and twitchy as he looks around, probably hoping for a way out. "I lost Benedetto's money. Half a mill on the tables. The guy who owned the casino offered me a way out. I sell some powder on my streets, and he clears my debt."

"What guy?" I ask, and he shrugs. I take the first punch and my stress eases slightly.

Diego stumbles back and cups his jaw. "I just wanted to pay the debt. He told me it would be simple."

"And you believed him?" Blu asks with a sarcastic laugh.

"I was desperate and not thinking straight. I knew I could shift the gear easily through my men, so I gave him shipping dates and locations. It was hidden amongst Benedetto's stuff."

"You used his ships?" I snap, my eyes wide. I glance at Blu, who looks just as amused by his audacity.

"It was easy. I was already in charge of what went on those boats. Look, it isn't too late, if you want in on the deal, I can make it work."

Blu punches him this time, and as Diego's head flies back, Blu growls deep in the back of his throat. "Don't fucking insult us," he hisses.

"So, if things are so fucking great, where's Mario?" I ask.

"He found out, got involved, and got himself killed."

I shake my head. "I'm not buying it. Bag him," I order. Gerry grabs him with Blu's help and they force him into a wooden seat. Gerry binds Diego's hands behind his back and then secures him to the chair with pull ties. I stand close, watching as he fights his restraints. Blu places a thick material bag over his head and grips a handful of hair, holding it back. Gerry gets a bucket of water, slowly tipping it over Diego's head. He gasps, trying desperately to catch a breath, but as his airways fill with water, he chokes.

I nod, and they stop. Blu pulls the bag, and Diego vomits down himself as he sucks in much needed oxygen. "The next time you lie to me, it'll be a minute, not twenty seconds."

"I caught him," he spits, his breathing heavy. "I fucking caught him with the dirty Colombian."

"From the beginning!" Blu yells.

"The casino was true. Mario was in on it. We were making good money, so we carried on. But then I walked in on him with Dante's brother. They were . . ." He trails off, looking uncomfortable.

"Should we try the bag again?" I snap.

"Fucking!" he yells angrily. "They were fucking!"

Having a gay son in a life like ours isn't good. It's seen as a weakness and that son would not be considered a leader to his family. He'd be an outcast. "So, what happened?" Blu pushes.

"I pulled my gun and shot him."

"Mario?" I clarify.

He shakes his head. "His lover."

"That doesn't tell me where Mario is," I growl.

"Dante found out. He knew about them, so he pulled Mario in and questioned him. He told him what had happened."

"Where the fuck is Mario, or I swear to God," I warn, snatching the bag and pushing it in his face.

"Dante killed him. He's on a mission to ruin my family."

"That's why he took Sofia?" I gasp. Diego nods, and I punch him, breaking his nose. "Have you seen the pictures?" I yell, hitting him again. He spits blood on the ground.

"It's not over. That's why I sent Sofia to you. He's coming for her."

"Why? He took his revenge."

"That was starters. He's coming for mains and he won't finish until he's had dessert. His words, not mine."

"Does he know where she is?" I ask.

He nods. "Yes. Recently, thanks to your little newspaper stories. He isn't scared of the Italians."

"You dragged me into your fucking war," I shout, hitting him over and over until my fist splits and I struggle to catch my breath. I stagger back as his head falls to the side. He's unconscious and unrecognisable. "We need more security," I mutter, heading for the exit. "Get me the best."

I storm into the house and head straight upstairs. I suck in a breath at the sight of Sofia sitting on my bed with her legs crossed, writing something. She looks up and a small smile tugs at her lips. "I was just filling the applications out." Her eyes fall to my bloodied fists. "You're hurt." She places the paperwork to one side and rushes over, taking my hands in hers and examining my knuckles. I allow myself a moment to enjoy her touch before snatching my hands away and heading into the bathroom. "Let me at least clean them up," she says, following me. It hurts to look at her, so I close the door, ignoring the shock on her face.

When I'm done, Sofia's nowhere to be seen, and I'm glad. I need space to breathe. As I go downstairs, Zarina is just coming through the door with Ash. "Stay in your room until dinner at seven," I tell her, and she nods, doing exactly as she's told without a question. Fuck, she's exactly how I expected Sofia to be. "Ash, keep her and Sofia apart."

Blu comes in, wiping his hands on a rag, and follows me into his office. "Are you gonna tell me what's going on?" he asks, pouring us each a drink.

"I've found Revenge." He stops pouring to stare at me. "It's Sofia."

He drinks his whiskey in one, then tops up before handing me mine. "What the fuck? Are you sure?" I narrow my eyes, and he nods. "Of course, you are, stupid question. Have you asked her why?"

I shake my head. "She isn't aware I know."

He takes a deep breath, his eyes full of questions. "What are you gonna do about it?"

"You know what I have to do, Azure," I snap bitterly, and his eyes widen. "Vinn, you can't." The Kings Reapers have rules and hurting women is against everything they believe in, not that I'd ever ask Blu to do it. There're some things only a capo should deal with. I drink my whiskey and slam the glass on the desk. "I don't have a choice. You know I don't. If this gets out, it will look like I can't handle my shit. If I can't keep my house in order, who the fuck's gonna do business with me? And then there's the whole disrespect she's shown. Defying stupid orders like what to wear is one thing, but trying to ruin me, telling people my business, I can't let that go. There are rules in this life and she fucking knows them all."

Silence stretches out between us as we come to terms with what needs to be done. "Since she came into your life, things have been crazy," Blu admits. "And with her father saying all that crap, it's about to get harder."

"Tell me about it," I mutter, sighing heavily.

"We could always let the Colombian have her," he suggests, and my heart twists. It would be the easiest solution—let him think he's taken her from under my nose and he can deal with her. But I know what he'll do when he gets her, and it will be so much worse than what I have to do.

I shake my head. "No. It needs to be quick and clean." Even saying the words pains me.

Blu sighs. "Gerry?" he suggests.

I shake my head again. "It's gotta be me."

"Shit, Vinn. Have you thought about how that'll stay with you? You love her. It ain't gonna be simple.""It has to me so it sends a clear message out that I won't tolerate betrayal. Not even from my wife. And I should feel the pain, every part of it. It will remind me not to be so stupid again. But first, I have to clear the space in the lockup."

Blu checks his watch. "Honestly, he'll be dead by the morning. I'd leave him to bleed out if I was you."

"Just a heads up," I say as he gets up to leave, "Gerry took Jessica Cole out last night. He made it look like suicide. She left a note saying she saw my interview and was left devastated that we'd never get back together. The police will come knocking any time now."

"Have you got an alibi?" he asks.

I nod. "Yes, I was with Zarina."

He groans. "Not with her in that way though, right?"

"No, but no one else knows that, including my sister. It stays between us."

SOFIA

I checked every news site, every social media outlet, and there's nothing about Jessica on there. Surely, the media would report on that just because of who she was. I glance across the table at Zarina. She's got her head down and hasn't said a word, again. Vinn still looks angry, chewing his food like it's about to be stolen from him. Gerry appears and mutters, "Boss, we have company."

Vinn nods. "Send them through." A man in a suit walks in followed by two police officers. "Good evening." Vinn smiles, standing. "How can I help you?"

"We have some bad news. I'm afraid Jessica Cole was found dead this morning in her apartment." I grab my water with a shaky hand and take a sip to distract me. "That's terrible," says Vinn, looking genuinely upset.

"Did she make contact with you at all last night?"

Vinn shakes his head. "No, I haven't heard from her at all."

"While we wait for the post-mortem results, can you confirm where you were last night between the hours of eleven and six?"

Vinn hesitates, glancing at Zarina. "I can, but maybe we should go somewhere private." I glare between the two of them, a realisation dawning on me. "No, say it here," I demand.

Vinn glances at the floor before looking me in the eyes. "I was with Zarina last night." The officer looks at Zarina, who nods once to confirm. I suck in a breath. It hurts so bad, I don't quite fill my lungs. "Thank you, we'll be in touch if we need anything further."

Vinn nods, and Gerry shows them out. I stand, bracing my hands on the table, while Vinn takes his seat, leaning back with a smirk on his face. "Sit, we haven't eaten." I want to laugh. He seriously wants me to sit and eat dinner like they didn't just confess to shattering my heart? "You said—" I begin.

"Sit, Sofia."

I swipe my hand across the table, sending the plate skimming to the other side. It smashes to the ground and food splatters the wall. "I don't want to sit!" I scream. Vinn doesn't react, but Zarina silently sobs, her shoulders shaking. "How could you?" I whisper in her direction. I half expected it from Vinn, it's the reason I tried to keep my guard up, but I didn't think for a second Zarina would act on her feelings. We were close, like fucking sisters. "You told me you love—" I begin again, cutting myself off with a sob.

Vinn sips his wine like nothing out of the ordinary is currently happening. "We both said things."

"Why?" I ask, my voice choking. I hate being the girl who doubts herself, but was it me? *Wasn't I good enough?*

"Betrayal stings, doesn't it?" he asks thoughtfully.

"I can't do this," I whisper, turning to leave.

"You will do this, Sofia, and you'll do it now. SIT DOWN!" he yells. His voice is loud and commanding. I've never heard him so angry and I almost follow his instructions, but then I remember what he's done and I run, taking off out the front door and around the side of the house. I hear Vinn yelling my name and glance frantically for a place to hide while I work out a plan. There's a door ajar, so I slip inside, pulling it to and staring down a set of stone steps.

I creep down, careful not to let my shoes make a sound so as not to alert him to where I am. As I get to the bottom, there's another door. This one is steel, but again, it's ajar. I wait, listening for Vinn's footsteps and working to steady my breathing, but then I jump in fright when I hear a cry from somewhere behind the metal door. It's a man, there's no doubt about that. I wince, wondering if I should stay hiding here or risk going back up to find somewhere else.

"Jesus, Diego, you're a stubborn bastard. Just go already," I hear Blu say. "We need this space. You're not Jesus, we're not expecting a resurrection or anything spectacular. Just let go."

The moaning continues. That can't be Papa, but I have to know for sure, so I push the heavy door and step into the dully-lit room. Blu has his back to me, but there's no mistaking my papa tied to a chair with his head hanging limply to one side and blood pouring from his face. The sound of my gasp alerts Blu, and he spins to face me.

"Shit," he hisses. My foot barely touches the first step before Blu's arms are wrapped around me and I'm hauled against his body. "Calm," he whispers as I fight against his hold. "Sofia, it's okay."

"Get the fuck off me," I scream, struggling harder. The top door opens, letting a stream of cold air in. Vinn fills the doorway, his arms across his chest, watching with interest.

"Did you leave the door open?" he asks dryly, and Blu nods. "Let her go." He releases me, but I stay rooted to the spot, my fists balled at my sides and my breathing heavy. I don't want to be down here, involved in whatever the hell's going off, but I don't want to be near Vinn either. "Come, Sofia, don't be shy," he drawls. When I make no move towards him, he sighs impatiently. "Bring her," he orders. Blu grasps my arms and marches me forwards and up the steps. At the top, Vinn snatches my wrist and drags me stumbling back into the house. We go upstairs, and once I'm in the bedroom and he frees me, I pull out a large bag from under the bed. Vinn watches me with amusement. "Where exactly are you going?"

"Away from you," I hiss, throwing it on the bed and pulling open a drawer. "Why is Papa in there?" I begin to cry at the thought of him tied up, dying. Tears blur my vision as I sit on the edge of the bed, burying my face in my shaking hands.

"Poor Sofia," he murmurs, but his tone is mocking.

"Did you kill Jessica?"

"I couldn't have," he says, leaning against the bedroom door.

"Because you were fucking Zarina?"

"At what point did I say I fucked your cousin?"

I pause, glancing over my hands at him. "You—"

"What I said was, I was with Zarina last night. I didn't mention fucking or anything else."

"So, you expect me to believe you sat talking all night? You've been acting weird all day, and she's been avoiding me."

"I expect you to believe me when I say I have an alibi. Don't get me wrong, given the chance, I think Zarina would definitely let me. She made it pretty clear last night, but I turned her away."

I stand, feeling hope in my chest, brushing my tears away. "So, you didn't cheat?"

He shakes his head.

VINN

Relief floods her face and she moves towards me. "I thought you'd cheated," she whispers, placing her hands on my chest. "So, she threw herself at you?" I nod. "I knew she liked you, but I never thought she'd do anything about it. I thought she was loyal to me." "No one is ever truly loyal these days, Sofia."

"I'm so relieved you didn't," she whispers. Her hands move to my face, and she cups my cheeks, pulling me down for a kiss. When I don't kiss her back, she pulls back, looking confused. "I'm sorry for flying off like that."

I take her wrists in my hands and lower them to her side. "I know what you did," I whisper calmly. Her brow furrows. "Zarina told me." She begins breathing faster, her eyes darting around, avoiding me, and when she tries to pull away, I tighten my grip. "So, I understand how you felt just then when you thought I'd betrayed you because it's exactly how I felt when I was told my wife had been lying and sneaking around with Jessica fucking Cole!" I yell the last bit, and she recoils.

Chapter Seventeen

VINN

I shove her from me, and she falls on the bed. "So, pack your shit, make it look like you've done a runner."

"It wasn't supposed to be like that."

"Don't tell me. I don't want to hear your bullshit lies. For once in your life, do as you're told and pack your bags."

I watch as she slowly begins to pack her clothes. She's going slow and it pisses me off, so I begin grabbing handfuls, angrily throwing them in. Once it's full, I zip it up and shove it back under the bed. "Now what?" she asks.

"Lucky for you, I have a second room out there. You can be with your papa."

"You won't kill me," she says, sounding sure.

I laugh, grabbing her upper arm and marching her back downstairs. Zarina appears in the kitchen doorway. "Say goodbye to your cousin," I snap, and Sofia smiles wide. She's hiding her fear well, and I admire her for that, but some sick part of me wants her to cry and beg for forgiveness. At least then I'd know she regretted fucking me over.

"Goodbye, Zarina. Look after him for me," she says sweetly, her voice dripping with sarcasm.

I roll my eyes and shove her outside. We go back down the stone steps. "Why did you do it?" I ask, passing her dying father and proceeding to the next room.

"I was angry. I didn't want to live this life." I push her to sit on a stool, and without me asking, she places her hands out front for me to tie them. She's far too confident that I'm not going to do this, which makes me more determined. She's not fucking immune because she gave me her pussy. "At least Zarina is a virgin," she says with a grin. "It's what you wanted." I pull the ties extra tight, pinching her skin, but she doesn't flinch.

"Shut the fuck up," I snap.

"I'm impressed you turned her away," she adds.

"Trust me, if I knew then what I know now, I wouldn't have."

"Will you get with her next?"

I laugh sarcastically, annoyed by her easy chat. You wouldn't think she was facing death by the way she's acting. "She'd be easier to handle than you, more compliant and grateful."

"You know, without my dead body, you'll technically still be married. It could stop you moving on in the future."

"I've instructed the solicitor to draw up the divorce papers. I'll forge your signature."

She wriggles like she's getting comfortable. "Right, so how are we doing this?"

It's enough to send me over the edge. I pull out my gun from the back of my trousers and push it against her head. She closes her eyes, and I see a flicker of fear for the first time. Good, she needs to be scared. "I was gonna give you everything," I hiss.

"At the time, I didn't know that. I was angry and hurt, scared of what the future held with a man I didn't know."

"I can't ever forgive you," I growl.

She looks into my eyes, seemingly calm again, and she smiles. Tears balance on her lower lashes making her brown eyes glisten. "I'm so sorry for hurting you, Vinn. If I could take it back, I would, but I was a naïve girl scared of living a life like my parents."

I push my face to hers and sneer. "You didn't hurt me, *cagna*. You gave me a reason to get out of this marriage."

SOFIA

My palms are sweating, and my heart is hammering in my chest. The look in Vinn's eyes is dangerous and I don't know if he's going to pull the trigger any second. His mood is unpredictable, but I know I have to remain calm because that's what you do in this life, my papa's words running through my mind. *Stay calm, don't react.*

I suck in a deep breath and close my eyes, preparing myself in case he does it before I've had chance to make peace with the world. "I'm sorry. I can't say it any other way, and now I don't have time to make it up to you. But please know that I tried to stop, but Jessica blackmailed me to continue." He frowns, clicking off the safety. My words aren't enough, he wants me dead, so I press my lips together in a tight line. "Okay, I'm ready," I say with a nod.

"You think I won't do it?" he whispers, and the metal of the gun digs into my temple.

"I don't think you have a choice," I say. "I love you, Vinn. It took me a while, but I do."

Silence stretches out and the ringing in my head turns up a notch until it's deafening. I begin a silent count.

One . . . two . . .

Suddenly, footsteps come racing down the stone steps and the door crashes open. "Gia, get out," yells Vinn.

I turn my head and watch with hope as she runs into the room and grabs Vinn's arm, trying to move the gun from me. "You can't kill her," she yells.

"Gia," I warn, "it's okay."

She ignores me, still clinging to Vinn's arm. "She's pregnant."

Vinn stares at me, shocked. "No, we did a test."

"She did another because her period didn't come. She's pregnant, Vinn. You can't kill her."

Vinn lowers the gun, putting the safety back on and tucking it away. His face is full of confusion and disappointment. After trying so hard for a baby, he's finally having one with the woman who hurt him. He takes a few steps back, and I growl angrily. I was ready. I accepted death and now he's pulling out. "I betrayed you. The families will expect you to kill me," I yell. "They'll say you're weak." Gia tries to cover my mouth, but I move my head. "They'll send someone to do it, and they might kill you."

Vinn doesn't bother to look at me. Instead, he takes Gia's arm, pulling her towards the exit. I shiver as cold air wraps around me, and I jump when the door slams and let out an angry cry. "I was fucking ready!" I yell but I'm met with silence. *Great, now what?*

VINN

I go to my bathroom and grab a test kit. Gia thinks love conquers all, and I wouldn't put it past her to lie just to delay Sofia's death in the hope I'll change my mind. But if she's not lying and Sofia is pregnant, it will change everything.

Sofia is shivering when I return, but I ignore the overwhelming need to wrap her in my jacket and hold her. I cut the ties holding her hands, and she wiggles her fingers as the blood rushes back to them. Pulling a bucket into the centre of the room, I pass her the test. She unwraps the packaging before pulling her jeans down without so much as an eye roll. Pulling out my gun again, I decide if it's negative, I'll pull the trigger. If it isn't, I'm screwed.

The sound of her pee hitting the metal makes her blush. She holds the stick there for a few seconds before passing it back. I place it on the side, watching as the results window changes colour. Sofia takes a seat back on the stool, wrapping her arms around herself. "Can I check Papa?" she whispers.

"No." He's still breathing, I can hear his gasps every so often.

"Can't you end him quickly? He's suffering."

"He deserves to." I groan when a faint line appears in the window, telling me she is in fact pregnant. I pick it up angrily and throw it across the room.

"Now what?"

"You just brought yourself nine months."

Sofia jumps up and runs from the room to her father. Rolling my eyes, I follow. She's on her knees, sobbing hard and grasping his limp hands in her own. "Oh, Papa, what did you do?" He groans, but he's too weak to respond. Sofia presses her hands over a wound on his leg.

It's no good—there's too many holes in the guy for her to cover. I ordered Blu to give him a slow death and bleeding out is exactly that.

"I hate you, Vinn Romano," she whispers.

I smirk. "The feeling is mutual, *cagna*."

"Papa," she murmurs, gently cupping his cheek. "I'm here. It's okay, you can go."

I roll my eyes. I hate drama. I pull out the gun I had loaded and ready to kill my wife and pull the trigger. Sofia screams, falling back into the pools of her father's blood. Diego's head flies backwards as the bullet penetrates his skull, spraying more blood and brain matter. Sofia keeps screaming until I place a hand over her mouth and haul her to her feet. I keep her back pressed against my front as I walk her from the room.

By the time we break out into the fresh night air, she's sobbing so hard, she's retching. I release her, and she falls to the ground, landing on all fours and coughing violently, then vomiting onto the trimmed lawn. I wait, letting her empty the contents of her stomach before grabbing her by the hair and pulling her to stand. In order for me to hate this woman, I have to treat her with the contempt she deserves.

SOFIA

I'm taken to the attic. I've never been up this far in the house because the stairs leading to it creep me the hell out. My limbs ache, and I'm so cold, my teeth are chattering together. It's the only sound that can be heard as Vinn unlocks the door and forces me inside. "What about my mama?" I ask hoarsely.

"I'll allow her to stay here and clean for me."

I nod. Mama will hate it, but once it gets out that I've betrayed Vinn, she'll never be accepted back in Italy, especially not without Papa. I see his broken skull in my mind and begin crying again. I can't stop the flow of tears no matter how hard I want to, because crying in front of Vinn makes me feel weak and vulnerable

"He deserved to die," says Vinn bluntly.

"According to you," I mumble, moving farther into the room and away from him.

It's a simple room with a double bed, cotton sheets, and a bedside table. There's a bucket in the corner, and when Vinn sees me staring, he smirks. "Your en-suite." I have nothing left for him, so I lie on the bed, keeping my back to him. "You can go now. I'll see you in nine months."

"You'll be seeing me before then, Sofia. I make the rules."

"From this moment on, I'll never respond to you again," I whisper, my heart cracking a little more. "And in nine months, when you take this child, I pray you see my dead, soulless eyes whenever you look at it."

When I hear the door close and the lock click, I cry harder. I never thought I'd feel disappointed to be alive. I bury my face into my pillow to muffle my sobs.

VINN

I stand outside Sofia's door, listening to her heart breaking, and rest my head against it. I close my eyes and take a deep, calming breath, building up the strength to walk away.

Gia's waiting with Blu in my office. He gives me a sympathetic smile, "Sorry, she insisted on waiting," he mutters, which earns him a glare from my sister.

"It's late, Gia. Go to bed." "What happened? Is Sofia okay?"

"She's alive, if that's what you're asking."

Gia sags with relief. "Can I see her, check if she's okay?"

I shake my head. "No. As far as this family is concerned, Sofia is dead."

Her eyes burn into me. "Where is she?"

"In the attic, safe and well."

"She's carrying my niece or nephew. I can't act like she's not a part of this family. You're married, for goodness' sake."

"Gia," mutters Blu in warning.

"Fuck off, Blu," she yells, and he raises his eyebrow in surprise. "This is between me and my brother, not your boss."

"Gia, it's best not to get too close to her. In nine months, it'll be like she never existed," I drawl, pouring a whiskey.

"Only that's not true, is it, Vinn? Because she will live on through your child and through here," she hisses, hitting me in the chest over my heart. "You don't stop loving someone." I smirk. "Who said I loved her? She was a pain in my arse. I'm glad to be rid of her."

Gia shakes her head and opens the office door to leave. "You stubborn men will never learn. You can tell yourself she's nothing and you can live without her, but we both know that's not true. She might have fucked up, but worse things happen in a marriage. If you kill Sofia after this, I'll walk away from this family forever."

"You can't just walk away!" I yell at her retreating back, and she spins to face me with a face full of rage. "You know the rules."

"What the fuck is that supposed to mean, big brother? Are you threatening me?"

"Gia!" yells Blu. "Enough!" She holds his stare for a defiant few seconds before leaving the room, slamming the door hard behind her. Blu lets out a breath. "Fuck, she could make me piss in my pants when she gets like that. Imagine her with a gun?"

"It's why women don't run shit," I mutter.

"Are you okay?"

"Better than okay. Put the word out that Sofia is dead along with her lying father. Make sure it reaches as far as Dante. And arrange for a video call with Benedetto tomorrow. If he wants to go to war with me over Diego, I need to prepare. Arrange for Josey to show Angela her new room first thing. She'll be sharing the staff quarters."

"Vinn—" he begins, and I know by his tone he's gonna give me a pep talk.

I open my laptop, interrupting him. "That'll be all, Azure."

He concedes with a nod and leaves.

Chapter Eighteen

SOFIA

Three days have passed and the only person I've seen in the whole time is Ash. She's been tasked with swapping my en-suite bucket twice a day and she also delivers me breakfast, dinner, and my evening meal. So far, I haven't touched any of them. I'm sick to my stomach and the thought of swallowing even the smallest amount of food makes me gag.

I hear the lock and open my eyes, not moving an inch from my foetal position on the bed. Vinn enters, filling the doorway with his huge, muscled body. It's wrong that after everything, he still makes my heart squeeze and butterflies take flight in the pit of my stomach. I remain still, staring back at his cruel eyes. It's the one thing I've noticed has changed since I saw him a few days ago. "Ash said you haven't eaten in days." He waits for a reply he won't be getting, then sighs. "Sofia, you need to eat something." He steps closer, pushing the door closed. "Think about the baby," he adds a little more softly.

I suck in a breath, the mention of my baby hitting me right in the chest. It's all I've thought about, that and the fact I'll never watch it grow up, that I'll have to hand it over to this monster. A lone tear falls from the corner of my eye and hits the pillow. Vinn crouches, and for a second, a look of regret passes over his expression before he remembers who he is and narrows his eyes. "It's not a polite request, Sofia. You will eat your next meal, or I will make you."

I stare past him to a spot on the wall. It's a scuff mark that I've spent hours wondering how it got there. Was someone else locked up here? Was it done when furniture was delivered here, and did the delivery driver know it would be used by a prisoner? "Sofia, are you listening to me?" Vinn waits a second before standing. "Your mother has been asking after you. Eat your next meal, and I'll let her visit." My eyes flicker, but I don't remove them from the scuff mark. *Mama.* She must be heartbroken to be cleaning for this piece of shit. Why did my Papa get involved with this man? What did he do so wrong to deserve a painful, drawn-out death? "Fine, Sofia, have it your way. I'll bring your dinner at seven. Be prepared."

VINN

"Would you like me to have a word?" asks Josey tentatively when I tell her to have Sofia's dinner ready by seven. "We got to know each other quite well, I think she might listen to me."

"No. She'll eat this evening."

"But . . ." She trails off when I glare at her.

"Seven," I repeat before going to my office.

I open my laptop to prepare for my second call with Benedetto. The first didn't go too well when I told him about Diego's betrayal to the mafioso. I should imagine most of his anger was because this went on under his nose and he knew nothing of it. It brings his leadership into question.

"Vincent," he greets, his face coming into view as the video call connects. I decided honesty was the best policy when it came to Sofia. I told him about her betrayal and her pregnancy, so he knew the reason for me not ending her just yet. However, he also knows what I plan to do once my child is here. It's expected. I don't need the Italians, I decided long ago I could be just as powerful here in London without their connections. And, ultimately, they need me more so they can do business here in the UK. But I told him out of courtesy, and I don't want to completely cut ties until I'm ready.

"Benedetto," I nod, "I trust you're ready to talk."

"Of course. Your news was not expected when I spoke to you last. I've done some checks and it seems you're right, Diego's dealings behind my back went deep. Shocking really, I misjudged him. I always thought he was stupid."

"He was," I mutter. "He crossed me."

"Vincent, I regret what happened, but the Grecos are your problem. You married their daughter."

"Dealings were done under your nose with an enemy," I snap. "You'll help me go to war with Dante."

"I made contact," he says, and I keep my face impassive even though I'm angry. I've been trying to make contact for days. "Diego's debt has been passed to you. The Colombians are not happy you took his life without speaking to them. You'll need to make a new deal with him directly."

"I'm not making a fucking deal with him," I growl. "Are you seriously going to brush this off like it isn't your debt?"

"I didn't marry the girl."

"Piece of fucking shit," I mutter.

"Careful, Vinn, you sound more and more British every day."

I laugh coldly. "Consider this fair warning, Benedetto. I don't take kindly to being screwed over, and I'll be looking at the deals we made just months ago after your father passed. As it stands, I have no choice but to freeze any boats you have coming into London, and I'll be disrupting your current distributions that my men are driving around as we speak." I disconnect and pick up my mobile. "Gerry," I snap the second he answers, "call the Italian's lorries back to the yard. Nothing moves until I say."

Blu walks in as I end my call, and I fill him in on my conversations. "That explains why we can't contact the Colombians. They'll be working on a new deal, new terms."

"They can come up with what the fuck they like, but I'll kill every single one of them before I pay a penny of that shithead's debt."

"Death is the only way to stop them," he agrees. "We need a plan."

Seven o'clock comes, and Josey presents me with a beef roast dinner. "It's her favourite," she announces proudly.

I climb the stairs and try to get my emotions in check because it's killing me to watch her so lifeless and broken. Gia was right, it's not easy to stop my feelings for her, and as soon as she's eating again, I can go back to pretending she isn't living in my house right above my bedroom. I've spent most of the day checking in on her using the camera I'd installed years ago. She hasn't moved from the bed.

When I open the door, she's staring blankly at the opposite wall. "Sit up," I bark, but she doesn't respond. "Sofia." I place the tray on the bedside table, hoping the smell will rouse something in her. "Please," I say, a little quieter, and her eyes flick to me. "Please, Sofia, don't make me force this food down your throat." I beg her with my eyes because I really don't want to make her eat like that. When she still doesn't make a move, I growl with frustration and snatch the tray. "Fine, have it your way."

I storm back into the kitchen, taking Josey by surprise. "Blend it," I order. Josey closes her eyes in a brief moment of sadness before taking the dinner and pouring it into the blender. She blasts it for a few seconds at a time until the consistency is smooth. She grabs a tall metal cup used for milkshakes and empties the mixture into it.

"Are you sure I can't just speak to her," she asks again. I snatch the cup and head back up the stairs. This time, I don't have to give myself a pep talk about being firm or hard on her because I'm angry. Angry that she's making me do this and she'll still hate me for it. She won't see it's for the good of my child.

I fling the door open, and it crashes against the wall. She doesn't flinch, which only angers me more. I grab her chin, forcing her to look at me as I tower over her. A flicker of anger passes over her face. Good, she needs to start fighting. I stick my thumb in the side of her mouth, pushing it to the gum right at the back. She coughs, gagging.

SOFIA

His thumb brushes the back of my throat, and I gag, my eyes streaming as I cough violently. He kneels on the bed, pressing his knee on my hand to stop me grabbing him. I use my spare to hit out, but it doesn't deter him. Instead, he wedges his fingers into my mouth so I can't close it and then proceeds to pour something from a silver cup down my throat. I cough, covering us both in blended food. He switches his hold on my mouth, clamping it shut. "Swallow," he yells. He then pinches my nose until I have no choice but to swallow the disgusting food. When he's satisfied I've followed his order, he releases me, letting me suck in oxygen. "Now, do I have to do it again or will you eat?"

I stare up at him defiantly, and he looks disappointed before beginning the process all over again. We must be halfway down the cup when the door opens and Gia rushes in. She seems to have a habit of rescuing me. "What the hell are you doing?" she screams, trying to pull Vinn from me. He releases me, and I roll onto my side and vomit all over the floor. We all stare at the undigested mush.

"Seven tomorrow morning," he hisses, storming from the room.

Gia bursts into tears, wiping my hair from my face. "I saw on the camera," she whispers. "I saw." I flop onto my back, suddenly feeling exhausted. "I don't know what to do," she adds. Any decent person would get me out of here or ring the police, but I know she can't, not without risking her own life. I stare at the ceiling while she strokes my hair. "Sofia, please eat something. I'll get anything you want, biscuits, fruit. I swear, ginger biscuits helped me with sickness during my pregnancy."

I roll onto my side so that my back is to her. I don't mean to be rude, but I'm done with this family, and if I died right now, I wouldn't care. In fact, I'd welcome it.

VINN

I sit at the dinner table, trying to regain control of myself. Gia storms in looking pissed. "What the fuck, Vinn?"

"Why were you watching the camera in my office?" I demand.

"You left the screen on, and I was looking for you. Do you think all this distress is good for the baby?" she yells.

Mother walks in with Zarina and they take their seats. I still haven't decided what to do with Zarina. She's everything I wanted in a wife, yet I can't get my head from Sofia. "Gia, either sit or leave," I say, shrugging.

"I'll leave. I won't sit here and pretend everything is okay."

My meeting with Riggs goes well later that evening. I know he'll have my back against the Colombians, just like I had his when going to war with his enemies. An alliance with the MC was one of my best decisions. Once business is out of the way, he refills my glass. I shouldn't drink any more, my eyes are already blurring, but it helps to take my mind from Sofia, so I take it gratefully.

"What happens between you and Sofia now?" he asks.

"Do we have to discuss that? I'm so tired of it."

"We don't have to, but I thought you might want to speak to the king of dick decisions."

"Getting her out of my life isn't a dick decision."

"Tell your heart that." "If you're gonna get all sentimental on me, Riggs, I'm gonna go," I warn.

He grins. "Let me say one thing and then I'll leave it. You'll need her around once the kid is born. It ain't easy having a newborn who screams for its mother. I know you're a cold-hearted bastard, it's why I banned Leia from dating you, but do you honestly think you can hold a gun to her head once she's given you something so amazing?"

"Zarina will take care of the child. And yes, I will be able to pull the trigger. There are no feelings."

"You sat right there not so long ago," he says, pointing to where I'm currently sitting, "and you basically admitted to falling for her, so don't lie to my face and tell me you feel nothing. Even when Anna drove me nuts, I wouldn't have been able to put a bullet in her and especially not after she gave me a kid. With Benedetto out of the picture, surely you don't have to prove anything."

"It's not about proving anything. It's about her making a fool of me, laughing while I declared war on the person responsible for trying to damage my name. All that time, she was in my bed. She crossed me, and I can't walk away and pretend she didn't."

Riggs smirks. "Isn't it punishment enough that she's trapped with you forever?"

"You cross the mafia, you face death. She knew that and she didn't care. Zarina told her how it would end, and she still didn't care."

"Zarina," Riggs repeats. "Her name keeps cropping up."

"And why shouldn't it? She's loyal, respectful, and compliant."

Riggs shudders. "Doormat."

"Wife material," I correct him. "Something I should have looked for more closely before I married Sofia." "But I bet Zarina doesn't get your blood pumping like Sofia does. I bet she doesn't challenge you. Isn't that boring for a man like you? It's why you wanted Leia and why you had Raven. Sofia kept you on your toes. Admit it, you liked that about her."

I smirk, draining the last of my drink. "It was nice to catch up." I stand and head for the door as Riggs laughs.

"You know I'm right. Nothing is more addictive than a challenge."

"Goodnight, Riggs," I say over my shoulder.

SOFIA

I'm woken by the lock of the door clicking open. It's dark outside, but I have no way of knowing the time. I know it's Vinn by the way he hovers in the doorway, and when I open my eyes, he's closer than I thought, causing me to jump with fright. Moonlight streams in through the rooftop window. There are no drapes or blinds, so it lights the room enough for me to see the sad expression on his face. "Sorry," he utters. "I didn't mean to wake you."

He sits on the edge of the bed, staring at me. Ash provided me with cleaning products earlier, but I've yet to find the strength to clean up the vomit from the floor. The smell is intense, and after a few silent minutes, Vinn reaches for the bucket of water and begins to clean up the mess. "There's a doctor coming to see you tomorrow. He'll check you over." I watch him scrape the crusty mess into an empty bucket using tissue. "Ash said you refused to leave this room to shower or wash," he adds. The fear of running into Zarina and tearing her face off is enough to keep me in here until I feel less angry and more stable. "I'm going to take you for a shower," he continues, but I shake my head. There's no way I'm going anywhere with him.

"Well, at least I know you can hear me," he mutters. He finishes cleaning the vomit and places the two buckets outside the door. "Walk or I'll carry you." It's a threat I know he'll carry out, and I don't want him to touch me, so I push the sheets from my aching body and slowly sit up. The room spins from me because I've been lying down for too long. He holds out his hands, but I make no move to reach for them. Maybe I'm resisting the connection because I'm scared those butterflies are still there waiting to zap me, or maybe it's because I'm equally as scared they're not and I'll feel nothing. I don't know what's worse.

I finally stand, holding onto the wall until I'm ready to walk. Vinn walks ahead, leading the way down the stairs towards his room. I stop at the room before, my old room. I push the door open, because I'd rather use this shower than his. "Sofia, no," hisses Vinn, trying to pull me from the room, but it's too late. I lock eyes with Zarina. She's in my bed. Right next to Vinn's room.

I thought I'd want to hurt her. I imagined ripping her hair from her head while screaming profanities. Instead, I simply stare, then my eyes fill with tears, which only embarrasses me. "Sofia," whispers Vinn, his voice full of regret, "it's not how it looks." I step back, taking a few shaky breaths. My heart twists and I wince. Why does heartache hurt so much?

I turn and slowly make my way back to the safety of the attic room. It hurts less there, where I can't see them or smell his scent. A choked sob leaves my throat and I curse, not wanting him to see me like this again. "You did this yourself," he says from behind me. "This was you. We could have had something so good."

I crawl into bed and wrap the sheets around me without bothering to respond.

Chapter Nineteen

VINN

When morning comes, I am in no mood to deal with Sofia, but I climb the stairs regardless and present her with a bowl of porridge. She keeps her back to me. "You will eat," I say firmly.

"I hate you," she mutters. I shake my head, angry with myself for breaking her to the point she won't take care of my unborn child. I hate myself right now, but I also feel a sense of relief that she's spoken.

"Are you trying to kill the baby?" I ask. "Is that why you won't eat?" She doesn't answer and it infuriates me that I might be right. "Sofia!" I shout, hoping she'll react, even if it's in anger. I growl, running my hands through my already messed-up hair. "Okay," I relent, "I get why you're mad. I understand why you hate me, but please, for the baby, just fucking eat something."

"I want her to leave," she mutters so low, I barely catch it.

"Who?"

"Zarina. I want her to leave."

"Will you eat if she does?"

"Yes."

"Fine, consider it done."

"It's a nice apartment with security," I tell Zarina as she fiddles with the key I just handed her. "Raven will take you."

Raven glares at me, her eyes burning holes into my head. Gia told her about Sofia, and now, all the women in my life hate me. "It's a great little fuck pad," she says with a fake smile. "Vinn takes all his women there."

I roll my eyes. "Just go."

"Right away, boss," she says, fluttering her eyelids and doing a little curtsy.

"Really, Raven? Yah know, I can sack you."

She scoffs, heading for the door. "And who would save your arse if I wasn't around?"

Gerry passes her as he heads into the office. "What's up with her?"

"The women in my life hate me right now, Gerry. Get used to it."

"Your day is about to get a lot worse. The Colombian's sent a message." He places a box on my desk, and I eye it warily. Gifts from enemies are never good news.

"Do I need to look inside?"

He nods, so I stand and lift the lid. A putrid smell assaults my nostrils and I scowl. Inside is a severed head. "Who the fuck is this?"

"Antonio. His body was left at the docks and his head was hand delivered to the front gate just now. He was on night watch at the container yard last night."

I close the box. "Any note?" He shakes his head. "Then I guess we'll wait and see what he's got for us next. The good thing is, we're drawing him out with our silence. Even if he isn't here himself, his men must be. Let's see if we can locate any of them, maybe pay a visit."

SOFIA

The doctor is a man. I guess they're easier to pay off than women, and he doesn't bat an eyelid when he sees me curled up on the bed. I smell, I know I do. It's also abundantly clear that I'm here against my will. Not only that, but I'm still covered in my father's blood. It's dried into my hair, my hands, and my clothes.

Vinn stands nearby, hovering like an annoying fly. Since I ate the porridge, I feel slightly better. I managed to keep it all down, which I'm surprised about.

The doctor checks my blood pressure, and Vinn hands him the sample bottle I was instructed to give right before the doctor arrived. He checks my pee, then feels my stomach. He sets about opening a bag and pulls out a portable scanner. "Any idea how far along you are?" he asks, and I shake my head. "When was your last period?" I shrug.

Vinn sighs impatiently. "Sofia, stop being awkward."

I ignore him. "I'm here against my will," I say as the doctor fiddles with the machine.

"I'm going to need you to lift your shirt."

I stare blankly at the ceiling, and Vinn mutters in Italian, calling me a stubborn cow before pulling my top up for him. "You're a doctor. You need to inform the police," I snap. "This man is forcing me to stay here. You have a duty of care for your patients."

The doctor squirts cold liquid on my stomach and presses the scanner to my abdomen. "If I were you, *cagna*, I'd pray this good doctor finds something growing in your womb or the police will be the last thing on your mind," Vinn whispers next to my ear. A thumping sound fills the room and we both stare at the doctor, waiting for him to speak.

"That's your baby's heartbeat. I'd say you're around six weeks, so still very early. I'm going to prescribe some folic acid and a multivitamin. You're very pale, maybe some fresh air each day would help," he says, looking at Vinn. "I'll also prescribe you an anti-sickness drug to help ease the nausea. That will be the reason you can't eat."

"The reason is because I am a prisoner here. I want to leave."

The doctor begins packing away his things. "I'll call back around twelve weeks for another scan to check growth."

"Is she gone?" I demand, and Vinn shakes the doctor's hand and asks Ash to show him out.

"Yes. She left this morning."

"For Italy?"

He frowns. "She's staying in London."

"No, you promised—"

"That she would leave this house but not London."

"Why is she staying here?" I hiss.

He smirks, tucking some of my matted hair behind my ear. "You're a mess, Sofia. Take a damn shower."

"Will she be your next victim?" He takes me by the hand, and I cry out. It surprises us both and he stares at me in shock. It shocked me when I felt the electricity between us, I thought it would be gone, but all it does is remind me that he isn't mine.

"Why did you kill him?" I sob. I can't get my papa's lifeless, bloodied face out of my head. It haunts me.

"I'll make a deal," he says, his face serious. "Shower and I'll tell you." I nod, and he gives me a satisfied smile. "Let's go."

Vinn takes me to one of the spare rooms and turns on the shower. He keeps his back to me, and I strip before stepping into the warm water. I groan in pleasure as it heats my skin. Vinn turns back, and I notice his dark expression and hooded eyes. He still wants me, and I'm thankful for the frosted glass of the shower screen. "Your father was involved with the Colombians."

I stare out through the top part of the glass, the part that isn't frosted. "No, he wouldn't have been—"

"He was. Heavily. He owed them money and found a good way to pay, but it involved working for them. Mario was involved too."

I think of all the times they were away on business. I never questioned them, even when they told me I couldn't tell Benedetto. "But that means Papa might have known—"

"Dante? Yes, he did."

VINN

Sofia stares at me for a long time. I can see her mind working overtime while she pieces it together. Then, a tear rolls down her cheek. "Was it because of him?" I nod. "Because he owed them?"

I shake my head. "No. It was revenge. Dante was getting your father back for killing his brother."

She goes quiet again. "It happens, doesn't it? Being in this life, we're all at risk," she asks quietly, like she's trying to make sense of it all. I nod. "So, you killed Papa because it was his fault I was attacked?" I shake my head, and she frowns. "Where's Mario now?"

"He's dead. Dante killed him."

Sofia cries harder, covering her face with her hands. She looks so helpless and exhausted, part of my feels bad for her. I sigh, moving to the shower and grabbing a sponge. "Your father and brother were in a mess. They played with fire knowing they'd get burned eventually. If Dante hadn't killed your brother, Benedetto would have." I run soap into her skin, and she remains still.

"Why did you kill Papa?"

"Did you know your brother was gay?" She nods. "He was in love with Dante's brother. That's what started the whole thing. Your father found them together and shot Mario's lover. Dante wanted revenge."

"Please, Vinn, tell me why you killed Papa."

I rinse the soap from her skin using the shower head, then turn it off. "He lied. He made me look like a fool. He used me to save you, and in turn, put me in the Colombian's firing line. He risked my family, my life, everything, for a daughter who's screwed me over."

"Send me back," she mutters as I wrap a towel around her. "Give me to Dante and he'll leave you alone." My heart squeezes. Why would she offer herself up for me? "Right before he sent me home, he told me he could easily fall in love with me. It's the only memory I have of that time. Maybe if you hand me over, all debts will be paid."

The thought of another man loving her causes me more pain in my chest. I'd rather her be dead than with another. "You're forgetting one thing," I say, leading her back to the attic. "For the next eight months, you're staying here with me. I'm not sure war can wait that long."

She nods, a sad look in her eyes. "Try not to get killed."

"Careful, I might start to think you like me," I say, using words we'd exchanged when we first began falling for each other. She recognises my reference, and her face hardens.

"If you're going to die, I want it to be on the blade I'm holding."

I laugh. "I'll make sure Josey cuts your food up so as not to give you a knife with your cutlery."

"Don't worry, Ash checks it's there each time she collects my plate."

More days pass and Vinn's upgraded me to a notebook and some pens. It sounds ridiculous, but I was so happy when he handed them over, I almost hugged him. I've also been eating. I can't manage a lot of food, but small amounts more often are working for me, and the anti-sickness pills help.

I'm drawing when Vinn visits with my evening meal. He lays the tray on the bedside table and glances over to see what I'm doing. He snatches the notebook and holds it closer to his face. "You can draw," he says, sounding surprised.

He hands it back, and I continue shading the portrait I drew of Papa. He messed up, but I love him, and Mama does too, that's why I'm drawing this, for her. "Maybe one day you can draw me," he adds.

"I only draw things I like," I mutter.

He sniggers, used to my snipes of hate towards him. "Would you like to give it to her?" he asks, and my head snaps up to look at him. "I'm sure your mother would love to see you."

"What do I have to do?" I ask suspiciously. Nothing is for free when it comes to Vinn.

He laughs, shaking his head dismissively as he leaves.

A few hours later, I'm wrapped in Mama's arms, sobbing against her while she strokes my hair. "It's okay, *figlia*," she whispers.

"Everything's such a mess," I sob.

She pulls back and wipes the hair from my face. "We'll work it out."

"How? Papa is dead, Mario is dead, and we're trapped here."

She smiles. "I know you don't see it right now, but we're safer here than in Italy. Your papa did some terrible things, and Benedetto would have sent us away."

"So, we should be grateful to Vinn?" I snap angrily. "He's a monster."

"He didn't have to let me stay. He could have sent me back, and I would have been killed. Cleaning might not be what I had planned, but at least I'm safe and I'm near you."

"Stop it," I hiss. "You're sounding grateful to be cleaning up after Vinn fucking Romano. I watched him kill Papa," I say, sobbing again. "I'm pregnant with his child."

Mama looks around, catching sight of the camera. She presses her lips to my ear like she's comforting me. "*Figlia*, it's so important you change his mind about you. Make him see what a good girl you are."

I shake my head, staring at her like she's lost her mind. "No."

"Don't you want to be here for your child? Don't you want to watch it grow? You can have that, just make him see it's worth keeping you alive."

"I can't do that, Mama."

"Do it for me," she begs, grabbing my hands. "I'll be alone."

"You'll have Zarina and this baby."

"None of it will be worth it without my beautiful girl." Her eyes fill with tears. "Please, Sofia. Fight to live."

The door opens and Vinn tells us our time is up. It angers me so much, I growl in frustration. Mama kisses me on the head. "Thank you, Vinn," she says politely as she leaves.

I scowl. I will not thank him for allowing me a measly few minutes with my own mother.

"Problem?" he asks, looking amused.

"I hate you," I say. I make a point of saying it every single day.

"Old news," he mutters.

"Like our marriage," I retort.

"Speaking of which," he says, pulling some folded paperwork from his back pocket. "I have these for you to sign." I stare at the offered document but make no move to take it. "If you don't sign it, I'll forge your signature, but I thought you'd want to read over the divorce."

"Won't this look suspicious when you've begun to tell people I'm dead?"

"I backdated it to the day you left. It's the reason you walked out, and you being dead is purely a rumour. I haven't confirmed anything ... yet."

"You've thought of everything."

"I'm organised."

"And when the divorce is finalised, will you be forcing Zarina into your bed?"

He smirks. "She doesn't need to be forced, *cagna*, she climbs in willingly."

I fly towards him. It shocks us both, but he catches my hand right before it meets his face. He twists my wrist and pulls my arm up my back, pushing me against the wall. I feel the warmth of his minty breath against my face as he nuzzles his nose into my hair. "Oh Sofia, you have no idea how much I want to fight you," he whispers, and I feel his erection pressing against my arse. The shirt I was wearing has ridden up and he trails his fingers over my lace panties. "You've gone very still, *cagna*, and that makes me think you want my hands on you." I shudder, breaking the spell he has me under, and I try to fight him off. He laughs, stepping back. "I'd never force you, Sofia, it's not my style. But if you ever need relief—"

"Fuck you," I snap. "And get out."

He adjusts his trousers, amusement in his eyes. "Pity."

Chapter Twenty

VINN

Back in my office, I stare at the camera image of Sofia in bed. She's got that defiant look in her eyes and she's staring right back like she knows I'm watching. "Don't do it, princess," I whisper to myself as she kicks the sheets from her body. "You're poking the lion inside me."

She parts her legs and runs her hand over her inner thigh, all the while watching the camera. My erection strains painfully against my trousers. Her other hand gropes her breast over the material of her shirt. My shirt. I gave it her after she showered, and fuck, it looks good on her. She closes her eyes and her head falls back, her mouth parts slightly, and her tongue darts out to wet her lower lip. I begin to loosen my belt. Fuck, she makes it hard for me to resist her. A groan leaves her mouth and I pull my cock free. What I'd give right now to be buried inside of her. Her fingers brush over her panties and she whimpers. I grip my cock, closing my eyes briefly.

"Oh, Frazer," she whispers all breathy and relaxed, and my eyes shoot open. "Did that get your attention, Vinn?" she asks, sounding amused as she pulls the sheet over her body. "Stop watching me, you creep."

I slam the laptop shut and tuck my now flaccid cock back in my pants. *Stupid cagna*.

At breakfast the next morning, I can't stand the thought of sparring back and forth with Sofia, so I send Josey up with her breakfast. Josey's been asking to see her, and since last night, I've done nothing but picture Sofia in various sexual positions. It's distracting and tiring.

I listen outside the door as they hug and whisper excitedly about how much they've missed each other. Am I the only one who sees this woman for the deceitful bitch she is? Everyone else seems to fucking love her.

Gia appears at the bottom of the stairs. I go down to where she stands, judging me with a raised brow. "Watching her from a camera, listening outside her room . . . I'm starting to think you're obsessed."

"Keeping an eye on the mother of my child isn't odd behaviour, Gia."

"It is when you proclaim to hate her so much. It's okay to love her, Vinn."

I scowl. "It's okay in a world where you don't lead a whole clan of dangerous men. Anyone who crosses me has to pay, Gia, you know that."

"You could change all that. Dad would never have killed a woman."

I roll my eyes at her naivety. She didn't know half the things my father got up to. He was a good capo, never letting the women in our family see the ugly side of this life. He sheltered them, something I try to do. Gia's married to Blu, so she sees too much these days, but that's his problem. "She made me look weak. Now, I have to work extra hard for the next few months to make sure men know I'm as strong as ever. When the time comes, they will know that even my own wife doesn't escape from my wrath."

"They'll see a cruel, cold bastard who killed the mother of his child."

"And they'll never cross me."

"Brilliant, and then what?" she asks, looking unimpressed. "You show them how big and bad you are so they never cross you, but they won't respect you. And what are you going to tell your son or daughter when they ask about their mother? Because they will, as they grow."

"They'll have Zarina. She's agreed to raise the child as its mother. Once Sofia is gone, Zarina will move back in."

Gia shakes her head. "I don't even know you anymore," she whispers. "No brother of mine would kill a woman over something so stupid."

"Stupid," I snap. "I have investors questioning if they should pull out of a multi-million-pound deal because they think I can't protect them from the law. If I keep Sofia around, they'll have no choice because they can't trust me with her writing that bullshit. My associates think she's corrupt, a spy for the cops, a snitch. You know how bad that is in our life. I've had to tell them she's already dead so they don't come to kill her with my fucking child inside of her."

"You're the boss. You have the say. You don't have to explain anything to them."

"Gia," I growl impatiently, "if you can't stay out of this, you'll have to leave."

She gasps. "You're kicking me out?"

"I'm saying you need to stop trying to save Sofia. It won't work. I've made up my mind. If you can't handle that, then leave."

She presses her lips together in a tight line and nods. "You're right. I can't live with the man I used to look up to. Not when he's making a huge mistake. Alfie and I will move out."

I didn't expect that response, so I follow her as she storms across the landing. "Will you move into the clubhouse with the Kings?" I ask.

"Like you care," she retorts, slamming her bedroom door in my face.

I sigh heavily. "Of course, I care. What about my nephew?" She ignores me.

Everything's going to shit.

SOFIA

I lie on the bed staring at the ceiling. After seeing Josey and Mama all in one week, I'm slightly happier. Josey gave the same advice as Mama—make Vinn see I'm a good person who just did a stupid thing. She insisted he's got a good heart deep down and she believes I can bring it out of him. I have no intention of pretending I'm sorry because I'm not. He's proved what a monster he is by keeping me here, by killing Papa in front of me, and by being a bastard since. But I do have a plan—follow their advice, get Vinn to forgive me, and when he trusts me enough to let me out of this room, I'll run. I'd rather live on the streets than for a second longer with Vincent Romano.

Vinn brings me my evening meal. It's the only way to gage the time—my meals are never late, and so I know it's seven o'clock. I feel his eyes burning into my exposed arse. The second I heard him climb the stairs, I laid down on my front to pretend to draw in the book he gave me. I pulled the shirt around my waist so he'd see my pink lace knickers.

When I've let him stare a few seconds, I glance over my shoulder and make a show of pulling the shirt down. "Sorry," I mutter, "I was lost in my drawing." I've been drawing his portrait and I hold it up for him to see. He moves closer and takes the pad, placing my dinner tray to the side.

"It's good," he says. "Really good."

He heads for the door. "Actually," I say, sitting up and crossing my legs. His eyes fall to where my shirt rides up slightly. "Can't you eat up here with me?" He shakes his head. "Please, Vinn. I'm so tired of eating alone."

I watch as he battles with himself and smile when he closes the door and shrugs from his jacket. "I'll stay while you eat."

"Won't yours get cold?" He doesn't reply, but instead takes a seat on the end of the bed. I grab the tray. It's pasta. "I love Lorenzo's pasta," I whisper, taking a forkful and putting it in my mouth. I close my eyes in pleasure and moan. "That's so good."

Vinn smirks. "Josey suggested I get you some books on pregnancy," he says.

"She did?"

"She suggested one about babies too, but I don't suppose you'll be needing that."

He wants a reaction, but I don't give him one. Instead, I groan again over another mouthful of pasta. "I should have married Lorenzo. The man can cook."

We fall silent while I eat as much as I can before placing the tray back on the side. I make no move to straighten the shirt, and Vinn stares at the gap between my legs. "Maybe you can take me to shower tonight?" I ask.

He grins, shaking his head. "No."

"But I'm too hot up here and you won't allow me to have the window open. Heat rises, so this must be the hottest room in the house." I give the shirt a shake as if to emphasise what I'm saying.

"Enjoy the rest of your night, Sofia." He stands and takes my tray. I watch as he leaves, angry he didn't fall for my flirting. I'll need to up my game.

It's dark outside and a few hours have passed since Vinn left me alone. I stare at the red light blinking in the top corner of the room. Vinn hasn't mentioned the camera, but I know it's how Gia saw him force-feeding me, which makes me think he watches me. He never mentioned me calling out Frazer's name either, and I definitely thought he'd react to that.

I take a deep breath. I have to do this if I want to get his interest again, but my nerves are crumbling with each passing second. I stand, making sure to face the camera as I unbutton the white shirt and drop it to the floor. I wasn't lying, it is hot up here, but my nipples still pebble as the air hits them. I lie back on the bed in just my panties and slide my arms behind my pillow. I need to remind him what he's missing.

VINN

She's perfect. Her breasts don't move, and if I didn't know better, I'd think she'd had plastic surgery to keep them so perfect. But I know they're real, I've felt them. That thought embeds inside my head and my fingers itch to touch them. She's doing this shit on purpose, I know she is. Asking me to stick around for dinner? She can't fucking stand me, so I know it's some sort of plan. But this teasing is taking it too far. I haven't fucked since she was in my bed and my cock is begging me to just go up there and sink into her.

I drink the whiskey I poured right before I opened my laptop to check on her. Part of me wishes I hadn't bothered. Sofia stirs, getting my attention. She moans, and I stare closer at the screen. Her hand is definitely under the sheet and she's moving it slowly. The sound of her breathing tells me she's touching herself, and I growl, she's making this hard. Her eyes are closed and she's moving subtly. Maybe she doesn't want me to see this. Maybe she's trying not to make it obvious. She stiffens, the outline of her body goes rigid, and she shudders, crying out as she brings herself to orgasm. It's too fucking much, and I slam the laptop closed and rush to her room.

When I unlock the door, Sofia is still on the bed with her cheeks rosy and her lips slightly apart. She watches as I move to her, and I see the sudden fear when I wrap my hand around her throat. I push my mouth close to her ear. "What are you trying to do, *cagna*?"

She bites her lower lip and blinks at me with innocent eyes. "I don't know what you mean," she whispers.

I apply more pressure, and she raises her hand to my face, brushing her fingers across my lips. Her scent hits me and I open my mouth automatically, tasting her sweet juices when she pushes them in. "Stop trying to entice me, Sofia," I whisper in a threatening tone. "It won't end well for you."

"I'm lonely," she mutters, wincing when I squeeze harder. "And bored."

"And you think showing off to the camera is a way to solve that?"

"You're here, aren't you?"

"No more," I hiss. "Fucking someone I hate always ends badly. Fucking you might end in your premature death."

"Sounds exciting." She smirks, reaching her hand out and brushing my cock through my trousers. "It's certainly got you going."

I push away from her. I've never had a woman behave like this and it's fucking with my head. She pops her fingers into her own mouth and hums in pleasure.

"And there I was thinking you were some shy virgin."

"I'm what you made me," she retorts.

It takes every inch of will power I have, but I leave the room, and for a fleeting second, I wish Zarina was still here. Maybe fucking someone else will make me forget about Sofia.

SOFIA

Vinn avoids me. Days pass and the only person I see is Ash. It's frustrating. How the hell am I supposed to get him to trust me if I never see him? The red blinking light on the camera has stopped flashing. He isn't watching me anymore.

I lose myself in writing, recording memories and remembering things from when I was younger. Playing with Mario, lounging in the pool, hanging out with Nono in his shed where he'd make little model trucks from wood. There are bad memories too. I can't stop them once they start, just like the tears that flow as I write them down. Papa yelling and hitting Mama until she could hardly stand. Me hiding under the dinner table, squeezing my innocent eyes shut and covering my ears. I hated it when they fought. Mario would often sit with me for hours because Mama would have to go and lie down and I hated to be alone.

Mario . . . poor Mario. I remember the day he told me he was gay. I was so angry because he'd been flirting with one of my best friends. We argued and he promised me it was all a show so Papa would stop getting at him. I was sixteen when he told me, and I didn't care. I loved him just the same, but I knew Papa would be angry, so we kept it a secret.

The door opens, interrupting my daydreams. I'm surprised to see Vinn. He looks agitated and there's blood splatters on his crisp white shirt. "Busy day at the office, dear?" I drawl.

He throws some trainers at my feet, and I stare at them. "Put them on," he orders.

I remind myself now is not the time to question him. I'm intrigued and possibly leaving this room, so I push my feet into them quickly. "You'll need a sweater." I grab it, pulling it over my head sharpish, then I follow him downstairs to the ground floor. He opens the front door, and I stare wide-eyed. "You want to go, right?" It has to be a trick, so I stay quiet. "That's your big plan?" I shake my head. How the fuck does he know all this? "I've spent days thinking about it, why you suddenly turned into this sex-crazed harlot. That's not you, Sofia. And then it dawned on me, you're trying to play me again. I'll trust you, and you'll leave."

I stare outside at the winding path. I'd never outrun him, and there's no way he'll let me go. Even if I was to reach beyond the gates, he'd have me brought straight back. So, I fold my arms over my chest and turn on my heel, heading back towards my room. Disappointment crushes my chest. "Wait," he barks, and I stop, keeping my back to him. "The doctor said you needed to take a walk each day. We haven't done that, so let's start."

I look back over my shoulder to where he's holding out his hand. Just to prove a point, I keep my arms folded over my chest and push past him, stepping out into the fresh air. I take in a lungful and close my eyes. I never thought I'd miss the cool British weather, but I have, so much.

We walk in silence for a good five minutes. The house is surrounded by a high wall topped with wire to stop intruders coming in or prisoners escaping, who knows. We do a continual loop around the house. "Was I wrong?" he asks. "About your little plan?"

"Yes," I lie.

"So the little show you put on?"

I shrug. "Maybe I'm losing my sanity locked away all day and night. I only ever see Ash, who isn't very talkative. Anyway, where would I go? And why would I leave Mama? It's not like I have family waiting for me. You don't give yourself enough credit, Vinn. Maybe you awakened something in me I never knew existed." We fall silent again, both thinking over my words. Maybe they aren't strictly a lie, because before Vinn, I'd never had an orgasm like that. I'd never felt a desire so strong towards someone. Those sorts of feelings don't just disappear, no matter how much you hate a person.

"You shouldn't try and pull me back in, Sofia. I'm not a good person, especially lately. Who knows what will happen if you distract me?"

"Who said I was looking for a good person?" I whisper, glancing at him.

He stops and assesses me with his dark eyes. "Sofia, stop."

I shake my head, a rush of emotions hitting my chest. I know this isn't real—it can't be because I hate him—but I step towards him anyway and slowly reach up, resting my hand against his cheek. "I hate you," I whisper.

He nods, his breathing shallow. "The feeling's mutual."

My lips are so close to his, I feel his every breath. "Glad we understand each other."

"If you kiss me, Sofia, it's an open invitation for me to fuck you right now."

Heat pools between my legs. Why does his dirty mouth make me feel so fucking turned on? I close the gap, gripping his face in my hands as our mouths crash together in a hungry kiss. He backs me against the wall behind a pillar so we're out of view, then he pulls away, turning me away from him and tugging at my leggings and panties. Once they're halfway down my thighs, he rubs his hand between my legs to check if I'm ready for him. I'm so fucking ready, it's embarrassing.

Vinn grips my hips and slams into me. I cry out, digging my nails into the wall as he continues a punishing onslaught. His fingers move down to my swollen clit, and he rubs circles while continuing to slam into me. I orgasm hard, so hard I almost collapse. Vinn catches me, wrapping his arm around my waist to hold me against him. His punishing pace continues until he slams one hand against the wall and buries his face into my neck, grunting through his release.

After catching our breath, we pull our clothes back into place in silence. He doesn't even look in my direction as he heads inside. I follow, trailing behind like a sad, lost puppy. Why the hell am I disappointed by his lack of affection? What did I expect? Inside, he stops at the bottom of the stairs, keeping his eyes downcast. "We shouldn't have done that," he mutters, and for some reason, his words cut me like a knife. "It was a mistake, and it won't be happening again. Would you like to shower?" His casual question throws me for a second, and I hesitate. He takes my pause as hurt and smiles sympathetically. "You know it can't go anywhere, Sofia."

I scoff, looking him up and down. "Christ, you're nothing to write home about, Vinn. I had an itch to scratch, that's all."

I storm up to the spare room to shower, not caring if he follows or not. When I step out, there's fresh clothes on the bed, his shirt and new leggings. On top of these is my notebook and pencils. I frown. I go to the door and try to open it, but it's locked. I smile to myself . . . I've been upgraded.

Chapter Twenty-One

VINN

Staying away from Sofia to break the pull I have towards her didn't work. I thought I was strong enough to see her again, but that went to shit the second she kissed me. I'm so fucked.

I sent Gerry to get Zarina, and she knocks on the office door before entering. "You wanted to see me?"

I nod. "I'd like you to stay here again."

She smiles, looking surprised. "And what about Sofia?"

"That's my business. Gerry will get your things. You'll be in my room."

Her eyes light up and something inside of me aches, forcing me to rub my chest, right over my heart. I need to do this to move on. I tried to stay away, but it didn't help. Zarina is the perfect woman to be a wife. "I'm not sure I should stay in your bed until we're married," she says quietly.

"What difference will it really make, Zarina? As soon as the divorce goes through, we can marry. It's being pushed through." It's a lie, because Sofia still has the paperwork.

Zarina nods. "I will stay in your bed, but we can't have sex."

"Of course," I say, smiling. Another lie. I need to fuck her to forget her cousin. "Go and get comfortable. I'll be there shortly."

Zarina is lying in bed in a full nightdress. It reminds me of something my nona wore. She's on her back, stiff as a board and staring at the ceiling. "Relax, Zarina, nothing's going to happen unless you want it to."

"I was thinking about Sofia actually," she says, sadness passing over her face. "Maybe she should know about our plans for a wedding. If I'm going to raise her child, she should know that."

"And what would be the point?" I ask, stripping off. She watches me cautiously. "There's thirty-one weeks left of her pregnancy. That's a long time." I climb into bed, and she stiffens further. I roll my eyes and flop back into my pillows.

"She's still my cousin."

"If you want to tell her, be my guest. I just think it'll make things worse between you. She's hardly going to be happy about it. She's eating well and resting. You might stress her out again, then she'll starve herself." I take Zarina's hand in mine. "Let's do it my way first. At least get her to the half-way mark."

SOFIA

Vinn brings breakfast and my heart squeezes. I have to remind myself this is a plan, that I don't like Vinn. He sits by the window as I tuck into my toast. When I'm finished, I stand. "I want to show you something," I say proudly. I take his hand, and he stares at where our skin meets. I lift my shirt, and his eyes move to the bare skin underneath. "When I was naked in front of the mirror last night, I noticed this." I place his hand over my tiny bump and turn sideways. "See?" Vinn's expression softens as he gently rubs his hand over the smooth skin.

"I'm practically a whale," I announce, laughing. Biting my lower lip, a sudden idea enters my head. "And these," I announce, lifting the top over my head in one swift movement. His eyes widen at my naked body, and I cup my breasts. "Are bigger, don't you think?" He nods instead of answering verbally. I move over to the mirror and pretend to admire my changing body. "I'm going to be huge. What if I get stretch marks and my breasts sag?"

Vinn suddenly shakes his head and blinks a few times, like he's trying to shake away the image in front of him. "What will it matter?" he asks coldly, and we both know the meaning behind his words.

"I don't want the only image of me that my child sees to be one of me covered in stretch marks."

"I hardly think he'll remember," he mutters.

I wince at his words and a look of guilt passes over his face. I force a smile. "You're right. I'll have so many more things to worry about after I've given birth. I was reading the book you got me. It says you can freeze breast milk. I thought after the birth, I could express some. They say it gives the baby the best start in life." He stares blankly, and I shrug, feeling stupid. "It was just an idea. I'm sure powdered milk is just as good, but I guess it's up to Zarina."

"No," he nods, "it's a good idea." I pick up the shirt and pull it over my head. "How long after I've given birth . . ." I begin.

"Sofia," he mumbles.

"I'd just like to know. And will I spend any time with the baby, or should I just hand it straight over?"

He stands, avoiding my eyes. "I haven't given it much thought. Have you signed the divorce papers?"

I shake my head. "The book says if you're giving up your baby, you should hand it directly to the new mother."

He nods, pulling open the door. "I'll speak with Zarina. She'll be at the birth anyway, so I'm sure it will be fine."

I suck in a painful breath but paste another smile on my face and nod. "Good idea." I knew the answers and I pushed for them anyway, so why is it crushing my heart? I'm going to fight to change his mind so nothing he's just said is final. I still have time.

Ash brings my lunch, placing it on the bedside table. "Ash, is Vinn home today?" I ask casually.

"I think he and Zarina went to the office today," she says, heading for the door.

"Zarina?" I repeat, and Ash nods. "She stayed here last night?"

She nods again. "She's moved back in," she adds as she leaves.

The news makes me smile. My plan is working. He's trying to stop himself from wanting me by moving her back here. I still have time. Zarina is a good Italian girl and wouldn't dare to have sex before marriage.

It's early evening when Vinn enters my room. "Ash will take you for a walk this evening," he says firmly.

I frown. "No."

"What do you mean no? The doctor said—"

"I know what the doctor said, but I'm not a dog that needs walking around the yard. I'll walk on my own."

He laughs, shaking his head. "No."

"Then I'll stay here." I go back to writing in my notebook, but he remains in the doorway. "Goodbye," I add bluntly.

"Why do you always have to be so difficult?"

"It's my prerogative. I'm on death row." He rolls his eyes like my statement is dramatic. "Speaking of which, I want to talk with Zarina."

"I don't think that's a good idea." "She's my cousin. She's in your bed. I want to speak to her." He looks momentarily flustered and is probably wondering how I know. I smile. "You look worried."

He stands straighter. "Not at all. Be ready in an hour and you can join her for dinner."

I didn't expect him to agree, but I nod to disguise the panic I feel. That backfired, I just wanted him to know that I knew she was here again.

Ash leads me downstairs and towards the dining room where Vinn is sitting at the table with Zarina to his side. I narrow my eyes. I assumed it would be me and her, but I should have known better. I take a seat and notice Zarina's hand on Vinn's. She keeps her head lowered, avoiding any eye contact with me.

"I expected you to pull a stunt," says Vinn. "It's so unlike you to follow instructions."

"Maybe I've changed."

"You wanted to speak with Zarina," he adds, smirking.

I take a sip of water, staring longingly at Vinn's wine. "I had a speech of sorts," I begin. "One where I begged you not to ruin my life, not to let Vinn take my child, and . . . well, yah know. But seeing you sitting here, in my seat, holding his hand, the hand that I once clung to, it hurts me, Zee. I can't lie." Our eyes finally meet and hers are filled with guilt. It's eating her alive. "I don't think you meant to take Vinn," I add. "I think you liked him, and I made it easy for you to turn his head because I fucked up." I move my eyes to Vinn. "I fucked up. I can't change that, but I'm the mother of your child. I know you love me, Vinn. I can see it when you look at me."

Vinn shifts uncomfortably. "Enough."

I lean closer towards him. "I know you do. You can't keep away from me. Your body craves mine, and you don't regret what we did the other day, I know you don't. You enjoyed it as much as me. We can have that all the time, Vinn. We can be together." I sound as desperate as I feel. "We can move forward together."

Vinn stands, grabbing me by the upper arm and hauling me to my feet. "Enough!" he yells. "Ash, take her back to her room."

"No!" I cry, grabbing onto his arm. "Just listen to me."

"Now, Ash," Vinn shouts. Ash steps forward, but I shove her back. I didn't plan this, and I'm being led completely by my feelings that decided to rush forward all at once to make me look like a fool.

"Zarina," I cry, "you're choosing him over me, over blood?"

"I'm sorry," she whispers, tears streaming down her cheeks.

Vinn tries to push me gently without hurting the baby. "Sofia, stop this. It's not good for the baby."

"Look me in the eyes and tell me it's over. Tell me I'm imagining it all and you don't love me."

Something cold switches in his expression, and I shiver. "I've made up my mind and this desperate behaviour is only pissing me off. We are done. Over," he says firmly.

"You didn't say it," I point out.

He sighs heavily before looking me in the eyes. "I don't love you."

I let the words settle between us before nodding. "I'd like to go for that walk now."

"Ash—"

"Alone," I add. "I can't go anywhere but around the house. You have men guarding the gates. I need some alone time."

"You're alone all goddamn day," he snaps.

VINN

I follow Sofia on her walk around the grounds. The agreement was I stay at least a metre away, but it's important she gets air, so I backed down. Choosing my battles with her is becoming a habit. I can still feel the way her hand gripped my arm so tight back in the house. She'd taken all of this well so far, but I knew a meltdown was coming. She's been in denial for weeks about how this is going to end. I'm surprised she went this long.

We do a couple of circuits before she sits on the front steps. "You can go inside. I'm just gonna sit out here for a while."

"No. You need to go back to your room."

"Why did you move me from the attic?" she asks.

I shrug. I don't know what made me do it, it just felt right. When we're getting along, I forget what she did and it's almost like we're okay again. But then I remember, and it hurts all over again. I sigh heavily. I'm Vinn fucking Romano . . . I don't hurt.

"Sofia—" I begin, but a popping sound behind me pulls my attention away and I glance back at the same time Sofia screams. Both my men are lying on the ground with blood spreading over the white stones. I pat my pocket, already knowing my gun isn't there because it's in the office. I growl, grabbing Sofia by the hand and dragging her towards the door.

"I wouldn't take another step if I was you, *escoria de la mafia*."

"Mafia scum?" I repeat, turning slowly with a smirk on my face. I gently pull Sofia behind me, keeping her hand tightly in my own. "I'm offended, Dante," I drawl, letting my capo mask slip into place.

"Imagine being so fucking arrogant that you left only two men on security."

"Imagine," I say dryly.

"Where's Blu and Gerry?" Sofia whispers.

"They left an hour ago, *mi pájaro hermoso*. Did you miss me?"

"Sofia, go inside, I'll be just a few minutes," I say, releasing her hand.

"I don't think so." Dante shakes his head. "She stays."

I run my eyes over the five men behind Dante. Sofia will never make it up the steps and be able to close the door without them killing her. Our last hope is that Zarina or one of the house staff is listening and will call for back-up. "What do you want, Dante? I have shit to do."

"I heard you were looking for me," he drawls.

"Yes," I say. "I'm going to kill you."

He grins. "Is that right? Firstly, I'm not as stupid as to leave myself unarmed and unguarded."

"Yes, that was a fuck-up on my part. I've been side-tracked lately." Distracting him with pointless conversation is my only option while I wait for someone to turn up and draw attention so I can get Sofia inside. "Women," I add.

"She is quite the distraction. It was hard for me to leave her on that boat looking so sun-kissed and goddess-like."

"I don't think it was as memorable for Sofia," I say dryly.

"Don't worry, she made all the right noises." He smirks. I bite my tongue to stop my reaction, and he sighs. "Anyway, this is going on for too long. I was planning on executing you right here on the steps of your beautiful home, but I have a better idea. Let's go."

I begin to walk towards him, and two of his men move forward, grabbing an arm each. Another man heads for Sofia. "Run," I tell her, and she turns a little too quickly, tripping on the step and falling to the ground. I try to go to her, but I'm held back. Dante reaches her and takes her hand, gently helping her to stand.

"Don't be scared, *hermosa*. It was never personal."

"Please let me go. I won't tell anyone. I hate Vinn. He's kept me here against my will."

I narrow my eyes, and Dante grins in my direction. "Is that right? Well, let's talk about that on the way." He leads her away from the house, keeping a firm grip on her wrist.

We're bundled into a van with three goons between us. Sofia keeps her eyes to the ground. Would she really have gone off without giving me a second thought had Dante let her go?

The van eventually slows to a stop and one of the goons moves towards me. I head-butt him square in the face, and he falls to his knees like a bitch. I laugh when the other two dive on me, both jabbing punches into my sides. When the van doors open, Dante joins me, laughing. Then his hand dashes towards Sofia and he pulls her from the van by her hair. "If you want your wife to stay in one piece, I suggest you stop trying to be the hero," he hisses.

I glance around as we're dragged from the van. We're in some type of industrial yard, and I can here banging and machinery. No one will be able to hear us around here, but I guess that's why they chose it. We're forced into a small lock-up where there's only one chair and a large hanging meat hook above it. I smirk as I'm jostled towards it.

Chapter Twenty-Two

SOFIA

My worst nightmare is being tied to a man I am madly in love with but hate just as much, yet that's exactly where I find myself. I stare at my left wrist where the metal cuff connects me to Vinn. The worst part is, Vinn's hanging upside down from his ankles with blood pouring from the wounds Dante's men gave him when they beat him for a solid ten minutes. My right hand is cuffed to a rusty metal bolt in the wall.

Dante smiles at my bewildered face. "This isn't the end. I haven't quite decided what to do with you. But your husband," he bends at the waist slightly to try and get a glimpse of Vinn's bloodied face, "this motherfucker will bleed to death, and then, I will take his little empire piece by piece." He looks pensive for a second, then grins as he whispers in Vinn's ear, "And maybe I'll keep your wife also, she was a good fuck."

Vinn's eyes shoot open, and he grins, showing his crimson-covered teeth. "You're wrong," he hisses, crashing his forehead against Dante's and taking him by surprise. I wince and turn away. "This is my wife and my empire, and no fucking Colombian is taking shit."

Dante punches him in the gut before storming from the lock-up. "What are you playing at?" I whisper. "Are you trying to get him to kill you now?"

"Maybe. Were you really gonna leave back there?"

I shake my head. "Of course not. I was hoping they'd let me run so I could get help. What do you take me for?"

"A desperate woman trying to save herself," he mutters.

"Unlike you, I have morals. I wouldn't sit by while my husband was being killed."

Vinn smiles. "Isn't a small part of you happy I took a beating?" I roll my eyes. "I did that for you."

"Because you had a choice?"

He winks, and my heart speeds up. "I'm going to kill every last one of them, *moglie*. I told you before, Colombia will burn for you."

I glance at the door, knowing they're all just outside. "And how do you plan to do that?"

"Remove my belt," he whispers, and I glare at him.

"Now isn't the time."

"Are you going to help me or not?"

I stand and the cuff on my right wrist clangs. "How? I'm cuffed!"

"Your teeth."

It's a task, but somehow, I manage to open his belt using my mouth and teeth. Biting the buckle, I'm able to tug it from the loops. I put it in Vinn's cuffed hands, and he feels along the leather. He uses his teeth to remove a small pin and holds it up with a grin. "Let's get these cuffs off." He wiggles the pin in the cuff we share and it frees me. "Now you take the pin and release me." I do the same and then I uncuff my right wrist. He takes the pin and swings himself up to grab an ankle. Within seconds, he's jumping to the floor.

The door swings open and Dante glares at us. "What the fuck?" he yells. The rest of his men rush to his side. "Gentlemen, join me. It's cosy in here," Vinn drawls, grabbing a metal pole they used to hit him with.

I watch as the men rush him and he begins swinging the metal pole like some kind of action hero. Within seconds, Dante's goons are laid out on the ground and Dante is moving in on Vinn. I glance at the open door, then back to the men who are exchanging threats. I look towards the door again. I have to take the opportunity to leave because staying will mean returning to that hell with Vinn, and yes, I love him—a small, stupid part of me wishes he'd change and be the man I want him to be, the man I know he can be—but we've done too much to each other. A scuffle breaks out and I realise Vinn's dropped the metal bar and they're fist fighting. I edge towards the door, slowly and carefully so as not to draw attention to myself.

"Don't do it, Sofia," Vinn says, and I freeze, looking back to where he's dodging hits.

My eyes fill with tears. "I don't have a choice."

"There's always a choice." He hisses when a fist connects with his chin. "Raven taught me that," he adds. "And I told her there wasn't. I told her I had no choice, that I had to marry you. I hated the idea, just like you."

"I have to leave. I can't let you kill me."

Vinn gets Dante under the eye and shifts his attention back to me. "I was never going to." I frown. "I decided to send you away."

"Lies," I yell as I move closer to the door.

"Not lies," he says calmly while dodging more hits from Dante. "No more fucking lies. Let's be honest for once, because let's face it, we haven't tried that since the moment we met." He hits Dante, causing him to stumble, giving Vinn the advantage. He pummels his fists into Dante's face until he's lying still on the ground. I turn to the exit and rush from the building. Seconds later, I hear a gunshot, followed by five more.

As I reach the end of the road, a lorry is pulling away from one of the factories. I wave my hands frantically and he slows to a stop. I climb into the large vehicle and slope down in the seat, hiding in case Vinn's behind me. "Drive," I hiss.

As he pulls away, looking confused and slightly worried, I see Vinn in the mirror, looking around in the middle of the road. It breaks my heart to see him so messed up. "Have you got a mobile I can borrow?" I ask. The driver nods, handing me his phone. I smile gratefully and dial Josey's number. I'd taken it from her when she came to see me before and I'd memorized it just in case. When she answers, I frantically ask for her to put Mama on. When I finally hear her voice, I break out into fresh sobs.

"Sofia, is that you?" she asks, sounding worried.

"Mama, you can't tell anyone I've called. You have to meet me. We're getting out of here."

"And going where? What happened? Where's Vinn?"

"He's alive. Don't worry about him. Mama, I need you. Please."

"Okay, where?"

I turn to the lorry driver. "Can we make a stop?" He nods. "Okay, Mama, go to the main road, we'll be there in five minutes."

She agrees, and I disconnect. "Where are you off to?" the driver asks.

"Wherever you're going," I say with a weak smile, and he laughs. "I just need to get away from here. There's a dangerous man who'll come looking for me."

"I'm heading to Ireland. Have you got a passport and money?"

I shake my head. "It's fine. Drop us at the ferry and we'll make our way somewhere."

"To be honest, at this time of night, they'll not be too vigilant. We can try hiding you in the trailer?" I nod eagerly. Anything is better than facing Vinn's wrath.

VINN

"Your face pisses me off," says Blu, and I drink the rest of my whiskey before refilling the glass. "It's been two weeks. She's gone. Let her go."

"With my fucking child!" I yell.

"You've had men scouring London. She's not here."

"She can't have left, she had no money and no passport."

"Because your psycho arse hid hers!"

"You're crossing the line," I warn.

"Well, someone needs to. I've had to watch your sister heartbroken because you basically pushed her out—"

"Not true."

"One hundred percent true. You loved Sofia and you treated her like shit."

"She lied to me!"

"It doesn't matter anymore because she's gone. Now, for the love of God, put the whiskey down and get a grip of things. You might have gotten rid of Dante, but that doesn't mean the war is over. The Colombians will come looking for him."

"And prove what? As far as I'm concerned, I never met the man. They'll spend eternity looking for him." We sent Dante and his little gang to the incinerator. They're ashes now. But Blu is right, I need to stop drinking and sort my shit out.

Zarina pops her head around the door. "I'm packed." I nod so she knows I heard her. Having her around is a reminder of the mess I made, so she's going home to Italy. I just want it all to be over and the world to go back to how it was before I met Sofia.

I watch from the office window as Zarina's car to the airport drives away and I feel a sense of relief already. Then, Riggs' bike pulls in, and I groan. Usually when he turns up here, it's bad news. I head out to meet him, and he's grinning like an idiot. "I have something for you," he says, handing me a piece of paper.

I stare at an address. "Is this what I think it is?"

Blu looks over my shoulder. "How the fuck did she get to Ireland?"

Chapter Twenty-Three

SOFIA

Ireland is beautiful, and I'll be sad when we have to leave here. Staring out at the busy town, I smile when I spot Mama crossing the road and heading into the cafe where I've been working since we arrived two weeks ago. "I thought I'd meet you to walk home," she announces. She's wary of our new surroundings, and I can't blame her. It's different to London—people here are friendly and kind, which makes her suspicious after being with Papa for so long.

"I told you, I'm fine."

"And I told you, it's my job to take care of you." She gives me a sad smile, and I know she's thinking of Papa and Mario.

"Sofia, get yourself home," says Charlotte, my new boss. She hands me fifty euros, and I stuff it in my pocket. She agreed to pay me cash in hand for temporary work. It's the holiday season and she's rushed off her feet, so she was willing to take me at any cost.

I hook arms with Mama and we step out into the cold. Charlotte said snow was forecast, and we're excited. We don't often get that in Italy. She also put us in touch with an elderly man who was looking for a housekeeper. Mama covers that, and he lets us both stay for hardly anything. I think he likes having company. He loves to cook, and I'm not surprised when we get back and there's two bowls of soup laid out. I hate that we have to move on soon, but I know Vinn will find me if we stay too long.

"Where will we go?" Mama asks as we climb into bed later that evening.

"One of the customers goes to France in his fishing boat. He'll take us in two days. That's when he's next sailing."

"And then what?"

I sigh. I know she's worried. We've never had to support ourselves because we've always had Papa. "I don't know, Mama."

"We can't run forever. He'll never stop because you're having his baby."

I run my hand over the now visible bump and my heart aches. I'd give anything to have a normal, loving husband. "What do you suggest we do?"

"Go back to Italy and beg Benedetto to forgive our family and take us in."

"He'd never risk a war with Vinn for us, Mama. You know that. Forget Benedetto and Vinn. Forget the mafioso. It's just us now." I turn my back and switch out the lamp.

VINN

"I don't know how this turned into a big trip," I mutter, moodily.

Blu shrugs, looking just as annoyed as me. "Are you kidding? We weren't going to let you stomp on in and scare the shit out of Sofia," says Gia.

"Besides, we care," adds Leia, giving my hand a squeeze. Chains mutters something, and she releases me with an eye roll in his direction.

When Gia turned up with Blue, Riggs, Anna, Leia, and Chains, I refused to get in the van they'd hired. Getting my pregnant wife back to London wasn't going to be easy, and now with this lot in tow, it'll be much harder. "You must take your time and be patient," says Anna. "No forcing her."

"And tell her how you feel," adds Gia. "If she can see you're being honest, she'll forgive you."

"I have rope," I say, holding up my bag, "and a gag. This isn't going to be a friendly reunion."

Gia gasps. "Vinn, you can't kidnap her."

"It's not kidnapping, she's my wife."

"If you talk to her, she'll come willingly. Isn't that better?" asks Leia.

"You're scared she'll reject you," states Chains with a smirk.

"I also have a gun," I warn, glaring at him in particular.

"Glad to see you've learned your lesson," he says, making reference to my lack of weapons which allowed Dante to take us. "Didn't you beat Blu for that same thing?"

"Blu let my sister get taken," I remind them all.

"Thanks for raising that again, Chains," Blu hisses.

I glance out the window at the dreary Irish weather. The grey clouds promise snow, and I pray we make it out of here before then. An hour later, Riggs stops outside a small cottage. "Just letting you all know, if I find another man in her bed, I'm going to kill them both," I warn.

"I think I should go in there first," says Gia. "You'll mess this up."

I roll my eyes and get out of the minivan. Gia rushes after me, trying to take the bag from my hand while hissing that I don't need rope. I knock loudly, and a few minutes later, an elderly man answers. "Where's Sofia?" I bark.

Gia nudges me. "Sorry," she cuts in politely. "We're friends of Sofia's and we were wondering if she's around?"

"Sofia?" he asks, looking confused.

I pull out a photograph. He narrows his eyes to look at it, then smiles. "Jenna? She's over the road at The Horse and Cattle." He points to a small bar that's heaving with life. "I'll show you the way," he adds, and I stomp off before he can get his coat.

SOFIA

Mama isn't impressed by the noisy bar, but I can't help smiling at the loud chants of the local rugby team. It seems they won the cup and they're very happy about it. I duck down as beer sloshes out of glasses around us. "Let's finish up and go," I say, and she smiles at my suggestion to end her torture.

"Don't rush on my account, *Jenna*," comes a familiar stern voice. I slowly look into the eyes of my husband and my blood turns cold. Mama stares wide-eyed, looking at me for guidance. "Aren't you pleased to see me?" Vinn asks, pulling up a chair and joining us. "Maybe you're surprised I'm still alive after you left me to die?"

I glance over the faint bruising on his face. "I knew you'd be okay."

"Let's find somewhere to talk," suggests Mama, standing.

"I like it here," I say, wanting the safety of these people.

"Sofia, don't be naïve. I can kill you here too," he mutters.

Vinn stands and holds out his hand, which I ignore, pushing past him and making my own way outside, all the while my brain is racing to come up with an escape plan. "How did you find me?"

"You knew I would." I thought I'd have more time. My heart is beating so hard, I worry he'll hear it. "Riggs and the others are with the old guy," he says to Mama. "Join them." She nods, heading over the road, and I'm suddenly angry. He always gets his own way. He bosses everyone about, and they all just do it.

"I'm not coming back to London."

"You are." He grips my jacket and tugs me closer. He unzips it and places a hand over my bump. His eyes are warm and he almost smiles. "Zarina went home to Italy."

"Good for her." I step back and refasten my coat.

"We both messed up."

"Some more than others," I snap.

He nods. "Crossing me wasn't your best idea."

"I'm talking about you, Vinn!" I yell, and he looks surprised. "You kept me hostage. Locked me in a room."

"You could have gotten me killed. You tried to take me down."

"But I failed because you're still standing here with that smirk on your face, bossing everyone around like you're the king." I take a breath. "You pointed a gun at me. You planned to kill me and take my baby."

"When you say it out loud, it does sound bad. I guess I could have handled it better."

"We can't salvage this, Vinn."

He nods. "I know. But we can come to an arrangement. Come home." When he realises I'm standing firm, he sighs heavily. "Look, you have no one here but me and your mother, and however much you protest, you know you have to come back to London with me. So, why don't we call a truce and work something out so we're both happy?"

I shake my head. "How can I trust you not to lock me away again?"

He reaches into his pocket and pulls out a mobile phone and a set of keys. "This is your phone and the keys to my house. You're not a prisoner."

"You made my mama clean for you!" I remind him, and he looks at the ground. "You locked me away from her after you killed my papa! You made me pee in a bucket!"

"I was angry."

"And so was I!" I yell, causing a few passing people to glance our way. "Too much has happened. A key and a phone won't make it better." "Then what will?"

I shrug. "I don't know."

I spot Gia heading our way and smile. "Hey, you," she says, embracing me. "Is my brother being nice?" She rolls her eyes. "In fact, don't answer that."

"Gia, we're talking," says Vinn firmly.

She links arms with me and begins leading me back towards the house. "It's cold out here, Vinn. Talk tomorrow."

"Tomorrow?" he repeats, following us. "We're not staying here."

"Yes, we are," she sing-songs.

Chapter Twenty-Four

VINN

It's been two days since we arrived in this god-forsaken shithole. The Kings returned home, leaving me, Gia, and Blu. I'm no closer to talking Sofia around and I'm getting impatient, which is why I find myself on an early morning run. I wasn't prepared for the rush of feelings that hit me when I first laid eyes on her after arriving here. The relief I felt knowing she was safe. Her small bump is obvious now, which surprised me. There's also been a steely look in her eyes, and fuck, it turns me on. She isn't taking my shit anymore, and a dark side of me wants her to push the boundaries so I can throw her over my shoulder and fuck some sense into her.

I shake my head. She can't even stand to look at me. The only way I'm getting near her again is by force, and that's already proven to be a failure. My eyes hone in on the female jogging in front of me. I know that arse, so I pick up my speed to catch her. Falling in sync beside Sofia, she pulls out one of her ear buds and groans when she sees it's me. "Expecting someone else?" I ask dryly.

"When are you going home?"

"Whenever you're ready," I say, smiling.

"I've told you, I'm not going back with you, Vinn."

"But you are, Sofia. You really are."

She slows to a stop. "I don't have time for this. Stop following me around."

She looks good, glowing in fact. Her small, rounded stomach shows under her Lycra vest. I place my hands on it and briefly close my eyes. "We're tied together forever, Sofia. That's a long time to hate each other."

"What happened to showing your enemies you can't be taken for a fool? You were more worried about them than me. Your reputation is so important, you'd kill me to save it. I can't have my child around someone like that."

I growl, pushing my hand into her hair and tipping her head back. Standing over her, I stare hard into her defiant eyes. She's turned on, and I smirk. "*Our* child," I correct her. "We worked hard making him, we should work hard to raise him together."

"So he can become like you and my papa and Benedetto?"

I nod, my lips dangerously close to hers. "Respected, powerful, rich."

"Arrogant, cruel, violent." My lips crash against hers and she allows the kiss for a few seconds before hitting on my chest. I step back and glance at my erection. She does the same, her face reddening. "Take a cold shower," she hisses, spinning around and walking away.

"You're inviting me to dinner?" I ask Blu, and he shrugs like it's not weird. "Why?"

"Because we don't ever do it and this feels like a holiday, so let's do holiday things."

"In case you haven't noticed, I'm trying to get Sofia to come home with me. I don't have time for dinner dates with my second in command."

"Humour me."

I groan, standing and grabbing my jacket. We found a hotel just around the corner from where Sofia and her mama are staying. It's quaint and very country, not at all what I'm used to, and the sooner I get out of here, the better. "Fine. But if this is some plan to talk me out of dragging Sofia back to London, it isn't going to work. My sister is not in charge."

"You don't think Sofia will come back willingly?" he asks.

I shake my head, following him outside. "No. I've booked ferry tickets home for tomorrow afternoon, and she's coming with or without consent. I've been far too lenient as it is."

This town is small and the only place we found to eat was a seafood restaurant with a romantic vibe going on. I glare at Blu as we're seated. He grins back and leans over to blow the centre candle out. "Relax, people might think we're having a lovers' tiff," he jokes.

"They'll witness a murder if you don't shut the fuck up."

"Why have you always got to threaten me with death? It's becoming a very bad habit of yours," he complains.

We're about to order drinks when Gia struts over, dragging Sofia behind her. "Fancy seeing you here," she says, winking at Blu.

"You promised me a Vinn-free night!" hisses Sofia.

"I lied," says Gia, shrugging. Blu stands, and Gia pushes Sofia to sit in his seat.

"I'll be at the bar in case shit gets out of hand," says Blu, slapping me on the back.

Gia pulls up another chair and sits herself on it. "Okay. It's clear you two need an intervention," she begins. For once, I keep my mouth shut because seeing Sofia in a fitted dress, with her hair pinned up and makeup enhancing her beauty, makes me want to hear out Gia's plan. "So, I'll be the judicator. You guys need to talk this out, and we're not leaving here until it's sorted."

"For once, little sister, I agree."

Sofia leans back in the chair, scowling. Gia places her hand over Sofia's. "I know you're angry, and you have every right to be, but you're having a child together and you know how this life works. You can't walk away with Vinn's child."

"He's treated me like crap, and he was planning on killing me."

I shake my head. "Not killing, relocating, *tesoro*."

"Bullshit," she hisses, and nearby diners glance our way. She takes a breath. "You wanted to take my child the second it was born and hand it over to Zarina."

"I felt like she was the only one I could trust at that moment," I say, trying to defend my decision.

"I messed up, I know I did, but as I've already explained, I tried to back out of the agreement and Jessica Cole began blackmailing me.

I was scared she'd tell you, and by then, I was falling—" she stops, shaking her head.

"It's okay," Gia encourages. "Be honest, it's why we're here."

"I'd fallen in love with you, Vinn. I was scared she'd mess it all up, and I thought, maybe if I did her one last story, it would be enough for her to leave me alone."

"Things were good between us," I agree, nodding. "That's why I was so angry when the truth came out. I've spent my life unable to trust anyone, but I trusted you, Sofia."

"You can't lock me up and threaten my life whenever I fuck up. People fuck up."

"It was a personal attack, and I was angry and bitter. When I found out you were pregnant, I panicked. It wasn't part of the plan, I wasn't prepared, and locking you up seemed the best solution to keep you safe."

"There are so many things wrong with that sentence. If you hadn't found out, I'd be dead right now. You had a gun at my head. But you did find out and you still locked me away."

"I didn't know how else to deal with the woman I love being pregnant with my child yet betraying me so badly. I needed time to calm down."

"And Zarina?"

"Was a way to hurt you," I admit. "It was childish and stupid. I didn't do anything with her."

"Not because you didn't want to, I'm sure," she mutters in disgust. "If hurting me is what you wanted, you achieved it, because you have hurt me, and now, I can't stand to look at you. It pains me to look at you."

We fall silent, and I notice Gia has tears in her eyes. I nudge her and nod towards where Blu is sitting. She takes the hint and leaves us alone. I grab Sofia's hands and hold them tightly. "And you hurt me," I confess. "I've never been in love. I thought I had, once, but it was nothing compared to how I feel about you. To find out you'd betrayed me from the start . . . I was so fucking angry and I wanted to kill you, but when it came down to it, I couldn't pull the trigger. When Gia burst in and announced you were pregnant, I wanted to shout with relief. I was so happy because a baby meant more time to come up with a plan. What I did was wrong. I see that now."

"If I refuse to come home with you, what will happen?" she asks, looking pleased with herself. She's backing me into a corner. "Because if you really believed that what you did was wrong, you wouldn't have our tickets booked to go back to London."

"Sofia—"

"Have you booked our tickets for London?" she pushes.

"Baby, I—"

"Cut the bullshit. Yes or no, Vinn?"

"Yes," I snap. "Yes, I have tickets booked."

"When?"

"Does it matter?"

"It matters to me," she cries, and we gain more curious glances. "You don't get it. If you want me to come back, it has to be on my terms."

"Then tell me the fucking terms so I can agree and you can come back to where you belong," I growl impatiently.

Sofia stands, giving me a pitying stare. "There's no point. I already know you won't agree."

I watch her march from the restaurant, then Gia rushes over. "What the hell happened?"

"She's trying to be in control!" I snap.

"Then let her."

I shake my head. "I can't."

"It's what she needs to trust you again, Vinn. Why are you so pig-headed?"

"I let my guard down once and look what happened!"

Gia takes my hand. "Vinn, you have to let it go if you want to be in your child's life."

"Why go to all this trouble?" I ask, standing. "She's coming home anyway, and if that means I carry her onto the ferry, I will."

"And she knows that, so why not humour her a little and try some give-and-take tactics. Relationships are about compromise, but so far, you're not compromising at all."

SOFIA

It's raining. I stepped out and the heavens opened. I walk over the road to a stone bridge that sits over a small lake. It's picturesque, and whenever I sit on the stones, dangling my feet over the bridge, I imagine it's like something from a movie scene. "Hope you're not thinking of jumping." I glance back at Vinn peering over the edge. "Not much chance of drowning in there though." I tip my head back and close my eyes. The feel of the rain hitting my skin relaxes me instantly. I know he'll force me to go home with him, and the scariest thing is, a small part of me wants him to. I hate making the big decisions for Mama and myself. I've never had this kind of responsibility, and soon, I'll have a baby to look after too. How can I raise a child when I'm constantly on the run? And then there's other things to consider, like him finding me once the child is born and him running off with it. What if this is my chance to make it right? We've both messed this up, but somewhere along the way, I fell in love with Vinn. Seeing him again made me realise just how much I've missed him.

"I still want to go to college," I announce. "And I want a career at the end of it."

"What about the baby?"

"Women work and have kids all the time, Vinn."

"Okay."

"I want to eat dinner when I feel like it, not at set times."

"What's wrong with everyone knowing when to sit down together?" he argues.

"And I want to redecorate. No more white walls or silk sheets."

"I like silk."

"I want to arrange plans and not have you ruin them or turn up uninvited. I want to make friends who are not scared of you."

"I can't help people feel intimidated by me."

"I want my own bank account and to earn my own money. If things ever go wrong again, I want to be able to provide for my child."

"Things won't go wrong."

"I want to have a say."

He's standing behind me, and for a fleeting second, I wonder if he plans to push me off this bridge, but his hands rest on my shoulders and I feel his forehead against the back of my head. "You do have a say."

"I don't. Not ever. I didn't when I was growing up, I didn't when Dante took me, and I didn't when I married you. I didn't with the pregnancy. I've never had my say and I've never been heard. I will not be like Mama."

"Sofia, you are nothing like your mother."

"I want to skip breakfast when I don't feel hungry. I want to turn down dinner invites if I don't feel like going. I don't want to feel scared of you." I pause, my mouth running away with me. I take a breath and turn sideways so I can see him properly. His eyes are dark and the rain water is dripping from the ends of his hair, down his chiselled face, and gathering on his perfect jawline before falling away. This man is so dangerously dark yet all I want is for him to kiss me. "If you ever pull a gun on me again, I'll wait until you're asleep and I'll stick a knife right through your heart because I refuse to be afraid of you."

He nods, running a finger along my own jaw line. "The thought of you straddling me with a knife over my heart does something to me," he whispers, a wicked look in his eye.

"I want a marriage, not a boss. You are not my boss."

He turns me so I'm facing him and stands between my legs. "You make a lot of demands."

"I'm not sure I've finished."

He licks his lips and my eyes follow the movement. God, I need him to kiss me. "We'll make a list. I'll get Raven to draw up a contract, and you can divorce me and leave if I break it."

I bite my lower lip to hide my smile. "Would you do that for me?"

"First thing in the morning, before we've stepped on the ferry."

"I'm serious though, Vinn. No more games. No more lies. We'll be honest and open."

"I'm deadly serious, Sofia. I just want you beside me. Not behind, not in front, just beside. And I'll get it wrong, I know I will, but I'll try my best to get it right and make you happy. You deserve to be treated like my queen and I've spent too long getting it all wrong. You leaving like that made me see how wrong I got it. Please, come home with me tomorrow."

"And if I say no?"

He glances around. "Then I guess I'll be moving to this little town of shitsville."

I grin. "You'd hate it here."

"I already do."

"But you'd move here for me?"

"I want to be where you are." I know it would never happen, that he's telling me what I need to hear, but it makes my heart happier this way. I'd never outrun him, though I'm not sure I want to, so why am I bothering to try?

I place my arms around his neck. "I kind of miss London anyway."

"There's more places to run and hide there," he points out.

I nod. "More places to hide," I repeat, gently pressing my lips against his. But I'm done hiding.

Playing Vinn was the worst thing I ever did, but falling in love with him was the best. It might not be perfect, and damn, we have a long way to go, but I love him, and after everything, I'm ready to move on. When we first met, we were forced into marriage, but this time, I'm choosing it. I'm choosing this man . . . this fucked-up, crazy man. And he chooses me. Everything else will work itself out.

Epilogue

"Let me have a go," I whisper, taking Mario from Sofia's arms and gently kissing my exhausted wife on the head. "Get back into bed." She doesn't need telling twice. I take a seat in the rocking chair placed in the corner of the room and stare down at my baby boy's moonlit face. Named after his uncle, with his second name being my father's, I feel pride swell in my chest. I wasn't prepared for the rush of instant love I felt for this tiny, precious human. I glance over at Sofia, already sleeping. She's an amazing mother, taking to it like a natural. But being a new parent and attending college three days a week is tiring her out. Luckily, she's got the help of her mama and my mother. In six months' time, she'll have finished her course, and she has a job lined up with Dave Cline. Since taking down Jessica Cole, we've become business associates, and he now handles a lot of my press for the club.

Our marriage has been better. It took a while after we returned from Ireland for us to relax around each other. But slowly, we've built trust again and we're getting along just fine. Better than fine. We never did draw up that contract. Sofia is very clear when she wants something her way, and I've learnt from Blu that giving in to the small things makes refusing the big things easier. It works for us.

One thing's for sure, I spent a long time thinking I loved Leia, then Raven, but it's clear I'd never felt love. Because what I have with Sofia, what we're building together, is real love. She's on my mind every second of the day. I'd do anything to protect her and Mario because they are my world. When I think back to how I treated her in the beginning, it hurts me. I've learnt to be a good husband and father. Some days, I realise, I'm still learning. I'll still mess up, just like she will, but I don't fear losing her like before. I know she loves me just as much as I love her.

I place a gentle kiss on my boy's head. One day, we'll have a whole football team's worth of kids running around, and I can't fucking wait!

THE END

Popular books by Nicola Jane

Riggs' Ruin https://mybook.to/RiggsRuin
Capturing Cree https://mybook.to/CapturingCree
Wrapped in Chains https://mybook.to/WrappedinChains
Saving Blu https://mybook.to/SavingBlu
Riggs' Saviour https://mybook.to/RiggsSaviour
Taming Blade https://mybook.to/TamingBlade
Misleading Lake https://mybook.to/MisleadingLake
Surviving Storm https://mybook.to/SurvivingStorm
Ravens Place https://mybook.to/RavensPlace
Playing Vinn https://mybook.to/PlayingVinn

Other books by Nicola Jane:
The Perished Riders MC
Maverick https://mybook.to/Maverick-Perished
Scar https://mybook.to/Scar-Perished
Grim https://mybook.to/Grim-Perished
Ghost https://mybook.to/GhostBk4

Dice https://mybook.to/DiceBk5

The Hammers MC (Splintered Hearts Series)
Cooper https://mybook.to/CooperSHS
Kain https://mybook.to/Kain
Tanner https://mybook.to/TannerSH